Joy Chambers was [...] Australia, the third [...] an Australian moth[...] age and has had a [...] Australia. She has appeared in numerous shows and has won awards over the years. Joy currently appears as Rosemary Daniels in the international television hit 'Neighbours'. She views her writing as a natural extension of her self expression, and describes herself as a proud Australian Anglophile who loves Africa. MY ZULU MYSELF is her second novel (following MAYFIELD, which is also available from Headline) and is the result of ten years of research.

My Zulu Myself

Joy Chambers

HEADLINE

First published in 1994
by HEADLINE BOOK PUBLISHING

First published in paperback in 1995
by HEADLINE BOOK PUBLISHING

10 9 8 7 6 5 4 3 2 1

ISBN 0 7472 4859 1

Typeset by Keyboard Services, Luton, Beds

Printed and bound in Great Britain by
Cox & Wyman Ltd, Reading, Berks

HEADLINE BOOK PUBLISHING
A division of Hodder Headline PLC
338 Euston Road
London NW1 3BH

HISTORICAL NOTES

My Zulu Myself is historically factual. I have woven my fictitious characters into the history of the colony of Natal, and into the history of the Zulu peoples. The majority of the places, and many of the situations, are real.

In the 1870s Isandlwana was spelt Isandlwhana. I have used the spelling of the times.

There is some dispute about the year of Mtonga's escape from Zululand. It took place in either 1864 or 1865. For the sake of my story I have used the year 1865.

From 1861 onwards I change the original spelling of D'urban and Pieter Maritzburg to Durban and Pietermaritzburg.

I have taken licence with Captain Theopolis Shepstone Junior's return to the Isandlwhana battlefield. I have him returning to the battlefield only days after the event, when in fact it was some months before he did so.

The following people were real. All lived/worked in the colony of Natal/Zululand and a great many played a distinguished part in the formation of the colony of Natal, and in the history of Zululand.

Brevet Colonel Anthony William Durnford
Bishop John William Colenso
Frances 'Fanny' Colenso
Theopolis Shepstone
Theopolis Shepstone Jun.
Captain George Shepstone
Henrique Shepstone
John Wesley Shepstone
Lord Carnarvon
Sir Henry Bulwer
Dick King

Lieutenant-Governor Robert William Keate
Lieutenant-Governor Benjamin Chilly Campbell Pine
Sir Garnet Wolsley
Sir Henry Bartle Frere
Sir Michael Hicks Beach
General Frederick Thesiger, Lord Chelmsford
Colonel Richard Thomas Glyn

Colonel Henry Evelyn Wood
Lieutenant-Colonel Milles
Lieutenant-Colonel Amiel
Brevet Lieutenant-Colonel
  Henry Pulleine
Major John Dartnell
Major Henry Spalding
Brevet Major Stuart Smith
Commandant Rupert
  Lonsdale
Captain Charles Cavaye
Captain George Wardell
Captain Reginald
  Younghusband
Captain William Mostyn
Captain William Degacher
Captain Edward Erskine
Captain Geoffry Barton
Captain W. H. Stafford
Captain Charles Barter
Captain Allen Gardiner RN
Captain T. B. Hill
Lieutenant John Chard
Lieutenant Gonville
  Bromhead
Lieutenant Charles Raw
Lieutenant Charles Pope
Lieutenant Francis Porteous
Lieutenant Horace Smith-
  Dorien
Lieutenant Francis George
  Farewell
Corporal Cooke
Elijah Kambula
Simeon Kambula
Jabez Molife
Paul Brickhill
President Thomas Burgers
Paul Kruger
Cornelius Van Rooyen
Sarah Frances Colenso

Agnes Colenso
Francis Colenso
Robert Erskine
Michael Gallwey
Reverend Otto De Witt
James Rorke
Sergeant Clarke
Trooper Bond
Trooper Potterill
Henry Rider Haggard
David Dale Buchanan
Father Jean Baptiste Sabon
Missionary Schroeder
George Cato
Mrs Dawney
Port Captain Bell
Warwick Brookes
Border Agent Joshua
  Wamsley
Border Agent Finney
Charles Norris-Newman
Jack Joss
Reverend Nesbitt
Dr Lindley
Mqhali
Chief Langalibalele
Chief Dube
Umkozaza
Umbilini
Sekukuni
Ngosa
John Byrne
Liam Nel
Editor Sanderson

Zulus

Cetshwayo
Mpande
Dingane
Shaka

Mbuyazi, half-brother to
    Cetshwayo
Dubalamanzi, half-brother to
    Cetshwayo
Usiwetu, half-brother to
    Cetshwayo
Gihlana, half-brother to
    Cetshwayo
Uhamu, half-brother to
    Cetshwayo
uSicwelewele
Umgoza
Tshingwayo
Mavumengwana
Maphoko

Mtonga
Mkungo
Mbilini
Mundula
Vumandaba
Matshana Ka Mondisa
Meleseli
Sihayo
'Chief' John Dunn, Jantoni

Real animals
Prince, Colonel Anthony
    Durnford's dog
Chieftain, Colonel Anthony
    Durnford's horse

BIBLIOGRAPHY

Ahrens, F. W., *From Bench to Bench*, Pietermaritzburg, 1948

Ashe, Major Waller and Wyatt Edgell, The Hon. Captain E. V., *The Story of the Zulu Campaign*, 1880

Barthorpe, Michael, *The Zulu War – A Pictorial History*, Great Britain, 1980

Becker, Peter, *Dingane, King of the Zulus 1828–1840*, New York, 1965

Berkovitch, Barry M., *The Cape Gunsmith*, 1976

Binns, C. T., *The Last Zulu King (The Life and Death of Cetshwayo)*, London, 1963

Bird, John, *Annals of Natal 1495–1845*, Vol. I, Cape Town, 1965

Bird, John, *Annals of Natal 1495–1845*, Vol. II, Cape Town, 1965

Buchanan, Barbara, *Pioneer Days in Natal*, Pietermaritzburg, 1934

Caffrey, Kate, *Great Emigrations: The British to Southern Africa*, London, 1973

Colenso, Frances Ellen, *The Ruin of Zululand*, London, 1884

Colenso, John William, *Langalibalele and the amaHlubi Tribe*, London, 1874

Dicke, B. H., *The Bush Speaks (Border Life in Old Transvaal)*, Pietermaritzburg, 1936

Durnford, Lieutenant-Colonel Edward, *A Soldier's Life and Work in South Africa*, London, 1882

Edgerton, Robert B., *Like Lions they Fought*, New York, 1988

Elliott, Aubrey, *The Zulu Traditions and Culture*, Cape Town, 1986

Elliott, Major W. J., *Victoria Cross in Zululand*, London, 1898

Ellman, A., *South African Anecdotes*, Johannesburg, 1914

Emery, Frank, *The 24th Regiment at Isandlwhana XXIV, The Zulu War 1879*, 1978

Galbraith, John S., *Reluctant Empire (British Policy on the South African Frontier 1834–1854)*, California, 1963

Giese, Toby, *The Men of The Zulu War of 1879*, Missouri, 1987

Gillmore, Parker, *The Great Thirst Land – A Ride Through Natal, Orange Free State, Transvaal and Kalahari Desert*, London, 1880

Harford, Colonel Henry C. B., *Zulu War Journal*, Connecticut, 1980

Hillegas, Howard C., *Oom Paul's People*, New York, 1899

Hurst, Colonel G. T., *Volunteer Regiments of Natal & East Griqualand*, Durban, 1945

Junod, Henri A., *The Life of A South African Tribe*, Vol. I, USA, 1962

Junod, Henri A., *The Life of A South African Tribe*, Vol. II, USA, 1962

Kidd, Dudley, *The Essential Kaffir*, London, 1925

Krige, Eileen Jensen, *The Social System of the Zulus*, London, 1936

Laband, John, *Kingdom in Crisis (The Zulus' Response to the British Invasions of 1879)*, Manchester, 1992

Laband, J. P. C. and Thompson, P. S., *Field Guide to the War in Zululand and the Defence of Natal 1879*, Pietermaritzburg, 1979

Ludlow, Captain W. R., *Zululand and Cetewayo*, 1882

Lyster, Lynn, *Ballads of the Veld-Land*, London, 1913

Mason, G. H., *Life with the Zulus of Natal*, 1855

Mitford, Bertram, *Through the Zulu Country, Its Battlefields and People*, London, 1883

Morris, Donald R., *The Washing of the Spears*, Great Britain, 1966

Morton, H. V., *In Search of South Africa*, London, 1948

Narrative of the Field Operations Connected with the Zulu War of 1879, prepared in the Intelligence branch of the War Office, London, 1989

Norris-Newman, Charles L., *In Zululand with the British Throughout the War of 1879*, London, 1880

Nyembezi, C. L. A., *Learn Zulu*, Pietermaritzburg, 1957

Lakeman, Sir Stephen, *What I Saw in Kaffir-Land*, London, 1886

Pakenham, Thomas, *The Scramble for Africa*, New York, 1991

Picard, Hymen W. J., *Gentleman's Walk*, Cape Town, 1968

Reader, D. H., *Zulu Tribe in Transition*, Manchester, 1966

Russell, George, *History of Old Durban*, Durban, 1899

Struthers, Robert Briggs, *Hunting Journal 1852–1856 in the Zulu Kingdom and the Tsonga Regions*, Pietermaritzburg, 1991

Tyler, Revd Josiah, *Forty Years Among the Zulus*, Cape Town, 1971

Whybra, Julian, *The Roll Call – Men Killed in Action and Survivors of Isandlwhana and Rorke's Drift*, Durban, 1990

Wilkinson-Latham, Christopher, *Uniforms and Weapons of the Zulu War*, London, 1978

Williams, Basil, *Cecil Rhodes*, London, 1921

Wilmot, F. R. G. S., *A History of the Cape Colony*, Cape Town, 1883

Windrow, Martin, *The Zulu War*, London, 1976

Young, John, *They Fell Like Stones – Battles and Casualties of the Zulu War, 1879*, London, 1991

Additional Source: Reading Room, National Army Museum, London

Dedicated to my darling husband,
Reg Grundy OBE,
my very own editor, whose constant interest in all I write,
I treasure.

Darlengi = Reginald

With deepest thanks to my sister, Coral, and brother, Jack, and my marvellous family and wonderful friends who continue to support me.

Special thanks to David Rattray of Fugitives' Drift Lodge, Zululand, Natal, South Africa: a splendid historian who took me through the battlefields and brought the battles of the Zulu War of 1879 to life for me.

Enlargement of Tugela Farm

PROLOGUE

Zululand, South Africa, 16 July, 1838

Between the Umlatoosi River and the Ungoya peak, the early morning sun, fighting through sliding grey clouds, cast a meagre winter light upon the kraal: large and circular, surrounded by an eight-foot-high fence, its hive-shaped thatched huts strung, in usual fashion, around the inside, the main kraal entrance facing east. A few women, wrapped in capes as protection against the wind, huddled, muttering softly, outside one of the biggest dwellings.

It lay opposite the main gate on the far side of the kraal, and that alone designated it as the abode of the headman's Great Wife. In the smoke-filled interior, the occupants stamped their feet as they moved back and forth in attendance on the woman who lay by the fireside. A rasping cry of pain escaped her lips as her mother's veined hand reached out to pat her gently on the tight, black, wiry curls of her head.

'Hush, my darling, it will come soon,' the old lady said, bending forward on her knees to kiss her daughter's wet forehead. As her mother's lips touched her the woman on the cowhide mat shook her head from side to side. Her eyes were glassy and full of fear. She panted audibly, and as her full breasts lifted her swollen nipples skywards, grunted in the strain to push downwards once more.

The mother turned to the induna who sat at her side on the floor of rock-hard polished clay. He was one of the headmen who practised the magic arts, and they had sent for him earlier in the day when the birth had become increasingly difficult. 'Can you do no more?' she asked. Her eyes pleaded, filling with tears. 'This is terrible. It has been going on for two suns now. I fear for her. I fear for her. She is not strong enough.'

He shook his head and his heavy brows rose unhappily. 'The

1

will of our ancestors cannot be changed, Oola. I understand your fear for your daughter, but there is little more I can do.'

'Oh, why oh why is it that Mattana is not here?' the distressed woman cried. 'Why is she not with us in our hour of need?'

A look of affront passed briefly across the induna's face and he turned away.

One of the younger women who bent heating water over the open fire exclaimed, 'Mattana did not expect Nadi to bear before her time was ripe. I heard her say she was sure Nadi would go her time.'

'She is supposed to see all things,' wailed the mother, leaning forward over Nadi. 'Why did she not foresee that my daughter would fall in the field?'

'Ah yes, why?' croaked the induna, lifting his eyes upwards. 'It appears to me she does not see everything as clearly as she claims.'

The young woman spoke again. 'My eyes are watering from the smoke!'

'Quiet, you tiresome girl,' answered the woman beside her. 'Poor Nadi's water in agony.'

There was another strangled sound of pain from behind them.

'I think it comes at last!' called Oola, as the two women who held her daughter's arms in support helped her bear down.

'Oh, Mother! Help me . . . it's . . . killing me.'

Minutes later, they lifted the child from Nadi's perspiration-covered body, and she collapsed back, her limbs racked by violent tremors.

'You have a son, my darling,' whispered Oola, as the women in attendance moved away with the tiny crying form, but there was no response from her daughter as the trembling ceased and she lay still.

The adviser to the chief moved forward on his knees, his head ring shining in the firelight. He took the limp hand that lay on the mat. Oola, panic in her eyes, kneeled beside him, watching him feel her daughter's pulse.

'Nadi? Nadi?' he said softly.

There was no response. Nadi's body was unmoving and she lay with unseeing eyes.

2

He turned sadly, sympathetically, to Oola. 'She is with her ancestors.'

Oola sank forward on to the inert body, her old arms, garnished with the stringy muscles of decades of mealie-making, clinging to the spent form of her daughter. Her grief welled over her lids and ran down her face. 'No ... no ... no ... it cannot be, my Nadi, my only daughter!'

The women who held the soiled infant looked over to Oola, their faces expressing dull acceptance. What could they say? It was oftentimes a woman's destiny to die in childbirth.

The induna rose. 'I will tell Shiambi, ancient one. I am sorry.'

Oola made no reply, and the sound of her weeping followed him as he bent double through the single small opening of the hut and scrambled out on his hands and knees. The women clustering round the hut entrance watched as he stood up, and sighing, pulled the thick hide cape more tightly around himself before he ran swiftly in the biting wind across the dust of the central pen and out of the kraal entrance.

A hundred yards away lay a larger, more important kraal, and to this he hastened. He entered and ran to the chief's hut.

The babble of voices ceased as he entered, and the faces of the chief and his wives and indunas turned towards him.

This hut too was filled with smoke, for as in the one he had just left, there was only the single low entrance that gave air. But this dwelling was larger still, and grander, the walls being decorated with war shields and the floor covered with numerous intricately patterned mats of woven grass and hide. People could move around upright instead of bent over. Those gathered were wrapped against the cold.

The newcomer bowed to the chief and repeated his praise names – the chief's many titles which must be used when addressing him – then he turned towards the young induna who sat at the chief's right hand. He was a handsome man of thirty-five years, wearing the headband of the uDlambedhlu regiment; these warriors had been given permission to marry by Dingane, king of the Zulus, only two years before. The young induna looked up hopefully at the one who practised the magic arts, and then, unravelling his long body and gaining his feet, advanced across the floor towards him.

'The news I bring is mixed, Shiambi. You have a healthy son

– he is already airing his lungs, but I am sorry to tell you Nadi was not strong enough. She is . . . gone.'

Shiambi's shoulders sank. He was brave and fierce in battle. He had a long assegai scar down his right buttock and another smaller one on his hand to prove his courage; did he not carry the pure white shield of his regiment's master warrior? He had known Shaka and was a favourite of Dingane and feared throughout all the Zulu kraals. But now he felt weak like an old woman, for he had loved Nadi, she was his Great Wife. He had only one other, his first; she, he had taken merely according to convention. He remembered Nadi's gentle smile on the day she had told him she was to bear his child. How proud she had been. He heard her say, 'And he will be strong and brave like you, my love.' He remembered the ecstasy of their times entwined together on the floor of their hut.

And now he had lost her. This baby had killed her. This boy child had done that. Children were important . . . yes, very. Yet there would be other sons. It was easy to have children, but there never would be another Nadi. His dark eyes filled with tears and as some of his friends moved over to comfort him he turned quickly away so that none would see and hurried to the hut opening and out into the chill air.

He looked briefly, painfully, up at the sky before he ran to the hut where her dead body lay. Inside he moved to her and gently removed the shining white stone that hung on the strip of leather around her neck.

Ah, Nadi, my beautiful Nadi, my tender delight. How I want you back. I hurt like a thousand spears were twisting in my entrails. I hate this child who has killed you . . .

Two hours after Nadi's death, and five and a half thousand miles to the north, a young woman in fine russet silk turned from the window of The Grange where she had been looking down across the cool green meadows dotted with summer daffodils, scanning the miles of open countryside for the dust that would announce the approach of a carriage.

'I'm afraid there is still no sign of the Colonel, Doctor.'

The doctor lifted his head from where he attended the woman in the big four-poster oak bed. 'I see.' The sound of his voice was grim.

The woman in the bed opened her eyes. They were large in

4

her ashen face and she perspired freely. A midwife wiped her forehead with a white cotton towel.

'I . . . I . . . feel as if I am being torn in two, Doctor. I cannot fight much longer.'

'Hush, hush, m'lady,' he answered gently. 'This is not your first time in childbed. You have brought five fine girls into the world. There's no reason why you cannot do it again.'

A weak smile broke across her thin mouth. 'Ah . . . you try to cheer me . . . but . . . I know . . . I cannot. It has been forty-eight hours and it still has not come . . . this one's killing me.' She grunted in pain then, and her head lifted from the pillow as the second midwife hurried forward to grasp her arms in support.

The doctor sighed and applied another leech to her.

It was an hour later that the woman's young sister-in-law, Jane Harrison, again turned from the window. It was a beautiful midsummer twilight and the fields radiated a burnished yellow glow from the setting sun.

'At last the carriage comes,' she said in a voice barely above a whisper. Her face was drawn with worry and she twisted her hands together anxiously. 'My brother is here.' She came swiftly to the bedside. 'Joanna, dearest, he comes.'

As she spoke the woman on the bed screamed again, and lifting her tormented face, looked with glazed eyes at the girl.

'Bear down, m'lady, bear down,' said the midwife at the bedside, and as the poor, weary, life-drained woman attempted once more to do so, the doctor urged, 'Good, good, keep pushing, m'lady.' A minute later, his blood-soiled hands urged the tiny form out from between her legs and lifted it in the air. 'Thank God! It's here. You have a son at last!'

A second midwife took the child from him as he cut the umbilical cord.

The cries of the infant filled the bedroom and his mother turned a glassy stare towards the sound. Her voice came in a whisper from her dry throat. 'A son, you say . . . please . . . Can I see him? Don't clean him or I fear it will . . . be too late.'

The doctor nodded vehemently. 'Yes, yes. Give the child to his mother.'

The midwife hurriedly wrapped the child in a towel and placed the bundle in the woman's arms as a glimmer of a smile came to her exhausted face. She looked down at the infant and touched his bloody cheek with her hand. 'My son . . . my son . . .' It was a heart-rending acknowledgement and those in the room with her looked fearfully at one another. Then Joanna's eyes lifted to her young sister-in-law. 'Jane . . . promise me . . . you'll love him.'

'Oh, darling, of course I will, but . . .'

The mother's gaze returned to her son, becoming a fixed stare upon him, her eyes bulging; then suddenly a heaving shudder ran through her and a sound like escaping air came whistling from her throat.

'Doctor!' cried the second woman in attendance. 'My Lord, is she . . .? Oh, dear God!'

Swiftly, the doctor returned the child to the arms of the midwife and leaning forward, took up the inert wrist to check the pulse he knew was not there. 'M'lady? M'lady?' He shook his head sadly and placed her hand gently across her breast. Then with another tired shake of his head he put his hands on her gaunt face and brought her lids down over her blind eyes.

Seven minutes later, Colonel James Harrison dismounted from his coach, and leapt up the stone steps to his front door, where he was met by two liveried servants. Behind them stood the doctor.

'Well? Well? And what has transpired? Is my wife finally delivered of a son?'

'Please come with me, sir,' answered the doctor, turning and leading the way into the drawing room.

The door closed behind them.

'Well, what is it?'

'My news is mixed, sir. Yes, you have a son. A strong healthy boy, but . . . you have no wife, she was not able to . . . I'm sorry, Colonel, but your wife died within minutes of the delivery.'

Colonel Harrison nodded. 'I see . . .' The words were pushed out along with a sigh. But inside his heart raced. He had a son! At last! A thrill of joy ran through him. Poor Joanna finally had given him a son. He was sorry she was dead; he really was. But what could he do about it? Nothing. They had been a mismatched pair, he and Joanna.

For a moment he felt sad for the marriage that might have been. Yes, there was a time when Joanna had been beautiful . . . He remembered the first day he had ever seen her. It was

6

June then, a glorious sunny day at Ascot. He had returned to his box for the running of the second race and there, to his amazement and delight, had seen a vision in pink lace sitting beside his cousin Myrtle. He had fallen immediately in love.

His family had never approved of her: an American, a Harrison wife! Why, his father had never forgiven them for the War of Independence. But James Harrison would have his way, and thus against all their opposition the vision had become his wife. Yet her beauty had faded quickly, just as his love for her had faded years ago. He knew that was why he had remained in the army. The army was his second wife, the one he truly loved. In the fifteen years since they had married, he had been away with the army for more years than he ever had been at home.

Momentarily, a heavy guilt, nauseating and leaden, settled across his mind. Perhaps he should have tried harder. Then, following the life-long habit of never finding fault with himself, he shook the guilt away in unison with the shaking of his shoulders, and faced the doctor. He could feel that the medical man did not approve. His eyes were casting judgements upon him; saying he should have been here when his wife was dying. But then how could the doctor understand all the intricacies? It had been impossible for him to get here in time. He had tried; he really had.

But he did not have to explain himself to anyone. 'Well, thank you, Doctor. I'm sure you did everything possible. Could you leave me alone now, please?'

He walked to the window and looked out on to the wide stone steps leading to the ivy-covered colonnade and the rolling lawns beyond. The pond at the bottom of the steps was reflecting the afternoon sun and the lily pads gleamed a deep, dark green. In the first weeks of their marriage he and Jo had run hand in hand down those steps and nearly fallen in the pond with laughter. He hadn't thought of that since the very day. Why would he think of it now?

His hand was unsteady as he opened the window. *I'm sorry, Jo, I really am. Perhaps I should have realised you were not strong enough to bear this last one; but after all, I'm not Solomon.*

There was a movement behind him. He turned to his youthful sister's sceptical gaze and formal greeting.

'Good evening, James. Jo is dead, but you have what you wanted, at last. Your son is ready for viewing.' Her voice was weighted with sarcasm. 'But no doubt you will want to see poor Joanna first.'

'Jane ... don't. That's not fair. I'm very sorry she's gone.'

'Really? If I believed that, I would have to ask you why you turned a fragile woman into a baby-making machine ... Even you must have known it would kill her in the end.'

He turned away. 'Leave me, Jane, I don't need your company. Go, before I become angry.'

There were tears in Jane's eyes. 'She was like ... a big sister to me, a friend. If *I* knew she was not strong enough, why didn't you?'

He did not answer, but continued to stand with his back to her.

He heard her sigh and the rustle of her silk skirts as she moved to the door. Her parting words came between sobs. 'I know the answer, James. It's because you did not care; but I did, I loved her. All along, nothing mattered to you but to have a son. Well, congratulations.' Then the door slammed and he was alone.

How dare she? Trust Jane to be so bloody rude; an obnoxious girl grown into an obnoxious woman; the only daughter and the youngest child. She continued to get away with appalling behaviour.

He walked outside into a beautiful day. He could not contain his feelings any longer, he smiled ... smiled and smiled.

He had a son! After all those daughters poor old Joanna had given him a son. It was a miracle. *Oh yes, I do thank you for that, Joanna. I truly do.*

Ah! How I will love the boy!

Eight years later: April 1846, Cleveland, Ohio, USA
The evening sun filtered through the curtains on to the tranquil lines of Victoria McLean's face. She sat reading the Lord's words from St Matthew and her eyes lifted in contemplation. *Blessed are the merciful: for they shall obtain mercy.* She tried so hard to understand and live by the words of the Lord, but she wondered if she would ever have the fervour to impart God's message the way Frank did. Her husband inspired all those around him, and had such a way with people

that he could uplift their spirits even when they were in the depths of misery. Yes, his was a true calling, and he was so very good and kind and caring and wonderful. Her life was quite perfect. She smiled, a smug smile, and then quickly remonstrated with herself for being so sinful.

She put down the bible on the velvet seat beside her and moved gracefully out on to the porch and down across the lawn. Her parents had built this lovely house for her and Frank when they had married two years before. It was a long way out of the town itself but that did not matter to Victoria. For a few minutes she stood looking at the tranquillity of the trees around her and listening to the song of a goldfinch in the sycamore tree that bent under the weight of its hundred-year-old branches. She felt so at peace with the world today.

She moved down to sit on the seat some feet from a walled garden, and there she remained until the evening shadows fell. She often sat like this, meditating on the words of the saints or the Lord, but this evening other things, worldly things, were on her mind.

She and Frank had often spoken about going to Africa where there was a desperate need for missionaries. If anyone could make a difference to those poor needy heathens so far away; if anyone could bring goodness and care and the ways of the Lord to them, it was her husband. And she would be his faithful helper. It was causing a rift with her parents, for they would hear no more about it; but they didn't understand. Yes, one of these days they would go as missionaries, she was sure.

'My own darling.'

She turned with a rapturous smile to run into her husband's arms. Frank McLean kissed her as if he had been away from her a month instead of a day.

'I have something to tell you,' she said, an awkward, shy smile playing around her pretty mouth, and she took up his hand and led him to the bench, where she sat him down and turned to him with shining eyes.

Frank McLean was a good-natured, good-looking man of thirty-six. He had been a pastor of the Methodist church for a decade and he had met Victoria when he had been sent here from Baltimore four years ago. He loved her deeply – perhaps too deeply, for he knew he should save his greatest love for God. Sometimes he felt guilty about that, but not today, not

9

looking into the depths of her round hazel eyes here in the shadows of the warm Cleveland night, with the wind playing a love song in the sycamore tree.

'What is it, Victoria sweetheart?'

'It's what we thought, my darling, I'm positive now.'

His strong features broke into a delighted smile. 'You mean it truly?'

'I do.'

'Oh how wonderful.' He hugged her to him, kissing her forehead, her eyes, her hair.

She looked up into his dark blue eyes. 'And do you know, I'm sure, somehow so sure, it will be a girl.'

He kissed the tip of her nose. 'As long as it's like you.'

Now a tiny frown formed between her pretty eyes. 'Oh no, Frank, not like me ... like you.'

Then he laughed and took her in his arms again, and deep in the rustling leaves of the sycamore the goldfinch began his tune once more in the swiftly falling night.

Six months later, in October, while Frank and his in-laws waited to hear the news of the birth, Victoria's father took Frank aside.

'Son,' he said, looking down his long, straight, patrician nose, 'now that you're beginning a family I'm hoping this missionary nonsense will be put aside. You cannot take a child into the wilderness. It's not fitting.'

Frank took a deep breath. It was not that he disliked his wife's father, he did not; it was just that the man seemed so ungodly. 'Mr Lawrence, sir, on the contrary. While we will wait a few years before we go, so that the child is walking and talking, we have given our word to God, and we hope in time you will understand that such a promise is not lightly made.'

A look of distaste covered his father-in-law's features as he turned abruptly and walked away.

Frank put aside the attitude of his wife's parents and rejoiced in the thought of the child that was soon to come. If it were a girl it would be Phoebe; if it were a boy, Peter. Frank did not care about the sex of his child; he would love it dearly ... whatever it was.

CHAPTER ONE

Six years later: 16 October, 1852
For two weeks the seas had been huge and the *Regent Three* had fought its way, plunging and rolling, all the endless miles down the west African coast towards the Cape of Good Hope. And now, as the clipper made its way into Table Bay and the passengers saw the distant lights of Cape Town, this thriving outpost of the British Empire, the angry waters, at last, gave way to blessed calm.

Jane Harrison removed her long white hand from where it rested on the forward bulwark. For some time now she had stood alone, watching the distant twinkling lights that represented her future across the inky fluid mirror that was Table Bay. She felt great relief, for she had brought her two charges safely to South Africa after over six weeks at sea with only Mannie, her maid, as helper. Tomorrow when they went ashore, Edgar, her favourite brother, would be waiting. She smiled to herself at the thought of seeing him again.

Edgar was of the pioneer spirit, enterprising and adventurous. Even as a child he had been interested in faraway places and peoples. She saw him now in her mind's eye in the schoolroom, a map of distant lands, India or the Americas, open in front of him. He was her big brother of nine or ten, leaning from his desk towards her, his blue eyes shining with visions she could not see, telling her of the things he would do and the places he would go. He had a saying that he repeated over and over to her. 'When I grow up, Janie, I'm going to ride on an elephant, shoot a lion and sail across the seas to new places, primitive places.' And her inevitable reply had been, 'Oh no, I don't want to come.' Until she was a little more grown up, when she had answered, 'Well, dearest boy, you'll have to change the sequence of your dreams: for you will have to sail across the seas first, in order to do the others.'

The army had finally fulfilled his wish, for it had sent him to Canada and then to South Africa, where in 1843, as a captain of the 45th Regiment in the Cape Colony, he had been sent by the Governor, Sir George Napier, with a detachment of the Royal Artillery to Port Natal under the command of Major Smith. Sir George was anticipating a time soon to come when the newly acquired territory would become a British colony.

Edgar had never loved the army, but South Africa pleased him immensely, and when he gained his discharge the following year, he left Port Natal and went into Zulu country, living for many months with these simple but fascinating people, and learning about them. Probably he realised his other dreams, to ride on an elephant and shoot a lion. He certainly saw his primitive lands and peoples. Jane recalled the letters he had written to her telling her of his meeting with Mpande, the Zulu king, who was intrigued by the English, while retaining his half-brother Dingane's distaste for the Boers. Edgar maintained a sort of friendship with Mpande and had actually spent some time at the king's kraal.

So here she was, Jane Harrison, thirty-five-year-old spinster, facing a new life over there in the twinkling lights of Cape Town. She sighed as she took her eyes from the firefly flashes across the black water and moved away from the bulwark. As she did so, in the dull glow of the ship's lanterns a black shadow fell across her path and a form jumped down from the rigging to stand in front of her.

'John Lockley Harrison,' she exclaimed, 'how you startled me!'

'Sorry,' said the boy, dragging his mouth down at the edges and looking up at her with a wry expression, 'but you're such an easy one to frighten, Aunt Jane, that I cannot help but take advantage.'

'You try me! Honestly you do; you try me! Why cannot you be like your sister Ellen? There's not a more well-behaved girl anywhere, I'm sure.'

He smiled at her, a mischievous but completely beguiling smile. He was a beautiful boy set to become a beautiful youth and, to follow, a beautiful man. His eyes were the colour of that line along the horizon at sea, blue and yet not blue, perhaps closer to the colour of indigo heightened with Tyrian purple: and already at fourteen he had an indefinable quality, something that made a person look again at him, and listen to what he said. In spite of herself she put her arms around him lovingly and ruffled his hair. 'Off you go, there's a dear! You're the most high-spirited child I ever did see! And you get away with it!'

'That's because you let me!' he replied, and ran ahead of her, sidestepping two sailors and the coil of rope which lay on the deck.

'Yes, I do,' she said aloud to his retreating form. 'What an insight into me.' She shook her head in disappointment with herself. John Lockley was right, she did let him get away with these things. Her excuse, of course, was that she loved him so; there never was a child more loved than John Lockley, she was sure of that. Perhaps it was because he had arrived after five girls, and because poor Joanna had died giving birth to him. And yet, he was loved for himself, she was sure of that.

She made her way forward towards the companionway, past the men and women who were coming above and milling to and fro on deck in the excitement of seeing the twinkling lights of their destination.

It had been a very difficult voyage. And there had been nasty trials, like the hordes of cockroaches that roamed the vessel, up and down the cabin walls and in every nook and cranny; and the objectionable taste of the stale water. She shivered now and her nose crinkled in distaste. The cockroaches alone had made her feel physically ill. And the clothes she had been compelled to wash in sea water felt so uncomfortable. She recalled her reaction to the embarkation order issued by the shipping company. It had read: 'As no fresh water can be allowed for washing while on board, a considerable stock of clothing is essential to comfort.' That was all very well, but as she refused to wear the same clothes multiple times, her stock, 'considerable' as it was, had not lasted the six weeks.

She was about to go below when she saw her friend, Victoria McLean, the missionary. Victoria had been the one person who had made the voyage bearable for Jane. She was a delightful woman, articulate, intelligent and understanding; the perfect wife for a man of Mr McLean's calling.

As Jane stopped to speak with her friend, the woman was

frowning. 'Jane, I'm looking for Phoebe again. She was with me playing with her doll in the cabin a minute ago. I turned round and she was gone. I'm worried, it's so dark.'

Phoebe was known as the ship's wanderer. She had become a favourite with the cooks and was often to be found in the galley sitting on the bench amongst the vegetable peelings. That was the first place they looked when she went missing. The child seemed to be fearless and was bright, pretty, eager and inquisitive, and Mr Blake, the ship's mate, had asked the missionaries more than once to watch their daughter more closely.

Soon John Lockley and Ellen had been seconded into helping to look for Phoebe, not an uncommon pastime for them in recent weeks.

'She's a pest,' Ellen stated, but because John Lockley was going to look she accompanied him. After a few minutes, though, she had had enough. 'I'm getting a headache from all this.'

'Ah, Nell,' he said, using his pet name for her. 'Go and lie down awhile. I'll just pop aft and see if she's down there.'

John Lockley liked the little girl, with her bright round eyes and funny tinkling laugh that made him laugh too.

As he headed aft along the newly holystoned deck, there was a silence hanging in the air, for most of the people were forward where they had the best view of the lights of Cape Town.

Running his hand back through his hair as was his custom when exhilarated or concerned, his clear young eyes darted this way and that, looking for the child, as he hurried past the covered life rafts aft of the main deck. Suddenly he heard a tiny voice singing, the childish pronunciation blending the words together. 'We are merry little cooks, smart in acts, and smart in looks . . .' He halted. The singing went on. 'We will show you how to bake, whitest bread and sweetest cake . . .' Where was it coming from? Inside the lifeboat? Surely not, the canvas was sealed down on all sides. Then he realised it was above him. He looked up. There in the dim light was the dark form of Phoebe, climbing in the rigging!

He went cold with shock, for she had to be at least fifteen

14

feet up, but somehow he stopped himself from shouting at her. Calmly, he called her name.

The singing stopped and the little face looked down. 'Hello, Jan Larkley.'

She appeared quite unconcerned, smiling at him in the benign light of the lanterns, but the boy's heart raced, for she was so precariously balanced, a little girl up there so high.

'Everybody's looking for you again, Phoebe. Stay there, don't move. I'll come up and get you. We'll come down together.' And the boy stepped up to take hold of the ropes and hoist himself up, saying all the while, 'Just stay there, Phoebe, don't move.'

But she had been diverted now from her climb: below was John Lockley whom she liked; he had often played a game of hopscotch on the decks with her. She tried to turn round, giving a happy laugh, but the laugh became a scream as her foot slipped and she toppled, hurtling like a lead weight down at the boy. He had only an instant to react as the form dropped towards him. He stepped swiftly underneath her and put up his arms to catch her if he could. She hit him with a thud and they fell heavily to the deck.

His body had broken her fall but she was crying loudly, and as they attempted to disentangle themselves from one another John Lockley felt strange sensations of pain in his left arm. He watched with surprise the swelling forming rapidly before his eyes. His wrist was broken.

Phoebe soon realised she had not hurt herself and she ceased to cry as she stood up and turned to John Lockley.

'I've surely broken my arm, Phoebe,' he said, and the child, realising this was a bad thing, began again to cry.

They made a sorry pair when they went below and found Jane and Victoria. Jane was all solicitude and rushed John Lockley away to the hospital where his wrist was soon expertly strapped by Mr Fleet, the ship's doctor.

In her cabin with her husband, Victoria was feeling remorse. 'It's terrible about John Lockley's arm. I'm responsible. I should have kept Phoebe by me.'

Frank took her hand and kissed it, then drew her to him in an attempt to stop her thinking about what had happened. 'No, it wasn't your fault, my love; it was an accident and the boy will heal quickly. Try and think of tomorrow when we land in South Africa. I think the *Wanderer* sails for Durban by the end of next week, so all being well we'll be on the last leg of our journey soon.'

'Ah yes ... Zulu country.' Victoria's eyes brightened. How lucky the Zulu heathens would be to have her wonderful Frank bringing them the one true message, Christianity. She put her arms around his neck. 'I know you will be wonderful with the native people, Frank, but were the six months we spent in England sufficient for me? Do I know enough to be a missionary?'

Their own church fathers at the Wesleyan Methodist Church in Cleveland had arranged for them to work with the London Missionary Society, the organisation which arranged to send missionaries of various denominations all over the world. Frank had been quite clear for years that he wished to go to South Africa, so they dealt with the British organisation and its established mission stations there.

Her husband kissed her, with a deal of passion. 'You know enough, my darling.'

They anchored that night not half a mile off shore, and the following morning, as the smell of bacon and eggs emanated from the breakfast saloon, Victoria, Phoebe, Frank, Jane, John Lockley and Ellen stood looking over the *Regent Three*'s side towards the town. It nestled at the foot of the table-shaped mountain which was half-hidden by a frothy covering of slate grey that sat over the upper part of the two-mile-long face.

John Lockley had slept fitfully, and he looked rather pale in the morning light, but he was in his usual good spirits as he turned to his aunt and said, 'There's a tablecloth on the mountain.'

'Whatever do you mean?'

'The second mate was explaining yesterday about Table Mountain. Because it's flat-topped, when the wind is in the south-east the cloud cover forms rapidly on the top, and thus, dear Aunt Jane, the local folk say you have a tablecloth on it!'

Ellen pointed to the distant buildings. 'There it is, Cape Town! They have fellows as black as night here, don't they, Aunt Jane?'

'Yes, Ellen, the indigenous people are the Bantu, I'm told, though perhaps they shall not be so black as brown, dear. And perhaps there shall not be many in the town.'

16

'Of course there shall be.' There was scorn in John Lockley's voice. 'Don't you see, Aunt Jane? They'll be the servants and the labourers in the colony. It stands to reason. That's what happens in these places, the local folk do the manual work.'

'Oh, why yes, that's true, I suppose.' She turned to Victoria. Her friend had yet another voyage ahead of her.

'How long will it take to Durban?'

Victoria looked thoughtful. 'Well, as it's nine hundred sea miles from here, a week or so if the weather's fair.'

Jane's eyes turned skywards. The very thought of another week at sea made her feel ill. How very pleased she was that she did not have to continue on to Natal as her friend did. Although at the same time she knew she would miss Victoria very much, for she was so kind and dear and caring.

'I can hardly wait to be ashore,' came Ellen's excited voice as she hung over the bulwark.

Her brother turned to her. 'And nor can I, for it will be as different from Mother England as it is possible to be. Why, there're elephants and great herds of wild beasts and lions; they roam around, you see! And are known to kill men.'

His sister's mouth arched in distaste.

Half an hour later they drew up the anchor and long boats towed them into the wharf. There were hundreds of people there to meet the ship, all manner of hustle and bustle; people calling greetings, and traders and pedlars and wharf labourers, and folk simply watching the spectacle.

Pulleys had been mounted all along the shore bulwark of the ship to hoist and lift barrels and commodities down to the wharf.

John Lockley watched the wharf labourers excitedly, for as he had predicted, they were mostly tall, beautifully proportioned black men who seemed to lift the heavy boxes effortlessly in their massive muscular arms.

'Aren't they wonderful?' he whispered to Ellen.

'I ... I'm not sure,' she answered, looking at him with uncertainty.

'Oh, Ellen.' There was disapproval in his voice.

Wishing to please him, she quickly added, 'But they certainly are the most unusual men I've ever seen.'

'That's the spirit,' he said as he moved away towards Jane,

who was looking steadily along the rows of faces upturned towards them. Ellen's eyes followed her brother until he joined their aunt and the three McLeans.

Jane shook her head. 'I cannot see Edgar anywhere.' Then, with an enveloping gesture, she motioned the two children towards the gangplank, saying, 'Come along down to the pier. The luggage follows.'

'Aye,' agreed Mannie, Jane's maid and helper, 'after six and a half whole weeks on this Godforsaken craft I cannot wait to have solid ground beneath my feet and all.'

'Where's Uncle Edgar?' John Lockley asked, as the four of them bunched at the opening in the ship's side.

Jane shook her head again. Then she exclaimed gleefully, 'I think I see him!' and began to push them ahead of her. 'Now carefully, please, take small steps, John Lockley, and be watchful of your wrist.'

As John Lockley followed his sister he felt a little hand slip into his right palm and he looked down at Phoebe's upturned face.

'Jan Larkley, I . . . I'm sorry you hurt yourself.' She looked so serious, frowning up at him with her little brow so very puckered with concern, that he could not help smiling. 'I'm all right, Phoebe. Mr Fleet said it'll be good as new in eight weeks.'

Suddenly the child did an odd thing: she took his bound wrist in her plump little hands and kissed it gently. Then lifting her six-year-old eyes up to his, stated, 'Phoebe make it better.'

To John Lockley, a boy of fourteen, it was a funny, childish gesture, and was soon set aside, but it was something that would return to his mind now and then and somehow it would give him strange comfort.

The McLeans followed down the gangplank, and when they were all on the wharf Jane forced her way through the crowds towards a tall man looking up to the ship. As she came closer to him, her smile faded; it was not her brother.

'There must be someone here to meet us,' reasoned John Lockley. 'For even if Uncle were held up with business matters, he would send someone in his stead.'

Soon Victoria and Frank were met by the superintendent, the Reverend Adrian Charles, who arrived in a four-wheeled

18

dray. He was the leading Methodist cleric in the colony, so the McLeans were being treated royally.

Victoria was loath to leave Jane and the children but Jane insisted. 'Please, my dear, don't be silly, Edgar will be along at any second.' She clung to her friend to say goodbye. 'And you will write to me care of my brother's firm here, won't you?'

Victoria smiled. 'Of course I will.'

'Now, go . . . Go.'

The McLeans and their boxes and trunks soon departed and so too did most of the other immigrants. Now the foursome stood together on the wharf, looking expectantly this way and that. After half an hour, Jane was becoming very concerned.

'P'raps he didn't know we were comin' and all,' commented Mannie, her sharp features darkening in dismay.

'Really, Mannie dear!' Jane's exasperation showed as she tapped her toe in a determined way on the wooden spars beneath her feet. 'Of course he knows! He was informed months since.'

'Well, he ain't here,' came Mannie's irrefutable reply.

And so the minutes passed until they became an hour and more and the wharf was decidedly less frequented. It was around twelve noon now and the sun shone vengefully down from a cloudless sky. The temperature was climbing close to eighty degrees, and the humidity was higher than it ever reached at home. The lonely foursome sheltered in the shade of a warehouse veranda, still looking hopefully for the invisible relative.

'This is terrible,' announced Ellen, who had removed her gloves and was fanning herself with them. She sat on one of the trunks, crossing and uncrossing her legs. 'I think I'm going to faint.'

'Now don't give me that nonsense,' replied her aunt, opening her handbag and taking out a small bottle of laudanum. 'Here, smell this, there's a dear, and stop complaining, please, for we are all hot.'

'And the light . . . I mean, it's so bright,' the girl continued woefully, while sniffing the laudanum, 'it hurts my eyes.'

'I think the reverse,' spoke up her brother. 'The light is wonderful, I've never seen the world with such clarity before . . . it's exceptional.'

'Oh,' replied Ellen in a small voice, 'then I suppose it's not so bad.'

John Lockley patted her shoulder approvingly and she gave him an imitation of a smile.

'Well, I care not whether it's the most wonderful light in God's universe,' declared Jane. 'It's of little consequence when we're in such a predicament. How I wish I hadn't sent the McLeans so swiftly on their way.'

'Oh, what can we do?' wailed Mannie. 'And home so far away.'

John Lockley looked to his aunt. 'We can't wait here forever, can we? We must do something. You do know where Uncle Edgar lives, don't you, Aunt Jane?' He was looking at her sceptically.

'Of course I *know* where he lives!' Jane began, and then noticed a man running along the wharf towards them, waving his arms.

'He's here at last,' exclaimed Ellen, jumping from her seat on the trunk.

But the closer he came the more sure Jane was that the man was not her brother. He ran right up to them, a sun-browned, good-looking individual with a solid, well-defined jaw below an aquiline nose and handsome hazel eyes.

'Miss Jane Harrison?' he queried, removing his white hat.

'Yes.'

'I'm Christopher Nelson, your brother's partner.'

'Oh, thank goodness, we thought we were stranded.'

The newcomer's face was serious and there was a concerned expression in his eyes. 'I did everything I could to get here on time. There's much to tell you.'

'Where's Edgar?' Jane asked.

Christopher Nelson's head bent momentarily, allowing a lock of his sun-lightened hair to fall over his forehead as he lifted his hand to hold his jaw. Then he met her eyes. 'There's no easy way to answer that, Miss Harrison. I'm so sorry to tell you, Edgar died last week in Grahamstown from a fever that attacked him a month since. I was with him. Subsequently, I've travelled at speed to be here to meet you.'

Mannie immediately began to cry, while Jane looked with disbelief at the man in front of her.

Now Ellen too began sobbing, and John Lockley, standing

in shock at his sister's side, automatically lifted his arm in a comforting gesture around her shoulders.

'I . . . I don't believe it. It cannot be.' Jane was stunned.

Christopher Nelson shook his head sadly. 'I'm only sorry that it is so.' He took her by the arm and steered her across to one of the travelling trunks. She sat there staring up at him with eyes that begged him to say his message was not true.

John Lockley left Ellen's side and came close to the man. He swallowed hard. 'Sir, did our uncle say anything? Did he . . . give you any instructions about us?'

Christopher ruffled the boy's hair affectionately. 'Well, lad, he was most concerned for you all, yes, most concerned. In his final moments he asked me to tell his sister here of his true devotion. I have been his companion, his friend and his partner, and I was privy to his innermost thoughts, and there's no doubt that he provided for you all, very clearly and very well.'

Jane shook her head. 'I must try to steady myself. Yes, I need time to reflect. Nothing needs to be done in a hurry.'

Mr Nelson crouched down on one knee in front of Jane, looking sympathetically at her. 'Unfortunately, I have to tell you that we do need to do some things rather swiftly, Miss Harrison.'

'Why? What do you mean?' asked John Lockley, for his aunt, who in her dismay could not utter a word.

'I mean, there's much which needs to be done, and, unhappily, done in a hurry. You see, Miss Harrison, your brother and I had decided to leave Cape Town and go to Durban; that's in Natal . . . the colony to the north. I actually met him up there years ago before it was a colony. He sold his house here in Cape Town, where no doubt you thought you were going to live, before we set out for Grahamstown. We'd already purchased new properties in Natal a year ago. We have the start of a thriving building business up there. He was very partial to that part of the country.'

Jane could not believe her ears. She forced herself to speak. 'What? Sold his house? Where on earth are we to live?'

Christopher sighed. He had regarded Edgar as his true friend and had fought hard to keep him alive, but the fever had been one he had never seen before and he had lost Edgar to it.

Telling this lady and her charges about the new plans in store for them would have been difficult even had Edgar been alive to do it himself. He strove to find the right words. 'Miss Harrison, the truth is, you have an excellent property to live in: a fine, large house and many, many acres of ground, and in addition there is more land in Pietermaritzburg and upcountry too. I'm sure the house will be to your liking; don't be concerned, it's a very nice place. Edgar saw to that.'

Jane's eyes widened. 'But I'm not following you, Mr Nelson. No, not following you at all.'

'I'm not either,' wailed Ellen.

'I think I am, Aunt Jane,' spoke up John Lockley.

'Are you?' Jane was incredulous. 'Well, there's a dear, tell me.'

'He means we have a house in Natal, Aunt Jane.'

Christopher Nelson could see the consternation and panic in the woman's eyes. He remained kneeling in front of her and nodded calmly. 'Yes, that's right. The properties in Natal are yours, and you can live comfortably in the house near Durban all right. Your brother had made arrangements for you to go there with him, you see. That was the plan. He'd intended to be back in plenty of time to meet you at the ship and then to transfer with you to Durban. And Miss Harrison, I understand that you don't wish to talk of your brother's will, but nevertheless everything of his in its entirety goes to you and your other brothers. And as you are here, the abode in Durban is now entirely at your disposal, and therefore I suggest . . .'

'Houses? Properties? Durban?' interjected Jane in a voice of alarm.

'Yes, that's right.'

'And my brother's dead.'

'Unfortunately, that is so.'

'No. I don't have the strength. I simply cannot go to this Durban place. Not without Edgar. It's unthinkable. I brought the children here on the understanding we were to live here in Cape Town until the arrival of their father after his Indian service. He wants to live here, in South Africa, with Edgar. But now there's no Edgar because of this horrible fever, and . . . and I . . .' She put her head in her hands and finally the tears came welling to dampen her palms.

Ellen and Mannie began to cry again, and even John Lockley's face had crumpled unhappily.

Mr Nelson stood and touched Jane tenderly on the shoulder. 'I'm so sorry, but everything will be all right. I shall accompany you all the way.'

Jane could not believe this was happening. She looked up into Christopher Nelson's face, appearing almost child-like in her grief as he smiled reassuringly down at her.

CHAPTER TWO

It was close to three weeks later, when, nine hundred sea miles away from Cape Town, a cannon sounded at Fort Natal on an overcast day in early November, alerting the inhabitants of Durban that the schooner *Wanderer*, under the captaincy of Jack Joss, had anchored beyond the bar and safely deposited the royal mail and fourteen immigrant passengers into the cargo ship which in turn was to set them down on the yellow beaches of Durban in the colony of Natal. The fourteen passengers for the cargo boat consisted of two couples, each with a baby, and Jane, Christopher, Ellen, John Lockley, Mannie, Victoria, Frank and Phoebe. They had peered attentively from the decks of the *Wanderer* upon the long bluff, the high ridge, the sandy point, and the mountains in the distance. They, in fact, looked with even more interest than had Vasco da Gama three hundred and fifty-five years previously: for while he was the first European to see this place, he was not, as they were, about to make it his home.

Christopher would have preferred to bring his party on the new screw steamer *Sir Robert Peel* which had just begun to ply between the Cape and Durban, but it was not due to make the run again until December.

Victoria and Frank had been amazed and delighted to encounter Jane and the children on board the schooner; although consequently they had been sorry to hear the reason.

Now, as John Lockley climbed carefully one-handed down the narrow side ladder from the steamer to the rocking and bouncing cargo ship, his eyes sought the opening between the sandhills of The Point and the long green-covered Bluff. He strained to catch sight of the settlement, but could make out nothing, though he could clearly see the breakers defining the bar, which left only some ten to fourteen feet of water over

24

which they must cross. As far as his eyes could see the entire yellow-sanded shore was edged with continuously rising foam and spray.

His heart was beating rapidly. He looked back up to the schooner to see Ellen peering over the bulwark at him with frightened eyes. 'Don't be afraid, Nell,' he called, as he bumped against the side of the ship. 'Look at me, I'm not concerned.' But his sister's eyes did not lose their alarm, and when she was hoisted out in a chair fashioned from a cask, and deposited in the bobbing boat, she was trembling. Her brother put his arm around her shoulders to comfort her, and she smiled weakly in an attempt to hide her fear. Little Phoebe, however, who was carried down in her father's arms, seemed to enjoy the adventure as much as did John Lockley.

The boatmen gave the word to let go from the *Wanderer*, hoisted the jib, dropped astern and sheeted home the mainsail to head for the breakers. They were all seasoned 'crossers of the bar', which according to the wind was not always reached without tacking.

Suddenly the cargo boat was surrounded by a large school of skimming albacore, resembling their cousin, the mackerel, beautifully marked and powerful in the water. John Lockley hung over the side of the boat enthusiastically. 'Look at them, Nell . . . Aunt Jane . . . aren't they wonderful?'

Phoebe pointed excitedly. 'Look, Dadda, look!'

As they neared the breakers on the bar, and could see the height of the waves, John Lockley lost some of his confidence and edged closer to Jane, who was already clutching Ellen in her arms. Victoria's eyes had been closed since they dropped away from the mother ship, and now her husband, who held their little girl, put his free arm around her.

Christopher Nelson was eyeing the waves. 'We shall have to go below,' he informed them. At the same time one of the sailors shouted, 'All below deck now, please, like sensible folk . . . It be for your own good as we shall take on a few heavy slops as we cross today, no doubt about it.'

The hatches were lifted and a dark hole was exposed in the deck.

'Down there?' said Victoria. 'I'm not going down there.'

Christopher looked sympathetic. 'Mrs McLean, you must, for the boat will swing and jump as she crosses the bar.'

'Aye,' shouted one of the sailors, a toothless old salt with skin leathery and sun-darkened. 'Ye don't want to be water-logged or taken overboard to drown, do ye? No, madam, it's down ye go and sit low, arms around yeer knees, make yeer centre of gravity low.'

'Do you mean you've done this before?' Jane was looking at Mr Nelson incredulously.

'Yes, Miss Harrison, I have, as you must. Please go below, so we can cross over safely. It's the only way.'

'Oh my God.'

Now Mannie's eyes filled with tears as she turned to Jane. 'I didn't know we was to be locked up in this place or I tell ye, Miss Harrison, I'd not a come, no, not for anything in this world.'

Jane put out her hand and patted the woman on the shoulder. 'Me neither, Mannie dear, me neither.'

So down they went, into the hot, stuffy darkness of the floating cellar, all protesting.

The old salt's face appeared above them. 'It's only for a few minutes, to keep yeer things dry and so as we land all fourteen of ye, none missin', as we are meant to do.'

Then, complete and stifling blackness as he fixed the hatch over their heads.

Frank held Victoria and Phoebe close while Jane put her arms around Ellen and John Lockley and bent forward. Mannie, in crouched position, kept mumbling, 'Lord save us.' Christopher, the experienced, sat grasping his knees.

Thud ... the cargo boat jumped.

Thud ... it turned around to face the way it had come.

In the blackness the fourteen souls had no way of orienting, and the craft seemed to take terrible plunges, almost turning over, bringing them falling on to each other. As they rallied to regain their seats and bemoan their bruises, they heard the cry, 'Here comes another!' and were again lifted high in the air and dumped unceremoniously down.

'We'll sink,' sobbed Mannie. And the groans from the others showed that they believed her.

Never again, thought Jane to herself as an elbow caught her in the face and she tumbled forward. Then, righting herself, she remembered John Lockley's broken limb. 'Be careful of your arm, John Lockley.'

Now the two babies were crying loudly and Ellen joined Mannie in sobbing.

The boat continued to rock violently, jumping high in the air as if leaving the sea forever, then smashing heavily down again.

John Lockley was almost pleased they were in jet blackness, for he was truly frightened, and as he heard little Phoebe's scared voice near him, 'Too dark, Dadda, too dark', tears were breaking silently from his eyes. Once more they lifted up as the boat turned completely round, before crashing down to be hit by another wave tipping them all again to one side.

'Our Father, who art in Heaven...' began Victoria in a high-pitched voice.

Then through the thunderous noise of the surf, the wailing and crying, came Christopher Nelson's calm voice. 'It's nearly over now ... I can tell. Don't worry, we'll soon be across.'

Frank answered him steadily. 'I'm sure you're right, Mr Nelson. You've experienced it before. Be calm, everyone.'

Groping around her, Jane found Ellen and clutched her, then felt for John Lockley's hand and held it tightly.

She was thinking, *No ... never again. I will have to stay in this Natal, no matter what ... whether I hate it or no, I shall have to remain. I could never live through this torment a second time. Lord in Heaven, I never wish to be on the sea again as long as I live.* She joined Victoria in the Lord's prayer, 'For Thine is the Kingdom, the power and the glory, For ever and ever, Amen.'

The boat dipped again.

Then, quite suddenly, it had righted itself and they realised everything was on an even keel once more. Then came the solace of daylight upon them as a cheerful voice sounded above. 'So we're over the bar. Wasn't too bad, eh? And ahead lies Port Natal.'

Jane released Ellen, and looking to her other side, dropped the hand she held in shock. 'Oh, my! I ... excuse me, Mr Nelson, I ... beg your pardon. I thought I held my nephew. Oh dear.'

Christopher Nelson said nothing. He was smiling at her, an odd smile, saying something that she failed to interpret.

They stood up and strong arms reached down to help them

climb once more to the deck. They were all a little shaky on their legs, but the sight of the mild green bushes on the lofty bluff gliding gently by calmed them.

And now, as the boat turned into the harbour, shutting the bar and the *Wanderer* from view, they gasped in admiration, for they were rewarded by one of the most beautiful sights they would ever see: a brilliant, aquamarine landlocked bay, some seven and a half square miles in size and twelve miles in circumference, delivering one unbroken sheet of glistening water framed by shimmering, brilliant yellow sand and fringed all round with glossy, gleaming greenery, emerald bright.

'Oh, isn't it wonderful?' shouted John Lockley. Forgotten was the episode in the darkness below deck, and he could not contain his pleasure at the sight. He stood to gain a better view.

'Yes,' agreed Christopher, 'it always is.'

Two tiny trading vessels and two cargo boats were at anchor and a few lighters and rowing boats rested on the beach.

Soon they could see the port office flagstaff, and the harbour groyne of stone at right angles to the beach, then the port captain's wooden cottage half hidden in the bushes, and finally an imposing gable-ended structure of brick with a slated roof, a red-coated sentry walking back and forth in front. It was the Custom House, one of the few brick or stone buildings in the colony; many were yet wattle and daub and thatch, for they were the most easily available building materials.

The crew took in the sail and soon the cargo ship bumped upon the beach beside the skeleton of a jetty presently being built.

'Oh dear!' Victoria turned to her husband. 'How on earth will we get ashore?'

'I'll carry you, my love.'

'No need for that, sir, no, not at all.' One of the sailors pointed to a group of natives standing by a small man dressed in white with a manila hat sitting jauntily upon his head. 'There's yer transport, missus.'

'What?'

The natives, all tall, with muscular long legs and perfect proportions, wore only the mutya, a belt of oxhide, from which hung a fringe of monkey tails. Their marvellous physiques called for admiration, but to the newcomers their scant attire was bewildering.

'They shall bring ye in sedan-chair fashion. It be part of their job.'

'Oh my Lord,' exclaimed Mannie.

Along the beach ranged all sorts of curious folk come to see the new arrivals. Resident wives with their children, ox-wagon drivers and their natives, merchants, one or two longshoremen and a small party of off-duty soldiers from the blockhouse.

Soon, on the shout of one of the sailors, the stalwart black men, laughing and joking, ran into the water to stand beside the boat, ready for their first passenger.

Victoria McLean was fascinated. How different all this was. It was primitive, but she had known it would be. They were here to do God's work, and she was prepared to accept it would not be accomplished easily. Rewards would come in time. She turned to smile at Jane just as Christopher took her friend's arm, saying, 'Come along, Miss Harrison.'

Jane had been quiet for a long time. Events had picked her up and swept her along. Cape Town had been outpost enough for an English lady used to the tilled green fields and civilised security of The Grange in the heart of England. But the events since hearing of Edgar's death had frightened her. Once more she had been on a voyage, ever farther from home. And now they had arrived, after that frightful boat ride, the most fearsome event she could ever recall, into what appeared to her a very unsophisticated backwater. She was surprised to see the native people were veritably naked; she was not shocked, for she understood that the entire world did not conform to her code of respectability. But she did not like Ellen and John Lockley, at fifteen and fourteen, exposed to these things.

Why had Edgar decided to sell up and come here? It had been wrong of her brother to assume so much with her life and those of her charges. Ah, but she was here and here she would stay, for she would never cross that bar again . . . no, never in her life. She managed to smile at Victoria as, with Christopher's aid, she climbed reluctantly on to the side of the boat and tentatively stepped into the arms of a native. In a few seconds she stood safely on the sand and shortly all the women were beside her.

The men took off their shoes and hose and waded ashore. Then began the long wait to unload their trunks and cases of luggage and numerous items of furniture.

29

The small man in the manila hat came forward with a smile to greet the new arrivals. He introduced himself as George Cato, the agent for J. C. Byrne's Emigration Scheme, which had recently been instigated by the businessman John Byrne, and which brought the settlers out from Great Britain. He immediately recognised Christopher. 'Mr Nelson, you've returned, eh? Where's Mr Harrison?'

'Ah, good day to you, Mr Cato. Mr Harrison unfortunately won't be coming. I'm afraid it's very sad news of him I bear.' Christopher explained in low tones about Edgar's death, and the agent doffed his hat and offered his condolences when introduced to Jane, then made his way to the other passengers, whom he in fact had claim upon, for they had come to Natal under the emigration scheme he represented.

There to meet the McLeans was the Reverend Jonas Fitch with his wide, almost toothless smile; he had lost five of his front teeth to a drunken Matabele warrior's spear in Griqualand seven years before. He had come today from the Wesleyan mission, which was a snug little house encircled by large wild fig trees at the beach end of a long, straight path leading from the Market Square. He greeted Victoria and Frank amiably, lifting little Phoebe high in the air. He would help organise their travels out to their own mission station over a hundred miles to the north-west beyond the Tugela River.

Ellen stood close by her brother, watching Christopher instruct the black carriers in the loading of the luggage into long covered wagons, each pulled by six or eight oxen. As their muscular arms twined around the trunks and boxes, raising them easily to the ox cart, she spoke softly in her brother's ear. 'These people are so strong,' and Christopher, overhearing her, replied, 'Yes, they are, Ellen, wonderfully strong. You see, the natives here have never had canoes or boats of any kind: they know naught of their workings. Sometimes I think they fancy a boat has a sort of will of its own. So they keep away from craft of any kind, and employ their strength in hauling, lifting, pushing and loading. They're pretty good at that.'

'Sir? Where is Durban?' asked John Lockley.

'A mile and a half that way.' He gestured along The Point with his left hand.

30

'Oh dear, haven't we come far enough already?' groaned Mannie.

'Won't be long now,' Frank consoled the maid. 'God will give you the strength to get to your destination, young lady.'

And Mannie, who had not been called 'young lady' for twenty years, beamed at him.

It seemed ages but finally the ox wagons were loaded.

Christopher supported Jane as she climbed up into the cart. It was such an uncomfortable, awkward conveyance, but then nothing else would be able to travel along the extended beach. The bush growing down to the sand was like a solid wall filled with huge cactus trees and caster-oil plants and what looked like gooseberry bushes intertwined with endless strong, sweet-scented creepers with little white and yellow flowers.

Just as Christopher climbed up into the cart there was a shout. 'Helloa there, Nelson,' called a rotund man in a blue hip-jacket, his large stomach poking from beneath to rest on his white trouser band.

'Yes, Port Captain Bell?'

The man had been along the beach, hands behind his back, stepping out a short quarter-deck walk, and listening to the talk of the sailors who had brought the cargo ship in over the bar.

'I've just heard the terrible sad news, sir ... about Mr Harrison. Now that's a damn blow to us all, that is. I do commiserate, I do.'

'Thank you very much. Let me introduce Miss Harrison, Mr Harrison's sister; this is Port Captain Bell.'

Jane leant forward from the wagon and the sailor took off his cap. 'I'm very sorry, ma'am, for yer brother were a credit to this community. He and Mr Nelson here have made work for folk as what thought the end had come.' He turned again to Christopher. 'Ye won't be closing the brickworks and things will ye, I ask?'

'No. We shall keep them running as Edgar would have wanted.'

And to Christopher's great surprise Jane had an opinion on the matter. 'Yes, Port Captain Bell, we shall endeavour to do just that.'

The ox wagon lurched forward to bump along the sand

around the line of the bay where the ever-breaking surf continued its rhythm.

John Lockley was thrilled and delighted. His exuberance bubbled out of him as he turned this way and that, watching the black men with their long, loping strides running ahead of the wagon, and concentrating on the bush growing to the sand's edge in the hope of seeing a wild animal. Ellen's feelings varied from her brother's. She was neither averse to her surroundings, nor enamoured of them. It was far too hot, that was certain, the whole country was. The heat seemed to rise up from the ground, encompassing everything like a net. But the whole place was extraordinary, so why not the climate?

Just over two months ago she had been reading Shakespeare to Mr Luton in the schoolroom of The Grange and counting the stocks of crisp starched linen with the housekeeper. Now The Grange was so remote to her, it was as if it were on the moon. She had been transported to a different world, where the sun was like a golden fury in the too bright sky; where black men did the housework and the cleaning; and where, it was said, wild animals strayed up to the back doors of houses on the edges of settlements. It was all so fundamental ... primitive ... raw. She was somewhat confused by it, but she did not dislike it She knew she was fascinated by the long, semi-naked, fluid black bodies moving ahead of the wagons. They were getting near the real Africa, as John Lockley called it, she could feel that.

She looked sideways to her brother and at that moment he took her arm with his good hand, pointing to a movement in the trees. 'There, did you see that, Nell? It was probably a small monkey or a local ant bear.'

She smiled at him. Her brother was so clever, so knowledgeable.

The wagon driver, a stocky man with a broad back and thick neck, turned from where he walked at the side of the cart and looked up at the brother and sister. 'There are some deadly fellows in the rivers, you know – alligators. Ugly great lizard things that regularly kill horses; and the python is prevalent hereabouts too, caught one eighteen feet long just before you left here the last time, didn't we, Mr Nelson?'

'Oh my God!' exclaimed Mannie. Her outburst expressed the shared feeling of them all.

Christopher shook his head at the man. 'For heaven's sake, Thomkins, it's not that bad.' He turned on the seat beside Jane and smiled at them all. 'Don't take that too much to heart. They don't come into the town. Thomkins is over-telling it a bit.'

'But it seems they are in the countryside.' Jane spoke haltingly. She had not imagined a snake could grow that long, and she was thinking with concern of her friend, Victoria, who was heading into the inland.

'Miss Harrison, don't be worried. Why, as long as people are careful, there's no reason for concern at all.'

When the entourage finally entered the settlement, they realised that the streets, too, were of sand; there was no paving of any kind. Jane sighed. It came from the soul of her. How could Victoria, who was so gentle and ladylike, be going on past this Godforsaken settlement into a positive wilderness to live with poor savages? She actually turned round to peer at her friend in the following dray as if observing her might somehow explain the workings of the missionary woman's mind.

Ten minutes later, they were in Smith Street, which ran the entire length of the community. They had passed a few stone buildings, but most were houses of wattle and daub and some huts of thatch, usually with a good-sized trench running around them to carry off the rainwater. Some had a light trellis porch of reeds, and a wide slab of stone for a doorstep, with a scraper of hoop iron beside it. There were some stores and business premises, all primitive-looking, and, under large shade trees, some cattle wandered about.

Here Victoria, Frank and little Phoebe waved goodbye, for they were staying with Pastor Fitch for a few days before commencing their onward journey. 'I shall come and see you before we leave,' Victoria called after Jane.

As the wagon turned into Gardiner Street, Christopher pointed with his slender, sun-browned hand. 'That's where the other two families from the *Wanderer* will spend their next few weeks. It's the Emigrants' Barracks.' He was referring to a rough wooden building surrounded by a group of tents, affording temporary accommodation to those arrivals whose allotments of land were subdivisions of the original farms granted to Byrne and Co. Invariably, the surveys of their allotments were not completed when they arrived in Durban,

33

and thus they spent their first weeks, and sometimes months, in this rude fashion. 'It's partitioned off inside, but not too private, I'm afraid.'

'Poor things,' commented Ellen.

'Yes, Miss Harrison, I'm afraid the immigrants are often disappointed with the lack of comforts when they arrive. I'm not an enthusiast of our emigration schemes. So many colonists arrive and, in fact, never see their allotments of land, losing their initial deposits altogether.' Then he smiled. 'But you're different. We have a proper house for you. Mr Harrison saw to that.'

And yes, it was a proper house, certainly by Durban standards, though nowhere near the beauty and opulence of The Grange, so far away back in England. But it was large and substantial in comparison with the others they had seen, and was built of bricks with a slate roof. There was still work being done, and from where they stood at the front, they could see a number of men, both black and white, toiling on a wing which ran westwards.

The house stood in the beginnings of a lawn, a mile beyond the edge of the settlement, on a tiny incline between the roads to the Umgeni and Pietermaritzburg. A line of well-cared-for mimosa trees ran from the wide veranda across the property, their fluffy yellow flowers adding a splash of welcome colour to the scene.

John Lockley spoke optimistically. 'Well, I think it's a marvellous house in marvellous surroundings with a marvellous view, eh, Nell?'

'I . . . suppose so.'

'We had many plans for this property.' Christopher lifted his hand towards the house. 'Give us time, and we shall make it as Edgar Harrison envisioned it.' He walked ahead up the stone steps to stand under the roof of the wide veranda. 'Welcome to Mimosa. Mr and Mrs Veldbron, your caretaker and house-keeper, await you inside.' And with a wide sweep of his arm he motioned them through the open door.

In the long hall stood Matilda and Dirk Veldbron: she, small and rotund, with a wide face, warm, friendly eyes and a matching smile; he, big with a round face and sun-etched wrinkles around his eyes. He had been one of the Voortrekkers who had left the Cape Colony in 1836 and gone on the great trek, but had finally found himself in Durban working for Mr Harrison and Mr Nelson, an easier life than the hardships of farming in often hostile territory.

Mrs Veldbron curtsied. 'Welcome to Mimosa. I'm so sorry it's such a warm day and all.'

Jane smiled and took her hand.

John Lockley spoke up. 'I'd call it *hot*, though I'm not complaining, don't misunderstand.'

The woman beamed at him. 'Yes, young master,' she answered. 'I suppose it is more correct to say hot, although this being only spring, it's going to get much hotter, don't you know.'

'Oh dear,' remarked Ellen.

Four black men had appeared to help them with their luggage. They wore slightly more than the scanty mutya of the beach natives and each had feathers braided in his hair.

It was not long before Mrs Veldbron had made a 'cuppa', as she called it, and they felt better for the refreshment, but even with the help of the natives and two young men from the brickyard, it was hours before they were finally unpacked and settled in their new abode.

Mrs Veldbron prepared their evening meal and, after eating, the new arrivals retired early to their rooms.

Ellen and John Lockley had become used to sleeping under the mosquito nets during the week they spent in Cape Town, and while it was a hot, steamy night there was a strong breeze reaching them from the bay. It had been a day of exertion and by half past nine all the house was quiet.

But one oil lamp still burned and one of the new arrivals sat late into the night by the window, thinking, her head resting from time to time on her hands. By the light of the moon Jane fancied she could see the small settlement on the edge of Natal Bay. Night had fallen early as it did in the southern lands, and it had been dark for hours. She was in her nightgown and had plaited her long hair in two braids to hang down across her shoulders. Her handsome mouth was set in a meditative line, and she tapped with her smooth oval fingernails on the wood of the sill. She was thinking of the last weeks and what had brought her here to this outpost, so detached from all she knew and understood.

When Joanna died Jane had been only twenty-one, and the

only adult female at The Grange, her mother having died two years before. She smiled wryly, as she recalled James's speech of entreaty to her. It had been about three weeks after Joanna's death. She had been cutting roses in the stone colonnade when she heard his measured steps behind her. He had worn an expression of uncertainty as he spoke. 'Janie, I know you loved Joanna well, and she you. I must go back to the regiment next week. Well, as you've no prospects of marriage at present, would you . . . could you help? I mean, will you look after my brood for a while? There's plenty of help, what with the servants. I'd just like to know they were taken care of by the family.' He coughed. 'I think dear Mother would have wanted that, you understand?'

She realised this was a blatant manipulative use of their mother's wishes. He cared little for herself, she knew that well. She was his only sister, but their natures did not blend. Even so, she could not refuse him; it was for the children's sake that she agreed.

Now, fourteen years later, the four older girls were all settled in their lives. Kate and Mary were married and Dorothy and Constance lived with their Aunt Conn and Uncle Andrew in Tralee in Ireland.

Yes, Jane had done as she had been asked; to such an extent that her prospects of marriage had diminished, and while there had been one or two gentlemen who had paid attention to her, she never allowed the relationships to develop. Her excuse was that she had no time to spare; the real reason was not one she acknowledged, for it sat deep within her consciousness and had to do with excitement and heroes and not with dull English squires.

And while she had felt capable of taking care of John Lockley and Ellen in Cape Town, this place was entirely different. Cape Town was exactly that, a proper town, settled for almost two hundred years, Europeanised, with character and beauty in its graceful streets. There were decent shops and carriages and parks and gardens. During the short time she was there she realised it had not only the necessities, but the niceties, of life, with twenty-three thousand people living there. Whereas here, she estimated, there were only a handful, perhaps six, eight hundred! Dear Lord, what was she doing in Durban?

And while she had been told this was a frontier settlement she had not been capable of understanding what that meant. Not until she had arrived here and experienced the place. Oh yes, now she knew what a 'frontier settlement' was. Here was a tiny township on the edge of a primitive country, with Pieter-maritzburg the only other settlement for hundreds of miles. No proper shops, no sealed roads, no parks or gardens, no carriages, no culture, no refinement. When she saw just how small Durban was; when she saw the cows and oxen roaming across what passed for the main street; when she saw the streets were all unpaved, all sand, and most of the houses wattle and daub; and finally when she had been told of the kraals of the Bantus on the distant hills, yes, then she had realised they were to live very close to what to her was primitive and savage.

Jane Harrison felt very out of her depth.

She had promised James she would look after his two youngest children; had promised to bring them to Cape Town and wait for him to come to them after his Indian service; but she had not promised to come to this miserable spot. Her eyes filled with tears and she sobbed to herself. How she had loved Edgar, and now she was never to see him again ... never. Because of his dreams, dreams so alien to her own, he was dead and she was here in Durban, Natal. And it was Christmas next month. What a Christmas.

Bitter tears ran from her eyes. She was about to leave the window when she stopped. Down below someone moved across the front of the house. Then she recognised him. It was Mr Nelson. She watched as he walked across the yard to stand looking towards the bay. Somehow she felt comforted knowing he was down there, and she wiped her eyes and moved over to her bed.

Just before she fell asleep she thought of Victoria, elegant and ladylike, who was continuing inland with a six-year-old child to some place called Fantele's Drift, near the Ibabanango Hills – wherever on God's earth *they* were – and she gave a long sigh in awe of her friend's courage.

At the very same time, in the Wesleyan mission house close to the pristine sands of the beaches of Durban, the subject of Jane's sigh stood over a crib covered by a mosquito net and listened to the steady breathing of her daughter. As she watched the small pale form through the net she felt the arm of her husband go about her and she turned to look into Frank's eyes.

'Well, my darling, Fitch tells me that our guides will be here next week.'

Victoria smiled, 'Good,' just as Phoebe stirred, giving a small moan. Her mother lifted the net to soothe her, absent-mindedly drawing the sign of the cross on the little one's forehead. The child was deep in a dream about sleek, muscular black men and oxen carts and long white beaches and lapping waves and her friend with the broken wrist, John Lockley.

In the solid house on the far hill, John Lockley dreamed too, of similar sleek, muscular black men, but in his dreams there were lions and wild beasts and alligators; though they were not frightening dreams but good dreams, happy dreams.

CHAPTER THREE

There was one school in Durban, a government boys' school in Field Street, in a new building only finished some months before, and run by the Reverend Nesbitt, an elderly, unmarried gentleman who had already acquired a reputation for ready use of his cane. There was no girls' school at all; and while Ellen was fifteen and, some would say, needed no more schooling, Jane disagreed.

So she decided to tutor the children herself until a suitable substitute could be found. Fortunately she had had an excellent education, so often neglected in females of her time; her father, the old General, had seen to that. She had been included in the schoolroom with her brothers and as each boy went off to Eton she continued on until she was seventeen, and her father had decided she was 'finished', as he put it.

Jane was well versed in the arts, and confident of her mathematic standard, but she was not sure of her capabilities in science. Thus some nights would find her poring over *Habberfield's Science Lessons* to prepare for her next day's teaching, which almost invariably John Lockley would dominate, for he had a natural scientific aptitude.

The threesome worked in an alfresco 'schoolroom', on the east veranda of the house where it was cooler. At the end of the lessons they would go their separate ways. Ellen loved to read and draw; and once his arm was healed, John Lockley found a new friend in Port Captain Bell and a new pastime in fishing.

In the first months after their arrival there had been many days of rain, for while it was summertime and very hot it was the wet season of the year, but by February the skies were clearer and by April the days were cooler and soon they were heading into their first southern autumn.

It was the end of April, a fair afternoon, when John Lockley passed swiftly down the sandy road that led to Durban. He rode his horse, Isiwukulu, which he had so named after hearing one of the boys in the kitchen say the word. He had had no idea at the time what it meant, he had simply liked the sound of it. Now he knew it meant 'goat' but he didn't care, he still liked the word, and sometimes if Isiwukulu misbehaved, John Lockley would lean forward and say in the animal's ear, 'It's true, you really are a goat, Isi!'

He was heading for the beach and a fishing trip with the Port Captain, and on his way he passed long, straggling groves of Hottentot figs, the branches dripping small, grey monkeys with black faces. He loved the little fellows. They would eat anything, and particularly liked fresh fruit, not that he could give them that too often, for that commodity was mostly dried. Fresh fruit was a delicacy rarely seen in the colony and coming only from the few trees that the colonists had planted and tended with loving care.

After a quarter of a mile, John Lockley found himself in the sandy streets of the settlement. He waved to the newly arrived Father Jean Baptiste Sabon, who lifted his green-lined umbrella in response as he wandered by in his rusty-coloured cassock and napless silk hat. He had already endeared himself to all the people of the settlement with his benevolence and simple piety, and he had quickly come to know all the children, Catholic and Protestant alike.

John Lockley continued on by the Market Square, a field filled with scrub, coarse grass and bushes, and dotted with clumps of wild date palms and strelitzia, the wild banana. Taking a short cut past the few tents of the latest group of immigrants, he rode diagonally through the centre of the square to come round the side of the Wesleyan chapel and into Smith Street. As he trotted by the mission he saw Mrs McLean and Phoebe in company with Dick King, who in 1842 had made one of those marathon rides of history when he had ridden six hundred miles south to Grahamstown in ten days to get relief for the English settlers of Durban who were being besieged by the Boers.

He shouted and waved and all three came towards him. Victoria McLean was a regular visitor at Mimosa and the friendship between her and Jane was now quite cemented. The McLeans had experienced ill luck since their arrival in the colony; for just when they had been ready to leave for their mission, the minister had been out in a violent storm, and had an accident where his horse had fallen on him. He had broken his collar bone, his leg and several ribs, and had been ill for a long time. It was only lately that he had been up and about again, and only as recently as last Sunday that he had finally felt well enough to visit Mimosa, where he had played cricket with Mr Nelson and John Lockley and some of the kitchen boys. John Lockley smiled now as he remembered how the American had thrown his hands in the air and shouted, 'Praise the Lord,' when he had caught out Mr Nelson for a duck.

John Lockley knew they would be leaving very soon for Zulu country where, at last, they would establish their mission.

Phoebe ran forward excitedly, shouting, 'Jan Larkley, Jan Larkley!' He halted and leapt down to the child.

'You take me to ride, Jan Larkley, please.'

'Phoebe,' her mother remonstrated, 'you shouldn't ask such a thing.'

But the boy did not mind for he had plenty of time before the appointed hour with the Port Captain, so Dick King lifted the child into his arms and while Victoria watched they rode in tandem a hundred or so yards down the road. Phoebe laughed and pointed and John Lockley, who always found the child's laugh contagious, began laughing too. As he pulled Isi's head round to trot back, Phoebe touched the boy's wrist. 'Your broken arm is better now, and so is Daddy's leg.'

When he handed her down to her mother, Victoria raised her steady gaze to the boy's. 'Would you please tell your aunt I shall walk over to Mimosa with her after church on Sunday, as she suggested.'

'I will,' he called as he rode away and Phoebe waved after him. He increased the pace as he rode, unconsciously stroking Isiwukulu's mane as he continued by Cato's flagstaff – a landmark raised by the Cato family – and out of Durban to cross the creek and pass through the natural archway formed by two huge 'waterboom', or red milkwood, trees.

A mile later he turned right off the path, and passing down through thick bush and a clump of palms that had been growing there for centuries, arrived on the beach where he found Port Captain Bell scraping the bottom of one of the small lighters that rested on the sand. Bell stood from his crouching position and rubbed his lower back. 'Age is a troublesome thing, Master Harrison, aches and pains and what all comes with it.'

John Lockley dismounted and ten minutes later they were pushing a rowing boat out through the shallow water into the bay.

The boy enjoyed the Port Captain's company; he had shown him how to find bait in the sand for fishing and had taught him to swim. 'I'm unusual, John Lockley, think a mite differently to others, eh? But I deem it necessary and all for every man who is in touch with the sea to learn to swim. And first ye must know how to float.' And he had shown the boy how, though it was a somewhat easier task for the rotund sailor than for the stripling boy. Nevertheless, John Lockley was becoming quite proficient and yesterday he had swum right round the lighter they used for fishing in the bay.

The Port Captain was a garrulous gent who needed only an interested ear like John Lockley's upon which to pour his revelations. He told the boy many stories, about his own life in the Royal Navy and the ports and places he had visited.

He told John Lockley, too, his version of the founding of Natal. It was from him that the boy learnt of Lieutenant Francis George Farewell and his party, the first settlers in 1824. 'See that there island just out in the bay.' The sailor pointed with a gutting knife. 'Salisbury Island, named by Lieutenant Farewell, after his brig, eh? Good ship, the *Salisbury*, but subsequently wrecked, ye understand.'

So John Lockley heard the tales of the Lieutenant and his companions, Nathaniel Isaacs, Henry Fynn and Lieutenant King. 'And some of me associates knew Farewell, they did, though 'twas before my time. Murdered he was, in Pondoland in thirty-one, eh? After he'd been trying to find an overland route to Grahamstown and all. They found him with his heart ripped out, lying at his feet.' He stopped here a few seconds for emphasis, so that his young listener could be properly horrified, then he nodded his sunburnt head in the direction of The Bluff, adding, 'And John Lockley, my boy, we still have Mr Henry Francis Fynn living up there on The Bluff, and being the native magistrate for Durban, eh? Long after his companions of those days are dead and gone.'

All the Port Captain's stories were detailed and long, and

John Lockley listened greedily. Later he would repeat them to his poor startled sister.

When the sailor had told his account of the Zulus, it took days. John Lockley was fascinated by the warlike Zulus and the bloodthirsty Shaka, the Zulu who had bound the tribes together in terror of him.

'Now he was something, my boy, thirty years ago he was something right enough. Organiser of the Zulu nation as a military power, eh? Banded 'em together good and proper. He swept through Natal, he did, eating up everybody and everything. Place was a waste almost as far south as the St John's River. Torture and killing were his delight.'

'Even of his own people?' John Lockley asked in surprise.

'Aye, even his own.'

John Lockley's eyes were glued to his companion. 'And what did he look like?'

'Ah now, he was fine-looking and tall, over six feet they say, and not an ounce of body fat.' Here he laughed and his stomach shook with his mirth. 'Not like me, eh, sonny? Oh yes, Shaka had a terrifyin' eye, was cruel and keen of killing. Made a feast of death he did. They say he made a temporary settlement up there when his impies came this way.' He pointed with his knife to the Berea Ridge behind Durban. 'His own people called him "The Hyena Man", which gives a clue as to his nature, don't it? Rivers ran red with blood.'

The Port Captain had filled the young boy's ears with numerous ghastly exploits of Shaka; stories of killing and more killing, long and gory; how the Zulu king murdered whole tribes of thousands of people by burying them alive; how he killed those who could no longer cry after they had been made to weep for days over his dead mother, Nandi; how his delight was to impale his enemies alive. John Lockley sat wide-eyed, at times revolted, but always fascinated; feasting on the fiendish, fantastic yarns. 'Oh yes, and Shaka was followed by another of the same mould, don't ye know, Dingane by name, eh? Liked a spot of war he did, too, as all them Zulus do. Knew how to terrify his own as well as his enemies.' This last piece of information the Captain had imparted to John Lockley only the previous day, and the boy had been thinking about it ever since. Today he had a question for the sailor.

It was a tranquil afternoon, pleasantly cool after the long

stretch of torrid summer heat, and the two companions enjoyed the weather almost as much as the expedition. They fished with that zeal which comes over true fishermen. They were baiting up their hooks when John Lockley half turned to face his friend. 'Sir, yesterday you said, about the Zulus ... you said they were all warlike. But we have Zulus at Mimosa and they are not warlike at all. They are quiet folk like Adanta who does the washing, and Thulmi and Umslopagas who work in the garden and the kitchen.'

'Ah now, different kettle of fish, Thulmi and them.' He patted the fishing tackle near his right hand for emphasis. 'They are the refugees, and children of the refugees, eh?'

'What's a refugee?'

'One who wants to get away from war, one who seeks sanctuary. The Zulus at yer place are like all the others in town. They came here deliberate like to ask us folks for protection from their own ... from being killed. They were frightened of the others, John Lockley, of being eaten up by the impies.'

'I see.'

'There were many of them before we were here who were in hiding and scraped a bit of food here and there. Some even took to eating fish, and ye know what that means to a true Zulu, eh?' John Lockley did. He had learnt that much since being here. Zulus abhorred fish. It would need to be a starving Zulu without hope who would eat fish.

'Oh yes, they hid in what crevices they could find. Terrified of Shaka and then Dingane, they were.'

John Lockley nodded, eyes and ears wide open. 'Tell me about Dingane.'

'Ah, Dingane, half-brother to Shaka, and one of those who sank their assegais into Shaka at the end.' The Port Captain threw his line far into the water, rolling his eyes to emphasise his coming revelations. 'Now Dingane did in Retrief, ye've heard of him? Boer leader along with Maritz. That's where we have the name of the town Pietermaritzburg coming from, eh? Pieter Retrief and Gerrit Maritz. Well, close to eight thousand of them Boers had trekked out from Cape Colony. Retrief and a number of Dutch farmers were massacred by Dingane only fifteen years back, February, eighteen thirty-eight. Retrief and his party were tricked into leaving their guns behind at

Dingane's kraal. Well, the slaughter at Weenen followed, when Dingane attacked the Boer laagers and murdered and disembowelled Boer women and children ... all manner of horrors perpetrated on the bodies. So, Blood River was the Boers' revenge. It followed Weenen and those Boers got their own back, eh? All in the same year, thirty-eight. They killed thousands of Zulus. I reckon your man Dirk Veldbron was in that little lot. There's no love lost between the Boers and the Zulus.'

Then another story occurred to him. He made a clucking sound of satisfaction. 'Ha, that reminds me, it was old Dingane that the Patagonian Martyr tried to convert.' Here he laughed and his stomach laughed too. 'Yes, the Patagonian Martyr tried his best to establish a mission among the Zulus, but the old Dingane was not interested in religion. No, merely wanted to know how to use a gun, he did.'

'Who was the Patagonian Martyr?'

The sailor didn't answer, for his attention was taken by a fierce tug on his line. 'Whoa, boy! Whoa, I've got one.'

And so he had, a foot-long sea bream. When he had removed the hook and put the fish in a bucket of water near at hand, John Lockley repeated his question. 'Who was the Patagonian Martyr?'

'Ah, him. Captain Allen Gardiner, Royal Navy, like me, eh? A missionary and kindly fellow. Hung around here for a while in the thirties, was a magistrate and all. Named the Berea ridge of hills behind town, didn't he?'

'And why was he called the Patagonian Martyr?'

The Port Captain folded his arms across his mighty stomach and nodded knowingly. 'In consequence of his being starved to death in that bleak, unsociable country, Patagonia.'

'Why, sir? What happened?'

And his enigmatic reply, 'He got into trouble with them disagreeable Patagonians, John Lockley, sonny, that's what happened.'

There was silence for a short time, during which John Lockley also caught a fish, longer by three inches than the Port Captain's. 'Mrs Veldbron will love this.'

When they were settled again the boy looked to his companion. 'Wasn't Dingane killed?'

'Ha ... assuredly. Those who live by the sword leave this

45

mortal coil by the sword; well-known maxim, eh? He was done in, in Swazi territory, by some of his own, eh? And that's how we got Mpande as king of the Zulus now, or Panda as we are wont to call him. He was Dingane's half-brother by a different mother. Mind you, he seems to have trouble of his own at present, for two of his sons, of which he has twenty up to now – bein' for a change a fertile Zulu king – are vying for his crown. They being Cetshwayo and Mbuyazi. They're always having a good time when they're blood-letting, that lot.'

'Really?'

'Really indeed, but the Zulus tend to keep their distance from the settlements now, though there was the odd scare in the early days. Some people are still fearful, eh?'

John Lockley was enthralled, and the Port Captain added, 'I've a friend, H. H. Garner by name; tall, stately bloke, lives way upcountry now, knows them Zulus and Hottentots and Bushmen and the like better'n any man alive. Lived with 'em for years, he has ... was here and abouts in the thirties; has many a story to tell, eh?' Here he stopped and a thought came to him. 'Now ye'll be able to ask him to tell ye a few yerself as ye'll be watering at his place on yer way towards the Tugela, no doubt.'

John Lockley looked amazed. 'What?'

'Well, as it's across the border into Zulu country ye're goin' in no time, eh? And what'll your aunt think about that, I wonder?'

'What? What's that, Captain Bell? Me? Going into Zulu country?'

'Don't ye know, laddie?'

'I know nothing of such a thing, sir.'

The sailor rubbed his chin. 'Oh, methinks I've spoken out of turn, eh? It appears ye have not been informed of such.'

John Lockley's face was radiant. He ran his hand back through his hair as he thought of it. The Tugela? Zulu country? What was this all about?

'Oh, Captain, do tell me, please. What do you know?'

The man did not know what to do now. He had been told yesterday by George Russell, the Harrison Nelson company manager, that Mr Nelson was going up to his property inside the border of Zululand and had thought to take young John Lockley for experience.

'Now, John Lockley, laddie, I'm sorry, for it is speaking out of turn I've been doing, eh? I must ask ye to say nothing about it until Mister Nelson makes it known to ye.' He shook his head. 'Promise me, laddie.'

'Can't you tell me any more?'

'Lord's breath, laddie, I've said too much already. Now promise me.'

It was a delighted boy who, carrying two fine sea bream, raced home on Isiwukulu to find that Mr Nelson was actually there speaking with his aunt.

At six o'clock Christopher had arrived at Mimosa. He usually did not leave the brickyard until the hour of seven or later and only occasionally ate dinner with Jane and the children, usually on a Saturday night.

Jane was wearing a pale blue gown, the skirt decorated with flounces and the fitting bodice topped with a deep blue collar. Her hands lay a little nervously in her lap. A messenger had come from the offices at noon to ask her to be home to meet with Mr Nelson. She had been wondering all afternoon what it could be about.

She had liked him right from the very first. And then liking had changed to something more . . . more personal. Sometimes, to her delight, she thought she noticed little meaningful things: like when he held her hand a mite longer than was perhaps proper when they said goodnight; or when she caught him looking at her in a sort of earnest way, earnest but tender.

For the last few months Jane had not seen a lot of him. He had been very busy with the building of a new brick police office, the old one being housed in a wattle and daub cottage with a cluster rose fence in Central West Street: and, too, he had been away from Durban in Pietermaritzburg where he was building a brickworks. He had not been to dinner at Mimosa on a Saturday night for weeks and she waited for him this afternoon with a little trepidation.

The blue frock she wore looked particularly lovely with her dark hair, streaked here and there with grey. She had taken more time than usual to dress, although she would have denied it, and she had chosen the frock specially; but she would have denied this too. She looked much younger than her years as she stood to greet him when Mannie showed him in.

They sat as Mannie moved out to get some tea and Jane

called after her, 'Ask Mrs Veldbron to make it, please.' Matilda Veldbron's tea was exceptionally good.

She met his eyes. 'Well, Mr Nelson, what brings you here?'

He moved in the chair and a serious expression crossed his face. 'I must go to the inland property, the one given to us by Mpande. And on the way I'll look in on the brickyard and the building in Pietermaritzburg.'

She nodded. 'I see.'

'Your brother had special relations with the Zulus. He even spoke Zulu with some fluency. I have a few words, but have never had the understanding he had. The large tract of veldt given us by Mpande is north of Pietermaritzburg, some sixty odd miles up on the Tugela, about twenty-five miles away from a township they are presently laying out on a Boer farm. If I do not go and survey our property and mark it out and put some sort of boundaries up, I'm afraid it will be forgotten that it belongs to us and ours. Actually I'm intending to build a dwelling there, perhaps start a farm.'

'I understand. How long will you be gone?'

'Some months. Four or five even, there's much to do when we get there. Also I will have to use ox carts to carry the tools and supplies from Pietermaritzburg, and the ox, while strong and willing, does not move at speed. Things will be slow.'

She was looking doubtful. He smiled, thinking he understood her expression.

'But don't worry, for Russell will be here to supervise things and is a good chap, knows the business sideways. And while Dirk Veldbron wants to come with me, you have Mrs Veldbron and Mannie and the servants with you. There's little to concern you.'

'I ... yes, thank you.' She was feeling quite sad. He was going away and appeared so matter of fact about it.

'Now there's one other thing.'

'Yes?' Her heartbeat quickened.

'John Lockley. It would be great experience for the boy to come with us. He's fascinated by Natal and I think it would be good for him to see Pietermaritzburg and the countryside.'

The disappointment she felt sounded in her voice. 'You do?'

He took her tone to mean she did not want the boy to go, which in fact was also true, although that particular feeling was not the cause of her regret.

He was smiling at her and she could feel herself going pink. Why was she beginning to flush? This was dreadful.

He leant a touch closer to her. 'Is something wrong? Really, the boy will profit by it. I think it'll be very good for him to learn about Africa and things African, but if you don't want him to come, then . . .'

'Oh, it's true, I don't want him to go.' Not want him to go? She absolutely detested the thought of his going. And for many months? But then she looked into Christopher's eyes and heard herself say, 'But if you so strongly think it will be good for him?'

'Yes, Miss Harrison, I do think it will.'

She came to a decision. 'All right, I agree he should go and I hope it proves as much of a benefit to him as you say.' Then she asked the question she really wanted answering. 'When will you leave?'

'I would like to be on my way next week, Thursday. I'll stay through the dry, the winter; to return before the next heavy rains and the rivers rising which usually come in high summer. I'll attempt to be back by October.'

She felt awful. 'Next week is . . . soon.'

'Yes, but I don't wish to delay now that I have decided. Do you want to tell John Lockley or should you like me to do so?'

'No, you tell him. It's your idea after all.'

He stood. 'Then I shall say good evening to you. I'd like to go back to the yard for a little time yet.'

She, too, stood. 'Will you have an evening meal with us before you leave? I have noticed you seem to have business or . . . somewhere else to go, these last weeks.'

He did not answer immediately. His handsome eyes weighed her. Then he smiled. 'I should be delighted to do so.'

'Oh? Then I'll make a special dinner of it. On Monday night? The children would like it, I'm sure.'

'Yes, that'd be perfect.'

He bowed from the shoulders and left her standing there, watching his departing back, and thinking what a conundrum he had become for her.

He was crossing the veranda when he turned to a shout from John Lockley.

When the boy had realised his aunt and Mr Nelson were in conversation he had gone to Ellen full of the information he had learned from the Port Captain. His sister had been feeding her rabbits, six wonderful, white, fluffy fellows that lived in a large hutch on the west side of the house and had been given to her by Mr Russell, the brickyard manager. When he imparted his news, she turned her lovely round, green eyes to him. 'What? But you never are going, are you?'

'Yes, I think so. Oh, I hope so.' His eyes were glowing with the light of dreams, just as his Uncle Edgar's had in the schoolroom of The Grange a generation ago. If he had realised it, he was very like his uncle. Jane often thought so.

Ellen felt a surge of unhappiness, and a peevish, fretful expression turned her pretty mouth down at the edges. 'But I don't want you to go.'

John Lockley hardly heard her. He knelt down and in his joy hugged her to him, making her drop the vegetables she held in her hand as she and her brother fell backwards in a childish embrace. She laughed then, but merely because he was laughing, she felt no happiness at all.

Then he had bounded to his feet and run around the front of the house to await Christopher.

When Christopher turned on the veranda to the boy's wide grin and cheerful greeting he spoke briefly. 'Hello, lad. I can't stay, I must be getting back to the brickworks.' And with that he mounted Caledon, his roan stallion, and rode out, calling, 'Goodbye, now,' over his shoulder.

The boy had been so sure that Christopher would say something. He stood, a disappointed look on his appealing young face. Then it hit him. He almost sagged forward with the weight of it. Mr Nelson had indeed asked his aunt if he could go into Zulu country and his aunt had said no. He turned with heavy steps and went to find Nell; good old Nell, she would understand his bitter unhappiness.

If Christopher had known, he would have put the poor boy out of his misery, but of course he did not, so he had no reason to speak before he had planned to do so, which was the following day, when he had decided to get John Lockley over to the offices and show him the route map.

That evening, Jane thought John Lockley abnormally quiet. He was usually full of his afternoon fishing exploit, or some wild animal he had seen, or a happening in the town.

She suspected too that she saw sympathetic looks pass from

50

sister to brother, and Ellen, always considerate of him, was this evening positively doting.

'You can have my piece of cake too.' Ellen pushed her plate towards her brother.

Jane was baffled. 'What on earth is going on here? John Lockley, you look as if you lost sixpence and found a farthing, and Ellen, really your behaviour towards your brother passes from normal charity to a confusing solicitude.'

The two young faces turned to her.

Silence.

'What's going on?'

The children looked at each other.

'I'm waiting,' Jane continued. 'Has something terrible happened to you, John Lockley?'

'May I be excused?' the boy asked.

'Oh, for heaven's sake . . . how you try me. Yes, you may be excused.'

He stood and left the table and now Jane faced accusation in every nuance of her niece's attitude.

'What have I done?'

And then it came tumbling out of Ellen, for she could not help herself; now, as tomorrow, as next year, as always, she must defend her brother. All that John Lockley had told her she repeated angrily. '. . . And so it's not fair. For if Captain Bell had not told him, he at least wouldn't have known and so it would not be so bad for him – but he does know, and you have denied him the experience he must so have enjoyed.'

'Child . . . child,' her aunt began, and Ellen's face clouded even more.

'I'm not a child,' she retaliated.

'Well, you're acting like one; for I haven't denied your brother anything. The two of you have had your heads together, and like children have assumed much, and while Port Captain Bell has a mouth like the rest of him, I don't know why Mr Nelson didn't mention it to John Lockley this afternoon, for it was certainly not because I had objected.'

'You . . . did not object?'

'On the contrary, I said your brother could go.'

Ellen leapt from her seat and threw herself into her aunt's arms. 'Of course you did. Oh, you are so good, dear, wonderful Aunt Jane.'

And before Jane could respond the girl had run from the room, calling loudly to her brother.

Jane sat nonplussed, and when Denna, the serving girl, came in to see if she wished for something else she replied, 'No, Denna dear, I've had more than enough tonight.'

It was Sunday afternoon and the straggling company made easy progress out of Durban towards Mimosa. Victoria and Jane, carrying parasols, walked with Phoebe between them, and behind came John Lockley and Ellen, accompanied by Daisy, one of the Zulu girls from the Wesleyan mission. They had reached halfway on the forty-five-minute walk in the ever-bright afternoon sun, when, in the distance, they saw Christopher riding towards them.

'Oh look, here comes Mr Nelson,' said Ellen, waving her gloved hand.

He was on Caledon, and leading Isiwukulu and Cambo, one of the mares. He carried a rifle and wore a pistol in his belt.

'Good heavens,' Jane said as he reached them, 'you look like an arsenal.'

He smiled at her and dismounted. 'I've come especially to find you all. I don't wish to alarm you, but there's a dead foal on Mimosa and I have just now followed lion spoor from our home across to Springfield Flat, where lion were seen on Cato's farm.'

'Oh dear,' exclaimed Victoria, as Daisy's eyes widened in fear.

'Lions!' whispered Ellen, looking around as if she expected one to appear beside her. 'How awful.'

'I want you all to ride home to Mimosa, then I'll ride over to Cato's farm where they're preparing to track the animals. I shall come back later in the afternoon for you and Phoebe, Mrs McLean, and return you to the mission. So come on, mount up. John Lockley, you take Daisy, I'll take Mrs McLean and Phoebe, and Ellen, you take your aunt.'

The children and Daisy moved swiftly, but Jane hung back.

Christopher pointed to Cambo. 'Now, Miss Harrison, up behind Ellen.'

Jane looked fearful. 'But I cannot ride . . . I never have.'

He dismounted and in one almost continuous movement lifted Jane in his strong brown arms and put her up behind

Ellen. 'Now simply hold your niece round the waist all the way home.' And he slapped Cambo affectionately on the buttocks as the horse moved off.

When they reached Mimosa he dismounted and helped Victoria and Phoebe down, then turned to Ellen and Jane. He lifted Jane out of the saddle and her face brushed his as he brought her to the ground.

'Now, inside, please. Everyone here is warned.'

Ellen was first up the steps and into the house, past Mannie at the door.

'Can I come with you, sir?' asked John Lockley. 'Please.' Christopher looked to Jane.

She was still feeling quite strange from brushing Christopher's face with her own, the spot was burning, but this question brought her to her senses. 'Oh no, John Lockley, you mustn't.'

'Please, Aunt Jane, please. There'll be no danger. I'll be with Mr Nelson and the other men.'

Jane was confused. She hated to refuse him anything. She had agreed to letting him leave her for many months. She trusted Christopher to look after him then, so why not now?

'All right,' Jane said, before looking up to Christopher, who stood a foot taller than her. 'Look after him.'

It was then that he smiled so very gently at her, and to her surprise bent forward and lifted her gloved hand to his mouth and kissed it. 'I will always do that,' he answered.

At that moment, Mr Veldbron issued from the stables carrying a Cape gun and leading his horse.

Soon the two men and the boy had mounted and moved away. Christopher turned in the saddle as they reached the fence. 'Stay close to the house until we return.'

Mannie touched Jane on the arm. 'The lions have killed a foal right here this morning. Isn't it terrible, Miss Harrison?'

'Yes, Mannie, it is.'

'And two horses on Cato's farm as well, and the natives in the kraal just beyond on the Berea Hills were attacked more than once this week. They're mourning a child who was carried off two nights ago and a young cow herder who was badly mauled last night and died this morning. Mr Veldbron told us.'

'Oh my Lord,' said Jane, watching the riders disappear

round a clump of waterboom trees in the distance. 'Mr Nelson didn't say anything about that.'

Then Victoria spoke as she lifted Phoebe up in her arms. 'Perhaps he didn't wish to alarm you more than necessary. I saw the way he kissed your hand, Jane . . . didn't kiss mine.'

Jane said nothing as she followed her friend into the house, but there was a small, tender smile playing on her mouth.

The riders soon met up with a number of other men and were at George Cato's farm within half an hour. There they were joined by the owner and his brother, their three sons, about John Lockley's age, and six other farmers, one of whom was Tom Murphy the choirmaster. In a body they rode over the Berea to the kraal where the child and cow herder had been killed, only to find out that the same lion had been trouble-some in the past.

'I know him, he very big; long, black mane and black hairs in tuft on tail,' said the headman in a frightened voice.

'Seems we have a man-eater here,' said George Cato.

'Probably got lionesses with him,' added Dirk Veldbron.

Several of the men from the kraal joined them, carrying spears. They followed the spoor for two hours to broken country. Then along a donga where they found three animals: two lionesses and a large black-maned male, resting by a half-eaten carcass of a reedbuck. The male was downwind of the horses and he stood and turned towards the newcomers. He was massive, close to seven feet long from nose tip to hindquarters, and his tail with the black tuft stood up aggressively. Underneath his body hung a copious fringe of hair. He watched them unmoving.

'Stay behind me, son,' said Christopher to John Lockley.

The men from the kraal spread out with the farmers on horseback between them, some down in the donga, others up on the plain. When the line of men was about fifty yards from them, the animals began to move away along the donga.

John Lockley's heart accelerated, and in an effort to miss nothing, he edged Isi up between young Liben Cato and another farmer.

Tom Murphy fired the first shot. It hit one of the lionesses and she gave a horrible screech and fell to the ground, then rose again, staggered a few steps, then collapsed.

Now a number of things happened in unison. The second

female leapt sideways up the donga and, scrambling over some rocks, tried to escape. The male roared, a bold, defiant, incensed sound, and momentarily appeared to turn to follow the female, but instead, in a mighty leap, came out of the donga and bounded fearlessly towards the horses and riders. Liben Cato's horse sensed the danger and shied, throwing the boy to the ground. And Isi, right next to it, shied as well; but John Lockley, who was a good rider, dug his knees in and kept his balance. Rifle shots filled the air and there was shouting and noise all around.

The huge cat was hit by three bullets and a spear struck its shoulder; and now it turned towards the fallen boy, who was rising, screaming. Its mighty jaws opened as it gave a horrifying roar that ended in an audible sigh before it bounded some seven feet in the air straight towards the terrified boy.

The only man who had not yet fired was Christopher. Caledon held steady beneath him as his mouth set in a resolute line, and he took aim and fired. The bullet hit the massive cat in the face and it fell dead, on top of Liben Cato.

The weight of the lion broke the boy's right leg in two places. And in the ensuing mêlée the female that had scrambled out of the donga escaped. The other was dead.

On the way back to Mimosa John Lockley rode silently. He kept seeing the huge lion leaping on top of Liben.

They were close to home when Christopher turned in his saddle and said, 'Listen to me, son. Those cats were killing humans and domestic animals and thus had to be dealt with. There are many hunters in Africa. Men who slaughter animals for the sake of it. Don't become one of them. I approve of killing for food; people must eat. Now, I took you with me so that you would have the experience. I told you to remain behind me, but you did not. Do you realise it could have been you lying on the veld grass instead of Liben?'

A deeply repentant boy replied, 'Yes, sir.'

'And will you ever disobey me in any such situation again?'

'No, sir.'

Monday night's dinner was a huge success.

They ate in the large dining room, seated on the handsome Sheraton chairs that Christopher had brought out from

England years before. Their view across the veranda they used as a schoolroom encompassed the line of mimosas and the few twinkling lights of Durban.

It had been decided that Victoria, Frank and Phoebe would accompany Christopher to his destination on the Tugela River and then continue from there farther into the interior.

John Lockley had a curious feeling when he was told about the McLeans joining them. He could not quite voice it; it had to do with little Phoebe, and her laughter, and not having to leave her just yet. He was enjoying the party; he smiled at everyone, and ran his fingers through his hair, and talked loudly.

Christopher, too, was enjoying himself. He talked to everyone, and during dinner, when he sat at the opposite end of the table to Jane, his eyes rested on her gently from time to time. And Jane glowed, for she was aware of Christopher's gaze upon her.

The five courses were not those she would have served at home, but they were of Natal and therefore quite suitable. They began with a soup that Matilda Veldbron had taught the natives to make. She did wonderful things with mealies, which were abundant and cheap. For the soup she mixed mashed mealies with pumpkin, which was one of the only plentiful vegetables, and onion and some salt and spices. The second course was lightly fried fish which John Lockley had brought home, followed by roast fowl with sweet potato, rice and beans. Blancmange and native wild fruit pie were dessert.

Victoria and Frank were in good spirits at the prospect of leaving Durban at last, and little Phoebe was having a wonderful time, as her bedtime had long passed by.

Only Ellen was not as cheerful as the others. Her sentiments were mixed. Oh, she was pleased, thrilled even, for her brother to be going on this wonderful adventure, for she knew it was just what he wanted; but it was taking him away from her. They had only been apart twice in his whole life, and that was when Father had taken him alone to Ireland, to Uncle Andrew. She had been six the first time and ten the next. It had not been so bad the first time, but the second she had cried almost every day he had been gone. So while she was happy for him, she was sad for herself, and the worst thing was that he would be gone for her birthday, when she would turn sixteen, in May.

56

After dinner they had a concert. Ellen and Jane sang the popular song, 'Flowers of the Field', harmonising quite well; Victoria and Frank played a duet on the piano and Phoebe sang her favourite song, 'We are Merry little Cooks'. John Lockley recited Wordsworth's sonnet, 'Composed upon Westminster Bridge, September 3, 1802'. Hearing it made Jane sad, and for a few moments she was homesick for England and the sophistication she had left behind.

For the last act, Christopher told a true story of a tame springbuck, on a farm outside Grahamstown, that had believed it was a dog. It lived amongst a litter of Alsatians, desporting with them and chasing them. The tale was so absurd that everybody laughed loudly.

But finally the night was over and Jane found herself, candle in hand and alone, at the bottom of the wide oak staircase on her way upstairs.

She was thinking of how Mr Nelson had leant over her hand and kissed it as he said goodnight. Suddenly she turned back and putting the candle down on the hall sideboard opened the front door and went out into the darkness. It was another clear Durban night but there was a cool wind blowing. For a moment she thought to go back in and get a visite to throw around her shoulders, but then any feelings of chill disappeared as she saw the figure which moved towards her around the corner of the house. She stood still in the light of the moon.

'Is that you, Miss Harrison?'

'Yes, Mr Nelson, I thought to get some air.'

'Indeed, it's a beautiful night. I mostly walk a little before I go to bed.'

'I know.' It seemed to slip out of her mouth before she could stop herself. Of course she knew, didn't she watch him regularly from her bedroom window? Oh, but she had not meant to say it; she must have taken too much wine.

'I know you know.' He said it with the suggestion of a laugh.

Jane took a step backwards. 'Whatever do you mean?'

He took a step closer. 'Miss Harrison,' there was amusement in his voice, 'I know you know that I take nightly walks, for I have seen you sitting at your window, watching.'

'Oh dear, it's true. I'm very much afraid I'm out of my depth.'

He had kissed her before she realised he had moved.

He held her close and his mouth brushed tenderly across hers. When he released her he said, 'Dear Miss Harrison, you're so beautiful, and so very appealing in all you say and do.'

'I am?'

'Yes, you are.' And he kissed her again. Then to her disappointment he moved away. He was six or seven steps from her before he turned and said, 'Please, if you are able, call me Christopher, for I would very much like to call you Jane.'

She felt hot, she felt cold. Then a determined look came to her face and as she spoke she did not know whether it was herself or the alcohol talking. 'Mr Nelson, you have just asked me to call you Christopher and you have kissed me . . . twice. Told me I was beautiful. Months, weeks ago, I thought you cared for me, yes, I did. But then you stayed away, went to Pietermaritzburg, remained late at the brickyard, when I . . . wanted so much to see you. Are you trifling with me?'

In the moonlight she thought she could see that smile he sometimes wore. It said that which she did not understand, as if he found her amusing and yet as if he were considering her earnestly at the same time.

He reached a decision and came swiftly back the few steps to her and took her hand. 'I'm the youngest son of a bishop, Jane Harrison, and while the church holds no interest for me I am not unfamiliar with bibles, and if I had to swear on one, I'd say I'm not trifling with you. You are beautiful, and yes, I did kiss you and want to kiss you now. I did avoid you for those weeks because I needed time to consider things, to be certain of how I felt, and now I am. I'm going away, so I must tell you. I'm in love with you, Jane Harrison, and of course I want you to call me Christopher. Shouldn't engaged people be on first-name terms with their betrothed?'

'You . . . engaged?' Then the implication hit her. 'Oh dear, are you asking me to marry you?'

'I am.' He took her other hand. 'Would you be kind enough to do me the honour of marrying me, please?'

Jane was at sixes and sevens . . . eights and nines even! This handsome, capable, courageous man was asking her, Jane Harrison, thirty-six-year-old spinster, to marry him! Here in the glow of the moon on this warm, wonderful night. She could not believe it. She would wake up in a minute and realise all this was a dream.

Jane took a deep breath to calm herself; her eyes were locked with his.

'Oh yes, Christopher. I would very much like to marry you.'

Somewhere in the clump of seringa trees that grew at the edges of the lawn sounded the chirpy chattering of a monkey. To the two figures there in the night it was a distinctly jubilant sound as Jane stepped into Christopher's arms to be folded close, and thoroughly, very thoroughly, kissed.

CHAPTER FOUR

The party of sixteen riders and eight pack horses made slow progress over the Berea Ridge on the sandy track walled on either side by dense forest. It was still before eight o'clock in the morning and the sky was devoid of clouds, with a light so pure that every detail of the country seemed etched on the world.

John Lockley's eyes darted left and right, continuously seeking signs of animal life, and were rewarded many times by sounds of chattering and the sight of leaves being pulled aside by tiny fingers to expose the pert, inquisitive little black face of the ever-present grey monkey.

At the front of the company rode Christopher on Caledon, whose fine chestnut and white head actually gleamed as he lifted it high in the morning sun. Behind him rode Dirk Veldbron who was a master carpenter and would help raise buildings on the inland property. Following him came John Lockley on Isiwukulu, and then Victoria, and Frank with bright little Phoebe perched on the saddle in front of him.

The McLeans' clothes and personal items were carried on three of the eight pack horses and Christopher had advised them to wait until arrival in Pietermaritzburg before buying any furniture and household items to take on to the mission. In the party were four men from the brickworks, and four Hottentots to do the cooking, riding two to a horse. Bringing up the rear were Umslopagas and Thulmi, two loyal Zulus who had fled from Zulu country seven years before and had been working for Christopher and Edgar since they arrived in Durban. They had horses of their own, almost unknown for Zulus, but Edgar and Christopher had always worked on the principle of rewarding good service.

On the far side of the Berea Hills, the densely wooded country thinned, and the party continued on slowly, for there was now hardly even a track on which to ride. The hills were low and undulating and here and there sat kraals, edged by fields of Indian corn – mealies – and herds of cows and goats.

As he rode, Christopher was thinking of Jane. In his heart he had known ever since he saw her on the dock in Cape Town that he wanted her for his wife. They would be married when he returned from Zulu country.

Behind him rode John Lockley with thoughts of his own, and not such contented ones as Christopher's. He had been so excited about going into Zulu territory that he had not really thought of leaving Matilda and Mannie and Aunt Jane and Nell; not until this morning, when suddenly he had realised. It was especially hard with Nell, for she had clung to him and cried and cried. He had whispered in her ear, 'Nell, don't worry about me, and I shall miss you too.'

Her eyes had filled with entreaty. 'Will you really?' she asked, tears still brimming.

'Of course I will ... and, hey? Have you noticed I'm taller than you now?'

She sniffed and eyed him and tried to smile. 'Oh goodness, so you are.' Yet the dejected expression had remained on her face long after the troop had ridden out.

Close to two hours after leaving Mimosa they came to German House, or the German Hotel, as it was alternatively called, some eight miles from Durban.

It had turned into a warm morning, for the sun was in a cloudless sky, and they halted briefly for the horses to drink at a brook which ran through the thick trees surrounding the verandas of the long, low thatched buildings. Hens and chickens stalked across stacks of firewood, and a man came out to greet them. Some of the party followed him into a taproom filled with rough, home-made furniture, where a strong aroma of coffee lifted from a coffee mill attached to a slab of wood beside the steps at the entry.

Along the far side of the buildings rested a team of oxen, and after a few minutes the animals began inspanning, the process of yoking them into a team. It always intrigued John Lockley, who had seen it often in Durban. As he watched now, the voorlooper lined the animals up while two other men, a Boer and a Hottentot, each stood holding on their arms a bundle of riems, long thongs of undressed leather, ready to throw skilfully over the horns of the great beasts. When its name was called, each ox left the line to join the span order.

John Lockley looked to Mr Veldbron. 'Isn't it marvellous?'

'What's that?'

'The way the oxen know their names?'

'Well now, John Lockley, seeing as they are so stupid I suppose it is.'

The boy was surprised, for he thought the animals were clever to recognise their names, and he admired the way they hauled huge wagonloads great distances without complaint. He liked the oxen, with the strange humps upon their shoulders and their marvellous curling horns.

When the party was on its way once more it wound round hills and over rugged country: there was no road, merely cart tracks running straight from farm to farm, for there were no settlements as such. They passed trees quite unfamiliar to John Lockley and he was fascinated by the variety of birds and beautiful wild flowers.

As the sun began to descend, Christopher chose a campsite on the side of a gently sloping hill with a small rivulet about a hundred yards distant. They were about eighteen miles from tiny Pietermaritzburg, with no bush in front of them, only open land, with the occasional clump of trees.

It was a beautiful night, and the temperature remained comfortable, only dropping in the early hours of the morning. There was no trace of wind, the air simply lay around the tents, balmy and still.

The pot was soon boiling over the fire and the food was prepared. As John Lockley sat watching the cooks, his fair hair shining in the fireglow, he looked round to see Phoebe standing beside him.

'Phoebe, you're not wandering again, are you?' And the child shook her cherub's head and laughed.

He stood. 'Come on.' Taking her hand he walked back with her to the small sleeping tent belonging to the McLeans. Victoria raised her head from where she knelt smoothing out their bedding for the night.

'Phoebe,' she said, a look of real impatience on her face. 'I thought you were with your father getting water at the creek.'

John Lockley spoke quickly. 'Don't be angry, Mrs McLean, she has been in no danger, really.'

Phoebe crinkled her pretty brow. 'I only went over to see Jan Larkley.'

Victoria pulled the child to her. 'Now stay here. Thank you, John Lockley, you seem to be her keeper.'

Phoebe looked up at him, her little smile turning the corners of her mouth, and he felt a rush of affection for the child. 'I don't mind, honestly I don't.'

When they retired a lookout was mounted; they took an hour each.

'Yes,' approved Dirk Veldbron in his heavy accent, 'it's best, Mr Nelson, for a lion or other big cat – even a buffalo – can become inquisitive occasionally.'

Nevertheless, they slept without incident and woke to another characteristically clear, uncloudy South African day. It was, however, a cooler day, for a wind had risen.

They traversed the open country and from the top of Usy Doorn's Hill saw Pietermaritzburg in the distance. The small town, with buildings predominantly white, nestled at the foot of distant hills. They could make out Fort Napier at one end, and much unrestricted grazing land all around.

Before noon they were crossing a wooden bridge which brought them into the town. Immediately across, they passed two cemeteries, one Dutch, one English. Christopher turned to the others. 'I don't think much of the town planning,' he smiled. And yet the town itself was delightful, filled with hedgerows of figs, roses, quinces and pomegranates, overlooked by weeping willows and seringa, interspersed with oaks and eucalypts and fruit trees. 'An oasis,' Dirk Veldbron called it.

They entered by Commercial Street into a settlement of wide thoroughfares, perhaps ten principal ones running from end to end, crossed by about six others, equally wide. Water channels, sluits, cut between the footpaths and the horse roads, brought water from the neighbouring hills.

Redcoats and ladies and merchants and Bantus wandered about and there was a general air of peacefulness abroad. The entourage crossed Burgher Street and Loop Street and turned into Long Market Street. Down past a number of mercantile and public buildings they rode to the Market Square, where they halted to watch a company of the 45th Regiment march by, the band playing 'Sprig of Shillelagh'.

John Lockley turned to Christopher. 'Don't they look grand?'

'Yes, they do.'

'I'm going to join the army.'

Christopher turned slightly in the saddle. 'Are you?'

'Oh yes, it's expected. When I'm seventeen I shall go home to the Royal Military Academy.'

Christopher's eyebrows rose. 'I see.'

The McLeans found a small inn where they could live while the party prepared for the onward journey. They would be at least two weeks here, for Christopher needed to inspect the brickyard and plan the construction of a hotel on some erfs – half-acre blocks – he owned in Long Market Street. Victoria and Frank did not mind the wait; they preferred to travel on in Christopher's company.

There were many articles to purchase for the upcountry property, though they had brought from Durban a load of stumps for any building they might erect; for as Dirk said when John Lockley questioned him, 'Stumps must be from the salt-grown mangrove, lad – the only one free from white ant.'

By nightfall the following day new packing cases of goods were stacked up next to the double-barrelled smooth-bore Cape guns and coffee grinder brought from Mimosa. There were spades, saws, pickaxes, brooms, hammers and nails, food supplies, tents and cooking utensils, as well as three large cases of sharp French short swords which would be traded. There was even a set of glass windows which Christopher had ordered months before.

On a fine May morning in 1853, at the hour of seven in the morning, four ox carts trundled out of Pietermaritzburg. John Lockley rode in front with Christopher, Isiwukulu's hooves throwing little splatters of mud to right and left, for there had been rain overnight and the streets were soggy. The boy looked up at Christopher as they trotted along. He liked Mr Nelson; felt very secure with him. There was a competence and efficiency surrounding Christopher which no one could fail to notice, and to the boy of fourteen it imparted a feeling of well-being.

They rode by Government House, a straggling construction covered in flowering vines, with a few oak trees in front and scarlet geraniums in bloom at their feet. Christopher had been there to dine the previous night with the Lieutenant-Governor, and now, as they rode by, a tall man in the uniform of a grenadier of the 45th Regiment stood under one of the oaks. He waved to Christopher, hailing him with, 'Goodbye, Mr Nelson, sir.'

John Lockley's eyes came round to Christopher. 'Who was that?'

'One of the Governor's men ... Jeremy Coopman, decent young man, though not happy in the army. He's pleased to be helping the Governor's office for a time, gets him away from day-to-day army life.'

'Really?' The boy looked amazed.

'Until recently he was fighting with Major-General Cathcart, south in Kaffraria ... in the war which has just been concluded. Yet he confides in me that he has no more stomach for fighting. Some men do not fit into the ways of the services. It's a hard, strict life and too often dangerous.'

'But that's the fun of it,' replied the boy, running his hand back through his hair. 'My father says it is. He says it's fun in India and Burma.'

'Does he? And is that what you believe, John Lockley? Do you think it would be fun to be knee-deep in the mud of a rain forest with a Burmese spear in your stomach?'

The boy's mouth turned down. 'Of course not. But if you're a good soldier that wouldn't happen. It's never happened to my father.'

Christopher's lips stretched to trace out a thin smile. 'Oh yes, I see. But then your father's a general, and generals are rarely in the front line.'

'But Mr Nelson,' countered the child, 'he wasn't always a general.'

Christopher sighed. 'Yes, that's true, lad ... of course that's true.'

They were soon on the veld, continuing slowly north, and during the morning they saw herds of various bucks grazing and even an elephant trudging away in the distance, which delighted John Lockley and Phoebe. The child shouted her glee to the distant animals. And the birds were wonderful; perhaps the strangest of all were the ravens, each so exactly alike, dozens of them sitting side by side on the branches, grave, melancholy creatures all with their matching white neckties.

They looked down into a huge valley which seemed to be surrounded by a thousand hills. It was the most extraordinarily beautiful place. There was a green and lavender and soft olive wash over the world. John Lockley sighed at the marvellous, mystical beauty of it, and Christopher remarked, 'This was your uncle's favourite place.'

'Oh sir, I can understand why.'

For four days they continued trudging along valleys and over hills. They forded streams and rivers where there were drifts and sometimes the horses and oxen were three and four feet into the water. Late on the fourth day they were on a ridge overlooking another beautiful green valley.

Christopher and Frank rode side by side in front of the trailing ox wagons, and the leader lifted his finger and pointed to the north-east. 'Over there was a farm owned by the Boer, Liam Nel. They've laid out a town upon it . . . Greytown.' He brought his arm over in a small arc and pointed to the north. 'And up there, some twenty-five miles distant, is our land, approximately eighteen square miles of it, running north from the Tugela, sitting in a great U-bend . . . beautiful.'

Frank sat eyeing the landscape intently. 'How is it Mpande gave you the land?'

A faint smile hovered on Christopher's mouth in remembrance. 'Well, Frank, he really liked Edgar Harrison, was somehow impressed by him right from the start. I believe Edgar's fluency with the Zulu tongue had a lot to do with it. It was odd, for Mpande was taken by a jar of macassar that Edgar possessed, just as they say Shaka was about twenty years before. And when we added a few guns to the macassar, plus several axes, a crate of daggers, three fillies and two of the finest stallions I ever had the luck to own, he seemed quite satisfied with the exchange. Cheap, I suppose, when you look at it from this vantage point.'

Frank nodded appreciatively and Dirk Veldbron said, 'You're right there.'

They crossed many small ravines and watercourses and on the fifth day they forded the shallow Inadi River at a drift which was remarkably clear of the ever-present crocodiles. Five miles later they stood at last looking across the Tugela

River at the piece of the South African interior that belonged to the Harrisons and the Nelsons.

They forded the river, this time very carefully, as it was infested with the saurian reptiles, and pitched camp well north of it, on a long, low hill fringed by acacia trees. In the distance were other hills with kraals nestling on their slopes, while across the Tugela to the south the land dropped away to peaceful veld. Herds of wildebeest and bucks fed in the distance.

That first night they slept in their tents, and the very next day, while Victoria and Frank prepared for their onward journey, Christopher began the laying-out of a small house halfway up the slope, about a mile from the Tugela with a fine view of the surrounding country.

After lunch he called the men together.

'I'm going to visit the largest of the near kraals.' He waved his hand westward. 'We certainly must make friends with those living on our land. The Zulus will be very aware that we're here, and while none of them have come down to look at us, as is often their habit, they will be watching us. Umslopagas and Thulmi will accompany me, for if we can convince some of them to give us a helping hand it will make a difference.'

'May I come, sir?'

'Yes, John Lockley, a good idea.'

It was not the first time John Lockley had been to a Bantu kraal. They had stopped at many on their way here: strange, dusty, bare compounds that they were, with the thatched beehive-shaped huts lying inside the perimeter and the tribe's most prized possession, the herd of cows, fenced in the centre.

John Lockley thought the Zulus quite the most perplexing people, for while they were no doubt unsophisticated and primitive in the way they lived, he had seen on their journey that they were proud, and sometimes haughty towards their white visitors.

The night before they arrived at the Tugela they had spent at the most peculiar outpost, north of Liam Nel's property, where the new town was being laid out. It was a small trading station in the foothills of Mount Allard, also known as Invelweni, and the owner, H. H. Garner, traded with the natives in everything from ivory to tobacco and chickens.

He was a sandy-haired, fair-complexioned man who looked

incompatible with the African landscape. But his looks belied him, for he was as at home with the country and its inhabitants as any European would ever be. He had called a welcoming greeting to Christopher's party from under his 'wide-awake' hat.

There were children playing around the house and a number of native men and women were lounging in what struggled to be a garden of proteas and orange and lemon trees.

H.H. smiled and doffed his hat as he came forward to stand by Christopher's horse. 'Well now, Christopher Nelson, it's you I see. And what brings you this far north again?'

Christopher had leant down and shaken hands with the man before he dismounted. 'I'm back to make some demarcation of my land along the Tugela lest those who gave it forget, and resell it to a Boer . . . or to you!'

Both men laughed.

H.H. spoke in a clear, educated voice. 'That's true, for if a man doesn't hold on to what is his own in this part of the world, it'll soon be taken away. It's possible to say possession is *ten* points of the law here.'

Before they moved inside his dwelling of sandstone, thatch, and wood Christopher introduced H.H. to the McLeans and the rest of his party. When it came to John Lockley's turn to be introduced he looked up into the sun-paled eyes of the country dweller and said, 'I know of you, sir, from my friend Port Captain Bell. He says you know more about the Hottentots, Bushmen and Zulus than any other white man.'

H.H.'s face creased into a wide smile. 'So, my old friend Dicky Bell has been telling tales about me, and a fine tale he tells, if I recall.' And the boy nodded, replying, 'Oh yes, sir, he still does.'

While Dirk Veldbron and the men saw to watering the horses and outspanning the oxen, the McLeans, Christopher, H.H. and John Lockley entered the strangest room the boy had ever seen.

It was large, with a fireplace at one end where a huge mat of zebra skin lay in front of the stone hearth. Rifles and other guns were neatly formed in two lines in a large ornate display cabinet, inlaid with old-silver mounts. It would have looked at home at Mimosa but seemed inappropriate here, with the arrangement of assegais and spears and knobkerries hanging on either side of it. Two skin rugs still retaining lions' heads were centred on the wooden floor, and all along the far wall, above rows of huge tusks of ivory, hung most intricately woven native baskets. And standing incongruously beside the tusks was a rosewood music stand with a page of music open upon it.

H.H. motioned Christopher to sit on a stool as he eased his spare frame into an old round-backed fauteuil armchair with padded elbow rests.

H.H's hand came up to rub his chin in thought. 'I heard about Edgar Harrison ... bad business. Fever, was it?'

Christopher nodded. 'Yes. In Grahamstown. I think he was bitten by something.'

'Ah, that's bad.' He looked to Victoria and Frank. 'Unfortunately many things bite in this country, from the huge lion or croc down to the minute mosquito.' Then he leant forward to John Lockley who stood beside Christopher. 'You remind me in looks of your Uncle Edgar, and that's a compliment, for not only was he a fine-looking fellow but spoke Zulu as well as myself ... understood them fast ... got to know them fast. Yes, Edgar Harrison, an excellent chap to resemble.'

Once more he turned to Victoria, who was restraining Phoebe from sitting on the huge elephant tusks. 'Mrs McLean, some refreshment?'

Before Victoria had time to reply the door beside the row of ivory tusks opened and in glided a Zulu woman. Her skin was the colour of russet gold and her black hair was twisted into many small knots with feathers interwoven. She was so lovely that John Lockley could not take his eyes from her.

'Ah, my love,' said H.H., standing and holding his arm open in an arc into which she glided. 'You know Mr Nelson, but let me introduce you to his travelling companions.'

The visitors stood and it was only Victoria whose eyes widened slightly when H.H. introduced the woman as his wife.

John Lockley noticed that Mrs Garner's 'k' sound was like a 'g', and so 'John Lockley' became 'John Logley' and 'welcome' was 'welgome', but otherwise her English was very good. She motioned for all to be reseated and H.H. said, 'Now some refreshment for our guests, please, my love, and the others too, who are outspanning and watering the animals.'

As she left the host watched her away with a gentle

expression, then turned back and asked, 'So you go to the land old "Panda" gave you, Chris? It's about fifteen miles from here, isn't it?'

'Yes, close to that, directly north. It's across the Tugela, around twenty-five square miles of it; most of it sits in an arc of the river about five miles from the junction with the Buffalo.'

'And we're getting a new town to the south of here, they're laying it out on old Liam Nel's farm, eh?' H.H. laughed. 'We'll be positively overcrowded.'

Christopher nodded. 'I hear they certainly did their fair share of arguing about the name of it . . . Boers wanted to call it Pretorious, but the government has named it after the Governor, in the end.'

H.H. smiled. 'Yes, Greytown, I believe.'

Frank had been watching their host with undisguised interest, and now, when H.H's gaze turned to him, he said, 'We travel on further to the mission at Fantele's Drift.'

'Yes, not a bad area. My wife's kraal is not far from there. Though I hope you've plenty of oil? The ticks along the rivers will like the child's blood, and the boy's.'

Victoria, Frank and John Lockley looked in amazement as Christopher replied, 'Indeed I have, H.H.' Then he turned to the McLeans. 'Don't worry. There are ticks, and the Zulus wear fat and oil to ward them off . . . effectively, I might add. They're much worse after the rains, and we're well prepared for them.'

At the thought of having to oil herself and Phoebe against ticks, Victoria's face sagged. Then she felt Frank's strong arm around her and she turned to him as he kissed her forehead and allayed her fears.

They remained at H.H. Garner's overnight. Little Phoebe fell fast asleep in her mother's arms at the dinner table, and soon the McLeans retired while H.H. and Christopher talked long into the night.

Before he was sent to bed, John Lockley asked their host many questions, which H.H. answered enthusiastically. 'For you see, young man, there are many ways, wondrous and different, to live a life in this world; and the Zulu? He's different.'

John Lockley was sopping up the information. 'Where did they come from, sir?'

'The Zulus? In reality the name is patronymic, for there was actually a man called Zulu. It's known that late in the seventeenth century Mandalela, a Nguni chieftain, the Nguni being a Bantu tribe, wandered down from what is upper Natal. He had very few in his tribe and finally settled inland on the White Umfolozi River. It was his son who was called Zulu, and by the time he died the few had grown into a small clan and adopted his name. It means "the heavens", and they called themselves amaZulu, "the people of the heavens". Zulu was followed by Punga and he by Mageba. Then came Ndaba and Jama and his son was Senzangakoma.' Here H.H. stopped and, looking quizzically at John Lockley, asked, 'Do you know the great significance of Senzangakoma?'

'No, sir, I'm sorry I don't.'

He winked at Christopher. 'Shall we tell him?'

Christopher nodded soberly. 'As he's so interested in them I think it's best.'

H.H. grinned. 'Senzangakoma was the chieftain of the Zulus who, around the year seventeen eighty-seven or eight, had a son by a strong-willed girl of the eLangeni tribe, the eLangeni being closely related to the Zulus. It was a scandal at the time, for Senzangakoma's mother was from the same tribe and thus he could not marry within it; nevertheless the child was born and he did ultimately marry the mother, Nandi. She became his third wife. He was to have sixteen. This child of Nandi's was called iShaka, named after an intestinal beetle which makes the belly swell. Thus came into the world "Shaka the hyena man", who took a clan of about fifteen hundred souls and made it into the most feared tribe in all of southern Africa.'

John Lockley was fascinated. 'I know about him. Dingane succeeded him. Dingane was Shaka's half-brother and then Mpande came along and he's king now.' And then John Lockley asked something he had wanted to be sure of ever since the Port Captain had mentioned it. 'And sir, is it true that they can run forty miles without stopping?'

H.H. cocked an eyebrow. 'Well now, I cannot say about the not stopping part, but shortly after I first came to Port Natal some sixteen years ago in thirty-seven, I wandered up this way and got caught up with a fellow . . . Chief Dube, leader of the Qadi, a vassal clan living north of the Tugela. Dingane was king of the Zulus then, a bloodthirsty chap like his half-brother Shaka ... lived in a huge kraal called Mgungundhlovu in the heart of Zulu country. Chief Dube was taken in by Dingane. He tricked Dube into sending over a thousand of the Qadi to their own massacre at Mgungundhlovu. This was April first, I think, and I was actually there when Chief Dube found out. Now here is the stamina of the Zulus ... It had taken the bringer of the news just thirteen hours to come nigh on *sixty* miles, and within two hours more a Zulu impi had followed him to kill old Dube, who, incidentally, had slipped across the Tugela near Middle Drift. That was the first time I noted how far they could run. So, yes, son, they can run forty miles when they have to, and more.'

John Lockley's eyes were shining. 'And what happened, Mr H.H. sir?'

'Eh? What happened?'

'Yes, to Chief Dube?'

'Ah lad, they caught him in the Nongoxi forest and put him to death ... as is their way.'

John Lockley's face dropped. 'Oh.'

Then H.H. leant forward and patted the boy on the shoulder. 'Though the heir apparent to Chief Dube got away to Port Natal, as did many fugitives from military kraals and family settlements at that time.'

John Lockley listened enthralled. 'Are they dangerous now, sir?'

H.H. smiled. When he smiled he looked very much younger than his years, which must have been fifty odd. There was that in his smile which was youthful, boylike. He looked across at Christopher. 'How do we answer that, Mr Nelson?'

Christopher looked thoughtful. 'Perhaps we should say they are much more dangerous to their long-standing enemies than to us.'

'Yes,' replied H.H. 'That's true. They're at present fighting their hereditary foe, the Swazis, and as Mpande has a liking for Englishmen I'd say he will leave us all alone for now.'

But John Lockley realised that the two men had left much unsaid, and that they meant the Zulus were always potentially dangerous.

The boy continued to watch H.H. with evident fascination. When he went at last to bed, he lay there thinking. He very much liked H.H., who lived out here as a trader in this singular fashion. Why did he like living out here? Perhaps he liked the danger? After all, he was all alone with only his Bantus for company . . . and had been here many years.

When they were all preparing to depart the next morning, in his innocence he asked some of his companions, 'Do you think Mr Garner will ever go back to living in a town? Though he knows and understands the Bantus, it appears to me that somehow he misses the company of white men.'

Mr Veldbron cast the boy an oddly disapproving look, and some of the men laughed. Thulmi and Umslopagas dropped their eyes and moved away. Christopher was inside at the time and it was finally Travers, a small Scot who had come out to the colony under one of the deceptive emigration schemes and had never seen his allotment of land, who enlightened him. 'Young Master Harrison, this man has made his . . . own selection. Has decided to differ from others. He married a nigger, oh, right and proper like, in a ceremony by a missionary, but that doesn't count with his fellow white men. He never can live in a town now. Not with her, no never.'

'But she's beautiful. Far more beautiful than any white lady I've ever seen. Well other than Aunt Jane . . . I suppose.'

'That counts for naught, son, she's a kaffir. Have you seen any man in Durban or Pietermaritzburg married to a kaffir? They have them as servants, lad, and sometimes more than servants.' He coughed. 'But never as wives gone and married in the sight of God. It's not the done thing.'

Tanner, another of the men from the brickworks, nodded vigorously. 'Yeah, H.H. done himself in. After all, it ain't proper.'

John Lockley knew that at only fourteen he did not understand how grown men thought. But he truly felt there was something wrong in the way men reasoned, for they, all of them, the whole party, had eaten H.H.'s food, slept under his roof and accepted his hospitality. And yet it was obvious that they did not really accept him or approve of him. He didn't understand it, but he knew he didn't like it.

When Christopher came outside the party began to mount up. Suddenly John Lockley dropped Isiwukulu's reins and ran back to the house just as H.H. was coming out the door to see them off. The others at the oxen and the horses were too far away to see or hear what occurred between the two standing at the door.

'Hey, John Lockley, what brings you back?'

'I want ... to thank you, sir, for having me to sleep and eat with you. It was one of the very best nights of my life. I enjoyed it ever so and also I want to thank ... Mrs Garner.'

The strangest look came over H.H.'s face and he bent his head forward to look deeply into the boy's eyes. They continued looking at each other for a few seconds; then, as if H.H. saw what he had sought to find, he gently shook his head and his eyes clouded momentarily as he put out his hand and took John Lockley's. 'Ah, you, John Lockley Harrison, are welcome in my ... in *our* home any time; any time at all, do not forget.'

'I will not, sir.' The boy smiled up into the steady blue eyes that held his own steady lead-purple ones.

It was later on the ride that he asked Christopher what he thought about H.H. and Mrs Garner.

'How do you mean, son?'

'I mean their being husband and wife. Mr Travers told me it is not the done thing.'

'Well, that's certainly true, but, John Lockley, the "done thing" isn't necessarily the right thing. H.H. treads a differing path from his fellow man, but he's an intelligent fellow who has chosen to show others his life is his own, and he lives it that way.'

'Then you approve?'

Christopher was unaware, but the boy's heart was begging for affirmation.

'I don't disapprove. Most men are too quick to judge those who deviate from the accepted path, and while it would not be my choice to live as he does, I like him and greatly respect him.'

'And Mrs Garner, sir?'

'Yes, I like her very much too.'

John Lockley sighed audibly. He was so glad to hear Mr Nelson talk this way. He admired him so much. He had always thought Christopher good and fair-minded and once more he had proved so. He turned in the saddle to the man. 'I like her very much too.'

Christopher laughed then, deep and mirthful, as they rode on together.

So John Lockley and Christopher's sympathies differed from those around them, and while it would matter only in a minor way to Christopher, it would matter immensely to John Lockley.

But the boy had not yet taken his first steps along the different road on that day in May 1853, when the troop of four – Christopher, himself, Umslopagas and Thulmi — made their way to the largest of the kraals along the Tugela from their property. As they rode up to the kraal, a cluster of about thirty huts on a hillside overlooking the Tugela, a number of Zulu boys wandered through the maize fields, and further beyond others tended cows and goats. The flies were bad and the horsemen were flicking at them constantly.

'Even in cold, flies bad round cows and goats!' Umslopagas stated philosophically.

It seemed that all of the kraal's occupants were outdoors to meet them as they rode through the opening in the fence that served as protection and border for the thatched dwellings. Some children wrapped in skins were playing in the dust and a few women continued mashing mealies on stones.

The kraal was structured in the orthodox manner: cattle kraal fenced in the centre, huts in a ring encircling that, and outer fence surrounded by the crop fields, in this case maize, growing waist-high. The headman, neither petty nor important, judging by the size of his kraal, came forward with his four wives hanging behind him, three of whom were no more than girls. About a dozen young men, tall and perfectly proportioned, their skins shining in the sunlight from the fat they used on it, watched with interest.

Christopher turned to John Lockley. 'Mpande is not the war-lover that his brother Dingane was, or at least he's not these days. He grows fat in the company of his many wives, that's why you see here a number of men of warrior age. He doesn't keep up the fighting regiments in the strict form of those before him.'

'Are there any regiments now?' the boy asked.

'Yes, there are, for it's a major part of the Zulu culture, but they don't train the impies in the rigorous way of ten years ago, thus the men are in their home kraals more often.'

'They still fight good quickly ... no time,' added Thulmi decisively. His understanding of English was thorough enough to follow Christopher's explanation.

Christopher nodded. 'Yes, Thulmi, doubtlessly they could reorganise in a short time.'

They dismounted to sounds of admiration for their horses. The headman stepped forward. He wore a skin mutya and a long skin cape, round his neck hung a necklace of animal teeth and on his head sat an intricate headdress incorporating leopard skin and ostrich feathers which he had quickly put on when he saw his visitors coming. Beside him stood his 'adviser on the magic arts', Yangaani, the tribal witch doctor, dressed even more elaborately with a necklace of buckhorns around his neck, numerous bracelets on his arms and legs, and an apron of cat tails peeping from under his zebra-skin cape. On his head was a matching zebra-skin cap to which was attached the gall bladder of a goat.

Christopher hailed the chief in a loud voice. 'I see you! *Sa ku bonum ngani!*' he said, and raised his hand solemnly, and the old Zulu replied, '*Yeh bo,*' lifting high a long ebony stick he carried in his left hand.

The formal greeting over, the newcomers followed the headman to a spot inside the kraal fence near the gate, where he sat to hear tribal disputes. Seating himself was a lengthy procedure, for each of his wives repeated his name, 'Unondo,' followed by his praise names, and at each repetition he raised himself from the seat again. Finally he was settled with his witch doctor beside him, while behind stood his wives.

It was then that Christopher, with the aid of his own Zulus, asked for help from the men of the kraal. 'For we will build a house on the land bought from your great king and protector, Mpande, and will mark some boundaries with signs and, in some places, fences. We would like your help. We need strong men. You will be well rewarded.'

And now an extraordinary conversation took place.

Unondo looked up from under his heavy lids and, raising his ebony cane, pointed it at Christopher. 'Why do you come here to my country? Why do you leave your home to come here?'

While Thulmi helped translate, Christopher understood enough Zulu to follow most of this and he explained that he had worked for men far away who had sent him to live in Cape

Town, a big town a long way to the south; and that was how he came to Africa.

Then the old Zulu harangued him with, 'Was the Englishman's country so bad that he had to come to this? . . . If not, why leave a better country for a worse one? . . . How long do you mean to stay in this country? . . . Why do the English not drive the Boers out of this land? . . . Are you here to "eat up" the land? . . . Have you ever seen the Great White Queen? . . . Is she greater than Mpande? . . . Is she as beautiful as Unondo's wives?'

Christopher replied satisfactorily, but when it came to the last question he hesitated. He needed Unondo's help to build his fences, dig his channels, clear his land and lop his trees. The wives were all fat, a quality of beauty in Zulu eyes: to call a Zulu woman 'a lump of fat' was high compliment. There were a few seconds of silence before Christopher spoke. He thought of Queen Victoria who was still relatively young and slender – 'Unondo's wives are all beautifully fat, the Great White Queen is not so fat as Unondo's wives.'

The Zulu, beaming, seemed quite satisfied with this and before he could drag out of his quite remarkable curiosity another question, Christopher produced two blankets from the bag he carried and put them at the chief's feet.

Unondo's attention was taken. He leant forward intrigued and felt the quality, rubbing a blanket against his face. He made a sound like 'Hau!' which seemed to show surprise and pleasure. Now Christopher took a finely decorated pipe of whalebone inlaid with ebony. The Zulu looked confused until the tobacco had been pushed into the bowl and he understood what it was. As the only pipes Unondo possessed were made of cow horn and very primitive, he was elated. This was an excellent gift indeed. The whole tribe made a sound like 'Eeeeoo.' He smiled and asked how many men Christopher needed and for how long? And did they have any cows to give him?

Christopher smiled in return, replying that he had no cows, but once the work was all completed Unondo and each man who laboured would receive a short sword like the one he wore. He lifted his out of the scabbard at his belt and swung it in a circle above his head to the same sound of 'Hau!' from all the tribe.

At this point Umslopagas bent down to the ground and unrolled a leather parcel he carried. Inside were dozens of pockets with a pair of shining Sheffield scissors in each. Thulmi took out a pair, and taking a piece of paper from inside the leather waistcoat he wore over his bare skin, cut it in pieces, while Christopher explained that each man and woman of the entire tribe would receive one after the work was completed. 'Hau!' was repeated with even more gusto than before.

Later that night John Lockley was to overhear Mr Veldbron ask Christopher why he gave the natives so much, merely to work. 'For they'll think you a fool, Mr Nelson, if you are too kind. It's strength they admire.'

'Perhaps you're right, Veldbron,' Christopher answered. 'But my way is to pay a man fairly for his day's work whether he be white, black, yellow, or brindled.'

And so in this way Christopher enlisted twenty Zulu men and youths to work for him for six days of each week for two months. It was difficult to make them understand how long they would be needed but finally Umslopagas had succeeded and every one seemed satisfied.

When the dealings with Unondo were completed they rode away, passing the witch doctor, who now had taken to sunning himself on a grass mat under a euphorbia tree some yards away from the kraal gate. Only his eyes moved to follow them as they rode by.

They were well away from the kraal, riding close to the river bank where at times there were thick reeds, a habitat for crocodiles, when just ahead of them, around an outcrop of rocks, a Zulu boy about John Lockley's age appeared screaming, '*Imamba! Imamba!*'

'It's a snake!' interpreted Christopher.

The boy was waving his arms to stop the riders. He shouted something else, which to Christopher was incoherent, but Thulmi said, 'He says it has just bitten his sister.'

'Where is she?' shouted Umslopagas in Zulu.

The boy pointed frantically to the rocks on the bank of the Tugela, and there, in the shade near an antboar hole, they found a girl of about twelve or thirteen.

When they reached her she was alive but perspiring freely and breathing heavily. Her brother knelt and cradled her in his arms, pointing to her foot. A yard away lay a puff-adder, its head crushed with a rock.

The girl was crying and Christopher acted swiftly. He took some cord from his saddle bag and tied it around the top of the girl's thigh. He removed the sword he wore in the scabbard at his belt.

The girl's eyes widened in terror and her brother cried out, lifting his hand towards the man. 'No! What is it you do?'

Christopher looked pleadingly to Thulmi and Umslopagas. 'Tell them I must cut the wound to remove the poison. That I will suck out the poison. It's the only way or she will die.'

Her heel was already swelling where the bite was.

Thulmi did as he was told and the naked fear in the Zulu boy's eyes faded slightly. 'Yes,' he said.

The water of the Tugela was flowing quite fast here and Christopher dipped the blade into it before he swiftly cut a cross through the wound, wiped it and put his mouth to it. He sucked and spat out the blood alternately.

John Lockley was watching the girl and boy on the ground together. They were nothing like he and Nell, but there was something in the obvious closeness between them that reminded him of himself and his sister. The boy was evidently distraught and the girl kept looking up into his eyes. Slowly she became calmer and stopped crying.

She was the same lovely honey colour as Mrs Garner, and she was quite naked under her skin cape except for her mouche and some decoration around her neck. Her hair was short, boyish, her nose was perfectly straight and her lips were a deep maroon colour, and full, the top one pushing up to her nose in a perfect swollen cupid's bow. Her cheek bones were already defined in her youthful face and her eyes above them were ebony black. As her cape opened he saw that between her small, pointed, pubescent breasts lay a tiger's tooth on a leather cord.

A strange sensation came over John Lockley. He felt a sort of thrill run through his limbs. He turned completely away for a few moments and looked down the river. The girl's brother was saying soothing things to her. John Lockley could tell by the tone of his voice.

As Christopher spat out the last of the blood and took his

water bottle from the saddle bag to wash out his mouth, John Lockley turned around.

'You will be well now,' Christopher said to the girl in Zulu, and she smiled wanly up at him. Then he added in English, 'She's very lucky. She had only just been bitten, otherwise . . .' He looked to Thulmi and Umslopagas. 'Tell her brother to make sure she lies here still, no moving, until there is no more bleeding and then to take her home and keep her quiet. It may help to give her a little of this.' He handed the boy a tiny bottle of spirits of ammonia, called Eau de Luce. 'She should take a few drops in water now and then. It helps with snake bite.'

The Zulu boy stood and said something, which to John Lockley sounded like, '*Umntwana wakeethu dumella. Darlengi, umntwana wakeethu Jettama.*'

Thulmi translated. 'My sister thanks you and so do I. My name is Darlengi and my sister's name is Jettama. You are good men.'

For the first time the Zulu boy looked straight at John Lockley. '*Sa ku bonum ngani.*' And John Lockley, who understood the greeting, replied in kind.

Christopher then asked them where they were from, and they told him they were from Unondo's kraal.

The boy explained. 'Though our father is not here, Darlengi and his sister live here. Our father is a great induna who lives near the king's kraal. And we were brought here by a powerful magic one called Mattana.'

Now this was ammunition for scepticism, and the two Zulu adults looked at each other dubiously, but Christopher merely smiled gently and nodded at the brother and sister.

They left the children together beside the river and turned and waved to them a number of times; the boy always responding and standing watching them until they were out of sight.

It was as they came near to their camp that Thulmi spoke. 'Boss, what you did to girl, good medicine. The necklace of magic one at kraal was made of buckhorns. In one he keep the head of puff-adder. The magic one make a powder from heads, heads of killer snakes, keep powder in necklace in buckhorns. Sometimes add crushed crocodile tooth or fluff from lion's mane. If he had girl he make girl drink powder and put powder on bite.'

John Lockley listened in amazement but Christopher knew of this sort of treatment. 'Yes,' he said, 'and unfortunately that would have killed her.'

'*Yeh bo*,' 'indeed', answered the pragmatic Thulmi.

CHAPTER FIVE

The day after Christopher had gone to Unondo's kraal the McLeans moved on. The mission station lay over forty miles to the north across the Tugela, deep in Zulu country.

Phoebe sat perched up on the ox cart beside her mother. The child wore a warm jacket and clutched a little red ball that John Lockley had given her. Her solid little legs were covered in oil against insects, and her bright eyes looked out from under a wide-brimmed sun hat. Their goodbyes had all been said, and, abruptly, John Lockley had turned from the adults and run back inside his tent. He could not explain the feeling he was experiencing. All he knew was that he was very sorry to see the McLeans depart. To see little Phoebe depart.

But a few days later he was thinking of other things, when, on a cool but brilliantly sunny day, he rode north with Thulmi to deliver a message to Dirk Veldbron, who was away setting a series of markers proclaiming the northern boundary of the property.

There had been unseasonally heavy rain the two previous days, and no work had been done. But this morning the sun had risen into a cloudless blue sky, and Thulmi and Umslopagas had gone for the Zulus. There had been certain resistance to the labour at first, for the Zulu men had never seen picks and shovels, and in any case it appeared to be 'women's work' – it was the Zulu females who were the tillers of the soil and the workers. But when Christopher reminded them of the rewards, they picked up the tools and began.

John Lockley had an aptitude for learning languages. He seemed not to have to try, and had already some Afrikaans, just from listening to Dirk and his Dutch friends. And now, Thulmi and Umslopagas had been teaching him some Zulu phrases. He understood swiftly and all the men thought him amazing. Christopher put it this way: 'It's not amazing. John

Lockley's like his Uncle Edgar, they have an ear for it, pick up the nuances that I miss, even down to the Zulu click.'

John Lockley and Thulmi followed the Tugela until it met the Intalalala, which was swollen from the two days of rain. At times, they rode well above the surface of the smaller river, for the current had cut a deep channel into the land over the ages.

Thulmi was on the horse Edgar had given him the previous year, a distinguished grey mare that for some obscure reason he had named Palace. The two were talking about Zulu customs and ways and John Lockley asked Thulmi how he had come down to Durban.

'King Dingane made great fear amongst our tribes, slaughtered many, and after Mpande become king, Umslopagas and Thulmi still loyal to Gqugqu, one of Mpande's brothers. Gqugqu and followers captured and slain by Mpande's impies . . . eaten up. All our cattle taken to king. Many of us fled south. This now seven . . .' he held up seven fingers, 'years we in Natal. Durban now real home. Mr Nelson kind man.' Here he laughed and his thick lips stretched back over white teeth. 'Thulmi dress in English fashion.' He dropped the reins and put his thumbs inside the arm openings of the waistcoat he wore, lifting it out proudly. 'See.'

They were passing up a gradual incline, with long-stranded veld grass to the horses' knees. In the distance, ahead and to the right of them, a host of quagga and wildebeest grazed. Bird sounds came from all around and John Lockley was feeling euphoric. South Africa excited him. Being here was just the most wonderful, stimulating thing ever in his life. And even though he would not quite admit it, there were times he half thought he did not want to go back to England to become a soldier.

Suddenly, both Isiwukulu and Palace sensed something. Isi lifted his head in the air and whinnied: he was nervous. Palace shook his head and shied a little. The wind was blowing across the Intalalala to them and while the stream was no more than thirty feet wide here, it was higher than usual because of the rain.

'What is it?' John Lockley looked to Thulmi.

'I know not, young master. But something over there, sure as sure.' He pointed across the gently running current.

There was a straggling cluster of giant aloe directly opposite, with high veld grass to north and south, moving in the wind. It was obvious that the horses smelt something and suddenly a number of the quagga sniffed the air and without warning sped away to the east, followed a few seconds later by the wildebeest.

A high-pitched screech ripped across the air, followed by another, and a Zulu boy darted around the aloe across the river, running at speed.

The two horses whinnied loudly.

The boy on the opposite bank had dropped his cape and carried nothing, wearing only his mutya of cat tails; his awe and horror transferring itself like a real thing to the two people watching him. John Lockley felt a terrible shiver of fear rush through him.

Then they saw it. It loped around the trees as if it knew it had all the time in the world to spare. A large leopard, the rosette markings of its silky skin shining in the streaming sunlight; its fluid limbs propelling it inexorably towards the Zulu boy. The youth screamed again and backed towards the river.

There was something about the boy on the other bank that was familiar, as John Lockley's voice sounded stridently. 'Thulmi! What can we do?'

The horses were shying now and John Lockley almost fell off Isiwukulu.

'Dismount young master . . . quickly.'

As they did so, the Zulu boy came to the brink of the far bank some twelve feet above the water, his back towards them. He was shaking and John Lockley's limbs were all aquiver in sympathy.

The leopard made a terrible, awesome sound, his jaws wide, and Thulmi fired the Cape gun at the creature at the same time as the Zulu boy plunged backwards into the river.

Isiwukulu and Palace whinnied loudly, raising their front legs high in the air. All the bird life around them lifted from the grass at once and the leopard jumped sideways as the bullet shot by its ear. The animal, sensing the danger, did not stop moving, but kept turning and bounded swiftly away through the grass, soon to be lost to view; while his prey struggled for his life, splashing helplessly, his arms flailing the water.

John Lockley could see the boy was drowning. 'He cannot swim, Thulmi.'

'No Zulu can swim; we do not like water.'

Already John Lockley was pulling off his boots and hose.

'What you doing?'

'He's drowning. I must help him.'

'No, young master! Stop! You no do this! Please, stop. Crocodiles!'

But John Lockley did not hear the last word, he had thrown off his warm jacket and already dived into the water below.

The water was icy and the Zulu boy was drowning all right. By the time John Lockley reached him he was struggling no longer and was sinking fast. With difficulty John Lockley yanked him upwards and slipped his hand through the boy's cat-skin apron. Laboriously he began to swim back to the east bank, towing the now semi-conscious Zulu boy. Eventually he arrived at a spot where he could drag the almost dead weight of the body through the shallows to the dry ground. Thulmi was there to help him.

'Oh God! Young master ... if you drown, Thulmi kill himself. No go Master Nelson and get head cut off.'

Through his exhaustion John Lockley actually smiled. 'Oh, Thulmi, you do exaggerate, really!'

They laid the boy face down and John Lockley, not knowing why, pushed a few times beneath his shoulder blades. The boy coughed, spluttered and rolled over. It was then Thulmi recognised him. 'It boy from before.' The Zulus always used the word 'before' when they meant an earlier time, for they didn't count days and weeks. Although Thulmi, having lived under the European influence for seven years, could do so, and often did, in the excitement he had simply slipped back into the Zulu vernacular.

'Yes it is. Isn't his name Darlengi?'

And Darlengi recognised them. He looked up at them from where he lay, the water shining in his tufts of curly hair, his dark eyelashes dripping tiny sparkling drops. His words came in short bursts and he finished speaking with the word, 'Ngiyabonga.'

Thulmi translated. 'He says he thanks you for his life.'

'Yes, I think I understood that.'

The two boys' chests were heaving in unison. Darlengi

coughed and spluttered and John Lockley panted; and they both shivered. Then it was as if Thulmi were not there; as if the black boy and the white boy were all alone; here on this muddy bank of an inland river with the wind playing in the long grass of the veld in Zulu country.

They were both waterlogged, both tired from the great exertion, yet both delighting in being alive. Darlengi moved slowly upright, shifting himself up on to one elbow and then to a sitting position, all the time looking into John Lockley's eyes. They were meeting now ... for the first time: the deep, jet-black eyes and the eyes of deep purple-blue.

John Lockley ran his fingers through his hair and laughed, a wonderful laugh full of the exultation of life, and Darlengi laughed in kind; and at that perfect moment, their souls met.

From that day the two were constant companions.

They spent many hours of many days together. The English youth learned how to build bird traps, a favourite Zulu pastime. He learnt how to catch grasshoppers and to follow animal tracks. Darlengi showed him the way to hold a knobkerrie and how to aim it to get the fastest throw. In time John Lockley became adept and the two would compete; often the poor ground birds, plovers and nightjars, being the unfortunate targets; and the dogs, great, gaunt mastiff-looking animals, would retrieve them.

John Lockley learnt all manner of odd matters that are imparted only during long comfortable hours: that crocodiles like dog flesh in preference to human flesh; that the honey bird will lead you to the bees' nest if you are patient and simply follow it; that a giraffe can run two miles even when mortally wounded; that Zulu herd boys regard eating the uncooked lungs of a newly killed bullock as the greatest treat (something that John Lockley could never bring himself to try).

His Zulu language improved at a wondrous rate, and so too did Darlengi's English. He had difficulty with the 'k' sound, just as, John Lockley recalled, Mrs Garner had done. Thus at first Darlengi called him 'John Logley' and in return was affectionately named 'Darli' by his new friend. They spent so much time together that Christopher dubbed them 'Romulus and Remus'.

They sometimes played with the other herd boys, games from time immemorial like hide and seek, and leapfrog, but mostly they would go off alone, unless Jettama joined them, and then they would stay close to the kraal and try to catch insects in their fists, or race and long-jump on the veld. The threesome would be as happy in their play as any ever were on a village green. A favourite diversion when they were all together was to draw labyrinths or mazes in the dust with a long sharp stick.

Darli told his new friend of the origin of the Zulu race: how a huge basket of mealies had rolled down the side of the Drakensburg Mountains and its lid had fallen off, dispersing the mealies, which sprang into Zulus. John Lockley looked at him with disbelief. 'Darli, do you really believe that?'

'It is what Yangaani says.'

'Do you believe what Yangaani says?'

'All our tribe believes him.'

'You do not answer my question. Do you believe him?'

Darli looked down. He was sitting cross-legged on the ground. He began to draw with his fingernail in the dirt.

'Darli? Answer me. You don't really believe that the Zulus sprang from a basket of mealies, do you?'

'Where do you say Zulu comes from?'

Then John Lockley told him what H.H. had related to him. 'So you see, your race goes back to the Mandelela and so on before him.'

Darlengi lifted his finger and pointed at John Lockley. 'Where does Eenglish come from?'

'Well, the whole race of man comes from Adam and Eve. Two people who lived in a garden called Eden. The woman was made from the man's rib, and they were sent away from the garden for being duped ... ah ... deceived. They listened to a serpent and ate an apple which was forbidden fruit. It's from their children Cain and Abel that the race of man came.'

Darlengi pursed his lips, and a deep crease lodged between his eyes. 'You believe that?'

'I'm supposed to.'

'I like basket of mealies better.'

Then they began to laugh, and they laughed and laughed until they cried.

The two inseparables found a special place, a natural tiny

amphitheatre in a cluster of huge rocks, with a one-hundred-and-eighty-degree view across the Tugela River.

John Lockley had been teaching his companion the idea of time. Zulus really had no way of counting time. Mostly they counted only up to ten; after that it was called 'a lot' They measured the year in seasons only: when the flowers came into bud; when the sun was hot; when the preparation for the cold winds was made; and when the cold winds blew.

He had explained the clock to Darlengi and the whites of the Zulu boy's eyes widened in wonder as he heard of the minutes and the hours making up a day. Then John Lockley said, 'You see, I am fourteen years old. I will be fifteen years old on this coming Friday, two days from now.'

Darlengi had grimaced. 'What is that? Fiteen yers old?'

'It means that I have lived that long. Long enough for the cold winds to have blown fifteen times; long enough for the flowers to have come into bud fifteen times.' He had already shown him how to count to one hundred, and so Darli certainly had the concept of fifteen.

Darlengi frowned, for he had recalled something; and in a mixture of Zulu and English he explained, 'I have a stick that Mattana give to me ... before. When she bring Darlengi and Jettama – how you say? "south"? – from kraal of father long way back, before, long time.'

John Lockley was looking questioningly. 'Stick? What stick?'

'Mattana is special magic one, you call "witch doctor". She love Darlengi, love Darlengi much.' He smiled softly. 'Sometimes almost make up for father's hate ... and for lack of mother's love. Back long time she see many things; things grown Zulu man no see. She bring Darlengi here away from father, Shiambi.' Now his voice grew soft and wistful. 'I miss her. She no come plenty. She give Darlengi small stick made from tree you call ivory palm. This good tree, magic sometimes. Stick look after Darlengi and Jettama ... keep safe. Mattana say, "Keep this stick. Each year in cold of wind, cut it here." She ...' he searched for the right verb, 'had made other marks ... before. There ...' he stopped to think of the tense again, 'were ...' he held up seven fingers, '*seven* marks on it, and each cold wind time since I mark it again. Now ...' Here he stopped and thought, looking at his fingers. Then he said triumphantly, 'fourdeen marks on it and soon Darlengi put one more.'

John Lockley was listening with interest. 'Why?'

'Ah...' he smiled. 'Mattana tell me it in the cold winds that Darlengi born and now I live fiteen cold winds. It is fiteen of these yers you speak about.'

'Why yes, that's so. Oh Darlengi, then we are both *fifteen* years old soon. And as you were born when the cold winds blow and I was born when the summer sun shines, it means we were born at the same time, are both the same age. We may even have been born in the same month. Imagine, Darli, even perhaps on the very same day!'

John Lockley was excited and his listener was thunderstruck. Darlengi was looking at him as if he had gone mad.

'What is it?' John Lockley asked.

The Zulu boy shook his head, eyes closed. It was many seconds before he opened them. 'You say you born in time of summer sun. You say I born in time of winter wind. Yet you say we born same time, same day? I no understand.'

John Lockley laughed. 'Oh gosh! How do I explain the southern and northern hemispheres?' And though the English boy went to pains to prove it, Darlengi was unimpressed.

'It not so.'

And it was quite some time before Darlengi finally grasped that it was so. But he did grasp it, after Christopher had given him a lesson on the world being round and the distance of it from the sun, and how the earth moved round the sun, and rotated on its axis. And Christopher then explained how the axis was tilted, thus creating winter and summer. He drew a diagram which Darlengi insisted on taking home with him.

'I see your people know many things,' the Zulu boy said to John Lockley afterwards. 'Many things that I...' he searched for the word, '*want* to know.'

One day when they had left Jettama grinding mealies and sought again their hideaway in the rocks, Darlengi confided, 'Yangaani says I am too white.'

John Lockley frowned. 'Yangaani the witch doctor? What does he mean?'

'He means I am too much with you. That I am too... interested ... is that the right word?'

'Yes.'

'Too interested in your Eenglish ways.'

John Lockley nodded, his face serious. 'Do you know Mr Veldbron says the same of me. He says I am too black . . . too Zulu. That I spend too much time with you and that it's not natural. That it's wrong.'

Darlengi's brow puckered in thought. 'But Mr Veldbron is a Boer. Boer and Zulu don't . . .' He was searching for the word again.

John Lockley supplied it. 'Harmonise.'

'What is that? Harmuonice?'

'No. Harmonise. To agree. Harmony is peace, to live together peaceably.'

They were both silent for a few moments. Then abruptly Darlengi slapped John Lockley on the back, saying, 'Yangaani and Meester Veldbron not like Darlengi and John Logley to harmonise.' And they both broke into laughter and rolled around, mock wrestling on the ground.

And so came the birthday, a cold July day, when the wind whipped along the wide Tugela, sending the leaves of the trees to dance in the air.

The two boys spent the afternoon together at the farm. Darli wore his best clothes, an old singlet of John Lockley's and a pair of short pants, under his warm skin cape and a cast-off hat of Christopher's on his head. He thought it odd to celebrate the day of one's birth, especially as his people did not even know how old they were, let alone the day they were born. The cake was the first food sweetened with sugar that he had ever eaten.

Darlengi came close to the English boy, who was leaning on the partly built fence looking uphill to where the foundations of the house were rising. John Lockley turned to Darlengi's question. 'Do you believe what you said before . . . that you and me born on same day?'

John Lockley corrected his friend. 'You and *I were* born on *the* same day. Yes, I feel it, Darli. I want to believe it and I do.'

Darli smiled wide. 'Good. Then this is *my birthday* too.'

They had a splendid afternoon, riding horses and playing cricket. Later, Darlengi asked where John Lockley's father was.

'He's in India.'

'What is Indeeaa?'

'A country across the ocean. I will show you in that book we looked at last week, the atlas. He's a general in the army, or the impi, as you say.'

'What is *general*?'

'An important officer. If there's a battle he leads the army, a leader.'

'Mine too. But my father no love me. Send me here, with Jettama. He no love her either. I think because I do love her, he does not.'

John Lockley frowned. 'Darli, why? Why does he not love you?'

'Because of me, my mother die.'

'Whatever do you mean?'

Darli spoke slowly, trying to be grammatically correct. 'When I am ... no, *was* born, she died. My father said I am bad. He – how you say? – hates me.'

John Lockley's smooth brow wrinkled and the frown settled more deeply between his eyes. 'I cannot believe it. This is too much of a coincidence.'

'What is that?'

'Darli, when I was born my mother died too.'

'No.'

'Yes.'

Darlengi looked empathetically at his friend. 'Your father hates you too?'

The other boy shook his head. 'While this is all quite amazing, with me it's quite different. My father does love me, very much.'

Darli was perplexed. 'All this is very strange.'

Then John Lockley pulled down his mouth, hunched his shoulders, stomped around in a circle, and in a most ridiculous voice shouted, 'Hey! Look! Two motherless brats! Two motherless brats! Two motherless brats!'

And Darlengi, who did not understand, but who realised there was much humour attached to this display, threw his arms up and laughed. Within thirty seconds they were rolling on the ground in their customary wrestling match.

So the winter gave way to spring and in September six rooms of the farmhouse were finished and a small veranda had been added at the southern side. It was late one afternoon when Christopher called John Lockley to him. He stood looking down across the veld towards the Tugela, out of one of the two glass windows they had transported all the way from Pietermaritzburg.

Christopher turned as the door opened. 'John Lockley, I have completed my task here for the present. Four of our party will remain at the farm, and Mr Veldbron has indicated that by the coming Christmas he will return to Durban and bring his wife back here next February to run this property for me. I want to get back south before any heavy rains begin, and I have a wedding to go to. We leave on Saturday for Durban.'

John Lockley said nothing. He looked down at the floor.

Christopher shook his head and brought his hand up to rub his chin in thought. 'You've become very fond of Darlengi.'

'Yes I have, sir.'

'Son, I'm sorry, but you'll need to make your goodbyes. It's an odd liaison which you perhaps will further when you come again to the farm.'

John Lockley felt as if he were about to cry. He really did not want to leave Darlengi or the farm or the fun they had together, or Jettama and the herd boys. He stood up quickly. 'Sir, will you excuse me now?'

That night Christopher walked late, as was his habit. He looked up through the bank of clouds to the milky moon delivering only a modified and ghostly light. He did not go near the river, for while crocodiles usually moved in the daylight, there was the occasional night attack.

As he returned to the farmhouse he saw John Lockley sitting on the front veranda. The clouds opened to partially illuminate the youth's face in the weak moonlight. It was despairing.

Christopher spoke quietly. 'Thinking about leaving Darlengi, son?'

'Yes.'

For a full minute there was silence, and then Christopher came to a decision and put his arm around John Lockley's shoulders. 'Listen, lad. There's much for me to do in Durban and Pietermaritzburg in the next few years, and in the meanwhile I'm hoping that Dirk Veldbron will turn this place into a real farm, an inland property for our future. So I suppose there's nothing stopping us from taking Darlengi back to Durban for a time if he wants to come.'

John Lockley leapt to his feet. 'Oh sir, really?' His voice rang in the night.

Christopher sighed. 'No doubt I will get some resistance from Veldbron, but I think it can be arranged.'

'Oh, sir, thank you. I'm so happy. He'll want to come, I know he will.'

Christopher smiled. 'Now get to bed, for goodness' sake. Loitering around in the dark like this, you are beginning to remind me of your aunt.'

The reference was lost on John Lockley, but he did as he was bidden, moving with a spring in his step.

Christopher's doubts about Dirk Veldbron's approval were justified.

'Mr Nelson, he's a Zulu. Born and bred. They do not understand kindness. This is weakness to the kaffir. He's primitive, and his understanding is on a par with his social graces. It's folly to bring him to Durban like an equal of John Lockley's. No matter what John Lockley wants. Darlengi, or whatever his name is, is a nigger, sir! It's not God's way to make them equal, they're children. The best they can ever be are servants like Thulmi and Umslopagas. You should not treat this boy differently.'

Christopher sighed. Perhaps at the present time most native Africans were uncivilised to the European way of thinking, but they needed to learn, and some were already different, clever and sharp, and deserved more than Dirk Veldbron would ever be prepared to believe. He knew Darlengi was one.

Sometimes Christopher wondered if Dirk Veldbron were the right man to run things here at the farm, but he had no one else and he knew that Veldbron, even with his strong beliefs, was an excellent farmer, a master carpenter, and a skilful planner.

'Dirk, Darlengi will be accompanying us. I must keep my promise.'

Dirk began to move away.

'And Dirk?'

'Yes, sir?'

'Don't ever use the word *nigger* in my presence. It's derogatory and I won't stand for it.'

The next day when John Lockley told Darlengi, the Zulu

could not believe it. 'With you? With you? To this Durban? You make a joke, Darlengi think.'

But when he realised it was no joke, he was the most excited youth in all of Zulu territory. Until he thought of Jettama, then his joy faded. 'For while I want to come with you, I do not want to leave my sister.'

When she heard, Jettama's reaction was mixed, so very like Ellen's when her brother went away. Her generous mouth turned down with disappointment but then she rallied. 'Oh, yes, I am glad for you, Darli, glad for you are glad. I have friends so I will not be alone. I will live to rejoice when you return.'

Darlengi and his sister lived in the hut of Weena and Kenga, an old couple with no tribal status, so there was only chief Unondo to appease. Thus to him the two boys went with a corduroy coat of Christopher's and a shining new bowl and spoon for his mealies.

The chief was hard to convince, for he was thinking of a recent visitor who had come to him in the middle of the night; an induna. The visitor had come from the powerful Mattana and had asked Unondo about the boy, Darlengi. Was he healthy and strong? Was he able to throw the knobkerrie and was he a good herd boy? Unondo had answered that he was all these things and the messenger had told him that at the end of two cold winds Darlengi and any two of the other herd boys must go to join a regiment in Inkanhla across the Tugela. All of Zululand knew that Cetshwayo, and his half-brother, Mbuyazi, were vying to be heir to the throne. And while Mpande, the Zulu king, did not keep up the impies with the strictness of Dingane, for he allowed his warriors to return to their home kraals and to marry, he still maintained certain regiments, and Cetshwayo, his son, was building up his own.

Usually custom dictated that only herd boys close to the king's kraal were enlisted in the regiments. But Darlengi, who lived much further away, had been asked for by name. And now the English boy wanted to take him away for what Unondo knew to be a very long time.

He shook his head. 'Darlengi cannot go.'

But when John Lockley returned to the kraal with Christopher at his side and four new woollen blankets and a painting of the white Queen, Unondo's resistance collapsed. He liked the white man, Nelson; he had kept every single promise to Unondo and his people, and Nelson had said Darlengi would be back within the agreed time.

He held up two fingers. 'Darlengi must be back before this many cold winds pass.'

'He will be.'

Jettama met John Lockley outside the chief's hut. Her beautiful black eyes, framed with long, dark lashes, lifted to his. 'I will miss you, John Logley.'

He felt odd. 'I will miss you too.'

'My brother is in your care. You will bring him back, won't you?'

'I will.'

'I go now, have my hair braided.' She glided from him, her buffalo-skin cape brushing the dust behind her.

The hair braiding took hours and it was not by accident that, much later, John Lockley was back where the young maids gathered between the mealie garden and the kraal fence to beautify themselves.

Jettama rose from where she sat and came to him. She smiled and John Lockley felt embarrassed. The other girls were watching and giggling.

'Can you come with me? I want ... to be private.'

They mounted Isi and rode out past the large mealie garden over the veld to a donga filled with clumps of fern and orchids and aloe. He reined in and they dismounted.

'Jettama, I wanted to say goodbye, but not with those girls watching.'

Suddenly he felt peculiar; there was a hot feeling spreading and rising up through him. He was looking at her dark, innocent eyes upturned to his and he realised that they had never been alone together before. Oh God, it's the same feeling I had that day when she was bitten by the snake. I cannot stop it.

She took hold of his arm, her touch like silk. 'I no want you go.'

It was a cool day but he was beginning to perspire. She was so close. He was imagining her body inside her calf-skin skirt and cape. He could see part of her through the opening at the neck, golden and provocative. She was still holding tightly to his arm. She lifted her other hand and as she did so he swung his arms around her, pressing his lips to hers as she responded openly.

When they broke away from each other he continued to look in her eyes. 'Have you? Have you ever kissed anyone else like that?'

'No.'

He could feel his blood coursing through his veins. 'You're so beautiful.'

She smiled. 'Say it again.'

'You are beautiful. You are . . . like Mrs Garner.'

'Who Mrs Garner?' ·

'A beautiful lady I met.'

He leant forward to her again, and this time when he kissed her she pushed his lips open and ran her tongue along the inside of his mouth. It was the most exciting experience of his life and thrills ran in spasms through his body.

'How did you know to do that?'

She smiled, and when she smiled his heart raced. 'Zulu girl know things.'

'But you said you had never kissed anyone before.'

'Yes?'

'Well, how did you know to do that?'

'Oh, Logley. You are so funny.' She laughed again, and the world was shut out and there was only her laughter.

He was feeling so wonderfully strange, but scared too. 'Jettama, we must go.'

'Why?'

'Because we must. Come on.'

'But you go away. You take Darli. You never come back.'

'I will come back. I solemnly swear on my life, I will.'

And now the revelation came, swiftly and with a thud like weighted lead upon his consciousness. He had thought it was Darli alone he wanted to be with. But there was another. Another one his heart desired. One he wanted to be with always . . . Jettama.

Jane was on her knees in Mimosa's small garden, taking cuttings from the dahlias and chrysanthemums, when Thulmi arrived carrying a letter from Christopher. He was in Pietermaritzburg and would be home on Saturday night or Sunday. How wonderful! Her two dear boys home at last . . . and what was this? She must read it again. What? A friend of John Lockley's coming too. A Zulu? For gracious sakes.

When she informed Mrs Veldbron, the Dutch woman commented quietly, 'No doubt he comes without my Dirk's blessing.'

As the party arrived Ellen ran forward to John Lockley and he leapt down from his horse to hold her close. Then, holding her arm, he said, 'Nell, this is my friend, Darlengi. Darlengi, my sister, Ellen.'

Ellen gingerly offered him her pale fingers.

'Oh, I am so very pleased to meeting you.' He took her hand in both of his.

Ellen gazed into the shining ebony eyes, and Darlengi's mouth drew back into a wide, attractive smile. Then, for some reason, Ellen abruptly looked away and withdrew her hand.

And so it was that Darlengi arrived, was taken in, and joined the Harrison family. The youth blossomed in the company at Mimosa.

Ellen was so thrilled to have her brother home that at first she would not have minded had he brought a whole Zulu tribe to live with them, but she soon recognised John Lockley's deep affinity with Darlengi. She did not like her brother showing Darlengi so much affection; there was something about Darlengi that unsettled her, even agitated her, so that while she swiftly noted the Zulu's intelligence and humour, she determined to remain aloof from him.

Conversely, Jane took to him quite quickly, and was soon teaching him along with John Lockley and Ellen. Although his attention span, at first, was not very long, after about two months he would sit all the required hours doing his writing and drawing.

He learned to read well within three months, and before the year's end the children's books he carried had turned into *Pickwick Papers* and *The Vicar of Wakefield*. He avidly learned anything and everything. His English improved at a wondrous rate and finally he understood grammar as well. He was very taken by pieces of furniture and their various uses and would sit for hours with a book from Christopher's library called *The Cabinet Maker and Upholsterer's Drawing Book*. He would stand for ten minutes at a time just looking at the Sheraton escritoire, or the sideboard and chairs and table. But in all the time he lived at Mimosa he never slept in a real bed, preferring to spend his nights upon the floor. Though he did make one concession. The Zulu pillow was a wooden one a few inches high on little legs, but after the first few nights Darlengi became a convert to the soft pillow and was to use one for the rest of his life.

After their school day the two youths would ride and hunt together. John Lockley's old friend the Port Captain did occasionally receive their company. He even attempted to teach Darli to swim, but they could never induce him to fish. He retained the Zulu disgust for fish and was never persuaded to taste it, no matter how it was cooked.

Christopher and Jane's wedding took place in the limited space of the government schoolroom in Field Street, on 21 November, 1853. While the foundation stone of St Paul's Church had been laid on the church erf in the Market Square on 17 March, it would be two years before it was open for services.

Jane looked lovely in a long cream lace gown, her pretty eyes shining through the Nottingham lace veil edged with silk. Ellen was her bridesmaid, in pale pink. Darlengi thought she was the most beautiful thing he had ever seen, with her chestnut hair falling gently on her shoulders. The guest list was very small and select. Then of course there was Darlengi, the intrigued and most intriguing guest, dressed in a suit and tie and looking quite wonderful.

While Darlengi thought the ceremony particularly short, compared with Zulu weddings, which lasted days, he was interested in the ring that was placed on Jane's hand, and liked the phrase 'I now pronounce you man and wife.' For weeks afterwards he would mime the minister's face and actions, repeating the words in a deep voice and then bursting into laughter.

Darlengi was very happy in Durban, for the family that he had come into opened their big hearts to him; all but Ellen who had no inclination to do so. The months passed and eventually it was accepted that Darlengi would stay until he had to return for his formal training in the Zulu regiment.

There were many in the settlement who were outraged that Mr Nelson had returned from upcountry with a Zulu boy in tow, not as a servant, but as a guest, in his home. Of course none of this worried Christopher or Jane. And the people they saw on a regular basis – like Mr George Cato, who would be the town's first mayor in the following August, and Port Captain Bell, and the men at the building and brickworks, and the people of Mimosa – accepted Darlengi for himself, for his appealing self. Besides, there were so many Bantus coming and going all over the settlement that Darli certainly was not an unusual sight, except for his European clothes.

In January 1854, the steamer *Calcutta* brought for the first time to Durban the Right Reverend Dr John Colenso, the new Bishop of Natal. He came for a ten-week visit and, whether accidentally or not, a proclamation was issued at that time stating: 'All natives residing or passing through the towns of Pietermaritzburg, Durban and Ladysmith are required to be clothed with some garment from the shoulder to the knee. Blankets are not objected to.'

Ellen, Darlengi and John Lockley were passing Mr Francis Harvey's wooden auction room when he nailed the proclamation poster to his wall. Ellen's eyebrows arched as she turned to Darlengi. 'Well, Darlengi, you can stop wearing real clothes now, and wear a blanket instead.'

Darlengi frowned. Mostly he did not understand Miss Ellen. She was somehow so ... cold, and he certainly did not recognise the sarcasm in this remark, but John Lockley did and he took hold of his sister's arm, pulling her sharply and saying, 'Nell, don't.'

But she appeared innocent, her lovely green eyes half closed. 'Sorry, I did not mean anything by it.'

That very afternoon, Matilda Veldbron reacted to the noise and clamour at the side of the house and came down the two stone steps out of her kitchen to find the delivery man, Councillor Sanderson, arriving with his dray load of casks of rice, and boxes of dried fruit and bottled beer. Thulmi and two other kitchen helpers, Joseph and Henny, plus Mannie, were arguing over where to store the casks.

Councillor Sanderson smiled under his wide moustache and patted the cask closest to his hand. 'So, Mrs Veldbron, fruit from the Cape, beer from London and eighteen casks of rice, all the way from Carolina via London town, don't you know? Well-travelled goods, I do declare.'

As Matilda instructed them where to store everything, she

looked down past the store shed and saw Darlengi sitting beyond it, all alone.

While John Lockley had long been a favourite of Matilda, somehow, from the day Darlengi arrived, the Zulu boy had captured her heart. It was a strange liaison, for Dirk Veldbron had no time for the youth. But the childless Matilda took to him and when the two boys were with her she would refer to them as her 'brave young men'; and they called her 'Mrs Tilly' in informal fashion, which over the years simply changed to Tilly. Matilda was a Boer, and as a Boer she had seen and been involved in struggles against the Matebele and the Zulus. She had seen bloodshed and had been broken-hearted by it, but while her husband quoted the gospel, Matilda applied it. She was a Christian in the true meaning of the word and never judged any person by something as visible as colour. So, without her husband Dirk ever realising it, Darlengi spent hours in the kitchen with her when John Lockley was off on a fishing trip.

Now, as she saw Darlengi sitting alone, Matilda frowned. He was so still, his slim back to her. She moved across the grass and down by the shed to him.

'Where's John Lockley?' she asked.

He started slightly and looking around attempted to smile at her. 'He's gone to fish, Mrs Tilly.'

'Ah, true, you're not a one for fishing, are you? Why are you sitting here?'

Now he frowned. 'I was thinking.'

She ruffled his tight curls. 'Ah, and what about?'

'Miss Ellen. She . . . how do you say? . . . confuses me.'

Matilda smiled. 'Well, you're not alone in that.'

'She says things to me that I do not understand. And when Logley is with us he gets annoyed with her, so then I realise it must have been bad. She never speak, I mean, speaks to me the way you and all the others do.'

Matilda sat down on the bench beside him. 'Darlengi, why does it trouble you? Miss Ellen is short with most people. She doesn't mean anything by it.'

He shook his head. 'She *does* mean something by it.'

Tilly sighed. 'There's one thing certain, she dotes on her brother. I sometimes think she's jealous of you, the way you are so close.'

He nodded. Then he turned on the seat to face her, his lively black eyes glinting in the sunlight. 'Yes, that is part of it, but there is much, much more.'

Matilda chucked him gently under the chin. He was such a thoughtful youth, wise and quick to learn, but perhaps too serious at times. 'Now, Darlengi, Miss Ellen is a complicated young lady and I don't think you should let it trouble you as you do. Come on, let's go and see the stores being unloaded.'

When Matilda and Dirk left at the end of February 1854 to live on the Tugela farm, Darlengi was truly sad, and Matilda was to incur Dirk's wrath for many a week afterward because in front of all those assembled to say goodbye she wrapped the Zulu youth in her arms.

It was because of Matilda that Darlengi realised all Boers were not alike: that one simply could not label a whole race as a certain type. But the blinkered attitude of some was shown to him just after Matilda and Dirk left for the farm.

Letters were carried between Durban and Pietermaritzburg by horse and rider. They were brought from Great Britain, Europe and Cape Town by ship, and as there were months between sailings the day or two after a ship's arrival was an exceedingly exciting time.

Part of Matilda's routine had been to go to the post office to collect anything that might have come from home. When the clipper ship *Port Dennison* arrived early in March, it was John Lockley and Darlengi who rode down to the settlement to see if there were anything for the family.

A section of a store owned by Messrs Middleton and Wirsing was rented by the government, and downstairs on the ground floor a good-sized room was utilised as the post office. It was late in the afternoon when the two boys arrived and passed under the sign hanging above the door which proclaimed: '*Post Office Business Hours, From Early Coffee to Sundown.*'

The room was empty except for the post master, Piet Fischer, who was working behind the long wooden counter half turned away. Without looking round he delivered his routine statement, 'To 'Maritzburg thrippence for half an ounce, every additional half-ounce sixpence; letters for England and the Cape eightpence; newspapers tuppence.'

101

John Lockley leant on the counter top. 'We've come to see if there is anything from the *Port Dennison* for Harrison or Nelson.'

It was now that the post master turned, looking over his pince-nez. 'Harrison or Nelson . . .' He caught sight of Darlengi. 'What the devil is the nigger doing in here, dressed like that?'

'I beg your pardon?'

'Him . . . the boy. There are no boys allowed in here. Everyone knows that.' He lifted his arm and sharply motioned for Darli to get out.

At that moment the Widow Strydom came lumbering through the door. She was a bustling old Boer whose husband had been killed by the Zulus. Her mouth actually dropped open when she saw Darlengi standing there.

'You heard me, boy.' Fischer continued to gesture with his thumb. 'Outside . . . there be no letters for niggers, you don't write. Out you go!'

Widow Strydom's eyes widened as she pursed her large mouth and took an incensed deep breath. 'Well, I never . . .'

Darlengi gave them a disgusted look and started for the door. For a few seconds John Lockley stood rigidly, unmoving. Then he took four quick paces after Darlengi, shouting, 'Stop, Darli!' and, taking his friend's arm in a restraining movement, faced back to the counter.

'No, John Lockley, it's better I go.'

'No. Post master Fischer, my friend and I shall leave now, together. If there's no place here for him then there's none for me.'

'I don't care whether you remain or go, but he gets out!'

John Lockley was embarrassed, insulted, and hurt: all for Darlengi. The inside of his throat had a stinging sensation as if he were about to cry. He took a deep breath. 'You're both bad people,' he said, and putting his arm around his friend's shoulder, they passed out through the door together.

Piet Fischer and the Widow Strydom shouted something after them, but they did not understand it.

They were on their horses and riding away before Darlengi said, 'I don't like some people.'

'And I don't like some people either. I'm so sorry, Darli.'

The dark eyes came round to the lighter ones. 'Why are you sorry? You defended me.'

'I'm sorry there are such people in the world. I don't understand them.'

Darlengi was silent for a little while; then as they passed the Market Square and turned north, he spoke again. 'Perhaps there are more such people than there are less such people.'

The incident was followed by an addition to the sign hanging above the post office door, which now read: *Post Office Business Hours, From Early Coffee to Sundown. No Bantus.*

When the two youths returned to Mimosa John Lockley was still angry and Jane came down the stairs to hear him say, 'Damn and blast them. How can they act like that in conscience?'

Jane asked, 'What's that, John Lockley? Damn who?'

'Old Fischer and the Widow Strydom. They insulted Darli, told him to get out of the post office.'

'Why?'

'Because he's black, a Zulu, damn it!'

'John Lockley, there's no need to raise your voice. Tell me what happened.' When he finished, Jane sighed deeply and took Darlengi by the arm. 'Oh, Darlengi, I'm so sorry. I apologise for them.'

She was amazed by his reply. 'Mrs Jane, John Lockley is more angry than Darlengi. Perhaps it is because he's embarrassed. The post master and the woman are not important. My own father hates me ... I am used to hatred.'

Jane turned to her nephew. 'Would you leave Darlengi with me for a few moments, please?'

When they were alone she asked Darlengi to follow her into the sitting room. Jane knew of some of Darlengi's life: how he had come with his sister to live in a kraal which was a long way from his birthplace; how his mother's death had occurred; but very little about his father. As they sat she asked, 'Darlengi, what do you mean when you say your father hates you?'

The boy had come to trust her. He lifted his steady gaze to hers and replied, 'When I was born my mother die ... er ... died. He blames me. He says I am no good. He loved my mother very much; too much.' He looked down at the pink palms of his hands upturned in his lap. 'He ... I think the word is ... banished me to live in a distant kraal.'

Jane was moved. She felt a tremor of surprise at the similarity between the births of her nephew and this boy, particularly as she knew they both believed they had been born on the same day. For a short time she was silent. She felt hurt for him and disgusted by his treatment in the post office, for if Darlengi were treated so, then of course many of the other Bantus must be. She leant over and took hold of the youth's hand. 'Has anything like what happened today ever happened before?'

She was very close to him, her lovely brown eyes distressed and a crease of concern sitting on her brow. He did not answer her immediately for he was thinking of the other time when he had been very badly treated. It had been recently, at the brickyard, when he had been waiting for Lockley.

Three white men had come in and swaggered across to where he had been sitting on the office step. He had seen one of them before, an ox cart driver who often outspanned at the back of Market Square.

One of the other two took off his hat and, wiping his hand across his damp brow, asked, 'Hey, nigger, where's the boss?'

Darlengi pointed into the next yard. 'Over there, that's Mr Russell, the manager.'

'You speak real uppity for a boy,' said the ox cart driver.

'Why aren't ye at work?' asked the first man, and Darlengi smiled. 'I do not work here, I am waiting for my friend.'

The ox cart driver looked affronted. 'Well, get outa here. Why're ye hanging around? Ready to thieve somethin', I'll be bound.'

Darlengi simply stared up at him. 'I do not need to leave.'

'Well I say ye do. Get on yer way, boy.'

Darlengi did not move.

This did not please the ox cart driver. He stepped forward and cuffed Darlengi across the head, so that he fell sideways from the step. He had only been hit once in his life before, many years earlier, by Shiambi, his father. He retaliated immediately and came straight back to hit the aggressor in the face. The other two men reacted, attempting to grab him and hold him but he swung around and hit the nearest one in the ribs. The man stumbled back, cursing as the other took out his whip and smashed it against the side of Darlengi's head.

Mr Russell heard the noise and leapt the stone wall. 'What the devil's going on? Stop! Stop!' He tried to get between Darlengi and the others.

'This bloody nigger hit me! I'll kill 'im.'

Mr Russell pushed the youth behind his own body and faced the men. 'He's a friend of Mr Nelson's ... *lives* with him at Mimosa.'

The three intruders all knew of Christopher Nelson, of his money and influence. They looked at each other.

'Bloody funny having kaffir bastards for friends.'

The youth was still shocked and insulted. He wished he had been holding an assegai, they would have been sorry then, but when Mr Russell asked him to go inside, he turned from them and went into the small stone office.

Mr Russell had come to him later and asked him not to make a fuss. Not to tell John Lockley or Mr Nelson. 'Those men are customers, Darlengi, and it'd be most awkward.' And as Mr Russell had stopped the fight before Darlengi had sustained any real injuries, no one was ever the wiser.

Now Jane repeated her inquiry. 'Darlengi, has anyone mistreated you before?'

He stopped himself just as he was about to tell her the truth. Instead he said, 'No.'

She looked relieved. 'Oh, thank heavens for that.'

He was looking at her in the way he had of almost staring. When he had first arrived it had made her feel uncomfortable, but now it was simply his way.

'Some white men think they are ... superior.'

'Yes, dear, very perceptive of you. There are so many foolish people. All I can say is that there are others, different from those silly folk today, who don't feel this way, who care for people, no matter what race or religion they are.'

'Like John Lockley?' The youth continued to gaze at her.

'Yes, like John Lockley, and others.'

'Like Mr Christopher?'

'Yes.'

'And like you?'

'Yes.'

'Thank you,' he said. The 'thank you' was so simple, so honest, so sincere, that it tugged at her heart. She leant forward and hugged him, hugged him as she would John

Lockley, close and tenderly, just exactly the same; for in her heart he was the same and always would be. And while she hugged him he was pleased he had troubled her no more.

Later, when John Lockley recounted the post office incident to Ellen, his sister shook her pretty head, put out her hand and touched his shoulder. After eighteen months she knew a lot about the history of Natal. 'John Lockley, darling, the Boers have had bad experiences with the Zulus. Everyone knows that Widow Strydom's husband was killed with Piet Retrief in 1838, at Dingane's kraal. She hates them, I suppose. And in any case, Darlengi ... well ... because of you, he's more civilised. Mr Fischer would not have realised that.'

'No, Ellen, don't defend them. Fischer and Strydom were not interested in Darli as civilised or uncivilised. Their attitude was simply because he's black. And when you say "everyone knows" about her husband, what everyone knows is how she treats her black servants. She's an old ... pig!'

And Ellen nodded, for it was true. The widow and her friend, Mrs Dom Joubert, were renowned for their ill treatment of their Bantus.

By the second Christmas the incident was far in the past. Darlengi excitedly recalled the previous year when he had kept asking about the presents. What were they? Who would receive what? How would they know which belonged to whom? This year he knew, and looked forward to the celebrations again. They had such nice, civilised customs, these English.

It was Christmas Eve, and Ellen was in the back garden. She had just fed her rabbits and was cutting some tiny roses that Jane had nurtured all spring and summer, but now had reluctantly agreed to have on the Christmas table. She looked up to see Darlengi coming from the stable.

'Good afternoon, Miss Ellen.'

'Good afternoon, Darlengi.' The girl smiled, but somehow it was not a friendly smile. 'Where's John Lockley?'

'He's inside the house.'

The youth watched as she snipped the blooms with her tiny, ornate scissors.

'The ruses are lovely.'

'Roses,' corrected Ellen.

'Roses. I am liking Christmas.'

She looked at him and a small shiver ran through her. He did have this way of making her feel odd. 'Yes, Darlengi, tonight shall be such fun. We'll give out the gifts after dinner and then we'll have a concert.'

Darlengi knew about concerts now, and he had learned some songs to sing.

Ellen evaded his gaze as she asked, 'Do you have an item this time?'

'Yes, I have two songs.'

'Oh? What are they?'

'An English song and a Zulu song.'

'Good heavens! In any case, John Lockley is always the best. He can recite funny things and can sing too.' She turned deliberately away.

He was still watching her as she bent down. His English was constantly improving, and he could construct sentences correctly most of the time. 'You love him more than anyone, don't you?'

She did not look up. 'I don't know what you mean.'

The sun was beginning to descend; the sky was deep rose and the evening light seemed to make her fair skin gleam. He thought she was very, very lovely. He believed she must be like the water spirit that Yangaani spoke of, all glowing and pale, and very beautiful. He was in awe of her and yet at the same time not afraid of her at all: it was an ambivalent, disquieting, and yet such a strangely protective feeling he had for Ellen. He decided he must say the truth he knew.

'I see with a Zulu's eye. It's obvious to everybody that you love John Lockley. But I think I'm the only one who sees you love him too much. Not even he knows that. And you force all your love towards him for you fear to turn it elsewhere.'

Ellen stood up and rounded on him. There was ice in her eyes as she locked her gaze with his. 'Darlengi. One cannot love someone too much. And you don't know anything about me, or how I feel.'

'Don't I? I have a sister, Jettama, she loves me, but not too much . . . only enough.' He was still holding her gaze. 'You deny what is so, for you greatly fear to look inside your heart.'

She sniffed and tilted her head. 'What does all that mean? You talk such rubbish, Darlengi.'

He continued looking intently at her.

'Don't stare, Darlengi, it's rude.' She turned her stiff back upon him and bent back to her flowers.

He remained where he was, watching her a few seconds more as she continued snipping the roses. He shook his head in confusion. He did not know why she acted as she did. All he had done was to say what he could see, oh, so very clearly. He had watched her for over a year, studied her; she was his favourite subject. He was often surprised that no one else saw the way she pushed all her love at her brother; especially John Lockley himself, who was totally oblivious. Darlengi felt that somehow, sometime it might hurt her, and he never wanted anything to hurt this exquisite, pale creature ... his Ice Princess. How badly he wanted to lean forward and stroke her abundant curls, but he did not. Momentarily he focused on his black hand and then on her white one holding the roses. He made a sad, strangled sound and then in a quick movement he somersaulted backwards and continued somersaulting all around the perimeter of the grass.

Now she turned to look at him with enigmatic eyes. She almost caught herself admiring how agile he was. The fact was that he was like a trying child really: an intelligent, trying child who made such vexing statements.

By the time Darlengi returned to his upcountry life he had insinuated himself into all the hearts at Mimosa. All except Ellen's. And yet his opinion of her never altered. To him, she was his Ice Princess whom he could see into, and yet would never have access to. She mostly avoided him and when she was in his company she only answered his questions and never instigated conversation. Yet it altered nothing: he, the Zulu, understood her: complicated Ellen who did not admit her true feelings even to herself. He had access to her heart, even though she did not want it, or concede it.

On the Wednesday morning that was the first day of August 1855, Darlengi left Durban. He had spent almost two years there. Everyone gathered to say goodbye, from the kitchen boys to Mrs Russell, the wife of the manager of the brickworks. He would depart with Christopher, John Lockley and Thulmi, who were returning to the farm.

Christopher was aware, as was all of Natal, that trouble was brewing in Zululand, that the half-brothers Cetshwayo and Mbuyazi were vying to become Mpande's heir, and while

Christopher personally thought that any real trouble was probably still a year or more away, he felt it was time to go to the inland farm and make sure it was fortress-like and well laagered. He was not about to give up the Harrison-Nelson square miles. His was a romantic dream that when things were finally, totally, lastingly peaceful, it would be their country property; worth taking Jane to for a few months each year.

When Darlengi came to say goodbye to Ellen she put out her small, white hand in a haughty movement. He took it in his and held it, regarding her through thoughtful eyes. 'Goodbye, Miss Ellen.'

'Good bye, Darlengi.'

'I wish you . . . well.'

'Yes, thank you, Darlengi, I wish you well also.' She attempted to remove her hand but he tightened his grip and confused her by asking, 'Do you?'

A quick flush of embarrassment rose to her cheeks. She did not want to keep holding his hand. 'Oh! Of course I do, don't be silly.' Firmly she extricated her fingers from his. There was a sick feeling in Ellen's stomach. Darlengi was disturbing her, his attention always did. He had grown tall here at Mimosa, and was almost his full height of six feet and half an inch, though at seventeen he was still very slender. He looked down at her, wondering when he would see her again.

He said in a low voice, 'I won't see you for years; that makes me sorry.'

She looked up quickly and was just about to retort, 'It doesn't make me sorry,' when the expression in his mysterious eyes checked her. She did not like to admit it, but there was something about him that was fascinating. She merely answered, 'Yes, well, time passes.'

She was relieved when he had left her and taken away his mystifying gaze.

He moved across to Jane and held out his hand once more in the European manner. He had come to call Jane and Christopher 'Aunt' and 'Uncle', which they were delighted about. 'Goodbye, Aunt Jane, I am honoured to have been here.'

'My very dear Darlengi, goodbye.' She knew he had to return to some sort of military training. The similarity with what was ahead for John Lockley leapt to her mind. Their lives were somehow parallel, so similar, and yet so dissimilar.

Sometimes she wondered if they had really done the youth a kindness. For while his English was impeccable (she herself had seen to that), and he understood and accepted all their European ways, Christopher had told her he would be going back to live in a grass hut with people who were superstitious and uncivilised. And as she took him again in her arms and kissed and hugged him to her, she earnestly prayed that in opening their lives to him they had done him no harm.

As they rode away, Ellen walked beside her brother's horse down along the avenue of young pines to the road. She told him to be careful and not to do anything dangerous, that she would miss him badly. Then she stood and watched them along the road. Just as they disappeared around the bend, she saw Darlengi turn in the saddle and wave, and she deliberately stopped herself from raising her hand in return.

It was after dinner that night, when the sun had set in a flaring red ball behind the Berea range of hills, that Jane and Ellen sat by the warm fire, the one tatting and the other reading. Jane sighed and lifted her head. 'How I shall miss them all. Dear Darlengi, he was such a well into which to pour knowledge ... liked to learn and did learn a great deal. His English is almost perfect. I noticed again today how his "k" sound is no longer a "g". He says "John *Lockley*" now, though he continues to use "Logley" affectionately.' Then she voiced the thought that had been disturbing her for months. 'I wonder if he'll be satisfied with his life back with his own people.'

Ellen put her book aside. She felt mixed up tonight. Her brother had gone, Uncle Chris had gone. 'He was lucky to be here, that's all I know, and I'll never understand why John Lockley thinks he's so marvellous. He's simply a very intelligent Zulu, that's all.'

'A little more than that to your brother, dear. They both truly believe they were born on the same day, and at the time of each birth their mothers died. I think that makes them feel akin.'

Ellen shook her head. She felt irritated. For most of the afternoon, she had been thinking of Darlengi, and she failed to understand why. 'Lord, Aunt Jane, that hardly makes them brothers.'

'In their eyes it may. John Lockley saved Darlengi from

drowning, Ellen, remember that.' Then her voice dropped and she spoke the strangest thought. 'Though somehow I have the peculiar fancy there was kinship between this family and Darlengi long before we ever laid eyes upon each other.'

Ellen looked up sharply. 'What on earth does that mean?'

'I don't know, darling, but I feel it all the same.'

CHAPTER SIX

The purple-flint-coloured eyes opened to look into the ebony ones.

The September evening sun threw indigo shadows across the two naked figures under the blanket on the grass mat inside the cluster of massive granite rocks on the bank of the Tugela.

'Jettama, I love you so.'

Her fine black fingers cupped his face to drag his mouth back down upon hers.

In the beginning they had simply kissed and held each other close, but soon John Lockley had put his hands under her cape and cupped her breasts, and shivered with delight. And as he had become more bold she had moaned a small sound of love in his ear and he had felt the blood rushing in his veins. It was just a month ago that they could no longer stop themselves, and her lithe young body had taken his lithe young body, welcomed him, exulted in his love along with the pain.

Darlengi had gone to the Inkanhla regiment along with two other herd boys a week after they had come back to the Tugela farm.

Christopher had asked Darlengi for a private conversation and they had met on the straggling lawn in front of the farmhouse.

The man had taken the youth's hand in his and said, 'My boy, I have brought you back here because I made a promise to chief Unondo to do so. But that's all I promised. Now, I give you this choice. You have lived two years in our home, become part of our family. I took a Zulu boy to Durban for one reason only ... because my nephew wanted me to, and I thought I would humour John Lockley for a couple of months and then return his Zulu friend back to his kraal. But that did not happen; for along the way I found much to admire in that boy. He was honest and kind, an avid learner, and he behaved in an exemplary fashion. So the months went by and turned into years and I brought you back here reluctantly. My wife and I are very proud indeed of you. And we want you to know that you may keep the place you have made for yourself in our lives, if you so wish.'

'You mean to stay and live with you always?'

'I do.'

Darlengi was silent for many seconds. He understood and appreciated the extraordinary offer that was being made to him. But he was a Zulu and he had a little sister, and Mattana whom he loved and had not seen for years. He did not fully understand the consequences of his time in the civilised world, but he was so astute that he realised they were extensive. For now he knew he loved the Nelsons and the Harrisons. He had gone to Durban an excited boy, keen to spend time with his wonderful new friend, in his wonderful new world. He had come back to the Tugela changed, and perhaps knowing too much. He stood looking at Christopher, a man he now called 'Uncle Chris'; a man who offered him a place in his home forever: a way of life which allured him.

Finally he spoke. 'While I will always treasure this offer you have made me today, I must go to the Inkanhla regiment. I must see my good mother Mattana and take my place among the Zulus.'

The last time Darlengi and John Lockley had been together they had gone to their hideaway, and over an open fire had heated the head of an assegai until it was red hot. Taking it up in a piece of cloth, Darlengi stuck it into the ground shaft down, red-hot head up, and they knelt facing each other with the spear between them. John Lockley rolled up his sleeve and then in ceremonial fashion they stretched out their right arms and took hold of each other's elbows, pressing the insides of their forearms against the red-hot assegai. As the heat seared their flesh they said in unison, 'You are my brother for life.' After ten seconds of the scorching pain they let go.

It had been a strange parting between the two youths, for they were now seventeen years old and had been constant, familiar companions living their most formative adolescent years in intimacy. They knew it would be years before they would be with each other again; and now Darlengi had the concept of what a year truly meant. He knew a strange truth, knew it with the clarity of a disturbing but accepted fact; that the world was changing for them, that they would change with it, that the days of their carefree youth were ending. Darlengi took John Lockley's hand in the British manner, and tilting his strong chin said goodbye in English and in Zulu. Then John Lockley repeated it.

Afterwards their eyes dropped to the painful, blistered burn marks on the insides of their forearms, and they unclasped hands and hugged each other close.

'I want you to have Isiwukulu. He'll be kept at the farm for you to use any time you're home. I've told Tilly and made sure all the men at the farm know he's for you, especially Dirk Veldbron.'

'Thank you,' shouted Darlengi as he loped away to join his travelling companions, holding both his hands high in the air in an extended goodbye.

The very next day John Lockley and Jettama began their secret meetings in the rocky bower overlooking the Tugela where he and Darlengi had spent so many hours.

They did not meet every day, though they would have liked to do so. They were cautious enough to miss days now and then and even to wait three days at a time.

Jettama's strategy was to leave the kraal after her work day was finished, and making the excuse that she liked to be alone and think, to walk west then north along the Tugela. She passed through successive threads of acacia trees until she came to a clump of seringas pushing their large, emerald-green leaves in profusion to the sky. There she halted. On the far side of these the tall grey stones sat in several clusters, all Stone Age sentinels looking down upon the Tugela. It was in the first great pile of rocks that the trysting place lay. From all sides it appeared impenetrable, but there was an entry from the south, a narrow passage between two rocks about eight feet high to another that had foot holes in it; and, climbing up, the lovers would find a second steep passage which led between two flat-sided rocks up into the saucer-shaped nook ten feet in diameter.

John Lockley's pattern was to ride Isiwukulu to the north away from the farm and after a mile or so to strike west and come down to the meeting place. When they were not making love he would teach Jettama English words and grammar. She was like her brother, bright and eager, and while she would never speak with the fluency of Darlengi, she eventually had an adequate grasp of the language, enough to understand and be understood.

Today he had shown her a picture book of animals of the world, and how she had laughed at the whale. She could not believe such a large water creature existed. And when John Lockley spoke about the oceans of the world, she could not conceptualise the size. Her eyes were round with wonder.

As the sun sank she said, 'It grows late. I must go, Logley.'

'Yes, I know, but oh, Jettama.' And he covered her mouth with his own and ran his fingers hungrily along her body.

She spoke more urgently. 'No, Logley, late. Sun set soon.'

He knew she was right. He sat up and pushed his hand through his hair. 'When shall we meet again?'

And now, because she understood the days of the week, she was able to say, 'Saturday.'

He watched her dressing. She tied her mouche around her waist, the long threads of beaded skin hanging down in front. Then she put back on the old singlet that Darlengi had given her, the pert nipples of her teenage breasts pushing through. She still wore the tiger's tooth on the cord around her neck and she wrapped the antelope-skin cape round her body and fixed it at the throat.

She leant down in the shadows where he sat watching her, to kiss him again.

'Saturday, Logley.'

She was soon outside and running through the seringas. The sun was making its last attempt at illuminating the day when she passed the strings of acacia trees, and by the time she reached the high grass of the plain near the kraal, darkness had fallen. She slipped in through the kraal gate and was hurrying by the line of huts towards the one she shared with Weena and Kenga when a voice said, 'Will your eyes be on me tonight when I dance?'

She stopped short and turned in the pale light of the early moon. It was Nangeni, a warrior of the Umbonambi regiment who had returned home last full moon, after years away in Nodwengu, the king's kraal, and then in Cetshwayo's military kraal near the Umlatoosi River. There was enough light to see that he was ceremonially clad and as he bent towards her she could see the pale blue crane feather he wore in his headdress. He was admired by all the girls in the kraal and had come several times to Jettama's hut.

She remembered there was to be a celebration tonight to ensure that the good spirits of their ancestors would help nurture the growth of the corn and other vegetables in the coming spring planting.

She nodded. 'Yes, I will see you.'

'Where have you been?' It was an innocent question, for while he had noticed that now and then Jettama liked to go off on her own, he had no idea why and was merely making conversation. But Jettama felt guilty; too frequently of late she had been asked the same question by her friend Patha, who braided her hair. So her reply was too quick, too strong, too defensive. 'Why do you ask? I have been walking. It is my way. I like to be ... alone.'

His large brows drew together. He could see the whites of her eyes softly illuminated in the moonlight. 'Yes, you do,' he answered as she turned and moved quickly away. Everyone said Jettama was deep, hard to know, and probably she was. She was surely too lean; she would need to get fatter and then she really would be hard to resist. He would dance well tonight. He would impress her.

Three hours later, while John Lockley sat thinking of her on the veranda of the Tugela farm, his knees drawn up under his chin and his arms clasped around them, Jettama sat thinking of him. Nangeni's powerful body spun before her in the rites of the spring planting and while her eyes followed his long blue crane feather whirling around, she did not see him. She did not see his strong, sinewy legs, nor his strapping girth, nor his powerful arms, nor the gleaming sweat as it ran in manly rivulets between the firm muscles of his chest. She saw instead the long, lithe, sun-browned body and the debonair swing of the handsome boy's head as John Lockley ran his fingers through his hair. She saw the smooth skin of his face and the dark eyelashes framing the purple-blue eyes as his mouth came down to hers. She saw his strong, young mouth and she relived the caress of it on her own.

Why could she not with be him, instead of being here and doing what custom demanded? Custom ruled her whole life really ... all Zulu lives. It was custom to have this dance each

116

spring; custom to have Darlengi go off to the regiment; custom to beat drums on the night of the new moon; custom for the brother of a deceased man to take up with his widow; custom for cattle to be driven to the grave of a dead man; and custom to change your hairstyle into a beehive after marriage; custom for Yangaani, the witch doctor, to hold 'smelling-outs' to find evil spirits, and custom to roll a newborn babe in cow dung and pass it back and forth in the smoke of a fire.

When her first signs of womanhood had appeared about three years ago, she had asked why she must protect her face from sunshine. Why she was not to walk on a path nor to drink milk. And the age-old answer had come back to her, 'It is custom. And worst of all, it was custom for a girl to marry the man who paid the most lobola for her. Custom ... custom ... custom ... it was crushing her.

'So, what did you think of me?'

She looked up sharply, eyes finally seeing Nangeni as he sat down, his skin shining with dripping sweat from his great and splendid exertion.

'What did you say?'

'Did you like my dancing?'

'Ah ... yes. It was very impressive.' Then she could not help herself as she added, 'I'm sure the custom of dancing will make such a difference to the mealie crop this season.'

Momentarily he looked disconcerted; then his eyes flashed with anger. 'Why do you say that? You make fun of us.'

She sighed; it shuddered through her young body like a miniature earthquake. 'No, Nangeni, I do not. Forgive me. I did not mean it.'

Then he suggested she walk with him around the kraal fence and his big hand came towards her to help her rise.

She did not take it but turned from him to Patha who sat beside her, her gaze fixed on Nangeni. 'Patha will go with you, I'm tired.'

'But the feast is only beginning; the cow is just now being slaughtered.'

Jettama stood up and turned from him, saying, 'I'm sorry. Goodnight, Nangeni. Goodnight, Patha.'

He felt offended and turned quickly from her to Patha, as if Jettama did not matter. But the next day his eyes followed her round the kraal, and he took to seeking her out and making conversation. It was Patha who came to her aid in the most unsuspecting fashion. She was so enamoured of Nangeni that she was offering him more than he could refuse, and for a time it was Patha he met in the trees beyond the mealie garden, and in doing so, allowed Jettama to go about unwatched.

One morning Christopher came into John Lockley's room and sat on the edge of his bed. 'Son, I'm taking Thulmi and Umslopagas on a two-week expedition up along the Buffalo River and into western Zululand and the Boer Utrecht district, and I'd like you to come. You should see more of Africa.'

John Lockley did not answer immediately. He was thinking of Jettama and how he would miss her if he went, but he knew it would disappoint his uncle if he did not go. 'Thanks, Uncle Chris, I'd like to come.'

And while he did miss Jettama, he loved every minute he was away. They put up their tent each night and talked under the stars, and Christopher told him tales and stories. It was a memorable time for both of them and brought them even closer. On their first night together, Christopher told him of a Swahili word, 'safari', which meant an expedition like the one they were on. 'It comes from the Arabic and a lot of the natives hereabouts use the word.'

'I like the sound of it,' John Lockley said, repeating it softly. 'Sa-far-i.'

They camped one night on a rocky plain covered with clumps of yellow long grass. Over them towered a strange, sphinx-like mountain and John Lockley stood looking up to the eastern slope of it while the sun set behind, delineating its eerie, black shape. A peculiar feeling came over him and he shivered and felt suddenly quite lonely. He turned and hurried back to the camp where Thulmi was preparing the meal over the fire.

The Zulu looked up as John Lockley asked, 'What's this place called?'

'Isandlwhana . . . meaning, "something like a small house".'

'It looks more like a sphinx to me.'

'What's that?' asked Umslopagas, coming up behind them.

'A sort of hybrid monster that has the body of a lion and the head of a woman. This mountain's like one.'

Umslopagas pursed his lips as he looked back at the mountain. 'Mmm, strange place.'

When they rode away in the early morning mist there was something that made John Lockley look back at the mountain many times.

They had been back from their trip for only three weeks when John Lockley met Jettama with a look of despair. She had known this day would come. She threw herself into his arms, the tears flowing down her satin cheeks to drip from her chin. 'Logley, Logley, but I will love you always. Please do not go.'

'Jettama, we return to Durban. I must go to military academy in England. It has been planned for me. It's the custom in our family; all the males are soldiers.'

'Custom!' She spat out the word with such venom, he was startled. 'How I hate it all. You must go, for it is planned, I must stay, for it is planned.'

'Oh, my darling. I'm sorry. I know we're young . . . but wait for me, Jettama, please wait until I grow up. I'll come back.'

She looked at him and took his face in her hands, pulling his head down so that he could look into her eyes. She knew he had to go to this place called Military Academy far, far away in England where the White Queen lived. But always she had avoided asking him the question dearest to her heart, the question of how long he would be away. Sometimes she thought she might die being parted from him. Now she had to know. 'How long, Logley? Tell me true . . . how long?'

And he kissed her mouth and said, 'It will be years, perhaps four or five.'

For a second she thought her heart had stopped. Then the blood seemed to rush to her brain. How could she live that long? Four or five years without him. She closed her eyes and swayed backwards.

He caught her in his arms, brought her gently to the ground and kissed her softly on the cheek. 'I love you as I will love no other in all my life. Wait for me, Jettama.'

Her frightened eyes turned to his. He kissed her again and they rolled backwards on to the ground to join their youthful bodies once again. And when his breath came in glorious groans from his mouth and she stopped lifting her hips towards him, she took his face again in her hands and whispered into his lips, 'I will wait for you.'

Jettama dawdled on her way home. She lingered in the

acacia trees and it was with very little interest that she heard Nangeni call out behind her. She did not want conversation with anyone, let alone Nangeni.

But he soon caught up with her and his first words brought her eyes round to his in shock.

'I know where you go and I know who you see.'

Nangeni had followed her today. After weeks of every afternoon with Patha in the trees beyond the mealie fields, today he had been inclined to sit and smoke with two of his friends in the shade of a euphorbia tree instead. For even when he lay with Patha he pretended she was Jettama. And when he had caught sight of Jettama passing through the kraal gate and heading westward he had followed her.

He had stayed well back from her and found her quite easy to track; hadn't he followed the spoor of animals a thousand times? Jettama was easy game. But he had been mystified when suddenly he had lost her in amongst the great heaps of rocks along the Tugela. He was turning back to see if he had missed something when he saw the English boy on his horse; the one who had taken Jettama's brother to the place of Durban so far away. He had only seen John Lockley a few times, for he had not come to the kraal once Darlengi had gone away, but he knew him. Swiftly Nangeni concealed himself and watched John Lockley dismount and hurry to the great heaps of rocks, where he scrambled between two granite stones and disappeared. He needed to see no more, but nevertheless he waited the full two hours until Jettama reappeared and went wandering leaden-footed back towards the kraal. Then he had watched for the white youth to come out of the rocks.

Just as John Lockley had been about to mount Isi a voice halted him, shouting, 'Stop!' in Zulu.

John Lockley turned in amazement to see a fine, strapping Zulu of about twenty-five brandishing an assegai. As John Lockley's Zulu was almost equal to Nangeni's the conversation swiftly progressed.

'What do you want?' John Lockley asked.

The man came nearer; he was surprised that the white boy spoke such perfect Zulu. 'You have been with Zulu girl, Jettama. You have coupled with her.' Nangeni was only guessing but it was surely what he would have done in the same situation, so his attitude was one of certainty.

120

'I don't know what you mean.' While John Lockley had been very surprised to be challenged like this, and he did not like the fire in the eyes of the warrior, he was not afraid of him. 'Why are you so angry?'

'She is not for likes of you. She is a Zulu and is meant for Zulu man. You bring her only pain ... fill her mind with dreams she has no right to.'

Had John Lockley been older he might have seen the wisdom in Nangeni's words, but he was brimful of his teenage love for the girl. 'I must go.'

'You must not see her again.'

'Why? Do you think *you* can capture her heart?'

Nangeni's eyes narrowed and he came very close, menacingly close, and dropped the blade of his assegai to rest on John Lockley's shoulder. The point lay very near the jugular vein in the boy's neck. 'She will be mine in time. You stay away now forever.'

John Lockley's eyes dropped for some seconds to the spear before he lifted them back to Nangeni's. He sounded much more in control than he was. 'I will stay away, but for one reason only. I must return to Durban after this night, but I *will* be back. You can be sure of that.'

Nangeni's answer was quite simple, quite definite and quite chilling. 'Then I shall kill you.'

John Lockley's hand quivered as he reached out and took Isiwukulu's reins and Nangeni removed his assegai. Then the youth mounted his horse and met Nangeni's menacing gaze as if he felt no fear. For a few seconds their eyes locked, then he turned the animal's head and rode away.

On his ride back to the farm he had a great ache in his chest. It was a warm evening but he shivered, the spasms running in tingles down his arms to his fingers. He suddenly felt quite out of his depth. He had been threatened by a Zulu warrior and he could tell no one. He loved Jettama deeply, but he had been shocked into realising that he was yet a boy with a boy's thoughts and dreams. He felt terribly alone, terribly inexperienced. But as Isiwukulu's hooves pounded through the long grass of the veld, he resolved that he would be true to Jettama, no matter what. In his heart he knew his love would last; in his heart he knew her love would last, and when he did come back here to her, he would be a man.

It was not until later, in the safety of his bed, that he began to wonder how Jettama would deal with such a man as Nangeni.

But Jettama had started to deal with him that very afternoon in the acacia trees when he had confronted her with the statement that he knew where she went and whom she saw.

'What do you mean?'

'You lie with the English boy. You are disgusting. No good Zulu girl would do such a thing.'

In those seconds she suddenly became aware that while he was challenging her, she had the chance to control him, and her reply was most effective. 'Forget him, Nangeni. He goes away. I will see him no more.'

And then he frightened her. 'I know. He told me he goes to place of Durban.'

She started and her hand came up to her mouth. 'You spoke with him?'

'Yes. I told him if ever he comes back near you I will kill him.'

She felt sick with fear that he had harmed John Lockley. She attempted to speak calmly. 'Where is he now?'

'He rode off on horse. Nangeni scare him good.'

Somehow she did not believe that John Lockley would be scared, but she was relieved to hear he had ridden away. Inwardly she sighed with relief. Outwardly she looked impassively at Nangeni, tossed her head and walked swiftly away. While she walked she thought about the years ahead. She knew she was almost at marriageable age, and while Nangeni might think to become her suitor, who was he to pay lobola to? Her father was the one to receive payment and she had not seen him since she was tiny. And it was most unlikely that she would be chosen to join an iNtanga – a female guild which corresponded to the regiments and which sometimes were married off to the regiments – for she was too far from the king's kraal. It was different with Darlengi. Mattana was grooming him for the future.

Yes, she told herself, she was quite safe. And when the following morning John Lockley came to the kraal on the pretext of saying goodbye to Chief Unondo, her heart expanded with pride and love. She and old Weena were cooking mealies when he strode up. He said goodbye to Weena and then

Jettama stood to face him. He took her left hand and said softly, 'Jettama, I meant what I said to you yesterday. I will come back. Believe that always.'

She smiled up into his eyes. 'I will.'

He kissed her hand and walked away to where Isi was tethered. When he mounted and rode away she followed to the kraal gate, her heart racing. She did not see Nangeni, there was no sign of him, thank her good ancestors. Her eyes followed John Lockley until he disappeared. She would wait for him, he would come back; she knew he would.

Darlengi and the two other herd boys had walked thirty miles north-east the first day away from their Tugela River kraal. The induna who travelled with them found them billets in a friendly kraal near Inkanhla Mountain, and Darlengi slept soundly. When he woke it was to find Mattana at his side and the other herd boys gone.

'Mattana!' Tears rose to his eyes. 'I do not see you for four summers. At last you are here.'

She took him in her stringy arms and kissed him. 'I have missed the reality of you but I have watched over the spirit of you. Never doubt that.'

'I do not.'

Then she explained, 'Your companions were chosen for Mebe kraal; you are chosen for Inkanhla military kraal on the Uvulu River. You are to follow Cetshwayo.'

'Why, ancient one?'

'Because I see it is best.'

She travelled with him, and on the evening of the second day they stood on the brow of Inkwenkewe Hill, from where they could see a substantial kraal sited below, a mile to the east towards the river bank.

They descended to the plain and she turned to him and smiled, showing three broken teeth which she had sharpened to little points. 'Wait here.'

He sat watching flocks of birds crowding on to a number of shallow lakes fringed with reeds. Blue cranes lifted with great wings from the surfaces and many-coloured ducks swam in company with flocks above of large heavy brown bitrons. In the middle distance plovers and small bustards ran through the grass and a herd of duiker grazed. He moved his position once when he saw a python nearby, and patiently polished the knife he wore in a sheath at his waist, until, as the sun was setting, he saw Mattana hastening back to him, using her staff to travel more quickly.

She took him in her arms and hugged him close, saying strange words that meant nothing to him. Then she said, 'Go now in through the gates of the kraal, the induna, Kayo, waits for you. He will teach you and when you are fit to be a warrior I will come to you again. All this is necessary.'

His eyes begged her. 'But cannot you stay here with me?'

She smiled gently. 'Darlengi – I gave you that name, you know. They laid you down in the back of the hut and I knew Shiambi was leaving you there to die. But I took you and even he dared not go against me then. To answer you; it is not good that I am seen with you here in this place, just at this time. But Kayo is clever and is one of mine. Trust him.'

Darlengi knew nothing of the intricate politics that made up Mattana's existence; the queen of witch doctors, cautious and artful, judicious, diplomatic; expedient survivor of a hundred social ebbings and flowings; ally of three kings, and now shrewdly positioning herself as ally to the next. All the boy knew was that if she said it was so, then it was so; that she would never hurt him and he could trust her implicitly. This was enough.

He embraced her a few moments and after kissing the multitude of ridges on her brow, hastened away.

Her alert eyes watched him loping off down the hill in the twilight ... the boy soon to be a man. She sighed, an odd sound crackling from her throat. She felt the aches and pains of age though she was, in fact, only fifty years old. She knew she had some summers left, enough to place Darlengi close to the power centre. She had always loved the boy, just as she had loved his mother, the child of Oola, her only true friend. Oola had died not long after Darlengi's mother.

Mattana smiled as she watched his slender black figure racing across the plain near the river, then suddenly a tremor ran through her and the smile faded. For out of the river of recollections in her mind flowed the memory of the girl of sixteen summers who also ran across a plain near another river; ran in terror as the huts of her kraal burned behind her.

... It was a summer's day. She was a daughter of the Tembu

clan, and Ngosa, their chieftain, had stood this afternoon against an impi led by one called Shaka, who had lived with the Mtetwa and now was uniting the Zulus. Shaka's name was already feared from the Umvoloosi to the Tugela and beyond, but some brave men simply would not be slaughtered without a fight and so the Tembu, allied with another clan, the Cunu, had tried to hold the Buffalo River crossings. But now the river was running with blood; the blood of her mother and her sisters and all the women of the Tembu who had waited terrified in their kraal to know the outcome of the day's battle. When she saw the black wrath swarming through the gates of the kraal, screaming for blood, she knew she would never see her father or her brothers again.

While the old men and women and children around her stood like horrified statues, she had turned and run to the inner kraal where the cattle were kept. Sliding down in amongst them she had hidden there and watched through the fence the butchering of her relatives. She had vomited when she saw the twelve-foot-long spears raised to the sky with her old Uncle Nembo and her grandfather writhing on them, eyes gouged out, impaled against the evening sky. Stiff with terror she saw the Zulu warriors herding up the women and children, and as they lifted their assegais to hack them down she forced herself to action and pushed further into the frightened cattle that stamped their hooves and raised their own fearful wailing to the sky. On her hands and knees she crawled through the animals, hooves kicking, cutting and bruising her, but she felt nothing; her whole world vision only the terrified whimpering in her mind. She slid through a hole at the bottom of the fence on the far side of the kraal, away from the blood-letting, and on her hands and knees crept into the nearest hut.

It was empty and the noises of death were in the distance now. This was Tenga's hut, one of her friends she would see no more. She ran across the highly polished floor and snaked under a pile of grass mats against the wall to lie there trembling.

A short time later she heard wild cries coming closer, and then she smelt the smoke. The Zulus were setting fire to the huts! She heard the running feet and the insane shouting and then the crackling all around her. Flames were everywhere when she came out from under the mats and ran out through the door. Wildly, without plan of action, she headed between the leaping, twisting flames. And then she remembered ... there was an opening in the outer kraal fence which the women used to go to the Buffalo River. The main gate was on the south-east side of the kraal, away from the river, but the one she wanted was such an insignificant opening with a small gate, easy to miss. It was somewhere close by. *Don't get disoriented in the madness of the fires. Breathe slowly, stay calm.* She screamed as part of a burning hut wall fell towards her, but it did not hit her and soon she was at the outer fence and pushing open the small gate and crawling through into the long grass near the mealie garden.

It was almost dark now and a storm was brewing in the twilight sky, but she was only aware of the storm in her mind, of the howling of the men in the distance to right and left, their bloodcurdling wails filling the night, filling her consciousness. *Must get away ... must get away ... fast, fast, run through the grass, keep bent double past the mealie garden into the trees. Run, Mattana, run along the river away from the madness.*

She had run right into them before she saw them.

They stood there on the bank of the river, looking back at the burning kraal. Five of them, tall and lean with great muscles in their arms and legs and ostrich feathers in their headdresses.

One stretched out his hand to take her by the throat. A gurgling sound of terror issued from her mouth and, petrified, she lifted her eyes to meet the Zulu warrior's callous, impenetrable gaze. The firelight from the burning kraal glinted in his eyes as he spoke. 'What have we here ... a fleeing mouse?'

Then one of the others answered. 'I am surprised that one escaped. I thought we had them all, great Shaka.'

Shaka ... Oh no! She was doomed. He would rip out her entrails.

She did not quake with terror now ... the terror was over for her. Death would be her next companion. As the grip on her throat relaxed she stood there looking with resignation at the king of the Zulus.

No one spoke. The seconds were lives, little lives that began and passed and died before her. And then he broke the silence. 'Where did you get the necklace?'

It seemed such a bizarre question that for a moment it was as if she had not heard, but then she gathered herself and said, 'I made it myself.'

No one answered this statement and so Mattana thought to go on . . . why not? What was there to lose? 'When I was small I was playing in the Olasi Hills and in a crack in the rocks I found lots of baby bats, all dead. I took one and dried it. I have worn it ever since.' Then, extemporaneously without design, she added quickly, 'It's lucky, you know.'

An odd, inscrutable expression played around Shaka's mouth and then turned into a smile, displaying perfect teeth.

She wanted to scream, 'How can you smile? You animal, you have just murdered all those who meant anything to me.' But she said nothing.

His heavy, deep voice sounded. 'It *is* lucky.' And his eyes narrowed as he actually bent his head forward to look more closely at it hanging between her breasts. 'My mother, Nandi, wears exactly the same thing. I have never seen another.'

Something lurched inside Mattana's chest. *His mother wears the same . . . he has never seen another.* Oh, by all that is powerful, I have a chance! She had assessed from his reaction that his mother was important. She had assessed correctly, for the only person whom Shaka ever treated with any care in all his life was his mother, Nandi.

Mattana took a deep breath, and relying on the strong anthropomorphic beliefs of the Bantus, her words came tumbling forth, though she tried with all her might to sound calm and controlled. 'It is told that the eternal queen who rules the spirits of our ancestors comes in the form of a dead bat to lie between the breasts of the mother of the one who will be the greatest and most powerful in all history. It is said that when the great one sees a second bat lying between the breasts of another, then the queen of the spirits of our ancestors is set free and she will sit forever at the shoulder of the great one and none will ever come against him.'

At that very moment lightning flashed in a blazing white trident across the sky, and the storm broke.

Shaka started, his head jerking towards the lightning; the warriors with him cried out; the thunder rolled . . . and Mattana, the great witch doctor, was born.

127

CHAPTER SEVEN

At first Darlengi had been merely in an age grouping, an intanga, and had been taught finesse in what he already knew: how to best use an assegai and how to use the stabbing assegai, the iklwa, adapted by Shaka, and so named because of the sound it made when withdrawn from the unfortunate quarry's body. He was already adept at using the knobkerrie, but now he learnt how to propel it over great distances. He was taught how to construct a shield, and how to use it in battle: the Zulu warrior's stratagem of locking his shield under his foe's and ripping it back and away so that his opponent's ribs and side were exposed to the ramming-in of his iklwa.

There was only one other who was as swift as Darlengi, as adept at learning and as keen to do well. His name was Intongalu and he was the son of Nongalaza, a great induna who was close to Mpande the king.

Darlengi and Intongalu had been the first in the class to erect the temporary shelters of reeds or grass which were used while an impi was on the march. They did it in less time than induna Kayo took to sharpen his assegai, and showed so much promise that they received their first praise names, the izibongo, from Kayo.

They were made to run great distances, and always Darlengi would be first home, closely followed by Intongalu. Darlengi liked the spirited competition he received from the other boy, but to Intongalu it was serious: he needed to win.

Darlengi was aware of the two rival factions in Zululand: one the uSuthu, loyal to Cetshwayo, the other the iziGqoza, loyal to Mbuyazi. These men were half-brothers, sons of King Mpande by different mothers, and both were vying for position of heir apparent. The youth listened carefully when the indunas spoke and thus he learned that there was a rumour that Mbuyazi was actually Shaka's son, that his mother was

128

already pregnant when she was given by Shaka as wife to Mpande; but it was not openly said. He learned the uSuthu were three times as numerous as the iziGqoza; perhaps because the population around Cetshwayo's kraal was greater than around his half-brother's.

As the months passed, Darlengi became friendly with Mtonga, a boy a couple of years younger, another son of King Mpande by his favourite wife, and thus it was whispered that he was his father's absolute favourite son. Mpande had many wives and so many half-brothers filled the kraals near Nodwengu, 'Place of the Irresistible One', Mpande's royal kraal. But the only two grown to manhood who were candidates for kingship were Cetshwayo and Mbuyazi, for both had already shown they were strong, capable warriors who could be ruthless. The boy, Mtonga, told Darlengi of his fear of being killed because he was Mpande's favourite. He was a sensitive young man and did not take easily to warrior ways, and there were times when Intongalu would tease Mtonga for not being a princely warrior like his two grown brothers.

Always Mattana had managed to transfer her alliances skilfully from one king to the next: from Shaka to Dingane to Mpande, and now she had cast her lot with Cetshwayo: Mpande was still king but the unrest in Zululand was obvious, and one of his adult sons must soon hold title to his kingdom. He had even confided resignedly to Mattana, 'Two bulls cannot live in the same kraal.'

It was time to ally Darlengi, and Mattana had cast him with Cetshwayo's faction even though King Mpande seemed to favour Mbuyazi. Shiambi, Darlengi's father, was close to the king, but she knew, too, that Shiambi had also survived in Zululand by transferring his alliance at the right time. He had been favoured by Shaka and then been an induna to both Dingane and Mpande. His choices were as unfailingly sound as her own. She was sure he would fight for Cetshwayo when the time came.

When Kayo told Darlengi that he was to accompany him to an indaba at Nodwengu, the king's kraal on the White Umvoloosi River, the youth was full of excitement. He had never seen the king, though now and then he had seen Cetshwayo.

It was September 1856; perhaps Darlengi was the only Zulu

in all the land who knew this, for they talked in seasons or full moons. He liked to think in the European way and because of his knowledge of English he had been used as an interpreter when they dealt with white men – officials, hunters, traders or missionaries. This was an important role for a skilled apprentice warrior of eighteen years.

The indaba lasted two days. The impies of both brothers had been invited and it was said that Mbuyazi's people were to dance and Cetshwayo's men were to watch. Mpande had ruled this to be so. The great hatred between the two brothers was already apparent throughout the land and there had been small skirmishes between each man's followers. Kayo had told Darlengi that Mbuyazi had raided Cetshwayo's cattle on more than one occasion.

The royal kraal was huge – Darlengi had never seen anything like it – and the first day was filled with the slaughter of oxen and feasting and singing, all in the customary fashion of the great indabas.

On the second day the sun was setting and the fires and tall torches were casting a golden glow on the faces of the assembled when the whispering began.

'He comes ... Mpande is here.'

'The royal household ...'

The mass of bodies opened to make a path for the king and his entourage to pass through. Mpande, 'the root', was huge, a bear of a man in a long, intricately woven cape which dragged behind him raising dust. His two rival sons walked behind him, the last time they would ever be side by side on this earth, and the indunas followed, all in ceremonial regalia and each holding a small torch. Mtonga and his numerous younger half-brothers followed after the indunas. It was a magnificent sight, and when they mounted the dais and the praise names of the king were repeated, the people all fell to their knees in one graceful, seemingly choreographed movement: four thousand backs pointing to the twilight sky. When the great royal entourage sat, Kayo's watchful eye remained on Darlengi.

Only Mbuyazi's people danced, and while they danced well and the drumbeats filled the kraal and rang across the plain, Darlengi could not help thinking it was a strangely divisive thing for Mpande to have commanded. Were not the uSuthu and the iziGqoza already enemies enough? He heard the grumbling of his warrior friends that the uSuthu too should dance, and Cetshwayo's grim face grew grimmer as each dance began. Even the maidens leaping in exotic moves in front of his eyes did not bring a smile to his mouth.

All the while Kayo's scrutiny of Darlengi continued. Then suddenly the youth gave a quick intake of breath. The man who sat four places from the king was his father, Shiambi, and while he had not seen him since he had been seven years old, he recognised him. He recalled little of the days in his father's kraal, but one thing he recalled too well . . . a hot, still night and the loud voices breaching the darkness like a club to his head.

'I cannot stand the sight of him, or his sister who favours him. When I am away from here I am at peace and then I return and see him, and my anger floods my brain like the Umvoloosi in the wet.'

And then Mattana's voice. 'He is your son!'

'He will never be son to me. He killed my perfect Nadi.' He spoke her name like a prayer.

'He killed no one,' Mattana shouted. 'You fathered him, you fool. He did not ask to come.'

'Silence, Mattana. You may be a magic one, but the day comes when even they part ways with the mountains and the plain. The child is the living recreation of the evil ones who have gone before. I detest the very air he breathes.'

'I know you have spared him only because you fear my magic, and so you should, for it is powerful, Shiambi, remember that while you walk this earth. But now I shall remove the air Darlengi breathes from the proximity of your lungs, and he can be son to me.'

'Take him. Take him anywhere as long as I see him no more. And may your ancestors rise up to make you regret, for he has the heart of the jackal hyena.'

'You're wrong. He is good, like the sweet grass of the veld is to the thousands who are nurtured by it, and I, Mattana, shall reap his goodness.'

Suddenly Kayo spoke at Darlengi's side and his mind came back to the present. 'So you have seen him.'

'I have.'

Shiambi wore wonderful white plumes, an ivory necklace and a cape almost as beautifully woven as the king's, though

131

not as long. Darlengi could not help thinking that his regal carriage made him appear much more kingly than Mpande, who was so huge and fat.

The youth said no more to Kayo and Kayo said no more to him, but the following day, a cold day with mist hanging over the river and encasing the kraal in a damp blanket, Cetshwayo's warriors were preparing to depart when a summons came to Darlengi. He was taken to a large and important hut not far from the royal abode and told to enter. Inside he rose up to see his father sitting alone in the great hut. He wore no plumes now and his head ring gleamed in the firelight.

At the sight of him his father's face clouded. '*Sa ku bona*, I see you, Darlengi.'

'I see you, Shiambi.'

'You are with the Inkanhla and thus with the uSuthu, I see.'

'Yes.'

'The sight of you does not please me.'

Darlengi was silent for a few seconds, then he answered, 'It is you who have summoned me.'

His father stood. 'Where is your home kraal?'

'Where Mattana took us. Unondo's kraal. My sister is there.'

Shiambi nodded. 'I know. On the Tugela. Though I did not know for many years, which was fortunate for you. It was Mattana who informed me you were here.'

Darlengi's face changed. 'Mattana? She is here?'

'She was. She left this morning.' He noted his son's disappointment at this, and hastened to add, 'Perhaps she does not care for you as she used to.'

Darlengi had been looking closely at his father but at these words he turned his eyes away. He was hurt but he would not let his father know. He stood quietly waiting in the ensuing silence until it was broken at last by Shiambi. 'You have the body of a budding warrior, but the face of a woman.'

Darlengi knew this for the insult it was. He brought his eyes around to meet the haughty ones glinting with animosity. His voice was cold. 'That is because I have my mother's face.'

It was like an assegai cut to Shiambi; he actually flinched and his large hands lifted from his sides in anger. Darlengi thought he would lash out and strike him but he saw the man control himself as he spoke, his voice sharp with the cutting edge of scorn. 'It would be well if I see you no more.'

Darlengi turned and walked to the hut entrance. Just before he bent to withdraw he turned back to the man he did not know. His voice was strained when he spoke. 'For many summers and winters it has been well with me also. It will continue to be.'

His father made no answer and Darlengi left him standing there. There were no tears in his eyes as he made his way back to his brothers, just an empty ache in his chest and the pit of his stomach.

The first face he saw as he entered the cattle kraal was Intongalu's. The youth stood there looking closely at him, and as Darlengi passed, he said, 'My father tells me you are an outcast in your own father's kraal.'

Darlengi halted and turned back. 'That is not uncommon knowledge.'

'My father tells me that Shiambi would have killed you but the old Great One, Mattana, saved you.'

'Your father says a lot.'

Intongalu's eyes narrowed. 'Perhaps he does. I was merely wondering how it makes you feel to know that your own father wants you dead.'

There was a strange, hot feeling in Darlengi's throat as he looked at Intongalu's mocking expression, and yet he made himself smile. His perfect teeth gleamed as he answered, 'Intongalu, it makes me feel grateful.'

'Grateful?'

'Yes, to Mattana.'

They left in a long ribbon of men, wending their way out of the royal kraal and across the lush green veld. And as they came to the crest of a wooded hill about two miles from the royal kraal, Darlengi lifted his eyes to see the form of a small woman leaning on a staff silhouetted against the gossamer of the mist that was quickly evaporating under the morning sun.

'Mattana!' he cried in delight, and left his place to run the hundred yards up the hill to her.

When she saw the man break ranks and run towards her,

she smiled and hurried down the slope. He wrapped his arms around her and hugged her to him.

'Mattana, Mattana. I believed you had left without seeing me. I was heartbroken.'

'Would I do that? I made the journey to the royal kraal especially to meet with you, but it was not for others to know that.'

'It's more than a day's march from your kraal to the royal kraal! You should not have come so far.'

She made no answer, merely lifting her worn hand to his face. 'Did you see your father?'

'I did. It was not a good meeting.'

Mattana nodded. She had expected as much. Yet she had nursed a vain hope for reconciliation.

'What did he say?'

'Nothing I wish to repeat.'

She understood. 'Can you leave the regiment?'

'Why, yes, for a few suns.'

What a joyful expression rose to her face. 'At last we can stay together . . . tonight and perhaps tomorrow too. Nearby is a kraal of my blood relatives.'

Darlengi smiled. 'Good. Afterwards, I must go back to Cetshwayo's great military kraal. It is an honour to be chosen.'

And so they spent three days together and Darlengi was content. Later he was to compare it with his times with Aunt Jane. Although he loved Aunt Jane, Mattana was his 'good mother' and he had missed the essence of her. When she fussed about him, he was as happy as a mealie garden when the rain falls.

Mattana was well known throughout Zululand. Her magic was renowned and she was powerful, although she wielded a different power from that of the great indunas like Shiambi. And while Darlengi loved her dearly, after the two years with John Lockley and the white men he could not help but believe that a lot of her magic was luck, astuteness and bravado. He realised that somehow he had always thought so, just as he did of Yangaani's transparent 'magic' in his home kraal. Mattana was masterful at spectacle and pretence and when he had told her of his time in Durban she had simply nodded and lifted her finger to tap her temple. 'Mattana knew Darlengi had gone from the kraal for long time. Could feel his spirit with white boy's spirit.' The youth said nothing, simply smiling sceptically.

Her lined face came close to his. 'Mattana was bereft when she had to leave Darlengi and Jettama in distant kraal, but Mattana had to be at the centre of matters near Mpande.'

She held up six fingers. 'I saw you only this often in all the long time. But when I dream, I see it was destined. You were allowed to come to fruit away from intrigue ... that is good. I dream hard and my dreams have kept you safe, yet there are things I see and which I fear.'

Darlengi was patient. 'Thank you for your dreams, ancient one, but there is nothing to fear.'

She stood on her toes to touch him on both temples; it was a difficult undertaking, for she was small and he was over six feet tall. He bent forward to help her.

'For you there are many things to overcome but you are Mattana's strong one and while you suffer and bend you do not break. I have put much time and effort into your training. You have learnt many things since you came to Kayo's care and there will be a great battle very soon between Cetshwayo and Mbuyazi where you will wash your spear.' This was the Zulu euphemism for killing, and thus having been in battle and having blooded the spear. 'And you will be victorious, my healthy tree, victorious.'

On December the second, Darlengi did wash his spear, over and over again. The great and ghastly battle of Ndondakusuka took place at the mouth of the Tugela River on the Indian Ocean where Mbuyazi's people, with only seven thousand warriors, had proceeded, chased by Cetshwayo's twenty-thousand-strong impi.

The mouth of the Tugela was some seventy miles from the Harrison-Nelson farm but the whole country was alive with fear, and the farm, indeed the whole of Natal, remained on alert for months afterwards.

As the thousands of men, women and children poured down the valley and bundled together on the north side of the Tugela under the green hills, two Europeans watched. One was the very worried border agent, Captain Joshua Wamsley, and the other his young assistant of twenty-three years, John Dunn. Natal had been declared a separate colony from the Cape in July and Wamsley took his duties seriously. He knew that the

Natal Secretary for Native Affairs, Theopolis Shepstone, was on his way from Pietermaritzburg to try to stop the battle, but he also knew that the secretary would be too late. And while Wamsley remained south across the Tugela he gave young Dunn permission to go over to Mbuyazi with fifty armed Natal natives. Dunn and his men crossed the Tugela and joined Mbuyazi's army.

Both armies used the same battle strategy and faced each other in the form of the buffalo: regiments substituting for the horns, head and loins.

By noon, Cetshwayo's hordes were spreading out to attack, the centre led by Cetshwayo himself and his very own regiment, the Tulwana. Darlengi and Kayo fought in the right wing under Uhamu, another of Cetshwayo's half-brothers, and Shiambi too, at fifty-three years old, was there. He was one of Cetshwayo's advisers on strategy and he stood on a hill north of the river, watching. He had finally cast his lot with Cetshwayo, even though Mpande had tried to convince him otherwise. Nangeni was there too, fighting in the left wing under a renegade Boer who had tied himself briefly to Cetshwayo.

As the two impies faced each other and the front-line warriors on either side waited for the call to battle, a gust of wind lifted Mbuyazi's long ostrich plume out of his headdress and cast it on the plain before him. There was a loud wail of shock as his horrified army stood appalled, for to them it was a sign that they would be annihilated.

And annihilated they were, the iziGqoza in their entirety, and afterwards so too were the women and children, all twenty-four thousand of them. When John Dunn, the young assistant to Border Agent Wamsley, saw the hopelessness of continuing the fight, he struggled back through a frenzy of screaming women and children to plunge into the river and save himself. The killing reached a summit in numbers that perhaps had never been seen before in all of South Africa, not even in Shaka's day. Six of Mpande's sons perished with the iziGqoza and so too did the last son of Dingane. Thousands of bodies lay in hideous piles along the sands at the mouth of the Tugela and washed up along the coast for weeks. For decades afterwards the mounds of bleached bones remained a constant shocking beacon, and Ndondakusuka was ever afterwards called 'the place of bones'.

Darlengi had known that killing would not come easily to him. He had watched many times the slaying of oxen, a ritual which was joined in by most young men of the kraal with great enthusiasm, and had always thought it a very one-sided affair. And while there was always the chance of being gored along the way, the numbers were so uneven that the result was inevitable.

When he found himself shouting the battle cry of *uSuthu!* opposite his first opponent his heart pounded. He was a big man, larger and older than Darlengi, and he made grunting sounds as he attempted to pull Darlengi's shield up and away with his own. But Darlengi had been well trained by Kayo, and, holding his shield steady, blocked the attempt. Immediately the man lunged forward, smashing at Darlengi again with his shield and trying to slice sideways at his head with his spear. Darlengi leapt back and then rebounded forward, quickly stabbing with his own iklwa. There was noise and yelling and frenzy all around him. Something pushed him in the back and he stumbled forward into his enemy. They collided, their shields banging together at a moment when Darlengi's assegai was so angled that it went straight through the man's throat. There was a strangled scream as the man dropped to the floor, his eyes bulging out of his head like frightful, ugly eggs.

And as Darlengi stood looking down, stunned by the reality of delivering a death blow, he was suddenly slammed in the side by a falling body and had to turn quickly to defend himself again.

At first it was obvious who the enemy was, but as the battle wore on it was hard to tell, yet the carnage went on, until there was a moment when it was obvious again, for the iziGqoza were fleeing.

At one point, Darlengi had seen the young white man, John Dunn, who fought for Mbuyazi, forced into the alligator-infested Tugela. Intongalu was there on the bank screaming for his blood. But except for Darlengi Zulus did not swim, and he later learned that John Dunn had escaped back across the river to Natal.

When the uSuthu had gone on with the massacre of the women and children Darlengi had slipped back and hidden in the bush until it was all over. He had been sick that day, vomited alone there near the stream that ran down the slopes into the Tugela. This killing was wrong; it was an ugly thing.

There was a Zulu superstition – Darlengi knew it for a superstition, though he dared not say it – that if one did not cut open the stomach of a dead foe, the spirit of the dead one would rise up and enter the slayer. He was offended by the custom, and he knew it was the influence of John Lockley and his family that had made him so. The period of time he had been with John Lockley had come at the most impressionable stage of his life, when he had been a boy on the brink of manhood, and what he had learned and seen then had altered him for always.

After the battle, and before the impi disbanded and the men returned to their home kraals, as was the Zulu custom, Darlengi stood with Kayo and many of his comrades on the edge of the slaughter field. Cetshwayo, Uhamu, Shiambi and all the indunas and the renegade Boer had laughed and yelled and then Cetshwayo had lifted his spear high in the air and shouted, 'You fought well today. You have washed your spears. You are Zulu warriors.'

This was met by hails of victory and the cry of *uSuthu!*; there was rejoicing all about. Darlengi made his way through his comrades with Kayo at his side. Suddenly Intongalu was in front of him. His wide forehead shone in the glow of the many fires that had been lit and the excited glint in his eye reflected the flames. He had fought well and ferociously and had been commended by name.

'They say you know the white man's numbers. How many iziGqoza did you slay, Darlengi?'

'I did not count, Intongalu.'

'You should have. You were lucky it was Uhamu who led our wing today and not your father, Shiambi, or you too may lie now with the iziGqoza.'

Some of the warriors laughed but Darlengi brushed by him and kept walking. He did not answer or look back, he just continued westward along the Tugela, away from the battlefield. It was some little time later that he realised Kayo was at his side. They walked in silence until Kayo spoke. 'Take little notice of what Intongalu says. He knows you have all the prowess he has, and more. That makes him resent you.'

'Yes.'

'You fought well today, Darlengi. You have proved your worth, but why is it that you would not look in the direction of the slain after the battle?'

Darlengi turned his head. It was weak moonlight but there was enough for Kayo to see the cynical light shining in his eyes and the cold, penetrating points of his black pupils. 'I looked in their eyes when they were alive. That was enough.'

Kayo was not affronted by this reply; he knew Darlengi was different and he accepted that. Had not the powerful one, Mattana, said he would at times be distinctly unlike his brother warriors? But he continued with his point. 'And I did not see you when we were reducing the dependants.'

Darlengi halted and Kayo had to turn back to him.

'Kayo.' He spoke the induna's name with a frustrated sigh, and as he continued he sounded much older, more mature than yesterday. 'I was used as an instrument today, just as you were used. Cetshwayo is now the undisputed heir to the throne of Zululand. We helped him attain his wish. My stomach for battle does not extend to the murder of women and children. We go home now. We are friends.' He put out his hand and took Kayo's.

Kayo was indeed his friend and he was a good man and a brave warrior. But Kayo was a Zulu and the customs of his ancestors had served him well. He would not, could not, dispute them. Darlengi knew and recognised this but even as they clasped hands in friendship he could not help adding, 'We are *told* to rejoice that our leader will one day be king.' He said this in such a manner that Kayo, for the life of him, did not know whether Darlengi trifled with him or not; but, because he liked his charge immensely, he decided to leave the matter there.

'Good, Darlengi. Yes, we are friends and we will go home and rejoice.'

They camped together that night and left each other the following morning where the Inzuzi River runs into the Tugela. There would be no call back to the regiment for perhaps two summers, but because Induna Uhamu had asked for Darlengi there would come a time when he must return to Cetshwayo's great military kraal at Empangeni, eight miles from Cetshwayo's home kraal at Undi, south of the Umlatoosi River in the emerald-green country of eastern Zululand.

Kayo saluted him. 'I will come for you, Darlengi, when the time is right.'

'I will be waiting, Kayo.'

When he was alone he thought about the battle. He had not been ready for what killing meant. He queried how a person ever really could be. He wondered if his brother Logley had fought any battles yet. He thought probably not. John Lockley was at school in England and he suspected there were no battles being fought there. He guessed that the British probably taught their sons about war for a longer time before they sent them to wash their spears. He wondered just exactly what Logley was learning at the military academy so far away.

He was walking slowly and pondering these things when he saw the three figures standing near a clump of giant ferns ahead. They had appeared from nowhere and one leaned on a staff.

His mouth broke into a joyous smile and he ran forward, crying, 'Mattana!' He took her in his arms, half lifting her from the ground as her two companions melted away into the trees.

When he released her she looked serious. 'You have washed your spear.'

He nodded. 'It was a ghastly battle, Mattana.'

'They all are.'

She turned from him and sat on a rock, gesturing for him to do the same. She took up his right hand in her left, saying, 'You will be able to spend time now with your sister. This is good. When Kayo comes for you and you return to the uSuthu, I shall be living there, near the military kraal. We will be able to spend many sunsets together.'

She increased the pressure on his hand, clutching it very tightly, and her voice dropped so that he had to bend his head to hear her. 'What you did yesterday had to be done. It is the will of our ancestors that Cetshwayo becomes king of the Zulus. And while there were things that disturbed you, Darlengi, there always will be, for even I cannot change how your heart beats, although many times I have tried. I have dreamed much in the last two night skies and I see that you carry the lives of many in the palm of your hand. You will be powerful and mighty; but nothing of moment is gained without pain. Your heart and the hearts of those you love are

good. This will help to save you, though not always the others.'
Her eyes narrowed and she turned from him in concentration
for a few minutes, before she faced back round to him. 'I am
not truly certain, but I feel there is trouble in Jettama's love for
the one you love.'

Darlengi was taken aback. 'The one I love . . . who is that?'

'The one you both call Logley.'

'I do not understand.'

'Mattana can do many things, but Jettama's love for Logley
was not in my earlier dreams. I cannot change it, for it is in the
will of our ancestors, but I fear for her.'

Darlengi had told Mattana all about John Lockley and his
family. When he had related the events of his years in
Durban, she had listened carefully, the great crevices between
her eyes deepening as he spoke, but nothing he had said could
possibly have given her any reason to think there was more
than friendship between John Lockley and Jettama. He
listened now with a feeling of disquiet.

'Jettama's spirit is interwoven with the English boy's.'

'No, ancient one . . . no, that is not so.'

She shook her wizened head so that the braids of her unruly
hair bounced in the air. 'Mattana would like to be wrong, but
she is not. I salute you.' And she stood, and said his praise
names, many more than he had ever heard before. As he
opened his mouth to ask her about them, she added, 'In time
they will all be yours.'

Then she kissed the palm of his right hand, and with the
words, 'We will meet again soon,' she left him there.

He continued on his way with Mattana's words bouncing
around in his head. Her talk was all riddles just to confuse him,
to hold sway over him. He did not really think she could dream
and see things. But why would she say Jettama loved John
Lockley and that she feared for her?

He ran across country to the Magendi River and avoided
the crocodiles as he forded it. Making his way south-west
towards the kraal he came upon the sign that hung from the
tree branch next to a tall stone beacon. It read: '*Harrison-
Nelson Land: Bought from the King of the Zulus. North-eastern
Boundary.*'

Something gave a strange twist in his chest and he stood
quite still to read the sign, memories clouding his vision. He

was rolling on the grass in a wrestling match with his friend, the sound of their boyish laughter ringing in his ears. And while yesterday and the battle had somehow altered him, had not he lived amongst the Europeans? Seen and understood them with all the trappings that he knew they called 'civilisation'. So even if Mattana were correct and Jettama loved John Lockley, surely any love would die when they were parted so long? Then, though he resisted it, he thought of the white Ice Princess, the beautiful sprite who lived in his head; the one whom he tried to block out and to seclude in the caverns of his subconsciousness. He saw her extend her long white hand imperiously ... reluctantly, towards him. He had not seen her for a long time either ... but didn't he remember her and how he felt?

He ran home from the sign, speeding easily across the plains of tall grass and the deep dongas, over the hills and across the valleys. When he came loping in through the kraal gate everyone turned out to greet him. Jettama ran forward and clung to him as if never to let him go. How she had missed him.

He had grown now to his full height of six feet and half an inch tall, and while in the years to come the muscles of his chest and girth would expand and grow rock hard, he was already an extraordinary specimen of beautiful young manhood. The girls in the kraal who had thought him thin and puny years before now gathered around him with obvious admiration.

Kenga had died in the winter and Darlengi was now the only male in the hut. He felt like the head of the family for the first time and he basked in it. But he thought constantly about Mattana's words, and the next day while he sat watching Jettama grind mealies he suddenly said, 'Do you love Logley?'

She put down her stone and her lovely eyes narrowed as they returned his gaze. 'Of course I love him, do not we all? You, and Weena and me?'

'That is not what I mean ... do you love him as a woman loves a man?'

'Where has this question come from, my brother?'

He was staring at her. 'I have seen Mattana. She told me you love Lockley.'

Jettama came to him and took up his hand in hers. 'Oh,

142

Darlengi, I have not seen Mattana since I was a child and while she is a great and powerful witch doctor, how could she know how I feel?'

He continued to stare. 'Do you love him?'

She did not answer.

He dropped her hands and nodded, slowly rising to his feet. 'Mattana was right. I see you do. When did this happen?'

She watched his back as he moved from her. 'Oh, Darlengi, you of all people should understand . . .'

His voice was loud now with the hard edge of anger in it. 'I said, when did this happen?'

She sighed. 'When you had gone to Inkanhla regiment.'

His coal-black eyes were full of pain . . . anger and pain, and his voice was cold. 'How could you both do this? He has gone away for years. You are one Zulu who knows how long a year is. He will forget you. You are a fool.'

She shook her lovely head. 'No, he will not forget me. He loves me. He will come back to me.'

Darlengi knew there could only be great pain in such a love. The same pain he felt when he thought of the Ice Princess. John Lockley should have been more careful than this. He wondered if the European God and the spirits of his own ancestors were in league together and playing some bizarre game with the brothers and sisters of this planet. He felt ill.

He turned from Jettama and ran away, miles away, along the Tugela and up the Intalalala. His feet pounded upon the ground and the blood pounded inside his head. When finally he turned to come back he was drained; he walked most of the way.

When at last he returned, she was waiting for him, standing in the dusk, a lonely figure there at the kraal gate.

He walked right up to her and stood looking down into her swollen, puffy eyes. She had been crying all afternoon.

'Darlengi . . . please . . . I am so sorry.'

In an abrupt movement he enveloped her in his arms and hugged her tightly to him. She could feel the urgent beating of his heart and the iron-firm grip of his fingers pressing into her back. She heard his hoarse whisper, his lips resting in her jet-black hair. 'Oh God, of course you love him, why wouldn't you? Don't we both?'

CHAPTER EIGHT

November 1861

High-spirited laughter sounded, followed by the perpetrators, twenty girls in white lace, walking two by two behind their teacher, Miss Anderson. Out of Riebeek Street they floated, skirts swinging round their ankles, and then, keeping their formation, passed by the battery and along the waterfront.

It was a grey day and Table Mountain wore its cloth of cloud, but it was warm, being the last week of November. The pupils of Miss Anderson's Academy were on their weekly walk through Cape Town. Miss Anderson held up her hand and halted the feminine armada – ranging in age from seven to seventeen – alongside a brightly painted vessel.

'This, as you know, is a steamship,' she pointed with her umbrella as they broke ranks, clustering round her, 'and what was the very first all-iron steam ship called?'

'The *Aaron Manby*,' they replied in unison.

'And when was it launched?'

'Eighteen twenty-one,' came the singsong answer.

'Very good. Now, I want you to look closely at this vessel, for later I am going to test your powers of observation. So range along the quay and scrutinise it, please.'

As the girls, muttering and giggling, spread out along the wharf, two young men advanced from the far end of the quay towards them. One was in the army uniform of a lieutenant and the other wore fashionable mufti. They were returning to their ship for departure on the evening tide. The soldier had spent the morning at the castle with some brother officers and the afternoon with the new Governor of the Cape Colony, Sir Percy Wodehouse, KCB. He was to return to Cape Town as Sir Percy's aide after his coming leave in Natal.

They stepped out smartly, an attractive pair, but the soldier had the advantage of the uniform and he was exceptionally good-looking anyway. Six of the twenty girls were over fourteen, and all six pairs of eyes left the ship and followed the two young men as they passed. In counterpoint, the eyes of the two men roved over the girls. But while the soldier thought them quite lovely, in his mind he saw another, with ebony skin like silk and deep brown pools for eyes.

He made a subdued sound, mirthful yet not mirthful, as his polished boot lifted to the gangplank. The civilian beside him caught the eye of pretty Shirley, the eldest girl at Miss Anderson's Academy. He winked at her and she blushed and turned away.

'Come on,' said the soldier, 'you've no chance with these girls, Michael, they're obviously with that old duck over there carrying the parasol.'

His companion laughed, and, slapping the soldier on the back, agreed. 'You're right, let's go.'

The soldier was on the gangplank when an unusual tinkling sound of laughter caught his ear. It jolted something in his memory; was somehow familiar, belonging in the hazy oblivion of his boyhood. He halted and turned to look in the direction of the laughter at a girl of fifteen with lively eyes and long fair hair trailing over her shoulders to nestle in her white lace collar.

She was some ten feet from him, and as her gaze met his, she smiled at him and turned back to her friends. The soldier hesitated and then suddenly his eyes narrowed and he stepped back to the wharf and took a few paces after her. 'Excuse me, miss.'

The girl turned in surprise. 'Are you calling me, sir?'

'Do I know you?' he asked.

The girl's heartbeat quickened. Did he know her? This marvellously handsome soldier was actually asking did he know her. It was like a dream. He was without doubt the best-looking man she had ever seen. His wonderful eyes, almost purple in colour, studied her, and a smile broke across his classic mouth as she stammered a reply. 'I d . . . don't think so, sir.'

'Then what is it about you that's familiar?' He stared at her for a long moment. Then he laughed, lifting the forefinger of his right hand in triumph. 'Phoebe . . . it is you, isn't it?'

145

The girl was astounded. 'Why, yes, that's my name.'

He remembered the last time he had seen her at the Tugela farm, sitting on her father's lap in the ox cart and waving goodbye with her fat little hand. He moved a step closer to her and now the other girls all clustered around.

'I'm John Lockley Harrison. Do you remember me? I travelled out from England with you and your parents when you were only tiny.'

She smiled. Oh, yes, she did remember him. 'You are the one who saved me when I fell from the rigging.'

'Indeed I am.'

This soldier was her John Lockley, the one she had kept in her heart all these years. 'Often Mother has told me how I could have been killed except for you.'

He smiled. 'Really? Has she now? I believe your mother and my Aunt Jane still see each other when they can.'

Phoebe nodded. 'Yes, they do. And I've been to your home, Mimosa . . . and the farm; it's on the way to our mission.'

'So you're at school here in Cape Town?'

And now the ring of intent young faces around him, who had followed every word, replied for her. 'Yes, we're boarders.'

'Our school is Miss Anderson's Academy for Young Ladies.'

'We've just been to church.'

And breaking in on the chorus of voices came that of Miss Anderson herself. 'What's going on here?'

John Lockley turned, his lively eyes meeting Miss Anderson's insipid gaze.

'Excuse me, please. I've been conversing with one of your pupils.'

'That's quite all right.' Miss Anderson beamed at him; he was so good-looking even she could not fail to notice. 'But we all must be moving along. Do you sail on this ship?'

'Yes, miss, with the evening tide.'

'Are you coming back?' asked Shirley, who now stood behind the teacher's shoulder looking at him with unabashed interest.

'I'd like to,' was his gallant reply.

Phoebe decided it was time to assert herself again, after all he was her friend. 'John Lockley,' she said, 'are you on your way to Durban?'

He smiled. 'Where's your accent gone? You used to call me Jan Larkley.'

And now she laughed again, and it was still such an infectious sound that he, too, laughed, and so did all the assembled young women.

When they parted he took her hand and bent over it. 'Phoebe, I'll see you in Natal sometime.'

That night young Phoebe lay awake thinking about him and hoping that she really would see him in Natal. His eyes were the most beautiful colour imaginable and his skin was like clear, polished bronze. She saw him as perfection and her teenage heart raced. Soon she was to leave for Durban and Christmas at home. For the last five years she had always spent the first night with Aunt Jane and Uncle Chris at Mimosa. So, yes, she really would see the soldier again. A radiant smile spread across her face and she rolled over and went contentedly to sleep.

Five days later the steamer landed the two travelling companions in Durban.

Unlike the first time John Lockley had arrived here, he was transported through the bar by a steam tug which brought the mother ship smoothly along a channel into the wharf near the Custom House. Little did he realise that the port improvements had been a recent cause for dissent in the community and that his old friend, Dicky Bell, had only slimly held on to his position as port captain.

But as John Lockley was aware of none of this he was impressed as he steamed into Durban harbour to be thrilled once more by the fabulous beauty of the water and the beaches, and the deep, emerald foliage. He looked down at the wharf filled with people, black and white, and he ran his fingers through his hair and smiled with the happy thought of spending three months here on leave. His appointment to the Cape Colony was to be his first army post after military academy and a short stint in Scotland. He had always been near the top of his class and because he knew South Africa and made his home in Durban he had been given the posting as aide-de-camp to the Governor. He knew his father's influence had not hurt either. General James Harrison had been retired and living in Durban, at Mimosa, since early 1859; he was an intimate of the Cape Governor, had known him since school-days and John Lockley suspected that he had pulled a few strings and got him the posting.

He gazed across the crowded wharf and there amongst the throng he saw Jane and Christopher side by side. For a moment he wondered who the young lady with them was, then he recognised his sister, grown to womanhood. 'Nell,' he said softly to himself, 'dear Nell.' And Michael Tallant beside him asked, 'What's that, John Lockley?'

'Ah ... nothing. I just saw my sister and got a bit of a surprise.'

'Where, which one?'

'The one in white standing next to the lady in green with the big hat.'

'Lovely, truly lovely,' Michael murmured appreciatively.

Then the bearded man beside Ellen took her arm and moved her forward and John Lockley realised it was his father.

When the ropes had been tied and the gangplank put down the seafarers disembarked.

Ellen had been silently crying and now she broke from her father to push through the crowd and capture John Lockley in her arms. 'You're back, oh thank God, at last.'

'Nell, dear Nell.'

From Ellen he passed to his father, the man he had not seen for ten years. The last leave his father had taken in England had been in early 1851, the year before they had come out to Durban. He looked into his father's eyes, eyes that told him how proud he was that his son had done so well at the Royal Military Academy. 'My son, what a fine soldier you make.'

It was wonderful to feel his father's hand take his, and just for a second a sad place opened inside him and he missed never having known his mother; and then he saw Jane smiling indulgently at him and he felt comforted again.

He answered the General. 'Well, an engineer anyway, Father.'

After his two and a half years at the academy he had decided to enroll for a further two years at the School of Military Engineering at Chatham. After his training there he had done over six months at Fort George in Scotland, and then had received his posting to the Cape Colony. The General tapped affectionately on the insignia on his shoulder. 'Full lieutenant.'

His voice could not hide the pride. 'You'll be a captain in a few years, son.'

John Lockley's eyebrow raised sceptically as he replied, 'That's what one of my best friends and tutors, Captain Durnford, told me; I laughed then as I'm laughing now.'

And then John Lockley was being kissed and clasped tightly by Jane and seconds later found himself in Christopher's bear hug. 'Welcome home, my boy.'

All the while Michael had stood and watched this family reunion and finally John Lockley was out of the arms of his relatives and able to introduce him. 'This is my friend, Dr Michael Tallant, who has come out here to help set up the new hospital for the Lieutenant-Governor.'

Michael shook the hands of the men and bowed over Jane and Ellen's hands. As he took Ellen's long white fingers in his own, he asked, 'How do you keep so wonderfully fair in this heat, Miss Harrison?'

Ellen's green eyes had been resting on her brother and now she drew them round to meet Michael's gaze of admiration.

'I wear hats and stay out of the sun, Dr Tallant.'

Port Captain Bell was larger than when John Lockley had seen him last and just as garrulous; he rolled along with them to the railway station at The Point to see them off into Durban. The railway had only been inaugurated in June and was still the talk of the colony. On the platform stood Father Sabon, still in his same rusty-russet cassock. He lifted his green-lined umbrella in greeting to John Lockley. 'Welcome back, my son,' he called as they mounted the carriage. They rattled past a sugar plantation and John Lockley remarked, 'Who are those men in the cane? They look like Indians.'

'Oh, they are,' replied Ellen. 'They started arriving last year.'

'Yes,' added the General, 'brought in from Madras and Calcutta to work on the sugar. Our local natives don't take too kindly to them, though.'

John Lockley's homecoming was celebrated with dinners and parties and all of Durban society welcomed him back, a soldier and a grown man.

At the end of the first week he took Ellen to the horse races. She looked quite lovely in a pink lace dress with matching hat. Ellen was quite the most fashionable young woman in all of Durban, which really meant all of Natal. She had a standing order for the London periodicals which showed what modish young women wore and she and Jane and Mannie worked for hours to remake the designs.

A local character called Congella Charlie had set himself up to take wagers on some of the horses. He had his own horses in almost every race and a few Hottentots who rode as jockeys for him. John Lockley had decided he would wager and he left Ellen sitting in the rustic tea room under a great fig tree while he went to find Charlie.

Ellen was having a simply perfect time. After nine years she was used to Natal and hardly saw the primitive buildings and rude furniture and this makeshift race track. Today, she was blissfully content, for she was with John Lockley, just the two of them, alone, after all these years. Her mouth turned up in a joyful, gentle curve as she sat listening to the hubbub around her. Suddenly her tranquillity was broken by a hand on her shoulder and a voice in her ear. 'Ellen, fancy seeing you here.'

She looked around into Michael Tallant's blue eyes. 'Oh, hello.'

The fact was that Michael was here because he knew she was going to be here. He had been in Ellen's company as much as he could in the twelve days since landing in Durban. At the party given in John Lockley's honour by His Excellency, the Lieutenant-Governor, John Scott, he danced so often with her that Jane had remarked to Christopher, 'I think Michael Tallant is quite taken with Ellen.'

Ellen certainly liked him, but she had wanted so much to be alone with her brother that she could not hide the cool tone in her voice. 'I'm here with John Lockley. He's just gone to make a wager.'

Michael took off his hat and smiled down at her, oblivious to the distance in her voice. He was thinking how marvellous she looked.

'May I sit down?'

'Oh . . . ah, I suppose so.'

He sat. 'You look quite wonderful, Miss Harrison. Pink is your colour, though I should say you'd look good in any colour.'

'Thank you.'

'Lovely afternoon, isn't it?'

'Yes.'

'Would you allow me to accompany you for a stroll by the stables?'

'No thanks, I'll wait for my brother.'

'But he may be some time.'

'Nevertheless, Dr Tallant, I shall wait.'

If she wished to wait then Michael was happy to wait with her, and as time passed she found herself conversing with him. 'Where did you study medicine, Dr Tallant?'

'At the Edinburgh University School of Medicine ... and please call me Michael. "Dr Tallant" makes me feel ancient, and I'm only twenty-eight.'

This actually brought a smile to her face and Michael mistakenly interpreted this as a sign of happiness and so remained in the company of the brother and sister all afternoon, unwittingly marring the true perfection of Ellen's day.

That night John Lockley made an announcement to his family as they all sat around on the wide veranda of Mimosa enjoying the light evening breeze.

Running his hand back through his fair hair he smiled. 'I'm going to ride on up to the Tugela farm. I think I'll leave the day after tomorrow.'

Christopher took the statement calmly enough but James Harrison was surprised; he looked over to Jane whose brows drew together in thought. Ellen was so startled that she exclaimed, 'John Lockley, you've only just arrived. We've all been waiting years to see you. It's Christmas in three weeks. Why do you want to go up there?'

'Nell, you know how I like the farm. I'd like to see what old Veldbron is up to, and in any case, I'd like to see Darlengi.'

His sister's eyes hardened. 'I cannot believe you'd leave us so soon to go and see a Zulu!'

Jane turned to her, putting down the lemonade she had been drinking. 'Ellen, dear, please. John Lockley and Darlengi are close friends. You know that.'

But Ellen continued as if she had not heard. She stood up and moved to John Lockley who half sat on the veranda rail. 'I think it's unfair of you to leave me ... us ... so soon. We're your family; he's not.'

John Lockley took Ellen into the crook of his arm. 'Ah,

Nell, I'm glad to be home, don't misunderstand, please. I'll be up and back before you know it.'

Finally the General took a sip of his gin and spoke. 'Let the boy do as he wishes. Whatever he wants.'

Then Christopher lifted his spare frame from the bamboo chaise-longue where he sat beside his wife. 'I've an idea. The farm's comfortable. Why don't we all go? Accompany the lad. Spend Christmas there.'

It was not really such an unusual suggestion for they had been going up to the farm for a couple months of each year since 1858. Ever since the great battle of Ndondakusuka the country had settled down a little and people seemed calmer. The farm was now quite substantial and Dirk Veldbron grazed a few cattle and sheep and had men working the soil for him. He and Matilda lived in their own small wing off the main farmhouse which now extended to five bedrooms and two living rooms, as well as a separate kitchen and wash-house.

Jane was the first to reply to Christopher. 'Yes, darling, we could certainly do that.'

The General was more than happy to join his son, but he had learned a few things about the climate so he looked over to his sister and said, 'But the wet season will be here soon and it's best not to be travelling when the rivers rise.'

Jane looked to Christopher who shook his head. 'That may not be for another month, James, look at tonight, it's marvellous. Anyway we can remain there until the rivers go down, if we like. Russell and Thorn are good men; they can run the brickworks here, and our Pietermaritzburg operation goes from strength to strength.' He touched his wife on the shoulder. 'Actually Jane and I were playing with the idea of looking at property in Greytown in the New Year, so it's an opportunity for us to do that. Let's decide to go, shall we?'

Jane and the General, who had become more compatible in recent times, smiled at each other, and agreed.

Ellen was very confused. She really wanted to be with her brother, but she did not like the farm. It was so lonely and all her friends were in Durban and Pietermaritzburg; but then she really had no choice, for if John Lockley were going to the Tugela farm, nothing on earth could keep her in Durban.

Her brother was having thoughts of his own. He was thinking of the smooth, ebony skin of the girl he had dreamed of for years, and in his heart he knew he would stay at the farm as long as he could. He shifted his hand from Ellen's waist to lift it and drag it back through his hair as he moved from the rail to stand in the centre of the veranda. *Damn it!* He had hoped to go alone. Yet he hadn't seen his family for years either and he really wanted to be with them too. Unconsciously he dropped his hand inside his trouser pocket to touch the last letter he had received from Darlengi six months ago. In it was a message from Jettama, a message of abiding love, and as his fingers felt the paper, there on the Mimosa veranda, in the middle of his family with all their eyes upon him, he had a quick change of heart. 'Ah, I agree. It would be wonderful to all be there together. But I'll start tomorrow and get up there first.' He spun on his heel to face Ellen. 'So, what do you think, Nell? Christmas at the farm?'

Her smile was wonderful. 'Yes, all right. I think I'll like it.'

When, three days later, John Lockley arrived at the top of the long slope north of tiny Greytown and looked down to where H.H. Garner's trading post lay, his heartbeat quickened. And as he cantered across the open country towards the man who stood from shoeing a horse in the lean-to, John Lockley raised his arm hailing him, and the man responded in kind.

The usual collection of native women and children sat and played in the enduring sunshine, and the garden of proteas and orange and lemon trees was almost as scanty as it had been the last time John Lockley had seen it, but there was an avenue of young acacias rising along the side of the buildings.

The young soldier dismounted to H.H.'s hearty welcome. 'Is it you, John Lockley Harrison? Can I believe my eyes?'

'Yes, H.H., you can.'

The two men shook hands and H.H. slapped the young man's shoulder. 'What a grand surprise, and what is it brings you here?'

'I'm on my way up to our Tugela farm. I'm home for three months before I take up my posting in Cape Town.'

'Cape Town, is it? Did the General pull strings? Come in, lad. Mrs Garner will be delighted to see you.'

And so she was. Her beautiful face lit up with delight and surprise when John Lockley walked into her kitchen to be made welcome with mealie cakes and tea.

153

He stayed the night with them and caught up on Zulu happenings. And he heard again of the great battle of Ndondakusuka. He had first read of it in a letter from Darlengi. The letter had taken six months to reach John Lockley and when he had read it his hand trembled. It was in that very letter that Darlengi had told him, 'While now I have fought and killed men, I am not like my Zulu brothers. My people have customs that I cannot accept. I am neither one thing nor the other. There are times when I wish I had never met your family and spent time with you. Yet, when I think that way I remember John Lockley and I smile. For he is my brother always, and you know? I believe most men are troubled by confusing thoughts, so I am – is the word essentially? – no different to others.' It was in the same letter that Darlengi had written, 'I know of my sister's love for you. Mattana told me. Jettama does not deny it. I was angry with you and with her and with myself. But then I realised she sees what I see. And I understand.'

The words troubled John Lockley for a long time. He thought of them now as H.H. shook his head and his pale sun-bleached hair fell forward as he continued speaking about the aftermath of Ndondakusuka. 'It was a frightening time, for some thought that Cetshwayo's victorious warriors might go on a rampage across Natal and even attack Durban. But as you see, that did not happen. Though other things have.' He smiled across to his wife. 'This very year has seen Mtonga, a young half-brother of Cetshwayo, returned from sanctuary with the Boers. Gave him up after they signed the treaty of Waaihoek which changed the border between the Boer territories and Zululand. The southern border now runs to the headwaters of the Blood River to a point way down the Buffalo near Rorke's Drift.' He gestured in an arc with his arm. 'You know the Boers ... always after more land, and Cetshwayo after power, so he's learning to play off the Boers against the English.'

John Lockley nodded. Mtonga had been King Mpande's favourite son. Darlengi had written to him of how Mtonga had fled to the Utrecht district, away from Cetshwayo who wanted him back at any price. Darlengi had been Mtonga's friend and, while he was loyal to Cetshwayo, he feared for Mtonga. John Lockley thought it seemed the Zulu kingdom was no different from any other: anyone who could be a pretender appeared a potential danger to the coming regent. 'What has happened to Mtonga?'

'They say he's a prisoner at a guarded kraal in the heart of Zululand.'

'Why doesn't Theopolis Shepstone, the Secretary for Native Affairs, do something?'

'It would be difficult for him. He regards Zululand as a friend. He was recently at Nodwengu where he proclaimed Cetshwayo heir apparent to Mpande in the name of Queen Victoria. John Dunn accompanied him, at least for the initial ceremonies, it's said.'

'John Dunn?'

'Ah yes, I forget how long you've been away. He's our only white Zulu chief.'

John Lockley frowned. 'White Zulu chief?'

'Yes, he's had a chequered career. About four or five years your senior I'd guess, and has for years lived in southern Zululand bartering with the natives. He was assisting the Border Agent, Joshua Wamsley, at the Lower Tugela Drift when the battle of Ndondakusuka took place, and, do you know? he actually fought on Mbuyazi's side and lived to tell the tale. Afterwards he made friends with Cetshwayo. Amazing really. They say he impressed Cetshwayo with his courage for he went to Undi after the battle and faced up to him. Interesting, for it's paid off, as the heir to the throne has given him a tract of land along the eastern Tugela where he lives as a chief. They call him Jantoni.'

The sun had gone down and they were continuing deep in animated conversation when suddenly the noise of men and horses broke the silent night outside.

'H.H., are you there?' called a strong, high-toned voice.

They all rose to their feet and H.H. took up a lantern. 'Sounds like the voice of John Dunn and no other. What's he doing here?'

As they exited on to the small veranda in the wan lantern light John Lockley saw four men. The one who spoke first was a big, bulky man a few years older than himself.

'Evening, H.H.'

H.H. put the lamp on a wooden shelf. 'Helloa, John, what brings you down this far south?'

'Chasing a Boer trader called DeGroot. He's been cheating my people. Came this way, I believe. Seen anyone like him, H.H.?'

'Now, you know as well as I do, John, that Boers avoid me like the plague. I deal only with Englishmen and native Africans. Sorry.'

The newcomer nodded. 'Yeah, H.H. you're right, he wouldn't come here.' He looked pointedly at Mrs Garner who stood behind her husband. 'That's one thing we have in common, eh, H.H.? The Boers don't care for us.'

H.H. did not answer. He took his wife into the crook of his arm before he looked to John Lockley and said, 'This is a friend of mine, Lieutenant John Lockley Harrison.'

John Dunn leant down from his horse to take John Lockley's hand. 'Harrison? Anything to do with the Harrison-Nelson farm old Dirk Veldbron runs?'

'Yes, I'm one of those Harrisons.'

As Mrs Garner left her husband's side and returned inside, H.H. asked, 'Will you stay for a drink, John?'

John Dunn turned briefly to his companions before answering. 'Nah, thanks H.H. We've made camp along the track a bit, cook's got food waitin'. Just thought I'd call by and see if you knew anythin'.' He lifted his hand in farewell as he turned his horse's head and rode away.

The two men stood listening until the sounds of the hooves had died away in the blackness. H.H. took up the lantern and John Lockley looked keenly at him. 'So that's John Dunn. What did he mean by saying that you and he had something in common?'

A strange smile shaped H.H.'s mouth. 'It was a reference to Isman, my wife, and John Dunn's way of life. He has children by a girl called Catherine whose mother was a Cape Colony native, and from what I hear he's just recently taken up other liaisons ... Zulu girls. That's where John Dunn and I differ, for Isman is all I ever wanted, and Isman is my wife.'

'And I gather the Boers avoid you, sir, for they see all black folk, at best, as servants; never as friends, lovers or ... wives.'

H.H. laughed. 'They do not approve of me or John Dunn. As if we care!' Then he patted the younger man's shoulder, took up the lantern once more, and was turning away to enter his home when the sound of a hyena crying in the distance drifted to them and John Lockley made a decision, there in the heat of the black South African night.

'Ah, sir, just a moment, please.'

H.H. turned back to John Lockley's intense gaze in the lantern light.

'Yes, son.' He put the lamp back on the shelf.

'I want to tell you something.'

H.H. was silent.

'Well, it's about you and Mrs Garner and John Dunn ... and me, I suppose.' As he went on, the colour of his eyes somehow intensified in the lamplight. 'I have a Zulu girl ... I love a Zulu girl.'

H.H.'s right eyebrow rose, the only telltale sign of his thoughts.

'She's at a kraal on the Tugela, not far from our farm. Her brother's the Zulu boy who came and lived with us in Durban. You remember? We called in here with him. My girl's name's Jettama, and though I haven't seen her in many years, I know in my very soul that she waits for me now, this very minute as I stand here telling you this.' He ran his hand with his habitual movement back through his hair. 'I know you'll ... well ... understand, because of Mrs Garner.'

He waited in the lantern light as H.H. regarded him with an inscrutable expression on his face until finally he broke his silence. 'John Lockley, you are how old? Twenty-two? three?'

'Twenty-three, sir.'

'Twenty-three. And you love a Zulu girl whom you are sure waits for you as we speak. A girl you haven't seen for many years.'

'Yes, sir.'

'Son, can you imagine what her life has been these years you've been away?'

'I think so, sir, I understand the Zulu culture.'

'Ah, you do, eh?' He nodded. 'Then you'll understand that her life hasn't been one which sets her up to be the intimate of John Lockley Harrison, whether her brother lived with you a couple of years or not. And I'm making the great assumption that you tell me about her when you've told no others. Am I right?'

The young man nodded.

157

'John Lockley, it's quite likely she may even be married by now.'

The young man shook his head. 'No, sir, she isn't. I have her last message to me here in my pocket. It was written by her brother not eight months since.'

H.H. looked surprised. 'I see. Your Zulu friend actually *writes* to you?'

'Yes, he writes well. He's quite brilliant, sir. Since I've been away I've had a number of letters from him.'

'And do you reply?'

'Oh yes, I send them to Uncle Chris; he takes them to the farm and when Darlengi is at his home kraal he comes for them.'

'But you haven't told your uncle about the girl?'

'No.'

They stood surrounded by the sounds of the night: an owl hooting, the cry of a reedbuck somewhere, the sound of a hyena and then the lowing of H.H.'s oxen. John Lockley sighed. 'I'm telling you, sir, because I need to tell someone and I thought you'd understand.'

H.H. smiled. 'And I do, son. But even I must warn you about any liaison with a Zulu girl. It's a trap and a delusion. You may want her and you may love her but your family will never accept even the most tenuous bond with her. The Zulu boy is one thing, the girl, another. You're young, with your life ahead of you. You are not John Dunn, the son of a drunkard who lives off hunting and bartering and favours from Zulu leaders; you are not even H.H. Garner, who chose his own path from the beginning. You're from a wealthy family, a grand family by Natal standards. One day, I heartily pray it will be different, but it's eighteen sixty-one, and even *friendship* with a Zulu girl will not be tolerated.'

'But I love her.'

'Well, lad, I can only tell you it'd be best if your love faded.'

'But, sir, you of all people.' John Lockley's face sank in disappointment. 'I thought you'd understand.'

H.H. made a sound like a laugh, but it was not mirthful. 'My boy, I do understand . . . perfectly. But I must tell you the truth as I see it.'

'Yes, sir, thank you.'

H.H. picked up the lantern again. 'Now let's go in.' Then he turned to John Lockley and took hold of his arm with his free hand. 'And I hope you listen to me, but if you do not ... in case you do not ... if ever I can help you at any time, in any way, I shall.'

When John Lockley reached the Tugela farm it was after noon the following day. He had left the Garners at eight in the morning and had made good time over the remaining miles of undulating green country which made up the foothills of Mount Ilvelweni to the south of the Inadi River. He crossed the shallow Inadi and five miles later saw the Tugela.

And then he saw the sign: *'Across the Tugela River Lies Harrison-Nelson Land, Bought from the King of the Zulus.'*

He thought he could just see the farmhouse sitting through the trees on a slope across the river. About a hundred yards to his right men worked on a pontoon which was obviously the transport across the water.

As he rode up he recognised the Scot, George Travers, and hailed him. Soon he was surrounded by the workers and before long taken across to the other bank.

George Travers accompanied him. They passed through a gate in a five-foot-high stone and brick wall which ran around the house and a few large outbuildings.

'Put that up in early fifty-six when we were all worried about the Zulus getting overheated,' informed Travers. 'Laagered the whole place and stood lookouts for years, really, but nothin' came of it around here, I'm pleased to tell ye, Mister John Lockley.'

When Matilda Veldbron saw him she burst into tears, and pulling him into her sturdy sun-browned arms kept repeating, 'Thank God you're safe.' John Lockley had trouble understanding why she thought he had been in danger. But he was truly pleased to see her.

'I've come on my own, Tilly' – he used his boyhood pet name for her – 'but the family follows and I'm to alert you that they'll remain through Christmas and into the coming year, though I shall have to leave in the wet to get back in time to my posting.'

'Oh gracious ... the family coming. Then I'll have to get moving.'

His next words were, 'Do you know if Darlengi is at the kraal, Tilly?'

'He is and I'm the first one he comes to see when he's home, don't you know.' A gratified smile broke across her wide face, followed instantly by a frown. 'Though Dirk is bitter about it . . . always was. Some months ago Darli was back at Nodwengu, the Zulu king's kraal, when Theopolis Shepstone proclaimed Cetshwayo as heir to the throne at a great party. Then he went into Pondoland – guide to a white hunting expedition. Only came back last week. Was here to pick up Isi straight away. I'm making this for him.' She lifted a garment she was knitting, a warm outer coat, and held it up. 'You see, John Lockley,' her words sounded almost proud, 'he's close to Cetshwayo now . . . a sort of favourite, really, and wears white man's clothes as a kind of symbol; I wash and iron them for him when he's here.' She laughed. 'Not sure how he does when he's away. He says even the great Cetshwayo asks him for hats and things. But Darli comes and goes; and when he's not with Cetshwayo, he's home here or working as a guide.'

Then she added as an afterthought, 'Don't know if he brought his sister back this time, though. You know he's kept up his English and it's as good as mine, much better if the truth be told.'

John Lockley's smooth forehead was furrowed. 'Tilly, what did you mean when you said you don't know if he's brought his sister back?'

'Ah, now, there's some fellow at the kraal who is far too fond of Jettama, you know. Can't ever recall his name . . . has two or three wives already as well, strange custom, won't ever get used to that. Now if Darlengi's going somewhere, he always takes Jettama away to a friend's kraal for safety, he says. Then when he comes back, he pops and gets her and brings her home here. Now, I realise you'll want to be off to see him but you'll not be going until some refreshment has passed into that body of yours.'

John Lockley said nothing but the furrow in his brow remained as he followed Tilly on to the front veranda.

Dirk was not home, and when John Lockley looked to east and west, he had to admit that the Boer had made a good job of the place. There were fields of corn, and cows and oxen grazing beyond. The house was twice as large as he remembered it and an additional wing where Matilda and Dirk now lived had been added at the back. Stables and sheds and a number of outhouses for accommodation for the men working the property stood through the trees, and around the farmhouse was a neatly laid lawn.

While he was truly pleased to see Tilly, he hurried his eating and drinking, giving only monosyllabic answers to her excited questions. When he stood up immediately he had finished she smiled. 'Off you go, then, I can see there's no holding you now.'

'I'll be back for dinner.'

Minutes later he was riding at speed along the Tugela. When he saw the kraal in the distance he lifted his hand and ran his fingers through his hair as a smile of expectation mounted his perfect mouth. Oh yes, he was thinking of Darlengi, but the other one filled his mind too, the girl of his wild imaginings; the one to whom no pale European girl could ever hold a candle.

Outside the kraal small children played, and under the euphorbia bushes and trees men lounged; in the fields women moved back and forth. He halted at the gates and leapt down from his horse. He looked to the men who had been lying under the nearest tree and who were now standing to greet him. He thought he recognised Gorda, one of the boys he used to play with.

'Gorda, is it you?'

'I see you, John Logley.'

'I see you, Gorda. Is Darlengi here?'

'Yes.'

'Where?'

Gorda waved his hand in an arc. 'Around, somewhere. Hunting?'

'Is his sister here? Jettama?' His voice quivered slightly.

'In fields, I think, on far side kraal.'

Then Unondo the chief appeared at the gate wearing his ceremonial headdress. Fortunately John Lockley was regarded as a friend, so while he had to politely recite the formal greetings with the chief, he did not have to sit and talk as a stranger would be required to, and he was soon able to take his leave, promising to return on the morrow with gifts for the chief and the tribe.

He tried not to hurry, not to seem anxious as he greeted people right and left passing through the kraal to the far side.

But he was all agitation and anxiety and his head shifted in staccato movements as he searched for her. Even three of the oldest mastiffs remembered him and leaped around him barking in welcome. He came through the gate on to the grass of the plain. Oh God! Was that Jettama walking towards him? Yes, it was. He heard her laughter and saw the basket of mealies under her arm; the thread of coloured beads hanging down over her breasts; the long, colourful mouche to her knees and her piled and braided hair. She was a woman, grown. Well of course she was; wasn't he a man? But it was the girl who had lived in his head, not this exotic, beautiful woman.

She was in company with two other women and a man; they had not yet looked his way. Then suddenly he realised the man was Darlengi. It was too much . . . both of them together. He actually fell back the few inches between his body and the gate post as if he had received a physical blow. It was at that moment that one of the women saw him and halted, pointing to him.

Jettama and Darlengi brought their eyes round, following her finger.

The mealie basket fell from Jettama's hands. She leapt in the air, her shout rang across the veld and even down to the river.

'John Logley!'

She ran to him, straight into his arms.

And then he realised he was kissing them both; both of them were in his arms, their tears mingling with his.

Who cares if the whole damn tribe sees us, if my family and the whole damn world see us . . . God! how I love them both.

CHAPTER NINE

It was nine days before Christmas. Victoria, Jane, Ellen and
Phoebe sat on the wide veranda at the Tugela farm. The
Harrison family had arrived from Durban five days before, and
Phoebe, in Mr Russell's care, had arrived this morning.

When Jane had realised they were to spend Christmas
upcountry she had immediately sent Thulmi to the mission
with a letter asking Victoria to come to the farm to meet
Phoebe on her way home, rather than in Greytown, as was
usual. This would enable the two old friends to see each other
for a couple of days.

It had been three years since they had been together and that
had been when Victoria had come down to Pietermaritzburg to
buy a pair of spectacles.

They talked animatedly. Phoebe was not listening, her book
lay in her lap and her mind was filled with the thought that
soon she must see the soldier, John Lockley, with his wide
clear smile and his handsome eyes.

Victoria was tatting and her fingers moved swiftly forming
the lace. 'Frank was all for returning home when he heard
about the war. But as I said to him, what could we do there
that would be more valuable than what we do here?'

Jane lifted her eyes from her needlepoint. 'It's dreadful
right enough, with families divided, from what one reads.
Chris told me yesterday that the Southern General Lee has
invaded Maryland. Isn't that near Ohio, where you come
from?'

Victoria shook her head. 'No, dear, Maryland is north of
Virginia, Ohio is further west. Though in the most recent
letter from my mother they are worried, certainly.'

At that moment Phoebe interrupted. 'Aunt Jane, when will
John Lockley be home?'

John Lockley had been on Phoebe's mind ever since her

arrival in Durban. She had expected perhaps to see him at luncheon but he had not appeared, and while there were men coming and going all around there was no sign of him.

'I'm not sure, dear, though I think he will be home for dinner. I think he may join us on a ride out over the property tomorrow which Uncle Christopher has arranged to show you some of the improvements that we've made up here.'

Ellen, who had been silent until now, turned in her chair to speak to Phoebe. The peevish quality in her tone was unmistakable. 'You shall be lucky to catch more than a glimpse of my brother, Phoebe. He prefers to be with black people than white people. From what I've seen in the last five days, he merely sleeps here.'

Jane shook her head. 'Oh, Ellen dear, that's not quite right. He was here to greet us when we arrived, and he spent last night at home. And stop talking about black people as if they had two heads.'

'Where does he go?' Phoebe asked.

'He has a wonderful friend here,' replied his aunt charitably. 'A particular friend and part of our family, as he lived with us for years.'

'A Zulu?'

And once again it was Ellen who swiftly answered, 'Yes, a Zulu. He thinks more of him than of us.'

Phoebe looked surprised. 'Why?'

Victoria held up her hand to her daughter. 'Phoebe, don't pry.'

But Ellen was in full flight. 'My brother has some odd notion that he and the Zulu . . .'

'Darlengi,' interrupted Jane. 'Give him his name, please.'

Ellen went on, 'He has the ridiculous notion that he and *Darlengi* were born on the same day. When they were boys he saved *Darlengi* from drowning and we had to put up with having him in Durban at Mimosa for two whole years. Since then my poor brother seems to think they are somehow united. And because my brother just *had* to see *Darlengi* we must spend Christmas away from the dances and parties.' She stood up from her seat and moved swiftly down the veranda and around the corner.

Jane sighed deeply and Victoria commented insightfully, 'I fear Ellen is jealous of Darlengi.'

164

But Jane dismissed it. 'Oh, Victoria, believe me, Ellen always gets on her high horse about Darlengi. It soon passes. She'll be herself in no time. She misses Durban, and too, I think she's missing that young Dr Tallant. He made quite a fuss of her before we came up here.'

'Oh, how I hope John Lockley brings his Zulu here,' Phoebe said, her eyes bright with excitement. 'It sounds like a perfectly fascinating friendship. I like it.'

Her mother smiled as Jane replied, 'Yes, you'll probably see Darlengi. He was here the day we arrived and again yesterday.' She dropped her voice and it carried a thoughtful tone. 'Though he won't take a meal with us any more; strange, for I know he still eats the cakes Matilda makes for him. We all love to see him, everyone's so fond of him.'

But Phoebe saw neither John Lockley nor Darlengi that day, for she was sent to bed at half past nine and John Lockley did not come riding in until close to the hour of ten. He was very polite to everyone and when Christopher asked him what he had been doing, he raked his hand back through his hair and smiled. 'The usual things, Uncle Chris. Tonight Darlengi showed me how to make a war shield.' And as he saw his family were interested he explained it to them while they all had a sherry before retiring.

Shortly after the sun rose the following morning Christopher and John Lockley were tucking into an early breakfast when Phoebe appeared.

The breakfast room was also the luncheon and dinner room. It was on the east side; a large room with wide wooden panels that opened on to the veranda giving it a happy, airy aspect, and as the sun rose and found the farmhouse it was a spot which was warm and cheerful. John Lockley motioned the girl to a chair as Christopher greeted her. 'My goodness, Phoebe, you're up early.'

And while her reply was to Christopher, her gaze was on his companion. 'We all rise at six o'clock at school. I'm used to being up early, Uncle Chris.'

John Lockley smiled at her and Phoebe's small heart missed a beat, thinking she had never seen such a smile and such perfect teeth. She sat beside him and he asked her a question. 'Do you enjoy school, Phoebe?'

'Oh yes,' and she went into an excited explanation of all her lessons and pastimes; but her pleasure was short-lived, for he had soon completed his breakfast and rose from his seat, patting her on the shoulder and saying, 'Have a good day, Phoebe. I'll see you tonight.'

Her face dropped. 'Are you off again to see your Zulu friend, Darlengi? I would very much like to meet him.'

He left his hand on her shoulder as he turned questioningly to her. 'Would you now?'

'Yes.'

'Then you finish your breakfast and come and find Uncle Chris and me at the stable yard, for we're meeting Darlengi there in about fifteen minutes.'

And as Umslopagas popped his head round the door to ask what she wanted for breakfast she called animatedly, 'Just a piece of toast, please, and do hurry.'

When Phoebe came to the stable yard she was excited, for she had been invited there expressly by John Lockley. There were a number of men coming and going. She saw John Lockley and Uncle Chris studying a shoe on Uncle Chris's old horse, Caledon, and Mrs Veldbron deep in conversation with a tall man on the far side of the yard.

She moved quietly over to John Lockley's side and stood listening to the conversation. He was so handsome, and as he lifted the horse's hooves she noticed that the backs of his sun-browned hands had a fine sprinkling of light hairs on them.

Christopher looked up. 'Hello, Phoebe. Stand away from the hooves.'

She moved back a pace, waiting for John Lockley to greet her, but he was concerned only with the horse.

'He really needs to be reshoed.'

Christopher nodded in agreement as John Lockley stood up and called, 'Darlengi, come and look, Caledon needs reshoeing.'

The tall man talking to Mrs Veldbron turned around and came towards them, and Phoebe's mouth actually dropped open. It was a black man dressed entirely in white man's clothing. She had never seen such a thing before. Oh, she had seen plenty of Bantus wearing bits of clothing, like a hat, or a singlet, or short trousers, but never had she seen a man like

166

this, and what a man! He was wonderful! Stately and regal, he seemed to flow, not walk, across the yard. He was almost as handsome as John Lockley, with firm jaw line, straight nose, high forehead and black, black eyes that held a profound expression. The girl automatically stepped back as he passed. And then the next shock ... he spoke to John Lockley in impeccable English.

'Yes, I thought he did, poor old fellow,' he said as he drew his long, firm fingers through Caledon's mane. 'We'll have you right in no time.'

As the two young men stood there Phoebe was awestruck. They were somehow beautiful together. The size and the shape of them was similar, except perhaps that Darlengi was about an inch taller than John Lockley. She stood perfectly still, silently watching them; eagerly watching them.

John Lockley lifted his arm and placed it round Darlengi's shoulder. It was an involuntary movement, a brotherly act, and Darlengi turned his head to John Lockley and they laughed, their profiles inches apart. Phoebe's intake of breath was quite audible, except there was no one to notice. She had just received her third shock and observed what only Ellen realised and what Mattana had seen only in her dreams: their faces were alike, almost identical: they had the same strong, high foreheads; the same shape to the perfectly straight noses; the same smooth, firm cheekbones and resolute jaw lines and unflinching gazes; even their mouths were a similar shape ... one face faintly sun-coloured, the other a rich bronze.

At that moment Ellen appeared and called to her brother from the yard edge. He turned and moved to her with a smile.

Phoebe stared, fascinated, for immediately Ellen appeared Darlengi faced her, eyeing her in a strangely intense way, and yet Ellen never looked in his direction during the entire conversation with her brother. She held John Lockley's arm in possessive fashion as they spoke for some minutes, before he moved away, calling to Christopher inside the stables. And now Phoebe observed the oddest thing.

All about was hustle and bustle as Darlengi moved swiftly across to halt Ellen as she left the stables.

While the girl could not hear what was said she watched the

body movements of the two. Darlengi seemed somehow open to Ellen and Ellen seemed somehow closed to him. Had Phoebe been a dozen yards closer she would indeed have realised that her assessment was accurate.

'Excuse me, Miss Ellen, I have not seen you since the day you arrived. How are you?'

'I'm well, Darlengi.'

He smiled. 'How long will you stay at the farm?'

She folded her arms. 'I'm not sure.'

'Did you ask John Lockley to take you riding today?'

She arched her eyebrows. 'How did you know that?'

'I guessed. Is he taking you?'

She began to edge round him, but he too moved, and blocked her way. She sighed, an exasperated sound. 'He cannot; he has some other obligation. He has promised to take me tomorrow.'

He smiled again at her and her expression became increasingly irritable.

'I can take you.'

'You? Don't be ridiculous.'

He moved his head sharply as if he had been slapped. It was then he stepped back from her, gesturing with his arm for her to pass. 'I'm sorry you find the suggestion ridiculous. Good morning, Miss Ellen.'

For a moment Ellen's eyes locked with his and her hand half lifted from her side towards him, then she dropped it and hurried away towards the house.

Phoebe stood silently in the stable yard, feeling as if she had witnessed something she should not have. Darlengi remained motionless, watching Ellen's retreating back. His expression turned bitter, then wistful, all in the space of a few seconds. And his thoughts were of the locket and chain he wore round his neck beneath his shirt.

Last year, when the Harrison family had been here at the farm for two months and were leaving to return to Durban, Darlengi had come over to say goodbye.

He had heard from Tilly that Ellen had lost her favourite pendant. It was a small locket on a gold chain she wore round her neck. Darlengi had found it lying on the ground outside the brick fence near one of the gates. His heart was glad, for he knew she would be pleased to have it back.

168

She stood alone looking down towards the river and he came up to her with a wide smile.

'I have found the pendant you lost,' he said in a happy voice, holding it out towards her in his palm.

Her eyes widened and her hand went up to her mouth.

'Here,' he said, 'take it, Miss Ellen.'

When she spoke her voice was cold and distant. 'I did not lose it. I threw it away.'

He knew she was lying. She knew he knew. They stood, eyes locked. There were men with whom he dealt, both Zulus and whites, who toyed with people's feelings, but he was cleverer than they and immune to their tricks; none could wound him; none but this woman, his Ice Princess. For her it was always easy.

The seconds passed. He kept his eyes on hers, nodded his head, closed his hand over the locket, put it in his pocket, and turned from her and walked away. She had no idea he wore it. And as he stood now, thinking of the incident, he would have been surprised to know that as she hastened from him, it was what she too reflected upon.

The memory made her feel odd, sad, uncomfortable. But then she always felt like that when she thought of Darlengi, and unhappily she thought of him often. It annoyed her that she did, but she could not help it and most days a picture of his jet-black eyes would slip insidiously into her mind. She drew her fingers across her eyes as if to clear her head and by the time she had reached the farmhouse, she had deliberately repressed her thoughts and was recalling how sorry Dr Tallant had been when she left Durban.

Meanwhile, Phoebe stood quietly up against one of the stable doors and as Darlengi made his way back towards her he noticed her for the first time. She smiled at him in a guarded fashion and at that moment John Lockley issued out into the yard, leading two horses.

'Ah, there you are, Phoebe,' he said, as if he too had just noticed her. Then he called to Darlengi. 'This young lady is Phoebe McLean, she showed an interest in meeting you. Phoebe goes to school in Cape Town.'

Darlengi smiled and offered her his hand, which she took, saying, 'I'm pleased to meet you.'

'And I you, Phoebe McLean. I think I know your father. Does he run the mission at Fantele's Drift?'

Phoebe was delighted. 'Oh yes, he does, and my mother too.'

He nodded. 'Of course. She is well known among my people as a kind, good woman.'

Phoebe remained until the two young men mounted up to ride away together. They were off to do exciting things she was sure; things she wished she could do. And as she walked away with Uncle Chris she was aware that what she had seen and taken in here in the stable yard had been extraordinary. She was only fifteen years old, with little experience, but she knew that she had witnessed perhaps more than she really cared to know about.

But all those sorts of notions were dispelled when, after an early luncheon, she was again in the stable yard, along with her mother, Jane, General Harrison, Christopher, Dirk Veldbron and Thulmi. Ellen had decided not to come; she preferred to read. They were off for a few hours' ride to see some of the property, for tomorrow she and her mother must leave for the mission.

Christopher had taught Jane horsemanship, and thus she rode straddling the horse; so too did young Phoebe, who thought the other method very awkward, but Victoria rode sidesaddle, for she had been brought up that way.

They headed north from the farmhouse through the horse-breeding yards and over the hill. Dirk was keen to begin a stud farm for Christopher. They had begun with a few good mares and stallions and were happy with the results so far. The Tugela farm was breeding cattle as well and had a small herd already. They rode through a gate in a wooden fence and continued north for two miles. It was a hot summer day with a goodly breeze and pleasantly enough the flies were not too bad.

The Tugela farm was a spectacular piece of territory and as they reined in and sat atop a long hill looking south down through trees to right and left, the vista was quite breathtaking. The river here made a huge upside-down U, and all the land it encompassed belonged to the Tugela farm.

'The land extends over there as well,' Christopher informed them, waving his hand to the north-east.

Jane pointed to a flat-topped rock. 'Darling, let's stop and have some refreshment. It's in your saddle bags, isn't it, Thulmi?'

They were near a rocky outcrop that ran for at least a quarter of a mile. Large and small, the stones stood in massed formation along the hillside.

Thulmi spread a cloth from his bags on a flat stone and began to lay out the food. Christopher and the General removed their water bags and poured everyone a drink.

Jane smiled. 'It's hardly an English picnic.' And Victoria agreed, 'Hardly an American one, either.' They both laughed and so did Phoebe, the enchanting sound of her mirth ringing in the clear day.

The adults all sat around and talked while Phoebe moved a little way off, looking in and around the rocks.

'Don't go far,' called her mother.

'But I want to explore a little. I'm bored just being here.'

'You go with the young mistress,' Dirk Veldbron said to Thulmi, gesturing with his thumb.

'Oh, yes please, Thulmi,' added Jane.

'I go,' said the Zulu, rising to his feet.

Soon Thulmi and Phoebe were wandering away, looking at animals moving far below on the banks of the Tugela. Exotic birds flew in and between the rocks as they roamed on and a great eagle dived down before them, startling Phoebe into a shocked giggle.

They pressed on through the great and small stones for another five minutes before resting. Phoebe climbed up on a rock and sat there quietly humming to herself, and Thulmi squatted down beside her, quite comfortable with the girl.

She tapped the Zulu on the shoulder. 'Thulmi, tell me some more Zulu words. I can say a few things, but I'd like to know the words for all the animals. What's a monkey?'

Thulmi looked up and smiling widely said, 'One word is *inkawu*.'

They went on with this for a time, Phoebe listening keenly and repeating what Thulmi said, and then he stood and, waving his hand in the direction they had come, said, 'We should go back now, miss.'

Phoebe pointed to a natural rock passage a few yards away and about forty yards long. 'Yes, Thulmi we shall; I'd just like to see what's through there first.'

She walked ahead of him and he followed. The rock was smooth on both sides and sunlight stole through the top of the rock passage.

On the far side she stopped so suddenly that Thulmi almost cannoned into her. His mouth was open to speak when he saw what she saw.

Down below them on the hillside, past some trees and wait-a-bit thorn bushes, stood John Lockley. In his arms he held a Zulu woman and he was kissing her passionately on the mouth. The woman seemed to melt inwards along his body, fitting into the shape of him in the most sensual way, as he ran his hands over her. A few yards from them was tethered his horse.

Phoebe and Thulmi were transfixed. Neither said a word.

They watched soundlessly until the kiss ended and the two mouths parted a few inches. The woman said something and their laughter drifted up through the straggling trees along the hillside.

Without a sound Thulmi turned and led Phoebe back through the passage. It had been a day of surprises and shocks for the girl; and this last one had giant implications that even a fifteen-year-old could recognise.

She stumbled for the right words. 'I ... we must not ... Thulmi ... what we have just seen ...'

But the Zulu was no fool. He had survived tribal purges and lived by his wits until he found a niche for himself in a kind and respectable household. He esteemed John Lockley, who had never treated him as anything but a man and a friend. Thus it was Thulmi who spoke positively and decisively. 'Miss. We must forget what we see. Master John Lockley good man. Nothing to do with Miss Phoebe and Thulmi.'

Phoebe nodded. She was still having trouble believing what she had seen; her handsome, wonderful soldier kissing and fondling a black woman. It was not respectable or right; or at least that was what she had been taught. And yet there was a part of her that longed desperately to be that woman who somehow had the right to be in his arms.

'Yes, Thulmi, I understand.'

'So, we say nothing ... nothing to Mister Nelson, nothing to Mrs Nelson, nothing to your mother, nothing to any person.' He was desperately seeking her agreement; his dark eyes telling her this was not a matter for them to discuss, now, or ever, with anyone.

She managed a bitter smile. 'I will never speak about it to anyone, Thulmi. It's our secret.'

'Good.' His sigh was very loud indeed.

When they came back to the riding party, they were both lost in thought. Phoebe's brow remained furrowed for most of the ride home, and a tear trickled down her smooth cheek as she averted her face from the others. She thought she was in love with the handsome soldier, but she realised now that he hardly knew she existed. His love was for some exotic Zulu, all curves and velvet ebony skin.

That night John Lockley was home for dinner. He had been requested by Jane to be there, as Phoebe and Victoria were leaving the next morning.

It was a hearty meal made specially by Tilly, and all the diners were good-humoured and animated; all except Phoebe.

It was near the end of the meal when John Lockley looked across the table at her and smiled. 'You haven't laughed at all tonight, Phoebe, and I seem to recall there is something quite infectious about your laughter.'

'Yes,' her mother agreed, waving her finger at her daughter. 'You've been quiet all day.'

Jane, who sat next to the girl, shook her head. 'People don't always feel like laughing, do they, Phoebe?'

And the girl replied, 'No, they don't.' Her eyes were on John Lockley, who nodded politely and turned away to talk again to Ellen, who had monopolised him.

Phoebe could not help it; how she envied the Zulu woman; how she wished with all her heart she could take her place.

But even at fifteen, Phoebe had a side to her character that was innately wise. She saw that while she might want something badly – and being denied it might make her sad – if it could not be changed then it must be endured. And while John Lockley was the man of her dreams, she must accept that he hardly knew she was alive. So she made peace with her circumstances and the following morning said goodbye to him with a bright smile. She even laughed at something he said, and he in turn laughed with her.

She put out her hand to him. He took it. His touch was

heavenly and a tiny shiver ran right through her body to the very tips of her fingers lying in his palm.

She looked up into his eyes. 'Good luck with your posting.'

He squeezed her hand. 'And good luck with your studies.'

She mounted her horse with a happy feeling. She was, after all, very young and the touch of his hand had brought her such pleasure. But her happy feeling would have swiftly faded had she realised that they were hardly two hundred yards beyond the stone fence of the house when John Lockley was down in the stables throwing a saddle on his horse.

John Lockley was becoming daring. He came openly to the kraal and while he did not court Jettama in front of the tribe, he took her riding on his horse and sometimes they would be away many hours. He brought gifts for her, but was generous to many of the other women. In fact he was openly admired by all the females of the kraal.

Darlengi had long since decided to approve of his sister's association with John Lockley. He knew of men like H.H. Garner and John Dunn and others who had made decent lives for black women – good lives, certainly better than most Zulu girls could hope for – and the one thing he knew as a positive truth now that he had seen his sister and his 'brother' together was that they loved each other deeply. He was unsure what the future would bring, and he was concerned that the Harrison family would disapprove of the liaison when they found out. But tomorrow would take care of tomorrow; they were all together again and when he accompanied them out on to the plains or up into the hills, he simply basked in the sunshine of the joy that surrounded him.

Christmas Eve came quickly round.

At the kraal it was just another summer day. The rains had not yet begun and a hot wind blew down the Tugela. Darlengi went hunting with the understanding that he would meet Jettama and John Lockley in their hideaway late in the afternoon, around five o'clock. Darlengi knew all about clocks, although he could tell the time of day simply by the height of the sun in the sky.

At about the hour of three John Lockley took gifts to the kraal; and when he put the golden ring set with three red stones on Jettama's finger, she asked, 'What does it mean?' And when he replied that it meant she would be his always, her happiness burst from her and she leapt into his arms and cupped his face in her long fingers and kissed his mouth.

And old Weena rose up on her wobbly legs and gave the imitation of a dance.

As they sat and talked Jettama kept lifting her finger in the air to admire her ring, until she said, 'John Logley, Nangeni come again this morning.'

A deep crease formed between his eyes as he dragged his hand back through his hair.

John Lockley had thought often of Nangeni during his years away. His reflections had begun as those of the immature seventeen-year-old boy and had grown to those of the determined young man. He had decided to make Jettama his wife. He was aware it was unconventional and that most of his family would put up barriers, but he was young and hopelessly in love and therefore did not think of the widespread complications: he did not think of how he would be seen by his fellow officers; he did not think of the social conventions that would make him an outcast; he thought only of his love for Jettama.

Jettama's dark eyes turned to his for comfort. 'John Logley, Nangeni follow me and when you and Darlengi not in kraal, he come to me; say I will be his wife.' Her dark eyes clouded. 'And he have Patha and Yeli already.'

John Lockley kissed her cheek. 'I've done a lot of thinking, my darling. Don't worry. I'm going to take you to a safe place. A place where you can live in comfort and harmony with a friend of mine until we can be married.'

Her eyes lit up with the light of belief; whatever he said she knew was so. She did not tell him that Nangeni often waylaid her at night and fondled her and tried to kiss her. She did not tell him that she knew he had gone from the kraal to her father Shiambi to pay lobola for her. She was too fearful of telling John Lockley this.

An hour later they were walking hand in hand through the long grass and the trees north along the Tugela. They were laughing as lovers do and, as they came to the patch of tall seringa trees, suddenly in front of them appeared two Zulu warriors brandishing assegais and dressed in battle regalia.

Jettama immediately recognised Nangeni and his friend Ubi and her frightened intake of breath was loud on the hot summer breeze.

John Lockley's mind raced. He had only his short sword in his belt and no other weapon at all.

He pushed Jettama behind him. 'Go back, Jettama . . . run!'

'No . . . I stay with you.'

But it was too late anyway, for the Zulus were upon them. Nangeni spoke in Zulu. 'Before, I met you very close here to this place. I tell you something then. I tell you to stay away from this woman.' He pointed to Jettama. 'But long time passes and you come back and this woman still smiles on you when this woman mine.'

'I am not,' Jettama shouted from John Lockley's side.

'Nangeni.' John Lockley spoke in Zulu and held his hands out from his body in friendly fashion. 'I do not want trouble. Let us pass. We are on our way to meet Darlengi.'

For just a second the warrior seemed disconcerted. He did not want Darlengi anywhere around. He looked back the way they had come and then returned his gaze to his enemy. 'You go, leave woman here. She mine.'

John Lockley tried to sound calm. 'Nangeni, why don't we all go back to the kraal? Talk there.'

Jettama shouted, 'You have two wives . . . I not want you.'

The warrior pointed his finger at her menacingly. 'I have been and paid lobola for you. You are mine.' And he signalled to his comrade to grab Jettama.

As Ubi moved forward John Lockley pushed Jettama behind him, but immediately Nangeni jumped at him, assegai raised, and John Lockley was forced to draw his short sword.

'You get the woman,' shouted Nangeni to his friend. There was menace, cold and vengeful, in his voice. 'I told you before what I do to you; now I do.' And he stabbed with his spear at John Lockley who leapt back, trying to take Jettama with him, but Ubi moved in from the side, grabbing her while John Lockley's attention was on Nangeni. As the Zulu thrust his spear again John Lockley brought his sword down to parry the blow and the warrior jumped to the side; then he turned to retrieve his position and struck again at the white man who stepped sidewards, bringing his sword down across Nangeni's hand. Blood spurted from the gash on his knuckles.

Nangeni cried out, all his hatred and anger now bare as he rushed anew at his enemy who had wounded him. John Lockley stepped backwards and as he did so caught the side of

176

his boot on a stone and, losing his balance, staggered and went to one knee. In those seconds Nangeni lifted his assegai high in the air, the afternoon sun glinting on the razor-sharp spearhead as it poised before it began its plunge down into the fallen man.

A terrified scream rent the air. Jettama catapulted herself loose from Ubi and threw her body on top of John Lockley as the assegai was hurled down with all the might of the Zulu warrior behind it. He had no hope of checking his blow and he watched in horror as his spear sank deep into Jettama's smooth, soft back. There was a sickening crunching sound as the spearhead was driven straight through her ribs, plunging into her heart.

For some seconds there was only silence ... awful silence. Jettama's face was buried in John Lockley's shoulder, her body draped across his where she had thrown herself upon him.

He looked up and met the shocked, unbelieving stare of Nangeni. Neither could speak. Nangeni's eyes were wide with the dismal horror of what he had done. John Lockley's were incredulous. He stared at the spear sticking from Jettama's back – at the thick ooze of red blood running from it. It was as if he were not inside his own skin but outside, looking at the horrible scene. He noted that his left arm was thrown around the lifeless body lying like a great rag doll across him, and his right hand still clutched his short sword.

Nangeni and John Lockley did not move, the impact of what had happened still assaulting their minds.

It was Ubi who lifted her from John Lockley and placed her face downwards on the ground. Then he moved to pull the assegai from her.

John Lockley managed to scream, 'Don't! Leave her.'

Nangeni, still in shock, turned from the body to stagger awkwardly away. He had gone no more than four yards when a knobkerrie smashed into his left temple. Instantly he fell dead to the ground, his corpse thudding heavily face down.

Ubi turned in terror to see Darlengi standing like the reaper at the edge of the seringas.

'I did nothing,' Ubi screamed and ran for his life through the tall grass towards the river.

John Lockley was still on one knee as if frozen there, holding his sword. He watched motionless as Darlengi walked by the dead Nangeni, not even looking down, and came to Jettama. He pulled the assegai from her body and threw it into the thick grass.

Darlengi's long fingers reached down to the kneeling man. John Lockley dropped his sword and took Darlengi's hand automatically to regain his feet. They stood looking into each other's faces and there was silence for a long time as the wind rustled through the tall grass of the veld. Then John Lockley knelt again, and now as he lifted Jettama in his arms and kissed her, his eyes were distant, frozen, dead. He looked at the mouth that had so recently kissed his own and his tears fell on her stiffening cheeks.

He gazed up and spoke, his voice a cracked, strangled sound so alien, even to his own ears. 'I . . . loved her so. I was going to take her to live at H.H. Garner's . . . she would have been safe there. I . . . oh God, Darlengi! I wanted to marry her. Make her my wife. And because of me . . . she's dead.' He threw his left hand up to clutch his brother's arm. 'Forgive me.'

Darlengi shook the hand from his arm. It was the first time ever that he had not wanted John Lockley's touch, and the realisation alarmed him. He opened his mouth wide for air and stared at the horizon where the sinking sun threw a pink and orange glow across the sky. He turned to leave and then faced back again. When he spoke, his voice too was strained, unlike his own. 'I know the things you say are true. I know you loved her, but . . .'

He stood rigid for a time, listening to the wind continuing to rustle the tall grass of the veld. How could this be? His sister dead on the ground before him. Slowly he knelt in front of John Lockley and took up Jettama's inert hand and lifted it to his face. Then his gaze met his brother's and he spoke. 'There is nothing to forgive. She is the innocent victim. It was as much my fault as yours that she died here today.'

'I don't understand you.'

'If I had not been so enamoured with you . . . with white man's ways and the European life, perhaps she would not have cared for you.'

'Do you believe that?'

He did not answer and the silence between them lasted while a small herd of buffalo passed two hundred yards away.

Darlengi knelt back down and extending his hand turned his

178

brother's face round to look into his tear-filled eyes. He stared steadily at John Lockley for some moments and when he finally spoke his gaze dropped to the assegai-head brand on his arm and his words were pushed out along with a painful sigh. 'No, I don't believe it. She was . . . I am . . . bound to you.'

John Lockley did not answer.

CHAPTER TEN

Induna Indhlovu Shiambi bent his long body double and passed out through the opening of his hut into the balmy evening. He had many other praise names besides *indhlovu*, 'the elephant'; but that was his favourite, and how he liked to think of himself: strong like an elephant. Even though he was quite old by Zulu standards – he was now approaching sixty, had he known – the muscles of his chest and arms had remained hard and inflexible. And he still serviced his ten current wives almost as well as he ever had.

There was a rejuvenating breeze coming down from the Inhlazatye Mountain after the acute heat of the summer day. Shiambi's kraal lay on one of a number of round-topped foothills covered here and there with heavily wooded ravines. He had named it Ezulwini, which meant 'up in the heavens', and he turned around now to view it with pride.

He drew his hand across his eyes and smiled at Enle, his eighth wife, who sat playing an instrument made from a hollow reed and some gut. Enle greatly appealed to him, she had a way of making him forget his troubles; yes, he might pass tonight in her hut.

He strode down to the main kraal gate and passed out of the dusty interior on to the grassy hillside. Smiling, he moved across to a large flat stone in the meagre long shadows of an aloe tree and sat down looking south towards the river. He did not sleep well and many a night he came here and sat watching the sparkling spots in the night sky, letting memories flutter, like the great wings of the eagle, through his mind.

As he sat thinking, a plover, in the thicket of trees nearby, whistled shrilly and suddenly he thought of her. He pictured her coming towards him with a gourd filled with plovers' eggs she had gathered, a soft, adoring look in her eyes. She had been dead so long now, many, many winters, and yet he still

180

imagined the touch of her lips on his mouth and felt her fine fingers stroke his skin. Ah, how I loved you, Nadi. Your life was cut short before your time. Killed by he who should have died in your stead. And now he runs across the plains and has grown to manhood while you have been with your ancestors and I have pined for you all these seasons. The warmth of the bodies of many lovers and other wives has not erased my grief. You should be here at my side. You were my Great Wife. I even moved my people to this distant kraal after you died for I could no longer bear to look at the hills and valleys that we knew together.

And the snake, Mattana, had promised to be at the birth, but no, she was away. And when she arrived back too late she took the child that killed you and gave it succour, when all it deserved was bile. How she betrayed me, twice!

His mouth turned down with distaste as he thought of the witch doctor, and his anger rose up inside him, forcing him to speak aloud. 'I curse you. May the pestilence which ruins the harvest set upon you both, Mattana and Darlengi.'

And then a hissing sound burst from his throat, as, to his amazement, Darlengi ran out of the thicket of trees towards him, as if his curse had produced the reality.

Hurriedly he stood to face his son, a weird expression on his face, at the same time expectant and hostile.

Darlengi loped up to him.

Before any sort of greeting was spoken, Darlengi shouted at his father, 'Jettama is dead. My sweet sister is dead!'

Shiambi shook his head. Jettama dead? How could that have happened? Darlengi looked tormented, hurt, angry. That alone brought gladness to Shiambi's heart. An enigmatic expression curled his thick lip up to the side. 'What happened?'

'You took lobola from Nangeni. You knew he was a cruel bully. That he would not be good for Jettama. But you did not care, all you wanted were the valuables he brought you. You are despicable.'

'I said, what happened?'

'Nangeni killed her. In trying to kill another, he killed my sister instead. You should not have accepted his lobola. You are to blame as surely as if you had thrown the spear yourself.'

Fleetingly a strange expression crossed Shiambi's face, in it a

181

myriad of sadnesses. Then his eyes grew rock hard and his voice the same. 'And you killed your mother as surely as if you had thrown a spear.'

Darlengi's black eyes clouded and a sorry, desperate sound escaped his lips. 'How can you continue to say that?'

'Because it is so. It is you who should lie in the grave beside the Umbucungene Hills, not she.'

And now Darlengi's voice was hard in retaliation. 'I have come to speak of my sister, not my mother, curse you.'

Shiambi took a step closer to his son, his venom showing in his eyes as he threw up his hand and pointed back towards the trees behind Darlengi. 'Go from here. Get away! Even though you and that beetle, Mattana, insinuate yourselves with Cetshwayo, you are not welcome here and you never will be!'

But Darlengi did not move. 'My sister is dead. Your daughter is dead. Don't you understand?'

And now Shiambi shouted, 'Leave my kraal, I said!'

'I will not go!'

Neither man held a weapon. Shiambi was dressed only in his leopard-skin mutya, but Darlengi wore European trousers and had a short knife in a sheath on his belt. Shiambi stepped up to him and in one swift movement ripped the knife from the sheath and thrust it up to his son's face. Darlengi leapt back from the blade but Shiambi followed, waving it in his face and shouting, 'Listen to me, dung heap! Go before I kill you, as I have often wished I had done when you were born. I don't care that your sister is dead! She was nothing to me.'

A howling scream burst from Darlengi's throat. It exploded from his mind, from his heart, from his soul. It was misery, pain, frustration, outrage, hostility. And at the same moment he leapt at his father, throwing up his left hand and ignoring the blade which cut across his forearm.

Both men were six feet tall and powerful but Darlengi was only twenty-three. He was one of the fittest men in all of southern Africa and had run all the sixty miles from the Tugela, resting briefly only now and then. With his right fist he hit his father a blow across the head that sent him reeling and in another lightning move he seized Shiambi's wrist, but his father retained the blade.

They were grappling with each other, the razor-sharp dagger swinging crazily between them. The blood was rushing from the wound in Darlengi's arm and spattering across the limbs of both of them as they swung around each other.

Men and women came running from the huts, calling and shouting. But the two antagonists knew nothing but the fury of the battle. They pulled and pushed and attempted to over-balance each other, and again Shiambi tried to stab with the weapon he held, but Darlengi kept hold of his wrist, pulling the arm upwards. As the blade shot up it caught the side of Shiambi's nose and slid into his right eye.

A shriek of agony rent the sunset and the people from the kraal rushed forward in stunned silence as the blade dropped from the wound and fell to the ground. Blood was everywhere.

Shiambi sank to his knees groaning, and Darlengi bent down and picked up the blade, wiped it on his already bloody trousers, and shoved it back in the sheath on his belt.

One of the induna's wives ran to him and cradled his head in her arms, shouting obscenities at Darlengi. And the other men and women pressed forward angrily.

Darlengi stared at them defiantly as he stood over his wounded parent. Then looking down at the moaning form at his feet he spoke in a voice that was harsh and pitiless. 'A few minutes ago you told me it meant nothing to you that my sweet sister was dead. Now I tell you that your pain means nothing to me. I reject forever any blood of yours that runs through my veins.' Then he turned on his heel and left the way he had come.

As the sun set, he bathed in the Umvoloosi River, watching carefully for crocodiles. An hour later he had built a fire and sat holding his knees, thinking of all that had happened, of all he did not understand.

He had lost Jettama. He had avenged her twice: by killing Nangeni and wounding his father. Strange, but none of it brought any joy.

He knew that when he returned to the Tugela kraal, Logley would be gone; he had said as much when they parted. And that meant that the Ice Princess would not stay either. Somewhere Mattana was supposed to watch over him. Well, she had not accomplished any good for him on this day.

The eerie cry of a hyena sounded on the night air, ringing between the rocks nearby. The lonely sound echoed the emptiness inside his soul.

He sat there engulfed by the black African night. His stomach lurched when he thought of yesterday and Jettama's death. Today he had confronted Shiambi; he always thought of him as Shiambi for he could never think of him as his father. He did not understand the insane hatred Shiambi felt for him, but he had long ago decided it did not matter. Just for a moment, he wished his mother had not died when he was born. He would have liked to know her. He was sure she loved him, even though she was with her ancestors. Mattana had loved his mother, and Mattana had taken her place.

Yes, he was greatly loved by some and despised by others. A picture of the Ice Princess floated at the edge of his awareness and he gave a long, melancholy sigh. But wasn't Darlengi strong? Wasn't Darlengi resilient? Wasn't he indomitable? Couldn't he face anything and overcome it?

He sat staring into the firelight, concentrating on the dancing gold and scarlet of the flame, searching within himself for that place which remained optimistic and unhurt, confident and assured; and as he did a tear broke over his lid to run down his face; followed by another, and another, and another, and another.

CHAPTER ELEVEN

The late afternoon sun threw long shadows across the thick green growth on the hillsides of Ceylon. In the heat of the interior and ringed by mountains and hills, an artificial lake glistened, and around it the temples of the town of Kandy were illuminated in the sunlight.

Forty-one miles to the north-east, across the mountains and lush valleys, a troop of soldiers rode single file over a ford of the Mahaweli River, their red coats tingeing the verdant country around them with a rousing show of colour in fading sunlight.

The young second captain at the head of the column was thinking of the coffee plantations he had left two hours earlier. Brigands had been harrying the Tamil and Sinhalese workers on four plantations east of the Mahaweli and it was thought that a show of force would quell the disturbances. Hence he and his men had been sent from their temporary barracks in the town of Piakapitia. They had spent two weeks in the area and no raids had taken place. It appeared that all was quiet and that the robbers had dispersed.

He could now get back to his main occupation. Three weeks ago he had been appointed the Assistant Commissioner of Roads and Civil Engineer to the colony, and was to be transferred south to Trincomalee where he would take up his duties. It was a chance happening, really, for his friend and tutor from his Chatham days, Anthony William Durnford, had held the very same position here in Ceylon a decade earlier. The young captain had written to Durnford to inform him of the coincidence. He knew he was a good engineer, and he enjoyed that side of his work: erecting military constructions and planning fortified works and building roads and bridges.

The splashing of the water beneath his horse's hooves brought a smile to his face and he took off his helmet and drew his hand back through his fair hair before he turned his uncommon purplish eyes skywards. Yes, the sun was getting low in the sky; it was about two hours to total darkness, there was no twilight here. They would push on quickly and be through the pass up ahead in time to make camp. He urged his horse up the bank.

Half an hour later they were in the heavily wooded pass where wandaru monkeys watched them silently from the trees and iguana ran at the sounds of their hooves. Suddenly the captain lifted his hand and halted: the fifteen men behind reined in.

'What is it, Captain Harrison?' asked the sergeant, edging his horse up closely behind the leader.

John Lockley put his hands up to his eyes. 'I thought I saw movement up there on the left ... those rocks, through the trees.'

Sergeant Ingley followed John Lockley's finger as he pointed ahead. Then both men took out their telescopes.

'I see nothing, sir. Possibly monkeys ... and there are panthers and jackals in this pass.'

'I know,' replied the leader. 'But I don't think it was an animal. I have an odd feeling, Ingley. How far ahead is our vanguard?'

'Johnson and Coates would be about two hundred yards ahead, I think, sir. Can't see them for the trees.'

John Lockley turned in the saddle and looked at his soldiers. His voice was calm but his pulse had quickened. 'Men, we spent two weeks looking for brigands. I don't want to alarm any of you but we're now in the middle of Gasper Pass and I fear we may have finally found them ... or they us. Johnson and Coates have not warned us of anything, but take out your rifles, fit your bayonets, bunch up and ride two abreast, and keep your eyes to the rocks and trees above you.'

Urging their horses forward, the men did as they were told.

They had hardly moved when the first shots were fired, and suddenly they were surrounded by screaming and howling men.

A figure dropped out of a tree in front of John Lockley's horse. The man had the wild, fierce eyes of a zealot and the huge machete he wielded came with a rush of wind towards John Lockley's face. His horse shied and raised up on its hind legs as John Lockley brought his rifle down in one movement and fired point blank at the orange turban. There was a deafening report mixed with a scream and half the man's face disappeared in a bloody mess. But before he had time to even think of what had happened he saw peripherally another danger and turned in the saddle to face a long jezail musket being levelled at him. He tried to pull his head sideways as the explosion sounded and he felt the impact of the bullet actually grazing his collar and just missing his throat. He spurred forward, aiming his bayonet at his attacker who balanced atop a rock. The tribesman dropped his musket, tore a thick blade out of the thong of leather round his waist and jumped from the rock, lunging at John Lockley who countered the blow with his bayonet. There were loud clangs of metal even above the noise of the howling and shouting as the tribesman fought desperately, slashing up at John Lockley with the razor-sharp sword. Suddenly he stumbled and fell to the ground but leapt back on his feet hurling curses and blows at John Lockley's legs.

With every thrust the brigand gave a yell and John Lockley parried with his bayonet. Suddenly, in a swiping blow, the brigand stabbed the horse in the side of the neck. It was only a flesh wound but the horse thrashed his head around in terror and as it did so the brigand jumped sideways, but John Lockley stabbed forward with his bayonet along the side of the animal to meet the man's body. There was a crunch as the weapon entered his chest and the man curled forward in death on to the blade.

When John Lockley had retrieved his bayonet, he looked around. The tribesmen were thinning out and some had taken to the rocks and were climbing away. While the soldiers had been outnumbered by two to one, their weapons were superior, and being on horseback had given them an advantage. The attack was dying.

A few minutes later the remaining assailants had fled.

Eleven dead men lay on the ground. Nine were brigands. Two were soldiers. Two other troops had wounds.

Three hundred yards ahead they found the men in the vanguard, Johnson and Coates, lying in the pass. They were both dead. Both with spears in their backs and their heads hacked off.

That night Captain John Lockley Harrison visited all his sentries just before midnight. He spoke encouragingly to them and told them all would be well. He did not think the brigands would attack again – they were probably miles away now. But he knew the men were concerned. When he returned to his tent he sat in thought.

He heard Darlengi's words to him about the battle of Ndondakusuka. 'This killing is an ugly thing.' Yes, now he knew that to be so. He had never killed a man until today. It was strangely unreal even now to think he had. But when you found yourself placed where men were trying to kill you, there was no alternative but to retaliate. Man had been designed with survival as intrinsic: his quintessence. His mouth broke into a wan, enigmatic smile; perhaps the trick was to place yourself where survival was not an issue.

He felt quite ill as he held his head in his hands and sat on his makeshift bunk. He thought about death ... then about Jettama, remembering the day he and his brother had carried Jettama's inert body home. Darlengi had excused him from blame over her death. Darlengi had the capacity to do that. His brother's soul was always larger than those of the people around him.

He had only received four letters from Darlengi in all the four years since. The first had told of the confrontation and fight with his father, Shiambi.

He missed Darlengi, he really did. Ah, if only they were boys again, riding across the veld on Isi and laughing with the unadulterated joy of just being.

He slept badly.

The following morning they buried their dead and in the late afternoon rode along the river towards the barracks on the outskirts of Piakapitia. In the river the working elephants were bathing after the long day's work, rolling over in the water, their thick, tough hides gleaming. A short time later the troop turned from the river and after a few miles gained the barracks.

As the unit halted and the Tamil servant took hold of the reins of John Lockley's horse, a number of small children clustered around, eager to join in the excitement of the soldiers' arrival.

John Lockley dismounted, and raising his hand in brief greeting to the small upturned faces, turned to his wounded men and escorted them to the hospital. Ten minutes later, he passed along the wide veranda towards his office. He halted briefly to dust his clothes with his riding crop, then he turned and entered the offices.

A sergeant stood from his desk as he entered.

'Sir. I hear you were attacked.'

John Lockley returned the man's salute. 'Yes. Two weeks at the plantations, Morgan, and, do you know? we saw nothing. Then damn it all if we weren't set upon by the bloody brigands on the return ride. I've buried four of my men today. We'll need to file a full report first thing in the morning.'

The sergeant frowned. 'Bad business.'

John Lockley was tired. It had been a long day. He had been riding for hours and his back ached. He walked through to his own office with a grim expression pulling the corners of his mouth down. He threw his riding crop into the corner and, turning to his desk, picked up the batch of letters tied with string. He undid the knot and flicked through them. There were letters from Aunt Jane, his father, Christopher, Michael Tallant, Tilly, Nell (five from her) and one from Anthony Durnford. Then, right at the bottom of the pile, two from Phoebe. The child wrote to him often, though he found he never really thoroughly read what she wrote. Yet it was sweet of her to bother. He pushed the pile of letters aside and moved to the window.

The sun was almost gone and only a burnt orange glow reflected on the roofs of the huts and buildings. He had hoped to find a letter from Darlengi. He clutched the rock-carved windowsill and closed his eyes and thought of Jettama.

He wondered if he had chosen the right path. Although he was completely happy as an engineer, he did not know if he were a good soldier or even if he truly liked soldiering. He had simply been a general's son, and what did generals' sons do?

More than once his uncle, Christopher Nelson, had tried to talk him out of a life in the army. He recalled, when he was but a boy seeing Pietermaritzburg for the first time, Christopher had said that some men did not fit into the ways of the services. That it was a hard strict life and too often dangerous.

He even remembered his own reply. 'But that's the fun of it,' he had said. 'My father says it is. He says it's fun in India and Burma.'

And his uncle had answered, 'Does he? And is that what you think, John Lockley? Do you think it would be fun to be knee-deep in the mud of a rain forest with a Burmese spear in your stomach?'

After yesterday he knew what Christopher meant. Today he was lucky to be alive.

He knew his comrades thought him a morose disciplinarian. They called him 'Hostile Harrison' behind his back and said that the only time he ever smiled was when he was in his cups. But he didn't care. What the hell was there to smile about?

There was a knock on the door and he opened his eyes and half turned his head as his sergeant came in.

'Sir, I'm going off duty now. Do you require anything else?'

John Lockley did not answer immediately and Sergeant Morgan waited. While he waited he lit the lamps. Sometimes the captain's mind seemed elsewhere and yet he was only young, twenty-seven or eight at the most. Handsome and moody. Most of the daughters of the regiment in Kandy were in love with him, but he never seemed to notice them. The dark-skinned girls at Moab Sardi's bar got more attention from him than the officers' blue-eyed daughters. He worked hard and pushed his men to do the same. The mess talk was that he carried a secret of some kind and the weight of it lay heavily upon him.

John Lockley turned around to the sergeant, looking straight at him, yet seeing through him. 'No, Sergeant Morgan, I need nothing, thank you. Goodnight.'

When he was alone he turned back to his batch of letters.

Half an hour later he was still reading and had just opened the third of Nell's. It had been written in June and began with: 'Michael and I have finally decided on a date for our wedding. It will be Saturday the 11th of November, for we now believe that at last dear Bishop Colenso will have returned from England to Natal and will marry us.' John Lockley turned quickly to the calendar at his right hand. Today was Monday, the sixth. Good heavens! Nell and Michael were to be married in five days. Some time ago Nell had written to him asking his opinion of Michael as a future husband. He had replied that he thought it would be a fine match. Michael was going places in the colony and at age thirty-two was the Governor's protégé and soon to be in charge of the Pietermaritzburg hospital.

The last paragraph of Ellen's letter read: 'Vera Van Der Meer and Eva Barnes, Mary Mitcham and Phoebe McLean are to be my bridesmaids. And Michael says he will have difficulty choosing a best man as you're not here. How I wish you could be here for the occasion. I will miss you, dear brother, I really will. My wedding will not be the same without you.'

John Lockley rose and walked to the window. The monsoon season was all but over, yet there was rain tonight. He could hear the heavy patter of it out in the darkness. He stood there a minute or so listening, his profile in silhouette against the lamplight.

There was a gentle tap on his door and he turned to face a swarthy young man who glided into the office and bowed. He was John Lockley's appoo, his butler, Yani, and his face was serious.

'I heard of the tragedy. I'm sorry. Does Captain Harrison dine in or out tonight? Your bath is ready.'

Yani had the knack of always telling him a number of things at once. So John Lockley took a moment to consider what he had said before he replied. 'Thank you, Yani, for your condolences. I now recall I am to dine tonight with the merchant Rajhi Tinlar and I shall come soon to bathe away the dust of my journey.'

Yani nodded and silently disappeared.

John Lockley had forgotten until now that he was to join the merchant tonight. He pictured Rajhi's fine dark features and his long black hair held in place with the customary circular comb. John Lockley liked him and had learnt much about local customs and attitudes from him. He had attended the wedding of the merchant's son a few months ago, and a fascinating, alien, colourful event it had been, so different from a Christian gathering.

He crossed to his office door and sighed as he opened it, thinking of the other wedding soon to take place in Natal. Yes, he wished he could be there. He did miss his family and he missed Africa. His sister was to be a bride . . . and little Phoebe McLean a bridesmaid.

The afternoon sun beamed through the casement windows to throw its golden light on Phoebe as she spun around in front of the long mirror, her lovely fair curls bouncing on her lemon-silk-covered shoulders.

'Isn't it just perfect?' she asked her mother, and Victoria smiled as she answered. 'Yes, the dress is, and so are you. In fact you all look wonderful.' She turned to the other bridesmaids who swirled in front of mirrors along the length of the room.

'Mr Trimm should be here soon,' said Eva Barnes, and the girls all broke into giggles.

Mr Trimm was a government surveyor, and the single person in Pietermaritzburg who had a camera obscura, a simply wonderful invention which could actually make a photographic likeness of a subject. Today he would bring it along and would use it to make likenesses of the four bridesmaids. He was to attend the wedding on Saturday too, and there would use his camera obscura once again to make photographs of the bride and groom and the whole bridal party. Everyone was so excited about it. They just all hoped he would be sober enough to use his equipment, for while he was popular and friendly, he was well known for his heavy drinking.

'I cannot wait for Saturday. It's all so exciting, and I'm only a bridesmaid. Imagine how Ellen must be feeling with only five days to go,' spoke up Vera Van Der Meer, a pretty girl of twenty-two.

Jane bent to smooth one of the bridesmaid's skirts, and Vera's mother, who was intent on making a good match for her daughter, sniffed through her long nose and added her thoughts. 'A young woman's wedding day is the most important day of her life.'

There were murmurs of agreement and Jane stood up and replied, 'While that is often the case, Mrs Van Der Meer, I like to put more importance on the day of meeting the love of one's life; that, to me, would seem to be most important.'

There ensued a deal of good-natured argument after that, during which Phoebe moved over to one of the windows, a serious expression clouding her features. She agreed with Aunt Jane. The day of meeting the love of your life was the most important. She had met her love years ago . . . when she was a tiny child. He had saved her life and she would love him for ever more.

A tingle of emotion ran through her frame. Even with all the noise and chatter around her, she felt lonely.

John Lockley had not been home to Natal since the death of the Zulu girl. She wondered if he ever would return. Phoebe now knew the full story of John Lockley and Jettama.

Ignoring the laughter now going on behind her, she looked out across the green landscape and recalled the day a year after Jettama's death when she was home as usual for the Christmas holidays. She had been searching for her mother and had gone into the small annexe of the mission chapel which her mother used as a study. Victoria was not there but on her desk was her open diary with pen and inkwell to the side. She had obviously been interrupted whilst penning her most recent entry.

Phoebe shivered now as she thought of it. She had not really meant to read what her mother had written. It was just that John Lockley's name had leapt up off the page at her. She had read: 'It appears that John Lockley has not replied to any of Jane's letters, and it's a whole year since the Zulu girl he was seeing was killed last Christmas Eve.'

Phoebe could not believe what she read. The Zulu girl dead? The Zulu girl she had seen in John Lockley's arms, no doubt. Phoebe had not been able to help herself then: she had avidly searched back through her mother's diary and found three other references to John Lockley and the horrible event. Each entry appeared after a letter from Aunt Jane, and the unfolding story told how Jettama, the Zulu girl, had been accidentally killed by her Zulu lover. It appeared that John Lockley had thought himself in love with the girl; that he had been distraught and had left the farm immediately; that the girl's brother was Darlengi (and Phoebe remembered him with total clarity, even though she had only ever seen him once at the farm stable). One diary entry said that some time later Uncle Chris had found out that Darlengi had killed the Zulu who had killed his sister.

It had been a few weeks after she read the entries in the diary that Phoebe had brought the subject up with Ellen. Phoebe had been on her way back to catch the ship for Cape Town and the academy, and had stayed a few days at Mimosa. Ellen's piercing green eyes had closed in frustration at the mention of the event. 'Oh, Phoebe darling,' she had said, 'it's all too awful. The whole affair was dreadful and there was my brother rushing away from us without really saying goodbye. And now he's in Ceylon. I do miss him so. It was Darlengi's fault, I'm sure. For he should have kept his sister away from John Lockley, but no, he didn't. Darlengi has no sense of right and wrong.'

How it could have been the Zulu's fault, Phoebe was at a loss to know, but she did not argue with Ellen's rigid views.

Then when she turned seventeen Phoebe had left Miss Anderson's Academy for the last time and come home to help her parents. After almost twelve years at the mission station in Zululand at Fantele's Drift, they had taken over the small Wesleyan church near Greytown where Victoria had opened a mission school and Phoebe was now one of the teachers. They had forty students, children of refugees from Zululand, whose families lived in a kraal nearby.

The war that had ravaged their American homeland had ended this year. The northerners had a fellow called Lincoln in charge in the final years and Phoebe's father had always thought he would win. After the rejoicing was over, the family had discussed returning to Cleveland. Phoebe recalled the very day they had asked for her opinion. It had been winter and the wind had been whipping savagely down from the Umvoti Hills across the tiny settlement. Beside the open fire Victoria and Frank sat hand in hand.

Her mother smiled and beckoned her to sit with them. 'We know you are aware of the terrible civil war which tore our country apart.'

Phoebe nodded.

'Well, darling,' Frank said, 'your mother and I have been thinking. It's over fourteen years since we came to Natal. You've never really known your grandparents, and in that time two of them have left this earth. We think we should decide what our future . . . your future, is to be.'

'You see, Phoebe,' Victoria broke in, her lovely eyes shining with her thought, 'your father and I feel that perhaps, now the war is over, we should return home, to America. We can help to bring God's word back, to bring love back into men's hearts.'

Phoebe nodded. 'I see.'

Frank took up his daughter's hand. 'You're almost a grown woman, Phoebe, and we want your opinion too. Your mother and I are uncertain, for we have made Africa our home for many years, and we are happy here. But perhaps the time has come for all of us to plan a return to our native land.'

Phoebe nodded slowly. 'Thank you for asking me. While I'm sure my grandparents would like to see me again – and I don't wish to sound unfeeling – they have other grandchildren. And I don't think you could ever do better and more valuable work than that which you daily perform here. I'm so glad to be your daughter.' She looked from one to the other, still holding her father's hand. 'And while I know I'm American, and I am proud of that, really . . . you see I do not know America. My home is here in Natal with you. Some day I want to see the country of my birth, but this country will always be my home.'

Frank sighed and looked at his wife. 'Our daughter appears to be a child of Africa.'

'But Daddy,' Phoebe added, 'I don't want to be selfish.'

He leaned forward and patted her cheek. 'My darling, you are saying what you feel, that's not selfish. We'll discuss it again in the future.'

Victoria smiled and her gaze went from one to the other. 'I think our family decision is made. For now, we'll remain in Natal.'

What Phoebe had said was all true, but there was another reason why she did not want to leave Africa. One she could not admit to her parents: John Lockley Harrison's family lived here and she reasoned that he must come back sometime.

She stood in her bridal outfit, caught in the afternoon rays of the sun, picturing him: his Tyrian-purple eyes, his high forehead and sun-bleached hair, the light tan of his skin; the way she had last seen him four years ago. Sometimes she tried to force herself not to think of him. She set herself tasks of turning her thoughts elsewhere whenever he came to her mind, but it did not work very well.

'Phoebe, come over here,' called Vera Van Der Meer. 'We are all ready for the likeness to be taken.'

Phoebe sighed, murmured softly, and turned round.

CHAPTER TWELVE

Darlengi heard the details of the wedding from Tilly. He had made a rare visit to the Tugela farm in November.

He was now an intimate of Cetshwayo's, where once he had been merely a warriors' apprentice. Kayo had done his work well, and after the death of Jettama, and Darlengi's return to the regiment, the induna had continued teaching him under the steady guidance of Mattana. Darlengi had learned all the Zulu strategies and methods of administration. His prowess with the assegai made him a gifted hunter and his aim was sure. He was svelte and lean and hard and moved with the speed and skill of a young lion. In recent times his name had become renowned throughout all the kraals along the Umlatoosi river.

He was beginning to be involved in many of the decisions concerning the major kraals and important tribal matters. The younger men turned to him and soon he was high in the standing of all the uSuthu, and even Kayo and others who had taught Darlengi listened to him.

He now wore the head ring of the uSuthu warrior, though he had not shaved the rest of his head as many did. The ring was made in various ways, the most popular on the Umlatoosi being made from the tendon of a cow and twined into the hair along with beeswax and powdered charcoal; the whole was then polished to a glassy shine.

The ring was a great honour and granted to an entire regiment once they had washed their spears. And while often men were well into their thirties or even forties before this honour was bestowed, Darlengi and his regiment were granted the ring after the battle of Ndondakusuka and thus were still in their twenties. Warriors were allowed to marry only when they wore the ring and the custom usually was that the whole regiment married a like regiment of women in a massive ceremony. In Darlengi's case custom had not prevailed and when his regiment had married he was accompanying John Dunn on a hunt in Swazi country. It was only now that he was considering taking a gentle girl from a kraal on the Umvulu River as his wife. And while most indunas had six and seven wives – already Cetshwayo had many more than that in his isi Godlo – Darlengi had said he would take no more than sweet Thulile. Intongalu and his peers whispered that this was the European weakness in him, but he was so powerful, both physically and in his alliances, that none dared to reprove him.

On a damp, windy day in early November 1865, Darlengi had come home to his own kraal on the Umlatoosi River.

He travelled over tall, lush hills and a sweep of rolling grassy slopes. It had been raining on and off for a week and there was no golden glow settling in the valleys today. The cattle were stiff and cold in their pens and the kraals, boldly perched on spurs, looked grey and bleak while the verdant mealie patches around them swam in creeping mist.

He ran through tall, soaking grass hanging matted in the wind and while he ran he thought of many things: he wondered about John Lockley. He must write again soon to Logley in the island called Ceylon. He had only sent four letters to Logley in four years. One he had given to a trader to post in Pietermaritzburg, and the others he had taken to Tilly at the Tugela farm, but that was always difficult because of Dirk.

As often was the case when he thought of Logley and the farm, his mind turned to others. He imagined the face of the Ice Princess and wondered if she and Uncle Chris and Aunt Jane had been to the Tugela in recent times. A peculiar expression, neither happy nor sad, lurked in his eyes as he ran up the gentle slope to his own kraal gate, and there, standing like sentries by the wet palisade, were two of Mattana's apprentice followers. He hailed them, '*Saku bona.*' And they replied in kind, 'I see you.'

'Is Mattana here?'

'*Yeh bo*, in your hut.'

When he had bent his frame through his hut entrance he found Mattana there with Kayo. Darlengi had not seen Mattana for several months and took her in his strong arms, enfolding her to his heart.

'How wonderful to see you. What brings you here?'

At Darlengi's words, Thulile, who had been visiting and rubbing charcoal into an ibaru – the calf-skin petticoat that married women wore – stood to leave and moved to the hut entrance. Darlengi stayed her with his hand. 'Don't leave.'

Mattana's ancient eyes filled with alarm. 'Darlengi, let her go. It is better.'

Darlengi shook his head. 'No, ancient one, she stays. She is to be my wife.'

Thulile took hold of his arm with her small hand. 'My future husband, I wish to cause no difference between you and the Great One. I will leave.'

Kayo nodded. 'Yes, the girl cannot tell that which she does not hear.'

Darlengi's voice was cold. 'Thulile remains.'

Mattana sighed and, coming to a quick decision, lifted her deeply pockmarked hand towards the girl. (Mattana had fallen ill in the smallpox epidemic which had ravaged Zululand two years before, but she had survived when so many had not, and that remarkable consequence had cemented her reputation even more.) The long twisted talons on the end of her fingers came close to the smooth skin of Thulile's face. 'This girl is very young to be entrusted with some of the secrets of Zululand, but we will live in the belief that her future husband knows her best.'

Darlengi smiled. 'Thank you, my good Mother. Now let us sit.' When they were settled, he asked, 'What are the secrets you speak of?'

Mattana looked grim. 'We have found out where Mtonga has been taken.'

Mtonga, Cetshwayo's young half-brother, had escaped to the Transvaal some years before but had been returned to Cetshwayo by the Boers and was now serving his fourth year in a guarded kraal. He was allowed visitors once in a while and Darlengi was one of those who went to see him. Recently Darlengi had heard rumours that some of the more aggressive indunas in the uSuthu had been considering getting rid of Mtonga: that while he lived he was a constant threat, for it was now openly said that he was old King Mpande's favourite. On Darlengi's latest visit, Mtonga was not there and he had simply been informed the prisoner had been taken elsewhere.

Zealous followers of Cetshwayo had always believed that

while Mtonga lived Cetshwayo's claim as heir to the throne became more uncertain. Intongalu was one of these. Darlengi knew that Mtonga had always feared Intongalu and his clan, with good reason.

He well knew the gory stories Mtonga told about how his sisters and his mother had been 'eaten up' – the Zulu term for killed – by an uSuthu impi, and how Mpande had been powerless to stop it. And how one of his half-brothers had actually been murdered in front of Mpande himself, who could do nothing against the powerful uSuthu warriors who perpetrated the act, one of whom had been Intongalu.

Darlengi nodded thoughtfully and asked, 'Where is Mtonga, good mother?'

Mattana lifted her wizened arm, the loose flesh hanging down above her elbow, and pointed west. 'You are not going to like my answer, my strong tree ... Kayo has found out that he was taken by Intongalu to Shiambi's kraal in the foothills of the Inhlazatye Mountains.'

Darlengi shook his head. 'This is not good. They both know Mtonga is my friend. I have spoken with Cetshwayo and he promised he would never harm Mtonga. While he was here near us, he was safe, but now that he has been removed, I'm afraid others might do what Cetshwayo would not.'

Mattana answered, 'Yes, and Cetshwayo will still have kept his promise if Intongalu and the others eat up Mtonga for him. But we know he was alive last night.'

Darlengi looked at his good mother. 'You are perhaps Cetshwayo's chief witch doctor. I am one of his young indunas. Kayo is one of his chief indunas. Yet we must save Mtonga.'

Mattana gave the impression of a smile. 'While I need Cetshwayo's favour, King Mpande is my old friend and he has begged me to help his favourite son. But we must be very careful.'

Darlengi nodded. 'If we can help Mtonga to escape, what do we do with him?'

Kayo and Mattana exchanged glances before Kayo answered, 'Somtseu will take him, of that we are sure. He will provide sanctuary.'

Somtseu was the Zulu name given to Theopolis Shepstone,

the Secretary for Native Affairs for all Natal, who was trusted by the Zulus. Some time before, he had accepted another son of Mpande's who was now enrolled in Ekukanyeni, the Bishop of Natal's school at Bishopstowe, six miles from Pietermaritzburg.

Mattana's eyes half closed, hiding the mass of crisscrossed lines on the whites of her eyes. She gave a cackling laugh. 'Somtseu will welcome him, seeing him as perhaps useful in future negotiations with Zululand.'

Darlengi stood and walked a few steps in thought. 'Shiambi's kraal will not be simple to infiltrate. If we can free him, we must smuggle him across the Tugela.'

Kayo gave a growling sound of agreement.

Darlengi snaked his long body down on to the mat next to his companions and put his arm around Thulile. 'It is dangerous but we must formulate a plan and move swiftly.'

Mtonga sat by the fire. It was the middle of the night and all was silent, except for the occasional hoot of an owl. His meal still lay on the ground in the gourd in which it had been brought to him. He was frightened to eat in case the food was poisoned. He felt tired and weak but also feared sleeping. He could not remember how long he had been here, though he knew it was not many days.

He thought of all the people he cared for and how most of them had been eaten up. He wondered if he would ever see Darlengi again. He had told Darlengi on his last visit how he feared for his life, and Darlengi had promised to talk to Cetshwayo. They had brought him here blindfolded, and he knew it was a long way from where he had been imprisoned previously, though he did not know where he was. They would eat him up soon, he knew they would; that was why they had brought him to this place far from all his friends. Intongalu had been the leader of the ones that had brought him here. Intongalu was fierce and had killed many, he knew that.

It was hopeless. He closed his eyes and held his face in his hands as he drew in his breath in a long, quivering sigh.

He thought he heard the faint growling of the dogs – all kraals had dogs, great lurcher-like, mastiff creatures – then he thought he smelled something odd, like squashed grasshoppers . . . how strange.

Suddenly he sat bolt upright. Something had happened outside; distinctly he had heard a thud on the ground. Yes, followed by a second thud. The noises had come from outside the entrance to the hut facing the cattle pen. His eyes widened in alarm. He stood and backed away from the hut entrance. Oh no! This was it, they were here to eat him up! Intongalu would eat his heart. He began to shake violently as the wattle screen was moved aside and a body emerged through the hut opening and unravelled to stand upright. He almost fainted before the word came in elation and surprise from his throat. 'Darlengi . . .'

'Ssh, Mtonga. Come. We must be swift.'

Mtonga smelled the overwhelming aroma of the grasshoppers again and he realised it was coming from Darlengi, who grabbed up the blanket from the floor and, taking hold of Mtonga's arm, whispered, 'Kayo waits for us outside. We must cross the Tugela to safety. Are you strong enough?'

And Mtonga, enlivened by the very thought of escape, replied, 'Oh yes, Darlengi, I am.'

They were soon out in the moonlight with Kayo. The two uSuthu guards lay face down on the ground and while Mtonga waited, Darlengi and Kayo dragged them through the opening back into the hut. One moaned and began to return to consciousness and quickly Darlengi took out the special paste that Mattana had made for him, and wiped it across the guards' mouths, sealing their lips. It was made from mealies, sap from the ivory palm tree, hippopotamus oil and a secret ingredient Mattana kept to herself. It would seal a man's lips for at least three hours. In a few rapid moves Kayo tied their hands and feet.

When they rejoined Mtonga his eyes gleamed in the moonlight as he whispered, 'The dogs?' Obviously he dreaded that one would bark as they made their way across the kraal. Darlengi held his nose, pointing to his body. His reply was one word and it relieved the young man's concern. 'Mattana.' Now Mtonga realised what the grasshopper smell was: a preparation of Mattana's which they had covered themselves in and which worked somehow to keep the dogs calm and silent.

Darlengi had forgone his European clothes tonight and wore only the mutya and a leopard-skin cape, so that he looked like any other Zulu. Stealthily the three figures crept across the kraal towards the gate, past the silent huts. The moonlight threw long beams in their path and they could hear people snoring as they moved by.

This kraal, like many others, had a gate at the entrance and as they slipped towards it one behind the other, Darlengi, at the front, halted, and the others almost cannoned into his back.

The gate was open a little way! When they had come through fifteen minutes before they had been meticulous in closing it.

Darlengi lifted his finger to his lips. 'Wait.' He stole forward to the gate. The palisade was about seven feet tall and the gate about five. When he arrived at the gate he peered over. Ahead there was nothing, to the right there was nothing; then, as he looked carefully to the left he saw a dark form move, over near an aloe tree. Darlengi tensed in expectation as he beckoned his two companions to come forward.

Induna Indhlovu Shiambi had been unable to sleep. He had risen in the silence of the night, and clambering over his favourite wife, Enle, and her two small sons, had picked up his stick and his cape and left his hut to go out into the night.

There was a gentle growl from one of his mastiffs sleeping in the ashes of the fire by his hut door. It was an early summer night, the moon high and bright in the sky throwing a gleam across the hut tops, and a warm breeze drifting up from the river. He had always liked to be alone in the peace of the night, and he liked it even more since he had lost the sight of one eye at the hands of the snake-child, Darlengi.

He walked with a stick now; it made him feel more secure. Slowly he proceeded round the rim of the palisade of thorn bush to the gate. As he unlatched it and passed through he thought he smelled something odd, almost like squashed grasshoppers.

He made his way over the grass to his giant aloe tree, the stick in his right hand helping his balance. He sat down on his favourite flat-topped stone. The moon was so brilliant it illuminated the plain in the distance, and even with his one eye he could see the black line of the river wending its way below him.

He sat for a little time and then he felt a cool change in the air. He pulled his cape more tightly around him and stood to return to his home. In the moment he rose to his feet he was taken around the throat by strong hands, but even in his shock he reacted like a warrior and flung his heavy stick round at his assailant. There was a strangled intake of breath as the stick met Kayo's ribs and he loosened his hold. Shiambi swung around to face his attackers and in that moment, the gleam of moonlight showed him the face before him.

'You!' he said to Darlengi as his stick fell from his grasp and Darlengi took hold of him.

'Silence, Shiambi, or I will kill you.'

By now Kayo had rallied and he took Shiambi's arms and held them fast.

Shiambi realised what had occurred. 'You have released the one who would be king, I see.'

Mtonga answered, 'I do not want to be king.'

'Quiet.' Darlengi spoke again. 'Bind him, we must make our way from here.'

'But,' whispered Kayo from behind Shiambi's head, 'he knows who we are. Darlengi, you cannot let him live. We must . . . we have to . . . kill him.'

'Yes, we must kill him,' agreed Mtonga.

Shiambi gazed insolently at his son, replying, 'So, now you finish what you began before. I will not beg. Indhlovu Shiambi will not beg to the snake-child. Go on, eat me up and I curse you for it.'

Kayo urged, 'Hurry, Darlengi, for if you will not, I will.'

The voice in Darlengi's head urged, *Do it, he hates you, he despises you. Kill him and be rid of the bane that is your father.*

And there in the moonlight, he again lifted the blade which had taken out his father's eye. He raised it high in the night. And as he did so he met the look from Shiambi's single eye; the glint in its coal-black centre defiant, proud, unflinching; if only Darlengi had realised, it was so very like the light that shone in his own.

Darlengi's hand quivered. He stood there, knife raised, as the seconds passed. *I cannot kill my father*. Then he dropped his hand without delivering the blow.

Kayo made a frustrated sound and Darlengi held up his other hand to silence his friend. Then he looked at his father.

'Shiambi, all this hatred all these years. I fought you once near this very spot. We would have killed each other that day. But now ... If I spare your life, will you ... promise on the graves of your ancestors that you will tell no man of our identities?'

Shiambi stared at his son in silence. He was in shock. He had thought his previous breath would be his last. And he did not want to die, even though he would join sweet Nadi. He was not ready for that yet. He could hardly believe the snake-child hesitated to kill him. He would never have believed that his hand would falter this way. Why had it? He had despised Darlengi so long it was hard to accept that the boy was actually offering him his life.

The moon passed behind a cloud and then came out again briefly, throwing a weird, scintillating light that brightly illuminated the patch of earth where the four men stood. It was in that odd, vivid moment that Shiambi answered, 'I will promise.'

'But ...' protested Kayo.

'On the graves of your ancestors?' Darlengi repeated to Shiambi.

'On the graves of my ancestors.'

It was the strongest oath in Zulu culture.

A few seconds passed. 'I believe you,' answered Darlengi. Then finally drawing his gaze from his father's to meet Kayo's he added, 'Bind him.'

Mtonga's interest was in leaving. His voice quivered with alarm. 'We must go, Darlengi. What if someone comes?'

They sat Shiambi on his flat rock, his arms and legs bound beneath his cape.

Kayo did not argue with Darlengi. He understood how, perhaps, it might be difficult to actually kill a father, though he had known those who had. He tapped Mtonga on the shoulder and they moved off down the hill to the south.

As Darlengi moved to follow, Shiambi called, 'Darlengi?'

His son turned back to face him. 'Yes?'

'I have hated you all your life. I have blamed you absolutely for the death of your sweet mother. I tried to kill you in the fight in which I lost my eye. Had I been in your place, here, tonight, I would not have hesitated in eating you up. But you have spared me and while I am confused by it, I will keep my promise.'

Darlengi nodded slowly. 'I know you will.'

Then Shiambi almost smiled. And somehow Darlengi realised it.

'Goodbye, Shiambi.'

'Goodbye, Darlengi.'

Shortly after dawn Intongalu and two others found Shiambi. They had first come across the uSuthu guards who were bound in the prison hut.

Intongalu was furious. His rage furrowed his wide brow in a hundred lines. 'Who were these men who released the prisoner?' and the guards replied, 'We know not. We saw no one. We were unconscious.'

Then Intongalu turned to Shiambi. 'Do you know who they were, Great One?'

And Shiambi shook his head. 'I do not.'

Intongalu's brows drew together. He spoke hastily now, the edge in his voice sharp and persistent. 'We must find them, they cannot have gone far.' He turned again to Shiambi. 'Which way did they go, Indhlovu Shiambi?'

'West towards the Boer country,' he lied unhesitatingly.

At first Mtonga's desire for freedom kept him moving and allowed Darlengi to push him swiftly across the White Umvoloosi River, but as dawn broke he began to tire and his weak state became apparent.

Kayo was insistent. 'We cannot rest yet. We must go on in case they follow. Here, eat this.' He opened a pouch which hung from his mutya and took out a handful of berries. 'It will help.'

Mtonga gobbled them down.

'We can rest only briefly, Mtonga,' agreed Darlengi. 'While I think we left well before the kraal would have woken, they might have guessed we would make flight for Natal and thus would follow this way.'

Mtonga looked scared.

'But do not worry, for we will head towards Ewsthanwan Mountain, to the south-west, I doubt they would suspect we would do that.'

They travelled as best they could with Mtonga, avoiding kraals and keeping to dongas and valleys as much as possible.

They speared a small reedbuck and made a meal of it, and after that Mtonga seemed better prepared for flight.

Yet by the time night fell, after they had been fleeing for what Darlengi knew to be fifteen hours, they had not reached the southern end of the mountain. They were on a rocky divide covered with patches of tall grass. Herds of reedbuck and a few zebras grazed ahead and the three men built a fire inside a ring of rocks that afforded shelter.

They ate what was left of the reedbuck and they drank water from the hide vessel that Darlengi carried.

By dawn they were on their way again.

As they ran, helping Mtonga between them, the hills and valleys awoke. Hawks wheeled over them, and flocks of cranes and kingfishers hovered while beautifully coloured trogons sailed between the trees and monkeys scampered along the branches in the rays of the morning sun.

They forded the Magendi River and ran across the plain, then along the valley of the Intalalala River. Here the trees were mainly mimosa, aloe and acacia with an undergrowth of the menacing wait-a-bit thorns. They detoured to avoid them.

They had to take numerous respites but Darlengi was now sure they had not been followed. At the slow pace Mtonga moved, they would certainly have been overtaken by now.

It appeared that Shiambi had done more than keep his promise. It seemed he had also kept their direction secret. The knowledge of that somehow overwhelmed Darlengi, giving him an odd feeling in his chest.

It was early in the afternoon when they came to a hill within sight of the spot where the Intalalala met the Tugela.

Kayo smiled at Mtonga. 'Once we ford the Tugela, Mtonga, we are in Natal and then it will only be two night skies and you will be truly safe with Somtseu.'

Darlengi stood in thought as Mtonga rested. Then he turned to Kayo. 'My old kraal is near here and so too is the farm of my friends.' He pointed south-east. 'So let us go that way.'

About a quarter of a mile on, near a euphorbia tree with a baboon and his family in residence, was the sign: *Harrison-Nelson Land: Bought from the King of the Zulus. Northern Boundary.*

'What is it? What does it mean?' asked Mtonga.

Darlengi smiled. 'This is the edge of land that is owned by English friends of mine.'

'The ones you get the clothes from?'

'Yes,' answered Kayo for Darlengi. 'And the ones he used to live with.'

Mtonga's expression was one of awe.

They travelled another few miles before Mtonga halted. 'I must rest.'

Darlengi looked from Mtonga to Kayo. His mind had been full of the Ice Princess, ever since he had seen the boundary sign. It had been necessary to come south, but he had brought them to this point deliberately.

In the four years since Jettama's death he had only been back to the farm to deliver letters for John Lockley. On no occasion had John Lockley's family been here, though he knew from Tilly that they came now for months at a time. Luckily only once had he run into Dirk, and if Tilly had not been at Dirk's side when Darlengi arrived, he knew he would have been turned away.

But now that he was so close he must see Tilly again; it was an opportunity to discover how things were with her and the family ... how things were with John Lockley ... how things were with the Ice Princess.

They came to a barbed-wire fence three miles to the north of the farmhouse. And as they passed on found there were still one or two kraals inside this latest boundary. They avoided the kraals and when they came to the far side of the low hill a mile directly to the east of the farmhouse, Darlengi halted them near a huge solitary rock with a clump of small euphorbia growing by it.

'You can rest here. I will be back by the time the shadow of the rock covers all the euphorbia. I must visit my friend who lives near here.'

Darlengi was soon over the hill and running towards the farmhouse. He could see the buildings in the distance on the rise leading up from the bend in the Tugela. Between himself and the buildings lay a new cornfield and three men were working amongst the corn. Darlengi did not recognise any and they turned out to be taciturn Swazis, for his greeting and question of, 'Where is the Mrs Boss Veldbron?' received only shrugs of the shoulders and a gesture in the general direction of the house.

He walked down the gentle slope to the five-foot-high wall which laagered the house and some outbuildings, only now it had been extended to protect the stables too. There was a tilled area of grass, lawn even, about fifty yards wide outside the wall.

He entered the gate and had only taken a few steps when a thunderous voice sounded from a clump of trees near the stables.

'Who the hell are you, boy?'

Darlengi turned to face Dirk Veldbron, cigar in mouth, stomping towards him. Dirk had recognised him immediately but was not about to admit it.

'This is private property, boy,' he began, then, pretending to suddenly recognise the visitor, continued, 'Ah, it's you.'

Darlengi's tone disguised the disdain he felt. 'Hello, Mr Veldbron. I've come to see your wife.'

The frown between Dirk's eyes deepened. 'She's busy.'

'She may be, yet I'm sure she will see me.'

'I don't know why you come here when the family are away. There's nothing here for you. I run this farm and there's no place for you on it. I see you have given up clothes and wear the head ring now, a warrior, eh?' He pointed with his big hand to the gate. 'So back out you go to Cetshwayo and your mates.'

Darlengi did not move.

'Come on now, go quietly,' Dirk said. 'No hanging around here.'

'Mr Veldbron, I have not been here for nearly two years. I do not ever "hang" around here. And I do have a reason to be here. Isiwukulu is mine, as you very well know, so firstly I shall take him, please.'

Dirk's lip curled slightly and there was undisguised satisfaction in his voice as he said, 'The horse died months ago.'

Darlengi looked away from the Boer and his eyes closed briefly. 'I see.'

Then Dirk smiled. 'So, Mr fancy Zulu warrior, you are back to walking, as damn well befits your position.' He gestured to the gate again.

The news of Isi's death rankled. Inside Darlengi's chest a

hot place was widening. While he really did not want to pursue this, he was going to have to. He must see Tilly. To Dirk's great satisfaction he turned away, but the Boer's gloating expression faded as he immediately turned back and said, 'Get out of my way, Mr Veldbron, I have a right to be here and you know it.'

Dirk Veldbron threw the cigar on the ground. 'I run this place, boy, and I say you go.' He lifted his big thick hand and shoved Darlengi's shoulder.

Dirk was as large and as tall as Darlengi, but Darlengi was more than thirty years his junior, and as fit a man who had ever lived. When Dirk shoved him, he hardly moved. For a second all was still, then Darlengi brought up his own arm so swiftly to shove Dirk in return that the Boer hardly realised what was happening until he found himself staggering backwards. He regained his balance and in one sharp move pulled out the voortrekker's oxen whip which he wore in his belt.

Suddenly there was a shout, 'Darlengi!' and from between the trees came Tilly, apron flying in the breeze. 'Dirk, is that Darlengi?'

Dirk Veldbron loved two things: his wife, and this farm, which he had developed for Mr Nelson. Working steadily for twelve years, he had created an oasis from nothing but strips of veld, hills and rocks lying in the arc of a crocodile-infested river. But the order was definitely as stated; his wife first, then the farm. One of the overriding reasons for his constant and enduring hatred of Darlengi was his wife's affection for him.

Dirk turned towards her, whip in hand.

She hurried up, smiling widely, ignoring the heat in Dirk's expression and the whip in his hand. 'Darlengi, how lovely to see you.' Matilda Veldbron was artful, not in a bad or scheming way, but in the way she had to be, to curb her husband's temper. She acted as if she had not seen what was about to happen; this way Dirk could save face; this way she could save the situation.

Her voice was soothing and she put a gentle hand on Dirk's rigid arm. 'Dirk darling, your luncheon won't be too long; let's take it together on the veranda, shall we?' She extended her other hand to Darlengi. 'Come with me and we can chat for a few minutes. Well, if this isn't a nice surprise.' And with that she ushered the visitor past her husband, saying, 'Darling, I'll call you the minute I have things ready.'

Dirk looked quickly round to see if there were any witnesses, but there were none. He murmured acknowledgement to his wife.

Darlengi followed Tilly to the house. He had wanted to fight the Boer, wanted to hurt him, but Tilly had rescued the situation.

In the kitchen she turned and hugged him, standing on tiptoe to accomplish the feat. 'Oh, it's grand to see you, it truly is.' She pointed to his head ring. 'That's new.'

He smiled.

She began to cut a slice of tea cake for him and motioned him to sit. 'So, what brings you here now?'

'While I've come to see you, Tilly, I've also come to ask how everyone is.'

'Oh, we're all well enough. Mr and Mrs Nelson and the General were here in the winter. Miss Ellen did not come as there is so much preparation for the wedding.'

Darlengi felt quite cold. 'What wedding, Tilly?'

She handed him the cake and sat opposite. 'Well, you living up there in Zululand and all, you don't hear about things. You should visit me more often. It's Miss Ellen who's to marry, five days hence in Pietermaritzburg. Being married by Bishop Colenso, none less, in the cathedral. By all accounts, going to be as big a do as the celebrations they had in sixty-three for the royal wedding.' She sighed. 'We were meant to go, but Dirk's not a one for weddings and things. Anyway, it's nigh impossible to remove him from this farm.'

'Who is Ellen marrying?'

'A medical doctor, Michael Tallant. Came out from England with John Lockley in sixty-one, on the same ship. She brought him here last year, seems a nice fellow.'

Darlengi did not answer. 'Is he a good man?'

She pursed her lips before she said, 'Well yes, I think so. I doubt Mr and Mrs Nelson or the General would let Ellen marry a bad man.'

'Sometimes men are not what they seem to be.'

'So, you've found that out then, have you? What else have you learned? Are you still close with Cetshwayo? And how is your good mother, Mattana?'

210

He sat looking at her for a few moments before he replied, 'Yes, I am an induna of the uSuthu, Cetshwayo's forces; soon I will command a regiment of my own. I see Mattana often. She is old, but deep in intrigue as usual ... but I think happy, now that she has me where she can keep an eye on me.' He finished the cake and then looked over to her and met her eyes again. 'What time on Saturday does she marry?'

'Six o'clock, with a breakfast afterwards in a great marquee in the beautiful garden of Mr and Mrs Nelson's Pietermaritzburg home.' She sighed gently. 'Yes, I would have loved to be there. But I'm getting some excitement too, for do you know what? They're coming here during their honeymoon. I've done up the master bedroom quite proper for them, I have.'

He closed his eyes briefly, then took the last gulp of tea and stood. 'I must leave. I do not wish to stay too long.'

She knew exactly what he meant and she too rose.

'Wait,' she said, and disappeared, returning with some shirts and pants, a pair of shoes, socks and a hat.

'These are all yours. I've had the clothes ironed and waiting a year since, but no sign of you.' She began to pack them in a knapsack. 'Though the way you are *un*dressed today, I'd say as you might not want them.'

'I have a reason for looking this way.'

Tilly nodded, and delved no further. 'Then you'll take these?'

'Yes.'

She handed him the knapsack and then took two envelopes out of her apron pocket. 'And there are these ... from John Lockley. Came about six months ago.'

He took them greedily.

Her good-natured face wore a concerned expression. 'Where are you going?'

He patted her hand as if she were Mattana. 'I go to Pietermaritzburg. Don't worry. I am accompanying a friend there.'

'And now, I suppose, going to watch a wedding too?'

'Ah, Tilly, how perceptive. Is that the word?'

She was remembering how scornful Miss Ellen always was of Darlengi, but then she probably had a low opinion of all Bantus, and so had never given him a chance. And why on

211

earth Darlengi had always attempted to be pleasant to the girl was beyond Tilly, but he had, so that was that.

Before they left the kitchen she gave him some cooked meat and bread, and took hold of his arm and said, 'Please come back soon. I know Dirk is difficult, but I will talk to him.'

Darlengi smiled at her, a meaningful smile that said he knew she would, but believed it would make no difference.

Then as they walked through the house he asked over his shoulder, 'How long will Miss Ellen be here at the farm?'

'Oh, perhaps three weeks or a month, I'm told.'

She took him along the hallway to let him out through the front door. As they passed the parlour he halted to look in. His eyes roved over the lace antimacassars, the crystal lamps on the delicate tables, the sofa, the curtains, the pieces of porcelain. He pictured the Ice Princess sitting in here soon on her honeymoon. He imagined her tilting her smooth round chin and giving an imperious wave of her hand. He saw her proud green eyes and the way her lips curled in a delicate smile ... and he made a small sound. It was hardly discernible, but Tilly interpreted it as one of regret. She thought of how he lived now and compared it with the days when he was one of the household, and tears rose to her eyes as she could not help but ask, 'Darlengi, are you happy?'

Beneath this single question Darlengi thought there were numerous others: how did he truly feel? Did he miss life with the Harrisons? Why was he interested in Ellen? Did he miss John Lockley? Where was his life leading? Was he dissatisfied or content? And most of all, who was Darlengi, in the inmost corner of his soul? These were *his* questions which he overlaid on hers.

Darlengi looked closely at her. How should he answer her? Did he pay this good, caring woman the compliment of answering truthfully, whether she comprehended or not? He had spent the two most formative years of his life in a sophisticated European environment; not in a trader's hut, or on a mission station, but in the grand home of Christopher Nelson and the Harrisons, fed a diet of urbane graciousness and knowledge. The true answer to her question was an explanation of a massively complex series of emotions, as inexplicable to Tilly as the harmonious marquetry in a Sheraton escritoire would be to his friend Kayo.

He moved past her out of the door and on to the veranda. She followed him, believing he had preferred to remain silent, and accepting that. When they stood atop the steps to the garden he took up her plump hand and kissed it, as he always did. Then with one foot on the first stone step he said, 'As happy as it is possible for the Zulu, Darlengi, to be.'

He loped across the lawn and through the gate. She watched as he entered the cornfield. He was almost out of sight when she saw him stop and tear open a letter and stand reading it. And now the tears, which had hovered in her eyes, broke over her lids to roll unchecked down her cheeks.

CHAPTER THIRTEEN

When Darlengi rejoined his friends he insisted that Kayo leave. 'Return to Mattana, my friend. Tell her you left us on the border of Natal in safety.'

'But you may yet need me.'

'No, I am certain Shiambi kept his word. But Mattana will be worrying. It is best you relieve her concern.'

'When will you come back?'

Darlengi hesitated. In the back of his mind he had a dream of seeing the family ... of seeing ... them all. He knew Kayo understood numbers up to ten, so finally he answered, 'I am not certain, but in less than ten sunsets.'

Darlengi and Mtonga camped that night just north of Greytown and had covered the forty miles to within ten miles of Pietermaritzburg by the next nightfall. Once Mtonga had started to eat properly he came back to strength. And while Darlengi would have made the journey much more swiftly alone, he was pleased with the way Mtonga had revived.

The next morning they caught some quails and breakfasted off them, but Darlengi seemed unwilling to make haste.

'When will we find Somtseu?' Mtonga asked.

'After. While the sun is still up.'

Darlengi was deliberately not hurrying now. He was close to the settlement ... within two hours' travel, and yet going there had so many overtones for him. Delivering Mtonga was easy. It was what to do afterwards.

But by noon he had brought himself to a decision, and like two beautiful impalas they sailed across the rolling green hills and valleys towards Pietermaritzburg, with a soft afternoon breeze blowing the exotic smells of Natal into their nostrils.

When they came to the outskirts of the settlement Darlengi changed into some of his clothes and dressed Mtonga also, according to the law.

Mtonga, who had never seen a town, stared at the buildings ahead. They had passed Greytown in the distance on this journey, but it was a tiny cluster of houses and small buildings; to Mtonga Pietermaritzburg was an amazing place and, as they passed the first house sitting alone in a number of acres on the edge of the town, Mtonga said, 'I like this place, Darlengi.'

'Good.'

'Where do we find Somtseu?' and Darlengi, who recalled the layout of the town very well from his days with John Lockley, answered, 'We will go to Government House; they will be able to tell us where he lives. Don't worry about what that means, I know what I'm doing.'

And Mtonga smiled broadly, showing beautifully formed teeth that gleamed in the sunlight.

At Government House, there was a single sentry asleep in the heat of his sentry box. The building was brick, of one storey but with two wings. Two horses were tied to the rail and a barouche and a second carriage, less substantial, stood at the front door, but the drivers were not in sight. Darlengi traipsed down the side of the building with Mtonga in tow, leapt a small hedge and came to the back door of the north wing of the house, the kitchen door. It was open and inside was all activity. Soon a kitchen boy armed with a pail came to the door and headed to the well which was about twenty feet away.

Darlengi hailed him and he halted. 'Where does big boss Shepstone live?'

The man was a Hottentot and his grasp of English was reasonable. 'Don't know.'

'Tell kitchen boss important he come out here now, pretty quick.'

Two minutes later an Englishman with a large moustache and long grey beard came out. He looked Darlengi up and down. 'Now where did you get those clothes, and what do you two want here?'

The man's mouth actually dropped open when Darlengi replied in impeccable English, 'The clothes are mine. Would you be kind enough to tell me where Theopolis Shepstone, the Secretary for Native Affairs, lives?'

'Good God! Never have I heard a black talk like you. Sound like you've been rowing for Cambridge. Where'd you learn to speak that way?'

215

'Does it matter? All I need to know is where Mr Shepstone resides.'

The man was absolutely taken by Darlengi. 'Well, at this very minute he resides here in our dining room. Fact is he's dining with the Governor, the Bishop, Mr Nelson and a few other gents.'

Darlengi felt his pulse quicken. 'Mr Christopher Nelson?'

Now the man was absolutely nonplussed. 'You know Mr Nelson too?'

'Yes. In fact if Mr Nelson knows I'm here I know he'll want to see me. Would you do me the surpassing favour of getting a message to them that Darlengi is here.'

'Darlengi is here.' The man repeated it.

'Yes, that's it.'

He shook his head in wonder. 'Well, as they've just completed their dessert, and moved to the smoking room, I suppose I can ask the butler to inform the gentlemen.'

'I thank you deeply.'

The man turned on his heel and went back inside.

Six minutes later he was again facing the visitors. 'The gentlemen say they will join you in the library. Follow me.' Then he added, 'And please wipe your feet.'

Darlengi turned to Mtonga. 'Wait here. I will return soon.'

When he came to the library he found four men waiting. Christopher stepped forward and embraced him enthusiastically. 'My dear, dear boy, it has been far too long, how pleased I am to see you.'

A brief look passed between Theopolis Shepstone and the Bishop. While both men were known allies of the Zulus, and Shepstone had, in fact, met Darlengi in 1861 when he went to Zululand and obtained public recognition for Cetshwayo as Mpande's successor, they were mildly surprised at Christopher's emotional greeting to Darlengi. They were even more than mildly surprised when Darlengi replied, 'Yes, Uncle Chris, it's good to see you, too.'

Lieutenant-Governor Keate was a close friend of Christopher, and was more aware of the relationship between Christopher and the Zulu. Christopher had told him the story of Darlengi and John Lockley some time ago.

When Christopher introduced Darlengi to him, he stepped forward and took Darlengi's hand. 'How do you do, Darlengi.'

Darlengi bowed from the neck. 'How do you do, Your Excellency.'

The Lieutenant-Governor beamed.

Then Christopher introduced Darlengi to the Bishop and to Theopolis Shepstone, but Shepstone remembered him, saying, 'We met at Nodwengu?' and Darlengi replied, 'Indeed, sir. I'm pleased to see you again.'

And he was pleased. He was happy to be in the company of the Secretary for Native Affairs and John Colenso, the Bishop. Even Darlengi knew of the troubles the cleric had been having. Tilly had been his main informant, though he gleaned information from traders in Zululand from time to time. John Colenso was not popular with the High Church of England and in particular the Bishop of the Cape Colony, Robert Grey. Colenso had only just returned to Natal after an absence in England. He had always been liberal and kind to the Zulus and had written works which called into question some of the historical books of the Bible. The Bishop of the Cape had even put him on trial for heresy in his absence.

But Christopher had been one of those colonists who had stood by him, and they had been in communication often, and John Colenso had promised to be back in Natal in time to marry Ellen.

Both Shepstone and Colenso were greatly liked by the Zulu people, and both were very powerful men. A decade later would have seen their friendship cool but on this hot November day they stood united. They both spoke Zulu; and Shepstone, who had been in Natal since he was six years old, also spoke Xhosa as one born to it, while his Zulu was fluent.

Darlengi told them why he was here and the notable gentlemen listened carefully until he finished with the statement, 'So, I am here in the hope that you, sir,' he looked to the Secretary for Native Affairs, 'will accept Mtonga as you did his half-brother, Mkungo, and give him sanctuary.'

Theopolis Shepstone had long-term plans. If ever Zululand fell, Natal must have it, it must not go to the Boer Transvaal, and thus he had been thinking while listening. Another of Cetshwayo's half-brothers in the colony's hands could turn out to be useful as time passed. When Darlengi finished speaking he smiled. 'Where's Mtonga?'

217

'He waits outside.'

'Does he speak English?'

'No.'

Then Shepstone turned to Bishop Colenso. 'What about your mission school at Bishopstowe for the present?'

The Bishop was happy to help. 'Certainly we will take him. In fact I return there now. The lad can come with me.'

The Secretary for Native Affairs smiled. 'As it is only six miles I shall accompany you. I'd like to speak with him.'

Fifteen minutes later Mtonga rode out of Pietermaritzburg in the brougham. Beside him sat the Bishop, and opposite, Theopolis Shepstone. They chatted happily away in Zulu. Mtonga, in fact, would learn no English his whole life.

Darlengi joined Christopher, who waited for him as he waved Mtonga away.

It was a wonderfully bright day and Christopher put his arm around Darlengi. 'Now, I must return home, there is much to do. Our Ellen gets married on Saturday.'

'Yes, I know.'

'You do?'

'Tilly told me.'

Then Christopher's face brightened. 'I've an idea. Come with me. Jane will love to see you and I'm sure Ellen will too. Why don't you stay for the wedding?'

Darlengi hastily replied, 'Oh no, Uncle Chris, I won't do that . . . but . . .'

'Well even if you only stay a day or two. Please, I want you to.'

They stood looking into each other's eyes.

Darlengi thought of yesterday and what he had said to Tilly. He could feel the locket against his skin. Her locket which he never took off. He was tempted to accept even if only to stay for a day . . . to see Aunt Jane, to eat at a table and to wash from a porcelain dish . . . to see the Ice Princess and look into her eyes just one more time. But of course it was impossible. He must not . . . he could not . . . he would not accept.

He heard himself say, 'Uncle Christopher, it's been four years since we were together. Thank you, yes, I would like to come.'

Michael kissed Ellen on the cheek as they came down the steps of St Peter's cathedral. They had been into the church to see where they would place the various invited dignitaries.

'So, sweetheart, it's Wednesday. In three days you'll be Mrs Tallant.'

Ellen and Michael had chosen Pietermaritzburg as the city for their nuptuals for Michael was second in charge here in Grey's Hospital and this is where they would make their home; a modern stone dwelling built on the edge of the town not far from Fort Napier and given as a wedding gift from the General and Aunt Jane and Uncle Chris.

As the couple turned out of the cathedral yard to walk along the street there was a shout, 'Doctor Tallant!' and they turned to see Thomas Greer, Michael's assistant, hurrying towards them.

His freckled face was serious. 'The mayor's wife has taken a turn for the worse, Doctor Tallant, and she's asking for you.' Mrs Archbell had caught pneumonia and had been under Michael's care for the past week. He had removed her to Grey's Hospital only the day before.

Michael turned to Ellen. 'Oh darling, I'm sorry. Do you mind walking home alone?'

Ellen patted his hand. 'Of course not, dearest, it's not far. Off you go and I shall see you at dinner time. Remind your mother there's the rehearsal for the whole bridal party tomorrow.'

Michael's mother had come out from Edinburgh and she was delighted with the match he was making.

Michael kissed Ellen again and hurried off with Thomas.

It was about half a mile to the large house that Jane and Christopher kept in Pietermaritzburg and had named The Grange after the Harrison estate in England. Ellen set off towards it past the hedges of quince and pink button roses and erven of fruit trees.

It was a beautiful afternoon and for a short time she followed a sluit, a number of which carried the town's water supply. Then she turned at the corner of Longmarket Street and crossed to the far edge of town. As she walked she was thinking of many things: of Michael and how in three days she would be his wife; of John Lockley and how she wished he could be here. It was to her that he had written his first letter after his long silence when he went to Ceylon; not to Aunt Jane or

219

Uncle Christopher or their father, but to her. Eighteen months ago Michael had asked her to be his wife and she had sent a letter to John Lockley asking him what he thought. His reply had been that he thought Michael was an excellent choice. Since then her brother had corresponded with them all again. Yes, she had been the one to reunite the family.

Her step became almost jaunty as she reached the edge of town and turned to pass along towards the big house in the distance.

Suddenly she thought of Darlengi and she halted. Why would she think of him? Her brow crinkled. Probably because she was thinking of John Lockley; how she truly wished she would not connect them, but she couldn't help it. She often seemed to do just that.

She had not seen Darlengi in years, though word drifted to her through Matilda that he was becoming more and more important in Zululand. As if that mattered. She recalled the last time she had seen him shortly after the dreadful business with his sister and John Lockley. He had come to the farm to say goodbye. She had seen him coming through the window as he rode up on Isiwukulu and had watched Jemby, the groom, take the horse from him. She continued to watch him cross the yard and pass through the gate in the stone-wall fence up to the veranda. But when Aunt Jane came in to tell her he was here, she had said she had a headache and could not say goodbye to him.

Jane's good-natured gaze had narrowed. 'Ellen, are you really so ill you cannot come into the parlour and say goodbye to Darlengi? We don't know when we'll see him again and, after everything that has happened, it's a miracle he still regards us as friends and bothers to come at all.'

But she had been adamant. 'I cannot, Aunt Jane, my head throbs too much.'

Her aunt had been very put out and left the room with a loud slam of the door. That was when she had moved from the bed to the window again to watch through the curtain. Sure enough, some minutes later, Darlengi, with Uncle Chris and Aunt Jane, appeared on the lawn below and walked to the stone wall. There they hugged him goodbye. He left them and moved away a few paces before he turned back and, looking directly at the window, lifted his right hand and pointed at her, straight at her, calling out, 'Goodbye, Ellen.' She had started in fright. How could he have known she was watching? She was behind the curtain. He always managed to disconcert her . . . anger her . . . unsettle her.

Even now as she thought of him here in Pietermaritzburg she felt uncomfortable, and she shivered as she looked around before moving on across a wide empty erf filled with trees and long grass. Suddenly she decided to detour and go along a pretty donga covered in wild flowers and leading to a small stream. She wandered along for a minute or two and then halted to bend and pick some wild blooms and tuck them in her bodice.

When she stood up she had the peculiar shivery feeling again: it was as if she were not alone, as if someone watched her. She turned completely round in a full circle. The acacias held their arms out above her and the stream meandered by a little distance away; the grass was thick under her feet and bushes with tiny pink flowers grew in abundance. She was quite alone. Yet a prickling feeling ran down her spine, and her pulse quickened. Suddenly she was overcome by fear. She had no idea why but she lifted her skirts and ran, heart thumping, back along the donga, up into the field and across to the house.

She entered the front door quite out of breath and seeing no one went immediately up to her room where she wrote a letter to John Lockley. It was late afternoon when she descended the ebony wood staircase and came through the living areas to the wide stone patio.

Her eyes widened in disbelief and her face paled as she registered the long form stretched out on a chaise-longue reading a book. He was dressed in European clothes but he had that head ring thing the Zulus wore.

'Darlengi!'

He looked up and fleetingly she thought she saw tenderness in his expression, but she realised she must have been mistaken.

'What are you doing here?'

He smiled. Oh God, he was so like John Lockley it was uncanny. How she hated that he was like John Lockley. And yet she knew she was the only one who realised it. Perhaps she had imagined it all these years. How could he be like her brother? He was black, for heaven's sake, and his eyes were hot coals of intensity, where her brother's were a glorious purple colour, shining and noble.

'I am here at Uncle Chris's request. He is with Aunt Jane inside somewhere. Didn't you see them?'

'No ... I ...' And then the horrible thought struck her. Oh no, they had brought him here for her wedding. Darlengi would ruin everything. How could they? How could Uncle Chris be so insensitive?

Darlengi saw her expression change to dismay. 'What's wrong?' he asked.

She did not answer. She turned on her heel and went to find her aunt and uncle.

He shook his head and closed his eyes to her departing back.

Ellen found Jane talking to Mannie in the hall. 'We'll have afternoon tea on the terrace, Mannie. Please tell Cook. Then Mr Nelson has to go back to the brickyard.'

When the maid had gone Ellen's eyes filled with tears. 'Aunt Jane, how could Uncle Chris invite him here? I cannot stand the thought of Darlengi at my wedding. It's cruel and insensitive of Uncle Chris. How dare he not tell me that he was coming.'

Jane's answer was severe. 'Behave yourself. Dear, it's true, you're acting like a child. Your uncle met with Darlengi just this afternoon and invited him here for a day or two, that's all. In case you don't remember, Darlengi was a part of this family for years. Your uncle and I still think of him that way. We see it as a fine opportunity to be with him again, and I'll thank you to do the same.'

'Then ... then he's not coming to my wedding?'

'Not to my knowledge. Though if you were charitable, you'd ask him.'

Now Ellen's voice rose in anger. 'Oh God, Aunt Jane ... please ... a Zulu, a guest at my wedding, along with Natal society? How could you possibly suggest it?'

Jane put her finger to her lips. 'Hush, he'll hear you.'

'I don't care if he does! We haven't seen him for years and he turns up three days before my wedding. I won't have it. Do you hear?'

Jane quickly stepped forward and took up her niece's hands, her voice soothing and conciliatory. 'Now, hush, there's a dear. You're all nerves and I don't blame you, I was too before

I got married. Now, no one's going to ruin your wedding, I can assure you. So, shh. Let's go out to Darlengi together and try to make him welcome.' She kissed Ellen on the cheek. 'Please?'

Ellen nodded and hand in hand they went back to the terrace. But Darlengi had overheard Ellen's raised voice, overheard some of her words, overheard enough.

Yet he was bright and happy during tea, and when Christopher asked him about Zululand and Cetshwayo, he replied unselfconsciously.

'And we note you wear the head ring now,' Chris said as he took the last mouthful of his scone.

'Yes, as an induna I must; as a true warrior I must.'

When they rose from the table Christopher put his arm round Darlengi's shoulders. 'Will you come to the office with me?'

'Yes. I would like that. I remember how it used to be.'

Jane laughed. 'Well, it's bigger and busier now, I can tell you.'

Chris smiled. 'Then I'll just go and get my papers. I'll be back.' He turned to his wife. 'Where's my case?'

'Oh, I'll get it.' And they departed together.

Ellen had been quiet. She had listened and asked the occasional question, but she had hardly been loquacious. Darlengi had expected nothing more. She had always been this way. But now he turned to her, in his eyes a supercilious look and a smile playing about his lips. But it was not a pleasant smile, there was something cold and perverse about it. He was staring at her. Her pulse quickened. She did not like this.

'You need not worry,' he said.

'Worry?'

'That I will come to your wedding. I will not come. After all, I am not inviting you to mine.'

She started. He noticed, and was gratified.

'You're getting married too?'

'I am.'

She felt her face stiffen. She had a funny wounded feeling, followed swiftly by anger. Why did he tell her this? She didn't give a damn. She didn't give a damn what he did. Then a thought came ... a masterstroke. She gathered herself and managed one of her condescending looks. 'Oh, and how many

wives do you have already? You Zulus have multiple concubines, don't you?'

Darlengi had never heard the word *concubine*, but from the
inference he decided on the meaning.

He took a step closer to her and the look he gave her was so
cutting that she looked away. He was thinking of when he was
a teenage boy, and how all he had wanted was to please her. By
all his ancestors, he wanted to please her now; but she would
have none of it. She had always avoided him; avoided his
youthful advances of friendship and his adult advances of
more. But he had changed, where she had not. While she could
still cut him dead, and hurt him, he had learned many things,
and how to hide his feelings was one. He had discovered how
to play the Ice Princess at her own game.

'Perhaps you would feel happier if I answered yes, that I do
have many *concubines*. But the truth is that I will have only one
wife. A single one that I will give myself to. The woman I will
spend my nights with, in the warmth of her body and her
arms. I chose her for her great beauty and her sweet and gentle
mind. The latter of which, you would have no understanding
of at all.'

She stepped away: she had never liked to be too close to him.
She felt injured, and she hated that she did. She was angry and
frustrated. They stood staring at each other; glaring at each
other.

Suddenly Christopher's voice sounded. 'Are you ready,
Darlengi?'

The two people on the terrace did not move. There was a
cold, bottomless crevasse lying between them in the warmth of
the humid November afternoon. They both desperately wanted
to say things, to call out to each other across the frigid chasm
. . . but neither spoke.

'Darlengi?'

With a grim expression, he stepped back from Ellen. 'I'm
coming, Uncle Chris.'

He turned on his heel and left her there.

As her eyes followed him she had an uncanny feeling. It was
to do with this afternoon when she had felt odd over there in
the donga and run home. Had Darlengi been there, watching
her?

224

CHAPTER FOURTEEN

Of course it had been the talk of the town that Darlengi, the Zulu, was in the home of Mr and Mrs Nelson, and not as a new servant, but as a guest. There were even some who remembered him from a decade before. Liam Voight recalled, 'Used to come with Mr Nelson to the brickyard. Walking and talking like a white youth. Shocking. And apparently he's back again.'

Others called Christopher a fool.

And yet there were some who remembered Darlengi more fondly, and Mr Russell and George Travers at the brickyard welcomed him openly; happy smiles on their faces.

'Good to see you again, Darlengi.'

'You bin away too long for certain, young fella.'

Michael Tallant met Darlengi for the first time when he came to dinner at the Nelson home on Wednesday night. Dr Tallant was a fair man, and he was impressed by Darlengi's appearance, his superb grasp of English and the sheer force of his personality. He had known about John Lockley's friendship with Darlengi, in fact John Lockley had first mentioned it when they sailed out from England together.

There was no indifference in the way Darlengi watched Michael Tallant. He was to marry the Ice Princess; thus everything about him was of intense interest. He waited for the moment when he could dislike the doctor; feed his anger and resentment towards him, but no such moment arrived.

During the course of conversation, Michael spoke about a man called Joseph Lister who had taught him in Edinburgh. Lister had written papers on the coagulation of the blood and was now doing much research in antisepsis. Darlengi's dark eyes narrowed. He was fascinated by this and asked, 'So this learned man, Joseph Lister, writes to you?'

'Yes, we exchange letters fairly regularly.'

Darlengi nodded thoughtfully. 'And you say he thinks sepsis may be caused by a pollen-like dust in the air which affects the wounds of men?'

Michael nodded. 'Yes, Darlengi, up until now we have always believed that there is simply bad air which directly infects the wound. We call it miasma. You see, so many of our amputation cases die from sepsis. Professor Lister is unsure what really causes the sepsis, but he *is* sure it's not miasma, and he's continuing to experiment.'

Darlengi thought about this for some time while the conversation progressed. At a later point he turned to Michael and said, 'While I know nothing of medicine and real science, it seems to me that your learned Professor Lister is right to reject the belief in miasma. I can draw a parallel from my own life. I was a Zulu boy with no understanding of the rest of the world, then I was shown much of western civilisation.' Here he smiled at Jane and Christopher. 'And I realised that there is always more to know ... more that eludes every one of us. Hence, in my opinion, even without certain knowledge, the good Professor Lister is right to assume that there is more to sepsis than simply what men know now, which they call miasma.'

Michael leaned back in his chair, eyeing the Zulu carefully. 'Darlengi, I do not wish to seem rude, but you are wasted in Zululand.'

And Christopher, as if he were a proud parent, quickly said, 'Oh yes, Michael, you're right.'

Ellen's lovely round green eyes followed the speakers, looking from one to another, but she said very little. Michael noticed this, but he put it down to pre-wedding nerves and he was oblivious to the occasional extraordinary look that passed between her and the Zulu guest.

When Michael was leaving they all gathered in the front hall. The doctor offered his hand to Darlengi and smiled. 'I've truly enjoyed meeting you. If ever you are back here please do call on me.'

Just for a moment Michael thought he saw a sardonic expression as the enigmatic black eyes narrowed slightly and Darlengi took his hand, saying, 'Thank you, I shall remember your invitation.'

Michael took Ellen into the arc of his arm as he continued, 'When do you return to Zululand?'

Darlengi's eyes were on the bride-to-be when he answered, 'On Friday.'

Then, as Michael turned to Ellen to say goodnight, Darlengi spun on his heel and returned down the hall.

That night Christopher and Darlengi sat up late, for Christopher wanted to know all that had happened to the young man since he had last seen him. Darlengi obliged and found himself telling Christopher all about releasing Mtonga . . . even about Shiambi.

The older man listened silently during the long story, and when Darlengi ended his tale Christopher smiled and, leaning forward to pat the younger man's knee, said, 'So, even your father has finally recognised your worth. You're a fine man, my son, and I'm proud of you.'

'I don't think he wants to sup with me, Uncle Chris, but he did keep his word.'

As they made their way up the stairs to bed, Christopher put his arm round Darlengi's shoulders, and when they parted the older man said, 'It's good to have you here again, son,' and Darlengi replied, 'It is good to be here.'

Thursday morning Jane and Ellen went out early. There was to be a full bridal rehearsal later in the day.

Darlengi sat in the parlour off the terrace. He had Richard Burton's *First Footsteps in East Africa* open on his lap.

Opposite him was General Harrison, who was questioning him about Zulu military strategy. 'I believe you form in divisions shaped like the chest, loins and horns of the buffalo.'

'Yes, sir. The warriors in the chest draw the enemy forward in a feint and then the horns peel off and surround them, and the loins are in reserve and used when needed.'

'Old Shaka came up with the idea, eh?'

'Yes, I believe so.'

James Harrison made a clicking sound. 'Won't work with our armies, you know.'

'Oh?'

'Well you see, laddie, while our foot soldiers and some of our mounted soldiers might possibly be surrounded in your classic battle plan, there are others in any column of ours; others with long-range weapons: cannons, rifles, field guns – howitzers,

227

mortars. They wouldn't be drawn into the hand-to-hand combat.'

A smile hovered on Darlengi's mouth as he replied, 'Yes, General, I understand that. We might have to fight differently if ever we fight you.'

The General looked up quickly. 'Ah ha, and that could come to pass if your king-to-be is as ambitious as I suspect. I spent over fifteen years in India, Darlengi ... saw my discharge a year after the mutiny. I know how princes are always after a little more land to call their own. Cetshwayo might just want Natal as well as Zululand. And how would that affect you, lad?'

An inscrutable expression sat on Darlengi's face as he replied, 'General, I think there is a saying in your country that goes ... "I'll cross that bridge when I come to it".' Then he smiled widely and the General burst out laughing.

'Well said, laddie, well said.' He rose. 'And now I shall take my constitutional, for I believe you and Christopher are soon to go riding.'

Darlengi watched him leave. It fascinated him to know John Lockley's father. He liked him; there was something quite uncompromising about the General which Darlengi responded to. He was sure he would have been an able adversary in battle.

He turned his attention to Richard Burton but all the while at the back of his mind he kept thinking how he must pack his knapsack and leave tomorrow.

Eventually he put the book aside. It was a complicated, ambivalent feeling he had. He was an induna now, and becoming powerful. He knew that in this European world he would always be an appendage to the Nelsons and the Harrisons. He was a Zulu, damn it! Yet a part of him always longed for this sophisticated life, the European company; it had been ever thus.

At the sound of his name he turned his head to see a frothy white creature in pale silk hurrying through the door towards him. Swiftly he stood as she spoke.

'Do you remember me, Darlengi? I'm Phoebe. Phoebe McLean. I met you at the Tugela farm four years ago.'

She held out her hand and he took it. Behind her came Victoria.

'Of course I remember you, Miss McLean, and you, Mrs

228

McLean.' He smiled at Victoria. 'You were there for a few days before Christmas.'

Phoebe nodded. 'I was so sorry about what happened to your sister. I know it's a long time ago, but please accept my sympathy.'

Victoria's voice was scolding. 'Phoebe, Darlengi may not wish to be reminded of that.'

He spoke quickly. 'On the contrary, Mrs McLean, I appreciate Miss McLean's words.' He faced back to Phoebe. 'Thank you.' Then he looked to Victoria. 'It is said that you have been missed by many of my people since you left Fantele's Drift and went to Greytown.'

Victoria was touched. 'Oh, thank you, but we felt we could accomplish more there with the large school and the mission all in one.'

At that moment Christopher arrived. 'Well, look who's here.' He kissed Phoebe and her mother, then Victoria lifted her gloved hand to him, saying, 'Frank said you have a book for him. *Great Cathedrals*, is it?'

Christopher nodded. 'I do. And there's another I think he may like. Come, they're in the library. I'll show you.'

Victoria turned to her daughter. 'I'll be just a minute. Then we must be off to the Colensos, we must not be late for luncheon.'

Phoebe smiled; for her mother got along so well with Sarah Frances Colenso and so respected her husband, the Bishop, that she at times forgot she was a Wesleyan.

'And then we'll go, Darlengi,' Christopher called as he led Victoria away.

'So, are you here long?' Phoebe inquired.

'I leave tomorrow.'

'Oh.' It was a disappointed sound and Darlengi watched her closely. He thought how lovely she was, and somehow understanding. He smiled at her. And she smiled at him, thinking how very handsome he was in his black, gothic way; his features so much like John Lockley's.

She said, 'I only heard you were here last night. You're the talk of the settlement, you know.'

'Yes, I know.'

Then she laughed and the merry tinkling sound was so catching that he too laughed.

'Would you like to go out on the terrace?' He motioned to the door and she went through across to the stone railing and stood looking over the fields to the hills.

'Lovely, isn't it?' she said.

He nodded. 'Yes, Miss McLean, it is.'

'Oh please, call me Phoebe. I would like you to.' She faced him. 'When I knew you were here I wanted to see you.'

He smiled and she wondered what he was thinking.

Then she asked, 'Do you ever hear from John Lockley?'

They did not realise it, but at the mutual thought of him they wore exactly the same soft expression in their eyes.

He nodded. 'Yes. I receive letters. I have some now. I get them from Mrs Veldbron at the farm about once or twice a year.'

For a few seconds Darlengi saw envy on Phoebe's face, and suddenly he realised with a shock that this beautiful young woman was in love with his brother. Darlengi had only ever thought of Jettama with Logley, never anyone else. Disarmingly he asked, 'Why? Does he not write to you?'

'No ... well, yes, but not as often as to you, and they are not the ...' She broke off embarrassed and walked a few steps from him.

And he completed the sentence for her. 'The sort of letters you would like from him.'

She rounded to face him. 'I ... why, yes. How did you know?'

And then he smiled. Ah, how young and innocent and honest she was. A little like his wife-to-be, Thulile, in a way. 'I can see it, Miss ... er, Phoebe.'

'Oh dear, I did not realise I was so transparent.'

She was disconcerted by him. For while physically he reminded her of John Lockley, he was really quite dissimilar. He was more fluid when he moved, and his bearing was different; just a step removed from a swagger. And while at times there was an imperious look in John Lockley's eyes which the Zulu certainly had, Darlengi was somehow more regal. He was certainly overwhelming, and the odd thing was that she felt so comfortable with him. She knew she could confide in him; that he would listen and understand.

'He doesn't know I'm alive.' She said the words with such sorrow.

230

And then to her amazement he replied, 'I know what it is to love unrequited, Miss Phoebe.' He moved away from her. Oh yes, he knew what it was to be haunted daily by an image where there was only pain. He felt sorry for the girl and he turned and asked, 'John Lockley has no idea of how you feel?'

'No idea.' She said it with a sigh. 'He's in Ceylon. He may as well be on the moon. Mother says he will not be back for many years. I write often, but he rarely replies. I'm used to it. It doesn't matter.'

'You are strong, Phoebe.'

A determined look came into her eyes. 'Yes, Darlengi, I am. I have...' She broke off as her mother and Christopher reappeared.

'Ah, now, Phoebe, I have the books for Father, and there's so much to do before the wedding. We must be off.' Victoria held out her hand to Darlengi. 'Enjoy your ride and the rest of your stay, and if ever you pass through Greytown, please visit us.'

He bowed from the neck. 'Thank you.'

When Darlengi said goodbye to Phoebe he took her hand and looked steadily into her eyes. 'Goodbye, Phoebe. Remember to enjoy life. For while I do not necessarily follow my own counsel, I urge you not to have dark thoughts.'

When the two women found themselves in the street, Victoria asked, 'What did Darlengi mean by urging you not to have dark thoughts? Are you unhappy about something, darling?'

'No, I'm not unhappy. I'm not sure what he meant.'

'Strange he'd say such a thing, then, but I suppose he is quite strange, if the truth be told.'

Phoebe defended him swiftly, 'No, Mother, he's not strange at all, but he's complicated, I'm certain of that. Anyway, I'm ever so pleased I saw him. You know, I feel as if he's a friend.'

'Mmm, I noticed. He certainly talks to you as a friend. He called you "Phoebe".'

'Yes, I asked him to.'

At that statement, Victoria's tolerant heart merely allowed her eyebrows to rise.

Darlengi and Christopher rode out and rested for a time on the banks of the Umsindusi River. The birds were in abundance and multicoloured flocks flew all about. Across the river a family of hares ran in and out of fallen trees. There was a cooling breeze coming up the river and all about was peace.

'Beautiful, isn't it?' said Christopher.

'Yes.'

'When I first came here, Darlengi, this country struck me so, and over the years it has wended its way into my heart. I think of myself as more African than English.'

Darlengi looked at him through narrowed eyes. 'Really?'

'Mmm.'

'Did you meet Dingane?' The question came out of the blue and Christopher turned to meet Darlengi's gaze.

'Only once, when I was young, just before he was killed. Why?'

'Some of the older ones in my kraal say he was a bloody murderer. Is that what you thought?'

Christopher was silent for a few seconds. 'He looked at human life differently, yes. Life was cheaper to him than to Mpande.'

'But you thought he was a barbarian, didn't you? And you must really think the same of Cetshwayo.'

'Darlengi, where are these questions coming from?'

The young man went on as if he had not heard. 'So, Uncle Christopher, you must really think the same of me. They are Zulus and I'm a Zulu. Last night you said you were proud of me but you must think me a barbarian. I fought at Ndondakusuka, the place of bones. I have killed men.'

Christopher did not reply immediately and when he spoke his voice was stern. 'Listen to me, son, and listen well. Admittedly, the Zulu culture is not the same as we would find in London or Paris or Vienna, or even here in Pietermaritzburg. There was much blood spilt by Shaka and Dingane, yes, and they took human lives without caring; but in fact so did Caesar and the vicious Napoleon and Robespierre and a hundred other supposedly *civilised* men. You? A barbarian? If you were not so serious I would think it funny.' He moved close to Darlengi. 'I haven't seen you for nigh on four years, and yet you come into my home for a couple of days and you are as urbane and damn-well polite and cultured as any blue-blood thinks he is. I don't know why you say what you do, but I can tell you one thing. Of course Zulu life is more primitive than

232

European life, but it's just as valid a way for men to live as any other.'

Darlengi did not reply.

Then Christopher took hold of the young man's shoulders. 'What's going on in your mind? Look, you don't have to go back, you know.'

Darlengi met his companion's eyes. 'What do you mean?'

'You know what I mean. I've said it to you before and I'll say it again. You can stay here. You're welcome to live with Aunt Jane and me. Always have been, always will be.'

For a long time Darlengi just stared into the frank, honest eyes in front of him, and when he spoke he had decided to try to explain something that he knew he had been hiding even from himself. He moved out of Christopher's hold and stood looking downriver. He felt the breeze through his thin shirt and he was aware of the movement of the air on his face.

He did not turn round as he said, 'Uncle Chris, I know your suggestion is motivated by good intentions. But I must leave tomorrow as I said I would. You say I am damn-well polite and cultured, and perhaps I am when I'm with you or Aunt Jane or Tilly or . . .' He had almost said the Ice Princess, but checked himself; for perhaps, with her, he felt raw, sensual. '. . . or others. I am a Zulu who is tainted with *civilisation*. You asked me the very same thing ten years ago and perhaps I should have accepted then; but not now. I have washed my spear, though there was no joy in it for me. In fact it made me sick. I am an induna. Many years ago Yangaani, a witch doctor, said I was too white. The part of me that is too white is hard to control at times.' Then he took a deep breath and spoke very quickly, giving Christopher the information he had withheld until now. 'I'm going to marry a Zulu girl; a trusting, sweet, naïve, simple child by your standards.'

Christopher stood silently watching Darlengi's broad back. 'I see.' He had not thought of this.

The breeze was wafting the fronds of the willows along the bank and all was so peaceful here. A large wading bird stood sentinel at the water's edge as he continued, 'Darlengi, I do understand, and I have often wondered if we really did you a kindness all those years ago. Having you with us as we did. All I hope is that we did not make things too difficult for you now.'

There was a long silence, while each man lived with his thoughts; then Darlengi turned to face the older man and his voice seemed to come from a long way off, as if it had to make itself heard down the tunnel that led from his heart. 'When I am with the Zulu, my affinities are with Europeans, and when I am with Europeans my affinities are with the Zulu. I am who I am and I blame no one. You did what you thought best at the time. Truly, I am grateful.'

They stood looking at each other. Christopher's expression was infinitely sad; Darlengi's was reconciled.

'I am a man-bridge between two races, Uncle Chris, and I understand neither of them. Yet I would not change my life for any man's.'

Christopher stepped forward and took Darlengi in his arms. He held him a long time, close to his heart, before he said, 'My dear, dear boy,' and released him.

They mounted the animals in silence and as they moved off Darlengi spoke; now his voice was light and cheerful. 'Oh, by the way, I have read about Caesar and Napoleon, but who was that Robespierre you mentioned?'

That night, Ellen and the General dined with Michael and his mother, and Jane visited Mrs Archbell, the mayor's wife, who was still in hospital and disappointed that she would not be at the wedding. Christopher and Darlengi waited at the brickworks until Jane came by from the hospital, and so it was after nine o'clock before the three of them sat down to the dinner table.

They talked of many things and when they rose to move into the parlour for tea and coffee, Jane broached the subject she had been wanting to raise since Christopher had told her that afternoon. 'So, Darlengi, you are to be married. Tell us about her.'

'There is little to tell, Aunt Jane. She is about twenty years old, I suppose. I paid a fine lobola for her. She's the daughter of a petty chieftain from across the White Umvoloosi River. She's what you would call pretty, I think.'

'What's her name?'

'Thulile. It means soft and gentle. And she is.'

Jane pursed her lips and looked keenly at Darlengi. He wondered what she was thinking, but he had to wait until

Mannie had poured the tea and disappeared before she said, 'Darlengi, I know enough of Zulu custom to realise that you can have any number of wives.'

'Yes, Aunt Jane.' He was not going to make it easy for her.

'So?'

'So what, Aunt Jane?'

Christopher was leaning back in his chair, watching them.

'Oh Darlengi, don't exasperate me. You know very well what I mean. So do you intend to follow custom?'

He did not answer immediately. He looked over her head to the far side of the room, as if deciding. Then he looked at Christopher before he brought his eyes back to hers. 'I could tease you, Aunt Jane, and perhaps you deserve it for asking such a question. You should know better. Don't you remember thoroughly Christianising me when I lived under your roof? Do you forget so easily?'

Jane looked abashed and Christopher broke his silence. 'Just like a woman to be inquisitive.'

Jane sniffed. 'Now don't you two be so supercilious. I merely inquired because I care about Darlengi, and he knows it.'

An enigmatic smile formed on Darlengi's mouth. He was thinking of Thulile, in Zululand, an eternity away from this parlour and these people who were just as large a part of his life as she would be. It was very strange.

An hour later Jane and Christopher had retired and Darlengi walked alone in the garden.

He had seen Ellen and her father come home a short time before and had watched them step down out of the carriage and walk to the front door. He had heard her laugh at something her father said, and he had backed away and gone further into the night.

Twenty minutes later he returned past the huge marquee sitting sedately on the lawn. He looked in through the open flap; tables and chairs were stacked inside in readiness for the big event on Saturday.

He thought of *her* and how beautiful she would look.

He stood looking up at the sky, at the stars, at infinity. Suddenly he made up his mind and strode across the lawn to the back of the house. He leapt easily over a row of rosebeds and came up to the veranda. Most of the bedrooms were upstairs but Ellen's was not. It lay here at the back of the house and its doors opened out on to the veranda.

Yes, there she was. He could see her through the glass. Her dark hair fell over her shoulders and halfway down her back. There was a blush of pink in her cheeks and her pale creamy skin showed at the top of her delicate nightgown. He felt his pulse quicken as he looked at her. He moved across the veranda and up to the door.

Behind her on the huge walnut wardrobe hung a long white dress with a scalloped hemline, covered in tiny pearls. A long piece of lace fell from the waistline to lie upon the floor, and a veil with sparkling stones around the top lay over a chair and shimmered in the lamplight.

He watched her slender fingers pick up a silver snuffer and put out the candles on her rosewood dressing table. Two lamps still illuminated the room and she moved to the one on a table near the door. As she did she looked up and saw the figure on the veranda. Her hand went to her mouth in fright as the door opened, but just as she was about to scream she recognised him.

'Darlengi!'

'Good evening, Ellen.'

'What are you doing here?'

He did not answer.

'How dare you.' Her hand went to the bare skin of her chest and neck as if to cover herself.

'I have come to say goodbye because I know that when I depart tomorrow you'll have such a bad headache that you'll be unable to leave this room. That is, until I'm gone, and then miraculously you will recover.'

She backed away from him and her hand went out to pick up a wrap to cover herself, but he moved as swiftly as a cat and dragged it from her hand. 'Don't be ridiculous, Ellen, I know what a woman looks like.'

Her eyes grew hot with anger. 'Yes, a black savage.'

For a moment she thought he was going to strike her, for he raised his hand, and she even turned her head to ward off the blow, but he checked himself.

His voice was hard and cold. 'When I think of you and her, I know who the savage is, and it isn't Thulile.'

'Get out of my room.'

236

Always, always it was like this with her.

She lifted her hand imperiously and pointed to the door. 'I said, get out of my room.'

He moved so fast she did not realise he had, until she found herself in his grasp. He pinned her two small wrists in his large right hand and his other arm went round her, bringing her face to within inches of his. 'Listen to me, Ellen. I shall leave your room when I want to. I could break your neck with one easy movement. I'm no longer the sixteen-year-old Darlengi who allowed you to torment and confuse him. Remember that.'

Just for a second he saw fear in her eyes, real fear, and then try as he might he could not help but be proud of her as she rejoined, 'But you will not hurt me, Darlengi. You never will, even though I hurt you.'

He continued to hold her. His mouth was so close to hers she could feel his breath as she looked into his ebony eyes, deep into his ebony eyes. *Oh, Darlengi, why have I always wanted to hurt you? Why?*

He thought he saw contempt in her eyes. He was wrong, but it served to finally betray his long years of buried emotions. And so he said it. He spat the words into her face, and as he said them he let her go with such force that she hurtled across the room and, hitting the bed, slipped to the floor.

'Damn you, Ellen!'

She looked up at him. Her nightgown had slipped from her shoulder, exposing the fullness of her left breast, the nipple taut. She did not bother to cover herself now.

She sat there on the floor, her eyes locked with his, and she did not move as she replied in almost a whisper, ever so gently, 'And damn you, Darlengi.'

Their curses were their love words, their ultimate embrace.

He moved slowly closer to her, the flickering flame of the lamp throwing his shadow across the floor and on to the bed. Somewhere outside night birds called, but still they stared at each other.

He came right to her, and stood touching her gown with his shoe. Her pulse raced. Her heart thudded in her chest. She was admitting things now that she would have preferred to die without acknowledging.

It was no revelation to him; he had always known.

He dragged his eyes from hers to look up at the white lace

237

gown mocking him from where it hung glimmering in the darkness.

Then slowly he knelt and the admission flowed between them without a single word.

They were unaware of time passing, and then finally he spoke and the words caught in his throat. She saw his lips move and heard him say, 'My own beautiful Ice Princess,' and she tried to answer but no sound came.

Abruptly he stood, and turning from her was gone through the door and across the veranda into the soulless night.

She did not move. She just sat there on the floor staring at the place where he had been. Oh God, the world would never be the same again. Everything was different.

When she began to sob, it was almost as if she looked from afar at the poor creature on the floor breaking its heart ... breaking its heart and repeating over and over the love words from the core of her soul, 'Damn you, Darlengi, damn you.'

Time passed, Ellen did not know how long, and finally she managed to raise herself and fall on to the bed.

She lay there trying not to listen to the torment in her head. Then she became aware of movement behind her and a hand on her shoulder.

She turned over and lifted her eyes. Darlengi!

He had been unable to bear the thought of her anguish. He had tried to stay away but he could not. He had to comfort her. To stop the pain.

He leant forward, and as his hand moved from her shoulder to touch her tear-stained face the top of his shirt opened and out fell the locket ... her locket. The one she had claimed to have thrown away when he had brought it to her years ago at the farm. It hung there glinting just inches above her face.

He wears my locket next to his heart.

Then she was in his arms and he was kissing her hair, her face, her eyes. She clung to him and he could feel her trembling. His senses were filled with the smell of her, the nearness of her, the reality of his Ice Princess in his arms at last. All the years of dreaming and wanting and aching for her were over.

And Ellen responded. There was no turning away now. They were living what Ellen had at last acknowledged. They

238

were not in this bedroom of The Grange in the little town of Pietermaritzburg; they were in Darlengi-Ellen country where Ellen rejected all the constraints of her past. She loved Darlengi. She had always loved him. She would always love him.

Somewhere amongst the spiralling sensations of desire, along with the brief pain, Ellen felt the coolness of the locket between them on her skin, but it was soon lost in the overwhelming knowledge of his body joining with hers. Her skin glowed in the lamplight as the Ice Princess melted into her primordial reason for being on the planet . . . to love the Zulu, Darlengi.

Later when she lay with her head on his chest where she could hear the steady beating of his heart, he whispered, 'Forgive me.'

And her love for him found voice in her reply, 'There is nothing to forgive.'

Before he left her, he took her hands and held them tightly. He had revelled so briefly in his consummate love for this woman, and now he had to leave. 'My darling one, I must return to Zululand. I do not know whether we have been right or wrong this night. All I know is that I have loved you as I will not love again, in this or any other world.'

'Did you always?'

'From the first second I saw you, the day I came to Mimosa so long ago.'

She gave a small, gentle smile, and then a look of fear crossed her face. 'I cannot bear to think of life without you.'

'They will not let you think of life with me.'

She nodded. 'I know.'

She lifted her long white fingers to caress the locket hanging around his neck before he stood and moved reluctantly across the room.

He halted at the door and turned back to her. 'I love you, now and always.' he said.

'I love you, now and always,' she replied.

CHAPTER FIFTEEN

Phoebe laughed as Lieutenant Benjamin Fielding of the Greytown Mounted Rifles took her hand for the Pride of Erin on the lamplit terrace. He looked smart in his reddish-brown moleskin uniform with black braid on the collar, and he contrasted elegantly with Phoebe drifting at his side in delicate swathes of lemon silk.

The small orchestra consisted of Mr Russell, who played the accordion, Eben Lewes, who played piano, and young Gert Vermeer, who was becoming adept on the violin. In the population of three thousand Europeans there were very few musicians; they were lucky to have these three who had been playing with gusto for hours, taking hardly a break.

Ben was a bright young man who had been talking animatedly to Phoebe and her new friend, Frances 'Fanny' Colenso, the Bishop's daughter. Phoebe had taken an instant liking to the fragile, pretty teenage girl, and they had been monopolising each other until Ben had broken into their conversation and danced with each girl in turn.

And now as he moved gracefully along with Phoebe he looked into her eyes. 'So, Miss McLean, have you enjoyed your stay here in the capital?'

'Yes, it's been quite diverting.'

'Allow me to say that you look radiant.'

'Thank you. And how does your father after his awful accident?'

Ben's father had been on the commissariat staff until on a hunting trip a cobra spat in his eye and for a time he was almost totally blind. He had been forced to resign.

'Oh, he's happy enough now, thank you. Been granted a pension of eightpence halfpenny a day for life, and the sight in his left eye is partially returning.'

As Phoebe and Ben swirled across the floor, she thought she caught Ellen's eye and smiled, but Ellen did not respond.

Ellen danced with her new husband. Her chestnut hair was tied up and hung in little curls at the back of her head, crowned by her Nottingham lace veil. As she danced, she carried the five-foot-long train of her skirt over her arm and her new husband beamed down at her. Her left hand rested gently on Michael's shoulder and she seemed to be staring at it with a faraway look in her pale eyes.

Everyone said it had been a splendid wedding. The breakfast, in the largest marquee ever made in Natal, had been an exquisite six courses by candlelight before the dancing had begun. All the dignitaries of Natal were present and Bishop Colenso had read the marriage service in a fine, strong voice. The bridesmaids looked radiant, and as Ellen and Michael had walked down the aisle after the ceremony Aunt Jane and Victoria had cried, and so had some of the other women. But no tears had fallen from Ellen's eyes.

She had married the man John Lockley had said was right for her. For as long as she could recall, she had wanted to please John Lockley, and once more she had done what he said. But amongst the violent revelations of the last forty-eight hours had come the unhappy admission that her brother's choices were not necessarily hers.

But what else could she have done? Until Thursday night she had been happy to let John Lockley choose for her. Until Thursday night she had lived in a cocoon, never admitting what lay buried inside her. Until Thursday night she had been a child, believing what she saw and not what she felt. Until Thursday night she had *never* been herself.

There was laughter all about her as she looked up at her husband and he smiled at her. He was respected and good; a good man, a good doctor, listened to and admired. She was his wife. Oh no! What had she done? She had married him in the sight of God. She was irrevocably his.

He asked, 'Are you all right, darling?'

'Yes, thank you, I'm perfectly all right.'

'Perhaps you'd like to sit down, it's been an emotional day, sweetheart.'

'Yes, I think I will.'

On the other side of the terrace Mrs Van Der Meer sipped

her champagne and talked with her friend, the mayor's cousin. Her austere features were mirroring her thoughts as she picked up her fan in her gloved hand and said, 'I suppose you know they had a black, a Zulu, staying here this week. I cannot understand Mrs Nelson. She seems so sensible and yet I'm told the same fellow actually lived with them years ago. And now the word's about that he's close to that savage, Cetshwayo. I wouldn't say it to her, but I think it's disgraceful.'

'Yes, apparently Ellen's brother, the soldier, was like a brother to the Zulu. Imagine an uncivilised Zulu allowed to befriend a white child like that.'

Mrs Van Der Meer sniffed through her extensive nose. 'And he a general's son! How could General Harrison have allowed it?'

'Well, he wasn't here, was he?' pointed out the mayor's cousin. 'John Lockley was in the charge of Mr and Mrs Nelson. It's they who are to blame. And if the truth is told they're to blame for a jolly sight more, for I've heard the rumour that the soldier was more than friendly with a Zulu girl as well, though one hates to believe it.'

Mrs Van Der Meer looked around the grand gathering: the dancing couples in the golden lantern light; the waiters in their black and white, carrying trays of champagne; the copious baskets of flowers resting on the stone walls; the orchestra; the glitter and excitement. 'Some people's only saving grace is their wealth,' she observed.

Suddenly from behind her a young voice sounded, 'And some people are devoid of any saving graces at all.'

The two women turned sharply around to see Phoebe McLean give them an indignant look before she turned to her partner, Ben Fielding, and led him away.

The young man was startled. 'Gosh, Phoebe, you certainly aren't afraid of people, are you?'

'Oh gracious, Ben, Mrs Van Der Meer is a horrible snob. I feel so sorry for Vera with a mother like her. And how dare she talk of Darlengi like she did, as if he were nothing. He's a fine man.'

Ben looked surprised. 'You know him? You know the Zulu they were speaking of?'

'Yes, I do. And I'll thank you to speak well of him, Benjamin Fielding.'

Ben laughed. 'I wouldn't dare not to.'

At the same time, down the steps and across the lawn, the General was in discussion with Victoria and Bishop Colenso.

'Until Darlengi left yesterday, I had a feeling he might even remain for this wedding.'

Victoria smiled. 'Well, the way that Jane and Christopher dote on him, I would not have been surprised, but Ellen apparently was extremely vehement that she did *not* want him here. It appears she never could abide Darlengi. You know, I've always thought she was a little envious of her brother's devotion to him.'

James Harrison frowned. 'Perhaps. She's always been possessive of her brother.'

'Do you think John Lockley realises?' asked the Bishop.

'No, I don't think so; but he adores Ellen, always has. For a brother and sister they're extremely close.'

Victoria looked across at the bride. She looked lovely, but very calm and controlled. But then Ellen always had been. When everyone had been weeping at the cathedral this evening, Ellen's eyes had been dry. She had been calm all day. In fact Ellen seemed to have been that way all her life.

Just then Jane and Christopher moved by and took the floor together. Jane looked up at her husband. 'Doesn't Ellen look beautiful?'

'Yes, she does.'

'How I wish her mother could see her tonight.'

Christopher's arm went round his wife. 'You're a wonderful lady, Jane Nelson, and I think Ellen's mother would thank you for bringing her up such a fine young woman.'

Jane kissed him on the cheek. 'Why thank you, darling.'

Over his wife's shoulder Christopher saw Mannie, all dressed in blue satin and deep in conversation with George Russell, his manager. Looking at her Christopher was reminded of yesterday.

He was always first down to breakfast, often eating just after the hour of six and off to the brickworks well before seven. Yesterday was no exception and when he had come to the breakfast room Mannie had met him with a note in her hand. It was from Darlengi, and it was brief.

Dear Uncle Chris and Aunt Jane,

I have left early for I do not wish to say goodbye. I shall come to see you sometime at the farm. Thank you for these memorable days.

Darlengi.

He had left the note for Jane and gone off to work, not returning until late in the evening when Jane and Ellen had already dined. He had a quick supper while Jane told him about the day's events and afterwards he went to his study. A little while later Mannie had knocked softly on the door and asked if she could speak with him.

Apparently just after he had left for work that morning Ellen had appeared. She had requested a cup of tea and when Mannie brought it she had asked, 'Where's Darlengi?'

'He's gone, dear . . . went early. Left us a note.'

The blood drained from Ellen's face. 'He's gone?'

'Yes, Miss Ellen, as I said, went before half five of the clock 'cos I was up by then.'

Ellen stood from the table, her tea forgotten. She looked at Mannie in a strained sort of way, and for a few seconds Mannie thought she was going to cry. This only served to confuse the maid, for all she could ever remember was Ellen's disdain for Darlengi and how she always avoided saying goodbye to him.

'Ellen, dear,' she said. 'I've known you all your life, and I cannot believe that you are concerned about Darlengi. You don't even like the man.'

Then, Mannie said, Ellen shook her head and in a controlled voice replied, 'Mannie, you're wrong about that.'

She said that Ellen had gone back to her room, and had been withdrawn and quiet the rest of the day. Mannie had said it was probably just 'wedding nerves' and she had not even been going to tell Christopher about the matter but felt it her duty to do so as it was such a peculiar happening.

Christopher had gone to Ellen's room and knocked gently on the door. When he entered, she had been sitting up in bed, reading.

He had moved to her and sat on the edge of the bed, saying, 'I just wanted to bid you goodnight, darling. Tomorrow is a big, exciting day.'

244

Her eyes lifted to his. He had been shocked at the sadness in them as she replied, 'Yes, Uncle Chris, it is.'

He had taken her slender, pale fingers in his big warm hand, noticing with surprise that the book she was reading was the Bible. 'Darling, is everything all right?'

'Yes, of course. Why wouldn't it be?'

He lifted her hand and kissed it. 'Sweetheart, I'm your uncle and I like to think my two best girls are always happy.'

She answered, 'You don't need to worry about me, Uncle Christopher, I'm all right.'

'Well, if ever you are not all right, remember you can tell me.' He had kissed her goodnight then and she had responded in kind, and as he had turned to leave her she had said, 'Marriage is forever, isn't it?'

He had come back to the bed and taken up her hand. 'Darling, what's this? Wedding nerves?'

She tried to smile. 'Yes, I suppose so.'

'You don't need to have them. You're marrying the best of men. And a happy marriage is a fine thing.' Then he had kissed her again and added, 'Look at your aunt and me.'

He had gone to bed a little concerned about Ellen, but all had gone swimmingly today.

And now, as the band drifted into a waltz, he wished John Lockley could have been here. The thought of his nephew brought back the ghastly Christmas Eve four years ago, when John Lockley had come back to the farm acting like a madman; telling them he was leaving for Durban immediately; that the girl he loved had been murdered and her murder avenged. Only later did they find out the girl was Darlengi's half-sister. John Lockley had managed to change his posting to Ceylon and they had not seen him since.

Half an hour later, with Jane at his side, Christopher informed the guests that the phaeton awaited to take the newlyweds to Nelson's Hotel around the corner.

Everyone laughed, for this was Christopher's new hotel, which had just opened recently, bringing competition to the Crown, the North Star and the Orion. Ellen and Michael were off to the Tugela farm on their honeymoon the next morning.

Ellen smiled at all her guests, hugged and kissed her father, who wore his uniform for the occasion, and kissed her mother-in-law and all her bridesmaids. As she hugged Phoebe, the girl said, 'Oh, Ellen, I'm so happy for you. Married to the one man of your dreams.' Suddenly, just for a second, Phoebe thought she saw something die in Ellen's smile, but, just as quickly, Ellen threw back her head and laughed, and Phoebe knew she had been mistaken.

Then Ellen was in Jane's arms and Christopher's and everyone was laughing and throwing rice and soon the married couple were waving goodbye in the balmy night air.

And when Michael turned to his new wife in the darkness of the carriage and kissed her passionately, she kept saying over and over in her head, 'It will be all right. It will be all right.'

Five minutes later Michael helped Ellen down from the phaeton, and as they walked hand in hand across the little bridge over the sluit and into Nelson's Hotel, a tall, lithe figure moved swiftly behind the cluster of acacia trees near the door. Ellen started and Michael turned abruptly to her. 'Darling, what is it?'

'Oh, nothing. I just felt a little odd, that's all.'

He kissed her forehead. 'Too much excitement.'

She smiled. 'I expect that's it.'

I must control myself. Yesterday he went back to Zululand.

And yet as her husband took her hand up the wide staircase, thoughts of the hours with Darlengi piled like dealt playing cards upon her mind.

She heard Michael speak to her and she saw his hand on the polished brass knob as the door swung back to reveal a room lit with long white candles and small pink lamps. Then she watched his shadow as it moved across the room and turned back to her and lifted its arms and beckoned her forward.

She forced a smile as she crossed the bridal suite to join him, but her heart pounded and she knew she must stop thinking of Darlengi or she would go insane.

Michael kissed her and when his hands found her breasts through her lace gown she pretended it was Darlengi.

Her husband was talking about their future life together; his hopes and his dreams. He put out the candles and most of the lamps and he called her beautiful.

At last she found herself lying at his side and he was

whispering love words in her ears. She felt his hands on her breasts again and then as he kissed her mouth and his fingers moved between her legs, she stiffened and said, 'No, don't! Michael, stop.'

Michael drew back. 'What is it, darling? What's wrong?'

She sat up. 'I ... I don't know ... I just don't want you to do that.'

He recognised the unnatural tone in her voice. Michael Tallant was a doctor, a caring man, and he realised that Ellen's sensibilities might be disturbed.

'But darling, come now, we're husband and wife. It's all right. This is quite proper. Lie back, I love you. Let me show you.'

'No!' She moved off the bed. He could see her rigid form in the pale light. He told himself there were women who had trouble with loving the first time. He must be gentle. He came to her but as soon as his hands touched her arms she stiffened. Then she began to shake uncontrollably. He was out of his depth.

'Ellen, darling, please tell me what's wrong?'

'I don't know ... I don't know ... I'm so sorry.' She stood there trembling in the warm autumn night.

After half an hour of coaxing, pleading, cajoling, threatening and begging, Michael was in absolute despair.

The newlyweds spent the night in the same bed; both in their own hell; both at a loss to understand.

On Friday, Darlengi had run nineteen miles without resting. When he did halt it was on one of those thousand green hills north of Pietermaritzburg which Edgar Harrison had so loved.

During the afternoon he forded many small rivers and streams and like an animal of the veld raced across the plains, along the dongas and through the grasslands. He remained on a straight northerly course and spent the night just south of the Tugela River, opposite the Inkanhla Mountain.

The next morning he travelled slowly and stopped at a small kraal south of the Emlalazi River where one of the inhabitants was an old friend from his apprentice days under Kayo.

'So what brings you here, Darlengi?'

'I move about a lot. I like to see what is happening in Zululand.'

The younger members of the kraal looked at the newcomer with wonder. They had never heard of anyone doing such things.

When he left they all came to the kraal gate to watch him lope away.

He knew it was close to six o'clock when he came to the long, gently slanting hill that looked down through the trees to his own kraal nestling half a mile away on the rise up from the Umlatoosi River. All looked quiet; the afternoon was dying and birds were taking off and landing in great flocks all along the water's edge. Far in the distance he could see a herd of giraffe moving down through ferny reaches to take their evening drink. Some small animals scuttled among the rocks a few yards away and he sat down on a sizeable flat stone, drawing his long legs up under his chin.

She was getting married now. It was about six o'clock. She would be wearing that white dress and that gleaming veil, and the doctor would put a ring on her finger and say 'I do'. There would be a celebration like there had been when Aunt Jane and Uncle Chris were married. The guests would be mingling in that marquee on the lawn and people would laugh and sing and everyone would be happy. And then Michael Tallant would take her away . . . No, he could not think of that.

He leapt off the stone and his feral 'No!' rang across the valley, echoing, echoing, echoing.

For a long time he stood staring at the orange-gold ball as it sank in the western sky. During the moments of love he had spent with her everything had been perfect.

Sometime there would be a world where a Zulu warrior could live in love and harmony with an Ice Princess: but not now; not here; not for him; not for her.

When he moved, his legs were leaden but they took him inexorably down through the trees to cross the river to his responsibilities, his life, his home.

It was almost dark as he passed through the kraal gate, but a child sitting near the first hut recognised him and gave a cry of joy to the returning leader. Soon everybody turned out to welcome him. People shouted with delight and Thulile ran forward into his arms.

248

'I have missed you,' she said.

He looked down into her childlike, innocent eyes. He could not speak, he simply held her close, his lips resting on her forehead.

CHAPTER SIXTEEN

As the rays of the morning sun found the unhappy bedroom on the day after their bleak wedding night Michael Tallant attempted to speak with his wife about her rejection of him. He took her pale hand and kissed it and asked her why, but all she offered him were her distraught eyes and a stammering, 'I ... I'm sorry.'

He moved from her to the window and, gathering all his compassion, said, 'It's not just your problem, darling, I will share the load. You need time and I understand. Truly I do. I will wait.'

Ellen's stomach turned. She had spurned him and here he was trying to understand. How could she do this to him? She felt so sick, so guilty.

They continued with the plans that had been laid – what else could they do? – and embarked on a honeymoon where the second night and the third passed like the first. With friends they were polite to each other but when they were alone they did not speak and Michael took to walking late at night and never retiring until after the clock had struck one.

The newlyweds had been in company as far as Greytown. Phoebe, Victoria, Frank and Benjamin Fielding had been in the cavalcade, as well as Mr Travers and Thulmi, who had been down from the Tugela farm in Pietermaritzburg and had been sent along to take care of the travellers. They had three nights on the road, the first two at farms, the third at a disbanded mission house.

The fifth night of their married life, Ellen and Michael spent in Greytown with Phoebe and her parents before leaving the following day to journey on.

They had completed dinner around ten o'clock and moved into the sitting room afterwards where the men were soon talking colony politics.

Victoria, Ellen and Phoebe were looking at one of the fashionable periodicals that came out regularly from Great Britain when Victoria was called away. Ellen watched her retreating back and then turned briefly to glance at her husband, smoking a cheroot and deep in conversation with the missionary, before she took up Phoebe's hand and with a strange look said, 'Phoebe, love, come, let us walk outside together.'

Soon the two young women were out in the invigorating night air and for a time they said nothing as they passed along the veranda, the sounds of the dark bush drifting to them.

Then Ellen turned to face her friend. There was a strained sound in her voice as she said, 'Phoebe, you were my bridesmaid, and while you are very young ... next to Vera, I count you as my dearest friend.'

'Thank you,' Phoebe answered.

'I ...' Ellen began, and then turned away, grasping the wooden railing.

'Ellen? What's wrong?'

'Nothing. I just wanted to come out into the night air. It's good for the complexion, they say.'

But while Phoebe might be young she was not stupid and she could see there was something greatly troubling her friend. 'Ellen, you seem different. Are you ill?'

'No. Yes. I might be. It could be called an illness, I suppose.'

Phoebe looked alarmed. 'Oh dear, what is it?'

Ellen was hopelessly lost. She did not know what to do. She was married, irrevocably and forever. She was on her honeymoon and she did not want to be here. And where she wanted to be, she could never be. She was powerless; life seemed untenable and there was no one to tell ... except perhaps this innocent girl with her here in the darkness. She turned back to face Phoebe and in the pale light of the heavens she could see her friend watching her with concerned eyes.

'Phoebe, love, I ... am married and ... Do you recall how upset I was to learn of John Lockley's intimacy with ... with Darlengi's sister?'

Everyone remembered how violently upset Ellen had been

to learn that her brother had been in love with Jettama. Phoebe recalled plainly how Ellen had been vitriolic in her comments about it.

'Yes, Ellen, I remember.' There was a tightness in Phoebe's chest as she answered, for thoughts of John Lockley and Jettama always brought sadness.

Ellen went on. 'Well, perhaps I should not have been so harsh in my judgement, for I think the Lord has decided to make me do penance. Penance that makes me want to die.'

'Whatever do you mean?'

'Oh Phoebe, please help me. Please understand. I have no one to tell. No one but you.'

Phoebe took Ellen's cold, shaking hands in her own. 'Oh darling, what is it? What on earth can make you talk this way?'

'I love Darlengi.'

Phoebe thought she had heard wrongly. 'What?'

'I'm married to Michael and I love Darlengi. I do not want to live if I cannot be with him.'

If Phoebe had wagered her life on what Ellen was going to tell her, she would have lost it on this disclosure. Her lovely eyes widened. What Ellen was telling her could not be true. White women did not love black men. Society did not allow it. It was so improper . . . yet why it should be she was at a loss to understand. She felt quite sure that Jesus would not have judged in this fashion. People should be able to love whomever they chose. But Ellen and Darlengi? She recalled all the times Ellen had made bitter references to the Zulu. She remembered the day years ago in the stable yard at the Tugela farm and the way Ellen had treated him.

'But Ellen, you have always hated Darlengi.'

'I have never hated Darlengi. Oh Phoebe, it's so complicated. I appeared to hate him, yes, because I suppose deep inside my heart I always knew how I truly felt. Don't you see? Love and hate are somehow akin. I told myself I hated him. I acted as if I hated him. All because I did not.'

This was too great a philosophical revelation for Phoebe. 'This doesn't make sense, Ellen. For years you've been courted by Michael. You only married him a few days ago. How can you suddenly say this?'

'Phoebe, please. It all happened last Thursday night. And the wedding was Saturday. What could I do? Everyone was

252

invited. Mrs Tallant had come all the way from Scotland. Father and Aunt Jane and Uncle Chris had spent so much money. Michael expected to get married. I couldn't hurt them . . . disappoint them. Oh Phoebe, I nearly went mad. I really thought I loved Michael, until . . . until . . . And then I knew I had loved Darlengi always.'

Phoebe could hardly accept what she was hearing but Ellen looked so pathetic that she enfolded her in her arms. 'Oh Ellen, I'm so sorry. What do you mean, "it all happened last Thursday"?'

And now Ellen began to cry. Her eyes brimmed with tears and she sobbed in Phoebe's arms.

The girl looked around and guided Ellen further round the veranda and down the side steps into the night.

'Ellen, Ellen darling, please. Don't cry. Everything will be all right.' But even as she said the words, there was a cold leaden feeling in her chest that prophesied that everything would not be all right. 'Do dry your eyes, please.'

Ellen attempted to control her sobs, but it was useless. She shook and quaked as the tears rolled down her cheeks.

Phoebe steered her to a seat under a clump of the mission's ubiquitous blue gums and there in the dark night, poor, wretched Ellen poured out her tale of Darlengi's visit to her bedroom two nights before her marriage.

Phoebe listened silently. She had only turned nineteen last month and while she knew she was inexperienced, she also knew she had to try to help her wretched friend. She tried to think what her mother would do and say. All the troubles of the small community of Greytown affecting both Bantu and European were brought to Victoria McLean to solve.

The lamps from the interior of the house threw a wan light to the seat where the two young women sat, and through the blue gums trickled a glimmer from the moon as Ellen completed her tale. 'And so you see, Phoebe, my life has been irrevocably altered. He forced me to acknowledge my love for him . . . forced me to see the world as it is. And oh God! How I love him to obsession. And he loves me. Yet we can never be together.' Suddenly Ellen turned round on the seat and grasped her friend by both arms. 'There I was, disapproving of poor John Lockley and Darlengi's sister, when all the time . . . Darlengi's going to be married too, you know. I know nothing can ever come of how we feel. It's not acceptable . . . to anyone. But you won't judge me, darling, will you?'

'No, Ellen dear, of course not. You cannot help it.'

'The whole thing makes me crazed.'

Phoebe drew gently from the hold and taking up her friend's hand patted it soothingly. 'Now, Ellen, I do understand, listen to me. You see, we share something in common. I have a secret too. I love your brother. It seems I have loved him all my life as well . . . and he doesn't know it, or want to, I suppose. So there. We both have sadnesses which we must face. I know I'm not married to another man so perhaps it's different for you. But only in a way, darling, for I'm as thwarted as you, really. Don't you see?'

Just for a moment Ellen forgot her own despair to sympathise with her friend. 'Oh poor Phoebe. But you've never told me this. I didn't know.'

Phoebe nodded. 'Ah, darling, it is not something I talk about. So please, dear Ellen, realise you are not really alone.'

Swiftly Ellen's thoughts returned to herself. 'But I can never have Darlengi. Not in this world. Whereas, you might . . . you could. It would be possible for you to have John Lockley.'

Phoebe thought there was little likelihood of her getting John Lockley in this world either, but she said nothing.

Then Ellen's voice dropped to a whisper. 'I cannot bear for him to touch me.'

'What? Do you mean Michael?'

'Yes.' It was a hopeless sound.

Phoebe was not worldly. She knew she was not, but she realised that this announcement had impossible implications. 'Oh dear Lord, this is terrible.' Then, with her natural optimism, she kissed her friend on the cheek and spoke authoritatively. 'Darling, believe me, time alters many things. My mother always says that and she's right. How we see things today may be very different tomorrow. So please don't be getting yourself in this state. You may alter, truly you may.'

Ellen's answer was given with closed eyes and a shake of her head.

Phoebe did not know what more to say. She sighed and

patted her friend's shoulder. 'Now, darling, at least you've stopped crying. That's good.'

'Phoebe, let me tell you something. I have been physically loved by the one man in all the world I want. It has magnified my soul. I regret nothing and would not want it any other way.'

Phoebe nodded. 'I understand.' Then she locked her arm through her friend's 'Someone may soon come looking for us. We'd best go inside.'

They crossed the yard. As they mounted the steps the girl said gently, 'Ellen, remember I'm your friend. I truly think things will turn out right. But if you need someone to confide in, then write to me. Let us console each other. I will help you if I can. Don't feel alone.'

'Oh Phoebe, you are so good. Thank you.' Ellen hugged her close.

At that moment Frank's voice sounded along the veranda. 'Ah, there you are. Michael and I were beginning to wonder what had happened to you. It grows late. We must retire.'

That night Phoebe lay awake thinking. She remembered the day last week when Darlengi had said to her, 'I know what it is to love unrequited, Miss Phoebe.' Oh, poor Darlengi. Now she knew what he had meant. It was fantastic. Ellen, who had always ignored Darlengi when he was present and heaped disdain upon him when he was not . . . in love with him! And he with her!

The next morning, Phoebe and her parents waved the newlyweds off into the gleaming daylight. Sitting in the Cape cart, in front of the bags of sweet potato and rice they were taking to the farm, Ellen appeared calm and Michael was quiet; but now that Phoebe knew her friend's secret she could see behind the reserve the two imposed upon themselves. Phoebe's heart was heavy for them all. For Ellen and Michael . . . and Darlengi.

As the horses disappeared Phoebe put her hand into her apron pocket and touched the three letters that Ellen had secretly given her with the words, 'Read the one for you and keep the others.'

Phoebe felt she was an unwilling conspirator in a plot she wished she had never heard about. But later, in her room, she read the short letter addressed to herself.

Darling Phoebe,

The two letters I leave with you are for John Lockley and Darlengi. We plan to return here for a night on our way back to Pietermaritzburg. If I do not come back then I ask only that you please make sure the letters reach their destinations.

Darling, I have no one to trust but you. I beg you with all my heart to please tell no one of this and I thank you forever for your goodness.

You are my true sweet friend.

　　Love

　　　Ellen.

Phoebe felt numb. She was grievously sorry for Ellen, yet she felt she was being manipulated and had no idea what to do about it. She sat for a long time looking at the words, 'If I do not come back'. Surely Ellen would not do anything to herself. Phoebe was so worried that for days her natural sunny nature was overshadowed by her worries.

Ellen and Michael arrived at the Tugela farm to a rousing welcome from Matilda and Dirk and all the inhabitants of the property. And during the days to come Matilda saw a different Ellen from the one she had known. Michael spent most of his time with Dirk or the men and Ellen joined Matilda, wanting to help her in the kitchen or the house. It appeared to Matilda that the young woman hated to be alone, whereas the Ellen of the old days had been happy with her own company, unless of course she could have John Lockley's.

Matilda could not help but think it strange that a new bride and her husband would be content to spend most of each day apart.

In the second week of their stay, Michael accompanied Dirk on a stock count. When the men had gone, Matilda expected Ellen to join her, and after an hour or so without a sign of the young woman, she went searching for her. Ellen was not in the house, or the stable yard or the fast-expanding garden. Then Needy Ned, one of their kitchen boys, said he had seen Mrs Tallant.

'She go right along.' He pointed to the river.

'What do you mean? Along the river?'

'*Yeh bo*. She go walk . . . right along.'

'On her own?'

'Yes.'

Matilda frowned. She did not like the idea of Ellen out along the Tugela on her own. Nevertheless she waited another half-hour before she sent for the foreman.

He had just come up to the house when the young woman returned home. She was quiet and distant, but that was nothing new these days. The bottom of her dress was damp. Matilda's eyes widened. 'Oh, Miss Ellen, you never should have gone close to the river, please. Things can happen. This is not Durban or Pietermaritzburg. There are crocs in the river as will attack anything, and many a wild beast on the land that'll do the same. Please, Miss Ellen, promise me you'll not go out alone again.'

Ellen smiled, an odd, somehow ambiguous smile. 'I'm sorry to have concerned you, Matilda.' But she made no promise.

So the days passed at the farm. Ellen spent much of her time reading alone on the veranda, working in the garden or helping Matilda. In the older woman's company she was either vague and quiet, or overly talkative and stimulated. Michael spent his time reading on the long bench out under a clump of mimosas away from the house, or at Dirk's side as he worked in the stables or attended to the cattle. Ellen and Michael ate breakfast and dinner together and occasionally luncheon. When Matilda waited on them, they were civil and courteous to each other. But by the third week of their stay, the Boer woman felt all was not right. The newlyweds seemed too restrained, too polite, as if there were a tension between them.

It was two evenings before their departure and Ellen walked on the veranda. Between the house and the river great flocks of birds swept across the sky, all colours and types: crested eagles, cranes, hawks, honey-coloured pigeons. The birds always flew along the river around sundown and were wonderful to watch, but Ellen's eyes did not see them. Not only was she suffering but she had brought agony to one of the best of men; it was not Michael's fault that she was unable to love him. She heard his voice in her head saying, 'Hell, Ellen! Don't you realise a man cannot bear this treatment?' A sigh shivered from her as she moved along the veranda, even the rustle of her skirt a melancholy sound.

In the distance she noticed her husband and Dirk exit the stables. Michael had been out all day with the farm manager, she did not know where. The day was fast declining and the buildings threw long shadows over the two men as they came across the yard. And as Ellen watched them she finally made her decision. Her pulse quickened as she did so; and she felt ill, but she would be resolute and follow it to its conclusion. She had no alternative. She owed it to Michael; she would try.

For the first time since before his wedding day, Michael saw a convivial Ellen at dinner. When she smiled at him across the table, hope quivered inside his chest. And after dinner when she took his hand he actually began to believe that perhaps at last the agony and the frustration might end.

That night when he turned to her in the bedroom she accepted his mouth on hers and when he came to her in the bed she did not resist. She loved him to the edge of violence and while at first he was confused, then startled, and ultimately amazed, he was soon delighted. Finally his wife *was* his wife! He had waited for her and been rewarded.

Yes, of course some women took longer to understand the role of wife. He analysed it no further, accepting that time alone had changed her. Rippling with ecstasy he took her for the second time, saying, 'Oh God, I love you. Thank you, thank you, my sweet darling.'

He fell asleep smiling.

But then Michael did not know whose eyes she had looked into, or whose mouth she had kissed, or whose hands she had felt upon her, or whose body she had encompassed with her own.

The following day was all bustle for the coming departure.

Matilda was preparing a special farewell dinner and through her kitchen window she noticed a slight rainfall. It was just after the hour of three in the afternoon when she lifted her eyes from her pie plate to see Ellen standing at the kitchen door.

'Well good afternoon, Miss Ellen. All packed, are you?'

'Mmm. It's been raining.'

'Yes, and Dirk's out in it somewhere. Trying to get the orchards going, he is. We've had a few figs and peaches the last couple of years. Now we've just planted apples, quince and oranges, so we'll see what happens. Very first time oranges have been planted in the interior, we believe.'

Ellen murmured a reply and came a few steps into the kitchen.

Matilda looked closely at her. This morning she had noticed a difference in Dr Tallant. He seemed exhilarated, jubilant. At breakfast he had kissed his wife. Matilda had never seen that before. And yet Ellen appeared unchanged. There was not the sparkle and sharpness that the unmarried girl had shown.

Matilda smiled welcomingly. 'Where's Dr Tallant?'

Ellen pointed through the back door. 'He's just now been called down to one of the yards; he's very interested in medical treatment for animals and one of the oxen has taken ill.'

'Good man, your husband.'

'Yes, he is, a very good man.'

Ellen lifted a cup from the dresser, turning it round in her hands and staring at it. She seemed to be deciding something, then she said, 'Matilda, how often do you see Darlengi?'

Matilda's eyebrows rose. Fancy Ellen asking about Darlengi, how surprising. It had forever been the other way round.

'About once a year, I suppose it turns out. Though I hadn't seen him for about eighteen months until he came here a month or so ago.'

'Oh? He was here so recently?'

'Yes, that was when I told him you were getting married.'

Matilda saw the interest spark in Ellen's tired face.

'What did he say about it?'

Matilda was surprised. 'Miss Ellen!' Her voice was slightly severe. 'He was eager to hear, as he always is at the mention of your name, though why I'll never know.'

Ellen looked hurt. 'Whatever do you mean by that?'

'I mean, you've never been anything but discourteous towards him.'

Suddenly Ellen was animated. It surprised the older woman. 'But I never meant that. Don't you understand? I never meant it.'

And honest Matilda replied, 'No, Miss Ellen, I don't understand. I've known you since you arrived in Natal thirteen years ago, a young girl, and I've known Darlengi almost as long. And while he tried to please you both as boy and adult, you would have none of it. And why you tell me differently now, I have no conception.'

Ellen's eyes welled with tears and the good Boer woman felt dreadful. She came swiftly round the table to her visitor. 'Oh, Miss Ellen, I had no idea I would upset you. Forgive me. I'm sorry.'

'Oh Matilda, please, do not think ill of me. I ... I estranged Darlengi only because I was frightened not to.'

Suddenly Matilda realised Ellen was trembling. What was this all about? 'Miss Ellen. Are you ill?'

'No ... I ...' And now there was an edge to the light in her eyes; she appeared overwrought, anxious. Tears ran down her cheeks. She took Matilda's hands in hers and stared into her eyes. 'Matilda, please, tell me you understand. You see I want you to ... for all the others that won't. Please.'

Now Tilly really was concerned. The look on the young woman's face frightened her. She took a handkerchief from her apron pocket and dabbed Ellen's cheeks as she answered soothingly, 'Dear Miss Ellen, yes, of course I understand. Whatever it is, I understand.'

Ellen pulled sharply from Matilda's grasp. 'Don't patronise me, Matilda.' And for a moment the older woman was pleased; this was more like the Ellen she knew.

But just as quickly, Ellen was fretful again. 'Oh please, Matilda. I never meant to hurt Darlengi. God, no! Don't you see? I didn't want to ever let my true emotions show ... to him. I was afraid, if I were to acknowledge him, I would not be able to control myself. But he made me confess ... made me admit. Oh, that's exactly what has happened, don't you see?'

Matilda certainly did not see. But she was bright enough to realise that this confusing talk made sense to Ellen. It was all incomprehensible to her. Ellen was on her honeymoon. She was leaving tomorrow to return to her married life with her husband, and here she was hysterically asking Matilda to understand that she had never meant to hurt Darlengi.

'Sit down, Miss Ellen, and listen to me.' She drew the young woman to a chair, patting her gently on the shoulder and smoothing her hair. 'I think I see that you're telling me you've never held bad feelings towards Darlengi. That in all the years you didn't mean to hurt him. Yes, dear, all right. I understand that.'

There was still a strange expression on Ellen's face as she answered, 'Thank you, Matilda, thank you. So you're sure you understand?'

To pacify her the good woman answered, 'Yes, yes, love, I do.' Then she went on, 'Look, let's have a cuppa. Remember I make a jolly fine cup of tea, I do.'

Ellen attempted a wan smile. 'No, Matilda, thank you. I shall go and lie down for a time.'

'Now there's a good idea, and I shall come and wake you later for afternoon tea.'

When Ellen had gone Tilly stood for a full minute trying to make sense of what had just occurred, but, admitting she was at a loss, she shook her head and returned to her pie.

She would have been very worried indeed had she seen Ellen slip out of the side door on to the veranda and run down the steps and across into the trees to make her way round the back way to the stables. There she took a horse and ordered the only person around, Jemby, the Swazi groom, to saddle it. He had enough English to ask, 'You take boss man, missy?'

'No, Jemby, I go alone. Don't worry. Everyone knows.'

As she rode away to the north-west, out of the line of sight of the house, Jemby's eyes lifted from stacking hay and noted the direction she took.

Mattana and Kayo were as happy as Thulile to see Darlengi back home. They celebrated his return with the killing of an ox and all the kraal danced and sang and life returned to normal.

Each evening, Darlengi unwittingly aped his father and went outside the main gate and by the mealie field across to a stone some three hundred yards distant, and sat and watched the sunset. He thought of the Ice Princess and her honeymoon and his heart ached.

He had been home over three weeks when a messenger came to tell him to join Cetshwayo for an uSuthu indaba at a great military kraal at emaNgwene on the upland two miles from where the Uvulu River met the Umlatoosi. He was requested to come in the number of sunsets on one man's hand.

That evening as he sat staring down to the river with the picture of Ellen's face in his mind, a hand clutched his shoulder. He knew who it was. 'Mattana, Great Mother, you startled me.'

'I did not mean to.'

She sat down beside him though there was not much room and he had to almost forfeit his seat to allow her her position.

Mattana's voice was subdued. 'I leave tomorrow. I must return to Undi.' Undi was Cetshwayo's huge kraal about fifteen miles away.

Darlengi managed a smile. 'Ah ha, you fear to stay here too long else your position as Greatest Magic One in Zululand be usurped.'

Mattana showed a row of broken teeth. 'Perhaps.' Then she dropped her voice. 'The time you spend here each evening is time when your heart twists.'

He stood and moved a few feet away before turning back. Eyeing her steadily, he replied, 'You are guessing.'

'If so, am I guessing correctly?'

'Mattana, Mattana, I am not the child you used to impress, nor the youth you could confuse. Nor am I as other Zulus are, you know that.'

'So. What you are saying is that your own mother's magic does not impress you any more.'

And now Darlengi laughed. 'Great Mother, believe me, you will always impress me. Have no fear of that. I am merely saying – and I say it only to you where no others can hear – that I am aware you *guess* more than you *know*. Mind you, you are more accurate than others, as you have made a lifetime study of watching and listening, and that in itself is magical.'

'If anyone else dared to challenge me this way I would put a spell on his cattle forever.' Then she wagged her finger at him. 'And don't think you can take my mind from my original statement. I said, when you are here on this rock at sunset, your heart is twisting.'

Now he nodded and, coming back to her, patted her gently on her bony shoulder. 'You are right. It is.'

She was silent for a time, then she said very slowly, 'If you love another, why are you going to marry Thulile?'

He met her eyes. She was challenging him as she always did . . . making him explain himself to himself.

'I don't know if I am.'

'You will break her heart if you do not.'

'Yes, I know. And she is too good to hurt.'

Mattana nodded to herself and lifted her hand to clutch his arm. 'Then who is the other one? She has lived a long time in your heart, I know that. Lately there is something that troubles you more about her. I am guessing that you saw her on your visit to the Europeans?'

He nodded. 'She is white and beyond my most delirious dreams.'

'I suspected as much. She is from the Harrison family, isn't she?'

'Yes. She is my Ice Princess ... unattainable. But I shall love her all my life.'

'And what thinks she of you?'

'The same.'

'She loves you?'

'She does.'

'This is a great sadness.'

'It is.'

They were silent a little time and Darlengi squatted down on the ground to look down the hill.

'She has just been married.'

'Then perhaps she loves you no more.'

'No ... the opposite is true.'

Mattana thought about this. Could Darlengi be wrong? She asked, 'Are you sure?'

'As sure as I am of your love for me.'

'Then there is no doubt. Something tells me you are considering going to her. Where is she? Is she not in one of the white people's towns?'

'She is at the Tugela farm of my friends.'

Mattana stood up behind where he squatted. She bent forward and took him by both shoulders, her long scrawny fingers clutching him like claws. Her mouth came down near to his ear. 'So ... the white boy loved your sister and you love his sister? It *is* his sister, isn't it?'

'Yes.'

'And you are thinking of going to the farm. Darlengi, I do not have a good feeling about this.' She turned her head and kissed the top of his. Then he stood up and faced round to her.

He smiled. It was a movement without mirth, and it drew his perfectly moulded lips back in almost a grimace. 'Good mother, the first time I saw her she offered me her slender white fingers, and as I held them I knew her heart was intertwined with mine ... though she had no idea of it.'

Mattana nodded and her matted locks shook. 'You are right. You are no longer the boy whom I could manipulate. Thus no matter what I think of this, and I do not like it, I cannot tell you what to do.' She tried to smile. 'I cannot, for you will not listen. So, I leave tomorrow.'

'I leave tomorrow also.'

'But the indaba is not for five nights.'

'I know.'

She did not answer immediately, and when she did she nodded to herself. 'I see. Then remember to be careful, my strong tree, remember to be careful.'

CHAPTER SEVENTEEN

Ellen reined in near a great clump of seringas. There were a number of large rock formations here, huge grey boulders. A flock of hawks screeched from their resting place atop the nearest group, but Ellen was oblivious. The strained expression still lived in her eyes, and she nibbled unknowingly at the edge of her lip as she climbed down from the horse and mechanically tied it to a branch.

A family of baboons eyed her from amongst the rocks, but she did not go in their direction so they did not deem her threatening. She walked slowly, automatically, towards the Tugela, thinking of last night and knowing she could not go through life pretending that Michael was Darlengi.

She halted at the river's edge, the hem of her dress soaking up the water on the muddy slope of the bank. Out of the keepsakes in her mind came the memory of the Christmas Eve so long ago when she was a girl and Darlengi had been at Mimosa with them. What had he said? Something like: 'You deny what is, for you are frightened of looking inside your heart.' Even then he knew.

She began to edge across the mud to the deeper water. 'Help me keep my resolve,' she prayed. Suddenly, peripherally, she saw the length of scale slide into the river beyond the reeds to her left. She turned towards it with a sharp sound of fear. The saurian shape was followed by another and another . . . a nest of them.

She stifled a scream and ran back to the bank, her pulse racing and tiny beads of sweat gathering on her temples. She hastened to a cluster of the great rocks, leaning back upon the nearest, unaware of the heat of the stone through her dress.

She looked up. The granite tower above her was at least sixty feet high. Slowly she moved between the rocks further into them. She saw what seemed to be a passage leading upwards behind one of the great stones. If she could make her way to the summit, this would be an alternative to the river, an easier way.

To her surprise it was not difficult to climb and soon she came into a natural small amphitheatre of stone where grass grew beneath her feet. To the west she could see clearly across the Tugela and to the south-east she looked over the clump of seringas where she had tied her horse to some high ground about a quarter of a mile away.

She was so frightened that her dress shook across her breast from the thumping of her heart. But no matter how terrified she was, she would do this.

She stepped up on to a little ledge of stone and clambered up to the flat top of one of the large boulders. She stood rigidly up in the afternoon sunlight facing west, her shadow falling back behind her across the granite beneath her feet. The edge was only about seven feet away and with small, deliberate steps she moved shakily towards it.

She did not want to hurt anyone, and this way she would not. They would believe this had been an accident. She would simply be gone.

She thought of Uncle Chris and Aunt Jane: Jane had been the only mother she had ever known and she loved Uncle Chris dearly. He was somehow more of father to her than the General. She thought of little Phoebe holding the letter for John Lockley; she could trust Phoebe, the letter would get to him.

She had loved her brother intensely all her life. Her earliest memory was of his third birthday when she was four years old. He had worn a little azure-blue silk pinafore. She could see his bright eyes now reflecting the vibrant colour. How happy she had always been in his company and how she had always tried to please him. She had married Michael because he had said he thought she should. John Lockley only wanted what was best for her, she knew that. She saw his face: his beautiful eyes and the perfection of his classic profile and the tilt of his head and she shuddered as simultaneously she pictured that other face so like his, only pigmented with the deep bronze of the Zulu. Oh God, how she loved these two men as one: her brother and her true love.

She stared out into the endless infinity of the sky, lifting her

foot, ready to step into nothingness ... and then she heard,
'No, Ellen! Stop! Stop!' and in that second she hesitated and
turned.

By mid-afternoon, Darlengi had arrived at the border of the
Harrison-Nelson land. He stood deep in thought with the lacy
grey shadow patterns thrown upon him from the acacias above.
He did not really have a strategy; all he knew was that he
would make his way to the farmhouse and watch it under
cover of the night. He was here to look upon his Ice Princess
from afar; to see her just one more time before he took up his
life without her.

The remainder of the daylight hours he would spend in
the amphitheatre of stone in the huge rock boulders near
the river, where he and John Lockley had spent so many
happy, boyish hours together. Their old hiding place would
be perfect.

Through the tall grass he ran, over hills and along dongas,
leaping narrow ravines like a cheetah. At the crest of a low hill
he halted. He could see cattle in a pen and men moving on
horseback in the distance to the south. The farmhouse was
over there about three miles away. In front of him to the north-
west stood the seringa trees and beyond them the great clusters
of rocks near the river and his place of concealment. Down the
hill he ran.

As he came through the seringas he saw the horse. It was
tied loosely to a branch and it leisurely ate grass at its feet. He
halted, looking around for the rider. He saw no one, and
advanced slowly on to the clearing near the great boulders.

Then, as he edged out on to the open ground he saw her, up
there where the hideout in the boulders was. She stood on the
edge of the rock. She was about to jump!

He screamed, 'No, Ellen! Stop! Stop!'

He saw her hesitate and turn, putting her foot back behind
her and looking down to him.

She cried, 'Darlengi!' And at that moment he put his arms
up and shouted, 'Ellen, come down. You must come down!'

She moved back from the edge towards safety. *Darlengi here!*
God has brought him. But as she stepped back, the heel of her
shoe lodged in a crack in the stone. She lurched sideways, and
in that second she realised she could not right herself.

He saw her stumble and totter and he screamed, 'No! No!' as she gave a long shriek of terror and falling sideways plunged over the side of the craggy mass. Down she came, smashing into the ground with a brutal sound that would haunt his nightmares forever more.

He was aware of nothing . . . nothing but her. When he came to her she did not move. He knelt down and then her eyes opened and he realised she was conscious.

She registered his face above her. She heard him say, 'Ellen. My darling, Ellen.'

She knew she must be broken in many places. There was pain everywhere and she could move none of her limbs.

She saw the locket hanging round his neck. How she would have loved to touch it just once more. She lifted her eyes from it and saw the tears running down his face.

He looked down into the soul of her. He had loved her without sanction from any mortal: perhaps that was why it had been so excessive. 'Ellen . . . my darling, I love you. Forgive me.'

And she managed to push out the words, 'I told you . . . there is nothing to forgive . . . I have always loved you . . . from the beginning . . . of everything.'

She did not feel anything as he lifted her in his arms. But she saw the infinite love in his eyes. No one on earth or in heaven could take that from her. A marvellous solace wafted over her and she smiled up at him, and whispered, 'There is a letter . . . for you . . . my darling. Phoebe McLean has it . . . in Greytown.'

The late afternoon sun glinted in his tears as he stood there with his Ice Princess dying in his arms.

She had no pain now, and there was a mellow, filmy feeling in her mind. She could see only him, his face, and even that was fading from her. Her universe was the knowledge of him, Darlengi, holding her forever in his arms. She knew these were the last words she would ever say and she must tell him the truth, the undisguised truth.

'I did not want to live without you.'

And now he bent to her and brought his lips down upon hers in the final moment of her life.

Matilda had gone to find Ellen for afternoon tea and when she was not in her room, she did not worry immediately. But when she had looked through the house and on all the verandas and down through the garden and the vegetable fields without sign of her, there was a tiny panicky spot in her chest.

She went down to the stables but she could find no one, they were deserted. Just as she was about to go back to the house she saw Jemby asleep under a side porch.

She woke him. 'Jemby, have you seen the Mistress Ellen?'

He nodded. '*Yeh bo*. I see her.'

'Where is she, Jemby?'

'She go on horse. Before.'

'Alone?'

'Yes.' And he pointed in the direction that Ellen had ridden away.

Now Tilly was deeply concerned. Why would Ellen do this without telling her? She tried to be calm and rational. Ellen had every right to go riding, and even though she should not ride alone, there was nothing so alarming in that. It was just that Ellen had not mentioned it; she had said specifically she would lie down until afternoon tea time.

She took Jemby by the arm. 'Come, we must find Dr Tallant.'

They found Michael easily. He was walking back to the house from one of the oxen pens.

'So what you are telling me, Mrs Veldbron, is that my wife has gone out riding alone.'

Matilda felt self-conscious. 'Yes.'

'And that you are worried about her.'

'Well, yes, I am. She was . . . agitated, this afternoon. I don't like the idea of her out in the bush alone.'

'No, I don't either. How long is it since she left?'

'I can't say exactly, but it's well over an hour since I saw her.'

Michael did not know what to think. 'Perhaps we should wait just a little longer. She might come riding in any moment.'

Half an hour later Dirk came home, but not Ellen. Within another fifteen minutes every man who could ride was mounted.

Michael was puzzled. What was this about? Ellen had been happy today, he knew she had. They had solved their problem last night when she had given herself to him unrestrainedly. Mrs Veldbron had misunderstood her mood, he was certain. Ellen liked to ride, she was an excellent horsewoman. Nevertheless, it was a worry that she had been gone so long.

A party consisting of Michael and Dirk and two foremen went to the north-west in the direction that Jemby pointed them, and the other party of four went directly north.

Michael's party came to the Tugela a little north of Unondo's kraal and followed the river. The evening sun threw long shadows as they passed along the river bank in the long grass up to the bellies of their horses.

Dirk Veldbron reined in, as he had done every now and then during the ride and scanned ahead with his telescope to some large seringa trees in the middle distance. Suddenly he said, 'I think that's the horse Miss Ellen took, up there.'

'Where?' Michael's voice was anxious now.

Pointing, Dirk handed over the telescope. Michael's heart-beat accelerated as he turned it to look further ahead to a number of boulders stacked near the river's edge. There was something lying on the ground. Then momentarily he thought he saw movement to the right in the evening shadows. Was that a person?

'I think there's something up there ahead.' A shiver ran through his chest as he threw the telescope back to the Boer and spurred ahead of his companions.

Darlengi had sat on the grassy floor of the world holding his Ice Princess in his arms for a very long time. The evening shadows had lengthened across him as he told her many things in death that he had been unable to tell her in life.

He had closed her eyelids and begged the Almighty of the Universe that she would be happy now.

How fragile human life was. How useless it all was in the end; how futile.

Then through his film of pain he noticed something and his head came up like one of the animals of the bush veld. With his perfect vision, he could make out movement perhaps two miles away. Horses and men were coming!

Anger surfaced briefly: *Why should I give her up to you?* He thought to take her and bury her where no one knew but himself; to keep forever secret where his Ice Princess lay. Then he recalled the man she had wed. He had no right to deny the good doctor a body to mourn over.

Tenderly, he eased her flat on the ground. He caressed her face before he stood looking down at her for the last time. A second later, he turned sharply away and left her lying there.

Michael knew she was dead before he jumped down from his horse. When he was on the ground beside her, he did not even lift her wrist to check her pulse. She was cold, but rigor mortis had not yet set in: she'd been dead for about an hour, he guessed.

As Dirk leaped down beside him he lifted his anguished face. 'She's dead, Dirk. Oh God in heaven, she's dead!'

Dirk had not realised, and now his big red face paled in the stream of evening sunlight.

Michael could not believe it. His wonderful wife dead. After last night when everything had been solved; when they had been so happy together.

Then Michael noticed that his wife's eyes were closed. Had someone closed them? The figure he thought he had seen through the telescope? Yes, perhaps. He looked around, but all was silent except for the screech of the river birds in the evening sky.

'It must have been an accident.' Dirk's voice broke into his thoughts. 'Looks like she fell, Dr Tallant. But why on earth would she have been climbing up there? What could have possessed her?'

For some seconds there on the grassy strip of land beside the waters of the Tugela, Michael Tallant was dazed. He thought of what no one else realised ... all the nights of maddening stress and the questioning of his very maleness. And then last night, when she had loved him so intensely.

He took her in his arms and wept. 'Why, Ellen, why?' he whispered. 'What happened?'

And as Michael Tallant nursed his dead wife in his arms the only man on earth who could have given him the answer ran at high speed northwards, while the wind blew hard in his face, and the picture of his Ice Princess blew disturbingly in his mind.

CHAPTER EIGHTEEN

Matilda, with mending lying idle on her lap, sat looking through her kitchen window down to where Dr Tallant had buried his wife. He had read the burial service in a dispassionate voice, and as he closed the Bible he wept. Tilly had cried again then too.

Yesterday morning at sun-up, before the poor doctor had left the Tugela farm, her husband had taken his hand and said, 'It was the most dreadful accident imaginable. We are more than sorry for you and we wish you all the best, sir.'

Ever since the troop had ridden in with Ellen's body, Matilda had been doing a lot of thinking. She could not help recalling the different Ellen; the tension she truly felt between the newlyweds; and most of all, she could not help recalling the afternoon Ellen died and the weird things she had suddenly, right out of the blue, said about Darlengi. Things like: 'Matilda . . . I estranged Darlengi only because I was frightened not to,' and, 'Matilda, I want you to understand . . . for all the others that won't,' and, 'I never meant to hurt Darlengi. God, no! I didn't want to ever let my true emotions show. I was afraid, if I were to acknowledge him, I would not be able to control myself. But he made me confess . . . made me admit.' The more she thought about it the more it all troubled Matilda. So much so that she wondered more and more about the 'accident'.

She would say nothing, how could she? But she possessed these questions now, and sometime . . . sometime, she would ask Darlengi if he knew anything.

She sighed and picked up her mending. What a sorry message the poor doctor had to take south to the Harrisons and Nelsons. And no doubt he would stop at the mission on his way and inform the McLeans.

Phoebe turned her head to look through the window into the hot December evening. The window was not glass, it was a board that lifted up and out and was held open during the daylight hours by two fitted poles. Yet every window of the mission house had pretty curtains; Victoria had seen to that.

The young woman drew her hand across her eyes in a limp gesture. She was thinking of Ellen. Yesterday Michael had brought the dreadful news of her death by an accidental fall.

He had buried her at the Tugela farm and was on his way to Pietermaritzburg and Durban to deliver the shocking news. After Michael had departed with his small, dismal entourage she had been sick alone in her room.

She knew she was the holder of two letters that she must deliver now. She had taken off her apron and walked down into the long veld grass, and standing under a great date palm had looked skywards, tears streaming down her cheeks, and said, 'Ellen darling, don't worry, I shall send the letter to John Lockley, though how I am going to get the other to Darlengi, I've no idea.' Then she quickly added, 'But don't worry, sweetheart, I'll think of something.'

She had decided to send it via Johann Street, a trader who came by in his ox wagon every December. He went up into Zululand around Christmas time and always saw Cetshwayo. Phoebe knew that Darlengi was close to Cetshwayo.

They were expecting Johann any day now and Phoebe had taken to looking out of the window constantly in anticipation of his arrival. She had Ellen's letter hidden in her room. She wondered how Darlengi would feel when he received it.

Suddenly she saw a figure running across the veld towards the back of the mission station. Good heavens! It was Darlengi. Her thoughts seemed to have given him existence.

She hurried through the house and on to the back veranda and down the steps just in time to arrive where he vaulted the hedge and came to land. He was dressed in shirt and trousers, though he wore no shoes. He looked wonderfully eccentric, but then she noticed that his eyes were bloodshot and his face was drawn and lined as if he had not slept for a long time.

A number of the mission pupils began to gather around and Phoebe lifted her hand to them. 'Away you go. This is a private conversation.'

They retreated to a polite distance, but still stood watching.

He had attempted a smile but it got lost before it mounted his handsome mouth. 'Hello, Phoebe.'

'Hello, Darlengi. I'm so pleased to see you.'

'You hold a letter for me . . . from Ellen.'

'But how can you possibly know about that? No one does.'

He did not answer, instead replying, 'Would you be kind enough to give it to me?'

'Of course. Please come in, my mother is over in the chapel but she'll be home soon and I know she'll be happy to see you again.'

He shook his head. 'I'd be more comfortable waiting here.'

Two minutes later she handed him the envelope. 'You must know about the accident. I'm so terribly sorry.'

He answered enigmatically. 'Yes, in the end it was just that.'

She took him by the arm. 'Please come up on the veranda, even if you won't come in the house. We can be private there, away from the children.'

He followed her up the steps and around the veranda to where it was sheltered by trees.

She turned back to him. 'Darlengi, Ellen told me how she . . . loved you.'

Momentarily he looked surprised, then he said, 'And I her. I was possessed by her . . . always was. Did she tell you anything more?'

'She told me many things, Darlengi. How you came to her a few nights before her wedding. That she went ahead with her marriage only because she saw no alternative. When she was here a few weeks ago she told me she did not want to live without you. That's why I've been sick with regret since I heard of the accident.'

He looked intently at her. 'Phoebe, I think you are sympathetically disposed to me.'

Phoebe nodded vigorously. 'Oh, Darlengi, I am.'

'Then I shall tell you something I can tell no other. I was there when she fell.'

Phoebe's intake of breath was quite audible.

'And while I do believe she may have meant to kill herself, when she saw me she halted. I had intended to go to the farm just to look at her, not even to speak to her, just to see . . . she was all right. I went to wait amongst the boulders until night fell. There she was on top of them. I called to her and she stepped back to come down, then her foot caught in something. It truly was an accident that she fell. She died in my arms. I am a Zulu. You were her friend. You know what a love like ours would have meant. I should never have done what I did.'

'What do you mean? What did you do?'

He looked away. 'Phoebe, I opened her eyes to what I had carried for years. I made her see. I was angry, hurt, jealous that she was marrying. I knew only that I had always wanted her. Ellen was my dream. And when I was in Pietermaritzburg, I was near her, under the same roof, with access to her. I took advantage of that. And in loving her, I killed her.'

She took his arm. 'No, you must not say that. She would not want you to. What happened was an accident, you've said it yourself.'

'But she would not have been up on the rocks otherwise.'

Phoebe faced him. 'Darlengi, what is, is. You opened Ellen's eyes to love. She participated because she wanted to, because she needed your love more than anything in the world. She told me that she regretted nothing and would have it no other way. So you must stop blaming yourself. For your sake and for the peace of Ellen's eternal soul.'

For a few seconds a cynical expression crossed his face. 'Christians always talk of souls; how I do wish I could believe in a blasted eternal soul.'

'Do you believe the Zulu teachings?'

He shook his head. 'No. I don't know what to believe.'

Then Phoebe surprised herself. She was pleased her mother could not hear. 'Nor do I ... at times,' she said.

And then he actually managed a small smile and the dying daylight shone in his coal-black eyes. And she smiled back at him and lifted her hand from his arm to touch his cheek. He turned his head into her raised hand and kissed her palm.

'I have only two things in this world to remind me of my Ice Princess. This ...' He held up the letter she had given him. 'And this.' He opened his shirt to expose the gold locket shining on his ebony skin.

'And your love for her.'

'And my love for her,' he repeated. 'Phoebe McLean, you are an exceptional young woman. Thank you and goodbye.'

He moved like a bolt of fluid black silk thrown down the steps, but she halted him with the words, 'Darlengi, do not leave it until something momentous happens to visit me again. I cannot come to you, therefore I would deem it a sign of our friendship if you occasionally came here, to me.'

He turned round and met her eyes. 'I will.'

It was almost dark as she watched his shape meld with the distant twilight.

When she moved inside, she went to her room and wrote a letter to John Lockley. In it she included Ellen's letter to him. As she sealed it, she decided she would not correspond with him again. He hardly ever replied and when he did his missives were short and remote. It was obvious he thought her an infatuated child. No matter how she felt about John Lockley, there was no commandment that could make him feel the same about her. She must face up to that. The world would not just conform to what Phoebe McLean wanted. Ellen's death had shown her that.

She stood from her writing desk and with a long sigh went out to find her mother.

In the dying light, three hundred yards from the mission, while hundreds of turtle doves cooed softly around him, Darlengi tore open Ellen's letter.

> Greytown mission, 15 November, 1865
>
> Darlengi, my Zulu, myself,
>
> I thank you, my dearest one, for opening my soul to my true feelings.
>
> Do not be sad, for I am not. I have no regrets.
>
> I prefer to be in the next world when I cannot share this one with you. Somewhere in the universe there is a planet where a Zulu man lives happily, in love and harmony, with a white girl. I will wait there for you.
>
> Ellen.

CHAPTER NINETEEN

May, 1870

The neat shadows of the blue gum trees planted by the settlers lay in a bar across the veranda where nineteen bright black faces lifted towards their teacher and laughed with her. Victoria had just turned from her blackboard where she had written the alphabet in perfectly formed copperplate writing and at the same time had dropped her chalk, which had given rise to the amusement.

She retrieved the piece of chalk and as she continued the lesson she glanced through the door in time to see her daughter returning home with Thulmi. The Zulu was devoted to Phoebe. Christopher had sent him to the mission after there had been some problem with Dirk Veldbron at the farm which had resulted in Thulmi's having a broken arm. He had turned out to be invaluable, and he and Phoebe did much of the hunting to help feed the many mouths at the mission.

Frank did not approve of his daughter's *acting like a man*, but there was no doubt she was a fine shot, spoke passable Zulu, and had the respect of all the natives at the mission and in the district. It was their white neighbours who were more difficult to convince.

Phoebe entered the compound on her horse, Sapphire, and turned to Thulmi, who led the horse which carried the hunt's yield. Her face was protected by a large sun hat and her sleeves were rolled up to her elbows. She wore boots when she hunted and kept her skirt to calf-length, another feature of which her father did not approve.

She had blossomed into a striking young woman; some, like Ben Fielding, would even say beautiful. Above her well-defined brows her forehead was smooth and wide, and the lips of her generous mouth were a healthy red-pink. She tilted her perfectly moulded chin and her fair hair swayed gently on her shoulders, shining in the sunlight. There was a precise quality about her, exuding dependability and sincerity, though there was a hint of humour, and even a provocative expression, lurking occasionally in her lovely earth-coloured eyes.

She smiled as she dismounted. 'Thanks, Thulmi, we did well. Take this lot to Fantasia in the kitchen, please.'

'*Yeh bo*, missy.'

As Thulmi led the horse away she crossed the grass of the mission compound towards her home. She was expecting Ben Fielding to arrive in an hour or so. He came to see her every Thursday afternoon around five o'clock. She would just have time to bathe and change.

As she came to the steps she glanced across the straggling Natal plum hedges to the dirt track they called the Greytown road, which led into the small settlement about two miles away.

She stopped and her eyes narrowed. There was a horseman coming. Goodness, Ben was over an hour early. She would only have time to go and comb her hair before he arrived. But as she put her foot on the bottom step, she hesitated. There was something in the aspect of the rider that made her pause and look back at him. No, it was not Ben. He did not ride like Ben. Yet in a way he was vaguely familiar.

Then it struck her. He rode like someone she remembered. But it couldn't be. It looked like John Lockley Harrison riding towards her.

Yes, yes, she was sure it was. Her heart started to pound. What in heaven's name was he doing here?

She had not seen him since she was a girl of fifteen . . . and now she was twenty-three. Embarrassed, she thought of all the letters she had written to him during her teen years. The last one she had sent him had contained Ellen's final message for him.

She watched him as he approached her. He was dressed in mufti: khaki twilled cotton shirt and trousers. He seemed larger than she remembered, his shoulders more square. Under his soft wide-awake hat his hair curled up at his neckline. He was an attractive sun-browned colour and he rode easily, as if he and the horse understood each other.

He came past the line of gum trees towards her and

dismounted, and now she had the presence of mind to finally put down the rifle she carried.

'Is it Phoebe?' he said, sounding surprised.

'Yes, John Lockley, I'm so pleased to see you.'

He stood looking at her. Little Phoebe was a woman ... a woman who exuded health and vitality under the wide brim of her hat. She smiled, and he thought how somehow she seemed to brighten this green African landscape.

She stepped towards him. 'Are you on leave?'

He answered as he took off his hat, 'Yes, over a year of it.'

Her heartbeat accelerated even more.

He forced a smile. 'Though I've agreed to act as an interpreter for the government whenever needed, and it seems the colony needs engineers for I'll take up duties here when my leave's over.'

He stood looking at her. 'So, I've come to see you.'

Now she felt quite heady with excitement. He had come home and he had come to see her. She could not help the tiny flush that rose to her neck.

He raked his hand back through his hair. 'To talk about my sweet sister, Nell, and what you know of her death.'

'Oh ... I see ... Yes, of course.' She bent down to pick up her gun. 'Please, come this way.'

She led him up the stairs and across the veranda into the wooden mission house.

Her mother and father were not at home, so she offered him some refreshment which he declined, with the words, 'Perhaps I will take something later, when we've spoken.'

'Yes, of course.'

She took off her hat and rolled down her sleeves and sat opposite him in the small parlour.

'Do you hunt?' he asked.

'Yes, it's a fact of life here. We must supplement our food. There are many refugees here at the mission kraal.'

John Lockley was having difficulty believing this confident young woman was his little Phoebe. 'Yes, I'm sure that's true, but it's unusual to find a ... lady handling a rifle.'

She sighed. 'A number of people, including my father, don't really approve.'

John Lockley gave a brief smile. It appeared that little Phoebe McLean had grown up with a mind of her own.

Slowly, he pulled his hand back through his hair and began, 'Phoebe, I received a batch of letters at my barracks in Ceylon on the eighth of May of eighteen sixty-six ... I'll never forget it. Four of those letters were concerning the death of my sister. One was from Uncle Chris and Aunt Jane, the second was from Nell's husband, Michael, the third from my father. The fourth was from you. I read them in that order and had I read only the first three I probably would not be here today, for they told of my darling sister's death as an accident. But when I read the one contained in yours, the one from Nell herself, I saw that she had decided to take her own life. Nell and I were always *very* close.

'There was no point in writing damn letters about it. Everyone seemed to believe Nell had died in an accidental fall. She was gone. I couldn't bring her back, but I could eventually find out the truth. You are the one she trusted with her letter to me, that's why I'm here.' He clasped his hands together. 'I've waited so long for this. Lived with it every day.'

Phoebe frowned. 'Have you spoken to your aunt and uncle ... or anyone?'

'No. While I've seen them briefly, I wanted to speak to you first.'

'Thank heavens you did. It'd break all their hearts to suspect anything different. And anyway it *was* an accident.'

He fell silent and she studied his handsome dusky blue-purple eyes; they had lost the lively quality she remembered; they were spiritless, clouded with his dark thoughts and grief. She wished with all her heart that she could make them bright and happy again. She leaned forward a little and said, 'John Lockley, I don't know what Ellen wrote in her letter to you. She asked me to send it to you, which I did.'

He put his hand inside his jacket pocket and touched a folded page. He was tempted to show the letter to Phoebe, but he did not want to draw the poor girl into it any more deeply than she already was. He could recite the damn words, he knew them so well.

Greytown mission, 15 November, 1865

My Darling Brother,

I write this letter to leave with little Phoebe. I have

confided in her and I trust her. She is good and will send it on to you, I know.

When you read this I will long have left this earth, for a better place, I hope. One which will give me freedom from my pain.

Oh, John Lockley, don't be sad. I am so confused. I am married to Michael irrevocably, and while I know he is fine and decent, I cannot live this way.

You, of all people, will understand, my dear, dear brother, when I say I love another, one I can never have on this earth. Just as you could never have had your Zulu girl. It is all unacceptable to everyone, everyone but you. You will understand.

I regret I will never see you again. For you I have truly loved, deeply and well. I am so proud of you, always have been.

Forgive me and forgive Darlengi. It was not something either of us could do anything about.

Your own sister,
Nell.

Phoebe watched silently as he sat with closed eyes for a few moments. Then he realised something. He opened his eyes. 'Why did you never write to me again after that?'

The question had caught her unawares. She took a deep breath. 'John Lockley, I realised that my letters were inconsequential. That I must have seemed childish to you, so I stopped writing them.'

How astute of her. Funny, though, for somehow he would now have preferred it if she had continued to write.

He looked closely at her for the first time. She was in plain working clothes and heavy boots and yet she was actually very lovely. Her fair hair fell in soft curls to her shoulders and there was a glow to her skin and an intrinsic honesty in her unequivocal brown eyes. Instead of saying anything he simply nodded, admitting that what she had said was true.

She continued to watch him intensely. She was thinking how similar his expression was to that of Darlengi and his melancholy black eyes.

'I'm so sorry, John Lockley. I still wake at nights and think of Ellen.'

'So do I, believe me.' He had been dumbfounded; heart-broken and dumbfounded when first he had read the letter. His sister Nell ... and his *brother* Darlengi. How could he have done that to her? Nell's death was not the tidy little accident that his relatives described.

Phoebe could see that he was controlling himself as he asked, 'I *know* she confided in you, Phoebe. What did she confide?'

Phoebe's heart was beating rapidly, now as much from his question as from the nearness of him. She stood up and moved a few steps across the room, her pale skirt brushing the zebra-skin upon the table.

'Well?' he insisted.

She started to speak as she turned back to face him. 'She was here, on the way to the Tugela farm, a few days after her marriage. She was strained, abnormal. She said that she never should have married Michael; that she did not want to live without Darlengi; that Darlengi had made her see things which she had denied all her life.'

'What did she mean?'

'I took it to mean she had always loved him, but never admitted it to herself.'

'And he *made* her admit it? How?'

'He went to her one night in Pietermaritzburg and then she knew.'

'What?' He stood up, his eyes clouded as if a dark shadow had fallen across them.

'No ... do not misunderstand. Ellen explained. She had always denied her love for him. Kept him at a distance, ignored him, resisted him, derided him ... until he confronted her alone ... with no one for her to turn away to, just the two of them and what they felt ... suddenly exposed. She said she knew then it had always been there. That it was Darlengi she truly loved, now and for ever more.'

'So ... she killed herself for it ... for this bloody love!'

'No. I do believe now it was an accident because...' She trailed off.

'Because what?' he questioned.

She did not answer. She feared she had said too much.

There was a menacing expression in his eyes. 'Tell me, Phoebe ... because what?'

She moved a few feet from him to where she felt more comfortable. Then facing back to him she replied, 'I believe that while Ellen did not want to live with Michael, her actual death *was* an accident.'

'Yes, I know you do. But why?'

She looked defiant. 'Because Darlengi told me.'

'How would he know whether it was an accident or not? Damn him in hell!'

'But how can you say that? He's like your brother.'

John Lockley forced out the words, '*Was* like my brother.'

Phoebe felt his torment. It filled the room like a tangible thing. She was frightened, it was so real. She knew how much he had cared for Darlengi. Everyone had said they were brothers, soul-mates. Her mother said they even believed they were born on the same day. And here he was denying Darlengi.

He moved slowly back and sat down.

'John Lockley,' she said, 'I understand your pain, but believe me, no one has suffered more than Darlengi. He deeply loved Ellen, in fact I think *worship* would be the right word.'

John Lockley's eyes were hard and cruel. She thought of Darlengi, her friend. He came to see her twice a year. He never stayed longer than an hour, and they would walk together under the trees and talk. The last time he had given her a letter for Uncle Chris and Aunt Jane.

Softly she asked, 'Did Darlengi ever write to you about it?'

'No.'

'Did you ever write to him about it?'

'No.' The answer was flat. He did not want to continue with this. He stood again and moved to the door. Then suddenly he could contain it no longer. 'He did not write for he knew what he did was evil. His guilt stopped him. I did not write to him for I had nothing to say.'

Her surprise showed on her face. 'I think you judge him far too harshly. His heart was broken too.'

'I hope so,' he said, and at that he walked out the door. 'I shall trouble you no longer.'

She followed him, her eyes riveted to him. He could never be any trouble to her. 'Where are you going?'

'I move on to H.H.'s place.'

'Then, please, before you go, do take refreshment as you said you might. I know my mother and father will be here soon and they'd like to see you.'

She did not notice Ben Fielding alighting from his horse below.

'No, thank you. I shall call in on my return and see them then.'

He held out his hand to her and she was intensely aware of the touch of his skin. She knew he felt nothing, that he stood here looking down at her but did not see her. She thought that in all her life, he had never really seen her.

As he released her hand she hesitatingly asked, 'Are . . . you going on to see Darlengi?'

His eyes hardened in the evening light. He certainly was; he had every intention of doing more than just *seeing* the man who had killed his sister. But he controlled his voice as he released her hand and answered, 'I might.'

Phoebe was fearful of what he would do. 'Darlengi is an induna now, and powerful. And you're in the British army. Your actions can have enormous consequences.'

He answered her as he moved down the steps. 'I'm aware of my responsibilities.'

He was riding away before she realised Ben Fielding was speaking at her elbow.

'Phoebe, Phoebe, what on earth was all that about? Who was that fellow?'

Phoebe kept her eyes on the rider as she replied, 'John Lockley Harrison, an old friend.'

'I heard you mention Darlengi.'

And now she turned to her visitor. 'Yes, he's on his way to Zululand.'

'Well he's jolly rude. I said good afternoon and he didn't even pay me the courtesy of replying.'

'Oh Ben, he's preoccupied today.'

'John Lockley Harrison? Isn't he poor Ellen's brother?'

'Yes.'

'Last I heard he was in Ceylon, in the army. Is he home on leave?'

'Yes, for more than a year.'

Ben Fielding felt the troubled green god of jealousy awakening. 'And you didn't realise I was here, even though I spoke to you while he was mounting his horse. You hardly registered my presence until I stood here beside you.'

Phoebe felt sorry for him and, placing her hand through his arm said, 'Oh Ben, don't be silly. Come on.'

But Ben was not to be so easily placated. He had been paying visits to Phoebe for years; in fact recently he had been courting her. He loved Phoebe McLean and had only been waiting on a bequest, from his aunt in Ireland, before asking her to marry him. He knew her father looked favourably upon him. He frowned as he took her hand from his arm and grasped it tightly. 'Phoebe? What did he want?'

'He just called in on his way north. I told you.'

But Ben had a very, very bad feeling about all this, and it translated into annoyance as he looked disapprovingly at her attire.

'You've been hunting again with Thulmi, haven't you? I wish you wouldn't do that. It's not proper for a lady to go out like that alone with a Zulu male.'

Phoebe's eyes met his. While she liked Benjamin Fielding and they had some really enjoyable times together, he was becoming far too possessive. What right had he to say what was proper for her or not?

He continued, 'Phoebe, I came here to ride with you. Now, are you coming or not?'

The evening sunlight showed a defiant glint in the eyes of Phoebe McLean as she answered, 'No, Ben, I'm not coming riding. I prefer not to be spoken to in such a manner. Good afternoon.'

He watched, abashed, as her straight back disappeared through the door. Then he slowly turned round and came down the steps.

He was about to mount up and ride away when Victoria and Frank rounded the corner of the mission school and came across the grass.

'Well, good afternoon, Benjamin,' said Frank, who always used the young man's full Christian name. 'Come to ride with Phoebe?'

Then they noticed the young man's crestfallen demeanour.

'What's wrong, Ben?' asked Victoria.

'I . . . oh nothing.'

'Where's Phoebe?' her father asked.

Ben's throat had turned scarlet. 'She's ... well, sir, she's not riding with me today.'

And now Victoria realised there must have been a disagreement. 'Ben, don't worry,' she said. 'These things happen. I'm sure it wasn't your fault.'

And suddenly Ben could not contain himself. 'No, it wasn't, Mrs McLean. Fact is, it was some damn fellow called John Lockley Harrison who is to blame.'

H.H. heard the horse coming a long way off.

He was standing on his small veranda with a shaft of moonlight falling across his face and a turtle dove cooing above his head when John Lockley reined in.

'H.H., it's John Lockley Harrison. I'm home on leave.'

'Well, bless my soul. It's great to see you, son. Come in.'

While he had occasionally corresponded with John Lockley in Ceylon, H.H. had not seen the young man since he had ridden in distraught over the death of his Zulu girl, many years back.

Inside, John Lockley looked around. The great ivory tusks were still in the same place against the wall and so too was the rosewood music stand with a page of music open upon it, just as John Lockley remembered it. Then he noticed that H.H. was much thinner and his hair had receded, giving his fine face a gaunter look.

'Where's Mrs Garner?'

'My wife died two years ago. Did I never write and tell you that?'

'No, sir. Oh, I'm so sorry. Mrs Garner was one of the most beautiful ladies I ever saw in my life.'

His eyes clouded momentarily. 'Yes, she was ... in every way. She wasn't sick long. It was swift.'

There was silence for a few seconds and then H.H. smiled and gestured to a chair. 'Sit down, lad. It's been a long time.'

'Nine years.'

'Yes, it would be. You've been in Ceylon, haven't you? You must tell me about it all. Are you on your way to the Tugela farm?'

'No, sir. I come to ask if you know where the Zulu, Induna Darlengi, resides.'

'Your friend? The fellow who grew up with you?'

286

There was the slightest hesitation before John Lockley answered, 'Yes, that one.'

'Well, I don't, but Dunn will know.'

'John Dunn?'

'Yes. He will be able to supply you with a guide into Zululand. I can tell you how to find him: it's straight along the north bank of the Tugela. He's now an adviser and confidant of Cetshwayo and has been given even more land. His wives and children grow in number each year and while he's hardly accepted in the drawing rooms of Pietermaritzburg and Durban, he's made a name for himself in Zululand.'

John Lockley ran his fingers back through his hair as he watched his host. He was thinking how even though society might not accept John Dunn, men could always make reasonable lives for themselves with black women. Hadn't his host done that very thing? He himself would have done it. But how in the Lord's name could Darlengi have believed that the other way round was possible? It was wholly unacceptable. The familiar hot, angry feeling rose inside his chest. His sweet Nell would have been here to greet him with her radiant smile if Darlengi had not been so bloody selfish. How could Darlengi have done this?

His face had dropped and a frown lodged between his eyes. This was not missed by H.H., who leant forward and patting him on the knee asked, 'Son, what's the matter?'

John Lockley did not reply immediately. He had not spoken to anyone except Phoebe about the nature of his anger, and to her he had held himself in check.

He looked into H.H.'s pale blue eyes, faded by over thirty years of South African sunlight, but the understanding and compassion in them still shone brightly.

'Can I help you, John Lockley?'

'I don't know if you can or not but . . .' He looked down at his hands. Then, coming to a decision, he lifted his gaze. 'I think you would know of my sister's death. She fell from rocks on the Tugela and died five years ago in November.'

H.H. nodded. 'I do.'

'Well, sir, I want to find the Zulu, Darlengi, because he murdered my sister as surely as if he had pushed her.'

H.H.'s attention was entirely on his guest. 'Now, son, why do you say that?'

And then it all came tumbling from him: all the anger and frustration and bitterness he had held for years. He told of what he believed; of Darlengi's selfishness and cruelty to Nell. Of how the Harrisons and Nelsons had nurtured him and how he had returned that care. He spoke of what he had learnt from Phoebe: of what Nell had said in her confusion and how Darlengi had gone to Nell, to her very room. 'He had no bloody right.'

And then he took the letter from inside his coat. 'Please, sir, read this. It came from Nell to me. She was even then contemplating killing herself for this futile love. You see, my family know nothing of this. They believe her death was an accident. That she was happily married. I am pained beyond explaining. I . . . looked on Darlengi as a brother, sir, and this is how he repaid me and my family.'

H.H. took the letter and John Lockley leant back in his chair and watched him read.

When H.H. finished he handed the letter back to his companion and said, 'It's a very sad note. To think your sister could feel so desperate. But there's no accounting for the feelings of folk in this world. She spoke from her heart, and loved you well to be so honest with you. I see you believe she would be alive and happy if it were not for Darlengi's actions. You think your brother has wounded you and your family, and perhaps he has. But I'm certain it was not deliberate.'

'That's not the point.'

'So you believe Ellen did, in fact, take her life?'

John Lockley slowly shook his head. 'I don't know, but the result has been the same.'

'You intend to find the Induna Darlengi. And what will you do then?'

'I'm uncertain.'

H.H. shook his head. 'No, lad, I'll not believe that. You have something in mind.'

John Lockley was silent and H.H. sat there watching him. The seconds passed and they heard some night sounds floating to them from the veld before the younger man replied, 'Yes, I have something in mind.'

And now H.H. stood and he moved over to John Lockley and patted his shoulder. 'Then let me say just a little more. This resentment against the Zulu has festered inside you for years, and that alone has built more anger, more enmity. You loved a Zulu girl and your sister loved a Zulu man. It's a complicated matter and you hold a grudge; doubly strong for it is against someone you cared for. Two things come to mind. Do you have the right to? And would your sister want you to? That's all I'll say.'

John Lockley looked up sharply and met his host's eyes. There was no ambiguity in what had just been said. H.H. had never played falsely with him. He stood up and took H.H.'s hand in his own. 'I respect what you have to say, sir. But my love had reality to it; Darlengi's was simply indulgence.'

The following morning, H.H. waved his overnight guest off with the words, 'Come back this way, lad.'

John Lockley had enjoyed the remainder of his night with H.H. They had caught up on a lot of things. H.H. had even confided that he might leave his little trading station and go back to England now that his wife had died.

'It was for her that I was here; she made it all quite bearable for me. But now that she's gone, there seems some argument to take up my life elsewhere.'

And now over the green hills and valleys of Zululand, eastwards to Middle Drift on the Tugela, rode John Lockley with all his unhappy thoughts ricocheting in his head.

He knew that H.H. did not approve of what he was about to do: whatever that was ... John Lockley did not really know himself. H.H. in his honesty had suggested that his own love for Jettama could be regarded as similar, but that was not so, not at all. He and Jettama had fallen in love virtually as children; had planned to marry in the heady days of their youth. Darlengi was an adult with a knowledge of the world and its workings, and still in his selfishness he had ruined Nell's life! His darling sister's joyful letters of impending marriage had been followed by the shocking notification of her untimely death and the realisation that the man he called brother had ruined her life so utterly. And he, John Lockley, was the only one in the world capable of making him answerable, for he was the only man who knew.

Suddenly he saw a lion and a lioness prowling in the

distance, and briefly he concentrated on this as he swerved his horse's head and detoured around a donga to avoid them.

By early afternoon he had crossed the Tugela at Middle Drift and now other thoughts played in his head. He found himself thinking of Phoebe McLean: her fair hair and pretty mouth and the blush of health in her cheeks.

By the time the sun had fallen low in the sky he came over a rise and found Mangete, John Dunn's principal residence; the man had recently built another in the Ungoya Mountains far to the north. A thick mist was rolling along the river valley and up towards him as he rode up to the five-foot fence. This was not a typical kraal, for the cattle pen was separated from the main houses by tall planted gum trees. Inside the fence were raised a number of small mud buildings and two or three larger wooden ones. About two hundred yards away stood a large conventional kraal.

John Lockley dismounted to the great interest of a dozen small children who gathered around him, and momentarily he was transported to Piakapitia and Trincomalee where the Indian children had always clustered around the soldiers' horses.

He led his horse through a wide opening in the fence to where two adult women stood from mashing the inevitable mealies, and four or five men came forward to him.

John Lockley said, '*Sa ku bonum ngani!*'

And they answered with the customary, '*Yeh bo.*'

'*Umnumzane uhlalaphi*, John Dunn?' Where is the headman, John Dunn?

The women began to laugh, but after he repeated his question, the men pointed to the largest house, some fifty yards away.

One of the men ran ahead of him into the house and John Lockley followed. Inside, on a bed against the wall, lay the white chief, and in attendance to him three Zulu women.

John Lockley introduced himself, but John Dunn remembered him. 'Met you that night many years ago at H.H.'s place. Weren't you in the army?'

'Yes, I was. Still am.'

'You're not in uniform.'

'I'm on leave.'

The host raised himself up and explained from behind his

closely cut beard that he was not his usual self, that he had caught some mild fever, but was very pleased to have a white visitor.

It was soon established why John Lockley was there.

'Yes, I know where Darlengi is, he's at an indaba at the Undi kraal. They discuss the Boers and I was meant to be there.'

'And will you be kind enough to supply me with a guide to take me there?'

John Dunn's shrewd features formed a smile. 'What do you want with Darlengi?'

John Lockley smiled in return. 'I'm not at liberty to say.'

'From what I read in your face, it could be trouble for the induna.'

John Lockley did not enlighten him any further, but he was invited to stay the night and was promised a guide.

He was offered food which he took, and women which he did not. John Dunn looked at him through narrowed eyes from where he remained on his bunk. He already had twenty-two wives and innumerable children, and when he was to die in 1895, would leave 49 recorded wives and 117 children; unofficial counts going much higher. He sniggered. 'Too proud to lie with a Zulu girl, are you, Harrison?'

John Lockley's eyes shone purple in the candlelight. 'No, Dunn, not at all. I was in love with a Zulu girl once. I find the race quite tantalising. They are more than acceptable to me.'

John Dunn burst out laughing. 'God! You've got a turn of phrase . . . *quite tantalising, more than acceptable to me*. Is that what they teach you bloody officers at military school?'

John Lockley refrained from answering by asking a question of his own. 'So, John Dunn, tell me more about the situation with the Zulus and the Boers. I know the events which have occurred in the past and I've heard a little from our friend H.H., but as I'm to go to Undi I'd prefer to know the present situation.'

And John Dunn, who was ever ready to air his knowledge, told him.

It was not until the following morning, when he was preparing to leave, that Dunn realised John Lockley was fluent in Zulu.

Dunn had lifted himself from his bed and was leaning against the door jamb as his guest prepared to depart. One of the white chief's Zulus came up to him and said in his own tongue, 'I am the one who will lead the white man through the Nkomo Peak Pass and to Undi.'

And before John Dunn had time to reply John Lockley replied in Zulu, 'Good. What is your name?'

Dunn's eyebrows rose in surprise. 'You've slept under my roof and I didn't discover you spoke perfect Zulu until now. I must really be sick.' Then suddenly he realised something and he wagged his finger at his departing guest. 'Ah ha, I remember now. You and Darlengi ... of course. You're a Harrison from the western Tugela. It's you that Darlengi lived with as a boy. He learnt English from you and you learnt Zulu from him.'

John Lockley merely smiled.

'And now,' continued Dunn, 'you go to find your old friend.'

'Something like that,' John Lockley said as he lifted his foot to place it in the stirrup.

John Dunn nodded. 'He's kept his British ways; still wears European clothing and has taken only one wife up to now, the foolish man.'

John Lockley almost missed the stirrup with his foot. 'What?' He turned to face John Dunn. 'He's married?'

'Yes, has been for a couple of years now; Thulile, a very pretty girl. No children yet, and for a Zulu that's damned odd.'

When John Lockley was led away from Mangete by his Zulu guide, his face was pale; his mouth was set in a stiff, unforgiving line and there was rage in his eyes.

CHAPTER TWENTY

Phoebe had risen early, and had written a letter to her friend, Fanny Colenso, before the dawn had really broken. Then, in the morning mist, with the first rays of sunlight breaking through, she took a long walk before returning to help the cooks feed the children who arrived early at the mission.

The night before, when her parents had asked the reason for John Lockley's visit, she had told them he was on his way to find Darlengi: which of course was true. How could she possibly have told them more?

During morning prayer under the large acacia tree, she wore a worried frown and it was not something that her father missed.

The children were soon filing into the little school house and as the cooks and maids and general help boys and cleaners wandered away, Frank called to his daughter. 'Phoebe, come here.'

She turned from where she was aiding a crippled child up the school steps. 'Coming, Father.'

When she was beside him and they were alone he lifted her hand through his arm and said, 'Let's walk around the mission, I'd like to talk to you about that contemplative expression my darling daughter has been wearing since yesterday.'

'But the children . . .'

'Your mother can do without you for a few minutes. Now, please tell me what troubles you. Was it your disagreement with Benjamin?'

'Oh, Daddy, no . . . I don't know.'

'He's a fine young man you know. His grain store is doing very well, not to mention the Crown surveying he's now doing, that being his trade; and his mother is a woman of excellent standing. Her grandfather was Lord Mayor of London, you know?'

'Yes, Dada, you've told me before.'

'I like Benjamin.'

And now his daughter turned to face him. 'You like Ben because he rides out here every Sunday to listen to you, and agrees with everything you say.'

Frank's eyebrows rose. 'Phoebe, it's not quite like that. I don't like to see you two having a spat. You usually get on so well. He seemed to think it had something to do with John Lockley.'

And now she turned round sharply to face her father. 'Did he say that?'

'Yes.'

'Just what exactly did he say?'

'Merely that. He said you were not riding with him and he looked so downcast that your mother said she was sure it wasn't his fault. To which he replied that he thought it was the fault of someone called John Lockley Harrison.'

They had halted near the fence line of the mission and now Phoebe looked away from her father to the horizon as she replied, 'Perhaps he was half right. Oh, Daddy, I know you would like Ben and me to become engaged. You've said as much on a number of occasions. But . . .'

'But what?' her father prompted.

She looked directly into her father's eyes. 'I don't love him.'

Her father sighed, then patted her hand and added, 'Then that's all that needs to be said.'

'Yes. Thank you, Father.'

Phoebe left him and headed back towards the schoolroom. She was some yards from him when he asked, 'And is there anyone that you *do* love?'

She halted and turned slowly around. She did not answer immediately. Then she said, 'Yes, there is.'

Her father nodded. 'I see. It wouldn't be just a young woman's infatuation with a good-looking man, would it?'

'No, Daddy. It wouldn't.'

'All right, darling, I'll try to understand.'

He smiled lovingly at her and she at him.

'Thanks, Dada.'

Some hours later, Phoebe was ending a singing lesson with the students she called the mission choir. They had been singing hymns and then popular songs, their young voices lifting to the blue sky, their bright faces happy. All the children were either Zulus, Basutos, Swazis or Hottentots, but their English improved daily, and the singing seemed to help their pronunciation. Phoebe took the lesson in the shade of a string of blue gums which had been planted some years before and had grown to quite a reasonable size.

The children finished singing 'Far from the old folks at home'.

Phoebe smiled. 'Now that song was written by a man called Stephen Foster. He was an American. The United States of America is the country in which I was born.'

'Does the White Queen own America too?' asked Lani, one of the brightest students at the mission.

'Her grandfather used to,' Phoebe said as she laughed, the children joining in. Then she gathered some of them together in her arms. 'That's enough for today. So who is off to the sewing bee with Jenny?' Jenny was one of the Zulu women who had been with the McLeans for a decade.

There was a loud chorus of assent from the girls and a negative rumble from the boys.

Soon the children had left her, and she joined her mother who was hoeing a small patch of ground alongside Thulmi. The Zulu was down on his knees in the dirt beside her. He looked up and smiled. 'We'll soon be plantin' potatoes, Miss Phoebe.'

Victoria took off her gloves. 'Let's have a little break now, Thulmi,' she said. 'Time we all had a cooling drink.'

The two women moved off together and Victoria took her daughter's arm. 'Darling, your father told me what you said to him this morning.'

'I thought he would. And, Mother, I really don't feel like discussing it any further.'

'All right,' Victoria answered soothingly. 'But when my daughter tells her father she's in love with someone and it's not the young man who has been calling on her, I think I have a right to ask about it, don't you?'

Phoebe did not reply.

'It's John Lockley Harrison, isn't it?'

And now Phoebe halted and turned surprised eyes to her mother. 'How did you know?'

Victoria smiled gently and lifted her daughter's hand in her own. 'My darling, I'm your mother. Mothers know things. I saw how you were last night after his visit here and I see how you react whenever his name is mentioned. You try so hard to seem neutral about him, but you're not, are you? I've known for a long time. But I've never said anything, for he was far away in Ceylon and with Ben so close ... well, I thought in time you might alter.'

Phoebe knew her lip was trembling but she took a deep breath and said, 'Mother, I've loved John Lockley ever since I can remember. That's not the sort of love that alters.'

Her mother nodded. 'You used to write to him regularly, but I don't believe you have in recent times. Why's that?'

'Oh, I thought it best, for I do believe he only saw me as a child, and I didn't want that.'

'Did he say anything yesterday?'

'Like what?'

'Well, anything that might show you he thinks differently of you now.'

She gave a tiny cynical laugh. 'No.'

'So this is a one-sided feeling?'

Phoebe hoped she would not cry. 'Yes.'

Victoria wrapped her daughter in her arms near the steps of their home and said tenderly, 'My sweetheart, he's home now. Let's be confident. While your father would prefer you married Benjamin, who knows?'

Tears welled in Phoebe's eyes. 'Why would Daddy prefer I married Ben?'

Victoria drew her daughter up the steps and across the veranda. 'Darling, he's only thinking of you. Ben is steady and reliable. I suppose it's just John Lockley's background.'

'What, with the Zulu girl?'

'I didn't say that, though I suppose it may be a part of it. Your father thinks that whole episode was very rash on John Lockley's part. But I think it's more that he simply sees John Lockley as a wealthy lad who is now a soldier, cavalier and dashing. He's so good-looking, I suppose your father has his doubts that a man like that could possibly be a good partner.

But your Daddy adores you and will fall in with anything you truly want.'

'Well, it's all academic at this stage.'

'Not for Ben it isn't. He's in love with you, Phoebe.'

'I know.'

Victoria leant forward and kissed her daughter's cheek. 'Well, we've said enough for today. Let's have a drink, and then I'll get back to Thulmi.'

Darlengi watched the herd boys bringing the cattle home from their evening watering. He had just come back from Mattana's kraal on the Emlalazi River. He had spent many days with her, for the Great One was fading fast; it broke his heart but he thought she did not have too long a time left. She had fallen ill last winter and as the summer had come on and advanced she had seemed little better, and soon winter would fall again. There were times when she was not lucid these days, but her retinue of disciples remained with her, tending her. Their methods were not always ones Darlengi approved of, but he could not be with her day and night. He had left Thulile with her now and would return to her as soon as he could.

The udubi boys waved to him and he lifted his hand in return greeting. Watching them herding the cattle reminded him of his own days at Unondo's kraal when he had done this very thing, and of how John Lockley used to wait for him and they would charge off on Isi together, filled with the cheer of boyhood and the happy laughter of youth. He drew his long tapering fingers across his forehead as his eyes narrowed contemplatively.

He had a letter to take to Phoebe next time he visited her: he had finally written to John Lockley yesterday, after all these years. At last he had found the strength to say to his brother what he had felt and what exactly had happened. He had never received another letter from John Lockley after the Ice Princess's death. He often wondered why.

The cattle came filing by, large, firm beasts they were. He smiled. Cetshwayo's herd was growing larger. The heir to the throne had begun to cull any coloured cows so that his herd was getting whiter, purer, all the time.

And while King Mpande was held in affection by his people, he was old and feeble now, rarely venturing from his kraal at

Nodwengu. He was so huge his belly had to be carried by servants when he moved. Zulu custom did not allow discussion of his illness, and the most that could be said was that Mpande was *dungezule*, indisposed. It looked certain that Cetshwayo finally would be king before too many years passed. Darlengi knew his own age, and so could judge that of Cetshwayo, who must be around forty-two or -three years. He even had a royal taster these days. Yes, it was just a matter of time before Cetshwayo was king of the Zulus.

He turned and walked through the gate into the Undi kraal, mingling with the lines of great beasts as they were herded through into their pen. He had come back to take his place in a meeting of the council. The heir to the throne had called his chief indunas to discuss the Boers. Cetshwayo really ran things in Zululand now. Relations were still grim with the Boers, always had been; whereas the Zulus were on far better terms with the English. The English had always kept their word. In all the years only the Tugela River had separated Zululand and the English colony of Natal and it had remained that way, whereas the Boers from the Transvaal were ever encroaching on Zulu lands and people.

Over the years, Darlengi had been instrumental in writing four letters to the Lieutenant-Governor of Natal on behalf of Mpande, Cetshwayo and the Zulu council to ask for attention to the border between Boer and Zulu. They had received no reply and the council members grew impatient. They had been called here to discuss what should happen next.

Darlengi moved through the huts towards the meeting place in the centre of the kraal and as he did so his eye caught Veele's and she smiled and called a greeting; he bent his head in answer. She was Mkosana's daughter. He was a powerful induna and since Darlengi had arrived here she had been overt in her attention to him. She was a pretty girl with high cheekbones and an abundant figure. At the same moment that Darlengi passed her, Kayo came from behind one of the huts and joined him.

'*Yeh bo*, you are here. How is Mattana?'

'Not good. She fades.'

Kayo nodded sadly. He had been Mattana's confidant over many years, and he was distressed to think his Great One and good friend was dying.

298

The two men walked side by side in silence for a short time and then Kayo looked round to his friend. 'Darlengi, I know your heart is full of Mattana and her sickness, but now that she is unable to guide you, perhaps it is up to me to do so.'

Darlengi looked sideways at his friend. 'What does that mean?'

'You have not yet taken a Great Wife.' Zulu custom dictated that the first wife was never the Great Wife, the one with the most power and the place of importance.

Darlengi stopped walking and Kayo halted and turned back to him.

'Kayo, I am married to Thulile.'

Kayo shook his head and the late afternoon sun glinted on his head ring. 'Even Mattana has urged you to follow custom and take more wives. You must not flaunt custom.'

The younger man's eyes grew sceptical. 'And why is that, Kayo, my friend?'

'Please, Darlengi. There are already those who do not approve of your European ways, your dress.'

'Do you mean Intongalu and his friends?'

'Yes. You often leave Zululand and go to visit white people. They are jealous that you can read English books: that you write letters for Cetshwayo. That you understand the English. And now that Mattana is old and sick, they are not as afraid of her magic as they used to be. Before, your alliance with her gave you automatic protection always. I have been at indabas where men have said that in your position you should have four or five wives at least by now. They whisper that you are not truly Zulu.'

Now a small smile formed on Darlengi's mouth. 'How can whispers hurt me?'

'Darlengi, I am your friend. I do not want anything to happen.'

'Like what?'

'I don't know. There could be moves against you ... I do not say now, but sometime ... unless you conform a little more.'

Darlengi nodded thoughtfully. 'And taking more wives, a Great Wife like pretty Veele, would make Intongalu's years of resentment fade?'

'Of course not, but it would help. His words may not carry

so much weight if only you would conform to custom more. And Veele is the daughter of Mkosana. It would be a powerful alliance.'

'Kayo, no matter what they say I *am* a Zulu. I am proud of that. I do not want to be anything other than what I am.'

The older man nodded. 'I know that.'

Darlengi patted his friend's shoulder as they entered the arena where the council sat. As they stood together inside the fence, he whispered, 'I hear you.'

Soon all the indunas were present.

'Darlengi, come sit by me,' Cetshwayo called.

Intongalu looked round quickly from where he stood. The distaste showed clearly on his face as he watched Darlengi stride across the grassless, dusty arena and bend his long body to sit beside the heir to the throne.

A hot shaft of envy ran through Intongalu's chest. He was as clever as Darlengi; as fast in the field; as accurate with assegai or knobkerrie; as thoughtful in council. And if he had spent as much time with the English, he too would be able to speak the language and write these messages as Darlengi did. He looked sideways to his close friend Inku and they exchanged glances.

When they were all seated Cetshwayo lifted his hand for silence. He was big man, with a large torso and massive thighs. He had smooth skin, with a wide unwrinkled brow, open round face and firm gaze. A thin moustache grew on his upper lip and a small beard covered his chin. A cheetah skin lay across his shoulders and around his neck hung an imposing necklace of crocodile teeth. He ruled Zululand in all but name and his was the power of the unopposed prince.

'My council,' he began, 'we have debated much today about what we should do. We, the Zulus, simply wish to be separated from the Boers. From the earliest our history with the Boers has been that of confrontation. We have heard nothing from the Lieutenant-Governor Keate after our last letter hoping for a settlement with the Boers. We had written others before, and to remind us of what was said in the last message, I ask Induna Darlengi to read the pertinent paragraph to us.'

Darlengi stood and began: 'The Zulus beg that the Governor will take a strip of country, the length and breadth of which is to be agreed upon between the Zulus and the Commissioners (for which they are asking) sent from Natal; the strip to abut on the Colony of Natal, and to run northward and eastward in such a manner, in a line parallel to the sea-coast, so as to interpose in all its length between the Boers and the Zulus, and to be governed by the Colony of Natal, and form a portion of it, if thought desirable.'

Having finished, Darlengi sat down.

'So,' said Cetshwayo, 'all we ask for is a strip of land to separate us from the ever-encroaching Boers. What is the next thing we should do?'

A long discussion ensued and the sun was almost set and fire brands had been brought to light the arena when finally Gihlana, a young half-brother to Cetshwayo, stood. He repeated the heir to the throne's praise names and then began, 'Baba, we have spent a long time in discussion and sent too many words in writing. We must speak directly with the Governor. Someone must go to Natal.'

This suggestion had general agreement.

'All right,' replied Cetshwayo. 'Who shall represent us?'

Dubalamanzi, another half-brother of Cetshwayo, suggested, 'Chief John Dunn.'

There was some murmuring at this suggestion. John Dunn was usually at these indabas but he had come down with some fever and so was not present today.

Cetshwayo scratched his ear in thought, and in doing so touched the tiny snick which had been cut out of his ear by the Boers thirty-one years before, so that they would forever recognise Mpande's chief son; one more reason for him to dislike them. He nodded. 'Any other suggestions?'

Kayo stood, and after the formalities said, 'While Chief John Dunn is almost one of us, he is still English. It should be a Zulu who speaks with a Zulu's understanding of our history with the Boers. And also someone who understands both tongues of Zulu and English; a man who is used to conversing with such as the Governor. I suggest Induna Darlengi.'

There was a mostly affirmative rumble at this suggestion.

Then Inku stood from his seat next to Intongalu and spoke. 'There is no one better to represent the Zulu cause than Intongalu. Did his grandfather not die at the battle of Blood River, and did not his father take an impi against our enemy the Swazis, and did he himself not fight at the battle of Ndondakusuka? I say Intongalu.'

This was greeted with mixed feelings.

The heir to the throne again raised his hand. 'Any more suggestions?'

There were no more suggestions.

'Then we must choose.'

They raised their assegais as each name was called.

Darlengi won the count.

Then Cetshwayo dismissed his council with the words, 'It is a good decision. We shall meet again when Darlengi returns from putting our feelings to the Lieutenant-Governor. Now let us partake of our waiting feast.'

The council rose and repeated the heir to the throne's praise names before the festivities began.

Darlengi put his arm around Kayo's shoulders and, bringing his lips close to his ear, said, 'It seems that I am not quite as unpopular as you thought, my friend.'

Kayo turned his head and winked. He had been taught to wink by Darlengi. 'Even they see you as our best representative in this matter.'

Three hours later rain halted the celebrations and Cetshwayo and Darlengi retired to the great hut to talk in the light thrown by six ten-inch cowdung and fat candles.

'Darlengi, when you go to the Governor for me, you should see Somtseu if you can. I had thought he might have come to see me by now as he is a regular visitor to us in Zululand.'

'Yes, he was along the Tugela a short time ago.'

The prince smiled, showing a line of pure white, perfect teeth. 'I have always liked him since he showed his courage when he came to my father's kraal to nominate me as heir to the throne at the great indaba. One of the men in his entourage, Umgoza by name, was found in my father's isi Godlo, alone with the women. There was much anger and resentment towards Somtseu. In fact at one moment our warriors called for his blood. But he did not flinch. This impressed me. He is a courageous man and has been a good friend to the Zulu nation.'

Darlengi remembered the incident well; it had been in 1861. He answered '*Yeh bo, Baba*, I was at the indaba too, it was the first time I ever met Mr Theopolis Shepstone.'

His companion nodded. 'So you will go to him first. Also I am thinking you should see Chief John Dunn on your way to Natal. It is best to alert him that we make representation to the Governor.'

'I shall do as you ask. Does Cetshwayo mind if I go to Mattana's side on my way south to Natal? She grows ever weaker.'

The leader sighed. 'All my life she has worked her magic. I am saddened that she is ill. I remember her when I was an udubi boy to my father Mpande, though he was never warrior like my Uncle Dingane or Shaka. She was the first to tell me I would one day rule all of Zululand.'

Then Cetshwayo lifted his hand and took hold of Darlengi's shoulder. 'Yes, you go to her. She is the one who saved your life and took you to the kraal on the Tugela where you met the white family.' Suddenly he looked questioningly. 'Do you still see the white family?' Cetshwayo had known Edgar Harrison and Christopher Nelson. He recalled their coming to Nodwengu when he was a young man. He went on, 'Did I ever tell you that I was there with my father when he granted the two men the Tugela land?'

'No, you did not, though I realise you knew them. And I have seen none of them for some years now.' Darlengi knew Cetshwayo understood what a year was, though most of his subjects did not.

The leader's eyes narrowed. 'Are you no longer welcome in their kraal?'

And now Darlengi smiled. 'No, it is not like that. The one I call brother is away from Africa in the British army of the Great White Queen. And while I will always think of the family as part of my own, I have no reason to see them. My life is here in Zululand.'

'Good. Good,' said the prince, as if the matter were settled.

The following morning, just before dawn ran its soft golden fingers down the Umgoya Hills to settle on the Undi kraal, Darlengi bent through the opening of a hut, and, carrying the paper which had Cetshwayo's mark upon it, and which told that he was the representative of the Zulu people, stood up to leave.

The night's rain had ceased and he was soon through the gate and running across the verdant country. An hour later he was passing the western edge of the Umgoya Mountain when he saw the figure that melted out of the dawn light and came towards him. As he drew closer he realised it was Globo, one of Mattana's disciples.

'*Saku bona*, Globo.'

'*Saku bona*, Darlengi. Mattana the Great One asks for you. She says to make speed.'

John Lockley had been led through Nkomo Pass by his guide, Yuni, who had pointed north-east and said, 'We go now to cross the Amatikulu River.'

They forded other smaller streams and by late afternoon they were approaching another river, the Emlalazi, when John Lockley's horse went lame. He examined the loose shoe on the left rear leg and stood to look around. They were on high ground and there was a kraal about half a mile to the right.

He faced his guide. 'Yuni, if I fix the horse's shoe plenty quick, will we get to Undi by nightfall?'

'No, boss.'

'Then I think we should bide the night at yonder kraal if they will make us welcome. There I can tend my horse's shoe at leisure and we can go on in the morning.'

And Yuni, who was hungry and ready for a rest, answered happily, '*Yeh bo*.'

The occupants of the kraal did invite them in. It was very rare for a white visitor to come here; one who was on a fine horse, even though it limped; all they ever saw were traders in ox wagons.

Everyone gathered around to watch John Lockley mend his horse's shoe, and while the mastiffs barked, there was not the usual laughter and chatter, or the general amusement which would normally have surrounded such a chance event. And while the children still played the games he recalled so well like labyrinth drawing and leapfrog, John Lockley thought there was a pall over the whole kraal.

Yet they made him and Yuni welcome and after a meal of plovers' eggs and mealie cake by the fire, and a chat with his host, a fine-looking man who wore a head ring, John Lockley was shown to his hut for the night. To the constant chirping of the cicadas he thanked his host, and bent through the opening to find a fire burning and a little water in a gourd beside it. He gave himself a cursory wash and placed his clothes and boots by the fire. Then he lay down on the reed mats upon the highly polished floor and covered himself with a warm zebra skin. He fell quickly to sleep, only to be woken by something and to see a woman standing in the centre of the hut illuminated by the weak light of the fire's dying embers.

'You startled me,' John Lockley said in Zulu.

And she replied, 'I did not mean to do so. I am here to request that you come with me.'

'Where are we going?'

'To the far side of the kraal. There is someone who asks for you by name.'

'But . . .' protested John Lockley, 'no one here knows my name. I have never been here before.'

'Are you Jown Log-ley Har-ri-son?'

John Lockley's eyes narrowed. What was going on here? He pulled his hand automatically back through his hair. 'I am. Though how the devil anyone here in the depths of Zululand knows it is beyond my understanding.'

The woman gestured to the hut opening. 'Then please come with me.'

He quickly put on his clothes and boots and followed her out of the hut and around the cattle pen past the lines of dwellings. John Lockley guessed it must be just before dawn. It was raining lightly and the temperature had dropped. He shivered; as much from the eerie request for his company as from the chill in the air.

His guide halted in front of the largest hut in the kraal and motioned for her companion to enter. She had a gentle expression and wore her hair in the cone-like shape of the married Zulu woman.

John Lockley bent through the opening and stood up inside the hut. It took him a few seconds to focus through the smoke that rose from a fire in the centre of the room, then he realised there were people standing silently all around. He looked at them but no one spoke and then they parted and made way for him to pass through. He moved slowly forward and there on the floor, covered by reed mats, with her head on an intricately woven wooden pillow, lay an old woman with matted hair and deeply wrinkled face. He could see she was fading fast and her breath came in great painful gushes.

He came forward to her side, and the woman who was tending her whispered in the ancient one's ear, then stood, and moved back.

And now the old eyes opened, and lifting her claw-like hand slightly, she beckoned the newcomer down to her.

John Lockley was feeling uncomfortable. He was not afraid, fear was not something that rose very swiftly in his heart, but he looked once more around at the still, ghostly figures before he bent down on one knee beside the prone figure.

Even though the eyes he looked into were clouded with approaching death, and one was covered in a white film and obviously blind, he saw surprise register as she looked at his face. Then she spoke.

'You ... even look like him,' she croaked. 'While he is black ... and you are white.'

John Lockley did not understand. He replied in Zulu, 'What is that you say?'

'I say ... you look like Darlengi.'

'Who are you?'

'Mattana. I ... am ... Mattana.'

Now John Lockley understood. He looked at her closely. 'You are Darlengi's good mother, the witch doctor.'

And she tried to smile, showing her line of broken teeth. 'I prefer to be called Magic One.'

And John Lockley managed a smile in return. 'I suppose you do.'

Then she waved her fingers to all those who waited around her. 'Begone ... I wish to speak to this one ... alone.'

The silent figures filed out one by one, and as they did John Lockley realised why the whole kraal had seemed so subdued: their great witch doctor was dying.

When they were alone, he asked, 'How did you know I was here? Your follower asked for me by name.'

She was breathing heavily and it was difficult for her to answer but finally she managed. 'Mattana has always known things ... others do not. I had ... a dream and in it ... I saw you come here. Though I did not see your face. I ... did not know ... how exactly like my strong tree ... you are.'

John Lockley was cynical about the answer, even though there seemed no alternative to it.

She closed her eyes briefly and when she opened them she

spoke again, though this time it was not much more than a whisper. 'I am dying . . . I have had a long life. And have been the intimate . . . of many kings and powerful indunas. I have devised some good . . . and much mischief . . .' She pushed out a strange mirthful sound, akin to a small cackling laugh. 'But always I have vigilantly watched over my strong tree, Darlengi, the son of my only true . . . friend.' She was silent while she tried to get her breath back. 'I can see . . . you come to your brother . . . with fury in your heart.'

John Lockley started, he was so surprised.

Then she tried to raise herself up, and he automatically leant forward and helped her. She took this chance to clutch his arm and to bring him even closer to her. 'I know what happened . . . to your sister. I know you have carried this pain many winters and have travelled far to bring it here . . . to Zululand. You believe you must . . . avenge her. I see that it is powerful, this . . . rage you carry, like the violent enmity the black eagle carries . . . for the dassie of plain and mountain. But it is misdirected.'

She could not go on and she lay back down, but she did not let go the grasp upon her captive's arm. John Lockley was amazed at how strong her grip was. There was silence except for the crackle of the fire. It threw weird shadows and the dying Mattana looked grotesque in the firelight. But she would not die yet. She had known this man, known him in her dreams all these years. She understood his heart as if he, too, were her own. She had much yet to say to him.

It was all like some fantastic dream to John Lockley. He had come to Zululand to take revenge on Darlengi; to make him suffer as Ellen had suffered. And somehow he had ended up here in the depths of nowhere at the side of the dying Mattana, the witch doctor of his boyhood stories and unreal imaginings.

Minutes passed while she clutched his arm and he knelt there watching her. When her eyes opened again her voice was a little stronger. 'John Logley Harrison, I understand . . . about your white man's years and . . . I first saw you in a dream over twenty-five years ago . . . before you came to Africa. I have waited all these years to see your face . . . to touch you.'

She fell silent and closed her eyes again, and John Lockley took the opportunity to say, 'Do not speak if you find it too hard.'

At this she opened her eyes and for the last time in her life accomplished some ferocity; there was a challenging glint in her good eye and her voice was raised ever so slightly. 'I may be dying . . . but I *will* speak.' Her words came in rushes of breath and John Lockley could not help but admire her. She raised her shaggy head aggressively towards him, there were beads of perspiration on her temples. 'Let Mattana ask you some questions . . . Did not Darlengi hurt inside when Jettama died? Could not Darlengi have wanted revenge?'

John Lockley made a frustrated sound. 'It was not the same. I would have married Jettama. Darlengi could never have married my sister. He is a Zulu. Hurting my sister was selfish, wicked. It is *not* the same.'

And now Mattana lifted her other wizened palm and held it towards her visitor's free arm, and mechanically, as if his will were hers, he let her hold his hand. She drew him even closer, looking deeply in his eyes, as she whispered, 'I believe . . . that you *believe* . . . what you say is true. But there would not have been a marriage . . . between you and Jettama. Your family . . . tolerant as my dreams tell me they are . . . could not have allowed it.' Her breath came in gasps and she closed her eyes, but did not let go of him.

After a minute or so she gathered herself again and now her voice came in a croaking sound. 'Your anger is only at yourself.'

He thought she mumbled the words 'ice princess' but he was uncertain. She lifted her dying eyes to his again. 'Darlengi and your sister were fated . . . there was nothing anyone could do . . . accept it.'

She was silent for a long time and she seemed to change colour; as if her face paled under her dark skin. She still held him tightly as if to take him with her, and now she whispered and he bent even closer to hear her. 'You and he . . . are extraordinary men. I fear what I see in my dying dream . . . a time when you both face death . . . face it as brothers.'

Then in a final, immense effort, she opened her eyes and concentrated on his face. A tear fell from the side of her good eye, yet she was smiling as she said, 'I have sent for my strong tree . . . but . . . he will come too late. It is you I must die with . . . John . . . Logley . . . Harrison.'

He felt her tremble, and heard the hissing sound from her

throat as her hands at last dropped from grasping him, and the one who had been the intimate and magician to three Zulu kings, and the one yet to come, slipped out of this world into the next.

CHAPTER TWENTY-ONE

John Lockley stood up from where he had knelt at the side of the dead Mattana and then he realised he was surrounded by her people again. As they began a low wailing sound, he moved slowly back through them to the hut opening.

He had never in his life had such a mystical experience. All the things the dying witch doctor had said to him ran through his head in wild succession.

Mattana, the great, renowned Zulu magic one, had died holding his hand. It was somehow unreal.

It had stopped raining and the clouds had opened. His fair hair glinted in the dawn light as he pushed his hand through it, and a shudder ran through him. He was moving through the huts when he saw Yuni coming towards him leading his horse. 'Well, boss, we eat breakfast and then go. *Yeh bo?*'

He was about to answer when he saw two figures run through the kraal gate. A thrill of pleasure tingled through him and he fought himself to hold it back as he stood stock-still watching the long, lithe body swiftly approaching. He had not been ready for this.

Suddenly, Darlengi saw him and halted. His face broke into an expression of delight, shock and disbelief. 'Lockley,' he said, coming forward, his heart expanding with joy. 'Is it really you?'

'Yes. None other.'

Darlengi opened his arms to take his brother in them, but John Lockley stepped aside, and pointing to the hut in the distance said, 'Mattana is dead.'

Darlengi's face stiffened and he turned from his brother and ran to Mattana's hut.

Yuni stood watching him and John Lockley walked on by with the words, 'Follow me, Yuni, I have something for you to do.'

He took lead pencil and paper from his saddle bag and, sitting near the kraal gate, he wrote:

16 May, 1870

Darlengi,

Ellen wrote to me before she died. I carried the knowledge of her pain for all these years.

I came to Zululand to kill you for killing her.

But Mattana fought one last great fight for you. Obviously she loved you as she loved no other on this earth. She said many things to me, one was, 'Your anger is at yourself' and perhaps it is true.

Our two sisters are dead. Let them rest in peace. I forgive you as you forgave me.

Once I called you brother; it is best we leave that brotherhood in the distant past that fashioned it.

If ever we meet again, and it would be best if we did not, we must meet as strangers.

John Lockley.

He folded the paper. Then he took the midshipman's dirk from the scabbard at his waist and handed it to Yuni. The young man's eyes widened with delight as he saw the white fishskin grip ornamented with gilt and the blue and gilt embossed blade.

'This is for you. You are a good guide. I leave here immediately. I know my way now. Return to your home kraal when you have given this paper to Induna Darlengi, the man I told of Mattana's death.'

He gave Yuni the folded paper and the young man smiled. 'Yeh bo.'

He took his horse from Yuni and was about to mount when peripherally he saw a figure standing alone by the palisade. It was the woman who had led him to Mattana in the night.

'Why do you leave before speaking with Darlengi?'

He pushed his hand back through his hair. 'It is too hard to explain. I have left him a letter. I must go.'

She watched him as he mounted his horse. She was a lovely, peaceful figure standing there beside the kraal fence in the morning sun. He had the most peculiar feeling he had seen her before; not just last night, but before. Did she remind him of

311

Jettama? No, it was not that. He had not been in Zululand for nine years, it was impossible for him to know her. He shook his head as he moved his horse forward.

She lifted her hand in farewell and he did the same before he spurred off down the hill.

Behind him Thulile continued to watch until she could see him no more, then she turned back into the kraal.

Darlengi held Mattana close to his heart for a long time and his tears fell in her matted hair. It was almost impossible for him to accept that his good mother, his magic one and mentor, had passed from the earth: that she would sit no more at 'smelling-outs' to find wrongdoers, or terrify chieftains into bending to her will.

'There was never one like you, nor will there be again,' he whispered into her hair.

When he stood up from where she lay on the mats, there was the conflicting emotion of joy in his heart. His brother was here, outside! It was what the Christians called a miracle. He had lost Mattana and regained John Lockley. To think he had a letter for his brother, here in the pouch at his waist.

He touched Mattana once more, ever so gently on her furrowed brow, and whispered, 'Mother, I will come back very soon. I must go now and welcome my brother home.'

He moved out of the hut into the morning sun and there stood Yuni holding a paper out towards him.

He looked around for John Lockley, but there was no sign of him. He took the paper and, opening it, read. And as he read his face changed and his hand shook.

He read it a second time before he lifted his eyes to Yuni who stood waiting. His voice sounded like someone else's as he said, 'Has the man who wrote this left the kraal?'

'*Yeh bo.* He rode away before.'

Then Darlengi turned away and walked around the perimeter of the kraal until he reached the gate. He passed through and crossed over to stand near the mealie field.

Mattana's dying deed was to stop my brother from trying to kill me.

Ellen wrote to Lockley. And he came to kill me.

Mattana, Mattana, perhaps you should not have stayed my brother's hand. But you did . . . and what is done is done.

312

His handsome face was set as he looked skywards to the impartial clouds.

I thought I had found you again, my brother, but it seems that I have lost you. You and Mattana . . . on the same day.

So be it.

He turned back to the kraal, and rapidly re-entered Mattana's hut where she still lay surrounded by her people. He moved through them and fell down on one knee to whisper again in the ear of his dead mother.

'I never really believed you could see things . . . I always thought you were simply very watchful, artful and clever; but now in death, you confound me once again. What could possibly have brought John Lockley Harrison to this one kraal in all of Zululand if it were not your magic?'

He stood up and spoke softly to those around him. 'I cannot stay to bury my good mother with her ancestors. I must go to Natal for Cetshwayo. Place her in the ground with pride, for she loved you all and was one of the greatest of all the Zulus.'

John Lockley rode at a steady pace south, resting his horse now and then. He reached the Middle Drift on the Tugela by early afternoon and there he bought food and drink for himself and his horse from a friendly trader named Arnold Richards who had set up in a wattle and daub hut by the river.

He walked along the river bank with a flock of starlings circling overhead, and relived over and over the weird hour of death with Mattana. He admitted that the things she had said had convinced him to face what was truly in his heart . . . an excuse to turn from revenge. He heard in his head her desperate breathing, followed by her thick whisper. *I saw you in a dream over twenty-five years ago . . . before you came to Africa. I have waited all these years to see your face* . . . While he didn't believe this, he had been influenced by it when she said it. He had been amazed she had known why he was in Zululand, and that had almost persuaded him that she really did have magic powers.

And when she had said, *Your anger is at yourself*, he had finally conceded that this was so.

Yes, he admitted, he felt relief. He did not feel happy; but he knew Mattana had shown him the truth.

313

And how in hell had he gone there? To the one kraal in the whole of Zululand that held the dying Mattana inside it? He could not help but give a wry smile, for while he was saying it was coincidence, he knew, wherever she was, Mattana was saying it was her magic.

Arnold Richards waved him off with an old blue kerchief in his hand and John Lockley arrived at H.H.'s just after dark as forked lightning played continually in the distance and a light rain began to fall. H.H. opened his last bottle of 1850 port wine and they talked well into the night while John Lockley recounted to H.H. what had occurred. He left the following morning with the understanding that he would come back to see his friend whenever he could.

When John Lockley rode through the green hills into the pleasant valley that was home to Greytown, he was once more reliving his experience in Zululand. He came out of his reverie to hear his name being called, and turned in the saddle to see Phoebe on a pale grey horse trotting towards him. The front of her saddle was covered in wild flowers and a rifle was strapped to the side.

Her expressive eyes looked at him from under her wide-brimmed hat. There was a soft colour in her cheeks and her curls blew back over her shoulder in the breeze. While John Lockley was preoccupied he still noticed all of this.

'What happened?' was the first thing she said.

'Nothing.'

'Nothing?'

'Well, actually nothing happened, and yet a tremendous amount happened.'

She watched him closely. 'Would you tell me about it? I've been very worried.'

'Have you?'

'Well . . . yes . . . Darlengi is a friend of mine.'

'Ah, yes, Darlengi. Well, your *friend* has not been harmed.'

'Thank goodness.'

'And what if I had been?'

'What if you'd been what?'

'Harmed.'

The corners of her mouth turned upwards the tiniest bit. 'I . . . would not have liked that.'

He sat gazing at her silently. Then looking around he

pointed to a grassy bank a short distance from the track. 'Shall we sit there and I'll try to tell you as best I can.'

This time somehow he told it differently from the way he had related it to H.H. He admitted more about what had been in his heart: more of his real feelings and of his true self.

She listened to all he had to say, and as he went on she thought that his pain had not really diminished at all. He had simply been released from taking revenge, from what he had seen as his duty. She thought there was still great sadness inside him and she believed it was because of the way he had left things with Darlengi.

'Did you have to say that?' she asked when finally he told her about what he had written in the message he had left for Darlengi. 'The part about leaving your brotherhood in the past, and meeting only as strangers in the future. I don't really see why you had to say that.'

'Phoebe,' he looked away as he answered, 'I was twenty-three the last time I saw Darlengi, yet I was still looking at the world like I did as a boy of fifteen. In the nine years that have passed since then, we, he and I, have lived lives as diverse as it is possible to imagine. We aren't the boys we were and the world we live in has taught me, and I suspect him also, some cruel lessons. Even Mattana on her deathbed made the mistake of thinking we are alike.'

'Don't you want to be like him any more?'

He looked sharply around to her. Why did she have this ability to ask such questions?

'I cannot be. And always the death of his sister and the death of my sister will lie between us. Impossible to pass over.'

They were silent for some time, both watching a small family of reed buck grazing in the middle distance.

Then she said, 'And will you be able to live with this rule you have made?'

'I will.'

'John Lockley, two days ago I said that Darlengi had told me Ellen's death really was an accident.'

He was staring at the reed buck and holding his hands around the tops of his polished boots. 'Yes?'

'Well, I think you should know . . . that the reason Darlengi knew was because he was there.'

'What?' His eyes came round to hers.

'Yes. It seems he had some idea just to look on her again from afar. To see the one he loved one more time . . . as we all might,' she added quietly. 'Well, he went to the rocks to wait until after dark and he found her there, already standing up on the boulders, and he does believe she had suicide in her mind until she saw him. Then she halted and actually stepped back away from the edge and was going to come down to him. That was when her foot caught in something and she fell. He was holding Ellen in his arms when she died. He left her when he saw Michael riding towards them. But of course no one knows that he was there . . . except me . . . and now you.'

'She died in his arms?'

'Yes. Where, believe me, I know for a fact, she would have wanted to die.'

He turned away and, resting his head on his knees, closed his eyes. 'What a bloody waste of my beautiful sister.'

'Yes.'

'I often think this world is an insane asylum. There's no reason in much of what happens here. So many die before their time.' He lifted his head and looked skywards.

She thought he must be thinking of Jettama and she said softly, 'You loved Jettama very much, didn't you?'

He did not answer for a few moments, then he said, 'Yes I did, very much. She was gentle and beautiful and strong and kind.'

Phoebe felt a twinge at his words. She was gazing at his profile, his perfect profile, in the peace of the afternoon. 'I saw you with her, you know.'

He looked at her in amazement. 'When?'

'A few days before she was killed. Thulmi and I saw you. We had been out riding with your family in the northern part of the Tugela farm. You were with her down through the trees.'

'Did anyone else see us?'

'No, just Thulmi and me.'

Then he said, 'Little Phoebe, you've turned into a lovely young woman and I hope you'll be a happy one.'

Why did she have a feeling of premonition?

'I had been sad a very long time, Phoebe; I carried Jettama's death like a shroud around me, and when I heard about Nell, I was worse. I soldiered and worked to the best of my ability and must have impressed some for they made me a major last year. There were times when I took too much liquor, an excuse to distract me from my troubles, and I eased my pain in other ways, with women.' He looked round at her. 'Tell me to stop if you want.'

'I'm listening,' she answered quietly.

'I loved many and yet loved none. I wore my pain like a veil.' He lifted his hands to his temples and leant forward with his elbows on his knees.

Suddenly Phoebe broke in. 'John Lockley, I'm twenty-three, the same age you said you were when you still saw the world as a boy, but I hope I can see more clearly than you did. Forgive me if I seem undiplomatic, but it seems to me you still enjoy being melancholy.'

His eyes came up quickly to meet hers as she continued, 'You must see it for what it is. There's so much human suffering that the whole world should be wailing. Look at those who are maimed and tortured in wars; the terrible battles that have left so many homeless and destitute. There are people still living in slavery in the Sudan and Asia Minor and the Orient and Arab countries; some are in vile prisons. Some poor souls never know their parents or a word of kindness their whole, miserable lives. We on the other hand are so lucky. I look at you and I see a man who ... perhaps indulges himself. There. I have said too much.'

He did not reply for a moment. Then he smiled, and looking up at a brilliant blue starling on a tree branch said, 'Phoebe, you have not said too much. Everything you say is very wise and I agree with you. But you see, I did face up to things, well over a year ago. Someone helped me to do that, and I have brought her home to Natal with me ... my wife, Kate.'

For some seconds Phoebe could not see, she could not speak, she could not focus. There was something hot expanding in her throat, choking her.

He was still looking up as he went on, 'When I found out Darlengi was married I was furious, then I saw I had no right. Hadn't I married to help me to forget? Each love is different, yet each is valid, and we all must find solace where we can.'

She did not speak, and he continued, 'And you're right. There's far too much unhappiness in the world, and you're doing something about it, you and your parents. Your work's to be admired.' Now he turned to her and smiled. 'You've been very kind to me, and you were right to speak your mind as you did.' Then he rose to his feet and held out his hand to help her up.

Somehow she took it and stood up beside him.

They crossed to their horses and he helped her into Sapphire's saddle and handed her the wild flowers which had lain on the grass. He smiled up at her. 'It'll be good to see your parents again. Are they at home today?'

She did not answer, and as he handed her the reins he touched her hand. 'Phoebe? Are your parents at home?'

Somehow she found her voice. 'Yes, they are.'

He leapt up into the saddle. 'Then let's go and see them.'

Ever afterwards, the ride back to the mission with John Lockley was an event Phoebe could not recall. She knew they travelled those miles together and she realised they must have talked, but she remembered nothing.

Her mother and father were in the mission yard as they rode up, and when they dismounted, and her mother invited John Lockley to stay the night, and he accepted, she made an excuse not to go into the house.

'I'm sorry but I have an appointment in Greytown and I cannot miss it for anything. Do excuse me, John Lockley.' Then she took her mother's hand. 'I must speak to you first, Mummy, please.'

John Lockley, oblivious to anything wrong, smiled. 'Of course. It's been grand to see you, Phoebe. And thank you.'

Her father gave her a questioning look as he retreated with John Lockley, then she quickly drew her mother along and around the side of the schoolroom.

A number of children playing in the dirt called greetings but Phoebe almost dragged her mother by them and on past a group of strelitzias to a hiding place.

Victoria was looking with concern at her daughter. 'Phoebe, whatever's wrong?'

'Oh Lord, Mummy!'

Phoebe looked so distraught that Victoria did not reprimand her for this language as she would normally have done. The young woman sank to the ground and tears welled in her eyes.

Victoria knelt down beside her. 'Darling, darling. What is it?'

Phoebe lifted her tear-filled eyes to her mother. She found it difficult to speak. 'I . . . oh, Mummy. He . . . h . . .'

'Darling, tell me.'

'He's married.'

'What? John Lockley?'

And then Phoebe managed to speak in a level tone. 'He told me . . . just like that. He's married to someone named Kate. He called me *little Phoebe*. He has no idea . . . none . . . of how I feel. I cannot stay here tonight, not while he's here. Please, Mother, help me. I must go to Phyllis. I can stay there.'

Phyllis May Muller was the wife of Graham Muller, the Greytown postmaster who was also the blacksmith. She was a dear friend of Victoria, and loved Phoebe, and was the one woman in the settlement who defended the young woman about her unfeminine pastimes.

Victoria was uncertain what to do but one thing was obvious: to her daughter this was a calamity; she was in shock. She wiped Phoebe's eyes and taking both her hands said firmly, 'All right, go to Phyllis May. She's absolutely trustworthy and will be ever so pleased to see you. Tell her you want to stay overnight with her. She's so kind-hearted she won't ask you why, so you don't need to tell her unless you want to. In time she might find out John Lockley was here, but we'll worry about that then.'

'Oh thank you, Mummy, thank you.'

'Now go and take Sapphire and ride into town. I'll come for you tomorrow when John Lockley leaves.'

Phoebe grabbed her mother's hand as she moved away. 'What will you tell Daddy?'

Victoria did not answer for a moment, then she said gently, 'The truth, sweetheart. That's the way this family is.'

CHAPTER TWENTY-TWO

Three years on, the last week of July
The Pietermaritzburg Club was a small establishment. Drinks were served until ten o'clock in the evening on Mondays, Wednesdays and Fridays, and on the other days of the week the bar closed at six o'clock sharp.

The great southern lands are places of little twilight even in the summer months and on this winter day, night was falling fast. The final glow from the sun showed faintly through the window on to the bar just before the hour of five in the evening.

The four men who chatted over a round of drinks had just completed a game of billiards on a table made in Natal by the Harrison-Nelson company, and now they had taken to talking about the coming coronation of the new Zulu king, Cetshwayo. Mpande, who had suffered, amongst other things, from gout and extreme overweight, had finally died the previous year and the Zulus had asked Somtseu, Theopolis Shepstone, to come and acknowledge the prince as the new king. They had also asked once again for the Natal Government to intervene between the Zulus and the Transvaal Boers: all their previous requests having so far come to nothing.

Warwick Brookes, the Superintendent of Education for Natal, patted John Lockley on the shoulder and looked across to Theopolis Shepstone. 'So, you two will be going into Zululand?'

'Mm,' answered the Secretary for Native Affairs, 'indeed we will, though I had to convince John Lockley to come with me, didn't I?'

John Lockley nodded. 'Yes, sir, you did.' Then he grinned. 'Actually *ordered* might be closer than convinced. For while I've been down to Griqua Land and Kaffraria and over into Basuto Land, I haven't been into the heart of Zululand for over three years.' He looked across to Christopher. 'Yet I shall stop off for a bit of leave at the Tugela farm on our return, so I'm happy about that.'

'Yes,' smiled his uncle. 'In his absence, I'll journey on up there with Jane and Kate and we'll wait for him. After years of trying, we've finally convinced Kate to come to the farm.'

Theopolis Shepstone looked at John Lockley. 'Doesn't your wife like the interior?'

''Fraid not, sir. She thinks Pietermaritzburg's the interior.'

The men laughed and a few comments on the sensitivities of women followed.

'You'll all be at Bishopstowe next weekend, for the soirée in honour of our new Governor, Sir Benjamin, won't you?' asked George Russell.

There was general assent and Warwick Brookes added, 'I'm bringing a major, newly arrived, along with me, an interesting chap I met in Cape Town. He's already met Bishop Colenso and they get on well. In fact I asked him to join me here this afternoon.' He looked over their heads to the door. 'Why, here he is now.'

The four men with him turned and John Lockley gave an exclamation of delight as he recognised the newcomer. 'Heavens, isn't that Durnford, Anthony Durnford?'

'It is,' verified Brookes. 'Do you know him?'

'I certainly do. We correspond regularly, but I didn't expect him yet, I thought he was still down in King Williamstown.'

John Lockley hurried across the room to the soldier who stood in the doorway looking around.

'Anthony!'

Anthony Durnford's handsome face broke into a wide smile. 'John Lockley, my boy, how are you? I hoped I'd find you here in 'Maritzburg.'

Warwick Brookes came over to them. 'Anthony, you didn't tell me you knew John Lockley.'

Anthony Durnford gave an amused grin. 'Brookes, I didn't tell you everything.'

After the other introductions were complete, Anthony Durnford turned back to Shepstone, the Secretary for Native Affairs. 'I'm pleased to meet you, sir. I've been with the

Governor for most of the afternoon. Apparently I'm to accompany you into Zululand for this coronation of the new king.'

'Good, Major, we leave a week on Sunday.' Shepstone smiled. 'I believe your uncle, Captain George Durnford, relieved us in Durban in forty-two when we were surrounded by the Boers.'

Anthony Durnford grinned under his wide moustache. 'Yes. In fact an old officer at the Custom House in Durban passed all my baggage on the spot without even looking at it, once he knew my name.'

They had consumed two more rounds by the time Sergeant Browne behind the bar called, 'Last drinks, gentlemen, six o'clock coming up.'

When they left the club and came out into Chapel Street, a cold wind was blowing. Christopher had previously invited Anthony to dinner and now they said their goodnights to Brookes, Russell and Shepstone. Then Christopher turned to John Lockley. 'Are you coming now?'

'No, Uncle Chris, I'll call home first and see if Kate's ready.' Then he took Anthony Durnford by the arm. 'Go with Uncle Chris. Aunt Jane will make you welcome. I'll be along shortly.'

John Lockley hurried off in the opposite direction and turned into Maritz Street, passing a number of small houses before striding across an erf of seringas to his own small garden.

When he had first brought Kate to Natal, they had lived at Mimosa and he had gone up to the farm as much as he could. But since his long leave had ended and he was involved with army matters again, he needed to be in Pietermaritzburg, which was the seat of administration for the colony. And while Christopher and Jane actually preferred Mimosa and Durban, they too, in recent years, had spent more and more time at The Grange in Pietermaritzburg, for it was forty miles closer to the Tugela farm where they went for some months each year.

John Lockley was enjoying his work in the colony. There was so much for an engineer to do, and now that Anthony had arrived they would be able to get on with a lot more. He hurried around the back of the neat house, made from Christopher's bricks, and into the scullery where Umslopagas was peeling potatoes.

'*Saku bona*, Umslopagas.' John Lockley spoke Zulu whenever he could. Umslopagas replied in kind and when John Lockley asked where his wife was he pointed through the house. 'In parlour.'

When John Lockley called his wife's name she answered, 'Yes, I'm here.'

As he entered the warm room where a fire burned in the grate, Katherine looked up at him from where she sat reading the *London Women's Monthly*, a periodical sent out from England.

She was dressed in green and the bare olive skin of her throat gleamed in the firelight. Her jet-black hair was piled on top of her head. Her animated brown eyes rested on him as she said, 'Good evening, dear.'

He bent down and kissed her forehead. 'Good. I see you're ready. It's pretty cold out there, so we'd better take a carriage.'

A frown creased her forehead. 'Sweetheart, what are you talking about? I'm going to the recital at the town hall with Sophie and Tom King. Don't tell me you'd forgotten. Where're you going?'

'Oh Kate, we promised Uncle Chris and Aunt Jane we'd dine with them tonight.'

'John Lockley! I didn't promise them anything.'

'Hell, Kate. You did the same thing to me last week, springing that play-reading on me, and it was Sophie and Tom King then too.'

'John Lockley, darling,' she pouted, 'they've been ever so good to me while you've been away in those Godforsaken places. They've looked after me so well. Sophie and her sisters have had me to stay and everything. You should be grateful.'

She dropped her magazine and came to him, putting her golden arms up round his neck and kissing his mouth.

He protested, 'But ... why didn't you tell me?'

'I did, my love, but you never listen. I'll be eating every night with Uncle Chris and Aunt Jane when I come to the Tugela farm. Please go alone, there's a dear. I'll be home by midnight.'

'That's late, isn't it?'

She shook her head. 'No, there'll be supper afterwards and I'll have to stay. It'd be rude not to. They'll bring me home.'

John Lockley said no more. Resignedly he patted his wife on the shoulder, turned on his heel, walked back to the kitchen, called to Umslopagas that he would be at his uncle's, and passed out through the door and down the steps.

By the time he arrived at Jane and Christopher's the smile had returned to his mouth. He couldn't really blame Kate. She was alone a lot of the time and it was good that she had made friends. Of late, he'd been away with the 75th Regiment almost constantly.

And his wife was a very social person. He remembered when he first met her in Ceylon how she had rushed him here and there, and somehow managed to take his mind off all his wretched thoughts. He had enjoyed the way she was then, so he should not complain now.

When he entered The Grange, Christopher met him in the front hall. 'Where's Kate?'

'She had a previous engagement. I'd forgotten.'

Christopher did not look surprised. John Lockley's wife seemed to have a routine that did not always include her husband; and as John Lockley did not seem to mind, why should he?

'All right, m'boy. Come through. Major Durnford's on the terrace examining the night sky.'

Jane's eyebrows rose when she saw John Lockley was by himself, but she said nothing until she was alone with him after dinner.

'So Kate had somewhere else to go?'

John Lockley looked at his aunt sceptically. 'Now, Aunt Jane, you know how Kate is.'

'I do. But as her husband has been away a lot of late, I would have thought she'd be delighted to accompany him tonight.'

John Lockley did not reply immediately; he shook his head first. 'And I'm to leave her again in a week. Off to Zululand, with Shepstone and the Major, to crown Cetshwayo.'

Now this greatly interested Jane, and she forgot to pursue the Kate matter. She said, 'Really?'

When he had returned from Zululand three years ago John Lockley had told his aunt and uncle nothing. They knew he had gone there to see Darlengi and that something had happened between them. That was obvious, but John Lockley said he preferred not to speak of it. All he had said was: 'We're grown up now. We follow totally divergent lives; have nothing in common. While I shall always respect his intelligence and his abilities, we can no longer be intimate.'

Christopher and Jane accepted this, but it saddened them. Darlengi would always be part of their family and it seemed wrong that John Lockley did not share their view. Nevertheless they did not pry.

But now that John Lockley was entering into Zululand again, Jane felt she had a right to ask, 'Will you see Darlengi?'

'I don't know. I might. He's an important induna, after all.'

'Then I shall give you a letter for him. Dear, it's true, it's so very long since we've had any contact.'

Her nephew eyed her speculatively. 'All right, Aunt Jane,' he replied as Christopher and Anthony saved him by returning to the parlour.

'So, John Lockley,' said Anthony Durnford, 'it's time I returned to my lodgings. Shall we walk home together?'

The two men said their farewells to Jane and Christopher and strode along the darkened street under the overhanging branches of oaks and quinces. They were perfectly comfortable with each other, and spoke of Natal and its affairs.

'Oh, and I believe there's been trouble with a fellow called Langalibalele and his tribe of amaHlubi up near the Drakensburgs,' Anthony said as they passed by two large euphorbias outside a rundown bar.

'Yes, some of his younger men have not been registering their rifles. Apparently they've been paid in rifles up on the diamond fields. It's trivial really, though the authorities are making a lot of it.'

'You speak fluent Zulu, don't you?'

'Yes, and Xhosa and a number of native dialects. Somehow I've always found them easy to pick up. They say my Uncle Edgar was the same.'

At the corner of Commercial Road and Berg Street they halted. Anthony Durnford was only eight years older than John Lockley but his attitude was paternal, perhaps because he had lectured him at Chatham Engineering School; whatever the reason, it was to be so always.

'Well, lad,' he said. 'Let's meet this week to go over our requirements for the Zululand expedition. Would Tuesday at the fort suit you?'

'Yes, indeed. Thank you, Major. Goodnight.'

By the light of the moon John Lockley thought his friend was smiling, though with his large moustache it was hard to tell.

'And good night to you, Major.'

The younger man saluted.

It was almost half past eleven o'clock when John Lockley climbed into bed. He drifted off to sleep, only to wake and look at the clock an hour later.

Kate was not there.

He lay awake for a time and then he heard the front door click and her soft footsteps on the staircase. She was very quiet, and as she undressed she did not light the lamp.

He did not speak until she eased herself into the bed beside him.

'Kate, it must be one o'clock.'

'Oh! I thought you were asleep.'

'Obviously I'm not. Why're you so late?'

She moved closer to him, speaking gently. 'Sweetheart, it took longer than we thought, and then the supper wasn't ready on time.'

He felt anger swell in his chest, and then she was close beside him, her arms around him. She was naked.

'Logley, darling,' she whispered. 'I'm sorry. I didn't know it would be this late. But I had a nice time.'

It was always amazing to him that her pet name for him was 'Logley', for that was how Jettama had pronounced his name, and too, it had been Darlengi's intimate form of address to him.

Kate was pressing into him, her breasts on his chest, her sweet-smelling breath on his mouth.

'Come on, Logley darling. Let Katy take care of you.' Her hand snaked down inside his pyjamas; her mouth covered his, wet and inviting, and her body nestled into him.

Fifteen seconds later his hands were moving over her skin and he was returning her kisses.

At three o'clock the following Saturday afternoon Phoebe watched Frances 'Fanny' Colenso add more sugar to the punch she was making for the evening soirée at Bishopstowe.

'Taste it please, Phoebe,' the young woman called across the room to her friend and Phoebe stopped placing sweetmeats in a dish and came over. Fanny handed her a spoonful of the mixture and she swallowed it.

'Perfect, darling.'

The two young women managed to see each other about three times a year, and these events were an exciting part of their annual calendar. Fanny had been away in England, but had returned recently, and so Phoebe had come down to Bishopstowe to be reunited with her.

'Guess who's first to arrive,' called Agnes, the youngest Colenso sister, peeping through the front curtain to the drive.

'I know,' laughed Fanny. 'Mr Trimm, the surveyor, he's always first, so he can "survey" the alcohol and drink more than anyone else.'

Agnes giggled. 'Yes, you're right. Oh, I do hope he's brought his camera obscura with him.'

'He's so funny when he drinks too much.'

Soon other guests were filling the large parlour, and Phoebe and Fanny were called away to help Martha, the Hottentot cook, to count the cutlery for the evening's refreshment.

As Phoebe's nimble fingers ran along the knives, tallying them, her friend said, 'He's coming, you know. They were invited.'

'Thirty-four ... Yes, I know,' Phoebe answered, bringing her eyes round to Fanny's. 'I've never seen her, so my curiosity will finally be satisfied, I suppose.'

'I told you. She's all black hair and eyes. If I didn't know she was an English general's daughter I'd think she was Ceylonese. He did meet her there in Ceylon, didn't he?'

Phoebe sighed. 'Yes, Fanny darling, you *know* he did.'

Fanny had known about Phoebe's feelings for John Lockley since shortly after the day in 1870 when Phoebe had learned he was married. Fanny and her father had called into the Greytown mission on their way to Helpmakaar, and Phoebe, full of the recent event, had told her friend everything.

Fanny smiled good-naturedly. 'When did you last see him?'

Phoebe sounded a little on edge. 'Fanny, you know very well I haven't seen him since April last year when he called into the mission on his way to his Tugela farm.'

'Well, I think it's awfully sad.'

'What?'

'That he married her instead of you.'

Phoebe looked annoyed. 'Fanny, stop. You're outrageous. You shouldn't talk like that.'

'Why? No one can hear me but you.'

'That's not the point. You know I'm becoming engaged to Ben as soon as I get home, and it's not proper. Come on, let's finish the count.'

As the two young women spoke, Mr and Mrs John Lockley Harrison arrived in their carriage at the gate outside.

Kate wore a fashionable warm alpaca jacket and her black hair shone under her scarlet feathered hat.

A servant took the carriage and another ushered them into the hall where they removed their coats and headed into the spacious parlour to join the other guests. Warwick Brookes and Frank Colenso, one of the Bishop's sons, were at a corner table engrossed in a game of chess; and the Bishop himself was explaining an ancient Roman game called 'Duodecim scripla' which, as the name implied, was played on a board with twelve double lines and was similar to backgammon. There was much happy chatter, and soon Kate was laughing with Tom King in the middle of a small group playing charades.

John Lockley spoke for a time with Theopolis Shepstone about their coming journey on the morrow, and, when the host requested a private word with the Secretary for Native Affairs, he passed through the parlour and met his friend Captain Pat Boehm, holding two glasses of champagne.

'Just in time, John Lockley. I had this for my wife but she's disappeared.' He offered a glass and John Lockley took it saying, 'Let's go outside.'

'Capital idea, a bit of fresh air will suit me. How's the new major settling in?'

'Very well I think, but you can ask him yourself, for here he is.'

On the wide veranda Major Durnford stood talking to Fanny.

They all greeted one another, and John Lockley introduced Pat to Anthony.

Fanny smiled. 'Major Durnford and I were talking about England.'

Fanny's was not a robust constitution – John Lockley knew she had seen doctors in London – and as there was a cool wind blowing here on the veranda he put his arm in brotherly fashion around her shoulders. 'Shouldn't you be out of this wind, Fanny?'

'Yes, probably.'

Suddenly there was a commotion inside. 'The Governor's here. Sir Benjamin Pine's arrived.'

'I shall take Miss Fanny inside,' volunteered Anthony, and he took her arm and steered her across towards the door where Pat's wife stood beckoning her husband. 'Pat, quickly, come.'

'You go, Pat, I was presented to the newly arrived Governor last week; he was here before in the fifties so he should know the place.'

John Lockley turned back to the view. It would soon be dark. He pushed his hand through his hair as he looked across to the kraal where some of the converts and other natives lived close to the Bishop and his family. The Colensos called their home here Ekukanyeni, which meant 'the home of light' and the natives had responded in kind and called their small kraal Esibaneni 'the place of the torch'. John Lockley knew that a lot of the colonists, and many of those in power, thought John Colenso's views too liberal, but John Lockley simply saw him as a man before his time, showing empathy for all men: Bantu, white, and all the colours in between.

He stood there thinking, his gaze fixed on the table-topped mountain in the distance as it disappeared into the gloom; then, as he turned to go inside, he noticed two servants coming down the veranda lighting lanterns and placing them on tables against the wall. Suddenly from behind them, around a corner, flowed a swirl of pink silk in a matching pink jacket. He smiled.

'Phoebe.'

'Hello, John Lockley,' she replied, as she advanced towards him.

The sight of him made her heart race: she would never be able to regard him impartially. It was about fifteen months since she had last seen him and he looked a little older. Though he was as remarkable to look at as ever, with his moody purple eyes and his strong, regular features.

'What a pleasant surprise,' he said. 'Are you here long?'

'Two weeks, though one has passed already.'

'Yes, I heard you and Fanny were good friends.'

They were both silent for a minute and then he waved his hand at the horizon. 'Beautiful, isn't it?'

'Yes, it is,' she said, her eyes on the back of his sunbrowned hand. 'But there is something almost daunting in the way the African night descends so suddenly.'

He laughed then: a peculiar sound, mirthful and yet mirthless. 'I suppose so.'

She looked at him and he turned his eyes to hers. Subconsciously, they both felt the comfort, the perfect harmony between them here on the Ekukanyeni veranda as the July wind blew in their faces. Then Phoebe drew her eyes from his and looking into the distance said, 'I see Darlengi now and then. He asks about you.'

John Lockley gave a strange, frustrated sound. 'Phoebe, why do you tell me this?'

Suddenly there was a voice behind them. 'Darling, I've been looking everywhere for you.'

John Lockley turned. He coughed. 'Ah, Kate . . . Come here and meet a young lady I've known . . . well, since she was a little thing of about six.'

Kate smiled as she joined them, melting into her husband's side and slipping her arm through his.

'Kate, this is Miss Phoebe McLean.'

Phoebe held out her hand and Kate took it gingerly in her gloved fingers. 'Pleased to meet you, Miss McLean. So where on earth did my husband meet you?'

'On the ship that brought us to South Africa, the *Regent Three.*'

Kate looked up at John Lockley. 'How old were you?'

'Oh, about fourteen, I think.'

Kate did a quick calculation. 'Oh, so you've known each other over twenty years: how very diverting.' Then she trained her eyes on Phoebe. 'Have you lived here ever since?'

'I live in Greytown, with my parents. We run the Wesleyan mission there.'

Now Kate's eyes glazed over with indifference: a missionary's daughter? Oh dear, trust John Lockley to know such a person. The Colensos were bad enough, with their discussions on the wrongs done in the colony and Christian apologetics, but at least they were intelligent and could turn their minds to other topics. She tightened her grip on her husband's arm.

'Well, do excuse us, Miss McLean, but I want my darling boy to come inside now.'

Phoebe stood beside the railing as they moved away, her eyes following them until they were out of sight. Finally she had met the woman who haunted her most troubled dreams: she was very beautiful, just as everyone said she was; well, everyone except Fanny, but Fanny was too loyal. It was easy to see how a man would be captivated by Kate.

What Phoebe did not realise was that as she stood there on the Colensos' veranda, with the lantern light bathing her lovely face and glinting in her gentle brown eyes and radiating golden highlights in her fair curls, she was an equal to all the Kates who had ever lived: an equal and more.

Later in the evening Phoebe learned that three of the men in the room were to leave the next morning for Zululand. She had been with Jane and Michael Tallant in the second sitting room during a solo by Sophie King on the harp. As the melody ended and Sophie took her bows and Michael moved away to get refreshments for them, Jane said, 'So, Phoebe, will you be coming to have a day or two with us? You haven't spent time with us in years.'

She did not answer immediately; she was uneasy. There was always the possibility of running into John Lockley at The Grange, and while one side of her wanted that, the sensible side told her to be prudent. She replied, 'While I really would like to, Aunt Jane, I'm ... uncertain what the Colensos have planned.'

Jane smiled. 'I shall have a word to Mrs Colenso.' Then she looked at the pretty ormolu clock on the mantel shelf. 'I wonder what time John Lockley has to leave in the morning? Perhaps he and Kate should be going soon.'

'Why? Where's he going?'

Jane turned to her. 'Don't you know? There's to be a deputation into Zululand to crown Cetshwayo. They leave tomorrow, led by Mr Shepstone. John Lockley accompanies him, and the new major too, I believe.'

This put a whole new light on matters and Phoebe said, 'Aunt Jane, if I come to visit you, would it be possible to bring Fanny?'

'Of course.'

As Michael returned with drinks, Phoebe excused herself

and moved quickly through the guests. She hurried past Kate in the hallway drinking punch and giggling with Tom King. They were oblivious to her as she mounted the stairs to her bedroom. There she wrote a short letter and then returned to the gathering.

In the front parlour, amongst a rumble of happy chatter, she found Fanny surrounded by John Lockley, Major Durnford, Theopolis Shepstone and David Dale Buchanan, the founder and editor of the *Natal Witness* newspaper.

'Darling,' said Fanny as she came over. 'Here, sit by me. Mr Shepstone is telling us about the new conditions he's to give Cetshwayo when he crowns him.'

Phoebe was most interested. 'What are they?'

Theopolis Shepstone turned his keen eyes upon her. 'You should know the Zulu penchant for blood-shedding; you have lived amongst them.'

She nodded. 'Yes, it's true of some of them.'

'Well, the British Government has certain terms for supporting the new king, a few well-timed and needy rules: that the indiscriminate shedding of blood is to cease in the land; that no Zulu can be condemned without open trial; that no Zulu's life can be taken without the knowledge and consent of the king; and that for minor crimes death will no longer be the punishment, but loss of property will substitute.'

'They sound only proper in my opinion,' spoke up Fanny.

Mr Shepstone shook his head. 'It'll take years for such measures to truly catch on, Miss Colenso. All I want to do this time is to get the king to agree to them.' Then he sighed. 'I know he'll want to talk again about Boer aggression, and the Transvaal. I'm uncertain what to tell him; it's so hard to juggle all these factions.'

'Perhaps you should think about annexing the Transvaal, sir,' expounded Mr Buchanan. 'It seems the Boer administration has no real power or resources, or credit. If it were part of the Empire, you could control it.'

Mr Shepstone looked hard at the newspaper man, but said nothing. Then he took a deep breath, and, dropping his eyes to his fob watch, announced, 'Actually, if we're to depart 'Maritzburg at eight in the morning, I think we should be moving.'

'Yes,' agreed Anthony and John Lockley together.

Anthony turned to Fanny. 'Would you excuse us, Miss Colenso?'

'Of course, I'll just go and find my mother and father.'

As Fanny moved away, the Major said something to Phoebe and she laughed. Then suddenly the Major and David Buchanan laughed too, and though he had not heard what was said, John Lockley found himself joining in, for Phoebe's mirth was still as contagious to him as it had been when she was a child. He recalled all the times she had made him laugh. He found it hard to believe that this lovely woman had been the tiny Phoebe: the one he had saved when she fell from the rigging of the *Regent Three*; the little one he had carried on his horse in Durban and who had travelled with him to the Tugela farm. He recalled the tiny, sweet face of the child under the hat all those years ago. And, too, he remembered her as the bright and happy teenage girl. He had always thought of her as 'little Phoebe', yet here she was, a lovely woman grown . . . and still a ray of sunshine.

When the Major went off in search of the coats and Mr Buchanan in search of his wife, Phoebe came to John Lockley's side. She noticed the thoughtful expression on his face.

'Are you all right, John Lockley?'

'I was thinking how infectious your laugh is, and I was remembering you as a child.'

She pursed her lips. 'John Lockley, I'm a grown woman.'

And his eyes weighed her. 'Phoebe, yes, believe me. I see you are.'

They stood together silently for a few seconds, and she wondered what he was really thinking. Then she asked, 'Will you see Darlengi?'

'It's possible.'

'John Lockley, do you ever think about him?'

'What sort of question is that?'

Her eyes were trained on him, watching him closely. 'Well?' she asked. 'Do you?'

He looked down at her and for a moment a barrier rose up inside him. Then he answered with the simple truth. 'Every day,' he said.

She nodded very gently, and now she amazed him with her insight. 'You cannot back down now, can you? You told him you must both leave your brotherhood in the past, and must meet only as strangers in the future. You placed him in the position of *having* to accept it, because it was written, and you had gone. I know you have avoided going into Zululand. You've been everywhere else but not there. John Lockley, what happened between you two was a mistake.'

He stood regarding her. Somehow this young woman always managed to be his conscience. Then he gave a sneering sound. 'Phoebe, Phoebe, your intentions are admirable, but let's leave it at that.'

'He's very dear to me. He visits the mission every four or five months. We have few secrets.'

'What's that supposed to mean?'

'It means I know how he feels about a lot of things.'

He did not say any more. He just watched her with a sceptical look in his eyes.

She handed him the letter she had just written upstairs. 'Would you be kind enough to make sure Darlengi gets this ... even if it's not you who actually hands it to him.'

'Ah, Phoebe ... you and Aunt Jane. She, too, gave me a letter for him. I shall see that he gets them.'

'Thank you,' she said softly.

He hesitated for a moment, as if he wanted to say more, then, putting the letter in his inside pocket, he gave a tired smile. 'I'd better find Kate.'

It was obvious to all who noticed, and Phoebe was certainly one of them, that Mrs John Lockley Harrison left against her wishes. Her husband had to bundle her down the steps and into the waiting carriage. Tom King watched her leave with open regret.

It was almost midnight by the time Ekukanyeni was silent.

Before the two friends had gone to sleep Fanny had whispered across in the darkness, 'Life has not been kind to you, my darling, but I'm praying that a miracle will happen ... and do you know what?'

'What?'

'I think Major Durnford is the most wonderful gentleman I've ever met.'

CHAPTER TWENTY-THREE

The state entourage did leave Pietermaritzburg at the appointed time on Sunday morning. The group wended its way from Fort Napier in a long line of mounted volunteers, bandsmen, pack horses and equipment, and a unit from the Durban artillery drawing two field pieces to salute the new king. They made only fifteen miles a day, and crossed the Tugela into Zululand on the eighth of August. Heralds proclaimed their approach to many kraals, and chieftains escorted them through the countryside.

When the expedition arrived at the appointed spot they found no Prince Cetshwayo. He had gone further north. They waited on a hilltop near Mgungundhlovu, Dingane's old kraal, where he had massacred the Boer Retrief's party in 1836. All John Lockley could see now were marks on the ground where the huts once stood, and burnt-out clay fireplaces, and cattle tracks deeply worn into the ground.

They had been joined by a Norwegian missionary called Schroeder when they passed his mission at Eshowe, and now they waited a week while diplomatic correspondence took place between Shepstone and Cetshwayo. There had been a misunderstanding, and some of the Zulu coronation ceremonies had already taken place.

Finally a message came from the prince apologising for having gone further north, and the expedition now moved on across the White Umvoloosi River to Mahlabatini, where some indunas presented a gift of six oxen as reconciliation to the Secretary for Native Affairs. There, on the twenty-fourth of August, the party from Natal set up camp, and the coronation day was set for September the first.

That evening, Anthony Durnford came to John Lockley's tent. He pushed his fine sunburnt face through the tent flap. 'John Lockley, while we wait for the big day, I've decided to make an excursion through the wild country to the north and up the Black Umvoloosi River. Do you wish to join me?'

'I'd love to.'

So the two men set off with some native levies, including two Basutos called Elijah Kambula and Tennyson 'Tenny' Rama.

The following day they rested for luncheon near a broad river, though it was not high and would be simple enough to cross. When they went to remount, Elijah's foot slipped from the stirrup and he fell heavily to the ground. John Lockley and Anthony were standing beside him. The man was badly winded and they both lifted him and carried him to where he could rest against a rock.

Anthony felt his pulse. 'Elijah, lad, are you all right?'

'*Yeh bo*, boss.'

But he was shivering, and beads of perspiration had formed on his temples. John Lockley took off his jacket and covered the man with it even though he protested, 'No, sir, don't, boss.'

'I'll get a blanket,' said Anthony, hurrying over to a pack animal.

All the other levies now gathered around. They brought water for Elijah and made him comfortable.

John Lockley knelt down beside him and patting him on the shoulder said, 'We didn't get far, Elijah.'

The Basuto smiled up at him. 'Elijah be all right, boss.'

'Well, we'll wait until you are,' said John Lockley.

As it turned out they remained there for the rest of the day, and camped there that night, for Elijah was still feeling poorly. Though the following morning he was well again and the party proceeded.

They were away six days, living off the game they shot. They saw alligators and hippopotami, hyenas, quagga and many varieties of buck, but no lion, much to the pleasure of the levies. 'Lion not predictable,' explained Elijah, and John Lockley agreed. He still clearly recalled the day on the veld when Liben Cato's life had been in danger from the huge black-maned male.

As he thought of that day now, he looked over to his friend, who was a crack shot and had proved it on this excursion. 'You know, Anthony, I've seen domestic animals treated in such an appalling manner by their owners that I try to believe there is a perverse kind of justice going on in the wild, where, if an animal attacks a human, it's some kind of retribution for all its fellow creatures badly treated in servitude.'

His companion smiled. 'Well now, I see your point.'

It was the last night before they were to return to the main camp. Coincidentally they were again camped near the river where Elijah had slipped from his horse. John Lockley and Anthony were playing cribbage by lantern light in the tent they shared.

Anthony pegged the scores on the board. 'It's been an enjoyable time with you, John Lockley. Rising at five, breakfasting in the darkness, then marching a few hours, halting a few, and marching again. And I've liked our nights beneath the stars. Lucky with the weather ... only that one night of rain.'

John Lockley smiled across at his companion. He too had enjoyed these days. He had found Anthony decisive, kind, tolerant, sensitive and thoughtful. They had similar opinions on most matters and had been entirely comfortable together. Anthony Durnford had treated the Basutos properly, in a way John Lockley approved of: he felt proud that Anthony Durnford was his friend.

'I absolutely agree. I'd like to repeat this again if we can.'

'John Lockley, lad, I seem to remember at Chatham you used to talk constantly of a Zulu friend. You mentioned him in your early letters to me and then you ceased. Did something happen to him?'

John Lockley stopped dealing. For a few seconds he looked undecided, then said, 'Do you really want to know? For the truth's a long and complicated story.'

'I wouldn't have asked you if I didn't.'

So John Lockley told him. The whole long story: his boyhood with Darlengi; his love for Jettama; his close relationship with Ellen; the deaths of these two women he loved; his marriage and his return to Natal, and his presence at Mattana's deathbed; the repercussions with Darlengi; his life since. They played no more cribbage that night, and John Lockley ended his story with the words, 'So you see, I came back to Natal to find out about Nell's death, to evaluate my life, and simply to just ... come home. And I managed to stay on when my leave was over.'

Anthony Durnford's long brow wrinkled sympathetically. He had listened carefully and well and had been silent until now. 'Ah, lad, thank you for telling me. I now realise all this carries with it many and complex emotions; a tale I suspect you do not often relate.'

'I've never told it like this before . . . to anyone.'

'Then I am indeed honoured, and I shall keep your confidence. I understand now that our visit to Zululand is much more to you than just the crowning of Cetshwayo.'

'Yes, it is.'

The tent flap shook as the wind rose, and somewhere a hyena cried.

'You're a man on a search, John Lockley. Some of us are.'

'You too?'

Anthony smiled grimly. 'John Lockley, let me say to you that my life is not necessarily as I wish it.'

'I will not pry, Anthony.'

"I know you won't. But for tonight I want to tell you a little: similar to you, there were things I did not tell you in our communications over the years. One thing you do already know is that I was married in Ceylon, as you were; though you at least waited until you were a captain, I was too young. Then I lost a son and daughter in infancy. The truth is that now my wife and I are alienated.' He sighed. 'Maybe we were too much apart; suffice it to say she found other interests. I'm left with one little girl whom I love dearly. My family are raising her in England.' He brought his eyes up to his friend's. 'I've never seen active service, in all my years in the army. Perhaps I want to prove something.' He smiled to himself. 'I'm a reformed gambler, lad, and here I am at forty-three in Africa.' Then he smiled directly at his companion, and his handsome, pale eyes narrowed. 'Perhaps we should leave it there for tonight.'

John Lockley nodded. 'Thanks, Anthony. I will hold your trust as you hold mine. It's been a good night.' He leant across the small table and extended his hand, which the other man took and held some little time, before he let go with the words, 'Yes, it's been a good night.'

Five minutes later John Lockley was taking a turn around the camp as was his way before retiring. A cool wind blew, chasing clouds across the bright moon. As he passed by a thicket of aloe and wait-a-bit thorns, he heard voices coming from the other side. They spoke in their own language but he understood.

'What sort of chiefs have we found? They do not despise us, like the others.'

'*Yeh bo*, Chief Harry-son gave me his coat. And Chief Durnford did not go off and leave me when I was sick. They are very different.'

'Yesterday, Chief Durn-ford said to all of us that we are the same as him, that we have the same flesh and blood, and that a man's colour is nothing; it's his heart that matters. And as he spoke, Chief Harry-son smiled and nodded his head. I could not believe this.'

'I could not believe this either.'

Slowly, stealthily, John Lockley moved on by. Before he entered the tent, he ran his hands back through his waving hair and smiled; a gentle, kind smile of gratification.

Two days later, Cetshwayo was crowned by the Secretary for Native Affairs, and Zululand once more had a strong and powerful king.

John Dunn was there, driving a carriage drawn by four grey horses. Around the huge pen he sped and took his moment of glory.

John Lockley stood close to Anthony behind Theopolis Shepstone, and several of Cetshwayo's indunas stood behind him. John Lockley looked for Darlengi, but he could not see him.

Now the five thousand Zulu warriors who were in attendance spread out over the arena and, as their king was led out to stand before them, raised their voices in a series of marvellous resonant chants; a Zulu war song. John Lockley had never heard one and his skin tingled at the raw power of it. He looked across to Anthony, who obviously felt the same way.

Then the prince walked along a carpet laid down for the occasion and Shepstone gestured for John Lockley to remain at the far end of it, which he did. At the other end was a chair of state and beside it a less pretentious one for the Secretary of Native Affairs. Shepstone took Cetshwayo inside a tent erected for the occasion, leading him back out a few minutes later with a golden and scarlet mantle on his shoulders and a crown upon his head. The prince was now a king.

They sat in the chairs of state and the Durban Artillery fired a seventeen-gun salute. There was much joyous shouting of the royal salute 'Bayete!', an abbreviation of *ma ba lete* which meant 'let them bring' and referred to *letting them bring* their troubles to the All-Powerful One.

Now the men on horseback rode in formation through the throng as the band struck up 'The Bay of Biscay'. They rode to the side of the arena where they dismounted and left their horses in a line to move up and stand either side of the red carpet.

Theopolis Shepstone stood again and, after praising the new king, took out his proclamation and read out to Cetshwayo the conditions which he had recited to his listeners at Ekukanyeni.

At the end of the reading, as Cetshwayo nodded his head and put his mark upon the proclamation, the five thousand assembled warriors suddenly stood and struck their shields with their assegais and knobkerries. It was such a sudden and sharp action and the rumbling noise was so ear-splitting that the unattended horses were startled into an instantaneous stampede. They broke to the left and charged towards the king and Shepstone.

There was a unified gasp of horror as the people realised the danger.

Only three men had a chance of acting: one was Corporal Cooke, the only man left with the animals, another was John Lockley, who stood alone at the far end of the long carpet, and the third was a Zulu induna who had been moving up from his brothers to present Shepstone with a gift of an ivory tusk.

The three men acted as one and dashed forward to leap on the three leading animals, grabbing at them and managing to turn their thudding hooves from trampling the alarmed king, Shepstone and their retainers.

Even as the animals came under control, there was a protective surge forward by the five thousand Zulu warriors, and noise and general mêlée all about. As the horses came to a standstill John Lockley came face to face with the Zulu induna who had helped him.

'Darlengi!'

'John Lockley.'

Their eyes met as John Lockley ran his fingers back through his hair. There was a second when they both acknowledged

340

what they had seen all those years ago on the banks of the Intalalala River . . . that glorious moment of sweet recognition. They began to smile, and then, as if a blind were thrust down simultaneously on the windows of their eyes, they both remembered the letter written after Mattana's death.

Each drew his eyes away from the other's face and turned resignedly and moved apart.

As the flow of bodies and horses moved around him John Lockley found himself being pounded on the back in admiration by Anthony Durnford and a number of the other men, and soon the assembly calmed down and order was called for.

This was followed by a huge feast, prepared by the Zulu women, and after hours of merrymaking, and eating, and drinking tshwala, a grain beer, the new king withdrew with his household to rest, and calm fell on the afternoon.

Around five o'clock, the Durban Volunteers gave an exhibition of horse-riding, and then some of them rode over to a small kraal to see a woman who was reported to be Shaka's sister. Later, as Mr Shepstone had predicted, Cetshwayo asked for a private discussion with him about Boer aggression.

That night, back in the British camp, Anthony and John Lockley sat drinking coffee. Anthony swallowed his last mouthful, and, turning to his friend, tapped his knee with his empty mug and asked, 'Was Darlengi there today?'

John Lockley's eyes lifted quickly. 'Yes, he was there right enough. He was the one who dropped the elephant tusk to help Cooke and me stop the stampede.'

His friend made a rumbling sound in his throat. 'Funny, I had a strange feeling about that man. So that was Darlengi. Do you realise there's something similar about you both, that you look alike?'

John Lockley's eyes met Anthony's. Mattana had said that, though he did not realise that Ellen had thought so, and Phoebe too. 'Perhaps we do, Anthony. Perhaps we do.'

'Did you speak with him?'

'No. It was brief. Brief and . . . awkward.'

The following day Theopolis Shepstone, along with John Lockley and Anthony Durnford, made a formal farewell to Cetshwayo, who arrived from his isiGodlo to say goodbye with a zebra skin around his shoulders and a smile upon his face. The coronation had been a coup for him. There had always been the chance that some of the other powerful Zulu chieftains could oppose him, but not so now that he had been given the support of the Natal Government and the Great White Queen.

He was followed by his entire council, amongst them Darlengi. Theopolis greeted the king and then Darlengi, whom, of course, he knew. And while Theopolis Shepstone was aware of the relationship that Darlengi had shared with John Lockley as children, he was unaware of the current circumstances.

John Lockley did not look at Darlengi; Darlengi did not look at John Lockley.

The farewell was conducted entirely in Zulu, for Shepstone and John Lockley spoke it fluently. The new king lifted his staff, which was intricately carved with replicas of fingers on the handle and was identical to the one Shaka had carried. 'Thank you, Somtseu. Cetshwayo rejoices that the English and the Zulus continue as friends and eat of the same oxen and join hands as brothers.' He brought his staff down to his side and spoke briefly to Darlengi and a half-brother, Usiwetu, before he faced back to Shepstone. 'And now that we have discussed the Boers that swarm over Zulu territory like the ants do across the dead carcass of the water buffalo, we have *again* attained your promise of action. Just as we did when my strong arm, Darlengi, came and spoke with you this many summers ago.' He held up three fingers. 'Unless something is done, I fear that soon blood may be spilt, my Father.'

Shepstone took a deep breath: this had all been addressed yesterday. 'Yes, King Cetshwayo, as I said yesterday, this is a delicate affair. I know and sympathise with the bitter feeling you carry towards the Boers. They frequently seize Zulu territory and we have formally objected to such a thing happening. Please do nothing rash. I repeat, I will do all in my power to approach the Transvaal government and to settle the matter.'

They bowed to each other and the British deputation left the great kraal.

As the party wound over the green hills of Zululand, Anthony rode up beside John Lockley.

'Did I hear the king mention Darlengi's name in that last speech he made?'

John Lockley turned in the saddle and, lifting his hand to shade his eyes, answered, 'Yes. He said Darlengi carried a message about the Boers to Shepstone three years ago.'

'They have a bloody history, don't they?'

'Yes, there's no love lost between the Zulus and the Boers. Our last governor, Keate, tried to help and was in touch with the government of the Transvaal but never heard back. You know how these things drag on.'

All the way back to the Tugela there was a wonderful showing of gratitude from the Zulu people to the whole expedition. Families came from many miles to give thanks to Somtseu and his brothers for the honour that had been bestowed by the British in crowning their new king.

On the sixth of September they crossed the Tugela and John Lockley left the party to continue on westwards to the farm.

Anthony grinned under his wide whiskers. 'When will you be back in 'Maritzburg?'

'Perhaps a month or so.'

His friend took off his wide-brimmed hat and slapped John Lockley affectionately on the shoulder. 'Good-o. Travel safely.'

John Lockley made excellent time without the trappings of the expedition and covered the twenty-five miles to the farm by just after dark. As he rode up over a low hill and brought his horse to rest on the crest he could see the gleam of the house's interior lanterns.

His mind had been on Darlengi for much of the ride. The way he had looked at him. He knew they had both experienced the same astonishing rush of kinship that had always been there. And he knew too that they had then automatically put up their defences. He had given the Norwegian missionary Schroeder the letters from Phoebe and Aunt Jane. The missionary said he would deliver them to Darlengi.

He rode very slowly down the hill and through the gate in the stone fence to the front of the house. He had only just dismounted when he heard the joyful call from Christopher.

'He's here! John Lockley's here!'

And out of the house came the General, Jane and Kate, followed by Tilly carrying a lantern and exclaiming, 'About time too. We've been expecting you a week since.'

The homecoming was a happy event.

Tilly presented them with a delicious dinner of pumpkin soup, roasted hen and corn dumplings, followed by a sweet sago pudding. They all stayed up late that first night, listening as John Lockley related to his fascinated audience the details of the coronation. They listened with rapt expressions.

No one asked if he had seen Darlengi, yet he could see that his father, aunt and uncle wanted to do just that. So, as he related his tale and arrived at the place where he had helped stop the stampede, he said, 'The induna who helped me, or whom I helped, whichever way one looks at it, was Darlengi.'

'Did you speak with him, son?' asked the General, voicing the thoughts of Jane and Christopher.

'There was no real opportunity, Father. He was soon swallowed up in the thousands of people who where there.' He looked down at his hands, and then up to meet Jane's eyes. 'Though I made sure he got your letter, Aunt Jane. Oh, and Phoebe gave me one for him as well.'

Kate had been yawning as her husband made his last statement, but suddenly her demeanour changed. 'When did she give you a letter?' she asked.

'At the Colensos, dear, the evening of the soirée.'

'Oh.'

Later, while Kate prepared for bed, John Lockley took his now customary walk in the night.

He moved across the side of the house and down past the stables to the little grove which had been cultivated around the white painted headstone.

He stood there as he always did when he came to the farm, and whispered, 'Nell, darling, I've seen Darlengi. He looks wonderful. I get more accustomed to . . . everything, as the years pass. Sleep well, my dear, dear sister.'

Then he turned and made his way slowly back towards the house, where he ran into his uncle who had been walking last thing at night for the better part of thirty years.

'John Lockley, I didn't know you took a stroll at this time of the night.'

'I have done ever since I first arrived in Ceylon, Uncle Chris.' Then he grinned. 'Must have caught the habit from you.'

Christopher laughed. 'Perhaps. By the way, your father and I like to check the fence lines now and then, so how about coming with us tomorrow?'

'I'd like to.'

'Dirk wants to accompany us, though he's really not well enough to ride far. George Travers is doing a fine job here these days.'

'Yes, Tilly told me Dirk has found it difficult letting George take over, but he's had no alternative.'

'True, I've let Dirk keep the title of farm manager for the time being, but I've given George the position in all but name.'

'I can't see old Dirk and Tilly ever leaving here, can you?'

'No, and they don't have to, ever, this is their home. Dirk just has to understand that running the place is beyond him now.'

'And does he?'

'He's coming round. He's older than your father, you know, and while he's a hardy old devil, his rheumatism just won't let him get about like he used to, and you can't run a property like this if you're not mobile. Anyway, I'll always make sure he has something to do.'

John Lockley nodded. 'And by the way, I'd like to spend some days travelling to the kraals and up the Intalalala while I'm here. Is old Chief Unondo still alive?'

'I believe so.'

Before they separated, Christopher put his arm around his nephew's shoulder. 'We all realise that you've become estranged from Darlengi. But I know that it's not just because you've grown up. I know you both better than that. You made that one journey when you arrived back in seventy. Told none of us where you were going, but I knew it was to see him. You've been back in Natal for three years and have avoided going into Zululand again until now. Perhaps sometime you'll tell me the real reason for your estrangement. It saddens me that the two men I regard as . . . sons . . . have become alienated.'

They had come round to the front of the house. There was a gentle breeze drifting up from the Tugela and peace was all about. In the light of the half-moon John Lockley turned to face his uncle.

'Funny, but I so clearly remember the night you found me here,' he gestured to the veranda, 'all those years ago when I thought I had to leave him and return to Durban. And you said there was nothing stopping us from taking him back with us. I was so very, very happy.' He made a short, sad sound. 'What a difference twenty years brings.'

'Why does it, John Lockley? Why?'

'Sir, I've never spoken of it, for there is something which I have never wanted you and Aunt Jane to know.'

'Why? Is it so bad?'

'You would not think so; you are so tolerant and ... fair. And no, it's not bad. It's what happened because of it.'

'Then why hide it?'

'There are those who would be hurt by it. I think, for one, Aunt Jane would be hurt.'

Christopher nodded slowly. 'Ah, then there's the rub. I have no secrets from your aunt. Anything you relate to me, she in due course will know.'

'That's just it, sir. I've always known that. And I truly don't want to upset her. She's lived with what she has thought to be the truth, all these years.'

'About what?'

'About my sister's death, Uncle Chris.'

'And it changed your feelings to your brother?'

'It did at the time. Because ... of what I believed.'

'And now?'

'I don't know.'

Christopher pulled the younger man down gently on to the steps beside him. 'All right, John Lockley. You've had your reasons for remaining silent. But don't you see that it hurts your aunt to think you and Darlengi are alienated?'

'Yes, I understand that. But there are others, too, to be hurt. Others who are not like you and Aunt Jane.'

'Would these ... others, ever have to know? You seem to have kept your secret pretty well so far.'

'No. They would never have to know.'

'Then perhaps you judge your aunt wrongly. She's a strong woman, has made homes in a wilderness and given them grace and beauty, and earned the respect of many. She's not easily hurt.' Then he patted John Lockley on the knee. 'But take your time, my boy, feel right about it. We've waited years, so what's a little longer? When, and if, you are ready, tell us when we're all together, eh? You and me and your aunt.'

Christopher Nelson had always been a father to him: given him the best of counsel, and, by example, taught him to be honest and fair-minded. He turned to him in the cool September night as the clouds chased each other across a half-moon, and answered as a son, "Yes, sir, I will do exactly that.'

Then they stood and mounted the stairs together.

Inside the long hallway Christopher stood alone after John Lockley had departed. He thought about the two young men and hoped fervently that one day they would resolve whatever it was that lay between them. It was strange, but Ellen's death had been on his mind tonight as well. But then it often was when he was here at the farm: Ellen seemed to be somehow closer to him here, and yet she had never cared for the place. For all these years he had felt something was wrong about Ellen's death. He remembered the night before her marriage when Mannie had come to him and told him that when Ellen had found Darlengi had departed from The Grange early that morning, the blood had drained from her face. Now why would that have been?

He remembered going up to his niece's room that night to find her reading the Bible. He recalled the strange look on her face and how she had asked him, 'Marriage is forever, isn't it?' It was such an odd thing to say.

And then the darling had died in that terrible way, falling from the rocks. The first time he and Jane had come to the farm after Ellen's death he had questioned Dirk and Matilda about it. There had been no hope of asking Michael anything, he had been too distraught. Dirk had nothing to say but Matilda had told him Ellen was 'not herself' the entire honeymoon. That there seemed to be a strain between the newlyweds and that the day before they were to go home Ellen had been acting very strangely. The housekeeper had said Ellen had asked her about Darlengi. This Matilda could not understand, as 'Miss Ellen had always been discourteous towards him.'

She said Ellen had surprised her by saying she never meant to treat Darlengi badly. That she had estranged Darlengi only because she was frightened not to.

Christopher stood for a time alone in the front hall. What did all this mean? And now John Lockley had intimated there was more to know about Ellen's death.

He sighed as he shook his head sadly and ambled along to his room.

A few minutes before, when John Lockley had pushed his own bedroom door open, his wife's voice had risen peevishly from the bed.

'Why on earth have you been so long? I've been waiting.'

'Oh darling,' he replied as he took off his shirt, 'I ran into Uncle Chris out there.'

'Well, I hope it doesn't happen every night. Here you are home, finally, after all these weeks, and I'm waiting here all alone.' She sat up slightly in the lamplight with her bottom lip protruding sulkily.

He came to her. She looked up at him with a severe expression, and then held out her arms saying, 'Logley, how could you do this to Katy?'

The roundness of her breasts shone golden in the lamplight as he bent down to her and her slim arms encompassed him.

'Sweetheart, I'm sorry,' he said, before he found her waiting mouth.

At the great kraal in Zululand, Darlengi moved gently from Thulile's side and lit a candle. She slept soundly as he took the letters which the missionary, Schroeder, had given him and opened the one from Aunt Jane and read it once more.

It spoke of many things: of the Tugela farm, of how their businesses in Durban and Pietermaritzburg prospered, of Christopher's bad back and of how good it was to have John Lockley home. But it was the last paragraphs which he had read over and over again.

We have not seen you since the day before our dear Ellen's wedding. Do you realise it is eight years? We know you have been once or twice since to see Matilda, and that Phoebe has your company occasionally, but do you avoid us? We have not had a letter from you in well over a year.

Your Uncle Christopher and I would truly love to see you again. Can you ever come to the Tugela farm? We will be there for August, September and all of October this year. John Lockley is coming too after Cetshwayo's coronation. And your Uncle Chris and I have decided

348

definitely to be there next year for June, July and August and possibly September.

Darlengi, the machinations of Zulu politics cannot be so consuming that you have no time for us.

Please come any time in the months mentioned above. We miss you.

> With much love,
> Aunt Jane.

Didn't she realise he was a Zulu induna? That things were not as simple as they used to be? How could she manipulate him so? To make him feel he *must* come to them?

He moved to the hut entrance and bending over passed out into the night air. There was a half-moon shining down on him. He walked slowly to the palisade gate. There he admitted to himself that Aunt Jane was not really attempting to manipulate him. She just truly wanted to see him.

Oh, Aunt Jane. I remember everything. It is etched into my brain. Of course I want to come and see you. Very badly. Yet I cannot come now. I cannot be there with John Lockley, as much as my heart wants to. I am not sure when I can come.

He let himself out through the gate and closed it behind him as a couple of the kraal dogs came running up to happily leap upon him.

He stood looking out through the clean, crisp night. He liked the darkness and the loneliness. Clouds chased the half-moon across the sky and there was a cool breeze. He found himself thinking of all those who had mattered to him. He thought of Mattana, his one true mother, who had nurtured him and brought him to manhood; he thought of Jettama, struck down before she had a chance at life; he thought of Thulile lying asleep, his good and simple wife, and he felt the comfort of her gentleness warm his heart. He thought of the Ice Princess dead and gone eight years since, and he was aware of the place that was hers in his heart; it still ached. He thought of Aunt Jane and Uncle Christopher and their compassion and care for him. He thought of Tilly, the one Boer in all of Africa he truly loved. He thought of Kayo, loyal Kayo, his friend. Then, finally, he thought of John Lockley, his brother, the stranger. He relived the short moment with him at the recent coronation.

349

Then he looked up at the sky and the immense endlessness out there. Humans were so insignificant, and yet attended to every petty detail of their lives as if it were actually important. He gave a grim smile. He supposed there was nothing else they could do. Men and women were trapped in the knowledge that life was a riddle without an answer.

He remained a little longer watching the silent valley and thinking, listening to the noises of the African night, before he returned to his kraal and his home.

CHAPTER TWENTY-FOUR

It was two weeks after John Lockley had arrived at the farm that Kate and Jane sat on the veranda together in the late afternoon. They waited for the menfolk to return from a day of inspecting the small herds of cattle and sheep.

Kate had been restless all afternoon. Jane knew she missed Pietermaritzburg and the happenings of the town, the gossip, and the night life. Finally she had started to read *Under the Greenwood Tree*, a novel by a new author called Thomas Hardy. Her friend Sophie King had brought it back with her from England last Christmas and had lent it to Kate to bring to the farm. Now she put it down in her lap, and turning her eyes to Jane asked, 'Why did you never have children?'

For a second Jane was taken aback. Kate had a way of doing that with people. The young woman often said outrageous things in company, which to Jane seemed intended to startle. She sometimes thought Kate's behaviour was attention-seeking.

But Jane was ever generous, and, while it was none of Kate's business, the older woman put down her knitting and answered calmly, 'Kate, I was thirty-six when I married Christopher twenty years ago, and he has always said to me that I was far too precious to risk on a mere offspring. Perhaps there may come a time when medicine is such that thirty-six, and older, is not too old to bear a first babe, but Christopher always thought it was. Dear, it's true, and we are perfectly happy as we are.' She smiled across at the younger woman. 'Kate, children don't make a marriage work. In fact, they often do the opposite.'

Kate nodded. 'Yes, I dare say that's true, and in any case you had John Lockley and poor Ellen to mother, didn't you?'

'Yes, I did . . . and Darlengi for a time.'

Kate looked amazed. 'Did you think of him like that? Like your own?'

Jane was silent for a few moments, her eyes on the Tugela where the evening sun threw its last rays. 'Yes. And I still do.'

'Well, I never knew that. I find that quite strange.'

'Oh, and why's that?'

'I don't know. I suppose because he's a Zulu.'

'He has always been just Darlengi to me.'

'You still write to him, don't you?'

'Yes.'

'Does he write to you?'

'Yes, though we've heard nothing for over a year. But Matilda has. A letter was delivered to her just a few months ago.'

Now Kate really looked surprised. 'Matilda? Your Boer housekeeper?'

'Yes, she and Darlengi have always been close.'

Kate stood and walked to the veranda rail. 'This is a very peculiar household.'

Jane spoke almost to herself. 'Perhaps it is, but I like it this way.'

A minute later Kate lifted her silk-covered arm. 'Look, here come the men. I'm going down to meet them.' She picked up her visite from the back of the chair and threw it round her shoulders.

Within a few minutes she was down at the stables and her husband dismounted into her arms.

'John Lockley, I've been so bored.'

'I'm sorry, darling, but guess what?' His eyes were shining. 'There are over a hundred cattle now, and the sheep. Why, they're almost ready for the spring lambing. It'll be soon. Won't you like to see the little lambs when they come?' He chucked her gently under the chin.

'I don't know. There's nothing to do.'

Christopher laughed. 'Kate, you could have come out with us today.'

Kate turned her seductive eyes to her uncle-in-law. 'I hate to ride out around animals where there are flies and stinging things. I'd prefer to stay home.'

'Well, Kate,' he answered, 'your choice.'

As Jemby led the animals away, John Lockley said, 'Come now, let's all go to the house and we'll clean up and then have a drink on the veranda watching the sun set. How's that?'

'That'll be great,' replied Christopher.

'All right,' said Kate.

Later that night, before retiring, John Lockley took a brief walk. At his wife's insistence, he had agreed to keep his late-night walks short. When he came back to her, she was sitting up in bed reading by the light of the paraffin lamp.

She put her book down and slipped out of bed as he began to undress. She came to him, and as he took his shirt off, stood behind him and slipped her hands under his arms and round to the flat of his stomach, kneading his skin with her fingers. He could feel the wetness of her tongue on his back.

'Katy,' he laughed, 'let me get undressed first.'

'Mmm, you smell so good,' she whispered. Then she moved back on to the bed and lay watching him remove his clothes.

'Your aunt told me the oddest thing today.'

'Oh? What was that?'

'That she thought of that Zulu, Darlengi, in the exact same way that she thought of you and Ellen.'

'Why was that odd?'

'Oh, no! Are you all the same? She only had him under her roof for two years. How could she possibly think of him like her own flesh and blood? He's black.'

John Lockley's eyes grew instantaneously hard in the lamplight. 'What has colour got to do with it? Kate, don't talk about something you don't understand.'

'For heaven's sake. You hate him. You told me you had grown apart. That your lives were so opposite that you had nothing in common. That he meant nothing to you now.'

'I lied.'

'What?'

Her husband came over to the side of the bed and stood looking down at her. 'Kate, sometimes people say the opposite of what truly lies in their hearts. They shouldn't, but they do.' He held out his forearm, showing her the scar on it. 'You've seen this many times and I have always told you it was a burn from when I was a boy. Well, that's true, but in fact it's a brand. Burnt into my flesh and Darlengi's flesh at the same time, by a red-hot assegai. To say to the world that we were forever brothers. Forever! We were mere kids, but the brand doesn't go away ... and nor do the feelings. So many things have happened, so very many things. But Kate, understand this. I may not see him, I may not speak of him, but I will *never* hate him. Even if I said I did, I didn't.'

Kate's eyes were wide in amazement. 'What things happened? Tell me.'

He was standing over her, looking at her with an enigmatic expression. He lifted his branded arm to take hold of the bed post and the scar gleamed in the lamplight. 'I've never told you, for it was impossible to talk about. Things happened that made me feel great pain, anger.' His look softened upon her for a moment and he leant forward and touched her hair tenderly. 'You helped me over it all, even though you didn't realise.'

It was obviously a struggle for him to speak of it now; but he thought the time had come to tell his wife certain things. She could see the fight going on within him.

'You see, Darlengi loved my sister ... And I loved *his* sister, and she was killed in front of *my* eyes, actually in *my* arms.'

'What?' Kate was speechless for some seconds, then she found her voice. 'You loved a Zulu girl?'

'Yes.'

'When?'

'I met her when I was about fifteen. She was killed when I was twenty-three.'

'What was her name?'

'Jettama.'

'She was killed ... in your arms?'

'Yes, with an assegai through her back, by a jealous man who meant to kill me instead. She gave up her life to save me.'

'Oh God. How awful.'

'Yes, it was.'

John Lockley turned abruptly away to pour water in to the bowl on the washstand. Silently he began to wash.

354

A minute later Kate's voice came sensuously across the room. 'John Lockley, did you . . . you know . . . did you? With her?'

He continued to wash and did not turn round. 'Kate, don't. This isn't the time. Not everything relates to sex.'

She was silent for a time, then she said, 'I want you to answer me. I have a right to know. Did you do it with her?'

He knew she would not let up on this and through clenched teeth he replied, 'Yes.'

She did not speak again and when he had finished and dried himself he turned around to see her standing naked. She had a near to perfect body and the lamp at the side of the bed reflected golden light across her flat stomach and down her smooth thighs and slender legs. The brown nipples of her high, full breasts stood out as she pushed them forward, hands on her hips.

'Was she as beautiful as me?'

'Don't, Kate. It's silly.'

'Was she as beautiful as me?'

He went to pass by her to his side of the bed, but she barred his way and put her hands up around his neck and kissed his lips.

'I knew you had plenty of women in Ceylon, but I never knew I had any real competition until now. Answer me. Was she as beautiful as me?'

Deliberately he removed her hands from around his neck, moved to the bed and climbed in.

She crawled across the sheets and leant over him, her breasts hanging down above his face.

'Don't, Kate.'

She remained where she was. 'I asked you if she were as beautiful as me.'

He turned away. 'You're similar.'

'Similar? In what way? Tell me?'

'I don't know. In shape, in size.'

Now she pulled him back to face her and straddled him.

'Did she make love as well as me?'

'Stop it, Kate.'

She bent forward enticingly. 'Come on, tell me. Did she make love as well as me? Did Jettama make love as well as Katy?'

Her hands were down upon him, and now her mouth was on his. Then she dragged her lips down across his chest, her tongue caressing his skin. 'Come on, Logley, did she make love as well as me?'

He did not answer. She moved back to kiss him again and to suck his earlobe and whisper, 'Come on. You love it. Answer me. Did she make love as well as Katy does?'

Suddenly he sat up and pushed her off his body. 'I said, don't! I won't allow you to make a mockery of her. The sex act doesn't fix everything, Kate. I think you need to learn that.'

He swung his feet down to the ground and pulled on his trousers.

Her dark eyes glowered at him from the bed. 'You'll be back. You can't resist it.'

'Can't I?' he said quietly, moving across the room. 'Sleep well, Kate.'

'You pig!' she called as he closed the door and walked down the hall.

Matilda was surprised the following morning, when at half past six she took John Lockley his usual early morning tea, and found only his wife asleep in the bed. Kate did not rise until ten as a rule, and Tilly backed out of the room and closed the door.

When John Lockley came into breakfast, his voice was artificially bright. 'Good morning, Tilly.'

'Well, good morning, and I suppose you'll be dying for a cup of tea?'

He looked sideways at her. 'Come on, Tilly, you know I slept in the spare room. You could have brought my tea in there.'

'I didn't want to embarrass you.'

'What do you think you're doing now?'

She did not answer as she placed his cup in front of him. Then, turning away, she said, 'I've trained Gladys to make the best bacon, tomatoes and eggs north of Pietermaritzburg. That's what you're having this morning, and a sausage too.'

He watched her pass into the kitchen and then turned to look out into the gleaming African morning. He thought about Kate and last night, and there was an empty feeling right through him. He had actually been going to tell her all those intimate, difficult things that lived in his heart, and she had understood so little about him that she had turned it into a stupid sexual contest between herself and a dead girl. He felt very disappointed about that. There was a loneliness inside him this morning for he recognised there was so much he could never share with his wife.

When Christopher and Jane arrived soon afterwards he forced himself to be animated, and by the time the General had come in for breakfast he was almost normal.

He did not see his wife until the evening, for he was out again with Christopher on the Tugela property all day.

Kate did not rise until after ten o'clock and then she was moody and uncommunicative. Jane knew there was something wrong, for while Kate was often this way, today she was positively sulking.

During the morning, Jane had been helping Matilda do an inventory of all the Manchester goods, and at lunch time she sought Kate out only to be told by her that she preferred not to eat.

'Kate, what's wrong?'

'Nothing.'

Jane decided not to persevere with this. 'If you want anything later, Gladys will make it for you. I'm going down into the storage sheds to grind some coffee.'

'I don't know why you do that when you have the Boer woman and the blacks here to do it.'

'Kate, Kate, I do it because I like to, and the *other folk* who work here have plenty to keep them busy.'

When Jane returned, she was informed by Matilda that Miss Kate was in her room. And there she remained until the hour of five, when she came out on to the side veranda and down the steps and sauntered over to the first of the paddocks where the General played golf. He was now over seventy, and had not gone out riding today. He had been playing golf since he had been a young man, when his mother's Scottish cousins had taught him the game. George Travers, the Scottish foreman who had worked at the farm for twenty years, had been playing with him for a couple of hours but had just departed to make sure that the evening milking was taking place.

Kate came up to where the General was putting his gutta-percha balls – which he had specially sent out from London –

along a piece of flat grass and into a four-inch-wide hole made in the turf.

'Well helloa, Kate. Haven't seen you all day.'

Kate's bottom lip protruded. She looked steadily at the General. 'I want to go back to Pietermaritzburg.'

'Oh, do you?'

'General, your son is out all day, every day, and I'm left here to fend for myself.'

He looked up before he hit the next putt. 'But you could go with him. I've heard him ask you many times.'

Kate sighed. 'I don't like riding.'

'But you'll have to ride all the way back to 'Maritzburg unless you go in an ox cart.'

'That's different.'

He swatted an insect with his left hand. 'So, you're tired of country life, eh?'

'John Lockley's being difficult. He was positively horrible to me last night.'

Now the one thing that General James Harrison could not entertain was that his son was horrible. He missed his next putt by a wide margin.

'Ah, Katy, I'm sorry to hear you say that. Are you sure you haven't upset him?'

Kate turned her eyes skywards. She should have known better than to attempt to make an ally of the General; his damn son could do no wrong. She did not even reply, turning on her heel and stalking back to the house.

The General went back to his putting.

On the veranda Jane sat knitting. Kate came stamping up the stairs and threw herself down into the chair opposite Jane, who looked up and smiled. 'Well, Kate, how are you feeling now?'

'Oh, I don't know. Aunt Jane, there's so little to do here.'

Now Jane had her own opinion on that, but she had to admit that from Kate's point of view, given the young woman's personality and attitude, that might be so. She nodded. 'Perhaps it was a mistake for you and John Lockley to stay so long. After all, we were here almost two weeks before he arrived from Zululand.'

'Yes, I've been here nearly a whole month.'

Jane nodded.

Kate sighed and made a small moaning sound. 'And Sophie's having her engagement party a week on Saturday. What I wouldn't give to be there.'

'Have you told your husband?'

'Oh, he's being awful.'

Jane's eyes narrowed. 'Is he now?'

'We had a fight last night.'

'Husbands and wives sometimes do. I'm sure he'll have forgotten it when he comes home.'

'Aunt Jane?'

'Yes.'

'Will you talk to him for me? Please. Will you ask him to take me back to 'Maritzburg? I just can't stay here any longer.' Suddenly she began to cry. The tears rolled down her smooth cheeks and she looked girlish and pathetic.

Jane rose, putting down her knitting, and came over to her. She embraced the young woman. 'There, there, don't cry. Yes, of course I'll ask him. I can understand that, for you, it's a long time to spend here. And whatever caused the fight last night, you forget it. Take it from an old married woman, just be sweet when he comes home and I'm sure everything will be back to normal.'

She took her handkerchief out and dried Kate's face. 'Now, look, here they come over the hill. Let's go down to the stables and welcome them as if nothing's happened.'

They stood up together and Jane smoothed Kate's hair. 'Dear, it's true, you look lovely, no one will know you've been upset. Come on.'

They walked arm in arm down the steps and waved to John Lockley and Christopher, who had been joined by the General, clubs under his arm, walking beside them.

As the two women approached the stables, Kate urged, 'You will ask him, won't you? You won't forget to say I must go home to 'Maritzburg?'

And Jane comforted her. 'No, I won't forget.'

When John Lockley dismounted, his wife threw herself into his arms. 'Oh Logley, I'm so glad you're back. I've missed you.'

Her husband looked over the top of her head to find his aunt eyeing him with an expression that told him to make up with his wife.

He kissed Kate's forehead. 'Yes, Katy, and I've missed you.'

Dinner was more than usually successful, and afterwards they congregated in the front parlour and played whist.

At eleven o'clock, Matilda brought tea and coffee, and while she poured Christopher walked out alone through the doors to the veranda. Kate took the opportunity to look meaningfully at Jane before she disappeared after Chris.

Jane turned to her nephew and took his arm. 'Darling, can I have a private word with you?'

'Yes, of course. What is it?'

'Sweetheart, I don't know anything about what happened between you and Kate, but I do know that the farm's not very exciting for a young woman. She's been here close to a month now. We arrived well before you came and I really think you should consider taking her home to 'Maritzburg.' She looked meaningfully at him. 'She's tired of the farm, John Lockley.'

His mouth twisted in annoyance. 'Damn.'

'You want to stay, don't you?'

'Aunt Jane, I love this farm. I could live here.' His eyes clouded wistfully for a moment. 'Fact is, I had hoped to do just that, in time. I've always loved Africa, from the minute we landed in Cape Town. And Natal? This is my home through and through. I'm African, Aunt Jane, and happiest here.'

'Mmm, dear, it's true, I suppose you are. But Kate's not, so there's going to have to be some compromising going on.'

In essence John Lockley knew that what his aunt had said was so, and while he did not wish to face it, he realised he must. So the following morning, when Kate nestled into him, he said, 'You're bored here, Katy, aren't you?'

'Oh darling,' she replied, 'it's not that, actually. It's just that it's Sophie and Robert's engagement party on Saturday week and I'd just love to be there.'

'So you're not really bored here?'

'Not really,' she lied, turning to him and kissing his cheek. 'But, oh, Logley darling, you know how I like a party.'

Yes, he did. So he came to a decision. 'Katy, I don't want to leave the farm just yet, so if I take you into Greytown, do you mind going on to 'Maritzburg with the mail cart? They usually stop overnight at Dalton's farm and at Kruger's too, so you'll be comfortable enough.'

Kate had stayed at these two farms on the way north with Jane and Christopher, so she knew what they were like. Elation rose up through her as she replied, 'No, I don't mind.'

Two mornings later, a smiling Kate left the farm with her husband and a pack horse.

As Jane kissed John Lockley goodbye, she said, 'Oh do call and see the McLeans while you're in Greytown. Frank hasn't been well in recent months. When we stayed with them on our way here he was quite ill.'

John Lockley nodded. 'I certainly will. I haven't seen them or Thulmi for a long time, though I saw little Phoebe at Bishopstowe.'

Jane smiled. 'John Lockley, *little* Phoebe is a woman grown, dear, it's true. She's twenty-six and just become engaged to be married.'

For some reason this news did not please John Lockley Harrison and he looked down at his aunt with a grave expression. 'Oh? And who is it she's marrying?'

'That nice, steady young man who's a friend of Michael. Actually he was at dear Ellen and Michael's wedding. What's his name?' She turned to her husband.

'Ben Fielding,' Christopher replied.

And John Lockley leapt up into the saddle without saying any more.

By evening they were in the shadows of Mount Allard, where they stayed the night with H.H.

Kate was so pleased to be on her way to Pietermaritzburg that she suffered in silence as H.H. and John Lockley talked about all the happenings of Zulu country.

At about eleven o'clock Kate went to bed and the two men kept talking until after midnight. Just before they turned in, John Lockley told H.H. about the stampede at the coronation and of seeing Darlengi. 'The two of us just stood and looked at each other, and said nothing but our names.'

'No conversation?'

'No. It was just too awkward. It wasn't possible . . . and there's so much that . . . I have put between us.'

H.H.'s brow wrinkled. 'John Lockley, for you to make that statement shows that you have recognised a great deal, and that alone is a step forward.' He patted the younger man's shoulder. 'Time . . . just give things time.'

John Lockley smiled wanly. 'Yes, sir, thanks. By the way, I notice you've never left Africa even though you mentioned it a few years back.'

H.H. shook his head and spread his hands palms upwards. 'Ah, laddie, sometimes I think I'll go and then I find I remain. Doesn't really matter. One thing I do know is that wherever I am there's no real peace or happiness without Isman. She was my life.'

John Lockley looked into H.H.'s pale eyes, suddenly realising that the man must be somewhere near his father's age. He had never thought of H.H. as an age before. He was somehow ageless; had always been so vital and lively and so sage and knowledgeable.

'Yes, sir, I understand. And you know, she was the most beautiful woman I had ever seen, and now I have suddenly realised she must have been quite mature even then, when I first saw her twenty years ago.'

H.H. smiled, and briefly a serene expression crossed his face. 'Thank you for saying that. It's true she was beautiful in her soul as well as her face. And when you first saw her, yes, she must have been close to her fiftieth year.' Then he took John Lockley by the arm and steered him towards his tiny bedroom. 'And, John Lockley laddie; while I'm here it's always good to share what I have with you.'

Kate was asleep when John Lockley entered, and swiftly he joined her. They awoke to H.H.'s call at six o'clock and by the hour of eight were on their way again.

When they came into Greytown, John Lockley went straight to Graham Muller's post office and blacksmith's shop. Graham was a big, handsome man who had been born in Cape Town and begun life in the field of law, but he had become disillusioned with courts and legal matters and had come to Natal to the frontier to get closer to the land and what he termed 'reality'. He wiped his hands on a piece of rag as he came out into the sunshine to stand beneath a gum tree filled with pigeons.

His face was damp with perspiration. 'Cart leaves tomorrow, Mr Harrison. Eight o'clock sharp.'

'Can it carry my wife?'

'Without you?'

'Yes, she wishes to return to Pietermaritzburg alone.'

362

The blacksmith eyed Kate, wondering why John Lockley was about to leave such a fine-looking specimen of womanhood. 'Well now, Al Baker's driving and I believe there's a Mr and Mrs Morpeth going back to 'Maritzburg. Aye, there'll be room for one more.'

'So there, Kate, you'll be in 'Maritzburg by Tuesday, in plenty of time for your Saturday party.'

Kate could not hide her delight, and a smile of absolute joy appeared on her mouth. 'Oh, yes.'

He looked at her through half-closed lids. 'And don't forget to miss your husband.'

She kissed him on the mouth. 'Of course I'll miss you. When do you expect to be home?'

'Well, darling, I've got to be back at the fort on the morning of October the sixth – that's about three more weeks – so I'd really prefer to stay another couple if you don't mind.'

She smiled. 'Stay as long as you like,' she said.

'So you'll be wanting somewhere to put up for the night?' asked Graham.

John Lockley nodded. 'Yes, we will. There's a small inn in the township, isn't there?'

'Flea-ridden, Mr Harrison. No place to be taking a lady like your wife.'

At that moment his own wife appeared, carrying her washing across the field beside the blacksmith shop, and her husband called to her. 'Phyllis May, darling! Mr and Mrs Harrison here need a night's lodging. The lady'll be taking the mail cart to 'Maritzburg tomorrow.'

Phyllis Muller was close enough to hear her husband clearly, but, fortunately, far enough away to give a start and for it to go unnoticed. For while Graham Muller knew John Lockley, his wife had never met him, so it was with great interest that she came over and put her basket down. 'How do you do. Yes, we've a free bedroom.'

'Why, thank you very much,' replied John Lockley.

'Put your horses in the stable,' she said, 'and then bring your things inside.'

When Phyllis May came into her kitchen and put down her basket of clothes there was a deep frown on her brow. John Lockley Harrison and his wife here in her house; now this was an odd turn of events, especially as she was expecting Phoebe and Benjamin this afternoon. How well Phyllis recalled the day three years ago when Phoebe had arrived and asked to stay overnight. She had readily agreed, for the girl was dear to her. She had not asked Phoebe any questions, but she could see that the young woman made a conscious effort to be cheerful and that underneath there was something troubling her terribly.

Graham had gone to bed early as was his habit and the two women had poured another cup of tea. Then Phyllis had suggested that they, too, get an early night, when suddenly Phoebe had not been able to contain herself and the whole unhappy story had come tumbling out. Phyllis May had comforted her and given her what advice she could, which was, when it boiled down, to forget John Lockley. But it had taken hours and the two women had still been talking when the clock struck twelve.

The next day, Victoria had come for her daughter and a red-eyed Phoebe had thanked Phyllis for her kindness and gone home to the mission. They had never spoken of it again and whenever John Lockley's name came into conversation they would pass over him as speedily as they could.

She sat down and took a deep breath as John Lockley's wife came through the door. She was very good-looking, with olive skin and dark eyes and long waving hair, and to Phyllis's way of thinking was overdressed for this part of the world.

'Well, dear,' she said, pointing to a whitewashed door behind her, 'that's your bedroom. Go in and pop your belongings down and then I'll make you a cuppa.'

'Thank you,' Kate replied as she wafted through the homely kitchen.

Phyllis May was folding her clothes when John Lockley followed a few minutes later, and she pointed to the same door. 'Your wife's in there.'

He took off his hat which had sat rakishly over his thick hair and passed by her and through the white door.

She watched him with as much interest as she had watched Kate. He was handsome all right. Very. Eyes a wonderful colour, sort of purple. He was clean-shaven and had a fresh, appealing look, somehow reminding her of the veld after rain. Yes, indeed, she could understand how Phoebe had fallen head over heels for this man. Mind you, Phoebe was a beauty in her own right: totally different from this dark, glamorous woman, but just as lovely.

A few minutes later, John Lockley came back. 'I'll take tea in to my wife if you don't mind. She would like to rest before luncheon. What time will that be?'

'Oh, I'll be making something in about another hour,' Phyllis said, rising to put on the kettle.

Then John Lockley surprised his hostess. 'I want to ride out to the mission this afternoon, to see the McLeans, and there's an old friend of mine with them now. Thulmi. Do you know him?'

Phyllis May turned back to him with a smile. 'Oh yes, he follows Phoebe everywhere. He's her shadow; turned up trumps for them the way he works so hard.'

'Always did,' replied John Lockley.

'So you'll be leaving to ride out to the mission at what time?'

'I'll go immediately after luncheon.'

His hostess nodded. He would probably run into Phoebe on the road at that rate. Ah well, life was like that. She bent to light the stove.

Phoebe came down the wooden steps of the mission house to the laughter of Treedy and Mary, two Hottentot girls of about seven who lived at the mission kraal with their grandmother.

Nearby, Thulmi stood holding Sapphire's reins.

Treedy's English was improving daily and she asked, 'Where you goin', Miss Phoebe?'

Phoebe patted the child on her tight curls. 'Off into Greytown, Treedy.'

'Wit' the soldier who own the grain store?'

Phoebe smiled. 'Yes.' And the girls got to giggling again.

At that moment Ben came riding through the open gate by the giant aloe tree and across to them. He wore a bright smile under his slouch felt hat. Things were going well for him these days. The grain store was in profit and he was sure they would soon make him a captain in the Natal Hussars. The Greytown Mounted Rifles had been absorbed into the Natal Hussars four years ago and he had been with the regiment since it was formed in sixty-four. And he had Phoebe, now. They were engaged at last. For years he had waited for her, and had not rushed her into anything. He knew her parents approved of him and he had finally got his own mother to accept that Phoebe was worthy of him. Funny, but for some reason, on the ride out here, he had been thinking of the day three years ago when he came to the mission and found John Lockley Harrison here.

He had seen Harrison a few times since in 'Maritzburg. He was a major with the Royal Engineers as well as some sort of co-operation officer between the Imperial forces and the volunteer forces here in Natal.

He hadn't liked the man the minute he'd seen him at the mission that day, and Phoebe had seemed so taken with him. For a long while after that she had avoided Ben and he'd put it down to Harrison's being back. Then a few months later, he'd been down in 'Maritzburg and found out Harrison was married. He felt the happiness surge through him even now as he remembered it. Well, he had begun calling on Phoebe again straight away. And while things had moved slowly, they had definitely moved. He felt quite confident of their future now.

'Afternoon, Phoebe dear.'

'Hello, Ben.'

'Should I go in and see your father?'

Phoebe shook her head. 'He's asleep. Best when we come home.'

Phoebe mounted Sapphire, and the children and Thulmi waved them off.

As they rode down the track that led into the township Ben asked, 'How's your father today?'

'Poorly. His cough is really bad. Much worse even than it was in the winter. Mother says he's always been susceptible to chills, ever since he had a bad accident when we first came to Natal.'

'Oh, what happened?'

'He was out in a storm and his horse fell. He broke his collar bone, a leg and some ribs I think, and you know, while I was only six at the time, I can remember he was sick for months.'

As they rode by, some bustards ran through the grass on the side of the track and then took to the air; and away in the long grass past the acacia trees, the little face of a vervet monkey popped up every now and then.

They had ridden about a mile when they saw a horse coming from the other direction. As the rider approached, Phoebe felt

366

her pulse quicken. She recognised the way this man rode. What was John Lockley doing here?

When Ben realised who it was, his pulse quickened too, but for a very different reason.

'Looks like that fellow Harrison,' Ben said.

'Yes, it is,' replied Phoebe.

John Lockley came trotting up, the dust rising gently behind him. He doffed his wide-awake to Phoebe. 'Phoebe, how are you? I'm on my way to your place.'

'Oh good. Ah ... this is Ben Fielding.'

John Lockley met a cool expression as he turned his eyes to Ben's. He smiled. 'Fielding? You're with the Natal Hussars, aren't you?'

'Yes.'

'Tommy Hill's in charge now, isn't he?'

'*Captain* Hill is our commanding officer, yes.'

John Lockley turned back to Phoebe. 'Where're you off to?'

'Into Greytown. We're visiting my friend, Mrs Muller.'

'Really? The postmaster's wife?'

'Yes. Do you know her?'

'Kate's there now. She's leaving for 'Maritzburg on the mail cart in the morning. We're staying the night at the Mullers'.'

How Phoebe wished she were alone here with John Lockley; that Ben were not beside her. But even as she wished it, she reprimanded herself. Her thoughts were dishonourable. Ben was the man she was going to spend her future with. Ben was her fiancé.

John Lockley met Phoebe's eyes. 'I believe your father isn't well.'

'Dada's very sick. He has been for a long time now. Mummy's so worried and ...'

'We all are,' interjected Ben. 'My *fiancée's* father's health is of concern to us all.'

Phoebe looked quickly at Ben but he was eyeing John Lockley.

'I'm very sorry to hear all this,' John Lockley said. 'I hope it's appropriate to see him this afternoon. I don't want to tire him.'

Ben went to speak, but Phoebe cut him off with the words, 'He'll be ever so pleased to see you. I'm sure you'll cheer him up.'

'But he was sleeping,' Ben protested.

'Ben,' Phoebe's voice was firm, 'how often does Dada see John Lockley? Of course he'll be pleased. John Lockley, thank you, I appreciate it.' She put out her hand to him, and watched as he edged his horse forward and lifted his hand to take hers. She noticed the sun-browned colour of it and the clear oval fingernails and the creases at his wrist. Then she was aware of the sensation of his palm on hers; the touch of his bare skin as she held on to him.

She looked into his eyes and somehow she was comforted. Then he dropped her hand and turned to Ben to say goodbye. But Ben did not give him the opportunity to shake hands as he pushed his horse on past, saying, 'Goodbye, Harrison.'

John Lockley nodded again to Phoebe. 'Nice to have seen you, Phoebe.'

'Nice to have seen you, John Lockley.'

When they were a hundred yards on, Ben's voice sounded tersely. 'I don't know why you're always so pleasant to that fellow. He seems a rum sort to me.'

'Ben, how can you say that? You don't know him. And this is only the second time I've ever seen him in your company, therefore how can you use the word "always"?'

'So,' Ben turned in the saddle to face her, 'I see. You've seen him when I haven't been around, have you? Did you see him when you went to the Colensos?'

Phoebe was looking steadily at her fiancé. 'Ben, what if I did?'

Now his voice was rising. 'Did you see him?'

'This is silly. Yes. But I cannot fathom why you're so angry about it.'

'I'm not angry, damn it! There you see, you made me swear.'

They rode on in silence until they came within sight of the blacksmith's forge and the house.

Phoebe put her hand out to Ben and touched his arm as they came closer. 'Ben, why are we feeling annoyed with each other? This is foolish.'

He took her hand. 'I'm sorry.'

'So am I.'

He lifted her hand to his lips and kissed it.

They spent a pleasant time with Phyllis May in her garden,

which was quite substantial, and later sitting around her little kitchen table and drinking tea and coffee and talking. They visited Graham at his forge as well.

Kate did not come out of her room until they had been there an hour. She only appeared then to be polite and to say a brief hello. But when she saw Ben, her sultry eyes lit up and she remained talking to him.

By the time they left, Kate was saying, 'Next time you're in 'Maritzburg, Benjamin, I insist you call on me.'

Ben had enough feelings for Phoebe to reply that he thought it unlikely he would be in 'Maritzburg for a long time, but he had rarely been the recipient of such overt female attention and he was cavalier enough to actually kiss Kate's hand when they left.

At Ben's insistence they rode home via his friend Andries Du Plessis's farm which took them north and around in an arc to the mission. Phoebe thought how very transparent Ben was: it was obvious he did not want to meet John Lockley on the road again, and he wished to make sure they would not arrive back until he had departed the mission. Why he should be in any way jealous of her tenuous relationship with John Lockley she did not understand.

Sure enough, John Lockley had gone when they rode in, though Thulmi was positively loquacious about his visit, and over dinner Ben had to sit through a detailed description of the afternoon from Victoria.

When Ben kissed Phoebe goodnight, he ran his hands over her body and squeezed her close. He had begun doing this since their engagement. But tonight, when he pressed her down on the veranda seat and his tongue ran down her neck and into the opening of her dress, she said, 'Ben, please, dear. Not tonight, I'm really tired after the long ride.'

'It wasn't all that long,' he whispered, bringing his hand up from her waist and cupping her breast through her clothes. She slid along the seat. 'I'm tired, Ben ... and I suppose I'm worried about Dada.'

'Oh, darling, yes, all right. I'm sorry. Another night.' And he kissed her again and stood.

She watched him ride away. He rode well and she felt a little pride at that. Then she turned and slowly walked along the veranda. The moonlight fell across her path and she sighed.

Suddenly she thought of Ellen and what she had said about Michael. She could see her poor dead friend's distraught face now, down there in the moonlight of the mission yard. She could see her trembling and hear her say, 'I cannot bear for him to touch me.' But she was not Ellen; she was Phoebe. She was strong and a realist. She liked Ben a great deal, and she was sure he loved her, so she felt positive that in time she would grow to love him too.

CHAPTER TWENTY-FIVE

Kate threw her head back and laughed and her black curls danced on her shoulders.

The party was going well. Sophie's mother had rented out the small hall that adjoined the Catholic church. All the people Kate enjoyed being with were here, and Tom gave her constant attention. Tom was delightful; he wrote verse and was light-hearted and handsome, and paid her compliments. He had the knack of making her laugh, and how she loved to laugh. And he was always ready to accompany her and Sophie and her two sisters anywhere. She couldn't help comparing him with John Lockley, whose priorities really were different to her own; four years of marriage had shown her that.

'Come on, Kate, it's a waltz.'

Tom leant down to her. His blue eyes glinted in the candlelight and he looked marvellous in a suit of chocolate-coloured velvet with a cream kerchief at his throat.

She took his hand and gained her feet and was soon swirling across the dance floor. They danced well together and as they swept around the floor they were watched by Sophie and her fiancé, Robert Wallace.

'Don't they dance just perfectly together?' squeaked Sophie with delight.

'They certainly do.'

'He's mad about her, you know.'

'That's obvious. In fact there are a number of rumours about them.'

Sophie nodded. 'I know. Quite diverting, isn't it?'

Her fiancé chucked her under the chin. 'You're wicked. But I love you.' And he took her by the hand and led her into the waltz.

Kate had a splendid evening and at one o'clock in the morning a number of guests left to walk home through the streets of Pietermaritzburg. She was one, and not far behind her walked Tom. Captain Charles Preston, a friend of John Lockley, had offered to walk her home, but she had put him off by saying she was going with the group. There was laughter and chatter as they avoided potholes and sluits, and at each corner some departed from the main body.

When they came to Maritz Street, Kate and some near neighbours said goodnight and five minutes later she was inside her front hall where Umslopagas stood with a candle in his right hand.

'Do you wish for anything, mistress?'

'No. Thank you for waiting up. Go to bed now.'

Kate hurried up the stairs. She threw off her clothes and put on her best nightgown. She brushed her jet-black hair in the lamplight and pinched her cheeks to redden them. Fifteen minutes later she crept back down the stairs and unlatched the front door. She stood trembling with excitement until the door was gently moved ajar.

She whispered, 'Is that you, Tom?' and the answer came back, 'Yes, darlin', it is.'

Four hours later, just before the dawn, Tom slipped out of bed, put on his clothes, and kissed her waiting lips one more time before he left the way he had come.

Some weeks later Kate lay beside John Lockley as the morning sun filtered through the trees outside their window and threw subtle patches of light upon them.

He lifted his hand from behind her head as he sat up. 'Come on, Katy. If we're going to church we'd better move.'

'Darling, I really would prefer to stay home.'

'I promised Anthony I'd go this morning. Bishop Colenso's sermon is going to be about this Langalibalele business and we should be there.'

'What Langalibalele business?'

'Katy, it's been going on for years. Everyone in authority's known that some of Chief Langalibalele's men have been acquiring arms and not registering them. Langalibalele was asked to enforce the ordinance of registration but didn't. Naturally enough, I suppose; it's a difficult situation for him: government on one side, his young men on the other. Finally, Sir Benjamin Pine and Theopolis Shepstone – do you know

372

they're calling him the Supreme Native Chieftain now? – well, they've become pretty much alarmed because there are over three hundred thousand natives in this colony, and only fifteen thousand Europeans, and I suppose natives with unregistered guns are a concern.'

'Where're they getting them from?'

'On the goldfields: they're being paid in guns up there. And of course there are always traders in guns. Some say John Dunn's one of them. Anyway, they've called Langalibalele in to stand trial and he hasn't come. In fact, word is he may try to escape over the Drakensburgs to Basuto Land. Sir Benjamin's taking it very seriously and it looks like a force will be sent to stop old Langalibalele.'

Kate's eyes narrowed behind his back. 'Will you be going?'

'More than likely. Anyway, come on, or we'll be late. I want to see what the Bishop has to say.'

'You go. I don't want to come.'

'Kate,' his voice was stern, 'I want you with me.'

Two hours later they had heard the Bishop, who had called for temperance in the colony's dealings with Langalibalele, and they stood outside St Andrew's with Anthony, the General, Christopher and Jane.

Kate's eyes wandered as the others reviewed the sermon. Tall native men in an array of clothing, from sacks with armholes to trousers with shirt hanging out, strolled by, many with white babies in their arms. Kate still thought it curious how the men were often nursemaids here, for Pietermaritzburg had a serious lack of native females, hence much women's work was done by the men.

She sighed as her eyes roved; there was no point in looking for Tom here. He rarely went to church and he was Wesleyan anyway. It was a strange situation in his family, for their mother was Roman Catholic and their father a Methodist, so all the girls were Catholic and the one boy, Tom, a Wesleyan.

'So, we'll meet you at The Grange for luncheon,' she heard her husband say, and Christopher replied, 'Yes, and then we'll all take a ride out to the Colensos' as arranged, and see you there, Anthony.'

'You will,' Anthony's level voice answered. 'I'm going out to

Bishopstowe directly. Just returning to my lodgings first to get Prince, and then we'll go on out.' Prince was Anthony's large dog. Anthony had found him down in King Williamstown, and the animal had been devoted to him ever since. His landlady was a kindly Scottish woman who happily took care of Prince while Anthony was away.

As Anthony departed Jane took John Lockley's arm. 'I'm not coming to the Colensos' this afternoon. I'm packing a few things. I'm going to Greytown to Victoria and Phoebe. Frank's seriously ill and from Victoria's last letter he has not much time left. I want to help her.'

'Who'll take you?'

'I'm leaving tomorrow with Mr Thorn. He'll go on to the farm. There are things he can do there for Christopher. So look after your father and your uncle for me, won't you?'

'Of course I will, and please tell Mrs McLean and Phoebe how very sorry I am. I saw him a few weeks ago and he was mighty sick then.'

As John Lockley and Kate walked home arm-in-arm, John Lockley thought about Phoebe. He hoped she would be all right. She was a fine, spirited girl, and while he was not very enamoured with her choice of fiancé, at least she had one, and he would be there to support her in her hour of need. Perhaps he should write a letter to her and her mother. Yes, he would give it to Aunt Jane to take.

At his side, his wife's mind was racing. Tom had said that if she could possibly get away he would wait for her on Sunday afternoon in the trees beyond old Lief Liam's disused hut. It sat in an overgrown area about a mile from Fort Napier. It was not as if she didn't love her husband – she did, and he was a marvellous lover – it was just that she needed more in her life than John Lockley could give and Tom was indefatigable, in every way. Oh yes, a shiver ran through her. He was such fun. Once she had called him 'Logley' when they were making love. He had been so mad; it had been positively sensually stimulating. She smiled now thinking of it.

'So, Katy,' John Lockley said as they entered their well-planted erf and walked to the front door, 'you're coming out to the Colensos' after luncheon, aren't you?'

'Sweetheart, a six-mile ride out in the heat and a six-mile ride back fighting the flies both ways is not my idea of enjoyment. I think I'll either stay home or go around and see Sophie.'

For a moment a crease lodged between John Lockley's eyes. He was remembering last week in the club. There had been a general discussion on why more young men were not joining the volunteer forces and there had been a point made that the forces did not offer the youth enough. Then some light-hearted talk had followed where it was remarked that the colony's young men were more interested in pleasures of the flesh than in joining armies.

Shortly after the discussion had taken place John Lockley had passed Joseph Trimm on the veranda. The surveyor had been at the club for hours, and as usual had imbibed far too much. He had leaned over and giggled as John Lockley walked by. Then he had slurred, 'Like Tom King and your missis. He'd rather be with her than be a volunteer doing all that parade work, now wouldn't he?'

They were alone and John Lockley had taken the man roughly by the collar. 'What the hell does that mean?'

'Now, John Lockley, laddie, no harm meant . . . no harm.'

'What are you saying, damn it?'

'Nothin',' he hiccuped. 'Just a few of us noted she sees a lot of him. Nothing meant, laddie.'

'Then keep your bloody tongues still. And occupy your thoughts with something useful.' He pushed Trimm from him and the man thudded into the wall. 'Go home and sober up, for God's sake.'

And now John Lockley eyed his wife, and like any man when the first seeds of doubt are sown, he hoped to discredit them.

'Katy?'

'Yes, darling?' she answered as she took off her hat in the front hall.

'It *is* just Sophie you go to see, isn't it?'

Her dark eyes found his. 'Now what on earth does that mean?'

'Her brother seems to spend a lot of time with you too.'

She laughed and came to him and put her golden arms up round his neck. 'My dearest. You're jealous.'

He took her arms down. 'No, Kate, I'm not. I would hope I have no reason to ever be jealous of my own wife.' He was looking at her with an expression she had never seen before. It was somehow cold and penetrating, and it thrilled her to her very bones.

Deliberately she placed her arms back up round his neck and brought her mouth close to his. He could feel her sweet breath as she spoke. 'I love you, John Lockley Harrison, and yes, sometimes Tom is with us, but so too is Robert and a number of others. I don't know why you're saying this.'

He continued looking straight into her eyes. 'You wouldn't lie to me, Katy, would you?'

'I would not,' she said and kissed him. She meant the kiss. And when she drew him up the stairs to make hasty love in their bed, she meant that too.

And after luncheon, when her husband left her at Sophie's front door and rode away with Christopher towards Bishopstowe, her blood coursed through her veins as she swiftly excused herself from her friend's company and mounted her horse and rode out of town past the fort. And when she passed Lief Liam's hut and entered the trees to find Tom waiting for her as he had promised, she trembled with the excitement and danger of it all.

The afternoon at Bishopstowe had been pleasant and John Lockley played a game of croquet with Anthony, Fanny and Agnes on the makeshift lawn. Some people from the Esibaneni kraal watched, and now as the game ended they all dispersed and the players made their way up to the house.

John Lockley looked across to Anthony, who was walking with Fanny. They seemed to have a lot in common and were always chatting to each other. He thought about Kate, and wondered what she might be doing. Then he shook his head and mounted the veranda where Christopher, the General, Bishop Colenso and his wife met them and they partook of cool lemonade.

For some time the General and the Bishop continued to discuss how to handle the Langalibalele affair, and Anthony said that he thought a force would soon be despatched to the Drakensburgs to bar the chief's escape route.

'The discussion at the fort yesterday was that Colonel Milles would be sent and I've volunteered to go as Chief of Staff. I think they'll send John Lockley as an interpreter. There's talk that Mr Shepstone and the Lieutenant-Governor will come along as well.'

James Harrison shook his head. 'They're pretty earnest about it then.'

Fanny's delicate hand lifted. 'I hate all this talk of soldiers going into danger. Please, Father, your sermon was full of all the trouble this morning, cannot we now discuss other matters?'

He smiled at her. 'Of course we can, darling. But we must not trivialise important issues.'

And Christopher, like a good guest, took his cue and brought up the subject of the water supply.

Some time later, after a number of topics had been discussed, and the large group had broken up into smaller ones, Fanny mentioned Frank McLean's illness to John Lockley.

'Yes,' replied John Lockley, 'Aunt Jane is going north tomorrow to be with them. Apparently he's dying.'

Fanny nodded sadly. 'I'm sorry I cannot be there with Phoebe. For while she's strong and capable, she loves her father dearly and there's so much pain attached to death. But I'm writing to her as often as I can.'

'That's good of you, Fanny.'

'It's the least I can do. She's my dear, dear friend.' Fanny was looking steadily at him when she added, 'In fact I think she's a wonderful person, and beautiful both inside and out.'

For some reason John Lockley felt this was a message for him. 'Yes, Fanny, I'm sure she is.'

Some weeks later the November sun burned down upon the roof of the mission house outside Greytown, forecasting the intensity of the summer heat to come. The folk from the mission kraal were gathered in long lines down the veranda and across the yard. Small groups sat by the large aloe at the gate, and most of them were softly wailing. The noise rose and fell in gentle cadence, a sad and woeful sound.

Inside the house Phoebe stood at her father's bedside, looking down at him. She could not believe it. He had died just minutes ago. She wondered if everyone felt this way at the loss of someone beloved. As if he would suddenly move and sit up and that it would all have been some ghastly nightmare.

Her mother's weeping and the tender voices of Phyllis May and Aunt Jane comforting her confirmed that it was real. Her father was dead.

She could hear outside the mournful voices of the people from the mission kraal. They had been keeping a vigil for him. They called him 'Umfundisi Khulu' – great teacher – and they would all miss him. All of them now had a concept of a forgiving Christian God and His goodness; of the importance of the individual; of caring about their fellow man with kindness and consideration. All because of 'Umfundisi Khulu' and his wife.

Her father had actually opened his eyes and focused briefly on her mother and herself a few hours before he died. And the smile he gave her would live forever in her mind. He had been a wonderful father, and unafraid of death. His faith had carried him through all the pain to the realm beyond human comprehension. Only a few days earlier he had said to her, 'Did not our Lord suffer? I am honoured to suffer.'

And while Phoebe admired her father for saying it, she could not quite give it credence. She just did not see the world the same way as her parents did.

She thought of the things she had done that her father had not approved of: the way she had learned about rifles and how she had gone out hunting for food; how she had helped the carpenters construct the school house and how she had stood up to the traders who tried to trick the people of the mission kraal. Yes, she had done all manner of unfeminine things. And even while he had disapproved, he had never confronted her or told her she must stop, as so many fathers would have done. He had tolerated so much. And when she had wanted to start a small hospital, he had helped and encouraged her to send away for books and medicines. He had even urged her to go and train with Michael Tallant for some months in the spring of the previous year. She remembered how gentle and wise he had been when she first discovered that John Lockley was married; how he and her mother had talked things through and had helped her to face what was so.

A wan little smile came to her mouth for she was so pleased he had seen her become engaged to Ben. He had wanted that for her. As he had put it, 'Ben is solid. He'll make a fine husband.'

She felt Ben's hand on her arm now, and looked round into his eyes. He kissed her cheek and said, 'Darling, come. There's no more you can do.'

She shook her head and knelt down at the bedside again, and taking her father's hand brought it to her lips and covered it with tears.

When Graham Muller arrived two hours later, they decided to bury Frank at the mission, forty-eight hours hence. And now as moonlight fell across the mission yard, the Mullers were gathering their belongings to ride back into Greytown.

Phyllis May moved across to Victoria and took her in her arms. 'I don't like to leave you, Victoria.'

'No, dear, you must. You've been here three days already. Your Graham needs you and I've got Jane and Phoebe and Ben.'

Phyllis May kissed her and moved reluctantly to the door.

'Don't worry, we'll be out again sometime tomorrow,' Graham called to them as they rode away.

'Now,' said Jane, taking Victoria's arm and turning her into the house, 'I'll make something to eat. And we must talk about your coming back to Pietermaritzburg with me, you need a rest.'

Phoebe moved to the top of the steps and picked up a paraffin lantern. 'I'm going over to the kraal.'

'Good heavens, why?' asked Ben.

'To see our people. To be with them a little while. They loved Daddy almost as much as we did.'

'Yes,' answered Victoria, 'they did. And tell them I shall come over first thing tomorrow. Oh, and check that Shinu has not taken his bandage off again.'

Shinu was only five and had badly cut his arm. He kept removing the bandage.

'I will,' replied Phoebe.

'I come with you,' said Thulmi, who had stood vigil on the veranda all day. He took the lantern from her.

'Then wait,' called Ben, 'I'll come with you, too.'

Momentarily Phoebe wished she could go alone with Thulmi, but she hastily dismissed that feeling. 'All right.'

They spent over an hour at the kraal. Everyone wanted to talk to Phoebe, and many of them cried. Some of the older folk set up a soft wailing as they had earlier in the day outside the house.

'Umfundisi Khulu with his ancestors now,' said Tokwa, who had set himself up as the kraal spokesman.

'With God, too,' corrected his wife Lila.

'Yes,' replied Phoebe, 'he is with them all.'

On the walk back to the house Thulmi led the way carrying the lantern. As they came within sight of the house Ben stopped near a large clump of trees.

Thulmi turned back to them.

'You go on, Thulmi,' Ben said. 'We'll be along shortly.'

'No, I wait for Miss Phoebe.'

'Thulmi,' Ben's voice had a hard edge to it, 'I said you go on, we'll follow shortly.'

'It's all right, Thulmi, do as Mr Ben says.'

Thulmi moved off reluctantly.

'That Zulu is so tiresome.'

'Oh Ben, don't say that. I've known him since I was a girl. He feels protective towards me.'

'Well, he doesn't need to be with me. It's ridiculous.'

'Forget it. Why did we stop anyway?' She took his hand in hers.

He wrapped her in his arms and kissed her. 'I love you, Phoebe.'

'Ben, dear, forgive me if I'm not feeling exactly romantic tonight.'

'Of course, darling, I understand, but it's hard being this close to you and not kissing you.'

She lifted her hand and patted his cheek affectionately. And he took her hands and kissed them. 'Sometime I want to love you properly, Feeb' – it was his pet name for her – 'you know what I mean.'

'I really can't think about that tonight, dearest.'

Two hours later Phoebe was in bed. Ben was staying the night, as he had done the previous one. He was in the small spare bedroom near the kitchen where they occasionally stored things.

Phoebe lifted the lid on the pretty box that lay on her bedside table and took out the folded paper. Aunt Jane had brought it when she came up here to them. It was a short letter from John Lockley and she read it every night before she snuffed the candles at her bedside.

Pietermaritzburg, 19 October, 1873

Dear Phoebe,

I hear that your father does not improve.

I am very sorry indeed and can only hope that somehow he recovers.

We all at times must face emotions that wear us down, but if I know you, and I think I do, you will fight back with spirit.

I spent the afternoon at Bishopstowe with the Colensos and as always had a most pleasant time. Fanny is a lovely person and a very good friend of yours. She said nice things about you, with which I concur.

It appears I am soon to leave with Anthony Durnford and to get up the Drakensburgs and hold the pass over them, through which Chief Langalibalele and his amaHlubi are taking their cattle and escaping. A soldier's lot I'm afraid. I'd rather be going up to Newcastle and building the fortifications; the thing I'm good at.

Well, dear Phoebe, please pass on my warmest regards to your mother, and Kate joins me in the hope that your father soon improves.

Sincerely,

John Lockley.

A tear fell from Phoebe's eye and dropped on to the page, running across the signature. She took out a handkerchief and blotted it.

Then with a long sigh she folded the letter and put it away, blew out the candles, and lay down with her thoughts.

CHAPTER TWENTY-SIX

The same hour that the Reverend Frank McLean died, John Lockley thought he was witnessing the death of Anthony Durnford. They were winding up the Drakensburg Mountains over the steep trail that was Giant's Castle Pass. They had been seriously misinformed about the ease of crossing the pass and once in it had realised that it called for experienced mountaineering. They had to lead their horses along narrow ledges and round tumbled rocks, frequently with sheer drops of hundreds of feet over the cliff sides. All around was scrubby, broken country.

They had been sent here by Theopolis Shepstone and Lieutenant-Governor Pine to cut off the escape route of Chief Langalibalele and his amaHlubi clan who were coming up another pass over the Drakensburg Mountains. Langalibalele had gathered his people and was attempting to move them out of their reserve in Natal over the mountains into Basuto Land where he would be out of the jurisdiction of the Natal Government and his young men could keep their arms.

For days now his clan had been straggling in their thousands across Bushman's River Pass in the Drakensburgs, bringing with them their women and children and herding their cattle.

The force sent from Pietermaritzburg to stop their escape and to return Langalibalele to the authorities had been split, half under Lieutenant-Colonel Milles and half under Anthony, with John Lockley second-in-command.

The men under Anthony consisted of a volunteer contingent from the Richmond Mounted Rifles and the Karkloof Troop of the Natal Carbineers, and twenty-five mounted Basutos under an induna called Hlubi. Two were Elijah Kambula and Tenny Rama, who had been with Anthony and John Lockley ever since the excursion up the Black Umvoloosi River, before Cetshwayo's coronation.

382

The November sun was searing down on them and some of the men had already fallen out from exhaustion when John Lockley, who was leading his horse, Horatio, watched in horror as Anthony's horse, Chieftain, stumbled and fell sideways over a rocky edge, dragging Anthony backwards with him.

'Anthony!' shouted John Lockley as his friend fell and thudded heavily down the rock face, Chieftain's reins pulled from his hand. The horse slithered, smashing through small trees and scrub, and Anthony followed him until he hit a broken tree limb about thirty feet down and caught on it and stopped.

To everyone's amazement Chieftain stood up at the bottom of the incline, unhurt, but Anthony was not so lucky.

John Lockley and Elijah Kambula, with ropes attached to their belts, climbed down to Anthony and brought him up. Then Elijah went back down for Chieftain.

It had been a miracle that neither the horse nor Anthony had been killed but Anthony's face and head were severely cut and he was bleeding freely. He had dislocated his shoulder and two ribs were broken. The tree limb had wounded his left armpit and his arm hung limply at his side.

They bandaged his head and strapped his shoulder and ribs as best they could.

John Lockley's face was full of concern as he looked at his friend. 'I'll take the men on, we must get you back to proper care.'

'No, lad. This is my command.'

'But you're badly injured and the wounds will worsen without attention.'

Anthony shook his head and his blue eyes gleamed in the sunlight. He took hold of his friend's arm and drew him down to where only John Lockley could hear him speak. 'Laddie, remember what I told you when we were on our little expedition together. This will be my first time in action. I cannot . . . I will not relinquish my command.'

Their eyes met and John Lockley nodded. He understood. His friend had to deal with his own ghosts in his own way.

So they persevered through the night until the going became almost impossible for Anthony; and Robert Erskine, one of the volunteers and the son of the Colonial Secretary, thought of a way to help him. They made a sort of sling from a blanket, and with two men holding the ends, and two men behind him, they pulled and pushed Anthony upwards over the hostile terrain.

It was a long and painful night for all, especially for Anthony.

The volunteers had already proved their inexperience by allowing their pack animals carrying the rations and ammunition to wander away in the middle of the night twenty-four hours earlier. Anthony and John Lockley had then needed to ask the Basutos in the Native Contingent to share their meat, biscuits and rum with the Europeans.

By dawn they were at the crest: hungry, tired and worn.

They caught a few hours' rest before they were alerted by the Basuto vanguard that twelve miles away at Bushman's River Pass some of the amaHlubi, armed with rifles, were issuing up over the edge of the mountain, herding their cattle and bringing their families with them.

'Wake the men and mount up,' ordered Anthony.

Sergeant Clarke, the senior NCO with the volunteers, shook his head. 'We can't go on yet, sir. The men are tired.'

John Lockley rounded on him. 'We're here to stop the amaHlubi from crossing the Drakensburgs, Clarke. Do as the Major says.'

By the time they reached the saucer-shaped basin where Bushman's River Pass emerged, there were about a hundred amaHlubi herders camped with their cattle. Most of the herders were armed and John Lockley's Basuto scouts informed him that there were many more armed below in the pass waiting to come up. As John Lockley rode back to inform Anthony, he was halted by Captain Charles Barter, the senior officer with the volunteers. The man looked tired and grim. 'My men are starving, sir. They haven't eaten since dawn yesterday.'

John Lockley met his gaze. 'None of us has, Barter.'

When Anthony heard the message, he stood up with the help of young Robert Erskine and lifted his good arm, to point across the depression. 'We should throw a line of men across here first, John Lockley, and then attend to some food for them. Help me on to Chieftain, Erskine, lad, I want to ride out and see for myself.'

Elijah Kambula who waited nearby said, 'I come with you inkosi.' He used 'inkosi' meaning chief, or leader.

As Anthony and Elijah rode across to a group of the armed amaHlubi who squatted on the rim of the basin, John Lockley immediately organised the line of men, leaving Sergeant Clarke in charge. 'Come with me,' he called to Captain Barter, and with a wave of his hand for six of the mounted Basuto to join them, he climbed upon his own horse, Horatio, and rode over to another group of the clansmen who stood along a ridge a hundred yards away, watching the proceedings.

'We are not here to harm you,' John Lockley called to them across a ditch of bracken. 'I just want to talk with you.' He held up his hand and forced Horatio through the ferny plants towards the amaHlubi. The Basutos followed closely behind him and Barter came after. 'We are sent to ask you to turn back and go down the pass the way you have come. We will not harm you and we ask you to tell all those here to follow you down. You must do this. We cannot allow you to go on.'

There was a general mumbling amongst the men.

'Where is Chief Langalibalele?'

'We do not know,' one answered.

'Is he down in the pass?'

'We do not know.'

John Lockley pointed back to the volunteers. 'Our men are hungry, we have not eaten for over a day. We want to buy a cow from you.' He turned and called to Barter. 'Pay these men for a cow, Barter. That should feed your volunteers, and us. I'm going over to Major Durnford.' Then he turned to the six Basutos. 'When the Captain has bought the animal, take it back to the men.'

He rode over to Anthony who came slowly back from having spoken, via Elijah, to the second group of amaHlubi herders.

'They look menacing,' Anthony greeted him, 'but I've asked them to go quietly.'

'I have too,' responded John Lockley.

Two hours later the men were cooking the cow when Elijah came to John Lockley. 'The amaHlubi back down in the pass will not allow the herders up here to descend, inkosi. They are coming back, followed by more, all armed.'

John Lockley hurried over to where Anthony lay, attended by Robert Erskine. Nearby some of his Basuto troops waited.

'We've got a problem, Anthony. The armed herders are returning, and others are joining them.'

Anthony stood up with young Erskine's help. 'Help me to mount Chieftain again, lad.'

Robert Erskine complied and as Anthony settled into the saddle, the young man said, 'There's more trouble abrewing, sir, for Captain Barter didn't pay for the cow we slaughtered. He said it's custom for the Natal kaffirs to feed Government troops free of charge. Some of the men say that the amaHlubi are angry.'

'What?' said John Lockley. 'I gave him specific orders to pay for it.'

At that moment Barter rode up.

'Hell, man,' spoke up John Lockley, 'why didn't you pay for that damned cow? Now you've caused more problems.'

Barter quickly defended himself. 'It's normal procedure, sir. I didn't think you were serious.'

'If ever I give you an order of any kind, Barter, it's serious.'

Barter looked abashed. 'I'm sorry, sir. But I've come with a more pressing concern. I feel I should tell you I don't think the volunteers can be relied upon, sir.'

'What?' Anthony replied. 'You're the senior officer of the volunteers and you are telling us *your* men might bolt.'

'Afraid so, sir. It's this order from the Governor holding us from firing the first shot. The men are afraid, sir. The natives are all around them now and they cannot defend themselves because of the order.'

John Lockley and Anthony looked at one another. It had been a strange order to be given, but given it had been, and they must abide by it: they could not fire first.

'So,' said John Lockley, turning to look across to where he could now see many armed herders of the amaHlubi moving slowly closer to the line of mounted volunteers. A few hundred yards away other armed amaHlubi were emerging in twos and threes over the side of the rim of the wide basin. 'We'd better get over to them, Anthony.'

'You're right,' agreed Anthony. 'I'll ask you to reason with them, John Lockley. Explain again that we mean them no harm, but that we are here to do our duty, which is to turn them back down the pass.' He looked to Elijah Kambula. In the distance the remainder of his mounted Basutos covered a trail leading to what they believed was another pass down the mountain. 'And if our Basutos see the Europeans bolt, they may not stay either.'

As they rode over, the amaHlubi were spreading out and moving down closer to the line of volunteers.

They were within fifty yards when they heard Sergeant Clarke shout, 'We're surrounded! We'll be killed!'

'Oh Lord,' said John Lockley. 'Clarke's lost his nerve. Quick.'

'Hold fast, men,' shouted Anthony as he and John Lockley, Elijah and Erskine, and a few Basutos with them, spurred up to the volunteers.

They rode to the front of the line and with shouts, threatening looks and rifles waving in the air, cleared the herders back through the scrub towards the rim of the basin.

The volunteers, under the poor leadership of Clarke, were now beginning to break formation.

John Lockley rode to the far end of the line of troops, calling loudly, 'Come men, hold fast. This is no way to act.'

But some of the men were already starting to move back towards the escape route leading across to Giant's Castle Pass.

'Will no one stand with us?' shouted Anthony.

'I will, sir,' answered Robert Erskine, and two others rode out of the ranks to join them. They were Bond and Potterill, friends of young Erskine.

Potterill looked over to Anthony. 'We'll ride down in amongst the natives, sir, show our men there's naught to be afraid of.'

'No, lad, it's not necessary.'

But the fear had set in and as the amaHlubi pressed forward through the scrub again, suddenly Clarke screamed, 'Form fours!'

John Lockley knew these men were not regular troops, but young, cold and tired volunteers, but he was alarmed enough to shout, 'Don't panic! Steady. I order you to hold your positions.'

But the amaHlubi were aggressive now and were shouting and coming on steadily. And as Elijah Kambula called to Anthony, 'Inkosi, the enemy look dangerous this time,' there was a single shot, followed by a volley, and all three young men – Erskine, Bond and Potterill – fell dead from their horses.

'Oh no!' cried John Lockley as he turned at the same moment and saw Elijah's horse shot from under him.

John Lockley attempted to restrain the Karkloof volunteers closest to him. He grabbed the reins of the nearest horse. 'Stop, man! Stop!' But they were now in complete disarray and the man pulled his horse around and galloped after his mates.

Fifty yards away, John Lockley could see Anthony trying to help Elijah to mount up behind him. He spurred forward to help his friends. But a group of the natives were already upon Anthony, screaming, 'Kill the chief!' and as he turned to fend them off an assegai was thrust into his side. At the same time Elijah was shot through the head and fell dead to the ground. As John Lockley charged closer another native threw a spear right through the elbow of Anthony's useless left arm.

Chieftain whinnied and lifted his forelegs in defence against the attack, and Anthony, blood all over him but holding firm with his knees, worked his revolver free and shot one of the men point blank. Then he fired again and a second man fell.

John Lockley came thundering up, firing at Anthony's assailants, who now were trying to drag him from his horse. He hit one, and the others backed away briefly.

'I must help Elijah!' Anthony shouted.

'No! Leave him, Anthony. He's dead!' John Lockley grabbed Chieftain's reins as Anthony balanced, holding his revolver in his right hand, his useless arm dangling at his side.

As John Lockley pulled Chieftain around to ride away he felt a thud in his left shoulder. 'Let's go!' he shouted and the two friends spurred away, followed by the amaHlubi running at speed.

They galloped up the broken ground to the rim of the basin and found Induna Hlubi and the rest of his mounted Basutos holding there.

'Good to see you, men,' called John Lockley. 'Let's get out of here.'

The Basutos fired a few more volleys into the mass of amaHlubi and then followed their leaders.

John Lockley was amazed that Anthony did not faint on the

long ride to Giant's Castle Pass. They had extricated the assegai from his elbow and while the wound in his side was not deep, it was bleeding badly and he was steadily losing blood. Yet all Anthony could speak of were the brave men who had fallen at his side. When he realised John Lockley had been wounded he said, 'I'm so sorry, lad.'

John Lockley shook his head in wonder. 'You're an amazing man, Anthony Durnford. And if I ever have the ill-fortune to go into battle again, may it be with you at my side.'

Kate's eyes opened. It was still dark. She thought about John Lockley. She hated to be alone and she had been alone so much since she had married John Lockley. He really was a hopeless husband, going away like this all the time.

He had only been home for two days after being wounded in the shoulder up in the Drakensburgs, and then he and Anthony Durnford had turned around and ridden back to Meshlyn, wherever on God's earth that was. Anthony had been really badly wounded in a number of places. Everyone said his left arm would never be any use again, but he hadn't even put himself on the sick list. And now they were gone again, back up the Drakensburgs to bury the men who had fallen and take stock of things, so they said. They were both mad!

So here she was alone again. It served John Lockley right, really. He had driven her into Tom's arms. Oh, and what arms they were. Tom really made her days here bearable. She so hated Natal; it was primitive. How dearly she would love to go back to England – or anywhere else really.

Tom had said he would take her to Australia. He said there were opportunities there. He had told her about Sydney and the goldfields. Australia ... it sounded so exciting. Oh, how she loved excitement. He had told her to just say the word, and he would up and leave here in a minute and take her with him. Now what a scandal that would be.

She gave a knowing little smile and stretched down into the warmth of the bed. She closed her eyes and drifted back into sleep.

When she rose it was ten o'clock and by the time she had washed her hair and sat in the sun and dried it, it was time for luncheon with Mrs Dawney, the chemist's wife. Carmen Dawney had large green eyes and smooth olive skin; she was the only other really good-looking woman in Pietermaritzburg, and thus the two had formed a sort of alliance. They met every second Wednesday.

'Come in, Kate,' said Carmen as she took her visitor's pretty hat and hung it on a peg by the door. 'How are you?'

'Quite well, Carmy, and you?'

'I'm as healthy as an ox, but guess what?'

'What?'

She drew her visitor by the arm into her parlour, where tea had been poured. 'Sit down and I'll tell you.'

Kate sat.

'I'm going to have a baby.'

A peculiar look crossed Kate's face momentarily, then she said, 'Oh, that's marvellous. When?'

'Dr Hayward says he thinks I'm into my fourth month. We're terribly excited. If it's a girl it will be Mildred; if it's a boy it'll be Kenneth.'

'Nice names,' agreed Kate.

When Carmen saw her visitor off at the door two hours later she was all smiles. 'I'm going out now to sit in the sun and knit bootees.' She handed Kate her hat. 'I feel so fulfilled at last. You know, you should follow my lead.'

'What's that?' asked Kate.

'You should have a baby.'

Kate did not answer. As she mounted her horse and rode away she felt very odd. Oh, she was excited, for she was going out to Lief Liam's disused hut again to meet Tom and they would have a wonderful afternoon together; but Carmen's news had definitely disturbed her.

She sighed, looking down at her stomach as she rode along. *It couldn't be, could it? No, it couldn't be.* She always made sure Tom was careful. But there had been that one time, about a month ago, after John Lockley had gone away on this Langalibalele business. Yet she'd been with her husband only a few days before, so . . .

Then when John Lockley had been home and wounded, he had not made love to her at all, and of course she'd been regularly with Tom again; but he was usually so careful. *No, no, I mustn't think this way. Everything will be all right.*

She had just turned into Berg Street when she saw Charles Preston, John Lockley's friend from the 75th Regiment. He called and waved to her and she responded warmly, then she saw the two women who rounded the corner behind him; Jane and Victoria. They carried sunshades and Jane hailed her as they came along. 'Good afternoon, Kate, how are you? We haven't seen you for weeks.'

Naturally Jane would take the opportunity to remind her of that! John Lockley on his brief visit here had told her that Mrs McLean had lost her husband. She looked down at the two women. 'Yes, good afternoon, Jane; I'm sorry, I've been busy.' She met Victoria's eyes. 'Mrs McLean, please accept my condolences. I didn't realise you were in Pietermaritzburg or I would certainly have come by.'

Victoria gave a small smile. 'Thank you.'

'Is your daughter with you?'

'No, she's still at the mission.'

Making conversation, Jane asked, 'Where are you going? I don't see you on a horse very often.'

Kate shook her black curls back over her shoulder. 'I ride more often than you think, Jane. In fact I like riding really; it's just that when I was up at the farm, the flies and insects were so much worse than here that I refrained. Anyway, I'd best be on my way. Nice to have seen you both.'

She pushed her horse on by, with a backward wave of her hand.

The two women were well down Berg Street when Victoria said, 'I wonder where Kate was going? You asked her but she didn't tell you.'

Jane nodded thoughtfully. 'Yes, I noticed that.'

'You're not sure of her, love, are you?'

Jane looked round at her friend's face. No, she was not sure of Kate, she never had been really. While Kate was beautiful and gregarious, Jane felt she was not the right wife for her nephew. Then the day she had brought Victoria back from the mission with her, Christopher had told her something which really troubled her.

Her husband had looked at her with his honest eyes and said, 'Jane, darlin', George Russell at the brickworks tells me that there's gossip abroad in 'Maritzburg about our Kate.'

'What are they saying?'

'That she's hot and strong for Tom King. The men at the brickworks were talking about it at lunchtime today.'

While Jane had never been enthusiastic about Kate, she was quick to defend her. 'Darling one, there's always gossip in this town. If it's not about one person, it's another.'

'That's exactly what I said to George, but all he did was shake his head and say he'd told the men the very same, but one of them swore he's seen Kate and King alone out on the Umsindusi River near Blakeley's place, and they weren't fishing.'

And now, as Jane looked at Victoria, she answered her friend's question with the words, 'Victoria love, let's just say I wouldn't have chosen Kate for my nephew.'

Victoria patted her friend's arm. 'Very diplomatic, dear.'

Shortly afterwards, the two women entered the Wesleyan church hall. A week earlier Victoria had met with the Reverend Dr Lindley and today he had sent word to The Grange that he would like to see her again.

Victoria had confided in Jane that she was tired; now that Frank had gone she felt her work here in Africa was over. As she put it, 'Jane, I feel twenty years is long enough. It's not the same without Frank. My mother asks for me in every letter and somehow I want to go home.'

When they came through the door, the Reverend Dr Lindley greeted them with the words, 'Since we spoke last week, it's almost as if we've had divine intervention. A letter came in from Durban yesterday: a new missionary will be arriving on the SS *Coral Sea* in January. And I should say he'll be ideal to take over from you in Greytown.'

Victoria was taken aback. 'So soon? You gave me to understand that it could be six months away.'

'Yes, indeed, as I say, a surprise to all of us.'

Victoria nodded. 'You see, Dr Lindley, I'm not speaking for my daughter. She loves Africa. She's engaged to be married, and will want to remain at the mission, she's so much a part of it. She started a hospital there, you know,' she finished proudly.

'Yes, I do, and I see no reason why she cannot stay on and continue God's work. I'm sure the new man, who, incidentally, brings his wife with him, will be happy to have help.'

Half an hour later the two friends sat in the small tea room alongside Jack Gedge's auction mart in Chapel Street. They could hear the lots coming up for sale and the voices and bidding. Victoria lifted her teacup and took a sip. 'I suppose while I'm here I should go to Durban and book passage home, as I'm so close.'

'Yes, we can travel down on Monday with Christopher. He's going for a few days.'

Victoria's sincere eyes lifted. 'Oh Jane, you're so good. Thank you for having me here these past weeks, with you and Christopher. You've helped me so much ... Coming up to Greytown and all. I know I've been full of nerves of late. I can never repay you and ...' She broke off as her eyes filled with tears.

Jane stretched her hand across the table to cover Victoria's. 'My darling, you've paid me all these years by your wonderful friendship. Let me tell you, when I came here and saw this place twenty years ago I wanted to turn round and go straight back to England. And there you were, so neat and lovely and confident about your work here ... well, you gave me confidence, inspired me to stay in a way. And now that you've lost Frank and made your decision to go home to America ... well, I'll miss you more than I can say.' Now her eyes too filled with tears as she sat there holding Victoria's hand.

They were both silent for a time while Jack Gedge announced another lot, then Victoria dabbed the corners of her eyes with her handkerchief. 'Thank you, my dear friend. It was a hard decision for me, as you know. But my father and both Frank's parents have died since we've been here, and my mother's old and missing me. You know, my father was so against our coming to Africa; and he died without ever seeing us again. So the time has come. I just hope the Lord won't think I've let him down.'

Jane made a rumbling sound in her throat. 'Goodness gracious, of course He won't. You've never let anyone down in your whole life, least of all Him. And if He has any sense at all He'll be making sure there are thousands more just like you born every month.'

Victoria's eyes came quickly round to her friend's. Then she smiled and suddenly they both laughed.

'There,' said Jane, 'it's so good to hear you laugh. Let's have another cup of tea.'

John Lockley lifted the flap of Anthony Durnford's tent where he sat writing at his desk in the campaign headquarters' camp at Bushman's River. It had been raining on and off for days and while the shoulders of the uniform John Lockley wore were damp, the smile he wore was wide.

'I've just heard the splendid news, you're a Lieutenant-Colonel. Congratulations . . . sir.'

Anthony laughed and his blue eyes twinkled. 'That news travelled quickly. I only heard myself a few hours ago.'

'You deserve it.'

'Thank you, but I think it'll not be long before you catch up with me and become a half-colonel yourself.' He moved round to face his visitor. The cuts on his face were still obvious and he wore his left arm in a sling. He was still suffering great pain, though he would not speak of it.

John Lockley looked carefully at him. 'You need some rest. You've never stopped riding all over the country since you were injured. Anyone else would have been on the sick list from day one. You intimidated me into not going on it either. How could I, with a mere shoulder wound, take sick leave if you, with all your injuries, did not?'

Anthony smiled as John Lockley shook his head, and, walking to a folding table at the side of the tent, picked up a newspaper. 'Are they still writing about us?'

'Yes they are, but that's the *Natal Colonist*. Sanderson, the editor, is the only one who does not vilify us, laddie. The rest are blaming me for the débâcle of Giant's Castle Pass. My crowning fault was to brand a portion of their volunteers with cowardice. They don't like that. It seems I have very few supporters indeed, other than one or two like good Bishop Colenso.'

'Everything you said in your report was absolutely accurate. It's a miracle that you and I are not lying dead at the top of Bushman's River Pass. Only our Basutos showed any courage at all.'

'Yes, and that makes them angrier still – that black men stood by us, when white men did not.'

'You've got that right . . . sir.'

Anthony grinned and patted the paper in front of him with his good right hand. 'And it looks like we'll be busier than ever, as they've asked me to undertake the position of Acting Colonial Engineer and to choose an engineer assistant. Would you be that man, Major Harrison?'

John Lockley's face brightened. 'I'll say I would. Thank you, I accept with pleasure.'

Just then the tent flap opened again and Sergeant Flannagan stood there. He saluted. 'Sir, information's just come in. They've caught Langa, sir.' 'Langa' was the troops' informal name for Chief Langalibalele. 'Apparently he wandered for six weeks on the high veld in the Drakensburgs, then some fella in another tribe betrayed him to a troop of our boys, the ones up from Kaffaria, I think. Anyway they've got Langa and four of his sons and they're being taken back to 'Maritzburg for trial.'

Anthony nodded. 'I see. Thanks, Sergeant.'

As the sergeant departed, John Lockley said, 'So, they've got the old bloke.'

'Yes, and from what I heard from Captain Pat Boehm of the Seventy-fifth this morning, there have already been reprisals against the amaPutini people for giving shelter and aid to some of the amaHlubi while they were escaping.'

'What?'

'I'm afraid it's true. Boehm said they've taken almost all the men of the amaPutini tribe prisoner.'

'But they are allied by marriage and kinship to the amaHlubi, naturally they would aid them.'

'I know that, laddie, I know that, and I fear the poor souls will need a champion before long.'

'What of the women and children?'

'God knows.'

The following day, John Lockley and Anthony broke camp to return to Pietermaritzburg for Christmas. The rain had stopped in the night and the sun sparkled on the plain.

They were packing the last of their equipment on Horatio and Chieftain when a man came up to them. He was of medium height and he wore a motley arrangement of clothing, from a soft felt hat with a red band to a pair of old boots that looked too large. There was something familiar about him as he doffed his old hat and stood there looking at the two officers.

'Yes,' said John Lockley. 'Do you want something?'

He nodded. 'Yes, inkosi.'

'Well, go ahead.'

His English was not good, but it was understandable. 'I would be soldier wit' you. Inkosi Durn-ford and Harri-son. I want be wit' you. My father say . . . you good chiefs.'

Anthony smiled. 'Are you asking to join our native contingent? Our Basuto mounted troop?'

'*Yeh bo*, inkosi.'

'Good man, we can do with as many as we can get.'

Just then Tenny Rama came by and John Lockley called, 'Tenny, we've got a new recruit. Come and take care of him.'

As soon as Tenny saw the man he ran over and hugged him, and the man responded warmly.

'Why? Do you know him?' asked John Lockley.

Tenny nodded his head quite fiercely. 'He son of Elijah Kambula. Die in mountain. He Simeon Kambula.'

'Elijah's son,' said Anthony quite softly. Then he stretched out his good right arm. 'Welcome, Simeon, laddie, welcome.'

CHAPTER TWENTY-SEVEN

It was the Saturday before Christmas and a drizzle of rain was falling on the parade ground at Fort Napier when John Lockley came out of staff headquarters and ran across to his office on the far side of the open space. As he mounted the few steps and brushed the drops from his uniform, Anthony appeared down the corridor and came towards him.

John Lockley could see immediately that there was something wrong. 'Anthony, you look troubled.'

His friend's brow wrinkled and he shook his head. 'John Lockley, lad, the enmity towards me has reached a new height. They've killed Prince.'

'What? Who has?'

'I don't know. Some of the colonists. They took out their chagrin on my poor old dog.' His eyes clouded. 'He was poisoned this morning. My landlady thinks it was done when she took him to the butcher's. He came in and died in front of me, John Lockley.'

'Oh hell, Anthony, the bloody cowards. Poor innocent Prince. I'm so sorry.'

'It's knocked the stuffing out of me a bit, laddie. I think I'll move out of the town and lodge here at the fort. I really don't want to live in the middle of a township where the hatred towards me is so great.'

'Hell, just because you told the truth about their faint-hearted sons. Why aren't they doing the same to me? I was your second-in-command and supported you in all you said.'

'Perhaps it's because you belong here, lad. I'm the stranger, and I was in charge of the expedition.'

John Lockley put his hand on his friend's shoulder. 'I'm deeply offended for you, Anthony. I wish we knew who the devil was responsible.'

Anthony shook his head. 'Wasn't it the Roman Terence who said, "Obsequiousness begets friends, truth, hatred"?'

John Lockley gave a wan smile, 'Whoever said it was unfortunately right. Come, my friend, let's go and have a drink.' He slapped him affectionately on the shoulder and they moved off towards the mess.

'Please don't mention this latest incident, lad,' Anthony said as they walked. 'It'll get around the fort soon enough.'

As they were the only two officers of the Royal Engineers in Pietermaritzburg, they were honorary members of the mess of the 75th. They were greeted at the mess door by Captain Pat Boehm. His strong face broke into a smile. 'Good evening, my friends, can I join you?'

'Certainly,' replied Anthony.

They came through the door into the smoky atmosphere of the interior and almost immediately were aware of the raised voices at the bar.

'Take that back, Redberry.' It was Charles Preston's voice.

'Like hell I will. It's common talk.' The angry reply came from 'Redberry' Waters, whose real name was John, but because of the dark red mole on his chin, his nickname was universal. He was known as a man with a sharp tongue, ready to pass on hearsay, and while as a rule he was not vicious, he liked to have a laugh at the expense of others.

Charles Preston was not a belligerent man, so it was surprising to hear him repeat, 'I said take that back, Waters. He's my good friend and I'll not have his wife slandered.'

A few other voices made conciliatory remarks but Redberry's voice came over them. 'I didn't slander her, all I said was I wish I could get as close to her as Tom King does. Everybody knows, so why the devil are you playing Harrison's protector?'

'Everybody knows what, Waters?' It was John Lockley's voice now.

All the men at the bar turned to the newcomers.

John Lockley looked to Charles. 'Thank you for taking Kate's part, Charles, but I'll attend to this now.'

Redberry Waters' hawklike features registered surprise and abashment, but he soon regained his composure and looking around the group of men replied, 'Look, Harrison, I meant nothing by it, damn it. It's just . . .'

'Just what?'

Waters gestured around the men near him. 'We've all heard it, Harrison: that your wife is overfriendly with Tom King.'

John Lockley's eyes narrowed. Anthony, at his side, could see the muscles in his jaw clenching and he took him by the arm. 'Come, laddie, let's leave this.'

John Lockley moved out of Anthony's hold and, stepping closer to Waters, said, 'So everybody's heard it, have they? And my friends have kept it from me, have they? So you're just doing a bloody service to the place by bringing it out in the open, eh?'

Waters backed away. 'Leave it, Harrison, I said nothing that isn't true.'

'Is that so?' It was obvious that John Lockley was only barely controlling himself; he looked as if he would lash out and hit Redberry at any second. Anthony and Pat Boehm moved as one, and, taking hold of him again, Anthony said, 'Come on, lad, don't waste your time on him.'

'Yes,' agreed Pat. 'He's not worth it, John Lockley.'

John Lockley struggled but a few of the others moved forward in front of Waters and hustled him away down the bar.

Charles Preston turned to John Lockley who still stood in the grasp of Anthony and Pat. 'Wouldn't have blamed you if you'd punched him; I nearly hit the bastard myself.'

'Come.' It was Anthony's voice of reason. 'Let's go somewhere where the four of us can forget this and have a quiet drink together.'

John Lockley shook himself free of his friends' hold and they all moved to the door. When they were outside in the corridor John Lockley was more calm. 'I suppose you're right, Anthony. Let's go to Nelson's. We can always get a drink there.'

'That's it,' agreed Pat. 'Your uncle's hotel will be good for a dram.'

When John Lockley came home he was a little the worse for wear. He had drowned his sorrows in more whisky than he had taken for years. When he found that Kate was not at home, he was inclined to drink more, which he did in the form of several gins. At eleven o'clock Umslopagas came in and found him asleep in the parlour. He helped him up the stairs to bed,

399

where he slept soundly until the following morning and woke with a dry mouth and a throbbing head.

He left before his wife was out of bed and spent the day drinking water and studying the plans for the new fortifications they were to build up north in Newcastle.

He escorted his wife to the Governor's Christmas party that night and said nothing about his confrontation with Redberry Waters. So the days passed until Christmas came around.

Phoebe and Thulmi stood up from where they had knelt beside Frank's grave. The evening sun was descending swiftly in a scarlet and golden ball and the African insects of the night were buzzing around them.

'Let's go home.' Victoria's voice sounded from behind them where she had been standing watching. She sighed. How could it be Christmas Eve without Frank? A tear formed at the edge of her eye and spilled down her cheek.

'*Yeh bo*,' replied Thulmi, standing up and putting out his hand to help Phoebe.

Seven weeks ago they had buried Frank here; down beyond the edge of the mission fence near an umbrella-like acacia tree. It was a pretty spot where he had often come to study his Bible and prayer book, and it looked out to the hills.

They moved off together and Phoebe took her mother's arm. Ben was arriving at seven o'clock. Late tonight they would sing Christmas hymns with their people from the kraal, and Ben would stay the night. Then tomorrow Phyllis May and Graham would come for Christmas morning prayer and remain for a quiet luncheon. Always on Christmas afternoon Phoebe and her parents had gone to the kraal where their people danced and sang and gave small gifts in the Christian way. They would do the same thing this year. Life must go on, and as normally as possible.

Ben's mother had invited them for Christmas luncheon but they had said they did not feel up to socialising. Mrs Fielding always asked a dozen or so of her friends over and had a very busy Christmas Day. She had pointed out that she expected Ben to come home for supper, for she did not want the whole day to go by without seeing him.

They came by the little hospital which was really no more than a shed, but it was pristine clean and it was Phoebe's pride.

Phyllis May was really showing signs of being a marvellous nurse and had helped her immensely with it. She rode out to help Phoebe every Monday, Wednesday and Friday.

Phoebe had been wearing a serious look of late. It was not only the death of her father that played daily on her mind: there had been a thoughtful expression in her brown eyes and at times the determined tilt to her chin became more pronounced.

Her mother's plans to return to the United States had been a topic of discussion even before she went down to 'Maritzburg for the few weeks with Jane. And then when she returned to the mission and told her daughter she had booked passage, Phoebe truly realised she meant to go: to leave the mission, to leave Africa. Her mother had said she was tired, that she did not have the inclination to go on without her father, that Grandma in Cleveland was asking her to come back. Phoebe had been remembering the day years ago after the awful civil war in her homeland had ended when her parents had suggested returning to America.

She recalled what she had said: '...while I know I'm American, and I am proud of that, really ... you see I do not know America. My home is here in Natal with you. Some day I want to see the country of my birth, but this country will always be my home.'

And now a new missionary was arriving in January and her mother was leaving in February.

When the trio arrived back at the house they made a cup of tea, and it was not long before Ben arrived. He stabled his horse and came across the little back garden to the veranda, where Phoebe stood waiting, lamp in hand, in the warm night air. The gentle beam of light bathed her youthful features, and her skin and fair hair glowed with a golden sheen.

Ben thought how pretty she looked but he wished she wouldn't wear her hair out on her shoulders like that, he preferred it neatly tied back.

'Good evening, Ben.'

'How are you, dearest?'

'Passing fair, come in.'

He followed her into the house.

The evening passed quietly, Ben and Phoebe playing chess while Victoria read.

After supper Victoria chose the hymns and Phoebe went to put out the musical instruments. They had a strange band, most of it percussion: with cymbals, a triangle, two small drums and the melody supplied by an old flute that Victoria and Phoebe could both play. Nevertheless the band had delivered music for many a resounding rendition of praise to the Lord and they expected it to do so again. Thulmi played the triangle, at which he was certainly adept, and thoroughly enjoyed himself.

From half past ten onwards the kraal folk began to arrive. Phoebe and Jenny, the housemaid, lit the lamps on both ends of the veranda and the moths began to circle the light in earnest.

By the hour of eleven everyone was seated, spreading along the veranda and down and around the steps. Lila stood and read out in her stilted but intriguing English the name of the first hymn.

'We will all be-gin by sing-ing "Hark the Her-ald An-gels Sing".'

And so one hymn followed another, until Victoria stood up in the lamplight with the moths and beetles and small insects playing around her. She remained silent for a few moments, looking at the people she loved, but whom she would soon leave. Part of her did not want to go, but there was the other part that wanted to see her mother again; to walk along the broad expanse of Superior Street and look in the exciting shop windows; to ramble east along the gentle eminence of Euclid Avenue to the gardens, smooth lawns and shade trees; to be back in a real city again. She understood that her daughter felt this country was her home; it was all she had ever known, whereas Victoria had lived the first thirty years of her life in America. Phoebe had Ben and would make their home here. It pained Victoria to leave her, but she accepted that Phoebe had her own life to live.

She looked down at her feet where little Shinu sat. His arm was better and out of the bandage now. He looked up at her and smiled. She felt the tears coming to her eyes but she managed to quell them.

Her voice quivered just a little as she began to speak and then it steadied and gained strength, echoing over her congregation in the African night:

'Lord, we cannot see you, we cannot hear you,
But we know you are there,
We live in the promise of your love and we believe in you.
For you are the rock of ages;
And suffer mankind to come unto you;
When our hearts are heavy you lighten them,
When our will is weak you make it strong: You give us the
courage to leave that which is dear to us,
And to walk upon the new road with steadfast tread,
We will be ready when you call,
Our Lord of Hosts,
Amen.'

And 'Amen' rang out from all the throats around her.

Then she lifted her arms to them. 'Goodnight to you all and tomorrow we will be happy for it is the birthday of our Lord . . . Christmas.'

The kraal people wandered off in groups, and Phoebe and Ben put out the lamps with the help of Thulmi.

When they came inside Victoria stood in the front room folding the hymn sheets. 'Thulmi,' she said, 'thank you for your help tonight, you played the triangle beautifully. Now, it's time we were all in bed, and would you please wake me at half past six in the morning.'

'*Yeh bo*, Mrs Victoria.' Then he turned to Phoebe. 'You go bed now, Miss Phoebe?'

Ben turned on Thulmi. 'Miss McLean and I shall sit here a minute or two first. Off you go, Thulmi.'

Thulmi stood his ground, looking at Phoebe. She was about to speak when Ben said, 'I told you to go. Go on.' And with a gesture of dismissal he pointed to the door.

Thulmi did not move, and Phoebe said quickly, 'It's all right, Thulmi. Do as Mr Ben says, please.'

With a backward glare at Ben, Thulmi moved out through the door and past the scullery, down to his little bedroom at the very back of the house near the other small room which Fantasia, the cook, shared with her husband.

When Victoria had gone Ben took Phoebe in his arms and kissed her. 'I love you so much, Feeb, I really do. We'll be married soon. How I wish we were married now.' He ran his hands across her breasts and kissed the side of her neck. Then he kissed her again, holding her body close to his and feeling the undulations of her through her clothing.

His voice was thick as he said softly, 'Please, let's ... tonight.'

'Let's what?'

'You know, Feeb, darling. Come on, please. Come to my room. It'll be all right. I love you so.'

He did love her, she was sure. They had even talked about their wedding day, sometime in April, when the heat was less and the winter winds had not yet come.

She closed her eyes and he kissed them: he kissed her forehead, her cheeks, her lips. 'Come on, sweetheart. We'll soon be husband and wife. I love you. I need you, please ... I really do. I've waited so long.'

She felt the warmth of him, and his young, virile body along the length of her. He asked her so often, and always she refused.

Phoebe could see his eyes in the reflected light coming through the open window from the Christmas moon. She hesitated, and then she took his hand in hers.

And now a change came over her, and with almost a detached expression, she allowed him to take her down the darkened hall to his room.

The following morning the mist rolled across the mission and hid the surrounding hills. Victoria was woken by Thulmi as requested and Christmas morning began.

When seven o'clock had passed and Phoebe was not out of bed, her mother went in to her, but she was not there.

The bed was neatly made as it always was once Phoebe had risen. Victoria went back to the kitchen where Thulmi was helping Fantasia by setting the breakfast table.

'Do you know where Phoebe is?'

'*Yeh bo*. She go walking with little Treedy.'

'In the mist?'

He nodded.

'Where?'

'To grave of Umfundisi Khulu.'

Victoria walked out of the back door and on to the veranda and stood looking across the yard for a minute or two, and then, sure enough, her daughter began to appear through the

404

mist in the distance, walking hand in hand with Treedy, the little Hottentot girl from the kraal.

She waved, and Phoebe waved back. Then Victoria heard someone come through the door behind her. It was Ben and he wore a wide smile. 'Good morning, Mrs McLean, and a happy and holy Christmas to you.'

'Thank you, Ben dear, and the same to you.'

He nodded down to where Phoebe came strolling home. 'Is that my darling coming through the mist?'

'It is.'

'I'll go and meet her.'

'Don't be long. Fantasia will have breakfast on the table shortly.'

Ben leapt down the few steps and stopped to pick a dahlia before he strode across to Phoebe. 'Good morning, darling, and a happy and holy Christmas to you,' he said. He handed her the flower and bent forward to kiss her.

'Run along, sweetheart,' Phoebe said to Treedy, patting her tight curls. 'If you go into the kitchen I'm sure Miss Fantasia will have a treat for you.'

At that moment Thulmi came out on the back veranda and called, 'Miss Phoebe, you come in now. Breakfast ready.'

Ben frowned. 'Really, Phoebe, you shouldn't allow that, you know.'

'What?'

'The way that Zulu speaks to you in such a familiar fashion. He should be asking you to come in, not telling you.'

Her lovely brown eyes met his. She shook her head.

'And once we're married there'll be none of this "Miss Phoebe" nonsense. In fact, it's a good thing you'll be parting company with him. My mother does not approve of his hanging around you the way he does.'

Phoebe sighed. 'Ben, I really don't care what your mother thinks.'

He looked offended. 'Phoebe, what an awful thing to say. When you're my wife . . .'

'That's the point, Ben,' she interrupted. 'There's no easy way to tell you and I'm sorry. But I'm not going to be your wife.'

Ben's eyes widened. 'What?'

'I'm sorry, Ben, please try to understand. I'm not going to become your wife.'

'But . . . but after last night . . . it was wonderful.'

'Yes, Ben, perhaps it was. But it was the final proof to me that I should not marry you. There are many reasons, but the main one is that I don't love you, Ben, and I never have.'

'But your father and mother approved, and I love you. Please, Feeb, many people marry without love. Love grows in time.'

'That isn't the sort of marriage I want, Ben.'

He took her hands in his. 'This is ridiculous. I know you don't mean it. You've had a lot of strain lately, what with your father dying and your mother talking of leaving. Come on, darling, let's have breakfast and forget all this. It's Christmas Day.'

'Oh, Ben, dear Ben, please, this isn't easy. I don't want to hurt you any more than I already have. I'm not proud of myself, I should have told you ages ago. I never should have become engaged to you.'

Now Ben looked truly mystified. 'Then why on earth did you . . . did you do that with me last night?'

She dropped his hands and took hold of his arms, looking right into his unhappy eyes. 'Ben, please try to accept this. In the last twelve hours I've understood a lot of things. I had a friend who married when she never should have . . . because she didn't know . . . about things. I thought that if we managed to find some excitement, some love, some compatibility, that way; then yes, I could go through with our marriage.'

His face dropped. Suddenly he comprehended. 'Then,' he said in a resigned manner, 'it wasn't the same for you as it was for me?'

'No, Ben, it wasn't, and I'm sorry.'

'But Feeb, sometimes it's difficult . . . the first time.'

'No Ben.'

'Feeb, I can't believe this.'

'Believe it, Ben darling, please believe it.'

He shook his head and moved out of her grasp. 'It's hard for me to take, Feeb.'

'It's hard for me to tell you; but a life together would have been far worse. I would have made you miserable. And you don't really approve of me; think about it. There's so much of

406

what I like to do which you do not regard as proper. In time those things would magnify.'

He stood looking at her without speaking. Then he shook his head again. 'You mean it?'

'I do.' She removed the ring she wore and handed it to him.

He moved away a few paces and stood looking at her, shaking his head. Then he said, 'In that case, I'll ... er ... get my things. I suppose I'd better be off ...'

'I'll come in with you.'

The sun was dispersing the mist as they walked across the yard and up the steps to his room.

'Ben, I'll go and tell Mum that you're leaving.'

His voice was strained. 'Yes, you do that.'

When Phoebe came into the kitchen her mother looked up from where she sat. 'Your eggs are getting cold. Where's Ben?'

'Mummy, please come into the parlour, I must speak with you.'

Victoria could see that this was important, that the cold eggs did not matter. She followed her daughter.

'Mummy, Ben's going home. I've just told him I won't be marrying him.'

Victoria's mouth actually dropped open. 'Not marrying him? Why?'

'I don't love him, Mum, and I never will. It would be wrong of me to marry Ben, truly wrong.'

Victoria took a loud, deep breath. 'Well, this is a surprise. Poor Ben. I hope he'll be all right. You're sure this is what you want?'

Phoebe nodded.

'What on earth are you going to do now?'

'I'm coming with you, Mummy, to America. That's what I'm going to do.'

When Phoebe saw Ben off at the front gate, he put out his hand towards her and she took it. He found it hard to speak and her heart was heavy for him as he managed to say, 'There's one thing I have to tell you, Phoebe. I'll always remember last night. I'm not sorry it happened. Not at all.'

'Nor am I, Ben. Goodbye.'

'Goodbye.'

He took her in his arms and held her close for the last time. Her eyes were damp when he turned and mounted his horse.

'I don't know what the devil Mum's going to say,' he said to himself as he rode off.

Phoebe turned from the gate and stood there alone for a time, watching Jenny picking something over in the vegetable patch: probably some sweet potato for the Christmas dinner. She lifted her gaze from the woman's bent form and her eyes narrowed as she saw movement in the distance. Someone was running across the velt towards the mission. It was Darlengi!

She ran forward and they met near the straggling hedge that formed part of the mission fence. He was dressed in his wonderfully eccentric manner: white shirt with a red kerchief tied round his throat, brown trousers, crocodile skin belt with a knife in a pouch attached, and today he carried boots slung over his shoulder on a rope.

'Darlengi, how grand to see you.'

His head bent towards her, and he took her hands. 'And to see you.'

'It's Christmas Day.'

'I know.'

'Of course you do. How are things with you?'

'Ah, the machinations of Zululand.' He gave a small laugh. 'Things are as usual with me . . .' He was looking squarely at her as he always did. 'Phoebe, I heard from some traders that your father had died.'

'Yes, seven weeks ago.'

'I am so sorry. I wanted to see you and tell you. He was greatly loved and respected. His life was one of those that make a difference to many people. I would like to speak with your mother, if she's here.'

'Yes, she's here'

They moved off together towards the mission house and Phoebe said, 'I'm very pleased you have come, Darlengi, for we're leaving Natal . . . Mother and me. We're going to America.'

There was surprise in his voice. 'When?'

'Well, soon actually. Mother has taken a berth on the SS *Kidde Halon* which sails from Durban in February, and now I shall go with her.'

'But what about Ben Fielding?'

She halted and he turned round to her. She pressed her lips together and closed her eyes briefly before she answered, 'I should never have become engaged to him. It was a mistake.'

He nodded. 'Yes, it was. Though I said nothing to you when you told me you were taking that course, for I believed you had resolved to move on with your life ... as you could not have the life you would choose.'

She nodded. 'And you were right. I came to the conclusion that a life with Ben would be acceptable. But I was wrong. I found out that I could not marry one man while I love another.'

At that second, they both thought of Ellen. They were standing looking at each other, both knowing the other's thoughts. The seconds passed and Phoebe lifted her hand and took his arm. 'How well I remember the first time I told you of my feelings. It was at The Grange in Pietermaritzburg.'

'Yes,' he said, 'a few days before Ellen married.'

At that moment Victoria came out on to the veranda and they moved forward in unison.

'Darlengi, a Christmas visit; how kind of you.'

'Hardly kind, Mrs McLean, it is always pleasing for me to see you. I learned of your husband's death. I am sorry; he will be missed by many.'

Victoria sighed. 'Yes, that's true, thank you.' She motioned for him to come inside and he and Phoebe mounted the steps.

Victoria's eyes followed him. He always fascinated her. His English was faultless and she conceded that Phoebe doted on him, but somehow she could never accept what this man was: a Zulu induna who advised Cetshwayo, and yet who at the same time had the authority and civility of the Governor. It was quite disturbing to her. While she loved and respected Thulmi and Fantasia and Lila and Tokwa and all the mission folk, they were what they were: native Africans who had received Christianity and with it some of the cloak of civilisation. She felt comfortable with them, trusting them and appreciating them, but Darlengi was something else all together.

He sat down and turned his uncompromising gaze upon her. 'I would like to offer my sympathy and also the sympathy of many of my fellow Zulus who have experienced your late husband's kindness. There are many who hide behind the guise of "missionary" and who are little more than charlatans,

409

coming into Zululand under the pretext of preaching the Lord's word, and taking advantage of my people and my country. The Reverend McLean was not one of these ... as you and your daughter are not. I have heard Cetshwayo say that a Christian Zulu is a Zulu spoiled, but I do not accept that point of view. If all humans adopted the attitudes of Jesus Christ, it would be a better world by far. And you and your family have enriched the lives around you.'

Victoria was in awe of him; she gave a small smile. 'Thank you, Darlengi. I'm well aware of those who are no more than traders or political agitators calling themselves missionaries, they make our job much harder.'

'But a job which you are leaving, I understand.'

Victoria looked questioningly at Phoebe.

'I have told Darlengi of our intentions,' Phoebe explained.

Victoria faced back to her visitor. 'The truth is that I can do my job anywhere. So while I'm leaving Natal I'm not leaving the Lord's work. And only in this past hour have I been informed by my daughter that she'll be accompanying me.'

Darlengi looked at Phoebe as he replied, 'You will both be greatly missed.'

'There's a new missionary arriving here in January, and from what I understand of him, he is a caring, dedicated man.'

Darlengi smiled. 'Good. Have you told your people you are going?'

Victoria shook her head. 'As you can understand, that will be very difficult indeed for me.'

'Yes, it will.'

Then Victoria asked, 'Would you like a drink? Some refreshment?'

At this he stood. 'No, I shall go over to the kraal for something, thank you. It is your Christmas morning and no doubt you have a service soon.'

He bent from the shoulders and Victoria almost tentatively offered her hand, which he took briefly before turning to Phoebe. 'If you have a few more minutes?'

'Of course I do, don't be silly. I'll walk over to the kraal with you.'

As they came out on to the veranda, Phyllis May and Graham were riding through the gate. They reached the steps and dismounted.

When Phoebe had greeted them she took Darlengi's arm. 'This is Darlengi, my friend.'

Now Phyllis May knew of him but Graham did not, and when Darlengi said, 'How do you do?' Graham almost fell off his horse. But he gathered himself quickly and his rejoinder came swiftly, 'How do you do?' And as he dismounted he was quick-witted enough to know that this particular Zulu probably shook hands as well, so he held out his hand, and was vindicated.

Thulmi appeared from around the side of the house to take the horses, and Phoebe gestured towards the house. 'Mummy's inside. Darlengi and I are off to the kraal but I'll be back for ten o'clock prayers.'

Darlengi smiled at them. 'Perhaps I shall see you again sometime. Goodbye.'

Graham watched them across the grass and shook his head. It was marvellous to see a Zulu as urbane as this. He supposed that in a hundred years there would be thousands like Darlengi. He liked to think so anyway. 'Admirable,' he whispered to himself, as he turned and followed his wife.

As they headed to the kraal Phoebe said, 'It's so very opportune that you came today, for how could I possibly have left without saying goodbye?'

'Yes, I would not have liked that. Are you sure you want to leave?'

'Oh Darlengi, I've been so muddled these last weeks since Daddy died. I was trying to imagine what my life would be like at Ben's side. I knew all along that I didn't love him in the same way he loved me. But I'd gone along with marrying him ... for Daddy's sake, really. And if Daddy had lived ... well, who knows? But he didn't and that changed things. So I had to know if I could truly live a satisfied lifetime as Ben's wife. Marry him, see him night and morning for always; bear his children.' She stopped walking and so did Darlengi. For some seconds she met his eyes, then, lifting her hands in a frustrated gesture, she walked on.

He followed her. 'So when did you decide you could not do that?'

'Last night.'

'I see.'

She was quiet for some time, walking at his side, the hem of

411

her dress pulling through the grass. Then she halted again and once more Darlengi stopped with her. Her eyes found the distant hills and then came back to his. 'My dear friend, we have said so many intimate things to each other over the years. You know I love John Lockley. I suppose I've loved him all my life ... from when I was six, anyway. He's married and I have no claim on him. I'm not practised in the ways of love, and I remembered darling Ellen marrying Michael, and ... so desperately wanting ... you instead. It drove her mad.'

A warm wind came whistling softly through the grass as they stood silently with their own thoughts for a time. Then Phoebe took a deep breath. 'And while I'm not Ellen, and I do really like Ben, I had to see if there could ever be more ... something deeper; some concord, some ... passion with him. So last night I attempted to love Ben as he did me.'

Darlengi shook his head and smiled at her. 'I said it years ago, and I say it again; you are a remarkable woman, Phoebe McLean.'

'So ... you don't disapprove?'

And then he laughed out loud. 'Disapprove of my good friend proving she could not bind herself to Ben Fielding? No, I do not disapprove.'

They said no more for a time and, as they drew close to the kraal, Phoebe paused again and turned to him. 'So I'm going to America where I don't have to run into John Lockley Harrison and have my heart torn all the time.'

Darlengi put out his hand and she took it. 'But you will continue to love him.'

'Yes, I will, as you do.'

'You think I still love him after all that has happened?'

'Yes. Don't you?'

He was still holding her hand and she lifted her other free one and touched the scar on his forearm. 'What's this?'

He gave a small sound which could almost be mistaken for a laugh as he gazed at her intently, his eyes weighing her. 'In truth, I think Mattana is not dead.'

'The great witch doctor?'

'Yes, only she could have asked such a question at that moment.' Then he turned from her. 'Look, the kraal people are coming out to greet us.'

Later they stood alone in the glaring sunlight near a cluster of small palms to take their leave of each other. It was a strange moment for both of them, and neither really wanted to admit it was goodbye.

'I have read a little about the United States of America,' Darlengi began, lifting his hand to shade his eyes. 'Tilly gave me a number of books a few years ago, one of which was called *Across America in a Covered Wagon*. I learned much from that, though I do not know a great deal about the state of Ohio.'

She looked up at him and smiled. 'You probably know more than me.'

They moved around into some shade and she gave a small sigh. 'I must leave Natal now; you know that, don't you?'

'I know you have decided to, and it's hard for me to say goodbye to you, Phoebe. While you are my friend in your own right, you have been my link, these past years, with that which is dear to me.'

'The Harrisons and Nelsons?'

'Yes.'

'But Aunt Jane and Uncle Chris ask after you all the time. They would truly love to see you. Their home is open to you. You do not need a *link* with them.'

'What you say is true. But it is not easy for a Zulu induna to socialise in Natal.'

'But you come to see me.'

He laughed. 'You have an answer for everything, but some matters are not easily solved.'

'Like the feud between you and John Lockley?'

'Ah, Phoebe, I will not take part in a feud. I simply accept things the way John Lockley prefers them.'

'But he doesn't prefer them that way. I'm sure of it. It's just his stupid pride. He finds himself in an invidious position which is of his own making.'

Darlengi looked squarely at her for some seconds before he replied, 'That is possibly so, but the result is the same . . . and so the years pass, and we live our lives.'

'But you could still be friends . . . brothers . . . you really could.'

He smiled mirthlessly. 'Yes, in a perfect world.' Then he moved a few steps into the sunshine and opening his arms in a wide gesture said, 'I will think of you often, Phoebe. You are like the African sunshine that nurtured you; radiant.'

413

She moved over to him and stood looking up at him and her eyes filled with tears. 'There's been so much that we've shared. And you mean a lot to me. I know you have a good wife who looks after you, and that makes me happy. I shall write to you care of Aunt Jane. You can always get your letters from Tilly. Will you please reply to me?'

He nodded.

And now the tears came and she lifted her hands up to hold his face. 'Goodbye, my friend.'

'I will not say goodbye to you, Phoebe, for you are Africa's, and it would be wrong if you never return. Tell me the date of your departure from this land.'

'The SS *Kidde Halon* leaves Durban on February the twenty-fourth.'

Then he enfolded her in his arms, holding her and resting his dark bronze chin in the golden nest of curls upon her head. They stood there close and still in the streaming light of Christmas morning, and when he released her his chest was damp from her tears.

He watched her as she hurried away across the grass and when she reached the mission fence she turned back once to lift her arm in farewell. He swallowed the sadness that rose in his throat and replied in kind before he turned and loped away.

CHAPTER TWENTY-EIGHT

As Christmas dusk turned swiftly into Christmas night, the people gathered on the terrace at The Grange lifted their glasses in a toast to the host and hostess and then turned from the giant moths that flew about them in profusion to pass into the welcoming glow of the interior.

'My husband should be here soon,' said Frances Colenso, sipping a light sherry and turning her eyes to Michael Tallant, who spent every holiday with Jane and Christopher.

'Yes,' replied Michael. 'Evening prayer will be over by now.'

Jane nodded as Christopher slipped his hand through her arm and asked, 'Do you need me to do anything?'

'No, my darling, everything's ready. We can sit down as soon as Bishop John arrives.'

'Then I shall go and finish my discussion with the General, John Lockley and Anthony.'

Kate moved to the window seat and sat down alone near the Christmas tree. She looked up at the pretty ribbons and fancy little cakes hanging from the branches and she wondered what sort of Christmas Day Tom was having. Her gleaming black hair was pulled tightly back in a series of plaits that wrapped around her crown. She wore russet satin which enhanced the colour of her eyes, and as John Lockley conversed with Anthony and his uncle, he was watching her over their shoulders. She looked particularly beautiful tonight.

He knew he had been preoccupied of late, yet so too had she. She did not laugh as readily as she used to and sometimes when he spoke to her she turned to him with a faraway look in her eyes.

'So it seems the poor amaPutini tribesmen will be made prisoners simply because they gave succour to their kinsmen the amaHlubi,' Anthony said with a frown.

Christopher agreed. 'It's a scandal really, the whole affair. And what with Langalibalele's trial set down for January, it's getting out of hand. And the way that you, as leader of the expedition, are getting vilified by the colonists is outrageous. I've spoken to the Lieutenant-Governor, and thank heaven the army is being rational about it and commending you.'

Anthony gave a wry smile. 'Yes, and I feel so damn sorry for the amaPutini. If they are taken into custody, as I suspect they will be soon, I'd like to give the poor fellows something to do. I have orders to close the passes over the Drakensburgs, so might take them up there to help me. What do you think, John Lockley?'

John Lockley had been listening, even though his eyes had been upon his wife. He now turned them to Anthony. 'I concur absolutely, and I'll help you do it. But you're always doing things for others. You should be on the sick list now, and doing something for yourself.'

And Fanny, who had joined them and overheard the last sentence, said, 'Yes, he should. His wounds aren't healing properly and nor is his arm. He's indefatigable and shouldn't be.'

At that moment Fanny's father arrived and Christopher excused himself and departed to greet the Bishop. It was then that John Lockley noticed the quick look that passed between Anthony and Fanny. Their expressions were tender, intimate and loving, and suddenly, with surprise, John Lockley realised that these two people were in love. He knew Anthony's marriage was over in all but name, but it was anathema for a commissioned officer in Her Majesty's Army to entertain a second marriage. Divorce carried with it an automatic dishonourable discharge. He watched as his two friends moved away together. Fancy that, Anthony and Fanny; they were both such good people and deserved happiness; but John Lockley felt the outlook for such an eventuality was bleak.

He shook his head as his mind turned to his own marriage, and he wondered if Kate could actually be unfaithful to him. Surely not; surely her actions had been misinterpreted by the townsfolk. She was lonely and needed company. Momentarily he felt guilty for leaving her as much as he did. He looked across at her again. She was now in conversation with Frank Colenso, one of Fanny's brothers. He wondered if resigning from the army would be the solution. He could certainly spend more time with her then. While he loved his work as an engineer, and working with Anthony these last six months had been marvellous, he would not really miss the soldiering part.

He had always nurtured a hope that Kate would grow to love the Tugela farm as he did. He fancied retiring there one day, but somehow he knew that was not likely; she liked activity and people and parties. In fact she had told him unequivocally after her one and only stay there that she did not want to ever go back. That saddened him, but there was something that was worse, and it continued to rankle inside him. He knew that if the officers' mess of the 75th was abounding with speculation about his wife and Tom King, then the whole of 'Maritzburg must be. He recalled when old drunken Trimm had said the same thing at the Pietermaritzburg Club. His gaze was on his wife as he made a dissatisfied rumble in his throat and turned away to the sound of his aunt's voice calling everyone in to dinner.

Kate took Frank Colenso's arm and he escorted her into the dining room. She met her husband's eyes as he sat opposite her at the table and she felt a little thrill pass though her. He was so wonderful to look at, he really was; but so was Tom, and Tom was happy and carefree, and he told her that if she were his, he'd never leave her like John Lockley did, never.

Kate was positively sure now of her condition; she was over five weeks late and guessed she was probably eight weeks gone. This morning she had felt quite sick and brought up her breakfast. Thank the Lord John Lockley had accompanied Anthony to a Christmas morning service. And for the life of her she didn't know whether it was Tom's or her husband's. She loved them both, she knew that, and she was in a horrible quandary. But it was John Lockley's fault for leaving her all the time and forcing her towards Tom. What was she going to do? It wasn't a bit fair ... nothing was. She should be in London going to soirées and parties, and being doted on ... well, even Cape Town would be better than this backwater.

At her side the General spoke and she turned her sultry eyes to him.

The meal passed pleasantly and at half past ten the party rose from the table and moved through to the parlour for tea and coffee.

John Lockley came to his wife. 'Katy, I think it's time we went home.'

She smiled. 'All right.'

As they took their leave Anthony shook John Lockley's hand, saying, 'Do you want to meet with the Bishop and me on Monday to talk about Langa and his men, and the Putini?'

'I'll be there. I'm on parade first and then meetings with Pat Boehm. How about after lunch in your office?'

'Good.'

Christopher saw the married couple to the front door, where he shook John Lockley by the hand and wished him a merry Christmas. Then, turning to Kate, he met her eyes before he bent to kiss her goodnight. During the entire day she had read from his expression that he was not happy with her and she was quite aware that there was no warmth in his kiss, but she smiled boldly at him and said, 'Thank you for a delightful Christmas Day, dear Uncle.'

Christopher stood at his front door as they strolled away arm in arm. He had been watching Kate a lot of the day and night; watching and thinking.

Just two nights ago, on the twenty-third, he had been at his hotel where the pre-Christmas trade was making it a very busy time. At around nine o'clock he was serving in the bar when they had run out of whisky and he had gone to the storeroom for more. A Christmas party was going on in the small room between the bar and the storeroom and some of the merry-makers were spilling into the little corridor along which he had to pass. There were smoke and laughter all about and as he came by a group of men who were a little the worse for their imbibing, he heard Kate's name.

'...was with Mrs Harrison, the black-haired beauty. They went into Lief Liam's old hut out past the fort. Kissin' and huggin' they were.'

There was some 'tut-tutting' at this and he pushed by the group to hear another voice add, 'I heard Tom's really fallen this time.'

'Well, fancy that.'

Christopher entered the storeroom and, lighting the lamp, closed the door behind him and stood in contemplation. He recalled what he had heard from George Russell last month when the men at the brickworks had been gossiping; how one said he had seen Kate and Tom King out on the Umsindusi River alone together. And now he had overheard this. He felt a responsibility to John Lockley. But it was all hearsay, and possibly wrong. Yet even as he said that to himself, he had the sober feeling that there was reality to these accounts.

As he stood at the door of The Grange, watching his nephew and Kate disappearing into the Christmas night, Christopher was in a dilemma. He had not mentioned this most recent event to Jane and he wondered what on earth he could gain now by doing so. It was enough that he had worried her by telling her of the brickyard talk. And broaching it with John Lockley was quite another, far more serious matter. As he turned and re-entered his home, he had a very bad feeling in his chest.

Meanwhile, John Lockley and Kate felt the warm December breeze on their faces as they sauntered along under the pomegranates and willows.

'It's been a nice Christmas,' John Lockley said, helping her to avoid a sluit outside the Prince Alfred Hotel on the corner of Loop Street.

'Yes, lovely.'

They continued on in silence, passing a few other people walking in the night air. Then John Lockley asked, 'Kate, you don't like my being away, do you?'

She turned her face to him in the weak, reflected moonlight. She could not see him clearly though she was very aware of his hand holding her firmly by the arm.

'No . . . I don't.'

'But I'm in the army. I remember when my father was posted to India we only saw him once in many years. I mean, at least you're here with me.'

'Yes, but you're hardly ever around.'

He did not reply and they walked on for a time until he broke the silence again. 'I could resign my commission, I suppose.'

Her heart began to beat faster. 'Would you?'

He halted and turned her to him. He ran his hand back through his hair and then abruptly took hold of her arms. 'Katy.' He could just make out her eyes in the faint night light. 'Would it make any difference if I did?'

'Well . . . yes, you'd be here, wouldn't you?'

'No, I mean, would it make a difference to you? Would you need to be out and about as much as you are? Spending time with Sophie and Tom King like you do? You told me that it *is* only socialising that you do with Tom King. That's true, isn't it, Kate?'

Kate could feel her pulse racing. This was so damn exciting. Too damn exciting. 'Logley, darling, yes, it's only socialising. You're away and I'm lonely.' Automatically she placed her hands on her stomach and spread out her fingers as she stood with him in the darkness.

Then he pulled her forward, his hand hurrying her along, and now his voice was cold and clipped as he said, 'Kate, I'm telling you as your husband to do less of it, because there's talk in 'Maritzburg and it's reached my ears, and I don't like what I'm hearing.'

So ... he had heard things! Damn and blast! And she and Tom were so careful. That was this little backwater all over. They were so narrow-minded they had to be gossiping all the time. How could she have any fun? Suddenly she felt sick. What was she going to do? There was only one thing she could do – no, it wasn't possible; she couldn't give Tom up. She couldn't. He wouldn't let her anyway, she was sure of that. He was always asking her to run away to Australia with him. But if she did that to John Lockley she would hurt him, and she truly didn't want to hurt him. Oh hell, what a mess it was.

Her voice came back in answer, abrupt and definite as his had been. 'This place is so damn small that they misinterpret friendship, my darling. You're intelligent enough to know that.'

He halted and pulled her up beside him. They were in Maritz Street now and outside the small Roman Catholic manse. There was lamplight glowing through the window of Father Connelly's room, which abutted on to the street.

She could see his face and his expression frightened her. He was holding her tightly by the arms, hurting her.

'I asked you this once before, Kate, and I'm asking you just once again. You wouldn't lie to me, would you?'

In the faint light from Father Connelly's room, she returned his gaze, looking unblinkingly into his eyes. 'No, I would not lie to you.'

'So there's no reason why I should heed these rumours?'

'None at all, my sweetheart.'

He remained staring at her for a few more seconds before he said, 'Then I suggest that you don't see Tom King again, unless I'm with you.'

'But darling ... but ... Sophie's my friend and he's her brother, I cannot avoid seeing him.'

Now his voice was sharp and hard. 'If you won't take my suggestion, Kate, I'll have to make it an order. You will not see Tom King again, unless I'm with you ... understand?'

She had never seen him like this and it thrilled her to her very bones. 'All right. Whatever you say.'

'Come, let's go home.'

They moved away and his hand was still clutched tightly on her arm, steering her along.

Kate almost smiled. This was so exciting. Her heart was racing. What was she going to do? What could she do? *Ah, well, I suppose he's made up my mind for me. What alternative do I have?*

They made vigorous love together that Christmas night, delivering sensations which bordered on pain. And they slept deeply in each other's arms until late on Boxing Day morning.

Two apple trees dominated the Harrisons' small back garden, and the husband and wife were having breakfast together in their shade when John Lockley leaned forward, elbows on knees, and smiled at her.

She did love him, she really did. She lifted her hand and touched his cheek. 'Did you mean it when you said you would resign your commission?'

He took a deep breath and sat upright. 'I'll be honest with you, Katy. I'm not a great lover of army life, but my superiors tell me I'm a good soldier and you know I love engineering – the building and planning – and working with Anthony's a joy. We've got to close the Drakensburg passes and Anthony and I are both keen to get justice for the amaPutini, but I can do that whether I'm in the army or not. We're supposed to start some fortifications up in Newcastle and to rebuild the old forts that have fallen down along the Zulu border.'

'When?'

He thought for a moment before answering. 'After we close the passes. But I'll be back and forth. I suppose it could all take a year and more.'

Her smile faded.

He leant forward again and took her hand. 'But I promise you that I'll resign my commission so that I'm free of military life in six months from now, no matter what. Look, we'll get out of Pietermaritzburg. We'll go and live in Durban. At Mimosa. I'll ask Uncle Chris if he'll let us have it; it's going to be mine one day anyway. Then you could go down to Durban while I'm away and organise Mimosa to your liking. We've so much to do, Katy . . . together.'

'Oh, yes, we have.' Her eyes were shining. Suddenly she thought of Tom. What would he say? But she was not to see him again. She was supposed to meet him out at Lief Liam's hut on Monday. But she couldn't afford to go, not now. Then she realised John Lockley was speaking about the Tugela farm.

'. . .and I know you don't love it, Katy, but could you try, please? We don't have to go up there a lot, perhaps just once a year until you grow more used to it. What do you say?'

She nodded placatingly; she wasn't going to get into that now. 'Well, darling,' she smiled and threw her mass of black hair back over her shoulder as she spoke, 'I think it's all timely, your getting out of the army and our going to live in Durban, because you'll be a father by July, I would think.'

He sat there looking at her. He did not speak. He just sat there looking: no smile, no frown, nothing. His face was immobile.

Her heart began to pound. 'John Lockley, darling, do you understand what I said?'

He seemed to shake himself into the present. He nodded. 'Yes, I do, Kate. I do, and while I know people have children all the time I'd never thought about our being in this position. Silly of me, I suppose.'

'Then you're not happy. You don't want it?'

And now, finally, he smiled and her heart lifted. He stood and drew her up into his arms. 'Ah Katy, darling Katy, of course I'm happy. So all these changes in our life are timely as you say.' He kissed her gently. 'I . . . I didn't hurt you last night, did I?'

She laughed. 'No, don't be foolish, of course not.'

'A father,' he said, hugging her to him again, 'and you a mother, Katy Harrison.'

Christopher was working alone at the brickworks. Everyone had finished on Christmas Eve, and they were not due back until Monday morning. He liked it when it was quiet, he got so much more done. He heard the front door open and close down the wooden corridor and then his nephew's voice calling, 'Uncle Chris, are you here?'

'Yes, son,' he answered.

Ten seconds later his nephew came through the door.

'This is a pleasant surprise,' said Christopher, putting down his quill pen.

'I wanted to see you, Uncle Chris ... to have a chat, if it's not an inconvenient time.'

'No, son, it's never an inconvenient time for you.'

John Lockley nodded. 'I know that, and rarely do I thank you for it. I never wish to be disloyal to the General, but you've been more of a father to me, as you're well aware.'

Christopher smiled. 'He had his job to do, son, and it took him from you. He's actually very generous; he has no objection to your filial feelings for me, which shows great character.'

'I know and understand that, and I too think it's magnanimous of him, but as it's easier to talk to you, it's to you I come.'

Christopher stood and came round his desk, motioning to a chair for his nephew and pulling one up for himself. 'So, what is it, son?'

John Lockley clutched his hands together for a moment, then lifted his right hand and pushed it back through his hair as he took a breath and brought his gaze up to meet his uncle's. 'A week or so ago, I walked into the officers' mess of the Seventy-fifth to hear my friend, Charles Preston, defending me against Redberry Waters who was insinuating that ... Kate was doing things behind my back; things of an unfaithful nature.' He paused for a moment and Christopher said nothing. Then he went on, 'He was implying, well, more than that ... he was *saying* she was clandestinely meeting with Tom King, Sophie's brother. I would have fought Waters except for the intervention of Anthony and Pat Boehm.'

'I see.'

'Well, the fact is, Uncle Chris, that I'd heard the same thing before, from old Trimm. He was drunk, as usual, one night at the club.'

Christopher rubbed his square jaw in thought. 'Have you asked Kate about it?'

'Yes. She denies it and I believe her. Certainly she sees Sophie a lot, and Tom's often there. I'm away, so he escorts them both to parties, dinners and the like. 'Maritzburg's entire population's only about five thousand or so; people gossip. Kate's beautiful and vivacious; she attracts talk.'

Christopher nodded slowly as if agreeing, and John Lockley continued, 'I feel it would be best if we left here, lived elsewhere. Thus I've decided to resign my commission so as to be free of the army in six months' time.'

'That's a big step. But one you know you'll get no argument about from me.'

'Yes, you see, I feel I should be with Kate more. She's not happy so ... well, do you think I should take her out of Pietermaritzburg?'

'To live somewhere else?'

'Yes.'

'Yes, I do.'

'In that case I want to ask you about Mimosa. Can we live there? That is, if it's all right with Aunt Jane and you and the General?'

Christopher leaned forward and patted him on the knee. He thought forty miles was hardly far enough away for John Lockley and Kate to outstrip the rumours, but it was better than staying here. 'Son, I think that would be perfectly all right with us. I'll discuss it with the others, of course, but can't imagine any objection.'

'Gee, thanks, Uncle Chris. There's a second reason why I'm resigning my commission.'

Christopher looked questioningly.

'I'm to be a father.' He smiled, but his words did not bring a smile to his uncle's face.

Christopher hesitated momentarily, then held out his hand and John Lockley took it.

'Well now, son, that's a bit of a responsibility you're taking on.'

'Yes, I know. But these things have a way of happening. It'll

424

be hard for Katy; her mother, as you know, died when she was a girl, so I'm hoping Aunt Jane will help and guide her.'

Christopher stood and moved over to the window. He heard his voice saying, 'I'm sure she will. How many months is Kate?'

John Lockley rose and came to his side. 'Only about two, she thinks, but she's positive. See, I want to have a real family. My father was away in the army so much, and I don't want to repeat that. Besides, I leave Kate too much as it is. She's not the sort of girl who takes easily to that.'

'No, she isn't.' Christopher attempted a smile. 'I suppose I'll have to put up with you in the business then.'

John Lockley looked thoughtful. 'I'd like that, Uncle Chris, but actually I've been thinking that some time in the future I'd prefer to run the farm. I know George Travers is doing a good job up there, but he's not all that much younger than Dirk.'

'Yes, that's true. And you'd be perfect for that. But while you and I would like it, I can't see Kate living there. Mimosa's one thing, the Tugela farm another.'

He nodded. 'I'm hoping she'll come round.'

Christopher thought hoping was a waste of time, but he said nothing.

'So, Uncle Chris, I've told you first, but when you've finished here I'd like to accompany you round to The Grange, and inform Aunt Jane and the General.'

'Shouldn't Kate be with you when you do that?'

'No, I've discussed it with her and she preferred that I tell you all, alone.'

Christopher thought perhaps he knew why, but he held his tongue. John Lockley appeared to be quite certain in his belief in his wife, so Christopher must attempt to gain the same confidence; for his nephew's sake. He nodded. 'I'll be about another half-hour.'

John Lockley waited and they left the brickyard and made their way to The Grange together. The young man chatted away at his uncle's side, content with what the future offered him, while his uncle walked with a heavier tread, thinking of all that he knew. How dearly he wanted things to turn out well for his nephew, and how right the young man was to think that he, Christopher, regarded him as a son. John Lockley's happiness was paramount, just as Ellen's had been. He sighed deeply, thinking of Ellen, and then he thought of Darlengi. Suddenly he was reminded that John Lockley still had never told him what had actually happened to estrange him from Darlengi.

He looked sideways at his nephew as they walked along. His three 'children'. He loved them all so dearly. One was gone forever; one he had not seen for many years and appeared lost to him; this one at his side was the one remaining legacy. He would do his utmost for him.

CHAPTER TWENTY-NINE

The afternoon sun streamed through the window on to the heads of Anthony, John Lockley and Bishop John Colenso. They were in Anthony's office at Fort Napier and the sonorous sounds of the drill sergeant's commands resounded through the window.

Anthony drew his hand across his high forehead. 'What are the charges going to be?'

'Treason and rebellion, certainly. I don't know what else,' replied the cleric.

'I heard murder, as well,' John Lockley added.

Bishop Colenso looked amazed. 'Murder? Who did Langalibalele murder? I suppose there's some sort of a case for rebellion, but murder? They were living quietly on their reserve until Theopolis made it so impossible for the old chief that he attempted to withdraw from Natal. It's been a disquieting revelation to me that Theopolis could be so hard and uncompromising.'

John Lockley's fingers lifted and pushed through his hair. 'He's been in a difficult position all these years, juggling the factions of Natal Zululand and the Transvaal; perhaps it's hardened him to any point of view but his own.'

'Yes, I was arguing with him for hours yesterday afternoon,' the Bishop replied, 'and I'm afraid it's put an almost impossible strain on our friendship.'

'I've heard that his brother John will prosecute at the trial,' said Anthony. 'Have you found anyone to defend the old bloke?'

John Colenso shook his head. 'No, and I'm afraid I won't. Yesterday Theopolis informed me the trial would be in Native Customary Law, with the Lieutenant-Governor, Sir Benjamin, sitting as Supreme Chieftain, assisted by Theopolis, four European magistrates and six native chieftains.'

'Well, that sounds fair,' commented John Lockley.

John Colenso shook his head. 'No, actually I think not. My feeling is that Theopolis wants it to be seen as fair, when he merely wishes to forgo the long formalities of a normal trial. He wants to get it over and to get a verdict which will be popular with the colonists and other native tribes, and that's "guilty", I'm afraid.'

Anthony nodded. 'The amaPutini will fare no better. Lieutenant-Colonel Milles told me yesterday that seven thousand four hundred head of their cattle have already been taken; and the rest of the tribe, other than those already in custody, have been scattered. I went upcountry before Christmas and had a look at the men in custody ... poor devils don't understand, and nor do I.'

John Lockley leaned forward in his chair. 'Anyway, we'll do what we can for them, Anthony, and taking them to help us close the Drakensburg passes is a great idea of yours.'

Anthony smiled wanly. 'Yes, my mounted Basutos are urging me to leave now, but I've told them I want to stay for Langalibalele's trial first.'

The cleric stood and walked to the window where the bright light outside made a silhouette of his gaunt features. 'I've been to visit Chief Langalibalele; he and his sons are being well treated, but they're very confused.'

John Lockley rested his elbows on his knees. 'So what do we do next to find someone to represent the old man?'

'I've exhausted the legal profession in 'Maritzburg,' the cleric answered.

'What about Durban? There's a chap down there called Ayres who's got a good reputation.'

'Yes, it's possible. I can probably go down there on Wednesday.'

Anthony asked, 'When's the trial starting?'

The Bishop turned from the window to face them. 'Sometime next week, I think.'

Anthony frowned. 'It appears we are three of the few people in Natal who think the amaHlubi and the amaPutini have been poorly treated.'

'Yes,' agreed John Lockley. 'And strange is the soldier's lot. For we were the ones who were ordered to the Drakensburgs to take the old man into custody in the first place. We ended up wounded in the process; you badly. And here we are doing our best to try to defend him.'

John Colenso smiled. 'Yes, I cannot imagine how you soldiers can fight for causes you don't believe in.'

'Causes are rarely black and white, Bishop,' replied John Lockley. 'And one can usually find a nuance of grey that earns approval. Nevertheless, professional soldiers can't afford to let their emotions run high.'

Anthony nodded. 'Let's just say, good Bishop, that being professional soldiers means we deliver professionalism at every level. Duty first, but carried out in a fair, honourable and consistent fashion.'

'Very hard to do,' commented John Colenso.

John Lockley stood and walked over to the cleric. 'We don't say it's easy, sir, but let's say it sure as hell builds character. Excuse my swearing.' He smiled widely at John Colenso and his eyes twinkled indigo-purple in the sunlight, and for the life of him, the cleric found himself unable not to smile back.

Anthony joined them at the window and as they stood looking at the red uniforms passing by in formation below them, he added, 'So you see, Bishop, we can still be compassionate. And thus we want to help Langalibalele and his people.'

John Colenso nodded, his grave face falling into severe lines. 'Yes, I know you do. And I think you're both most unusual men.'

At that moment there was a knock on the door and it opened to admit the duty sergeant. 'Excuse me, sirs, but Mrs Harrison is down in the duty office, wantin' to see you, sir.' He looked at John Lockley.

'Thanks, Sergeant. Are we finished?' he asked.

'Yes,' the cleric said, 'you go. I'll let you know what happens in Durban.'

Outside, Tenny Rama, John Lockley's Basuto sergeant, who had been with him since Cetshwayo's coronation, stood waiting for him. 'I'll be back soon, Tenny,' he said. 'Just going to see Mrs Harrison at the front gate.'

Tenny nodded. He would wait. He was happy to wait any time for Inkosi Harrison.

John Lockley followed the sergeant along the corridor and down the rock-hewn stairs to the duty office on the ground floor near the front gate. Kate rose and came to him as he entered.

She had lived through the most terrible morning. And finally she just had to come to John Lockley. She knew she really shouldn't do this when he was at the fort but she could not help it. Before Christmas she had made a tryst with Tom to meet today, in fact right now, at Lief Liam's hut. She had spent the morning in a quandary, wanting desperately to go out and meet him: one minute deciding to go, the next minute fearful of going.

She wanted so badly to see Tom; she loved him as he loved her, but she loved John Lockley too, damn it, and he had said . . . no, had ordered her, never to see Tom again without his being there.

She had been in such a state by two o'clock that she could not remain in the house any longer. She had donned her bonnet and taken her parasol and come walking out to the fort. She had to see one of them and John Lockley was the safer of the two.

'Kate,' he said as he came over and took her hands, 'what brings you here?'

'I . . . I just had to see you.'

He ushered her outside into the sunshine of the courtyard. 'Why, darling, what's wrong?'

'I know I shouldn't come here . . . but I just wanted . . . to be with you. Perhaps it's because I'm going to have a baby. I feel strange.'

He kissed her. 'Sweetheart, now listen to me. When you feel this way you must go to Aunt Jane, you know how kind and understanding she is.'

Kate almost smiled at that. Aunt Jane was not really her first choice of companion. 'I'm not sure I want to see Aunt Jane all the time, she might misunderstand, think I'm a nuisance.'

'Listen, darling, she'd never think that. You don't have a mother to fall back on so you must rely on Aunt Jane. She wants you to.'

Kate's expression bordered on the supercilious, but one thing she knew was that she needed friends. She asked tentatively, 'Do you think she really wants to help me?'

'I know she does.'

'But did she say she does?'

'Yes. When I told her of your condition, she said she would do anything we wanted her to, and so did Uncle Chris.'

Kate recalled the way Uncle Chris had looked at her on Christmas Day, as if he were condemning her. She took hold of John Lockley and looked up into his eyes. 'You told me Uncle Chris was happy about the baby. Is he really?'

'Look, what's all this? This child's going to be like their very own grandchild ... of course they're happy and of course they want to help. So will you promise me you'll go to Aunt Jane whenever you feel like this or when you are in any way distressed?'

'All right.'

He kissed her forehead. 'Good. So that means now. Will you go to The Grange now?'

She nodded and he kissed her again and accompanied her out past the sentry. 'Off you go, darling, and I'll be home before seven o'clock tonight.'

She waved as he disappeared through the stone archway. She stood there on the edge of the dirt road, tapping her foot. A mile beyond was Lief Liam's hut. She could simply head back down the road to the town and slip off into the trees and double back. She would be at the hut in about half an hour from now. Her pulse raced. She thought of Tom. He would be waiting for her.

But she had promised to go to The Grange. John Lockley would certainly find out if she didn't. Damn and blast! Why did she have to fall with this child? Everything had been going so well. She must give it a father, and John Lockley was the obvious one. But oh, how badly she wanted to see Tom.

She sighed and it shuddered through her frame, then slowly, with an expression of resignation, she began wandering back towards Pietermaritzburg.

Tom King lit another cheroot and sat back in the V of the trunk of the old waterboom tree. He blew smoke rings in the air and looked again at his fob-watch. Had he got the wrong time? Perhaps she had said three o'clock, not two. He hadn't seen Katy for a week, so it was possible he had mixed up the hour. Christmas had been positively dull without her. Trust her husband to be around at Christmas. Tom had been careful

431

to avoid parties he knew they would be attending: he didn't want to run into them.

She loved him, he was sure. He could always tell when he'd caught a woman and he knew he'd caught Kate. When he had suggested they run off together, she had taken him seriously. She really had, asking him when, and where would they go? She never got enough of him and never wanted to leave him.

He smiled, thinking of the places around 'Maritzburg that they'd got to doing it. Even in old Harrison's very own bed! Mind you, out here was his favourite place; nice and quiet. He thought of Kate's naked body; now she was something, really something, and he'd had plenty to compare her with. And she never got enough; she was insatiable.

Where the devil was she? He looked again at his timepiece: a quarter past three. She was never late. Fact was, she usually beat him to their trysting places. What had gone wrong?

Yeah, he used to be able to just enjoy Kate for what she was . . . a beautiful body with a delicious mouth and a great sense of fun; but in the last few weeks he had begun to miss the damn woman when she wasn't around. Never thought it would happen; amazing, really, considering the women he'd been through. Heck! He'd even admitted to a couple of his friends that he was falling for her.

When four o'clock came and went Tom knew he would not see Kate today. He felt angry . . . yes, and hurt. It came as a revelation; for he had never felt hurt about anything to do with a skirt before.

At half past four he mounted his horse and rode back into Pietermaritzburg, deliberately passing by the Harrison house in Maritz Street and looking intently at the windows to see any movement, but there was none.

When he entered the drapery store his father looked up in surprise. 'Thought you weren't coming back today.'

'Changed my mind,' remarked his son, stomping miserably through to the back room.

Kate stirred. What had woken her? She lay there in the dark listening. Perhaps she should have remained at The Grange, as John Lockley had wanted her to. She had to admit Aunt Jane had been positively friendly in recent weeks, and when John Lockley and Anthony had gone up to the Drakensburgs she had suggested Kate come and stay. And it had worked out better than Kate would have believed, but she had wanted to come home for a few days to get things in order before leaving for Durban and Mimosa.

John Lockley had left 'Maritzburg after the trial of that old chieftain had finished. They had sent him and his sons off to Robben Island, and John Lockley and Anthony had been very upset at the verdict. Apparently Bishop Colenso was even thinking of going to England to see the Colonial Secretary about it. Kate didn't understand it really, as the six native judges had been more than harsh on the old chieftain, one even calling him a dog who had bitten his master. Anyway, Anthony and John Lockley had decided to champion that Putini tribe and were doing all they could to obtain a pardon for them.

She rolled over on her side and then she heard a clinking sound. She sat up. What was that? She knew something had woken her.

There it was again. It was over at the window. She moved across to it and when she heard the sound again, she understood. Someone was throwing small stones at her window. Oh heavens! It couldn't be.

With a racing pulse she opened the window and leant out.

'Katy ... Katy, darlin', it's me.'

'Tom?'

'Yes, open the front door.'

Oh Lord! It must be the early hours of the morning. She could see his form down by the willow tree. Oh, this was just too thrilling.

'Go away, someone might come along ... see you. Go away.'

'I'm not going, Kate, not until you open the door ... please.'

She hesitated, looking down at his dark figure. This was just too exhilarating for words and she simply couldn't resist. 'All right, I'm coming.'

When she opened the front door he took her immediately in his arms and kissed her deeply. Then he whispered thickly, 'God, woman, I've missed you. You've been avoiding me, staying at The Grange. Why'd you do that?'

He ran his hands over her body, feeling her through the soft silk of her gown.

'Oh Tom, Tom.'

He kissed her again, and within another thirty seconds they were hurrying up the stairs to her bedroom.

John Lockley and Anthony stood by a large boulder up in a wide crevasse leading across to Giant's Castle Pass where Anthony had been so badly wounded.

John Lockley handed Anthony his water bottle, which he took in his right hand, his left lying limply in a sling.

'Hot work,' said Anthony.

John Lockley nodded. 'But come June we'll be working in snow.'

'That's true. And while we're this far from 'Maritzburg I'd like to take a first-hand look at the disputed territory between the Boers and the Zulus. You know it, don't you?'

'Yes, I do. I can take you up there. It's north of Newcastle, the Utrecht district. There's a lot of broken country between here and there, but we could still get to the southern end pretty quickly.'

John Lockley leaned back and took a drink from his water bottle. Then, looking carefully at his friend, said, 'There's something personal I'd like to discuss with you, Anthony.'

Anthony smiled. 'Mmm, what's that?'

'My Aunt Jane informed me before we came up here that our friends the McLeans are leaving Natal for America on the SS *Kidde Halon*. It sails from Durban to Cape Town on February twenty-fourth, and if you don't mind I'd like to take off for a few days and ride down and see them depart. Then I'll call in overnight on Kate who'll be down in Durban at Mimosa. I shouldn't be gone more than six days.'

Anthony nodded. 'Certainly, lad, you do that.'

'I'll take Tenny Rama with me.'

'Yes, do, you need a companion on a long ride and I can see how devoted he's becoming to you. And while you're down there, have three or four days with your wife. I can manage here. Young Simeon Kambula is turning up trumps. And my Basutos and the Putini are working very well side by side.'

'Yes, they are. Thanks, Anthony. I appreciate your suggestion of a few days with Kate. She's very excited about going to live in Durban. She's got all sorts of plans for Mimosa.'

'I'm glad you and Kate are leaving 'Maritzburg, lad. And while I truly wish you were not considering resigning your commission, I know that your marriage is very important and that you see getting out of the army as a necessary step.'

'Yes, I'm afraid I do. I've written my letter of resignation and shall hand it in at the fort on my way back from Durban. You see, Kate's not good on her own, misses me too much. That's why the tongues of 'Maritzburg were wagging, when she was merely friendly with that bloke King.'

'Mmm, small places are like that.' Anthony pulled on his long moustache. 'And we all miss those we care about. We simply deal with it in different ways.'

John Lockley met his eyes. 'Yes, we do.'

Anthony cleared his throat and clipped the top back on his water bottle. 'There's someone here in Natal that I ... care about.'

'I know.'

'You do?' Anthony looked amazed.

'Yes, my friend, I do, though I think I'm the only one who does. You are the souls of discretion, and I wouldn't have suspected, except that I witnessed a look pass between you both on Christmas night, a look of love.'

Anthony gave a brief, sad smile. 'Ah, I see we must be more prudent. We've told no one and that's the way it must stay. I'll admit to you, and you alone, my good friend, that I love Fanny Colenso, but I don't know what will become of such a love. She's the Bishop's daughter and I'm a professional soldier, an officer of the Queen ... and already married.'

John Lockley leaned forward to meet his friend's gaze. 'Yes, it's going to be hard for you; almost impossible. But I like to believe that a way can be found out of impossible situations. And ... I shall keep your secret.'

'Thanks, lad. Actually, I ... er, think you'll find Fanny there when you get down to Durban. She informed me she was seeing her friend Phoebe off on her long voyage.'

John Lockley lifted an eyebrow. 'Any message?'

Anthony gave a wry grin and pulled again on his long moustache. 'Not this time. I would prefer to tell her myself that you are my confidant.'

With his good right hand, Anthony put down his water bottle and patted John Lockley affectionately on the shoulder. He would miss the younger man very badly. The man was a fine character and an able and highly competent engineer.

Anthony found their days together so companionable. He honestly hoped that John Lockley's plans would run smoothly and that there would be no disappointments for him. Unfortunately Kate Harrison did not inspire Anthony with the confidence the lad apparently had in her. But it was none of his business. John Lockley was his friend and he would support the lad in any way he could.

Suddenly Simeon Kambula's face appeared round the edge of the rock. 'Inkosi, come please, we need you.'

And the two friends clipped their water bottles back on their belts and left their resting place to follow Simeon.

CHAPTER THIRTY

Darlengi stood watching the morning mist coming swiftly up from the broad valley of the White Umvoloosi River. The new royal kraal of Ulundi was soon surrounded by the swirling white vapour. He smiled as the dwellings seemed to disappear before his eyes.

Cetshwayo had decided he wanted his new headquarters to be even larger than his Uncle Dingane's had been, so he had sent messengers to Mgungundhlovu, the site of Dingane's burnt-out royal kraal, to take measurements. The outside circumference of Ulundi was enormous, about one and a third miles, and between the inner fence of the cattle kraal and the outer palisade were close on a thousand huts built in rows of three. Cetshwayo's dwellings for himself and his wives stood on the far side of the kraal opposite the main entrance, and nearby were the dwellings of his 'maids of honour'. It was the largest kraal ever in Zululand, and the new king was gratified.

Darlengi had been in council here for the last few days and he was about to depart from Ulundi and return to his own kraal south on the Umlatoosi River. He remained outside the main gate of the kraal, standing in the mist, watching the herd boys taking out the royal cattle to graze: pure white beasts passing through the pure white mist.

The king's herd had been greatly reduced in recent months; in fact the number of cattle in all of Zululand had been painfully depleted; about half had died, leaving only about fifty thousand. In October, Cetshwayo had demanded that all the cattle of the country, which were nominally his, were to be brought to Ulundi for inspection, and so they had been, all one hundred thousand of them. As the massive herd passed before the king, his subjects had rejoiced at the sheer size of the display but shortly afterwards, on their return to their home kraals, many of the animals had begun to die of lung sickness.

It was then realised that the mustering together of all the beasts had allowed for the spread of the disease.

This had been an unhappy start to Cetshwayo's reign, and consequently there had been a succession of rites carried out by the witch doctors to ensure that no more misfortunes would occur. Darlengi had smiled to himself, thinking how Mattana would have indulged herself at the ceremonies.

He passed through the main entrance side by side with the cattle, and then took a path through the centre of the kraal to the king's huts, where he approached the sentry.

'*Saku bo num ngani*,' he hailed the sentry.

'*Saku bo num ngani*,' the man replied.

'I come to see the king.'

'*Yeh bo*, he expects you.'

Darlengi entered the royal area and bent through the opening into the great hut. He stood up inside to find Cetshwayo being oiled by four of his wives. Three of Cetshwayo's children jumped up from where they played on the floor and crowded round Darlengi, who was a favourite with them.

With the king was another of his confidants: Induna Tshingwayo, a man approaching his seventies.

Darlengi repeated the correct number of praise names for the occasion and greeted the children as the king smiled and waved his massive arm. 'Come sit by me.'

When Darlengi was seated the king said, 'I think the Great Council made good decisions this time.'

'Yes, the matter of our young men avoiding conscription in the regiments by becoming witch doctors was handled well. Zululand's surfeit of witch doctors will now regain normal proportions. And even though the lung disease in the cattle was a bad thing, when the ceremonies were performed throughout the land, it allowed us to notice the disproportion in our witch doctors. So something good came out of something bad. There is an English proverb, "Every cloud has a silver lining".'

Cetshwayo thought for a second or two and then seeing the meaning smiled broadly at Tshingwayo. 'Ah, these English have some wonderful sayings, but what did you call it, Darlengi?'

'A proverb, my king, meaning a saying which expresses a truth in a concise way.'

'Very good . . . a proverb. Yes, I like that.' Then Cetshwayo rolled over on to his quite voluminous stomach as his wives now oiled his back. He looked up into Darlengi's eyes. 'So, how long will it take us to bring our regiments back to full strength?'

'My king, are you truly sure you wish to do this?'

'I do, as I said in council, and I want to create new ones. How large is your own regiment?'

Darlengi thought for a moment, and knowing that Cetshwayo would understand the numbers replied, 'I could raise five hundred men in an emergency.'

'Good. I want you to have doubled that three winters from now.'

'Why, are you thinking of washing your spear again?'

The king signalled to his wives to stop and they withdrew as he sat upright. 'Darlengi, you know as well as I do that when a new Zulu king comes to the throne it is expected of him to do so.'

Darlengi met his leader's eyes. 'And who would you fight?'

'Probably the Boers. Their aggression continues. They have the effrontery to tax the Zulu people living in the disputed territory. It enrages me.'

'Your friend Theopolis Shepstone, Somtseu, has asked you to hold steady. That he will help us regain it.'

'Yes, he has been saying that for more years than I care to remember.'

'European politics are convoluted. Changes are time-consuming, my good leader.'

'So you told us all today in council. Even Chief John Dunn, Jantoni, who was born one of them, agrees we should not have to wait year after year like this.'

Darlengi nodded but did not comment.

Then Tshingwayo asked, 'So what do you think about Intongalu's offer to bring us this Portuguese called Mqhali, who has agreed to make the gunpowder for the guns Jantoni will supply?'

'John Dunn will be supplying them illegally, as you know,' Darlengi replied. 'That is one thing; the king trusts him. Dealing with the Portuguese is another. But if you get the guns and wish to use them, then yes, you need gunpowder.'

'So,' questioned Cetshwayo, 'you will vote to use this man?'

439

'If my king wants weapons, and those weapons need ammunition, then yes, I will vote for what my king desires to have.'

Cetshwayo smiled broadly. 'Good. So you leave me now.'

'Yes, I depart to my home kraal.'

'You are wise and tolerant; some of my indunas are headstrong; and some, I think, have their own desires above the needs of Zululand. It has been ever thus. A king needs good counsel.' He smiled at the two men with him and stood up beside Darlengi. 'I value your opinions as I value Tshingwayo's.'

As Darlengi was about to leave Cetshwayo halted him with the words, 'How is your English family?'

'I . . . have not seen them for many years.'

'Did you know my father sold them the tract of land they own on the Tugela?'

Darlengi nodded. The king had told him before.

'Theirs is a genuine claim, the land is rightfully theirs, unlike the Boers. I remember the two men coming to Nodwengu when I was a young man. My father wanted a jar of macassar that one possessed. I believe my Uncle Shaka liked macassar too. From memory they traded a few guns and axes, a container of many knives and five horses; which were meant to breed others. There were a couple of female horses if I remember right . . . I think they did breed one foal, though there were never any more.' Then he broke into a wide smile. 'They made a good bargain, for I would not sell them the land for that today.'

Darlengi smiled. 'They are good people; they have helped the people in the Zulu kraals on their land. They give work to those that want it and they help the sick . . . with the witch doctors' approval, of course.'

'Yes, that is good, the English are a fair people. Though I am told there was a Boer in charge there for many years.'

'Yes, but his power has waned; and even when he was in control, he had to obey certain rules.'

Cetshwayo touched Darlengi's shoulder. 'Come back soon. Why not for the day of the new moon? By then we may have the guns from Chief Dunn and the gunpowder from Mqhali.'

Darlengi answered, 'I will return as you wish.'

The children came outside with Darlengi and followed him

some yards through the mist before he patted them on the head and told them to return inside to their mothers. He strode off round through the hundreds of huts towards the main gate. As he passed one of the larger huts a woman was bending through the opening. As she stood he recognised Veele, Mkosana's daughter, the one whom Kayo would have had him take as a Great Wife years ago. She had been here with her husband for the council meeting.

She smiled openly at him and he noticed she was large with child. 'Darlengi, I have not seen you for some time. I was not well enough to join in the festivities last night.' She gestured to her stomach.

'It is good to see you, Veele.'

'Thank you, and you also.'

At that moment Intongalu came round the side of the hut. His expression became grave when he saw his wife with Darlengi and he hurried up to them, looking at Veele and saying with annoyance in his voice, 'I told you to remain inside until I returned.'

She looked abashed. 'I was so hot inside, my husband, I came out to walk in the cool mist.'

Darlengi bowed his head to her. 'Goodbye, Veele.'

'Goodbye, Darlengi.'

He looked at Intongalu, and without speaking moved on.

Intongalu turned to Veele. 'You know he always disagrees with me in council. You should not fraternise with him, he is my enemy.'

Veele looked squarely at her husband. Her father knew she would have preferred to marry Darlengi, but as the years passed he had shown no signs of taking a second wife. Everyone said it was the British in him, that they had filled him with their customs when he was but a boy. Then Induna Kayo had finally told her father, it was true, he never would take another wife, even though Thulile still had not borne him a child. It was then Veele had accepted Intongalu's offer to make her his Great Wife; and Great Wives had a certain amount of respect owing, even from their induna husbands. So as Veele's eyes met Intongalu's she said, 'I would not go against your wishes, my husband, but I prefer to emulate the honey bee, and remain friendly to every flower.' Then kissing him gently on the cheek she returned inside the hut.

As Darlengi came to the wide front entrance the mist was beginning to disperse and the morning sun was breaking through. He waved goodbye to a few of his friends, who sat taking snuff on some small boulders along the outside of the palisade. Then he saw Kayo beckoning him from nearby. Kayo was still regarded as a great warrior and respected in council, unlike Shiambi, who since the loss of his eye twelve years ago had taken less and less part in the affairs of Zululand. And as his son's reputation grew, so did his diminish, and for many years now he had remained at his home kraal of Ezulwini, and no longer came to voice his opinion with the king.

Kayo hailed him, 'Saku bo num, Darlengi, you are leaving?'

Darlengi came up to his friend. 'Yes, I leave now. But I return to Ulundi on the day of the new moon.'

'Good, to do that you must pass my kraal. Will you visit me too?'

'I shall.'

Then Kayo seemed to be studying him as he asked, 'Do you ever visit your English family?'

'Kayo, I have not seen them for many summers. It is strange you should ask that now, my friend, for Cetshwayo just mentioned them and I have been considering going to see them sometime this winter.'

'And what about the English lady at the mission in Greytown?'

Darlengi smiled. 'She is not English. But, yes, I have been visiting her regularly for many summers. Though I will not see her in the future for she leaves Natal for her home country before this very sunset.'

'She goes away?'

'Yes. This is the twenty-fourth of February on the European calendar – the one I have explained to you, based on that of the ancient warrior race, the Romans. Remember?'

Kayo smiled widely, 'Yes, I remember about them.'

'Today, then, is the day my friend from the mission departs on a ship from the town of Durban.'

'Is Durban larger than Ulundi?'

Darlengi grinned and patted the older man's shoulder. 'While Durban covers more ground than Ulundi, it does not have so many huts.'

Kayo looked pleased at that.

As Darlengi left his friend and headed towards the river he was thinking of Phoebe on the ship sailing out of Durban. He recalled the harbour so very well. He sometimes went over to St Lucia Bay these days. He liked the water, which was unusual for a Zulu. He really should go down to Durban sometime; see Mimosa again. But even as he thought it, he realised it probably would never happen.

How he hoped Phoebe would find happiness in America so far away. She was such a superior woman: kind, charitable, courageous and so very lovely. He was pleased she had not gone ahead with her marriage to Ben Fielding; from all she had ever said about him, Darlengi had received the feeling that her heart was against it. He knew that her heart, in truth, belonged to John Lockley; that she had loved him all these years. A smile, somehow sad and cynical, came over his face as he ran towards the drift across the White Umvoloosi. Wasn't that the point? Wasn't that the irony of it? Hadn't everybody loved John Lockley all these years?

Kate rolled on to her back and opened her eyes. She looked at the small ormolu clock on the dresser: half past ten. Then she remembered that John Lockley had left before dawn to ride to Durban to see those McLean missionary people off this evening.

She had been so startled when he'd arrived home last night. Thank the good Lord in heaven she had been here at the time. He'd expected her to be in Durban at Mimosa with Jane and Christopher, who were down there seeing those McLeans depart. Her husband had called in to The Grange to see his father, the General, and had learned she was still in 'Maritzburg. How amazed she had been when he'd come through the front door. Her heart had positively raced. For a second she'd thought it was Tom. She wouldn't have been surprised if it had been, he was daring so much for her lately. But it had to stop.

Her pulse quickened just slightly as she lay there. It was all so dangerous; too dangerous. She was meeting him out at Lief Liam's place for the last time today. She had resolved to tell him about the baby. Gosh, if she didn't he would notice soon anyway. She had decided she had to think of her child. She was married to John Lockley, not to Tom King, and while she loved Tom, and always would, she loved John Lockley too. She really meant it this time; she would not see Tom again.

John Lockley would resign from the army, they would go to live in Durban, she would have their baby and she would be a good mother and wife; well, as good as she could be, that was. John Lockley would be a great help, she knew that. Mind you, she would never know whose baby it truly was. Then a horrible thought struck her. What if it grew up looking exactly like Tom? She sat up and got out of bed, pulling a wry face at herself in the mirror above the dresser. Then she winked at her image. She would worry about all that when it happened.

John Lockley and Tenny had made good time to Durban, stopping only twice in eleven hours to refresh Horatio and Tenny's horse, Nebus. They had come via Mimosa, which was on the road into town, and John Lockley had left Tenny and the horses there to recuperate for the long ride back tomorrow. The housemaid there told him that Mr and Mrs Nelson were on board the *Kidde Halon*, saying goodbye to Phoebe and her mother.

Picking up a fresh stallion he had ridden into Durban proper, and was walking the animal along Smith Street when he heard a faint rumble in the distance. About ten seconds later he thought the horse had stepped in a hole for it lurched beneath him. Then he realised the ground was shaking. It did not last longer than six or seven seconds but the people in the street were all calling and shouting to each other, and the basket of flowers hanging on a pole outside the Catholic convent fell to the ground.

'Good heavens,' John Lockley said out loud. 'I do believe that was an earthquake.' A few seconds later there was another vibration beneath his feet. Again it lasted only moments and was less severe than the first, but on the opposite side of the street the windows in the Natal Bank rattled and one pane fell out on to the footpath. Soon the street was filled with people rushing out of doors seeking open ground.

John Lockley immediately recalled Aunt Jane telling him of two separate earthquakes that had occurred while he was away at military college back in 1860.

'Well,' he again spoke out loud, 'I suppose if such an occurrence happens only every fourteen years, we can be

444

grateful.' And as if in appreciation of the statement, the stallion whinnied loudly.

He made his way through the now populated streets to the harbour. When he arrived there were two small clippers at anchor, and the SS *Kidde Halon*. Boxes and casks were being hoisted up from the pier, and there was activity all around.

When John Lockley mounted the gangplank he saw Phoebe immediately. She was coming towards him, picking her way through piles of ropes amidships. She wore a pale blue dress and as John Lockley stood on the deck looking at her he thought what a beautiful woman little Phoebe had grown into.

'John Lockley!' she exclaimed when she saw him. 'How wonderful. What on earth are you doing here?' Her delight was so obvious that he felt quite gratified by it.

'I've come to wish you a good voyage, of course. I couldn't let you and your mother leave without saying goodbye.'

'How very kind of you.'

'Did you feel the earthquake?'

'Oh yes. The whole pier shook and two old ladies fell down. At first I wondered what it was, but Uncle Chris realised straight away. He said there'd been one here years ago.'

'Yes, that's right.'

'I've never been in one before. Have you?'

'No.'

And now her face became serious. 'I do appreciate your coming, knowing how busy you are, and I know Mother will. Aunt Jane and Uncle Chris have been here an hour since. They went down to see our cabin. Oh, and dear Fanny's here too. She'll be along directly; she's back there speaking with someone she knows.' She pointed aft.

'I can't believe you're truly leaving South Africa,' he said, taking off his helmet and thrusting his fingers back through his hair.

'I can't believe it either. It's been the only home I've ever known.' She looked away. 'I'll miss it and I'll miss my friends so very much. Fanny and I have been weeping most of the morning. Aren't we silly?' she added.

He shook his head. 'No, I don't think so at all. But I must say I was mystified when Aunt Jane told me you were going with your mother. I know it's none of my business, but weren't you going to marry that Fielding chap?'

She lifted her candid gaze to his. What could she say? *Yes, I was, but I couldn't marry him because I love you. I was marrying him only as second best, and I finally acknowledged that I was cheating myself and him.*

He was so close to her and the proximity of him made her feel heady and happy. Why was he able to do this to her? He saw her only as a friend. He loved that dark, mysterious and beautiful Kate. This was possibly the last time in her life she would ever be with him. The knowledge of that altered her mood completely and she felt so sad, so defeated, that she looked away.

He took her silence to mean that he was prying and he said softly, 'I'm sorry, Phoebe, I really answered my own question; it *is* none of my business.'

She drew strength from somewhere, perhaps from her dead father, and turned back to him, meeting his eyes once more. 'No, it's as much your business as anyone's, John Lockley. And I want to tell you. I realised I did not love Ben enough to marry him. It's that simple.'

And then he surprised himself, and her, as he replied, 'I'm glad. For I didn't want you to marry him. I mean ... that is, I didn't think he was the right sort of husband for you.'

She tried to smile. 'Well, you were correct, as it turns out.'

He was thinking how beautiful and yet how sad she looked. He wanted to cheer her and he smiled. 'Do you recall anything about falling from the rigging when you were tiny? When I broke your fall?'

'And broke your arm,' she added.

He laughed. 'Yes, true.'

She nodded. 'Actually, I do remember a little. I think I was singing and then I saw you below and somehow I fell.'

'That's right.'

At that moment Christopher's voice sounded and they turned around to see him in company with Jane and Victoria.

'John Lockley,' his uncle said, 'how marvellous. We didn't expect you.'

And Jane added, 'Weren't you up in the Drakensburgs, darling?'

He smiled and greeted them all. 'Yes, Aunt Jane, but I rode into 'Maritzburg last night and left before dawn to get here.

446

Anthony didn't mind. I couldn't let Phoebe, or you, Mrs McLean, leave without saying goodbye.'

Victoria smiled. 'Thank you so much, it really is a wonderful surprise.'

Shortly they were joined by Fanny and they stood around chatting, mostly about the earthquake, until they heard the mate's loud call from forward. 'All visitors disembark, please. The *Kidde Halon* leaves with the tide. Gangplank comes up in five minutes. Thank you one and all.'

Fanny clung to Phoebe, and Victoria to Jane. There were tears running down Phoebe's cheeks as she kissed them all and at last turned to John Lockley and moved him aside a few paces. He felt very strange as he took her in his arms to say goodbye.

She looked up at him, tears running from her eyes, and as he went to say something comforting, she spoke first. 'Darlengi still loves you, you know. Please don't let the silly feud go on and on. He's not your enemy, never has been, never will be. Pride is folly.'

He shook his head. 'Phoebe, I know he's not my enemy, and I'm not his. I understand what you're trying to do, and I thank you for it. You are ... a marvellous person. I wish you happiness.'

He held her close and she clung to him, thinking how perfect this moment was, and how saying goodbye to him was breaking her heart. She had thought to depart without ever seeing him, and these moments together had been so bitter-sweet.

He kissed her hair and had the oddest impulse to kiss her mouth; which of course he restrained. He had never held her in all his life – well, only when she was a wee thing all those years ago – and the feel and smell of her made him think of the pristine spring flowers of the veld.

When he let her go he felt sad. And when they had all said their final goodbyes and he found himself standing on the wharf looking up at her, he felt quite sharply a sense of losing something unique.

And so the *Kidde Halon* drifted away into the harbour and beyond, and Phoebe stood at the bulwark until she could see Durban no more.

Later, John Lockley led his horse along Gardiner Street

beside Christopher, Jane and Fanny until, at the corner of Pine Street, they separated. They would all meet back at Mimosa later.

'I'll have to leave early tomorrow, Aunt Jane, as I want to get back to 'Maritzburg by tomorrow night. I'd like to spend a couple of days with Kate before I return to the Drakensburgs.'

Christopher and his nephew went together to the brick-works, and as they walked along side by side Christopher said, 'We were surprised when Kate decided not to come to Durban with us. A few weeks ago she was so keen to come and start things here, and then suddenly she decided to stay in Pietermaritzburg.'

'Yes, I was surprised too when I found her at home last night. But apparently she hasn't been feeling well, so preferred to stay there for the time being.'

Christopher nodded. He said nothing, but he knew that Kate had been to two race meetings this month, and to the Magistrate's Ball and the Corporation Public Dinner. Still, to be fair, he supposed it was not impossible for her to have been socialising and feeling unwell too.

John Lockley halted to speak to Father Sabon, who still, after all these years, wandered the streets of Durban doing good deeds for the inhabitants and wearing his rusty-coloured cassock and his napless silk hat. He was very pleased to see John Lockley and he remembered him clearly. He looked at Christopher, who nodded in agreement as he said, 'Doesn't he look well in this fine uniform?' Then he turned back to John Lockley. 'Now, I seem to remember it was ye and a Zulu lad as were fine companions in those days of yore. What was his name . . . Darlengi, was it?'

John Lockley nodded. 'You have a very good memory, Father, yes it was.'

'Are you still his friend?'

John Lockley was a bit taken aback by this. Phoebe's last words to him had been of Darlengi, and now Father Sabon, whom he hadn't spoken to in twelve or thirteen years, was asking about him. 'Yes, Father,' he replied slowly. 'I am still his friend, and, ah, how are you?'

The priest smiled and his sun-lined face creased in a hundred places. 'I'm well enough, son, thank you. Still able to get around. The Lord's work continues.'

As John Lockley and Christopher continued on their way, Christopher said, 'So, you're still Darlengi's friend?'

'What else could I say, Uncle Chris? I could hardly explain the intricacies of our relationship to the old fellow.'

Christopher faced round to his nephew, and the sun gleamed in his eyes as he said, 'Son, I've noticed that you don't explain the intricacies of your relationship to anyone.'

John Lockley did not reply to his uncle; but he thought deeply about the statement and that night, after Fanny had said goodnight and retired, and he sat with his aunt and uncle in the drawing room of Mimosa, he cleared his throat and, running his fingers back through his hair, said, 'Aunt Jane and Uncle Chris, I've something to tell you.'

Jane looked up from her knitting. She had almost finished a baby's blanket for Kate, and intended to make bootees and bonnet and coat to match.

Christopher put down the *Mercury* newspaper he was reading. 'Yes, son, and what's that?'

'Last year when I came home to the Tugela farm after Cetshwayo's coronation, you and I, Uncle Chris, had a conversation one night . . . about Darlengi. You asked me what had happened between us, and why we had become alienated.'

Christopher nodded.

'I said at the time that I couldn't tell you for I did not want to hurt Aunt Jane, and you said that she had made homes in a wilderness and earned the respect of many, and that she was not easily hurt.'

Jane looked at Christopher and smiled gently.

'Then you said, if ever I were ready to speak, to tell you when all three of us were together . . .'

'Yes,' responded Christopher, 'I did.'

'We are all together tonight.'

Jane and Christopher met each other's eyes briefly as John Lockley continued, 'In truth, it's what happened today that has brought me to this. You see, Aunt Jane, you weren't there but I met Father Sabon in the street; hadn't seen him for a dozen or more years, and he asked me about Darlengi. And I don't think either of you realised that Phoebe's parting words to me were also of Darlengi. So I've been thinking that perhaps tonight I'm meant to tell you about what happened between us.'

449

His aunt and uncle sat silently watching him, and Jane leant over and took his hand and kissed it. 'Don't feel obliged to do anything unless you want to.'

He smiled at her. 'Thanks, Aunt Jane, and while up to now I've thought it best to leave it in the past that created it, I also realise that it's not fair to you two, who have been real parents to me. It does concern you that Darlengi and I are not as we used to be ... and so ... you do have a right to know. I'm certain you will keep my trust and never speak of it to anyone.'

Christopher answered for them both. 'We will.'

'You see, my dears, there's one person who must never learn what I'm about to say. It would shatter his life if he knew.'

The questioning look in their eyes was answered as he declared, 'Michael Tallant.'

'Michael?' exclaimed Jane.

'Yes. It'll soon be nine years since Nell died, and still he has not remarried. He lives with the memory of her and comes to The Grange to see you all the time.'

They did not deny this, for it was so.

John Lockley took a deep breath, and pushing his hand again through his abundant hair said, 'I hope it's not too devastating for you to learn that my darling sister did not love him, but that she loved Darlengi.'

Christopher and Jane said nothing. Jane because she was completely stunned, and Christopher because for years he had suspected something and at last was having the concerns he had lived with verified.

Jane looked from John Lockley to Christopher and back to John Lockley again. She was amazed and disbelieving.

'I first realised it when I was still in Ceylon. Nell had written me a letter and left it with Phoebe. Phoebe sent it to me after her death. In it she said she loved Darlengi, that she could not live ... did not want to live ... without him. I was shocked and hurt, and angry. For the rest of my years in Ceylon, my anger with Darlengi festered inside me and I thought her death had been suicide. But my dears, I have since been convinced it was not. She did, in fact, fall accidentally. But there's no doubt that she was up on the boulders with the intention of taking her life.'

'I don't understand,' said Christopher.

'How can this possibly be true?' said Jane, breaking silence at last. 'I don't believe it. Ellen loved Michael.'

John Lockley shook his head. 'No, Aunt Jane, she didn't. It seems my darling sister denied her true feelings, but her soul ... her soul ... Aunt Jane, did not accept it. She loved Darlengi. I can tell you now because ... Phoebe has left these shores ... gone ... She too held Ellen's secret. Ellen confided in her on her way to the Tugela farm, to what was to be her honeymoon. She told Phoebe everything: how two nights before her wedding she and Darlengi had come together and acknowledged the truth ... which was the love they had always felt for each other.'

'But,' protested Jane, 'Ellen was always distant, even supercilious, to him.'

Christopher leaned towards his wife. 'My dear, that apparently is the point. She had never admitted the truth, even to herself, it seems ... until it was too late.' Christopher was thinking of the night before Ellen's wedding when the poor child had said, 'Marriage is forever, isn't it?' Now he recognised it for the cry for help that it might have been. Why, oh why, hadn't she said more? He just might have been able to help her.

Jane shook her head. 'That means that this acknowledging of their love happened at The Grange ... before the wedding, when Darlengi was there.'

John Lockley nodded. 'And I blamed Darlengi for what happened to Nell, absolutely. I thought he had been cruelly selfish.' He closed his eyes briefly. 'Though now I think differently. There was a time when I loved his sister more than anything, and he didn't judge me. These days I think I was wrong to act as I did. When I came home from Ceylon four years ago, I went to Zululand with the intention of harming Darlengi ... perhaps even killing him.'

Tears had risen to Jane's eyes and she sat shaking her head.

'In Zululand I had the weirdest and most mystical experience of my life. I came to a kraal where Mattana, the witch doctor who had been a mother to Darlengi, was dying. Strange that I should choose the one kraal in the whole of Zululand that held her. I was at her side when she died. She was holding on to me ... She convinced me to have no confrontation with him.'

451

He fell silent for a moment and Christopher asked, 'Did you see him?'

'Yes, I did. He arrived just after Mattana died. I could see he was worried about her, but ... overjoyed to see me ... knowing nothing of what had been in my heart. When he went into Mattana's hut I wrote him a note and left immediately.' He looked down at his clasped hands as he added, 'In the note I said we were no longer ... brothers. That too much had happened, and that if we met again we should meet as strangers.'

There was silence for a time and John Lockley stood up and walked to the far side of the room, his giant shadow stretching across the parlour in the lamplight. When he turned around his aunt was crying and his uncle comforting her.

Jane looked at her husband, tears rolling down her cheeks. 'So ... my dear Ellen was going to kill herself. It breaks my heart to think that.'

'Sweetheart,' Christopher replied gently, 'that's why John Lockley did not want to tell you.'

Jane shook her head. 'No, no, I'm ... glad he did.' Then she looked across to John Lockley. 'Why did you say you believe her fall was an accident after all?'

He came back across the room and knelt in front of her, the brilliant colour of his eyes heightened in the lamplight. 'Because Darlengi was there when she died.'

'What?'

'Yes, Phoebe told me. He had come to the farm ... I suppose to see her. He found her high up on the rocks and when she saw him she turned to come down, but she slipped and fell. My sister died in Darlengi's arms. He left her there when he saw Michael coming.'

Jane leant her head on Christopher's shoulder as she asked, 'How could Phoebe possibly know this?'

'Because Darlengi told her.'

John Lockley was still kneeling in front of Jane and now she sat upright and wiped her eyes. Then she took up his hands in hers and spoke in a voice breathy with emotion. 'I find all this hard to believe, but I realise it must be so. My heart is heavy for our long-dead Ellen, and for our Darlengi. What a wicked world we have created, when love between any man and woman must be concealed like some terrible stigma.' She looked round to her husband and then back to her nephew, still holding tightly to his hands. 'Darling, your brother Darlengi was not responsible. Love happens, with, or without, sanction. You know that.'

John Lockley said nothing, but, holding her gaze, he nodded very slowly.

Now Jane turned her eyes to Christopher. 'And poor Michael; he must never know; we must not shatter his illusion. He's such a good man.'

Christopher put his arm around his wife's shoulders as he replied, 'Yes, that's right.'

John Lockley kissed his aunt's hands and then rose to his feet. 'Strange, I remember most of the things Mattana said, but one plays on my mind. She said, "Your anger is at yourself." And she was right.'

And now Christopher rose beside him. 'John Lockley, life holds innumerable lessons. We cannot bring back Ellen, or the girl, Jettama. They belong to a part of our lives that was sweet, but which has gone. We must leave them there. I'm sure Darlengi knows that, and I think you do. Thank you for revealing all this. We know some of it hurt to tell. I won't say you should rekindle the lost kinship between yourself and your brother; that's for you to do, only if the need lies within you. Darlengi will always be part of this family. My real sorrow is that nine years ago he and Ellen felt they could say nothing of what lay in their hearts.'

He put out his hand to Jane and she took it and stood up beside him, saying, 'John Lockley, what you did tonight took great courage. Thank you, sweetheart.'

Then all three of them embraced and John Lockley whispered, 'Thank you for being the two most wonderful people in the world.'

As they said goodnight at the bottom of the staircase, Jane said softly, 'Sometime, and it doesn't matter when, could I see the letter Ellen wrote you? That is, if you still have it.'

CHAPTER THIRTY-ONE

John Lockley said his goodbyes and he and Tenny left Mimosa at seven o'clock in the morning, making good time on their return ride. When they came to Dick Baxter's Wayside Inn, which stood about halfway between Durban and Pietermaritzburg they brought Horatio and Nebus to a halt under the flowering laburnum trees at the side of the hostelry.

The stallions drank from the long water trough and John Lockley and Tenny entered the inn.

Two farmers sat near the wooden counter and the host put down his coffee cup and came forward, holding out his hand. 'Good day to ye, Major. Didn't I serve ye two just yesterday?'

John Lockley took off his white helmet and smiled. 'Yes, we've made a quick trip to Durban. We're on our way back to 'Maritzburg. We'll have whatever you're serving.' He looked at Tenny, who nodded in agreement.

'And just two glasses of water, please, no ale.'

'Good, I'll be gettin' that for ye directly, but ye're the first people we've had in from Durban today. How bad was yesterday's quake down there?'

'Oh, not too bad, really. Ground shook for a bit. Some panes of glass fell from buildings and some old folk were unsteady on their feet, but no real damage that I heard of, though it caused a lot of talk for the remainder of the day.'

Dick Baxter looked over at his two other customers. 'So it seems it was much worse in 'Maritzburg, then?'

'Aye,' replied one of the farmers. 'Daniel Boyd told me just afore I came in here as there were cracks in the walls of the police station, the government school and the colonial office; and that some poorly built private dwellings had their roofs cave in.'

The host turned back to John Lockley. 'All we felt here was a rumble and me favourite pewter tankard fell from atop the

454

fireplace.' He pointed to it hanging back in its precarious position on a nail on the wall.

'Was there anyone hurt?' inquired John Lockley.

'Daniel said a few folks were,' the farmer answered. 'He didn't know how badly, but one or two had been taken to the hospital, he knew that.'

John Lockley frowned and, running his hand back through his hair, looked at Tenny. 'Somehow I think I'd prefer to get on into 'Maritzburg, Tenny.'

'*Yeh bo*, Major, let's go.'

John Lockley looked to the host. 'We'll just have a swift cup of that coffee you're drinking, landlord. Forget the luncheon.' And he put down half a crown, much to Dick Baxter's delight.

As the host poured the coffee, one of the farmers asked, 'Got family in 'Maritzburg, have ya?'

'Yes, my father and my wife.'

They took up the coffee and drank.

'Hope yer relatives are all right,' Dick Baxter called as John Lockley put on his helmet and hurried out through the door, closely followed by Tenny.

'Thank you.'

When some hours later they arrived at the top of Usy Doorn's Hill and looked down on Pietermaritzburg, John Lockley was telling himself he was concerned over nothing. Chances were the General would have been at The Grange, and it was built like a fort so he'd be all right; and Kate had probably been at home, and their house was pretty solid too. And Umslopagas would have been with her. The farmer had intimated that the only people hurt had been in poorly built dwellings, so really he had nothing to worry about. He was just concerned about Katy's condition, that was all.

They rode straight to his home, and while Tenny held the horses John Lockley hurried in through the front door. 'Kate!' he called. 'Katy, are you here?'

The voice that answered was Umslopagas's. 'I come, I come.' And as he hurried out of the kitchen along the hall, John Lockley knew something was very wrong. The Zulu had a worried look on his face and was wringing his hands in agitation.

'Umslopagas, what is it? What's happened.'

'Mrs Katy.'

'What, man? What?'

'She in hospital. We have earthquake, she get hurt. She . . .'

But John Lockley heard nothing else: he was out of the door and calling to Tenny, 'We go to the hospital,' as he leaped upon Horatio.

Pietermaritzburg's Grey's Hospital was a long, low, one-storey building with climbing vines over the awning at the front. A number of native men habitually loitered here taking snuff and talking about the happenings of the day.

John Lockley turned to his companion. 'Tenny, Mrs Harrison is here. Perhaps you should go back to my house. Wait there for me.'

Tenny shook his head. 'I wait here, Inkosi.'

John Lockley patted his shoulder and, dismounting, ran through the group of lounging men to the door and inside.

Pietermaritzburg had one trained nurse, Miss Audrey Edness, who had been formally trained at St Thomas's Hospital in England. She had worked with the London Mission Society in Zanzibar before coming here, and she assisted Dr Tallant, who was now in charge of the hospital. She had been here for three years, and cared deeply about the community. It was she who had given instruction to Phoebe when she had come here in the spring of seventy-two.

As John Lockley entered the hospital Miss Edness came towards him, wearing her familiar grey gown and broad white band embroidered with S.T., standing for St Thomas, round her left sleeve.

'Miss Edness.' John Lockley halted in front of her. 'My wife . . . I believe she's here.'

Audrey Edness straightened her long white apron and looked sympathetically at him from under the white handkerchief which covered her pretty fair hair. She had always liked Major Harrison; who didn't? He was the handsomest man in the whole of Natal, and in his uniform he could make any woman's heart race. And while he was a friend of that strange Lieutenant-Colonel Durnford, she didn't hold that against him.

'Yes, Major, that's so.'

'Can I see her? Is she hurt badly? What happened?'

'I'm sure Dr Tallant will allow you to see her. He's with her now. Come with me.'

She turned and they walked back down the corridor together. 'Is she all right? She's some months into a pregnancy.'

'Major, I'll let the doctor inform you of the detail, but I'm afraid that . . . no, she's not all right.'

John Lockley halted. 'What do you mean?'

She sighed. It was really too dreadful. How did she tell this wonderful man that Tom King had brought his wife in here yesterday after the earthquake? That she had miscarried and that she was dying. How did she say it? She turned to him and hesitated, just as Michael Tallant came into the corridor.

Michael held out his hand. 'John Lockley, you've come at last.'

'I was in Durban, didn't know about it. Michael, tell me what's happened?'

Michael glanced at Miss Edness and she quietly withdrew. Then he took John Lockley's arm. 'There's never an easy way to say these things. Your wife's dying. In fact I don't think she'll last the night.'

John Lockley shook his head. No, this could not be.

'John Lockley, I'm so very sorry.'

He controlled himself to where his voice was calm. 'What happened?'

'She was in a hut a mile or so out of town when the earthquake hit. The hut collapsed. She was fatally injured. She miscarried even before she was brought here, I'm afraid.'

Now John Lockley's voice had an edge to it. 'What in God's name do you mean, Michael? In a hut? What hut? Where?'

'Lief Liam's old disused place out past Fort Napier.'

And even as he asked the question, he knew the answer. 'Who brought her in?'

Michael shook his head sadly as he answered, 'Tom King.'

'The bastard! I'll kill him.'

Michael took a firm hold on John Lockley's arm. 'Steady, my friend, there'll be time enough for all that. Right now, perhaps you should see Kate. She did regain consciousness briefly, earlier, and asked for you.'

He brought himself under control and nodded, then Michael

led him back to the room he had come out of a few minutes before. With his hand on the door knob the doctor said, 'We've made her as comfortable as we can. I've administered tincture of laudanum, it's all I can do.'

Inside, the evening light filtered through the single window on to Kate in an iron bed.

'Mrs Harrison, Kate, can you hear me?' Michael said softly, but there was no response.

John Lockley approached the bedside. Her face was swollen and there were cuts on her chin; her abundant black hair contrasted acutely with her pallid skin. Her right arm was hidden in an enormous bandage. 'Katy,' he said, 'it's me, John Lockley.'

She opened her eyes and he saw the flash of animation when she recognised him.

He sat down on the chair at the bedside and tenderly touched her cheek. 'Katy, Katy,' he whispered.

She tried to raise her left hand but it fell back, and John Lockley took it in his own.

Behind him Michael lit a lamp, and then, touching John Lockley comfortingly on the shoulder, left the room.

Kate just lay there looking up at him. Then she closed her eyes and he sat there holding her hand as the minutes passed.

Ah Katy, you were deceiving me all along. Why wasn't I enough for you? Why? Why? Why? Did I ever know you, Kate? No, I don't think I ever did. I'm so damn sorry . . . so damn sorry.

Half an hour later, Miss Edness came in and lit another lamp. She leaned close to his ear and whispered, 'Would you like a cup of tea?' And he looked up into her sympathetic eyes and shook his head. Then she dipped a small white piece of cloth into a bowl of water on the bedside table and moistened Kate's lips with it. 'Do this from time to time,' she said softly.

And so the hours passed and John Lockley looked at his fob watch now and then and Michael Tallant came in and out. At around nine o'clock Miss Edness prevailed on John Lockley to take some tea and toast. It was then he realised he had eaten nothing since breakfast in Durban; and he remembered Tenny.

He found his loyal Basuto outside where he had left him.

'Tenny, I want you to go home now, back to my house. Umslopagas will take care of you. Wait there for me.'

458

Tenny nodded. 'Mrs Harrison?' he asked.

John Lockley met his eyes. 'Not expected to live. Please go now, my friend, and wait for me.'

When he returned to the little room, Kate still lay with eyes closed, and her breathing was increasingly strained. At midnight Michael came in to say he was going to get a few hours' sleep and that his assistant, Thomas Greer, doing the night watch, was in the ward across the hall. 'He will get me if you want me.'

'Is there any more you can do for her?'

Michael shook his head. 'I'm afraid not.'

It was perhaps half an hour after Michael left that Kate stirred and moaned and opened her eyelids. Her eyes were glazed.

'Katy, Katy. It's me, John Lockley.'

He wiped her mouth with the damp cloth and she lay looking up at him. She could not see him properly but she knew it was John Lockley. Her husband had come to her. She felt very odd. Everything was unreal and there was pain at the edge of her awareness. She remembered meeting Tom out in the hut. She had just told him about the baby when the ground shook violently and she saw the roof fall in on top of them. She remembered the great wooden support that came down on her. Everything was black after that. John Lockley was so good and she did love him so. Why did she feel so strange?

'John Lockley . . .' She managed to say it.

'Katy, Katy, I'm so sorry.'

'No . . . not you . . . me. I'm sorry.' She saw him lift her hand and hold it to his cheek. Why the devil had he gone away so much? She wouldn't have needed Tom if he'd been home with her. She groaned as she felt a twisting pain somewhere that seemed to end right in the middle of her brain. She must tell him, she must. 'John . . . Lockley.'

'Yes, Katy, I'm here.'

'I love you . . . always. Just made . . . a mess of it . . . Wanted . . . more. Wanted fun . . .'

'Yes, Kate, I understand.' John Lockley held her hand to his cheek. It was so cold and yet perspiration beads were all over her face and her breathing was very laboured.

She had an awful pain in her head. It was hard to say the things she wanted to say. 'I . . . told him . . . wouldn't see him

459

again . . . going to be a mother . . . going to live in Durban. John Lockley . . . we . . . are going to live in Durban?'

She could hear him, but he sounded such a long way off. 'Yes, Katy, yes, dear. We're going to live in Durban.'

'Good . . . that's good.' She knew her eyes were open but she could not see him now. He had blurred away into a black shape. She could not see anything. She felt terribly frightened: cold and frightened. 'John Lockley?' Why didn't he answer her? 'John Lockley?' Black, everything was black, and there was a constant sound in her mind like the sea rushing on to the shore.

As John Lockley held her hand, he saw her slip back into unconsciousness. She did not wake again and an hour later, as he still sat holding her hand, her breathing ceased.

'Wake up, you bastard, and get out here!'

Jonas King woke to a thundering on his door, and momentarily he thought there was another earthquake. At his side his wife leaped up as their daughter Sophie shouted, 'Father, Mother, come quickly, John Lockley Harrison is trying to smash down the door.'

Sophie and her sisters huddled together on the staircase as Jonas King came downstairs in his nightshirt shouting, 'I'm coming! I'm coming!'

Mrs King appeared behind him carrying a lantern, and as Jonas opened the front door he encountered John Lockley in red coat, with glaring points of fury for eyes, and a short sword raised above his head. 'Where the hell's your bloody son?'

'He's not here.'

'Where is he, King? Don't trifle with me.'

And Mrs King, eyes wide in the lantern light, called, 'He speaks the truth. He came home last night and packed a bag and left. We've no idea where he's gone. None at all.'

'The bloody rat.'

'What's going on over there?' shouted Hans Kruger, the publican of the Plough Hotel across the street.

'Nothing,' answered John Lockley, dropping his sword to his feet.

Sophie and her sisters came gingerly forward from the staircase to cluster around their parents at the door.

Jonas King looked at the soldier standing in the moonlight

in the street in front of his house. He, too, had heard the rumours about his son and Mrs Harrison. He had faced his son with them on the very morning of the earthquake and Tom had replied, 'Father, they're not true. She's a friend of Sophie and I see a lot of her simply because of that. People gossip, you know what they're like.' But Jonas also knew what his son was like, and his answer had been, 'I'll not have a son of mine in an adulterous relationship. If there is something in what I've heard, then straighten yourself out now, and finish it. You might be a thirty-year-old man, but you're my son and as long as you live under this roof, I won't have it.'

And then the earthquake had happened and the whole town was talking about how Tom King had carried a broken and bleeding Mrs Harrison into the hospital. His son had come home and packed a bag, and while his mother and sisters had wept and wailed he had climbed on his horse and gone.

'Major Harrison, all I can do is abjectly apologise to you for my son's behaviour. I wouldn't have blamed you had you used your sword upon him. But like the coward that I now fear he is, he's gone.'

John Lockley stood there a few seconds longer, then bent down and, picking up his sword, pushed it into the steel scabbard hanging from his belt. When he spoke it was in a tired, defeated tone. 'I'm sorry I woke you, Mr King.'

'I would have done the same, lad.'

John Lockley swung round on the heel of his boot and walked away. The tears on his cheeks glistened faintly in the moonlight as he strode along. Life was insane. Phoebe McLean had the right idea in getting out of this bloody place.

Kate had been unfaithful all along, when he had trusted her and believed her. And now she had died for her infidelity. He wandered on from street to street, without design.

Darling Nell was dead. Darlengi was lost to him. He had given himself to two women: Jettama and Kate. Jettama had thrown herself in front of a spear so he might live; and Kate had thrown herself at another man.

He continued walking until suddenly he realised he was outside The Grange. It stood there in the moonglow looking solid and strong ... naturally it would; it had been built by Uncle Christopher. Thank God for Uncle Christopher and Aunt Jane ... but no, even they weren't here. They were forty miles away in Durban. No one he cared about was here. Even Anthony was up in the bloody Drakensburgs. *No, hang on, the General's here*. Dear old General, didn't know him really, but oh, how badly he needed someone tonight.

He wiped his eyes with the back of his sleeve and passing through the arch of climbing flowers knocked on the front door. It was Lacey, the Hottentot gardener, who opened the door, candle in hand.

'Lord in Heaven, Major Harrison, what you doin' here?'

'The General, my father, I want to . . .'

'What's going on, Lacey?' It was James Harrison in his pyjamas in the front hall. Then he saw his son. 'John Lockley!'

John Lockley entered the hall and stood looking at him. For some reason he thought about his mother. For the first time in his life he wondered if his father had loved her. He lifted his left hand and pushed his fingers through his hair. 'I . . . Kate's dead, and I . . . it's just that . . . I've got no one to go to . . . Father.'

The General hesitated. Then, stepping quickly forward, he wrapped his son in his arms, hugging him tightly. 'Come in, son, come in. Tell me about it, my dear boy, tell me about it.' And from a hidden place down deep within him came his next words. 'Just the two of us will talk, just you and me.'

CHAPTER THIRTY-TWO

Anthony looked up from where he knelt, fitting more branches into the windbreak of earthen sods that enclosed the camp fire.

'You've got icicles in your moustache,' laughed John Lockley, as Anthony ran his hand across his freezing whiskers.

'It's so cold I've got the men working in relays up there.' John Lockley pointed up a narrow gorge of rock about two hundred yards long and twelve yards wide.

Anthony stood up beside him. 'All right, lad. Will they be finished tonight?'

'Yes, should be. Though everything's frozen. Even a waterfall, it's a huge column of ice. I'm afraid there'll be more snow tonight. I've left Charles Preston and a few of the troops up there with our Putini fellows. I'm going back up soon, for they'll be ready to blast that main scarp of rock late this afternoon. We're lucky, you know, the Putini are some of the best "road workers" I've ever had.'

'Yes, they are. I've just written again to England to my father asking him to continue trying to persuade the Colonial Secretary to intervene on their behalf and have the pardon granted. And the claim has gone in to the government here for them to be considered loyal subjects. I'm of a mind to think that none of the colonists would have done the job they have these last six months.'

'You're probably right about that, and you've been their untiring champion,' John Lockley replied, blowing into his clasped hands. 'What with Bishop Colenso over in London on the same cause, something should come of it all.'

'I must get their land back for them, John Lockley. I *will* get it, and the twenty thousand pounds for all their cattle that the colonial government seized after the tribe was taken prisoner. It's a struggle for right over might, and I'm in the fray.'

'Well Anthony, we British are supposed to lead the world in

justice. It just seems that sometimes the path to justice is a little like these passes over the mountains; with obstacles, obstruction and impediments all along the way.'

Anthony nodded and moved across the white landscape, past picks and shovels and mats and pack horses, to speak with Simeon and Tenny and another Basuto called Jabez Molife, who all wore soldiers' greatcoats, and worked over large cooking pots, preparing the evening meal.

John Lockley regarded his friend as he reached the three men and fell in conversation with them. They received great loyalty from the Basutos; in fact from all the natives they had working for them. They were good, simple people who responded to being treated fairly.

On the journey up here to the Drakensburgs they had camped at the reserve and spent time with many of the Putini women and children. A woman called Umkozaza, a widow of a chief, had walked one hundred miles to see them, 'the inkosi who are helping us'. Anthony had an idea for the tribe to begin purchasing land for themselves. Apparently Lord Carnarvon himself, the Secretary of State for the Colonies, was in favour of native land purchase, believing it anchored them to soil. On the day they left the camp Umkozaza and all the women and children had formed a great circle around them and sung a song of thanks to the soldiers. And as they turned to ride away they shouted 'Bayete!' which was the royal salute and should be reserved for a king or the Governor of the colony. It had been a very moving moment.

John Lockley thought of it now as he moved by a group of slaughter cattle and sheep and goats to his tent. Inside he grabbed a pair of gloves. He would need them up in the pass. He smiled; they had done well, another month should see them finished. He and Anthony had worked incessantly to block access across the mountains; quarrying and blasting all over the Drakensburgs. He knew Anthony's arm had been badly affected by this extreme cold; it was absolutely useless now, and yet he worked like a man with three arms not one. John Lockley knew who the devils were that drove his own soul and made him work like a man possessed; but he was not sure what drove his friend.

Phoebe lit the lamp and lifted a long blue feather from her

dressing table. She moved across to the window, caressing the plume and touching her cheek with it. It had been such a pleasant summer's day and Cleveland was in bloom. All the trees and flowers were blossoming and summer was abroad. It was so strange to have summer in June and July. These months should be cold, with the chill wind of the veld rattling the windows and doors.

This morning she had sat in the public square in the city, watching the world go by, with her mother tatting lace doilies on one side of her and her grandmother reading the *Leader* newspaper and commenting on the politics of the day on the other. 'Garfield's in trouble, poor man,' she kept saying. In the few short weeks that she had been here, Phoebe had learned that James Garfield was a local congressman born here in Cuyahoga County. He was in trouble for accepting gifts of stock from a corporation called Credit Mobilier who were seeking favours from the government. Phoebe knew her grandmother was sympathetic to Garfield, for she had to listen almost on a daily basis to what a gentleman he was, and how people were so cruel.

Her grandmother's house was lovely. There were pretty lamps all over it and great brocade curtains and baskets of flowers and velvet chairs. Phoebe had never seen anything like it; even The Grange and Mimosa suffered by comparison, and she had thought them positively beautiful.

Her grandfather had made his money out of lumber. Many of the vast lumber yards along the flats of the river had signs that read: 'Lawrence Lumber'. Her grandmother and her mother's sister, Aunt Leah, had taken her to tour around one of the largest when she had first arrived.

She stood now looking out of the window on to the perfect lawn, and in her mind she saw that other grass so far away; tall grass blowing in the breeze under the bright sun of Africa, where the world sparkled. She thought of the Reverend Arthur Bradley, the new missionary. He had taken to the place straight away and Phyllis May liked him immediately. He had been so understanding. 'You will miss it all, Miss McLean, and I understand how hard it must be for you to leave.' Hard? It had devastated her heart to leave Fantasia and Lila and Tokwa and little Shinu and the others; and Thulmi, most of all Thulmi.

The night before they had left the mission he had found her down by her father's grave. He had stood and waited for her; she knew he was there, standing behind her as the short twilight came and went. And when she turned around and made her way back to the house he had fallen in beside her.

Quietly he had said, 'You go tomorrow, I know, but when do you come back?'

She had turned to him and met his soulful eyes. 'Oh, Thulmi, dear Thulmi, I don't know.'

He had looked surprised. 'But you do come back, Miss Phoebe? Yes?'

The lump in her throat prevented her from speaking for a moment and then the tears brimmed in her eyes. 'Oh Thulmi, I might not ever come back.'

The warm breeze blew gently across her face and she felt tears coming as he made his simple, explicit statement. 'I will wait.'

The next morning he had been standing by the giant aloe near the gate when they left on the ox wagon with all their paraphernalia. He had reached up to her as she passed him and handed her a magnificent, long, brilliant blue crane feather. She had never seen one this colour before, for the 'blue' crane was normally more grey. 'Oh, thank you, Thulmi, I will treasure it always.'

Then he had tried to smile and had said once again, 'I will wait.'

It had broken her heart.

Phoebe sighed as she touched the feather again to her face. Behind her the door opened and she turned to see Victoria glide into her room. 'My sweetheart, dinner is laid and Mother is asking for you. Come along.'

Dinner was three courses served by Trill, the maid, a stiff little person in a stiff little dress.

During the main course of duckling, Grandmother Lawrence raised her glass. 'To you both. I'm so excited to have you home.'

'Mother,' said Victoria, 'you'll have to stop drinking a toast to us, you've done it every night for almost three weeks.'

Her mother smiled. She was so pleased to have Victoria home. She had her other daughter, Leah, of course, and Leah was very dear and special, but she had not seen Victoria for over twenty years. And while Victoria did far too much reading of the Bible for her liking, she supposed that that was what missionaries did, so she'd have to accept it. Victoria had already been to see the Wesleyan church fathers and they were going to organise a lecture tour for her all around Ohio, to inform people first hand about her twenty years in Natal with the poor savages.

'So, darling, when is this lecture tour to begin?'

'Some time next month, if everything goes as planned. Mr Bright has already written to Columbus and Toledo and Dayton and Cincinnati, and it seems they're all interested. He says he's sure that dozens of the smaller communities will be too.'

Mrs Lawrence turned her grey eyes to Phoebe. 'And so you, darling, will accompany your mother, no doubt?'

Phoebe put down her knife and fork. 'Well, Grandmother, I'm not exactly certain, as Aunt Leah has said she'd love to accompany Mummy and ... I went to the Cleveland General Hospital this afternoon. Did you know they opened a training school for nursing just last month? There are hardly any in the country, so it's marvellous. Well, because of my background, having done some training in Pietermaritzburg and having run my little hospital at the mission, the superintendent informed me I'll only have to do two years' training instead of three.' She looked at her mother and smiled widely. 'And as I told you this evening, then I'll be a certificated nurse. Oh, and I need to supply satisfactory evidence of character and education.'

Victoria leaned across and took her daughter's hand. 'My darling, that's just wonderful.'

Victoria's mother finished the wine in her glass, then with a sigh asked, 'Why, oh why do you need to be a nurse, for heaven's sake?'

'Grandmother, I don't *need* to be, I want to be.'

'But we've sufficient money. You shouldn't do menial work, you shouldn't work at all. Girls of your class don't work, it's not right. How do you expect to find a husband, a man worthy of a Lawrence, if you step down out of your class like this?'

Phoebe clasped her hands. 'Firstly, Grandmother, I want you to understand that I'm not looking for a husband. Secondly, I don't want to upset you, or go against your values, but what about Florence Nightingale? She was born to wealth and did not need to be a nurse either.'

Her grandmother shook her head. 'Who's Florence Nightingale?'

'Oh, Grandmother,' said Phoebe askance.

Victoria shrugged her shoulders and turned round to her mother. 'Phoebe was brought up in a British colony, Mama, therefore her knowledge of things is more British than American, I'm afraid. She's referring to the lady who established the first school for nursing anywhere in the world. She's the one who actually began the improvement in the health and conditions of British soldiers. She's very well known over there.'

'Oh, I see.'

'And Mother,' Victoria continued, 'people won't think Phoebe's so odd, they'll simply think she's like me. Remember how you and Daddy and all your friends disapproved of my being a missionary. Daddy and Frank didn't see eye to eye on very much, if you recall.'

Her mother made a sound distinctly like a groan. 'I suppose that's true.'

So Phoebe was enrolled in the Cleveland General Hospital's school for nurses.

Her days were full and her evenings found her getting to know her grandmother. The old lady was actually quite sweet. Millicent Lawrence had been hidebound by her position in Cleveland's society, and Leah, her elder daughter, had followed in her footsteps. She did not understand her younger daughter's desire to cure human souls, nor her granddaughter's desire to cure their ailments. But she was more tolerant than many of her breed, and while she would never own up to it, she was really quite proud of both of them.

After her successful lecture tour, Victoria remained involved in Wesleyan church affairs, and there was talk about her going wider with her lectures into Pennsylvania and West Virginia. She seemed to settle back into life in Ohio.

Phoebe spent many Sunday afternoons walking along the shores of Lake Erie, looking out on what appeared to be an ocean, and thinking about her life. She became friendly with a pretty, red-headed girl called Diana Holmes who was training with her, but missed those others she cared about so far away on another continent. She slept under the blue crane feather. She had sewn it into the valance which hung over her bed.

It was a Wednesday in October, a half-day holiday, when Phoebe and Diana met Victoria for luncheon in Burrows department store in Superior Street. Phoebe's mother was quiet during the meal and when her friend left to go to the library, Phoebe asked, 'Mother, is there something wrong?'

'Today I received two letters from Aunt Jane. One written in April and the other in June, but both in this morning's post.'

Immediately Phoebe thought of John Lockley. 'Is everyone all right?'

Victoria shook her head. 'Kate was killed in an earthquake. It's the most dreadful story imaginable. She'd been carrying on with a fellow called Tom King. They'd been meeting secretly and the building caved in on top of them.'

'Oh, how absolutely horrible.'

'Yes, isn't it? Jane says John Lockley has been working like a demon ever since. He was up in the Drakensburgs in her first letter and still there in her second.'

'Poor John Lockley.'

'Yes, his choice of women seems to bring him only misfortune.'

Phoebe did not go home with her mother, instead she sat in the public square for a long time, thinking about John Lockley and home; Natal would always be home to her. What had happened to Kate was terrible, and she felt sad for John Lockley. No doubt he was pushing himself to forget, working so hard. She must write to him tonight; try and help him through this terrible time, sustain him, even though it all happened months ago.

She did write that night and she continued to write from time to time afterwards. They were hard letters for her to devise, for she was always wanting to say more than she should, but she tried to be honest and straightforward. She told him about her life and asked him about his, and occasionally she would diplomatically mention Darlengi. He must have appreciated the contact with her, for sometimes he would reply, and when a letter arrived from him, it made the whole of Phoebe's world a little brighter.

Phoebe worked hard and passed all her examinations, and in the first week of June 1876 her grandmother gave a party to celebrate the end of her studies and her certification as a Nurse, Grade One.

Cleveland was in bloom again and the soft June breezes wafted across the city. Millicent Lawrence had been one of the city's grandest hostesses forty years before but this was the first party she had held in over two decades, her daughter Leah doing the entertaining for the family these days. The whole of her wide front veranda was bathed in lantern light, and flowers seemed to be growing out of every container in the garden and the house.

Trill was having a marvellous night, bossing all the hired help, and rushing hither and thither organising food and drinks.

Millicent Lawrence sat in one of her fine Sheraton armchairs brought out on to the veranda for the occasion so that she could peruse both the garden and the house. Cleveland's first families were here, and on one side of Millicent sat her oldest friend, Jean Sheer, a grand lady with pearls wound round her throat.

As the small orchestra played a waltz Phoebe swung gracefully by her grandmother in a long yellow silk dress.

'Isn't she beautiful?' said Millicent to Jean, and Jean nodded. 'Yes, dear, she is, but she's getting on and there doesn't seem to be a special young man in her life. This business of becoming a nurse is all very well, but there should be a home and children.'

Millicent sighed. 'Ah, Jean, I've said it over and over, but she's of the younger generation and they have different values.' She took another sip of her wine and confided, 'Mind you, her mother told me once that there was a man in Africa whom Phoebe doted on, but he married someone else and it broke the child's heart.'

Jean shook her head. 'How very sad. There's usually a story like that when a girl's approaching thirty with no wedding ring on her finger.'

The night was a success and no one left before midnight. The last person to depart was Diana, hand in hand with her fiancé, Dr Gordon Campbell.

When Victoria came in in her night attire to say goodnight to Phoebe, it was the early hours of the morning. She smiled at her daughter lying beneath the blue crane feather as she sat

470

down on the side of the bed. 'Goodnight, sweetheart, and thanks for letting Grandma have her party. I was afraid she'd stay up all night, she was having such a grand time.'

'Yes, she did like it.'

'So, my dear, you're a trained nurse. Congratulations. What do you intend to do now?'

Phoebe sat up and took hold of her mother's hands. 'Mummy, I'm going to take my training where it can do good things.'

Victoria said nothing for a moment, and then she nodded slowly. 'And where's that?'

'Back to Natal. My heart's there, Mummy, you know that. And it always will be.'

At exactly the same time that Victoria blew out the lamp and left her daughter's room, seven thousand miles to the southeast John Lockley and Anthony stood in the morning sun saying goodbye.

In the cool morning air, their red coats conferred a flash of colour upon the Durban sea front as around them people milled about in expectation of the ship's departure.

The previous night they had spent quietly at Mimosa with Jane, Christopher and the General, and some of the Colenso family, in particular Fanny.

'How I do hope there'll be someone in England who can do something for your arm and your shoulder joint, my friend.'

Anthony smiled. 'At least I'll spend some time with my little girl ... ah, what am I saying? She's in her teens, she'll be a young lady.' Then he patted John Lockley on his shoulder with his good hand. 'So you're now Acting Colonial Engineer in my absence, John Lockley. Look after our men, they're all fine chaps.'

'I will. The Basutos and the amaPutini and the amaHlubi revere you, and rightly. You fought against all odds for them, Anthony; made yourself unpopular with the colonists and the government.'

'Always had a soft spot for the underdog, lad.'

'You make light of it, but I know how badly Governor Wolseley treated you, and still you didn't give up. It's mostly because of you and Bishop Colenso that the current Governor succumbed and gave the amaPutini their land back. Now

471

they've got money from the government as well, and the amaHlubi are pardoned too. You're amazing.'

Anthony smiled. 'You acknowledge me far too highly, my good friend.'

'No, I don't. You've built schools and wharves and bridges and public offices and roads all over this damn colony, and I can tell you, you leave with the love of the natives and the confidence of your brother soldiers.'

Anthony grinned. 'You've forgotten one thing. I also leave with continuing abuse from the colonial press.'

'The press are fools. You've been thanked by the court of inquiry into the Bushman's River Pass activities and you've been recommended for a CMG. What the hell would the press know or care about the truth?'

And now Anthony's blue eyes gleamed in the sunlight. 'Nothing, as far as I've noted.'

And the two friends laughed as the mate called loudly from above, 'All aboard, please. Visitors off, passengers on.'

'Hurry back, Anthony, you're one of the people who make this life of mine bearable.'

Anthony held out his good hand and John Lockley took it. 'Look after Fanny for me.'

'No doubt of that.'

They hugged each other briefly and Anthony turned and took two steps up the gangplank before he halted and looked back. 'Laddie, perhaps while I'm abroad there might be an opportunity for you to see your friend, Darlengi. If there is, why not take it?' Then he smiled gently and strode on up to the deck.

CHAPTER THIRTY-THREE

Early April, 1877

It was an unusually hot evening and Darlengi sat looking at Thulile, who was cooking their evening meal over an open fire. She turned from her task and poured cool milk from a calabash into a small vessel and handed it to her husband. He drank.

The kraal was noisy. Ulundi always was, with its thousands of people coming and going.

'Will you be back in council tonight?'

'Yes. Cetshwayo is determined to send another regiment to the disputed territory. He has taken heart from Chief Sekukini's victories over the Boers, and believes we should mobilise on the Transvaal border ready to follow up the victories of the baPedi people and Sekukuni.'

'Is it true the Boers have Swazi allies?'

'Yes, and they being our long-standing enemies makes Cetshwayo even more determined.'

After Darlengi had eaten his meal he moved into the hut and Thulile followed him. A small mirror was attached to one of the hut poles and he wiped his hand across his clean-shaven chin as he looked into it in the gloomy light. Then he bent down to pick up a short spear. They voted in council by lifting the weapon in the air. As he leaned, the gold chain and locket fell forward from his throat, and Thulile stretched out her hand and touched it.

'All these summers later, the woman of the gleaming locket still lives in your heart.'

Darlengi brought himself upright to meet his wife's eyes. 'Why do you say that?'

'Because I feel it. Why would you wear her locket if she did not live in your heart? I was not your first choice and I have disappointed you. There has been no child in our hut in all these summers. You should take another wife.'

He shook his head. 'My good wife.' He took her face in his hands and kissed her gently. 'You have not disappointed me. You may not understand this, Thulile, but your love is more important to me than producing a child. The world is full of children. I need you, only you. I do not want, nor will I take, another wife.'

He looked down into her trusting eyes. ' And as to the "woman of the gleaming locket", as you call her, her name was Ellen and yes, there is a part of my heart that is hers always. Just as there is a part of my heart that is Mattana's and a part that is Jettama's ... and the same for all the people I have loved. I truly need you to understand this, for it is so important to me. You are here with me now. No one can ever take your place, and the largest part of my heart belongs to you ... my wife, the only wife I want.'

Her black eyes were brimming with tears but there was a radiant smile upon her mouth as he leant down and kissed it.

Half an hour later he sat in council. It was so hot they were conducting the meeting outside the Great Hut and the indunas all sat round on mats. Attendants kept bringing drinks and most of the chiefs scraped the sweat from their brows with bone knives.

Beside Darlengi sat Kayo and opposite him the king. On the king's right were a number of his half-brothers and on his left sat John Dunn.

Cetshwayo lifted his great carved ebony stick exactly like the one his Uncle Shaka had carried. He spoke more and more of his uncle these days and constantly compared the quality of his warriors with those of Shaka's day. 'My chieftains, Chief John Dunn, Jantoni, tells me that Somtseu moves into the Transvaal. That he speaks with farmers and burghers. Sekukuni and his tribe have the Boers in retreat and their allies, the Swazis, have given up the fight. Now is the time for a Zulu impi to mobilise in the disputed territory.'

John Dunn nodded and dabbed his heavy face with a handkerchief. 'This is so, Baba. Somtseu arrived back from his voyage to England where he saw Lord Carnarvon, the induna who deals with all the colonies of the Great White Queen. It is told that he was shipwrecked in the south, off the Cape Colony, but survived.' He looked at Cetshwayo. 'It seems he is hard to kill.'

Cetshwayo and most of the indunas laughed heartily at this. Then Cetshwayo grew serious. 'So we know the government of the Transvaal is weak like a bird with broken wings: its people are disheartened and now we hear Shepstone, the man who was a father to the Zulus, moves through the countryside. I do not like that, so we too must be there, for now is our opportunity.' He pointed with his stick to Darlengi. 'What do you say about all this?'

Darlengi bowed his head to his king. 'All you say is so, my king, and what Chief Dunn reports is also true. Our own spies tell us the Transvaal coffers are empty, corruption is rife, the administration breaks down and in the towns many die from fever.'

'Good, the Boers are a nation of liars,' said Cetshwayo, rubbing the part of his ear where the piece was missing.

Darlengi continued, 'The Boers are dissatisfied with their own government and so Theopolis Shepstone, Somtseu, is there. Why?' He looked around the council. 'He is a wise man, he is an opportunist, he must be there for a reason. It could be that he hopes to take over the Transvaal for the British.'

Intongalu put down the bone knife he had been using to scrape the sweat from his face, and raised his assegai. 'Why would they want a country which is weak like a cow with lung sickness?'

Darlengi shrugged. 'Perhaps they see a whole united southern Africa, all under the one flag, and not small pieces pulling in separate directions.'

'Does that include Zululand, I wonder?' Cetshwayo queried. Then he looked at Darlengi. 'Whatever the reason, and I'm sure Somtseu has one, we too must be represented there. Would my Uncle Shaka have hesitated in this position? No. Now might be our opportunity to take back our land which the Boers stole from us many long summers ago.'

The whole council murmured in agreement.

'So,' continued the king, his head ring gleaming in the glow from the fire, 'we will send an impi to the disputed territory now. I wish four regiments to go.' He looked around his indunas and lifting his ebony stick pointed in turn to one of his half-brothers, Uhamu, to Intongalu, to Mbilini, a young induna who led a celibate regiment, and then to Darlengi. 'I choose you, my chieftains, to take your regiments there.'

475

'And who is in charge of the impi, Baba?' asked Uhamu.

Cetshwayo met the eyes of his old adviser, Tshingwayo, before he took a long drink and replied, 'Darlengi is the leader. He is temperate and I can trust him to do nothing before I order it done.'

When John Lockley rode into Fort Amiel near Newcastle, with fifty soldiers of the 80th Regiment Staffordshire volunteers; Sergeant Tenny Rama and a detachment of mounted Basutos; one field piece and a working party of Putini; followed by mules, oxen wagons and the like, it was late at night and a light rain was falling.

He found the commander, Lieutenant-Colonel Amiel, in his temporary office, little more than a hut, poring over his despatches.

'Lieutenant-Colonel Harrison, I was expecting you yesterday,' his brother officer said, standing from his desk and coming round to shake his hand .

John Lockley returned the formal greeting. 'Had trouble crossing the Buffalo. Lucky to be here now. Has Colonel Durnford gone through?'

'Received a heliograph message this morning. He's due in here tomorrow, the tenth.'

John Lockley grinned broadly. 'That's marvellous. I've been upcountry since his return last month. Can't wait to see him.'

'Yes, seems he's worried about our newly knighted Theopolis Shepstone up in the Transvaal on his own with only two dozen mounted police and a dozen of his staff.'

John Lockley shook his head. 'I don't think he needs to be. Amongst his many talents, Sir Theopolis speaks fluent Afrikaans, and most of the Boers respect him.'

Amiel nodded. 'There's a lot of speculation about why he's in Pretoria.'

'Indeed there is. No doubt we'll find out.'

'I've got the rest of the Eightieth Regiment here building the fort, and the Thirteenth Regiment is a mile away in Newcastle, ready to enter the Transvaal if Sir Theopolis does need us.'

'I should think Colonel Durnford will move the forces a little closer. This is thirty miles from the Transvaal border and two hundred and ten miles from Pretoria, and while I doubt Sir

Theopolis will need them, if he does, they won't be much help to him at this distance.'

Amiel nodded. 'You're here to build the laager and the cantonment in Newcastle, right?'

'Yes. How are you coming along with the fort?'

'Pretty well. Another few months should see it finished.'

'I've heard we've got other forts to rebuild too.'

Amiel nodded. 'I'll just organise for the sergeant to take you on into Newcastle. Major Peter Pinne's running things there; he'll find quarters for you, such as they are.'

'Thanks, my men are pretty tired.'

Amiel disappeared out through a side door. A few minutes later the sergeant arrived, looking decidedly unhappy about leading John Lockley and his men in the rain into Newcastle; but he had his orders, and an hour later John Lockley had bathed and eaten in his quarters in the temporary barracks of hastily built structures and tents.

Before retiring for the night, he walked outside. It had stopped raining and he looked up at a milky moon chased by fragmented clouds.

He had been in 'Maritzburg only once since Christmas and already it was April. In February he had been reconnoitring near the junction of the Buffalo and the Mangeni and as it was only twenty-five miles round the Ndeni forest to the Tugela farm, he left early one morning and paid Tilly a visit.

She had been thrilled to see him and had informed him of Aunt Jane and Uncle Christopher's planned visit to the farm. 'We're having them twice this year; for June first and then October and November too. Will you be able to have some leave with them?'

He laughed. 'If I can possibly arrange it I will.'

While he had been there George Travers had given him a quick tour of the place and he had been impressed with the large count of livestock on the farm these days. Later Tilly had taken him in to see Dirk. The old Boer's eyes were failing and he was getting frail, but he was still as strong-minded as ever and as forceful in his opinions. 'We should talk to your uncle about putting a bridge across the river. He can afford it and you could build it,' he had said, pointing his bent index finger at his visitor.

After Tilly had wrapped John Lockley in her arms and said

goodbye, she stood with pursed lips watching him mount Horatio. He had asked, 'Is there something else you wanted to say, Tilly?'

She nodded. 'Darlengi came to see me last November. So much easier for him to come now with no Dirk to have to avoid. He looks so grand and has a regiment of his own. I told him not to bring them down here and to keep his warriors well away from our place.' Then she had added quickly, 'Do you ever see him?'

'Tilly, no, I don't. As you know very well. But I accept that you ask only because you care about us both. So I'll tell you something that I've told no one else.'

'I'm all ears,' she said, looking up at him expectantly.

'Everybody I care about wants me to make peace with him. The division between us was entirely of my making and thus the reconciliation must be of my making as well.'

She said nothing but she was smiling as she lifted her hand and patted him quite vigorously on the knee.

He knew Tilly was right, he knew Aunt Jane and Uncle Chris and Anthony were right. Even Phoebe had said the same thing when she had left for America years ago.

He moved across the small barrack yard in the darkness and as he did so he continued to think of Phoebe. He knew she was back in Natal. He had thought about her a lot recently, and somehow it was right that she had come home; somehow she belonged in Natal.

He had received a letter from his aunt only last week in Utrecht. It had followed him around the country a bit, and had been written six weeks ago, but it told him of Phoebe's homecoming and how she had been to see Governor Bulwer about using nurses she had trained to staff the military hospitals he wanted to open in Natal.

He smiled at that. She was an amazing girl. A veritable Florence Nightingale.

He walked out past the army buildings and down the short gravel area they called a street, to within sight of the river. Well, it was called a river, the Incandu, but at present it was hardly a stream. He liked the smell of the night after the rain. He could stay out here for ages. Yet it was getting late, must be after midnight now. He turned back, passing through a small area of trees in front of the tiny wooden post office where he saw a woman carrying a lantern come out of a door nearby. As she walked towards him, there was something familiar about her. Then he realised.

'Phoebe!' he shouted. 'Is it you?'

She stopped short. In the lantern light he saw the delight on her face. 'John Lockley, oh, how wonderful to see you.'

He ran forward and swept her up into his arms.

'Watch the lantern,' she laughed, holding it high as he hugged her.

'I knew you were in Natal, but here? How is it you're here?'

'Put me down and I'll tell you.'

He put her down.

She was smiling happily at him. It was so marvellous just to see his face again after three years away. How often she had thought about him, dreamed about him. She acknowledged that she loved Africa and things African and that she had wanted to come back here because of that; but she admitted there was another reason. And that reason stood before her, looking down at her with his brilliant blue-purple eyes gleaming in the light of her lantern.

She sighed. 'It's like this, the Lieutenant-Governor wants to build a few military hospitals, and I . . . well, I'm trying to help staff them with my nurses. I'm starting a school to train nurses here in Natal.'

He was not sure, for it was hard to tell in the poor light from the lantern, but he thought she blushed as she said, 'I've already been shameless enough to ask Uncle Chris to donate to my cause. In fact it's through his and Aunt Jane's generosity that I have a place for my school in Durban.' Her face was aglow with the light of belief in her dreams. 'Remember the old neglected building in West Pine Street near the railway station?'

'The one that used to be the auction rooms?'

'Yes. That's it. Uncle Chris and Aunt Jane bought it and donated it to me. It's now the Phoebe McLean Nurses' Training School and Miss Edness and Dr Tallant in 'Maritzburg are being wonderful and helping all they can. I've got a skeleton staff, for I brought three nurses and a doctor with me from Cleveland.'

'Well, I'll be darned.'

'Governor Bulwer wants to build a military hospital here.

That's why I'm here, taking a look, you might say. The Army Medical Department is being helpful.' She pursed her lips. 'Well, mostly helpful, though I've had a bit of resistance in certain quarters.'

'I suppose you will have some opposition, but what you're doing all sounds good to me.'

'Oh, John Lockley, forgive me. Here I am going on about me ... and so much has happened to you since I saw you last. You're a Lieutenant-Colonel now, I'm told. That's marvellous. Congratulations.'

'Thanks.'

'I saw Anthony at Bishopstowe only two weeks ago. He was in high spirits to be back in Natal.'

'He'll be here tomorrow.'

'Oh, good. But they could do nothing for his arm. He has a leather piece that holds his dead hand in place. He's been so very brave about it.'

'He's brave about everything.'

They fell silent for some seconds and then John Lockley lifted his hand and raked it back through his hair. 'I'll say goodnight, Phoebe. It's marvellous to have you back in Natal.'

She stood illuminated by her lantern and he registered her smile as she answered, 'It's marvellous to be back here.'

He was turning away as she said, 'The Governor told me the Royal Engineers will be building the hospitals.'

John Lockley mock-bowed to her. 'At your service. We build everything else, so that sounds likely.' As he straightened up he heard a familiar voice behind him. 'Master Harrison? Is that you?'

He turned around to see Thulmi standing in the night.

'Thulmi? I thought you were at Mimosa.' He took the Zulu by the hand.

'I sure was, until Miss Phoebe come back.' He smiled broadly as if all were right with the world.

Phoebe touched the Zulu on the shoulder. 'Thulmi's driving me and my friend, Diana Holmes, another nurse, around the country. We have one soldier with us, Sergeant Gardiner, and he's very conscientious.'

As John Lockley walked back to his billet he felt so much better – well, actually so much happier – than he had when he came out on this late night stroll.

The following morning Anthony Durnford arrived as expected.

John Lockley stood under an awning with Tenny Rama, watching him ride in on Chieftain; a dashing figure in khaki with a slouch hat on his head, his wounded arm somehow heightening his glamour. Then John Lockley smiled in surprise as he noted the man riding immediately behind Anthony. He wore a brand new wide-awake upon his head, and carried a breech-loading carbine. It was Simeon Kambula, and following him, Jabez Molife and a whole company of Anthony's loyal Basutos.

'I see you at last, lad,' Anthony said when he dismounted to John Lockley's wide smile. 'And congratulations on joining the ranks of half-colonels.'

John Lockley saluted. 'Thank you.'

Anthony did not remain long in Newcastle. He took refreshment with Phoebe and John Lockley but was keen to get on to Pretoria to see Sir Theopolis.

'I shall go alone,' he informed John Lockley.

'Alone?'

'I just want to see if Shepstone's all right; he's been gone months now. The Boers might have taken him prisoner, you know. Have you a Cape cart and four horses I can borrow?'

'Yes, but it's two hundred and ten miles to Pretoria across broken country.'

'I know, lad. All I need's a driver who speaks fluent Dutch. There'll be a few of those here in Newcastle. Now,' he went on, his blue eyes shining with excitement, 'I'll be up there and back in a jiffy. I'll pretend I'm a land speculator if there are questions asked. Get Major Pinne to begin to move his troops up to the Transvaal border at first light tomorrow. And you support him if he needs it.'

John Lockley shook his head. 'I came here to fortify the place and now you want me to deploy soldiers to the Transvaal border.'

'Just in case, lad. Just in case.'

Anthony was packing items in a knapsack when John Lockley went to find Major Pinne, the senior officer in Newcastle. When he did so, his orders were brief.

'At dawn tomorrow, start for the Transvaal border.' He pointed to a spot on a map on the wall. 'The Colonel and I are

481

going into Pretoria to see the position with Shepstone. If he's in trouble and we need a force, we want you at the border.'

'Yes, sir.'

Anthony looked in amazement as the Cape cart came along to pick him up with John Lockley driving. 'John Lockley, lad, what are you doing?'

'I'm coming with you, that's what I'm doing, Anthony. My Afrikaans is passable, so I'm your driver.'

They made good time to the border and arrived there just after nightfall. They camped on a long rise and ate by the fire. It reminded them of their expedition along the Black Umvoloosi four years earlier, and they talked by the fire in an intimate fashion.

'So, lad, they could do nothing for my wounds after all. I went with my darling daughter to Wildbad in the Black Forest for the baths, and would have gone on to Switzerland, but I was ordered to Cork, which is a very different climate, and where my arm ached most of the time. At least I had some old friends from the Seventy-fifth Regiment there, which made it bearable.'

'Well, it's great to have you back here, Anthony, even if you do have me rushing off to Boer country when I should be building fortifications. And no doubt there were others pleased to see you home. How's Fanny?'

'Wonderful. I had the most marvellous week out at Bishopstowe. I don't know what we're going to do, lad. We'll just have to bide our time.'

'Do her parents know?'

Anthony lifted his blue eyes from his tin mug of tea. 'You know I have the highest regard for her father. He's a wonderful man, as is her mother, a fine woman. And while Fanny and I have never spoken to them of our feelings, I suppose they realise something.' He leant forward and touched John Lockley on his knee with the mug. 'And what about you? It's over three years since Kate died.'

John Lockley shook his head. 'You could say I'm disillusioned, my friend. I think from time to time about leaving the army and running the Tugela farm. Then I do nothing about it, and my life totters on.'

'Hardly that, laddie, you're making a sound contribution to this country. It needs a few more like you.'

482

They slept soundly in their tent and as dawn broke over the plains of the Transvaal they were on their way again.

They were virtually ignored on their journey, for the Transvaal was a country of self-made roads or none at all, a dry land of wide open veld. Towns were few and far between. They reached Pretoria on the fifteenth of April at eleven in the morning, to see the Union Jack flying over the capital.

They were met by Henry Rider Haggard, the twenty-year-old secretary to Sir Henry Bulwer, Lieutenant-Governor of Natal, who had been seconded to Sir Theopolis's staff.

'We're all right,' the young man announced. 'In fact Sir Theopolis has really been welcomed by the people here in Pretoria. They're fed up with the ruling body here, the volksraad. The country's bankrupt. We spoke to every shop owner and hotel keeper and farmer we could find on our way here. They were all disgruntled with President Burgers and his burghers, pardon my pun. Mind you, there's a member of the volksraad called Paul Kruger who has a pretty loud voice. He's dissatisfied with us but most people here pay him no mind.'

When they saw Sir Theopolis, he welcomed them warmly. He stood with a sheaf of papers in his hand in front of a huge map of the Transvaal hanging on the wall. 'I think everything will settle down. I annexed the Transvaal in the name of Her Majesty's Government three days ago and there's been no resistance whatever. The opposite actually. Mind you, it's good to know I've got troops close by if a time comes when I need them. Return and bring them forward into the Transvaal. I'll send a despatch to you a week from now to inform you of the continuing state of things here.'

On the ride back to Natal John Lockley speculated, 'I cannot see the Boers remaining happy about the Jack flying over the Transvaal. This Paul Kruger's no lover of the British, and he seems a determined man from everything I've heard and read.'

'Yes, you're probably right, lad. But Africa's been full of unrest since year one, and today's no different. I've only been back a few weeks and I note there's trouble south in the Ciskei and the Transkei, where the Fingoes and Gcalekas don't see eye to eye; and up here we've got the Zulus building their regiments back to full strength. Why are they doing that, I ask? And now we've gone and annexed the Transvaal where our old enemies, the Boers, will rankle under English rule. So what do we professional soldiers do, lad? Our jobs, eh?'

John Lockley gave a wry smile. 'Yes, we do. They say Carnarvon wants a united South Africa. I wish him luck.'

'I heard in 'Maritzburg that there's a Carnarvon appointee arriving as Cape Governor and High Commissioner for Native Affairs. He's Sir Henry Bartle Frere, the man who totally suppressed the slave trade in Zanzibar. He's strong and capable and someone who just might carry off federation.'

'If Africa allows it.'

'Well said, lad. If Africa allows it.'

They met only a few hunters and traders on their return ride and on the eighteenth were back at the border, where they met Major Pinne and his force half a mile inside the Transvaal at a place called Meeks Farm.

John Lockley was checking supplies when he realised that there was no reserve ammunition. Each man had only the sixty rounds which he carried himself. He called in Major Pinne, who knew nothing about it, and so down the ranks he went until he spoke to Sergeant Major Wellings.

The man screwed up his face as he answered, 'Weren't no room, suh. The wagons were full.'

'Yes, full of the bloody biscuits, salt pork, mealies, forage and rum I've been tallying. We're supposed to be here to lend support in the Transvaal if needed, and what if we have to fight? The Boers are dead shots at four hundred yards. Sixty rounds of ammunition a piece won't last an hour, man. It's incredible.'

Anthony shook his head in disbelief when John Lockley told him. 'So, someone will have to go and get it.'

'Yes, Anthony, someone will.'

'And as you're supposed to be building fortifications there, and I, more than likely, will be marching around the Transvaal on a wild-goose chase, I suggest you go to Newcastle and send wagons back here with the reserve ammunition.'

Half an hour later the two friends stood together beside Horatio as John Lockley checked his saddle and blanket. He smiled at Anthony. 'I'll be back if you need me.'

'No, laddie, I don't need you for the present. You get

Newcastle fortified as you were meant to do. And send Simeon and my Basutos on up here. Thanks for the company into Pretoria, I appreciated it.'

John Lockley rode hard and arrived in Newcastle around ten o'clock that night. As he came along the uneven stretch of ground that led to the temporary barracks he was heartened by the vision he saw through a window. He held Horatio steady as he watched Phoebe sitting by a lamp, head over some papers and holding quill in hand. She did not look up and would not have seen him in the darkness outside even if she had. He rode on with a smile.

Phoebe had been surprised when she had heard from Diana that Lieutenant-Colonel Durnford and Lieutenant-Colonel Harrison had driven away in a Cape cart. 'They were in mufti,' Diana explained, 'and the word is they were headed to the Transvaal.'

Later Phoebe had spoken with Major Pinne and he had implied that what Diana had said was true. Phoebe knew that Sir Theopolis Shepstone was there. Everyone knew that. So she assumed it must have something to do with him. She hoped her two friends were not doing anything dangerous, and she prayed each night for their safe return.

Meanwhile she had been studying the plan for the military hospitals. Sir Henry Bulwer had given it to her. It looked adaptable and could be built anywhere as long as it were close to a water source. Though there were a few changes she would like to make if she could. John Lockley and Anthony had said more than once that Newcastle was one of the most strategic positions in Natal, so having a hospital here, where there would always be a force stationed, made sense. It was positively thrilling.

She needed the hospital now for unfortunately she already had patients. One of the Basutos waiting for Anthony's return had broken his leg when part of a redoubt fell on him. She and Diana had set it. And today Thulmi and Sergeant Gardiner and two of the others were not well; some sort of dysentery. That was always rife in this part of the country.

At ten o'clock at night she was still poring over the plans. She must return to the capital soon, for there was so much to do, and Diana was keen to leave. She was missing Gordon

Campbell, her doctor fiancé. But while she was here Phoebe wanted to see as much as she could, so she must go north into the Utrecht district. Diana needed to stay to take care of all the sick, so as Utrecht was only about thirty miles' ride she would go by herself. The distance could be covered in a day.

She heard a horse pass by in the night and a few minutes later she stood and walked to the door. When she opened it she saw Thulmi, lit by the lamp beam from her room. He sat taking snuff on a bench a few feet away.

'Thulmi, you're sick. You should be in bed.'

'I feel a little bit better, Miss Phoebe.'

'I'm going to bed now, and you should too, please.'

'Yes, Miss Phoebe.'

She had half closed the door when he added, 'Master Harrison ride on by just a few minutes ago.'

The following morning, Phoebe and John Lockley were both up at dawn.

John Lockley had commandeered six wagons well before breakfast and as he exited the commissariat he saw Phoebe on a horse trotting through the yard.

'Phoebe! Where are you going so early?'

Phoebe brought the mare to a halt beside him. 'To Utrecht. I must have a quick look at the place while I'm so close.'

'It's mostly Boers. About thirty houses, from memory. Not much to see.' He looked around. 'Where's Thulmi?'

'Why?'

'He's going with you, I assume.'

'He's not well. I'm going alone.'

'What?' He ran his long fingers swiftly back though his hair. 'Why the devil are you doing that?'

'Why not?'

He shook his head. 'Phoebe, what the hell's wrong with you? You grew up here. This is Africa, not Cleveland, Ohio. I cannot believe you're so cavalier as to ride alone through thirty miles of countryside you don't know. Get down off that horse. I'll get one of my men to go with you.'

She looked down at him silently.

'I said, get off the horse. I'll find one of my men to go with you.'

'John Lockley Harrison, I'm not one of your soldiers. Don't

486

you dare speak to me like that.' And she spurred her horse and rode out of the settlement.

'Come back here!' he yelled, but it was no use, she was gone. He turned on his heel as reveille sounded, and ran across to the troops' sleeping quarters. The first person he came across was Corporal O'Hare. He was a reliable young fellow and John Lockley took him by the shoulders. 'O'Hare, I'm sorry, but I need you to saddle up and follow Miss McLean. She's ridden off to Utrecht on her own. Grab some supplies and follow her. Stay with her and return with her. There's a good man.'

O'Hare would have liked a hot breakfast first, but a ride out in the country sounded fine; it would get him away from the drill and the digging.

'Yes, sir.'

John Lockley would have preferred to have gone after the silly girl himself. But he had to get the wagons loaded with the ammunition and on their way up to Anthony.

He strode angrily across to the makeshift mess, and ordered his breakfast in clipped, formal tones.

Phoebe pushed her mare for the first quarter of a mile and then brought her back to a trot.

How dare John Lockley treat her like a child? He really had made her angry. But then he wouldn't have said what he did unless he cared about her welfare. That brought a small smile to her mouth. Still, he could have been more polite. He was used to giving orders, but she was not in his army, and didn't have to take them from him.

She had ridden about three miles and was coming down a long hill in broken country when she saw the lioness. It appeared abruptly up out of a donga over on her left. The big cat was long and lithe and so pale she was almost a silver grey. The mare whinnied uncomfortably as it picked up the animal's smell. 'Steady girl, steady,' Phoebe said as she took her double-barrelled Cape rifle from the side of her saddle.

A chill tingled through her as three cubs and another lioness appeared, following the first animal. Oh dear! Was there a male yet to come?

Perhaps she would have been wiser not to have become angry with John Lockley and to have let him supply her with an escort, but it was too late now.

She held the mare from galloping off and, pulling hard on the reins, continued to walk it forward. But then she saw the first lioness move swiftly in a wide arc around behind her. She had seen enough lions in her life; it was going to attack. She had no time. She dragged the mare around, but it was nervous and jumpy, and without taking proper aim, she fired, and missed.

The lioness did not falter, but came bounding on through the long grass towards her. She felt panicky. This one was coming in for the kill, smelling the frightened mare beneath her. And while the terrified horse backed and neighed in fear, she made herself aim and fire again.

This time she hit the lioness and it rolled sideways in the grass. Looking around fearfully for the other lions, Phoebe hastily reloaded.

Perspiration stood out on her forehead and temples as the wounded creature limped away. She could not see the other animals. They had disappeared.

Then she heard the shout.

'Hey! Miss McLean, I saw that! Jolly first-class shootin'. Ye should be in the Eightieth!'

She looked around to see a soldier bearing down on her.

'Morning, miss.'

'Who're you?'

'Corporal Sean O'Hare at yer service, Miss McLean. I've been riding mighty hard to catch up with ye as well. Orders of the Lieutenant-Colonel. He didna want ye ridin' up to Utrecht alone.'

Phoebe took a deep breath. She was quite glad to have company after all; and, too, she was secretly pleased that John Lockley had sent someone after her.

They rode along without further incident. Two or three times they forded shallow streams and occasionally they noticed buildings on the hills in the distance, but they sighted no people until they were about twenty miles into their journey and they saw a single rider coming in the other direction.

As he came up to them he hailed them. '*Goeie middag.*' He wore the usual Boer 'uniform': corduroy trousers, khaki shirt, wide-brimmed felt hat with puggaree, and soft leather-soled boots coming up to his knees. He was big, as most Boers were, with well-developed muscular arms and legs. Two rifles were slung on his saddle and he wore a bandolier of bullets over his right shoulder. He exuded that look of health which comes from a roving existence and life in the open air. Phoebe thought it would be difficult to find a race of people more physically perfect than the Boers, even comparing them to their natural enemies the Zulus.

'*Goeie middag*, good afternoon,' said Phoebe.

'I'm Roit Vos,' he said, showing a row of strong, white teeth. 'Where're you headed?'

'To Utrecht,' replied Corporal O'Hare.

'In that case, stick to the road. I saw an impi of Zulus on the far bank of the Ingcuba River, about five miles back.'

'Oh Lord!' exclaimed O'Hare.

'They seemed to be peaceful enough, but there must have been a couple of hundred of them, so I'm just alerting a few of my neighbours.'

'Thanks for the warning. I'm Phoebe McLean and this is Corporal O'Hare. We'll be careful.'

He touched his hat and with a flick of his right knee, his horse jumped forward.

'Thank you,' Phoebe called after him.

'Now, Miss McLean,' said the Corporal, tugging on his helmet. 'How necessary is it really to go to Utrecht?'

Phoebe thought for a time. She was within ten miles of the place. 'Corporal, that man, Roit Vos, said they were on the far side of the Ingcuba, and according to the map I looked at last night we shouldn't go anywhere near the river until we're within a mile of Utrecht. So as he said, if we stick to the track, and we will, we'll be all right. And anyway, we've nothing to be afraid of from the Zulus.'

'We haven't?'

'No, Corporal O'Hare, we haven't.' And with that she moved on and Sean O'Hare, shrugging his square shoulders, followed her.

They were about four miles from Utrecht when they came over a hill and around a forest of scrubby trees. There, only a hundred yards in front of them, was an army of Zulus.

'Oh no!' exclaimed O'Hare. 'Oh, no!'

And while the poor man sat stiffening with fear upon his horse, he could not believe his eyes as the woman next to him shouted with delight and sped her horse forward.

He watched, open-mouthed, as she rode right up to the Zulus and dismounted straight into the arms of one of them. It was the most amazing sight he had seen in his twenty-five years of life and he was to tell the story forever afterwards.

'Well, Colonel Harrison,' he said aloud. 'Ye sent me on to look after that gal, and she shoots lions and kisses Zulus! It's me what needs the lookin' after, not her.'

CHAPTER THIRTY-FOUR

Darlengi and Thulile had made their way back from Ulundi to their home kraal on the green hills of the Umlatoosi. There, Induna Darlengi had sent out his messengers to the kraals where his warriors lived, and within twenty-four hours his regiment of over seven hundred had assembled.

Amongst other things, Darlengi had taught Thulile the concept of dividing time into days, weeks, months and years; so after he had wrapped his wife in his arms and kissed her, he took leave of her with the words, 'I am uncertain of how long I will be away. But it might be weeks and even months. Do not worry, Thulile.'

'I will pray to our ancestors for your safekeeping. And I will wait impatiently all the days and nights until I see your face before me again.'

She walked with him out through the kraal gate to where the warriors were collected. There were many wives taking leave of their husbands here, and the udibi boys, who would follow behind the impi driving the slaughter cattle and carrying the karosses, the warriors' sleeping mats, were making ready to depart.

Thulile touched her husband's arm and pointed as a man came loping down the hill from the north towards them.

'I bring a message for Induna Darlengi of the Great Council. Which one of you is he?' he called as he came closer.

'I am he,' Darlengi replied. 'Who is the message from?'

'From Induna Shiambi.'

Darlengi glanced at Thulile and hesitated momentarily. 'What is the message?'

'If you wish to see the one who gave you life, before he leaves for all time to dwell amongst his ancestors, then come now.'

For some seconds Darlengi considered the import of the message. He was surprised Shiambi wanted to see him. Did he want to see Shiambi? He had not seen or heard from him since the night he had rescued Mtonga, and that was twelve years ago. Why should he go now, simply because the man was dying?

As he stood in silence he felt Thulile's cool hand on his arm and he turned his head to meet her eyes.

She nodded gently. 'Go to him. Ezulwini, Shiambi's kraal, is not far out of your way.'

It was true, the destination chosen to meet with the other regiments was west on Little Blood River in the disputed territory; he would only have to make a minor detour to the north. But did he want to see the man?

'I will think about it,' he replied to Thulile as the messenger stood waiting.

'Come a moment, my husband,' and she took his hand and led him aside a few yards. 'Darlengi,' her voice was tender, 'whenever you have mentioned his name you have told me his hatred for you is strong like the venom of the cobra. You told me of his cruel attitude to Jettama's death and the fight which followed where he tried his best to kill you and you stabbed him in the eye. It is true that malice and hostility lies between you as the veld grass does between the earth and the sky. But there was one single time when he could have harmed you and he did not. The night of Mtonga's escape when he kept his word and did not send Intongalu after you.'

'That was simply because I did not kill him. He was bound to keep his word.'

She lifted her hand and touched his cheek. 'Many would not have. He did. And now in his final hours he asks to see you. You find that surprising. But just as the Buffalo River rises in the Drakensburgs and slowly makes its journey of life across the valley and the plain to join at last with the waters of the Tugela, so Shiambi's life journey approaches the joining of the river of death. Go to him, finish whatever there is to finish.'

He kissed her forehead. 'I am undecided, but for you I will go.'

Then he gave instructions to his second-in-command, an induna called Maphoko, to travel to the appointed place, and told him that he would join them there.

Thulile remained watching her husband and the messenger running into the distance until she could see them no more.

Every three hours they rested half an hour, and it was about nine hours later that Darlengi and the messenger came up the hill to Shiambi's kraal. Clouds had floated threateningly above them for the last half-hour of their journey, and now as they ran by the large flat stone near the aloe tree where he had left Shiambi bound and gagged all those years before, it began to rain.

Darlengi could hear voices wailing in some of the huts as the messenger led him right to the opening of Shiambi's dwelling, and, pointing through it, hastened away.

Darlengi bent through the hole and stood up inside. As he did so two witch doctors slithered out of his way. They had been watching for his arrival and now moved nearer the man lying on a heap of skins by the embers of a fire.

Shiambi was conscious and five of his wives were in attendance around him. He looked up at his son. His good eye was bloodshot and he spoke with difficulty. '*Sa ku bonum ngani*, Darlengi.'

'*Sa ku bonum ngani*, Shiambi.'

'So you came. Why?'

Darlengi bent down on one knee. 'Because my wife thought I should.'

Shiambi managed to impart scorn even in his weakened state. 'You are told what to do by a woman?'

'Shiambi,' Darlengi's voice was strained, 'how I live my life and what I do is really no concern of yours. You requested me to come here. I am here.'

'So you are.' Then he pointed to the witch doctors. They were pouring a green powder out of two buffalo horns. 'They are useless. I have already filled my belly ... with their *remedies*. I will soon go to the plain that carries the spirits of our ancestors ... no one can alter that.'

He gestured to his wives that he wanted to sit up, but when they tried to help him he was too weak. He was quiet for a time and Darlengi squatted in silence beside him.

Then he said, 'You have many brothers and sisters, many more than a man has fingers and toes.'

Darlengi shook his head. 'No, Shiambi. You have sons and daughters. I do not have brothers and sisters.'

'So be it.'

He began to cough violently and for a time was too exhausted to speak. Darlengi sat wondering how it would have been to have known him well. He decided it did not matter. He had been given love by many in his life, and while he had never experienced the love of this man, he had still known what it was like to have a father. Uncle Chris had managed that.

Some time later, after the witch doctors had thrown their green powder on to the fire, causing a terrible stench, and giving Shiambi another fit of coughing, he lifted his right arm feebly towards his son. 'Darlengi?'

'Yes.'

'You know I loved your mother as I loved no other.'

Darlengi nodded.

'You were her only child ... She ... left me when you were born.'

'Yes.'

'Because you were her only child ... I have decided ... You are the one who must have ... this.'

Now Darlengi noticed that his fist was closed around something. It was an effort for Shiambi to lift his arm and now he opened his hand. In his palm lay a gleaming white stone on a leather thong. Darlengi knew it for the diamond it was, and so too did Shiambi.

'Nadi ... your mother ... wore this always. In my youth I did not realise what it was. Her grandfather had been given it many summers before over in the place they now call ... Griqualand. She always wore it ... and I have kept it all this time. Now it is yours. Take it. I want you to have it.'

Darlengi took it and Shiambi's hand fell limply to his side. Then he fixed his gaze upon his visitor and said, 'That diamond is the essence of her ... pure, shining, good. She was all those things ... as the sun is to the earth.'

And Darlengi replied, 'I have always known she was.'

Then Shiambi sighed. 'You should go now. I must die with my good wives ... and my people.'

Darlengi nodded and rose from his side. He did not know what to say to this man lying at his feet. He heard himself say, 'Goodbye, Shiambi.' Then he turned away and moved towards the hut opening.

'Darlengi?'

He turned back. 'Once I said you . . . had a woman's face. I said it then to hurt you. But today . . . I say it to praise you. You . . . are like my Nadi . . . your mother.'

Darlengi hesitated and then came back across the space between them and knelt down. For the first and last time in his whole life he reached out to Shiambi and touched him tenderly on the arm. 'Thank you.' He could not say *Father*. It was impossible. 'I am proud . . . to look like my mother.' Then he smiled at the dying man and the thought that welled through his mind was, I have never willingly touched you before. He held Shiambi's gaze for a moment longer before he rose and moved quickly out of the hut.

Soft rain was still falling as he ran at speed down the hill and across the veld thinking of Shiambi, and when he reached the drift over the White Umvoloosi, he halted and tied the leather thong around his neck.

He ran on with a smile on his face and the diamond and the gold locket gleaming side by side on his bronze skin.

When Darlengi met up with his warriors they camped on the Little Blood River until the other three regiments arrived.

The following day the leaders of the regiments met and discussed what they should do. It was early morning and they sat on a small kopje where the breeze lifted the clean smell of the veld to their nostrils.

'It will soon be known that we are here,' Intongalu said. 'We are four regiments, and our many night fires will glow like beacons.'

Darlengi agreed. 'What you say is true, but we are to do nothing unless Cetshwayo tells us otherwise. I have dispatched a runner to him this morning to tell him we are here.'

Then Darlengi waved his arm in a wide arc. 'We have not been here for many years. We should know as much as we can about where the Boers are and what settlements and farms are laagered. We should also visit all the Zulu kraals in the area and find out if they have paid the taxes demanded by the Boers. There are many Zulu kraals to the north near the upper waters of the Pongola. We will send out small parties to reconnoitre, and to bring back the information.'

'I shall take a party to the kraals of the Pongola,' said Intongalu.

'And I shall travel south-east towards Utrecht and then south to the Buffalo,' answered Darlengi. 'And others led by you, Uhamu, will go east and north-east into the disputed territory. You, Mbilini, will remain here in charge of those who stay behind. And they must be kept busy. They should build shelters.'

Intongalu shook his head. 'Those of my regiment who remain shall sharpen their weapons, and practise the arts of war.'

Darlengi stood up. 'Intongalu, we do not necessarily come here to fight.'

Intongalu stood up beside him. 'I think we will.'

Darlengi shook his head. 'That is not for you to decide, and I caution you to act as I request. Do not be aggressive.'

Intongalu's eyes were full of malice but he said nothing.

At noon Darlengi took two hundred of his own men and left the main camp. He would divide them into smaller groups once they were out past Utrecht.

They did not run, there was no need, so by the late afternoon they were just south of the small settlement of Utrecht.

They were about a hundred yards from a scrubby wood and crossing the dirt road leading into the settlement when into sight came two riders. One was a woman and the other a soldier. The riders halted briefly and then Darlengi, who was at the front of his men, realised who the woman was. He lifted his hand in greeting and when she saw him she came charging down to him, shouting with delight.

The next minute she slipped off her horse and into his open arms.

'Darlengi, Darlengi, how wonderful!' she cried as his men watched in amazement.

'Phoebe, when did you get back? What are you doing here?'

'Oh, I've so much to tell you. Where do I start? I wrote to the farm and told you I was coming home.'

And so there they halted for an hour, and Darlengi and Phoebe talked about all the things that mattered, while the two hundred warriors rested and watched the surprising fellowship between their leader and the white woman; and Corporal O'Hare did exactly the same.

As daylight began to fade Phoebe took leave of her dear

friend. She acknowledged his warriors with some phrases Thulmi had taught her and her words brought smiles to their faces. They lifted their shields in honour to her.

Then she took Darlengi's hand and said, 'John Lockley's in Newcastle right now. Where will you be in three or four days' time?'

'On my way back to our camp on the Little Blood River, I should think. Why?'

She met his eyes.

He gave her a knowing look. 'Now, Phoebe, don't you think you should leave all that alone?'

'Please, could you tell me a place you might be. Let's say four days from now. That'll be Friday. Please, Darlengi. It's worth a try.'

He gave her a peculiar look and the sun glinted in his dark eyes. 'All right. I shall wait from noon to dusk at the junction of the Buffalo and the Ingcuba. On the western bank.'

'I know you think I meddle. And I do. But thank you.'

'I do not do it for you alone, my friend Phoebe. I do it for myself.'

Phoebe and Corporal O'Hare rode away and came into Utrecht just as the sun was setting. There was no hotel but they knew that the best house in the village took in passers-by and so they went there to be greeted by Maria, a young woman in a man's wide-awake hat who made them welcome.

Late that night Phoebe sat looking out at the African moon as it threw a feeble silver light into the wide yard and up to her window.

It had been grand to see Darlengi. They had talked of many things, amongst them Darlengi's visit to the dying Shiambi.

Today for the first time ever his Zulu life had struck home to her. Today she had seen the induna with hundreds of warlike warriors ready to do his bidding. Always before he had been Darlengi, her friend, the man who visited her at the mission; the man who was John Lockley's estranged brother. Before, only the European in him was emphasised in her mind. She had somehow ignored that he went home to a life of kraals and mealie fields and warriors with assegais. Today she had suddenly understood some of his life amongst his people and she had acknowledged his responsibilities and his obligations.

He was still the Darlengi she knew and loved, but now she realised how remarkable he truly was; for he managed to walk two divergent paths. She could not guess whether he was successful, she could never be in his head to find out, but she felt there was no other person alive who could do it.

The night cry of an animal sounded somewhere out there in the untamed veld around Utrecht.

And now her thoughts slid from Darlengi to the man so like him and yet so unlike him, the man she had always loved, John Lockley Harrison. She had carried her love in her heart for so long; ever since she was a tiny child. She had watched him from afar while he had spent his life caring for exotic beauties like Jettama and Kate. He was a handsome, glamorous, red-coated soldier who rode through her life like the wind blew by the rivers and the trees and the hills. Well, she had managed to live without him, hadn't she? And she could continue.

She knew in some ways she had been a fool to come back to Natal. What if he had already found another dark, beautiful woman?

Then she thought of the words in the book of Matthew: 'Ask, and it shall be given to you; seek, and ye shall find; knock, and it shall be opened unto you.' How did she do that?

She stood up and leaned out of the window, breathing the clean fresh air. She had to be realistic. Life was what it was.

She must go to bed, it was late and she wanted to be up at first light. She could see as much as she needed to of this tiny place in an hour. Then she could be on her way back to Newcastle.

Holding firmly on to the sill she pushed her round chin forward and took a deep breath. She was in Natal to be a nurse; to help those who were sick and needed care. Her life could be full, with or without John Lockley Harrison. Yes, that was right. Get on with things, Phoebe.

She left the window and ten minutes later put out the lamp and went to bed.

She had so much to do ... yes, she really did. She must think about the things that really mattered, like her work. But even as she drifted into sleep her mind cheated her and her last thoughts were of her soldier. *At least I might be able to convince him to meet Darlengi. I will have accomplished something wonderful if I can do that.*

* * *

Phoebe and Sean O'Hare were back in Newcastle the following afternoon. The return ride was without incident, which greatly pleased the Corporal.

When they reached the outskirts of the settlement they found a body of soldiers and a contingent of Basutos and Putini working hard, digging trenches for John Lockley's fortifications; but there was no sign of him and as they came into the barrack yard Phoebe turned to her companion.

'Thanks for accompanying me, Corporal.'

He grinned. 'It were a most interestin' ride, Miss McLean. Ye're such a plucky gal I reckon ye must really be Irish.'

She went to look for Diana and Thulmi and found them at the side of the hospital tent.

Diana smiled in welcome. 'What did you think of Utrecht?'

'Even with the speculation about the Transvaal under British rule I doubt the Governor would be interested in a military hospital there. Still, I've seen it now.' Then she turned to Thulmi. 'You seem a lot better.'

He gave her a look of faint disapproval. 'Miss Phoebe. You go to Utrecht without me.'

'Thulmi, you were sick.'

'Not too sick to go with you. Never too sick for that.'

She smiled and patted him on the shoulder. 'All right, I'm sorry. I'll remember in future.'

That evening, as the sun was sinking and throwing a rose glow across the little settlement, she stood with Diana under a blue gum tree planted by the locals. They were talking about their return to Pietermaritzburg the next day.

Diana smiled. 'I'm pleased we're leaving, Phoebe. We've seen all we can up here.'

Phoebe laughed. 'You're keen to get back to Gordon. We'll go back via Helpmaaker. And though it's a little off the track, I'd like to call into Greytown. We bypassed it coming up.'

Diana nodded. 'You'll be able to see your old friends.'

'I only have two in the township; Phyllis May and her husband Graham, but I have a lot at the mission. And Thulmi will enjoy seeing them all again as well.'

A voice sounded behind them. 'Good evening to you.'

It was John Lockley. Phoebe's pulse quickened slightly. She

had been hoping to see him but he had been indoors with his officers since she had returned.

Diana smiled widely. She thought he was just the most perfect man she had ever seen, and as he stood here now in his tunic of scarlet with the gold lace round his collar, and his blue-purple eyes regarding them from under his white helmet, she felt herself blush. She wasn't being disloyal to her fiancé, she just couldn't help it.

'Good evening, Colonel,' Diana replied, 'beautiful sunset, isn't it?'

'Yes, it is. Would you ladies care to join me for a cup of tea at Duffey's?'

Duffey's was as close to a hotel as Newcastle could offer. It was at the other end of the settlement and was a rickety, one-storeyed building where there were three or four rooms to rent and where, in the small front parlour, they served the quaint combination of ale and tea.

'We'd love to,' replied Diana, unaware of the sidelong glance she received from Phoebe.

The three made their way through the township. In Duffey's front parlour a few soldiers and some locals sat taking refreshment, and John Lockley found them a table near a cracked windowpane.

It was not long before Diana realised to her astonishment that her friend Phoebe and the handsome soldier had known each other since they were very young.

'Phoebe, you sly one,' she whispered as John Lockley went over to get some sugar, 'you've never mentioned him and he's quite the most perfect-looking man I've ever seen.'

Phoebe smiled. 'I'll tell Gordon you said that.' For Gordon, Diana's fiancé, was quite good-looking himself.

'Don't you dare.'

By six o'clock they had been joined by Major Pinne and his second-in-command, Captain Peel, and had moved on from tea to the only bottle of wine the establishment could find; well, it was sherry, actually, but the proprietor presented it under the guise of wine.

As it neared seven o'clock Phoebe touched Diana on the arm. 'We must go and pack.'

Diana shrugged. 'Yes, I suppose we must.'

'Why?' asked Captain Peel. 'Are you going somewhere?'

Phoebe nodded. 'We return to 'Maritzburg and Durban tomorrow. We've accomplished all we can here and, while we enjoy your company, gentlemen, I'm afraid we'll have to leave.'

She stood up and Diana rose beside her.

John Lockley had not realised they were leaving Newcastle so soon, and he stood and accompanied them to the door, where he let Diana pass through, but halted Phoebe. 'Perhaps after you've finished packing we . . . could meet back here for a nightcap?'

Phoebe met his gaze. 'I'd like that.'

'What time then?'

'I should be packed by ten o'clock.'

'Good. I'll be here.'

As the two women made their way along the street Diana was chatting merrily. 'I know I couldn't do without my darling Gordon but there's something about a man in uniform, isn't there? And fancy your knowing Colonel Harrison since you were just a tot. He's a dream, isn't he? And do you know, Phoebe, I think he likes you. I really do.'

'Thanks, Diana, but he's just being polite. I'm very close to his friends and relatives.'

All the same, Phoebe hurried through her packing and was in her favourite muslin floral dress with her hair hanging in brushed curls to her shoulders as ten o'clock approached.

When she arrived at Duffey's it was much rowdier than earlier and someone was playing an accordian.

John Lockley waited for her on the veranda by the door. He had been thinking about Phoebe; remembering when she had left Natal on the SS *Kidde Halon*. That day he had thought he might never see her again and had been sorry. And the letters she had written him from Cleveland in America: he used to be so very pleased when one arrived. He was beginning to see that he had cared for Phoebe always; ever since she was a tiny child. He remembered the curly-headed little girl whose laugh was so infectious. And now she was such a beautiful woman; and a good woman. Funny that he was only just recognising her virtues when he had known her so long. Perhaps that was it; she had always been so available to him that he had not realised how much he cared for her.

He was so pleased to see her coming towards him, looking

fresh and lovely in her pretty dress with her fair curls falling to her shoulders. He pointed with his thumb to Duffey's. 'We won't be able to hear ourselves think in there.'

She smiled. 'Yes, it's loud. Shall we go for a walk?'

'Good idea.'

As they walked they talked of Aunt Jane and Uncle Chris and the Tugela farm and her mother in Cleveland and finally Anthony and Fanny. Phoebe brought them up. 'You've become very close to Anthony Durnford, haven't you?'

'Yes, I have. He's one of the best men I've ever met.'

She nodded. 'Fanny's in love with him, you know.'

He turned towards her, meeting her eyes in the wan night light. 'Yes, I do, but I didn't think anyone else was supposed to.'

'Fanny and I are very close. She hopes that one day he'll leave the army; that they may be able to do something.'

'What? Like his petitioning for a divorce?'

'I suppose so. It's so sad. They're such good people and deserve happiness.'

'Yes, they do. Though divorce is long and difficult and puts people through such agony. And I know Anthony. He wouldn't want to hurt anyone.'

Phoebe stopped walking and John Lockley halted at her side. 'You regard him highly. I suppose real comradeship's not something that comes along very often, is it?'

'No, it's rare.'

She took a deep breath. 'You used to feel like that about Darlengi.'

He was silent for a long time and she could feel her heart beating while she waited for him to speak.

When he answered his words were quiet, yet somehow to her they seemed to ring in the night air. 'I still do.'

'Oh, John Lockley, I know where he is. I saw him yesterday.'

'I know. Young O'Hare told me.'

'He said he would wait, on Friday, from noon to dusk at the junction of the Buffalo and the Ingcuba, on the western bank.'

'I see.'

'John Lockley, will you please go? Meet with him. I know it would mean so much to him.'

She waited for his reply and it seemed an age in coming.

'Yes, I will,' he answered as he lifted his right hand and drew his fingers through his hair.

She gave a cry of joy and jumped forward spontaneously to wrap him in her arms. And then suddenly he was kissing her mouth, tasting her for the first time, deeply, sensually, and, as he did, he slid his arms around her to hold her close along his body.

This was the culmination of her dreams. She felt the love she had carried all the years expanding up through her, engulfing her mind as she returned his kiss. *I'm in his arms. After all this time, I'm in his arms.*

She heard him whisper, 'Phoebe, Phoebe.'

They stood together in the darkness. She could just see him as he drew back and lifted his hand to touch her face. 'Phoebe Mclean, you're truly beautiful.'

She found it hard to reply. It was not really possible that John Lockley Harrison had kissed her; had told her she was beautiful; it was not possible.

While this dialogue went on in her head, she realised he was pulling her to him, kissing her again. The taste of him held the clean, vital essence of spring in the bushveld. He was Africa, and she loved him. She felt his hands move down her spine; over her buttocks. She felt him along the length of her. She had never experienced anything like this. It was raw, and earthy. She was slipping out of control.

She stepped quickly back and her voice trembled as she said, 'I'd better go.'

And his was thick with emotion as he replied, 'Yes, I think you should.'

She took another step back from him. 'How long . . . will you be up here, building the fortifications?'

'Many months . . . but I'll come wherever you are as soon as I can.' Then he could not help it. He crossed the space between them and took her in his arms again.

His mouth was hungry for her. Greedily he ran his hands across her body, feeling the undulations of her. She was womanly and warm and wonderful, and oh, how badly he wanted her.

She was not resisting; she could not. She did not want to. She had loved him all her life.

He lifted his hand to the opening of her gown as his mouth

moved down her throat, and then abruptly he broke from her and stepped back. 'Phoebe, you should go. You must go.'

She moved away a few paces and he remained where he was. She looked round and he said, 'Go, Phoebe, please.'

She hurried back through the trees, past the hubbub of Duffey's and along the little street that led to her room.

Outside on the seat sat Thulmi, taking snuff.

She tried to sound normal. 'Thulmi, we should leave tomorrow morning by nine o'clock.'

'Sure we will, Miss Phoebe.' Then as she opened her door he added, 'You have nice walk?'

'Thulmi, whatever do you mean?' Her voice shook a little.

'You went for walk, I think.'

Phoebe was in no mood to explore the conversation any further. 'Yes, I had a nice walk. Goodnight, Thulmi.'

'Goodnight, Miss Phoebe.'

She closed the door and leaned back on it. John Lockley Harrison had kissed her, fondled her, wanted her. Oh Lord! It had been so passionate. She wondered how she would ever face him again.

But she did. In the frank, sharp light of the following morning he came to see her off.

Diana was still inside and Thulmi was up on the wagon and Sergeant Gardiner was checking his saddle and bedroll when John Lockley came walking down the uneven street.

He came right up to her, smiling. 'Good morning, did you sleep well?'

'No, I tossed and turned.'

'I didn't sleep well either.' And now she thought he was saying things to her with his eyes. Or was she imagining it? 'Too much on my mind. I wish you a safe journey, and, from what Corporal O'Hare tells me, Sergeant Gardiner's in good hands.'

Oh dear, he was being flippant. Last night didn't mean anything to him.

Then she was so pleased when he took her hand. 'Thanks for telling me about Darlengi,' he said.

'I hope it goes well for you . . . both. Good luck.'

And now a serious look came into his eyes. 'Phoebe, I suppose you'll be busy now with your nurses' school in Durban.'

'Yes, I will.'

'I'll be stuck up here for months finishing the fortifications in a number of settlements. I have to go to 'Maritzburg once or twice for staff meetings with the Governor, and if I can get down to Durban to see you, I will. But if I can't, I know Uncle Chris and Aunt Jane intend to be at the Tugela farm for his birthday on the ninth of October.' He looked her straight in the eye. 'I know it's months away, but I'll make sure I'm there for it. Will you come?'

She was feeling quite hot even though there was a cool wind blowing this morning.

She seemed to consider her reply. 'Yes, John Lockley, I'll come.'

At that moment Diana came out, carrying a small case. She walked towards them but suddenly understood she was superfluous. She was a sensible young woman, so she simply turned, and put her case in the back of the wagon, and climbed up beside Thulmi.

A work party of the amaPutini led by Sergeant Tenny Rama came walking by with their picks and shovels, followed by Captain Peel, who halted beside John Lockley. 'Colonel Harrison, we're ready, sir.'

'Good, Captain, I'll join you down at the site of the outer wall.'

They marched on and he turned back to Phoebe, and taking up her hand said, 'Last night I realised many things. I saw that not only are you beautiful and so very desirable, but that you mean a great deal to me.'

She looked up into his eyes and smiled. Her reply was simple, for it was the unadulterated truth. 'You have always meant a great deal to me.'

CHAPTER THIRTY-FIVE

On Friday afternoon Phoebe and her entourage came rolling into Helpmaaker. They had camped the night before in the shadows of Insindumeni Mountain and had journeyed on here in the cool of the morning. Helpmaaker was a collection of five wooden houses, one pretending to be a store with the major item for sale being eggs, as a consequence of dozens of hens apparently considering the long open veranda a permanent roost.

As Sergeant Gardiner and Thulmi raised their tents, Phoebe left Diana and wandered across the dirt track that passed for a road. They would be in Greytown in another couple of days. Thank goodness; at least it had a couple of shops and was what passed for a township. But she had enjoyed her travels and she didn't mind the hardship.

She thought of John Lockley. Truth was she had thought of little else since leaving Newcastle. It seemed she had been thinking about him her whole darn life. How dearly she loved him. She remembered the other night. She had desperately desired him; and he, her. The following morning he had said she meant a great deal to him. But what did that really mean? Could someone mean a great deal to you if you simply desired them? Yet he wanted her to come to the Tugela farm in October, didn't he? That meant that he cared, didn't it? And he had said he'd even come to Durban if he could. She would have to stop this sort of thinking or she would very quickly drive herself mad.

She turned her mind to the encounter between John Lockley and Darlengi. They would be meeting some time soon, could even be meeting now. Oh, how dearly she hoped all would be well.

She recalled the day she had first seen Darlengi; the day she had first seen the two of them together and noticed the similarity between them. In her mind's eye she could picture them now, bending down side by side and attending to Caledon in the stable yard at the Tugela farm.

She sighed. *I should have remained in Newcastle to find out what happened. But Diana was keen to leave for Durban, and there was no reason to delay; well, except for a selfish reason.*

Out of her pocket she took the small gold timepiece that had been her father's. It was three o'clock. Darlengi and John Lockley would be at the meeting place.

But at three o'clock John Lockley had only just turned off the road to Utrecht. He still had almost fourteen miles to cover to the junction of the Buffalo and the Ingcuba. It was autumn and to be there by dusk he would have to average nearly five miles an hour. The way across country was not easy going and the damn horse beneath him was almost a donkey. He was not feeling confident.

It had been a series of disasters since he had risen this morning. He had planned to leave at six o'clock but had been informed by Tenny Rama, who had gone to saddle Horatio, that his gallant stallion had been lying on the floor with some sort of fever.

He had chosen another horse, Bleckney, a fast mare he had ridden often, and she had been saddled and ready waiting for him when a message had come in by helio to say the contingent at Adelsdorf needed more supplies. Normally that would not concern him but they had asked for a rocket battery to be sent up, and he, as the commanding officer, had to approve it. Not a large problem, but time-consuming, for he then had to find out why they requested it. This meant helio messages back and forth. He had finally left at eight o'clock and had made good time and was thinking about Phoebe, when Bleckney had thrown a shoe. He could not believe it. *Hadn't someone checked the damn horse's shoes?* And he said to himself, *John Lockley you should have.* He was ten miles from Newcastle, in the middle of nowhere.

He had walked Bleckney miles to a house on a distant hill. The Boer owner, a large, handsome man called Roit Vos, had been happy to help, but Bleckney had come so far without her shoe that she was lame.

John Lockley had turned to Roit Vos. 'Could I borrow a

horse? As you can see, my mare's a beauty. I'll leave her with you.'

Roit had only a few horses and he needed his best, but he wanted to help, so he gave the Englishman a roan mare called Lieber. John Lockley found out that Lieber did not like to be pushed, and while she would accelerate for a short period of time she would drop back to her own pace no matter what.

Three and four and five o'clock passed.

Twilight descended and he was uncertain how far he had yet to go. He still could not see the junction of the rivers.

Darlengi would leave at sunset if he hadn't done already. He'd told Phoebe he'd wait from noon until dusk.

John Lockley could see the Buffalo as he came down a long hill, but he could not see the other river. He would follow this one until it came to the Ingcuba, though he would not go right to the edge, for there would be crocodiles along the shore.

Darkness was swiftly descending as he tried to coax Lieber into speed.

After all these years, I'm going to miss him.

Night descended, but still he pushed on under the wan light of an early moon. When he came to the junction, it had been dark for some time, but by moonlight he could see the joining of the rivers a few hundred yards away down an incline.

He dismounted and stood beside Lieber near the dark shape of an acacia tree. He had been hindered and frustrated the whole day long; trying so hard to get here, all to no avail. He had let Darlengi down.

And his brother would have kept his word. He always did. He would have been here, and then left when it grew dark. There had been no reason to stay.

He stood there beside Lieber with his arm resting up on her saddle, his hand holding tightly to the cantle. He felt hurt and thwarted and rapped his fist in anger with himself on the saddle, but the complacent Lieber ignored him.

Then he walked a few paces to some rocky ground and halted, looking down to the rivers. On the long ride here he had been so hot he had taken off his jacket and rolled up his sleeves. He stood now, rubbing the assegai scar on his arm.

Darlengi had arrived at the river junction at noon.

He had sat for a long time under an acacia tree, looking

down the hill and thinking about all the years since he and John Lockley had played along the Tugela and laughed on Isi's back. He remembered when John Lockley had saved him from drowning and when their eyes had met.

It would be so good, so right, to be with his brother again. How dearly he hoped he would come. They would sit and talk and just be together again. Of course all these years had passed, but their spirits had not changed.

They had been apart for seven years. It was time for the healing to begin.

He thought of Jettama and how greatly she had loved John Lockley; enough to die for him; that was a powerful love indeed. Then he thought of the Ice Princess. He recalled their few short hours of love together; the perfection of her and her desire for him. But the Ice Princess had been fragile like the ice she had been made of. He could not help it; even after twelve years thoughts of her still saddened him.

His mind turned to Thulile. She was real, and lasting and stable; yet she was very gentle, perhaps too gentle. He loved her dearly.

He wondered if John Lockley would ever realise how Phoebe loved him. They would not be meeting here today if it were not for Phoebe.

He knew that the woman John Lockley had married had died. He had first heard of it from Tilly, two years ago.

And so the hours passed for Darlengi. He went down closer to the Buffalo and he ran for a little way along it, chasing a small herd of steenbok, before he turned back. He wandered in and out of rocks and boulders, disturbing a number of mongooses, and watched by black eagles. Then he sat for a time under a rocky outcrop and sharpened the knife which he wore in a sheath on his belt. His memories covered all the days of his life; all the important people of his past and of his present, those he loved and those he did not: Mattana, Shiambi, Jettama, the Ice Princess, Thulile, Tilly, Dirk, Aunt Jane, Uncle Chris, Kayo, Mtonga, Intongalu, Cetshwayo ... and John Lockley.

Finally, as twilight descended, he stood rubbing the assegai scar on his forearm.

He watched the distance for a sign of movement until night fell. He even remained while the early moon threw her insipid light across the veld. He would have to spend the night somewhere near here anyway. He remembered an area further on that had afforded quite good shelter. The disappointment dragged his handsome mouth down at the corners as with lethargic steps he moved away.

He had gone about three hundred yards when his acute hearing picked up the sounds of a horse. He stopped and looked back. Back some way, over there on the hilltop. He was sure.

He ran back as swiftly as the uneven ground allowed.

Yes, he was certain as he came closer . . . up there under that acacia tree. A man and a horse. In the pale moonlight the figure walked forward on to the rocky ground and stood there looking down at the rivers. It was John Lockley, of course it was!

He was about seventy-five yards from the dark figure when it heard him coming and turned towards him.

He called out, 'John Lockley! Is it you?'

'Oh, dear sweet Jesus!' John Lockley shouted. 'Yes, yes, Darlengi, I'm here!'

There was a moment of pure elation as they rushed forward to each other. Then they were in each other's powerful arms; hugging, laughing, shouting for joy, clasping each other like the treasure they thought lost forever . . . Even the moon shone more brightly.

They talked for hours and the night was kind to them; still and comfortable.

It was very late when John Lockley looked across the leaping flames of their fire and said, 'Darlengi?'

'Yes.'

'I'm sorry I've been such a damn fool. Wasting all these years.' He met his brother's eyes in the flickering light. 'I judged you, and now I know that sitting in judgement is in itself hypocrisy.'

Darlengi returned his gaze. 'You were hurt. I understand.'

'But I had no right.'

Darlengi smiled and his perfect teeth gleamed. 'It is over now. That is all that matters to me. I have my brother back.'

John Lockley maintained his gaze. 'I loved your sister very deeply.'

And Darlengi answered, 'And I loved your sister very deeply.'

They slept only briefly and awoke to the brilliant morning of a warm autumn day. They had said so many things last night, and still there was much to say; but they must leave each other soon.

John Lockley had brought a tin in his supplies, and he boiled water from the river and made tea.

Darlengi laughed. 'Drinking tea for breakfast reminds me of The Grange or Mimosa. Do please let Uncle Chris and Aunt Jane know I think about them.'

Then an idea came to John Lockley. 'It's Uncle Chris's birthday on the ninth of October. We're all going to the Tugela farm. Do you think you could come for a few days?'

Darlengi did not answer.

'Come on, Darli, it'll be like old times.'

It was the first time he had used this intimate form of address and Darlengi smiled just hearing it.

'I will think about it. I do not like to be away from Thulile more often than necessary.'

John Lockley almost said, 'Bring her with you,' but he stopped himself in time. It would have been so wrong. Darlengi could move between cultures, but it would be cruel to expect Thulile to, and Darlengi would have thought him a damn fool for saying it.

'I hope you can come,' John Lockley said, finishing off his tea. 'And, too, I'm hoping Phoebe will be there.'

He had explained last night his feelings for Phoebe, and Darlengi had been so happy to hear him say, 'I feel differently about her to the way I've ever felt about a woman before. I loved Jettama deeply, but it was youthful and vibrant and immature. All the other women in my life, of whom my wife, Kate, was one, I've been attracted to in ... well, in a very physical way. I realise now the predominant feeling in my relationship with Kate was sensual. I loved to make love to her. But with Phoebe, while I want her physically, and badly, believe me,' he smiled, 'I want to be with her, talk to her, understand her, protect her. Is that the way you feel about Thulile?'

Darlengi had nodded, and leaned across to him and patted his shoulder in the firelight. 'You've grown up at last.'

And then they had burst out laughing and had laughed so much they rolled on the ground like boys again.

When they were ready to depart they stood opposite each other in the clear, radiant sunlight. The soldier and the warrior, reunited. Life was sweet to John Lockley again. He wasn't carrying the burdens of yesterday. He was lighter, metaphorically and almost physically, for he moved briskly, energetically.

'One last question, and a political one,' he said. 'From what you told me last night Cetshwayo thinks he might have to deal with the Boers himself. Is that why he's building up his regiments again?'

'Yes, the regiments grow in size all the time.'

'How many men do you estimate he has?'

Darlengi thought for a moment. 'Some of the regiments are perhaps too old to fight. But real fighting men, I can tell you ... forty-five thousand and twenty.'

John Lockley shook his head and gave a small laugh. 'Hardly an estimate. Thank you.'

'Lockley, heed this. After all these years, the border question of the disputed territory is still unsolved. Cetshwayo grows impatient and so grows in his hatred of the Boers. And he has been king of the Zulus for four years and in that role has not washed his spear. He is almost beholden to do so. I know you British regard that as mere folly, and mystifying as well, but it is custom, and my people are ruled by custom. Some you can avoid, but others you cannot.'

John Lockley took his brother's hand as he replied, 'I should tell you that Somtseu, Shepstone, annexed the Transvaal in the name of Britain about a fortnight ago.'

Darlengi had thought this was possible. 'I see. That colours it all very differently. That means the disputed territory now belongs to Britain.'

'Darlengi, I'm going back to the capital for staff meetings with the Governor, and while I'm there I'll bring up the question of the border land again. See if we can do something constructive now the Transvaal is British. Please hold your warriors from doing anything foolish here. It would be best if they returned to their kraals.'

Darlengi still held John Lockley's hand as he answered, 'I agree. But I will have to wait for Cetshwayo to give the order.'

512

They parted and John Lockley mounted Lieber. He smiled down at his brother. 'Come to the farm in October. Thulile will understand.'

Darlengi shaded his eyes as he looked up at the golden figure on the horse. He smiled in return. 'Thulile always understands. I will come if I can.'

Then John Lockley said, 'I told Uncle Chris and Aunt Jane about you and Ellen. And also about my ... stupidity. They were perfectly wonderful about it, as they are about everything.'

Darlengi nodded slowly. 'We are lucky to have them.'

'Yes, we are.'

John Lockley pressed Lieber forward and Darlengi watched him, lifting his assegai in farewell.

When Darlengi arrived back at Little Blood River he was confronted by his second-in-command, Maphoko.

'I have waited for you to come, Baba. The men who went to the Pongola were in a skirmish with some Boer farmers.'

'You mean the warriors with Intongalu?'

'Yes.'

'Send for him immediately. I will speak with him.'

Intongalu was resting when Maphoko came to him. He sat in the shade of a clump of giant aloes, taking snuff from the long wooden spoon he wore through his left earlobe.

'Darlengi wishes to speak with you.'

'I cannot come now.'

Maphoko returned to Darlengi. 'He says he cannot come now. Yet he sits in the shade of the aloes taking snuff.'

'Maphoko, I must ask you to go to him again. Tell him that I was appointed by King Cetshwayo as the leader of this expedition, and that if he does not come to me now, I shall regard it as a rebellious act and shall be forced to act accordingly.'

Maphoko disappeared and soon returned with Intongalu.

'Sit down, Intongalu.' Darlengi pointed to a place opposite him.

The warrior sat, placing his iklwa beside him on the ground.

'What is this I hear of a skirmish with some Boer farmers on the Pongola River?'

The warrior's expression was sullen as he replied, 'It is

nothing. It happens all the time. The Boers get greedy like the leguaan and mongoose do for the crocodile's eggs and our people retaliate. There is trouble in the kraals of the Pongola. Our people are unhappy. There are taxes on their cattle. I had to defend a kraal against the Boer farmers.'

'What do you mean by defend?'

'It was just two Boers, they had been demanding cattle as payment for taxes Chief Redna had not paid; as if he should. There was a small fight.'

'What does that mean? Explain or I shall have to ask your warriors.'

Intongalu's eyes narrowed. 'They had been into Redna's kraal with their rifles. I simply went with a force when the Boers were away from their farms and took some of their cattle. It was fitting. They could not blame Redna, as I had done it. And I did not remain in the district.'

Darlengi leaned forward, his elbows on his knees. His voice was perfectly controlled as he said, 'Is that everything?'

'There were some bullets fired at us by two young Boers. No one was hurt. Two barns were burnt. They deserved it.'

'What you did was not defensive, it was offensive. You were sent there to reconnoitre, not to make more trouble between Boer and Zulu.'

Intongalu met his eyes. 'I did what was right.'

And now Darlengi's voice held an edge of anger in it as he answered, 'You did what was stupid. We were given specific instructions from the king himself that there was to be no aggression unless we received an order from him. What you have done reflects on Cetshwayo. You are an induna of his Great Council. You are a fool, and as of now, I relieve you of your command.'

Intongalu screamed with rage and leapt to his feet, thrusting his assegai at Darlengi. But Darlengi was still one of the fittest men in all Africa, and at the same moment he jumped up and threw himself sideways so that his opponent's thrust went wide. As Intongalu rounded to face his quarry, Darlengi hurled himself at his assailant's legs and brought him to the ground.

By now Maphoko and some others had rushed over to them. There was shouting and yelling and they held Intongalu as he hailed curses on Darlengi.

Darlengi stood in front of his captive. 'I shall inform the king of this. Until I hear from him, you will be kept under guard.' He turned to Maphoko. 'Bring Intongalu's second-in-command to me, and at the same time, Induna Uhamu and Induna Mbilini.'

CHAPTER THIRTY-SIX

It was just over three months later when John Lockley came rushing into The Grange on a cold winter's evening. It was already dark as he leapt down from Horatio and, tying him loosely to the rail near the arch of climbing roses, bounded up to the front door, which was always unlocked. Hurrying along the front hall, his brown polished boots thudding on the runner of carpet, he called, 'Aunt Jane, Uncle Chris, are you here?'

'Yes, son, in the parlour, come on in.'

Christopher had just arrived home himself and stood by the fireplace drinking a warm toddy.

'How grand to see you, son. You appear in a hurry.'

John Lockley took off his helmet and laid it on the Sheraton side table. 'Yes, sorry I can't stay, but I'm to be back at Government House for a dinner at eight o'clock. The High Commissioner, Sir Henry Bartle Frere, is here on his way to see Shepstone in Pretoria, and they have to feed him.' He laughed. 'I just wanted to tell you I'll be back here to sleep the night, if you don't mind.'

Jane had entered the room behind her nephew. 'Well,' she said, 'I'm sure we don't mind. We haven't seen you since March.'

'But I do write, Aunt Jane, I do write,' he said, turning and kissing her on the cheek.

'Yes, you do.' She smiled. 'Have you time for a quick drink?'

'Yes, please. I'll have whatever Uncle Chris's drinking.'

When the drink was in his hand he looked at his uncle. 'I want you to know that I'm coming to the farm for your birthday. And, well ... I was in Durban for two hours the day before yesterday accompanying Bulwer to meet old Sir Bartle and saw Phoebe.' He raked his hand back through his hair as

516

he continued, 'Well, fact is, if you don't mind, she's coming too.'

Jane answered for both of them. 'No, we don't mind at all. That sounds like it'll be a lovely celebration.'

He put his arm round his aunt's shoulders as he said, 'I'm hoping it'll be better than that.' He paused before he continued, 'because . . . I've got a feeling Darlengi will be there too.'

'What?' Christopher almost shouted in his delight.

'I was going to write to you,' John Lockley explained, 'but it was something I wanted to tell you . . . both of you, in person.' He hesitated and looked from one to the other, meeting their eyes before he said, 'A few months ago I saw Darlengi. The meeting was arranged by Phoebe, actually. We . . . well, the truth is, it was just like we'd never been apart. There was nothing awkward, nothing to be explained. He understood.' A faraway expression came into his eyes as he added, 'Just as he has always understood.'

Jane came over to him and took him in her arms, hugging him tightly to her. 'Oh, my darling, I'm so happy, so happy for you both.'

He met Christopher's eyes over the top of Jane's head, and his uncle smiled. 'Well done, son. Well done.'

When he had extricated himself from his aunt's continuing embrace he went on, 'We talked almost all night, and before I left him the following morning, I asked him to come to the farm for your birthday, Uncle Chris. I saw him again just recently near Blood River, where he's been for many months. We met with a number of Zulu chiefs and discussed again the never-ending boundary dispute. Anthony and I were present on behalf of our own Lieutenant-Governor Bulwer, who really is trying to get a clear understanding of it. Darlengi was there for Cetshwayo. Afterwards, Darlengi and I got together, had two days, in fact, and he said he'd come to the farm for the ninth of October.'

Christopher beamed. 'That's marvellous, son. It's hard for me to express how I feel, knowing that things are finally settled between you.'

John Lockley said nothing. There was no need. He gulped down the last of his drink and picked up his helmet.

Christopher looked at Jane and then to his nephew. 'Let's

make a house party of it. Why not invite Anthony too? If he can take a few days' leave.'

John Lockley nodded vigorously. 'Capital idea.' Then as if it were an afterthought, he added, 'In that case I'll ask Phoebe to bring her friend, Fanny Colenso. Fill out the numbers. It'll be the grandest birthday you've ever had, Uncle Chris.' And with that he was down the hall and out through the door.

Behind him Jane and Christopher hugged each other with delight.

Some few hours later, John Lockley and Anthony, in full dress uniform, stood in the smoking room of Government House. Dinner was over and Sir Henry Bartle Edward Frere, Governor of the Cape Colony and High Commissioner for Native Affairs, stood in the centre of the room, surrounded by his staff, public servants and army officers. He was a handsome man with a heavy moustache above a determined jaw. He was known to be resourceful and had been appointed by Lord Carnarvon with the understanding that a federated southern Africa was desirable. Opposite him stood Sir Henry Bulwer, Lieutenant-Governor of Natal, an able and uncomplicated man.

'Every newspaper I have read since I landed in Durban writes about the fear of the mounting menace from your Zulu neighbours,' Sir Bartle said, sipping his port.

Sir Henry nodded. 'Sadly the press excel in hyperbole. Although there's some truth in what they say. There are over three hundred thousand Bantus in Natal, and merely sixteen thousand Europeans, and the Zulu nation which sits looking down at us comprises hundreds of thousands, with a standing army of over forty thousand men. It's rare food for the press's insatiable desire to stir up trouble.'

Bartle Frere nodded. 'I've noticed the feeling of tension. It reminds me of the years leading up to the Sepoy Rebellion in India.'

'But you quelled that, sir,' spoke up his secretary, a loyal young man with mutton-chop whiskers.

Bartle Frere nodded at his aide before he turned back to the Lieutenant-Governor. 'And this Cetshwayo clamours for the land that he says the Boers stole.'

Sir Henry gestured to Anthony and John Lockley. 'Lieutenant-Colonel Durnford and Lieutenant-Colonel Harrison have been instrumental in asking the Zulu king to treat the disputed territory as neutral for the time being. It's gone on too long. I now wish to form a Commission of Inquiry into the matter so that once and for all the question can be settled without the Zulus coming to blows with *anyone*.'

The High Commissioner turned his cool blue eyes to the two officers. 'I have been told that one of you speaks fluent Zulu and knows the culture as well, if not better, than Sir Theopolis himself.'

Anthony motioned to John Lockley. 'You're speaking of my friend, Lieutenant-Colonel Harrison, sir.'

Sir Bartle asked, 'So what do you think? Are the Zulus a menace?'

John Lockley answered, 'I cannot give you a simple answer, sir.'

'Then give me a complex one.'

John Lockley smiled. 'The Zulus have a complicated military structure like no other race in Africa, sir.' He paused. 'Other than us, that is.'

The company around him laughed.

'Cetshwayo's father, Mpande, let the regiments disperse but they have been brought back to their former strength under Cetshwayo. The border agent, Mr George Finney, estimated their strength at forty-one thousand, nine hundred, but I have it on better authority that it's forty-five thousand and twenty. They're disciplined and efficient at man-slaying. And while there are always small disputes in Zululand there's no major fighting. Cetshwayo is proud, even arrogant. He regards the English as his friends and the Boers as his enemies. He's not a fool and while he does not understand the convoluted workings of British politics . . .'

'Who does?' broke in Sir Bartle, and the room laughed again.

'. . . he has been disappointed by Sir Theopolis's negative attitude to settling the border question. There's no doubt he's angry about that.

'We're living on a frontier here, Sir Bartle, and all sides have vital interests of their own. So in answer, while I agree with Sir Henry that the press is irresponsibly representing matters in Zululand by depicting Cetshwayo as a blood-thirsty despot who allows summary executions, I'd say the

Zulus have a war-machine and at present no one to make war against.'

Sir Bartle nodded thoughtfully. 'Thank you, Colonel Harrison ... enlightening.'

Phoebe walked through a ward in the little building that served as Durban's military hospital. It sat a couple of hundred yards behind the train station and was not far from her nurses' school, where she had spent the day instructing.

Thank goodness the school was close for she was back and forth between the two buildings all day long.

She had a number of patients at the moment. Some of the men in the 80th Regiment were ill with a fever not unlike malaria. She and Diana and her two other trained nurses, Coral-June and Patricia, were working double shifts. And Dr Campbell was indefatigable.

As she came down the ward she greeted her charges by name.

'I feel better when you're here, Nurse McLean,' called a young private as she passed the end of his bed.

'Then you should be well by morning, Private Masters, as I'll probably stay all night.'

He managed a smile and she came to the side of his bed. He was perspiring freely but shivering at the same time. She took down another blanket from a shelf nearby and drew it across him. 'There, I'll look in on you again in a little while.'

She found Diana out in the hall, writing up her patient notes by lamplight. The woman lifted her head as Phoebe came closer.

'Hello, Phoebe, I've almost finished.'

'Good. You go home then. Any new cases since I was in this morning?'

'No, none, thankfully. In fact a lot of the men seem much better.'

'That's marvellous. I'm positive that keeping things clean and using carbolic acid like Dr Tallant suggested is the way to kill germs. You know he corresponds with Joseph Lister, the man who discovered that germs cause fermentation and who first practised the methods we use. He's the one who informed Dr Tallant about antisepsis. He says that we must wash our hands a lot. It makes sense.'

Diana smiled. 'This building may be old, but it's spotless.'

Phoebe took a lantern from the top of a cabinet and lit it. 'I'll just go and check the other ward.'

As she moved along the hallway, she looked neat and businesslike in her long grey skirt and full white apron. In the nurses' fashion of the day, she had a red armband with the letters CGH embroidered in white cotton upon it. They stood for her training school: Cleveland General Hospital.

Things were going well. Her assistants came to each day with that spontaneous enthusiasm and caring that was so necessary when looking after the sick. She was very lucky to have them all.

The south ward was in another small building, and as she came out on to the veranda to pass down the steps and over to it, she looked up at the moon. She wondered where John Lockley was. She had only seen him once since Newcastle. He had been here in Durban just for a few hours meeting the Cape Governor, and he had come to the school to urge her to go to the Tugela farm in October. She had set his mind at rest on that.

She relived the moment when he had said goodbye. He had lifted her hand to his lips and turned it over to kiss her palm. She could feel his lips on the skin of her hand right this minute. A little thrill ran along her shoulders.

Her lantern was flickering, and the thrill turned into a shiver as she hurried on in the cold wind, thinking of the coming celebration at the farm.

Darlengi ran up from the river towards the kraal, where Thulile stood waiting for him. He carried a hare over his shoulder which he had caught for their evening meal.

She laughed as he came closer. 'You still run with great speed like the hare you bring. Except he shall run no more, poor thing.'

Darlengi put his free arm around her and kissed her and they continued on towards their home.

As they walked Darlengi spoke. 'Thulile?'

'Yes.'

'You know I am to go to Little Blood River for the meeting with Somtseu sixteen sunsets from now?'

'I do.'

'If I were to leave you sooner, would you mind?'

She laughed. 'My husband, you often leave me when the affairs of Zululand demand or Cetshwayo calls. I accept that you must go.'

'This is not only for the affairs of Zululand.'

'Then what is it?'

'Remember when I told you that my British brother had returned to me?'

'I do. And my heart was filled with joy for you both.'

'And I told you that I saw him once more some months ago when we met to discuss the disputed border lands with the British.'

'Yes.'

'Both times he asked me to join him and my English family at the Tugela farm for a celebration for the man I call Uncle Christopher.'

'Yes, then you must go. Is that not where you go to see the one you call Tilly? I know that and do not mind.'

He nodded. 'But when I go to see Tilly, I spend only hours with her and return to you swiftly.'

She stopped walking and turned to him. 'You were gone from me for months when you went before to the lands of the disputed territory. So I do not mind if you go to the celebration for the one you call Uncle Chris.'

He hugged her tightly and she laughed. 'The hare sticks into me.'

Later, when they had eaten their meal and lay entwined in each other's arms on the hut floor, Darlengi's head on a soft pillow – for he had slept on one ever since his time at Mimosa – she said, 'Darlengi, what is it that you celebrate for the man, Uncle Chris?'

'It is to observe the day of his birth. The British, and many other races, celebrate the day of a person's birth.'

'Yes, you have told me before and I think it strange.' She smiled gently. 'I remember when the cold winds blew not long ago you said you were thirty-nine years old. I think you are the only Zulu who knows the day of your birth.'

'Perhaps.'

'You look forward to seeing your British family, don't you?'

'Is it obvious?'

'Yes.'

'You are so good, Thulile, so understanding. Though it is only a small part of my life these days, it is still a greatly important part. I thank you for your acceptance of that.'

She turned and leant over him and kissed his forehead. 'It is part of your life I can never share. But it does not hurt. There was a time when I believed you wanted the lady of the golden locket back, instead of me. But for many summers now, I have known that for the false belief it was. You are my husband. You have given me what no other woman in the kraals of Zululand has. Yourself. I share you with no one. It makes me walk proudly through the land, for I am Darlengi's only woman.'

'You can thank the British family for that. Especially the woman I call Aunt Jane. To use an English word, she *indoctrinated* me.'

'What is that, in-doc-try-nated?'

And he explained and she laughed. 'It seems to me that we Zulus are in-doc-try-nated. As the heavy rain sinks into the earth of the plain so too do our customs sink into us.'

Now she moved and sat astride him, looking down.

'You are really very clever,' he said, gazing up at her. Then he stretched out and brought her head down to his and kissed her mouth.

'When do you leave me?' she whispered.

'Six days from now.'

'Then I must make you remember me,' she said, rubbing her hips sensuously across him.

'There is little fear of my forgetting,' he answered as he moved beneath her.

Seven days later, Phoebe, Jane and Fanny sat on the Tugela farm veranda. Jane was tatting lace; Fanny was doing petit point and Phoebe read a week-old copy of the *Natal Witness* newspaper. There were a number of articles and letters in it about Zulu mobilisation and transgressions, and the need for more soldiers in Natal. On all sides the colonists complained about the lack of defences, and there was a feeling abroad – and it was sadly quite valid, Phoebe supposed – that the surest means of preserving peace was to be perfectly able and ready to defend if attacked.

523

She did sometimes worry about the state of the country, for while John Lockley and Anthony were engineers, they were soldiers after all, and if anything went wrong they would naturally be involved.

She remembered when she used to be concerned about something her mother would quote to her from the book of John: 'Peace I leave with you, my Peace I give unto you: not as the world giveth, give I unto you. Let not your heart be troubled, neither let it be afraid.' It was a comforting prayer and one she repeated often.

It was Uncle Chris's birthday tomorrow and still there was no sign of John Lockley or Darlengi or Anthony. She put the newspaper aside and moved to sit on the top step of the veranda.

Jane smiled to herself as she watched the woman she had known since childhood. Two nights ago Fanny had retired early and Christopher had gone for his nightly walk, so she and Phoebe had been alone together.

Tilly had brought them tea, and when she had departed, Jane looked across at her lovely younger companion and said, 'When your mother stayed with me at The Grange after your father died, she told me how you have always felt about John Lockley. She told me in confidence, of course, and I've kept it.'

Phoebe put down her teacup. 'I see. I don't mind that Mummy told you. The truth is, yes, Aunt Jane, I suppose I've been in love with your nephew since I was six years old and the cause of his broken arm on the *Regent Three*.'

'Phoebe, I hope you don't think I intrude when I ask whether you would have remained in America if Kate had not been killed.'

Phoebe paused before she answered. Then she said, 'Aunt Jane, I had faced the fact that John Lockley was married to another woman and beyond my reach. It broke my heart but I faced it. Yes, I would have come home to Africa anyway. While I went with Mummy thinking to begin a new life, and I did, by becoming a nurse, I realised I am African. This is where I wanted to be, John Lockley or no John Lockley. And that he might care for me still seems unreal.'

'We've only seen him twice in the last two months but each time he mentions you he has a certain expression.'

524

'Aunt Jane, I'm not the nervous type but you're making me nervous.'

They had laughed at that and then Jane had leaned forward and patted Phoebe's hand. 'How I do hope he's got the good sense to be in love with you.'

And now as Phoebe stood up from the step and went down into the leafy garden, Fanny rose and hurried down to join her. They moved off hand in hand towards a group of tall eucalypts: two beautiful young women. Jane wondered if Fanny had a special friend. She suffered from illness of the lungs and was quite frail, but so lovely, and very dear to Phoebe.

At that moment she saw Christopher, the General, Matilda and Jemby come hastening round the side of the house, followed by Thulmi who had come up with Phoebe from Durban. Jane stood and waved.

'There you are, darling,' Christopher called, waving a telescope above his head. 'Quickly, come down. Jemby's good eyes have picked up movement to the east down near the pontoon. He says it's two horses being led and three men walking.'

He called to Phoebe and Fanny and signalled for them to follow. Out through the hedge and side gate they all went to stand looking over the two fallow fields to the east.

Christopher put the telescope to his eye. 'Ha! ha! John Lockley, Darlengi and Anthony. How is it they all come together?'

'Who cares?' replied Jane, laughing. 'As long as they come.'

John Lockley had been in Greytown when Anthony joined him. He was supervising the fortifications to the laager which had been begun in 1854 but had fallen into disrepair. On Sunday, 7 October, he was standing up on the earthworks, with his constant companion, Tenny Rama, beside him, calling orders to his Basutos, when Anthony rode in.

'Hallo, lad,' Anthony hailed him from under his great moustache. 'I've been riding hard to get here. Fort Williamson was in such an abandoned state that we've really had to begin again over there.'

Fort Williamson, near the Tugela mouth, was begun in 1861

and had been allowed to fall into ruins like most of the forts in Natal.

'Yes,' answered John Lockley, 'we've got our work cut out bringing them back to any standard.' He jumped down from the earth wall and came over to Anthony and patted Chieftain's mane. 'I was wondering when you'd get here. We must leave this afternoon to be at the Tugela farm tomorrow. And we'll stay tonight with my old friend H.H.'

'Suits me,' replied Anthony.

So that evening, as the sun set behind Mount Ilvenwini, the two friends rode in to H. H. Garner's remote dwelling.

John Lockley had spoken so often about H.H. that when Anthony held out his hand in greeting his first words were, 'I feel as if I know you, sir, John Lockley has told me so much about you.'

H.H.'s faded blue eyes twinkled. 'Ah, yes, well, I've known the Lieutenant-Colonel since he was a sprout of fourteen summers. We've come through a long and successful association, you might say.'

'We certainly have,' agreed John Lockley.

That night H.H. reminisced and his two visitors were happy to listen. He related his stories of the days of Dingane; of how he began his trading station. 'No one here then but me, no Greytown, hardly even any 'Maritzburg, just a few Boer farmers. Now I'm talking about the late thirties, you understand. Then Dingane, "the needy one", was murdered in forty, the year I married Isman.' His face softened and momentarily all the sun-etched furrows seemed to vanish and the two visitors caught a glimpse of how the young H.H. must have been.

Then he laughed and pointed at John Lockley. 'Met this young fellow in fifty-three, if I'm not mistaken. Took to him the very day I saw him, reminded me of his Uncle Edgar, a real pioneer if ever there was one.'

Later, John Lockley told him that he had seen Darlengi. 'The break between us was of my doing. I have mended that break.'

H.H. was delighted. 'That's marvellous news, marvellous.'

Then Anthony asked him what he thought of matters in Zululand.

H.H. nodded sagely and sipped his rum. 'What with the

goings-on in the Transvaal, the annexation, I think it's confused our Zulu king for the time being. He was, and is, mobilising, there's no doubt of that. But now his old enemies, the Boers, are part of that great British Empire, which he does not understand in detail but has a certain concept of. There's no doubt Cetshwayo wants to rule his kingdom in his own way, and my own sources inform me that he is disappointed in Shepstone and wonders why he agreed to the laws which were announced by Shepstone at his coronation.'

Anthony said, 'I thought most Zulus welcomed those new laws. They halted the indiscriminate blood-shedding.'

'Anthony, my boy, they did. But the Zulu king is the Zulu king and now he feels that he should be able to run his own country in his own way.'

'You mean bring back those barbaric practices?'

'Not necessarily, son. I mean, he's decided he doesn't like the fact that he *had* to accept rules placed upon him by what he sees as an outside government.'

John Lockley nodded. 'I understand. He wants to be totally autonomous again. That's worrisome.'

H.H. nodded. 'I'm told Cetshwayo sees himself as the successor to Shaka: that in itself is problematical, showing delusions of grandeur. He is proud, and, I would guess, arrogant. All that eventually adds up to a powder-keg for us.'

'But,' John Lockley protested, 'Darlengi tells me he likes the British.'

H.H. smiled. 'He might, son, he might. But he's building up a huge army, and that our government cannot continue to allow. So who in all the world will tell him he cannot be autonomous; he cannot rule as he wishes; that he must conform to certain standards? We will ... the British. And then, whether he likes us or not will be immaterial.'

They left H.H. the following morning.

He came out to see them off, wearing his sun helmet and standing in the middle of the assortment of adults and children who always surrounded his home.

'Goodbye, John Lockley, come again soon.'

They made good time and when they came to the Tugela, to the pontoon which was tied to a tree on the north side of the water, they dismounted and suddenly saw Darlengi appear over the hill to their right on the far side of the river and come running down to the pontoon.

'Darlengi!' shouted John Lockley.

'What amazing timing,' Darlengi shouted across the water, and Anthony turned to John Lockley. 'I'm always fascinated by his perfect English.'

'Well, he learnt from me, so why wouldn't it be perfect?'

Anthony slapped John Lockley on the back with his good arm. 'Modesty itself, laddie,' he laughed.

They led Chieftain and Horatio on to the pontoon and were soon across the water and greeting Darlengi.

As the two riders walked beside their new companion, leading the horses behind them, Darlengi said, 'To think Uncle Chris is sixty-two: how the years fly.'

'Yes,' answered Anthony, 'and you two fast approach the age of reason, I note.'

Darlengi looked questioningly to John Lockley and John Lockley laughed. 'He means forty, Darlengi. He thinks men have no sense until they reach that magic age.'

Darlengi smiled. 'I will not argue; perhaps he could be right.' Then he shaded his eyes and said, 'I think I see a group of people moving inside the laager wall.'

'What?' exclaimed Anthony. 'And I thought my eyes were good! I can't see them.'

'Darlengi will be right,' John Lockley said. And sure enough a minute or so later, as they walked on, they could make out the figures.

As they drew closer John Lockley laughed. 'It's a whole delegation. Uncle Chris and Aunt Jane, and Phoebe, Fanny and the General; and Tilly and Jemby too, if I'm not mistaken. Heck, Thulmi's there too!'

When the two parties came together there was mirth and shouting and shaking hands and hugging. Anthony even hugged Fanny and it went unnoticed in the general joy about them. Jane kept hold of Darlengi for so long that in the end everyone just stood and waited for her to let go of him.

When finally she released him tears of happiness flowed unchecked down her cheeks. 'At last,' she managed to say.

Then Christopher came to him and holding him close said, 'Son, you're the best birthday gift a man could have.'

And so the glad company wended its collective way back to

the farmhouse, all talking at once, to be greeted by George Travers and most of the household, who had been alerted to the coming arrival.

When the newcomers had settled in everybody took tea and coffee on the front veranda, and as the day waned into the coming night congeniality and contentment enveloped the Tugela farm.

Late that night, as Christopher took his walk, he saw a figure coming by the stable yard. At first he thought it was John Lockley, then he realised who it was and he called, 'Darlengi.'

'Yes, Uncle Chris,' the figure replied as it came to him.

'I'm so glad you're here.'

'I am too.'

'No, I don't mean at the farm, I mean out here, now, for I've something to tell you.'

'Yes?'

Christopher found Darlengi's eyes in the vague night light. 'Son, I feel obliged to tell you that I know about you and Ellen, and so does Aunt Jane. Finally, a few years ago, John Lockley explained how he caused the estrangement between you. And while many years have passed and what is done is done, I want to tell you how sorry I am that you and Ellen were both so alone at that time. I often think that if only I had known I could have helped you both.'

Darlengi was silent and they stood there as the moon went behind a cloud and came back out again.

'Uncle Chris, I fail to see what you could have done. It is far better that you did not know.'

Christopher shook his head. 'I loved Ellen and it broke my heart when she died. I just have to believe it was meant to be.'

Darlengi nodded slowly. 'Yes, I understand. I did not see clearly at that time, I loved her to distraction.'

Christopher placed his arm round the younger man's shoulders and they moved forward together. 'So, we go on, and we live with the living, son. We cannot go back.'

'No, we cannot. But we can still look back, Uncle Chris. Don't misunderstand me, I would not change my life now for anything. I am only sorry that Ellen did not have the chance to live to find the contentment I have found.'

The next morning Christopher entered the breakfast room

to calls of 'Happy Birthday', and two hours later the happy group began gathering in the stable yard for a ride across the property.

John Lockley and Darlengi stood reminiscing about Isiwukulu when Anthony joined them.

'We're talking about a great horse,' remarked John Lockley.

'Like Chieftain, do you mean?' Anthony asked.

'Yes, I must admit, Chieftain is remarkable.' John Lockley explained to Darlengi, 'He fell down the mountainside when Anthony was so badly injured and was hardly scratched. Then he was in the midst of an attack by the amaHlubi and he stayed pretty calm. Mind you, Horatio stood his ground too.'

'Yes,' agreed Darlengi, 'I can see that having a horse that does not panic and shy is of paramount importance to a soldier.'

'Makes the difference between life and death,' stated Anthony.

It was a most successful ride. The farm had large herds of livestock now and fences had appeared and there were even wide tracks leading over much of the property. They saw flocks of birds and many families of vervets, and baboons and hosts of smaller animals such as servals – the wild cat – and porcupines and hares and common duiker. They even came across an extensive herd of buffalo lying on the ground in their habitual mode of shoulder to shoulder.

'Africa,' said John Lockley, waving his arm in a wide arc, 'I love it.'

That night the birthday dinner was a delight.

Matilda had excelled herself and made five delicious courses, starting with a superb game soup and ending with a two-tiered cake that had 'Happy Birthday to a Wonderful Man' written on top. Matilda stood at the door, beaming as the candles were lit and Christopher blew them out to enthusiastic applause. They drank a toast and then called, 'Speech! Speech!' and Christopher rose to his feet. He paused to look around their expectant faces. 'Ladies and gentlemen, I've had a lot of birthdays, but none as happy as this one. I'm so pleased to share it with Jane, my constant and wonderful companion who brings me daily joy, and also my brother-in-law, General James Harrison, and lovely Phoebe and our friends, Colonel Durnford and Miss Fanny Colenso, and you, too, dear Matilda,' he added, looking round to her at the door. Then his eyes rested on Darlengi and John Lockley. 'For the first time in too many years "my family" has come together again. Our lives are busy and full of responsibilities but we have found time to gather together. Thank you all, for these are truly halcyon days to me.'

He sat down amidst as much noise as eight people could make, and Tilly took the cake away to cut it.

It was a splendid night and Christopher did not want to go to bed, so they ended up singing songs around the old harpsichord, which Jane played until the early hours of the morning.

The following day at six o'clock only one of the house party had risen. He made his way down the side steps of the house and passed along the garden wall to go through the gate and down by the stable and beyond to the white headstone glinting in the morning sun.

There was a heavy dew at his feet as he sat on the border of stone that surrounded the grave. He was silent for a time, then he spoke very softly, 'Good morning, Ice Princess. It is a bright, gleaming morning here ... like your soul, wherever it is. I'm sure you know I am reunited with John Lockley and that has gladdened my heart.' He leant forward and touched the headstone.

He remained where he was for a long time, just looking at the grave, and living with his thoughts, then as the sun rose higher in the sky he stood up. 'Sleep in peace, my darling Ellen,' he whispered as he turned away.

He made his way back along the path and there beside the stables stood Tilly. 'I've been waiting, I'd like to talk to you,' she said.

He led her to a seat under some she-oaks outside the stable yard. He brushed away the profusion of cones that had dropped from the trees, and as Tilly sat down said, 'That was a wonderful dinner last night.'

She patted his knee. 'Thank you. Mr Nelson deserved it right enough. He's a proper good man, of which there are few.'

'That's true,' agreed Darlengi. 'Now what is it you want?'

Matilda sighed and then she coughed.

'Tilly? What's wrong?'

'Well, nothing's wrong. But there's something I've been wanting to ask you these dozen years and more. And in the few

531

short times you've been here to see me ... well, I never have ... because I'm always so pleased to see you, and I don't want to spoil your visits.'

Darlengi had a premonition but he met Tilly's eyes. 'Ask me, Tilly. It seems you've kept silent too long.'

Tilly sighed again, and then she began in a great rush of words as if she had to get them all out at once. 'All those years ago, when Miss Ellen was here on her honeymoon, she acted awful strange. She was not herself, no, not at all, and I kept feeling a kind of tension between her and Dr Tallant. Then the day she died she said a lot of very peculiar things about you. I said to her she had never been anything but discourteous towards you, which was true, and that brought on such statements ... well, I wrote them down later so that I would always remember them.'

'And what were they?'

Matilda took a piece of paper from her apron pocket, and looking at it read out the things that Ellen had said about Darlengi all those years ago.

Then she turned to face Darlengi beside her. 'Now, Miss Ellen was crying and very upset. And I've thought a great deal on all this, and kept silent all these years, and then lo and behold where do I find you this morning? Down by her grave, that's where. Now one thing I know for certain is that you cared for her. I recognised it right from the start when you lived at Mimosa, but what did she mean by all that she said to me?'

'Tilly, I will tell you but you must keep your counsel, for there's a good man that could be hurt.'

'You know I will. Look at all the things I don't tell Dirk.' And she laughed gently.

He bent forward to her, looking into her kindly eyes. 'Yes, you are right, of course. I cared for her right from the minute I first saw her. She was beautiful and unattainable ... I thought. And then just before her wedding ... she finally admitted that she had always cared for me.'

'I knew it, I knew it,' whispered Matilda.

Then Darlengi took up her hand and softly told her enough to satisfy the good woman. 'So you see, dear Tilly, what I have told you must remain with us, for I would not have Dr Tallant hurt.'

532

She took him in her large arms and held him. 'Of course it stays with me. Poor Miss Ellen. I understand now. God bless you.'

They made their way back up to the kitchen together, and just before she left him she asked, 'But Thulile is a good wife, isn't she?'

He smiled. 'The best there is.' And Tilly left him with a firm, satisfied nod of her head.

The days passed too swiftly. The evenings found the General teaching Darlengi and Anthony to play golf over in the home paddocks, and phrases such as 'Champion putt!', 'Fine stroke!', 'Don't worry, everyone misses' floated across the paddocks. There were only three holes, which they played over and over, and often, before teeing off, the General lectured on battle techniques while Darlengi and Anthony listened tolerantly.

On the final day Darlengi and John Lockley rode alone to Unondo's kraal. As they came through the mealie field Yangaani was sauntering by. When he saw them, he jumped up and down and ran as fast as his now ancient legs could carry him to Unondo. What a welcome they received. Even the young men who did not know the two newcomers soon realised they were very special and went out and slew an ox and a feast got underway.

There were dancing and merriment and many questions before they handed out the gifts they had brought on a pack horse.

The entire kraal came to see them off, and as they rode down along the Tugela they turned many times in the saddle to wave goodbye.

Later that night, when everyone was gathered in the parlour after dinner, Darlengi stood up and walked to the fireplace. All eyes lifted to him.

'I wish to make one short statement. I once said to Uncle Chris that I was a man-bridge between two races and that I understood neither of them. That is still true, but I want to tell you that when I am with the Nelsons I have never felt I was anything except Darlengi, a son of this house. For here with you . . .' his eyes roved over Christopher and Jane and John Lockley, 'there are no races, only people; human beings.' And now he looked to Phoebe and Anthony and Fanny and the

General. 'For while we accept that reality which is evident in the material world around us, reality is also what one feels ... and I have always felt I was a member of this family.'

Everyone applauded loudly, and no one else said anything, for there was nothing to add.

Later, when some of them started drifting off to bed, John Lockley took Phoebe's hand and drew her on to the front veranda. When they noticed Anthony and Fanny at the other end they smiled and moved around the corner.

Behind them Anthony spoke with Fanny.

'I've been thinking, my darling. I'm forty-seven, and in another three years I could retire. I don't know what I can offer you, Fanny. I'm almost twenty years older than you and you're the daughter of a Bishop; divorce is ugly and people say evil things about divorcees. But I know one thing. I love you, and if you were willing...'

She stood on her tiptoes and kissed him. 'I'm willing, and I'll wait.'

The kindly sound of rain began on the roof above them, and around the corner of the veranda John Lockley took Phoebe in his arms. 'The time has gone so quickly, my darling,' he said.

'Yes, and so you go to Conference Hill on Blood River tomorrow?'

John Lockley nodded. 'Anthony and I travel to join Sir Theopolis. He brings some Boers to meet with a delegation of Zulu chiefs. Darlengi is one of them, so we shall all travel over together.'

'To once again talk about the Boer claims to the Zulu territory?'

'Yes.'

'Hasn't it been discussed to death?'

He took a deep breath. 'You're right, it has. But Sir Henry, the Governor, has requested Theopolis to have a last try at finalising it before he must set up a commission to look into it.'

'Seems to me a waste of time to meet yet again.'

'To me too, but we must attend.'

He bent down and found her mouth, which she offered to him. He held her close and she could feel his hands on her back and in her hair. He lifted his lips from hers, caressing her face with his fingers. 'I love you, Phoebe. Say you love me too.'

534

Say it? She had said it a thousand times, but never aloud before. She looked up at him. It was still unreal to her that he was here holding her. But he was and so she said it. 'I love you, John Lockley Harrison.' And then liking the sound of it she laughed, and said it again. 'I love you, John Lockley Harrison.'

'That night in Newcastle, I . . . wanted you badly.' He ran his right hand through his hair. 'I want you now. And while the army is keeping me away from you, building forts, and you're down in Durban with your training school, fate won't be able to keep me away from you forever, and then I won't be able to hold back. So I think there's only one way we can solve this, Phoebe.'

She was looking up at him, smiling. 'And what's that?'

He knelt down on one knee, and now he was looking up at her. 'Will you marry me, Phoebe McLean?'

They could hear the gentle sound of rain on the roof above their heads. She would remember these moments her whole life.

She seemed to be taking so long to reply that he said, 'Phoebe?'

She knelt down in front of him. 'Oh, yes, John Lockley, I will . . . I will marry you.'

And as they knelt together with the pleasing sound of the cleansing rain surrounding them he leaned into her and kissed her again.

The following morning, Darlengi was walking back along the path which led from Ellen's grave when a voice halted him.

'So you still come here, eh? Still playing lord of the manor? Still tricking the Nelsons after all these years.'

Through the trees came Dirk, resting heavily on a cane. He wore spectacles on his nose and looked a frail, sorry old man. The only remnant of his former self was the look of fire in his eyes.

'Good morning,' said Darlengi, moving off the path to pass by.

Dirk lifted his cane across Darlengi's chest. 'I haven't finished speaking.' And Darlengi, who could have picked the old man up with one hand and thrown him into the bushes, turned resignedly to him. 'Then finish, please, as my breakfast waits.'

'Bloody insolent. Things have deteriorated around here. Blacks are getting uppity. Never allowed it in my day.'

Darlengi nodded. 'That's true, and how you managed to deceive a good man like Christopher Nelson for years is beyond me. Now that George Travers is in charge, men get treated like men.'

'He's a fool, and for the last nine years he's been proving it. And you ... I knew you were an insolent upstart from the minute I laid eyes on your nigger's hide.'

Darlengi's eyes glinted in the morning sun. His voice grew cold and hard. 'And how a kind, decent woman like Matilda can have remained married to a bigot like you all these years is beyond me.'

Dirk was enraged and lifted the cane to strike a blow as Darlengi knocked it away as if it were a matchstick, and the old man overbalanced and fell to the ground.

Darlengi shook his head sadly. 'You will die with your hateful prejudices etched in your mind.'

And he strode away as Dirk called after him, 'Bloody Zulu nigger! We showed you at Blood River and we'll do it again.'

As Darlengi mounted the steps to the house, he paused and looked up into the sky. Then, abruptly, he smiled. Ah well, if he had not run into Dirk the five days would have been just too perfect; and that was not the way of things in this imperfect world. He wiped his long fingers across his brow and entered the breakfast room.

An hour later John Lockley, Darlengi and Anthony departed into the bold African sunlight, as Phoebe and Christopher and Jane and Fanny and the General and Tilly continued to call and wave to them until they disappeared into the distance.

CHAPTER THIRTY-SEVEN

The enduring summer sun of Pietermaritzburg made a bold path from the window across the carpeted floor of the office of the Lieutenant-Governor of Natal to rest upon John Lockley's burnished black boots.

Sir Henry Bulwer leaned his elbows on his desk and fixed his open gaze on his visitor. 'As Cape Governor and High Commissioner Sir Bartle wants to bring in more troops. We have a volatile situation in Zululand now. I'm becoming more concerned myself and believe many of the fears of the colonists are justified. Down in the Cape, Cunynghame, our commander-in-chief, has been replaced by General Thesiger, who will arrive in Cape Town any day now to deal with Chief Sandili and Kreli in the war with the Gaikas and Gcalekas north of King Williamstown. When that's over he might come here.'

He stood up and walked over to the window, looking out on the peaceful town. 'Sir Bartle has accepted the fact that I'm appointing a commission of inquiry to establish the truth about the disputed lands in the Utrecht district, and we'll all be duty bound to act and fix the boundary once and for all when the decision comes in. I don't know what he'll think if the court decides for Cetshwayo. I know he'd like to appease the Transvaal. Mind you, he'll have to ratify, if that's how you decide.'

'Me, sir?'

'Yes, Harrison, that's why I had you travel down here. I want you to be one of the court of inquiry. You know the Zulus, their customs and their language. Besides which, you're fair-minded, as are the others I've chosen.'

'And who are they?'

With a wide smile Sir Henry rose and came round the desk and John Lockley stood up beside him. 'There are three others and they're downstairs. I'd like you to meet them now.'

As they moved to the door the Lieutenant-Governor said, 'I'd like you to stay for dinner if you can, though I know you'll want to visit your relatives while you're here in 'Maritzburg.'

John Lockley smiled. 'And if it's possible to have a couple of days, sir, I'd like to ride down to Durban and see my fiancé.'

The Lieutenant-Governor put his arm round his visitor's shoulder. 'Certainly, my boy, can't stand in the way of love.'

Darlengi stood in the centre of the cattle kraal in the midst of the indunas of the Great Council, ready to read out the message that John Dunn had carried into Ulundi the day before. It had come to John Dunn from Sir Henry Bulwer, the Lieutenant-Governor of Natal.

Cetshwayo lifted his ebony stick in the air. 'After all these years of anger and bloodshed and dispute over the lands between the Drakensburgs and the Mzinyathi and Ncome rivers, the ones the Europeans call the Buffalo and the Blood, there is to be an outcome.'

He pointed with his stick and Darlengi read:

'The Lieutenant-Governor wishes to inform Cetshwayo that he has chosen four men as Commissioners to hold a definitive inquiry into the lands of the Disputed Territory between the Zulus and the Boers.

'These men are: Her Majesty's Attorney-General in Natal, Michael H. Gallwey Esquire; The Acting Secretary for Native Affairs, the brother of Somtseu, John Wesley Shepstone; The Colonial Engineer, Lieutenant-Colonel Anthony Durnford RE and his assistant, Lieutenant-Colonel John Lockley Harrison RE. These men will proceed to Rorke's Drift, the place you call kwaJimu, on the Buffalo River in the Colony of Natal and will open their inquiry on Thursday March the 7th, 1878.

'I ask the King of the Zulu peoples to appoint three or four indunas to put the Zulu cause at this inquiry, as the Transvaal Government shall be represented there by Boer appointees.

'The findings of this Commission will be accepted by this government as binding.

'Signed: Henry Bulwer, Lieutenant-Governor of the British Colony of Natal.'

'So,' said Cetshwayo, moving the solid bulk of his body across his seat and turning to John Dunn, 'I have a message for you to return to Sir Henry Bulwer.'

'Just a minute, my king,' Dunn said, 'I will get my lead pencil and paper.'

'You will not need it. Simply send this message: I am very glad to hear what you say. I shall now be able to sleep.'

And the indunas, realising the humour in this, gave a rumble of laughter.

Now Cetshwayo's alert brown eyes passed over his gathered chieftains. 'Who will represent our people and our claims?'

A hubbub of voices rose as each man gave his opinion. Then the king quelled the noise by raising his ebony stick high in the air. 'I, as your king, shall choose one, you as my chiefs can choose two, and then I will choose a fourth who goes purely to listen . . . just to listen . . . for me.'

Now he trained his gaze on Darlengi. 'You, Induna Darlengi, are my first choice, for not only do you speak their language but you are like the still waters of the Umvoloosi when no wind blows, you can stay calm and will present our arguments well. Now, who else?'

After a vote, Meleseli, an important, aged induna announced the choices. 'It is decided that Uhamu, the king's half-brother who accompanied Darlengi to the disputed territory before, will go again. And with them uSicwelewele, the leader of the youthful inGobamakhosi regiment.'

During the proceedings a sullen Intongalu had watched with disdain. He was not allowed to vote since he had come home dishonoured from the previous journey into the disputed territory. Cetshwayo had severely reprimanded him and taken a hundred of his cattle as a fine. He was only allowed to sit in council and listen now.

'There is one more thing,' Cetshwayo added, standing up to make his statement. 'I want all the missionaries removed from Zululand. A Christian Zulu is a Zulu ruined. For my whole life these people have come into this country without permission and attempted to crush my people's customs as the python does to the bushbuck. This is my country, not theirs! I will no longer tolerate these people. I shall send an impi to move across my land and tell these people to get out. The man I wish to lead this impi . . .'

Suddenly there was an uproar outside the main kraal fence and women began to scream. Children ran into the cattle kraal and began yelling and there was confusion all about. Someone shouted, 'The uThulwana are attacking the inGobamakhosi! They kill each other!'

These two regiments belonged to the two indunas just chosen to go with Darlengi: Uhamu and uSicwelewele.

The chieftains rose to their feet and rushed as a body out through the main gate to see a battle raging between the two regiments who had been camped outside on the Ulundi plain near the tents of Chief John Dunn's men. It was impossible to get near them or to stop them; all the indunas could do was watch as they trampled John Dunn's encampment in their rage. The noise was horrendous with the people of the Ulundi kraal shouting and screaming as the warriors continued their bloody dispute.

When the scene of anger finally calmed there were seventy-five dead warriors and twice as many carrying wounds. They lay in and about John Dunn's wagons, and many were draped over the crushed tents.

After numerous questions and much examination it was finally ascertained that some of the unmarried younger members of the inGobamakhosi had begun a stick fight with the older married members of the uThulwana; there had been angry statements made about the celibacy of the young warriors and it had turned to a bloody rage which swept through John Dunn's camp.

The king was furious. He walked though the dead bodies. 'What is this that we kill each other? Are the Zulus turning on themselves like the first chick of the tawny eagle does to its brother?' He now made a decision. 'I cannot allow the chieftains of these two regiments to leave them now. Both bodies of warriors need a strong hand. We must choose two new indunas to accompany Darlengi. Uhamu and uSicwelewele must remain to control their men.'

He waved his arm high in the air. 'Come, my indunas, we must return to the council and vote again, and then we bury our own.'

As he passed back through the high kraal gates he shook his

head and turned to Darlengi who walked at his side. 'My warriors are like elephant bulls caged together. They need a war!'

Eight weeks later, a light rain was falling on the tents that surrounded the stone mission house at Rorke's Drift, about half a mile from the Buffalo River valley.

Inside the house, in the first room off the small veranda, John Lockley lifted his eyes to his companions. They had been here for five weeks and the Swedish missionary, the Reverend Otto De Witt, had been kind enough to lend the members of the commission this room to work in. Thus, while they had slept and eaten in the tents outside, they had conducted their court of inquiry indoors.

Rorke's Drift had been a lonely trading station until the original owner James Rorke died in late 1875. The house had not been altered by the missionary, but he had turned James Rorke's barn into a chapel and had named the rocky hill behind it the Oskarberg in honour of the King of Sweden.

'So,' said Michael Gallwey, who had presided over the hearings, 'Mr Shepstone, you were saying about the Boer forgeries?'

John Shepstone looked around at his three companions. 'We've read every document produced by the four representatives of the Transvaal and listened to the verbal claims and refutations of both sides. We've been here five weeks and we've been very thorough. I believe that many of the documents presented by the Transvaal are fakes.' He held a discoloured paper in the air. 'This shows Mpande's mark of a cross ceding most of the territory along Blood River and is witnessed by a whole Boer commando of twenty-five men and no Zulus. And the document which told of the meeting at Nodwengu between King Mpande, Theopolis Shepstone and Cetshwayo on the sixteenth of March eighteen sixty-one is a patent forgery, as we know for a fact that Sir Theopolis did not arrive there until May the ninth.'

Anthony patted a pile of papers in the middle of the table. 'I think we are very sceptical about the validity of the constant additions and alterations made to many of the original Boer papers, aren't we?'

'I am,' said John Lockley. 'They're full of discrepancies and

I've just been re-reading this one.' He tapped on a yellowed document in front of him. 'It's signed by Cornelius Van Rooyen, a Boer farmer, and says that Cetshwayo granted him four hundred thousand acres for fifty head of cattle fourteen years ago. And yet the Zulus expressly state that Cetshwayo says no such bargain took place. That Cetshwayo distinctly remembers a gift of fifty head of cattle but it was made to him so that he would not slay Van Rooyen and his farmers after they finally handed the Zulu fugitive Mtonga over to him. The Zulus asked why Cetshwayo would have been so stupid as to have made such an impossibly poor bargain. And I agree.'

'And Cetshwayo wasn't even king at the time,' added Anthony, 'so in essence he didn't have the authority to enter into such a covenant with Van Rooyen anyway.'

The president of the hearings, Michael Gallwey, sighed. 'We have ascertained without doubt that the land originally belonged to the Zulus; the question has been whether in fact there was ever any concession of territory to the Transvaal Boers.'

The rain on the roof increased and a wind came up through the door lifting the papers on the table and making the flames in the lamps quiver. John Lockley rose and closed the door on the dark wet night.

Gallwey's pale hand lifted for attention. 'We've been told that our findings are to be unanimous. We've done all we can here. We'll return to 'Maritzburg tomorrow to write up our report and make our recommendation. Before we leave here, though, I will ask you to please raise your hand and say "Aye" if you see a case for the Boer claim.'

There was utter silence and no hands raised.

'All right. We will address all this formally once we're back in the capital.'

The following morning the rain had gone and the sun was shining when for the last time Michael Gallwey stood on the veranda of the mission house and, holding the thin rail, addressed the representatives of the Transvaal delegation and of the Zulus.

Otto De Witt's young children, who had taken a great interest in all the people who had camped here for many weeks, sat on the steps looking up at the President of the hearings as he spoke. 'Thank you for attending this court of inquiry. We have been painstaking and you have all been patient. Our findings and recommendation will now be placed in writing and given to Sir Henry Bulwer, the Lieutenant-Governor of Natal, who will forward them on to Sir Henry Bartle Edward Frere, the Cape Governor. The Transvaal Government and the King of the Zulus will be notified of the findings in due course. This hearing is now closed.'

People began drifting away and Henrique Shepstone, Sir Theopolis's son, who had appeared for the Transvaal, much to Darlengi's surprise, now came over to his Uncle John.

'All over at last. We'll leave for the Transvaal tonight. Do you have a message for father?'

John Shepstone frowned. 'Only that I hope he's in good health.'

'Nothing else?' asked his nephew.

'Nothing else. Tell him, he'll be informed in due course.'

Darlengi and John Lockley moved aside together. They had spent many hours alone in the last five weeks when the court was in recess. They had even been hunting for food a few times.

'So when do you leave, my brother?' asked Darlengi.

'I'll leave this afternoon. I have to get over to Fort Pine.' He pointed to the north-west. 'Up there.'

'I know,' smiled Darlengi. 'Our spies tell us you are building some forts along the Transvaal and Zululand borders.'

John Lockley smiled in return. 'There was some thought that we would have to send troops into the Transvaal to back up Shepstone, but that need seems to have passed.'

'And the forts along our border?'

'There aren't many, Darlengi, but the few there are are being raised because the governments of the Cape and Natal are worried about Cetshwayo. It's as simple as that. I know he hasn't washed his spear as king yet, and I'm afraid there are others who are aware of it.'

'Yes, I am told the newspapers of Durban and Pietermaritzburg carry stories which build fear of the Zulus in the colonists' hearts.'

John Lockley looked closely at his companion. 'Are they right to do so?'

Darlengi's gaze found his brother's. 'There is no doubt that Cetshwayo has grown confident in his role as king. He has built up his army until it is as strong as it ever was . . . stronger even. The whole structure of Zululand is based on regiments of warriors. I think my king was ready to wage war against the Boers, and then suddenly the Transvaal became British.' Darlengi smiled. 'You confused him with that.'

'Are you saying he has an army with no one to wage war against?'

Darlengi thought of the recent debacle at the Ulundi kraal. 'Unfortunately, Lockley, I'm saying just that. We are a warrior race with only ourselves to fight.'

John Lockley closed his eyes briefly. 'There is a new Secretary of State for the Colonies in London. Lord Carnarvon resigned. This new man is Sir Michael Hicks Beach and I don't think he's as keen on a federated southern Africa, so British policy might change. They might be willing to leave Cetshwayo alone.'

'Wishful thinking, my brother, for while Cetshwayo does not yet realise it, I cannot see how you British can allow him to keep a standing army of forty-five thousand men, divided from you by the width of the Tugela River. Especially as you make rules that say he cannot fight the Boers and he cannot fight the Swazis and his other traditional enemies.'

'So,' John Lockley said, 'unfortunately that's why I'd better go and check on my forts.'

'Yes, and I will return to the king and the kraals of Zululand.'

They walked a few paces together and John Lockley put his arm around Darlengi's shoulder. 'Before I leave I have something to ask you.'

'Yes.'

'Would it be possible for you to come to the Greytown mission on the last day of October?'

'I think so, why?'

'Phoebe and I are getting married there, on the thirty-first, Thursday. And well . . . I want you to be my best man.'

Darlengi's smile was so broad that his white teeth gleamed in the sunlight. 'Surely surely,' he said, slapping his brother on the back. Then as if they were boys again they both burst out laughing.

CHAPTER THIRTY-EIGHT

It was a golden spring day. Flocks of birds swarmed overhead, a gentle breeze wafted down from the mountains, and the trees and grass gleamed an emerald green. Looking out of the window of the mission house Phoebe thought she had never seen a more perfect day.

Mr and Mrs Bradley, the missionaries, had been wonderful. Jane and Christopher were staying in the house and they had given Phoebe her old room which she was sharing with Fanny. In their spare room they had put two beds, one for Matilda and one for Mannie, who had insisted on coming. She was seventy-seven and worried with rheumatism, but as she said, 'I brought that boy to Africa and I'm not goin' to miss his wedding day; missed the first one; but won't miss this.'

Phoebe's nurses were all here, and Coral-June and Patricia and Diana all slept on the side veranda which had been covered in with great lengths of canvas.

Phyllis May and Graham had responded in their own marvellous fashion and were being host to many, including John Lockley, and Anthony, who was a groomsman. He had recently been showing the country to the newly arrived Lieutenant-General Thesiger and had come for the wedding in company with Pat Boehm, the only one of John Lockley's old friends from the army who was still in Natal, and now a major on the staff of the Governor.

When Darlengi arrived he had said he would be happy to stay at the mission kraal but John Lockley insisted he stay under the same roof with him. So he moved into John Lockley's room. John Lockley had brought H.H. down from Mount Ilvenweni. The elderly trader had found a suit in a trunk, which he fitted into just as he had forty years before.

Thulmi and Umslopagas had found their way to the mission

and made up the ranks, along with all the folk of the mission kraal.

On the morning of the wedding day, Darlengi, John Lockley, Anthony and Pat Boehm went riding. Pat had heard about Darlengi, but he, like all who met Darlengi for the first time, was astounded. Natal was almost alive with a tangible fear of the Zulus; he had seen and met quite a few on his travels with the army, and Darlengi appeared as far removed from the Zulus he had met as the Governor was. As they rode along Pat turned in the saddle and asked, 'Darlengi, I don't mean to be rude, and forgive me if you think me so, but don't you find it hard to deal with your warrior brothers? You're so refined and aren't they ... well, savage?'

Darlengi smiled. 'I do forgive you, Pat, and the answer is very involved, but I'll try to simplify it. Yes, many of my warrior brothers are what you term savage, ruled by superstition and custom that at times I find repugnant. But whilst that is so, they live a plain, uncomplicated life, which carries with it none of the burdens of civilisation and that in itself is appealing. There was a time in my life when I was discontent, feeling as if I belonged nowhere, but now I know that I am who I am; and when I am with Lockley and his family and his friends, I am this Darlengi, the one you see; and while in my psyche I do not change, I do, in behaviour and action, when I am back with my own people. So to answer your question: I can deal with all of you: British or Zulu.'

'Amazing,' replied Pat.

Later, when they rested in a quiet wood beneath the green hills, they talked about many things. Here was an articulate Zulu induna and the men could not help but take advantage of the situation. Anthony lifted his hand to shade his eyes and looked at Darlengi. 'I have always believed that the Zulus don't want to invade Natal. I gained this view from my extensive travels throughout the country and of talking to many people, both Zulu and others. I still feel that way. Am I right?'

'Anthony, are you asking me as a man who lives in Natal or as a soldier?'

'I must be honest, Darlengi, I've been a professional soldier since I was eighteen, so ...' He shrugged. 'I suppose I ask as a soldier.'

'I appreciate your honesty,' Darlengi answered, smiling. 'So I must request you all to agree that anything said here today is not passed on to your superiors.' He looked at John Lockley, who responded, 'Will you promise that too?'

Darlengi hesitated momentarily. 'Yes.'

'I agree,' replied John Lockley.

'So do I,' said Anthony.

'Me too,' added Pat.

'In that case, Anthony,' Darlengi replied, bringing his dark eyes up to meet Anthony's light ones, 'I don't think Cetshwayo has ever really considered invading Natal. While he does not conceive the real vastness of it, he is very impressed by the Empire upon which the sun never sets. He also appreciates you as a magnificent warrior race. He is not a fool, so you are definitely not his first choice for a foe. In fact, he believes the English are fair and has always liked them, as John Lockley knows.'

His brother nodded. 'I do.' Then he leaned forward to Darlengi. 'But I think the government is fearful that Cetshwayo's impies are too close, too threatening. Look, Darlengi, we're already fighting Chief Sekukuni, who has risen up against us in the Transvaal. There's no doubt our superiors feel that if your impies ever did cross the Tugela, then other tribes already resident here, in their hundreds of thousands, would rise up too, and then it would be a bloodbath.'

Darlengi shrugged. 'Of course I understand that, Lockley.' Then he looked round all their faces. 'We know that General Thesiger, who fought the recent Ninth Kaffir War down in the Cape, has been in Pietermaritzburg since August. We have also been informed that Sir Bartle Frere has arrived. So now it is my turn to ask, do you intend to invade Zululand?'

'*Touché!*' exclaimed John Lockley.

'We haven't been informed of anything,' replied Anthony, 'but I will say just this, in confidence, here today. The colonists cry out in fear of you, Sir Bartle is listening, and Thesiger is here.'

John Lockley nodded slowly.

And Pat Boehm sighed.

They left the topic there; for they all knew what had really been said.

As they rode back into town they left the depressing subject of politics and were more like four men simply out on a day's ride. There was banter, followed by laughter and talk of the afternoon's coming event.

But later, when John Lockley and Darlengi were alone in their room getting ready for the wedding, Darlengi turned from where he stood at the window and faced round to his brother. 'Lockley, I should tell you that Cetshwayo grows impatient about the findings of the boundary commission. You sat at Rorke's Drift five months ago and still we have not been informed of your findings.'

'Darlengi, I don't know why Sir Bartle Frere has withheld our decision all this time. I can tell you that we wrote up our report, and on the twentieth of June we handed it to Sir Henry Bulwer to send on to Sir Bartle. He's had it since then.'

Darlengi nodded. 'I see.' He was silent as he looked back through the window and watched two children climbing the tree beside Graham's blacksmith shop, then he said, 'I am an intimate of Cetshwayo, and he has no great desire to fight you . . . the British; but there are certainly a number of our younger warriors clamouring to do so. You know we are mobilising, as we know you are, and we all know what that implies. If it precipitates into war, then, Lockley, you and I . . . will be on different sides.'

John Lockley put down the shirt he was holding and crossed the room to stand beside Darlengi. 'Yes . . . I know.'

They both looked down at their arms where the scars gleamed in the rays of the sun: the exact same shape on each man's arm: the shape of the tip of an assegai, made when they were mere boys over twenty years earlier. Then at the same moment they raised their eyes. They stood there in front of the open window with the sunlight delineating their profiles, both thinking the unthinkable. They had never appeared more alike in their lives as they surveyed each other's face. John Lockley was the first to speak. He shook his head. 'I could not fight you.'

'And I could not fight you,' replied his brother.

They remained there silently holding each other's gaze, then John Lockley turned round to the window, and grasping the sill looked out. 'There are forty-five thousand of you and a few thousand of us. We'll just have to count on the fact that we don't run into each other.'

Now Darlengi too faced the window, and slapped his soul mate on the back. 'Remember when Yangaani used to say I was too white?'

'And old Veldbron used to say I was too black.'

Darlengi smiled sadly. 'It's a damn shame there weren't a lot more like us ... more white-blacks and more black-whites.'

'Maybe in a hundred years,' John Lockley said.

'I don't wish to appear cynical, but maybe in two hundred years,' was Darlengi's reply.

And then, as if they were sixteen again, abruptly John Lockley laughed, 'Oh hell, it's all mad,' and he grabbed his brother's shoulders and mock punched his solar plexus; and Darlengi responded with a mock punch to the jaw and so they sparred, leaping round the room and shouting. They ended up grappling with each other and falling down wrestling. They laughed and laughed until they were exhausted, making so much noise that Graham and H.H. and Anthony came in to see what was wrong.

As four o'clock drew near and Phoebe stood before her mirror with Jane and Fanny and Phyllis May all crowded into the bedroom and fussing over her gown and veil, she could not help but think she was the luckiest woman in all Africa. She had turned thirty-two two weeks ago and had been in love with John Lockley her whole life. She had waited: and she had won.

'You look absolutely beautiful,' said Fanny.

'Oh you do, you do,' concurred Jane, kissing her on the cheek.

And she did. Her burnished curls were tied on top of her head and a Nottingham lace veil, which Jane had specially imported from England, hung from her crown down over her shoulders to the floor. A strip of tiny yellow silk roses ran round the rim of the veil and across her forehead. Her dress was cream silk; very simple, with a yoke of the same small yellow roses running across her bodice and down the sleeves.

At the hour of four everyone was in the small chapel, and the people from the mission kraal filled it to overflowing and spilled out all over the yard.

Christopher waited in the small parlour and when Phoebe appeared he smiled encouragingly at her. She looked perfectly beautiful. As he watched her coming towards him, he could not help thinking of that other bride he had walked to the altar all those years before. Momentarily Phoebe blurred and it was Ellen's captivating green eyes he looked into. He gave a short, sad sigh and refocused on the lovely woman in front of him.

'Oh, Uncle Christopher,' Phoebe said with that unique light that has shone in the eyes of brides since the beginning, 'I'm suddenly quite nervous.'

'So's John Lockley,' Christopher laughed, and then she laughed too, with that infectious sound from her girlhood that made Jane and Fanny, coming behind her, begin to laugh as well.

On Christopher's arm the bride glided down the steps and across the yard. The kraal people were waving and laughing and she answered most of them by name. They crossed under the wide branches of the acacia tree and advanced through the happy smiling faces to the chapel door. There, on the two small steps, stood Lila and Tokwa and Fantasia, and then from behind them someone appeared and stood waiting.

Phoebe halted abruptly; she could not believe what she saw.

It was Victoria standing at the chapel door!

'Mummy! Mummy!' she called as she left Christopher's side and ran forward into her mother's arms. 'Oh, how wonderful, how perfectly wonderful.'

And as mother and daughter embraced in a joyous extended greeting, all the people about them began to applaud with delight.

'Oh dear,' said Victoria when her daughter finally released her, 'we're in tears already.'

Christopher gave Victoria his handkerchief and she dabbed her daughter's eyes. 'It doesn't matter, darling, you still look beautiful.'

Phoebe was ecstatic. 'I can't believe you're here.'

'My darling, it was John Lockley's idea, but now that I'm back, I'm back to stay. Your grandmother understands. She has Leah, and she knew my heart was here, with you ... and Africa.'

Christopher coughed. 'We have a wedding to attend.' And, extending his arm for Phoebe to take, he walked her down the tiny fifteen-foot-long aisle with the five pews on either side filled to capacity with the delighted congregation.

When Phoebe saw John Lockley standing in his dress

uniform at the altar she held back the tears. She was about to marry the man she had thought she could never have; and out of nowhere, her mother had appeared. It was all too wonderful.

Just before John Lockley gave her his hand, she caught Darlengi's eye. He winked and she smiled. Then she seemed to be in a dream and the Reverend Bradley was reading the marriage ceremony and she was saying, 'I do,' and John Lockley was placing a wide band of gold upon her finger. Aunt Jane, Phyllis May and Victoria were crying, and H.H. was laughing, and Anthony and Darlengi were slapping her husband on the back, and people were calling greetings and little Shinu was jumping up and down, and Treedy and Mary, who had grown tall, were handing her flowers, and Phoebe McLean Harrison's whole world was complete.

The wedding breakfast was laid out on trestle tables under the acacia tree. The mission band played, with Thulmi back in his old position vigorously striking the triangle, and John Lockley and Phoebe danced while the home kraal people sang marvellous tribal songs.

Later John Lockley and Christopher and Darlengi all made splendid speeches, and Graham and Phyllis May and Fantasia and Jenny kept filling glasses and passing food. Fanny danced with Anthony, in the midst of dozens of dark swaying forms, and then, as night fell, Jenny and Thulmi and Umslopagas lit the lanterns that the kraal menfolk had hung in the trees earlier in the day. The party continued, and a warm, comfortable spring night settled around the celebration.

The talk and laughter was at its height when Phoebe left her conversation with Patricia and Coral June and walked alone into the middle of the yard to stand under the lanterns hanging in the acacia tree. The children noticed her first and came and sat at her feet as she stood there in her wedding dress with the flickering light gleaming on her hair. All around people fell quiet as they saw her, and a hush descended. She lifted her arms and slowly brought them down to where she joined her hands in front of her, then she began: 'Perhaps it is unusual for a bride to make a speech on her wedding day . . .'

'Not here,' called John Lockley, his arm round Darlengi's shoulders. 'We'll make our own rules, my darling.' And a murmur of agreement rolled around the people gathered.

'Thank you, sweetheart,' Phoebe replied as she took a minute to look around all their faces, to gaze into their eyes in the lantern light. 'Today I want to remember clearly all my life. I have married the man I love. I am surrounded by the people I love, and my mother has appeared. It's all some kind of miracle for me. The generosity of the Bradleys has been overwhelming, as too has been that of our true friends, the Mullers.' She looked down at the children, their cheerful, upturned faces watching her. 'This mission was my home for many years. It is, perhaps, where my soul resides.' She gestured down past the house. 'For my father lies here and I feel his presence with me now, this very minute.' Then she smiled an ethereal smile and finished with the words that all of them were to remember for many years to come. 'This is really an ecumenical gathering of the spirit. My dear people of my home kraal are with me, my family and my friends are with me, black and white, all of different creeds: people celebrating joyously, shoulder to shoulder; no judging, no discord, but true harmony of the souls, as Africa . . . as the world . . . should be. Thank you, each and every one, for this jubilant, memorable day.'

Then she turned and walked into John Lockley's arms as a thunderous applause and loud cheering and shouting began.

As John Lockley wrapped her in his arms he said, 'How truly blessed I am to have found you at last.'

Half an hour later the bride and groom were about to depart back to the Mullers' house in a Cape cart. They stood near the giant aloe at the gate of the mission while Christopher and Graham and Thulmi held lanterns, and well-wishers were all around, when someone shouted, 'A rider comes.' And sure enough, along the track that led into Greytown they heard the approach of a horse.

As he arrived at the gate, his red coat shone in the lantern glow. 'Is this the mission of the Reverend Bradley?'

'Yes,' called the cleric.

'And are Lieutenant-Colonels Durnford and Harrison, and Major Boehm here?'

'Yes,' they replied in unison.

'All leave has been cancelled. You're all to report to General Thesiger's headquarters in Pietermaritzburg by sunset on the second.'

552

John Lockley turned to Phoebe. 'That means I'll have to leave tomorrow.'

'Oh, no!'

And then, as he clasped Phoebe in his arms, he raised his eyes. There in the lantern light behind his uncle and aunt stood Darlengi. His eyes locked with his brother's while Darlengi slowly shook his head.

Forty miles to the south in Pietermaritzburg, a tall, almost gaunt gentleman of fifty years, whose pleasant face was hidden behind a rounded spade beard, was being addressed by Sir Bartle Frere.

'Lieutenant-General Thesiger, it's all here in these records.' He tapped on a large pile of papers in front of him. 'This year we've had numerous reports of out-of-hand slayings of people in Zululand. In April Cetshwayo precipitately turned all the missionaries out. In July, there was the case of two wives of a Zulu chief, Sihayo, who fled into Natal and were followed across the Tugela, kidnapped and returned to Zululand where they were summarily murdered. In September all the German settlers around Luneburg up north of Utrecht were ordered off their farms by Cetshwayo. And up on the Pongola there's a Swazi freebooter called Umbilini. Right now he and his brigands are terrorising everyone in the vicinity. They've been raiding Boer farmers and Swazi and even Zulu kraals. Just two weeks ago he savagely raided Swazi kraals, burning them, and carrying off women and children and killing a number of men. And he was given permission to live there by Cetshwayo.'

General Thesiger uncrossed his legs and leaned forward to tap his fingers on the desk between them. His brow creased in thought as Sir Bartle went on, 'Confederation of the southern African states *must* include Zululand. An absolutely independent, uncivilised nation with a standing army of well over forty thousand men, in the charge of a man who at a whim could send them invading anywhere across two hundred miles of frontier, is finally intolerable.'

The General sighed. 'Yes, you're probably right. Anyway, I've cancelled all leave, and brought the men back to 'Maritzburg. Colonel Wood with five companies of the Ninetieth is still up in Utrecht, and I have only six battalions of infantry in Natal. I've already requested two more and also two companies of Engineers. I've been studying what maps we have, though we've virtually none in detail of Zululand itself. But it seems to me that if I can get five columns in position, three offensive and two supporting, at various points on the border, then I could mount an invasion of Zululand quite swiftly and successfully.'

Sir Bartle nodded. 'Unfortunately I'm not receiving the support from London that I want ... not at all. Our new Colonial Secretary, Hicks Beach, is being positively difficult. The last message I received says...' he turned and lifted a paper from the shelf behind him, 'and I quote: "Her Majesty's Government are not prepared to comply with a request for reinforcement of troops." He goes on, "We hope that by the exercise of prudence and by meeting the Zulus in a spirit of forbearance and reasonable compromise, it will be possible to avert the very serious evil of a war with Cetshwayo."' He lifted his eyes to his companion.

'So what are you going to do?' asked the General.

'I'll continue to try and convince him otherwise. And if I can't I'll have to demand reinforcements simply to ensure the safety of the colonists if we're invaded. But Hicks Beach, sadly, is not Carnarvon.'

'That's true, and I doubt you'll convince him. Remember, it looks as if he has an unavoidable war in Afghanistan bearing down on him. He doesn't want one here as well.'

'That may be so,' replied Sir Bartle in clipped tones. 'But I'll not lose sight of my dream. There's no land set aside for the natives in the whole of southern Africa, except here in Natal, which is grossly overcrowded. They've been totally ignored in the Transvaal and most of the Cape. I need a centralised government, then I can stop the continual warfare between the tribes and begin to redistribute the land. And to do it successfully I must bring Cetshwayo and his hordes to heel.'

There was a rap on the door and both men turned to it.

'Yes?'

An aide entered, carrying an envelope. 'This has just arrived from London. Marked urgent; for Lieutenant-General Frederick Thesiger.'

'Thank you.' The General took it and scanned the paper contained inside then looked up at his companion. He had difficulty speaking. 'My father's dead.'

'Oh, I'm terribly sorry,' Sir Bartle said, rising and coming round the desk to put his hand comfortingly on his companion's shoulder. Then a thought crossed his mind and he said softly, 'That means you've inherited the title. You're Lord Chelmsford now.'

'Yes,' his companion answered with tears in his eyes. 'I suppose I am.'

Back in the little bedroom in the Mullers' house in Greytown the moon threw a silver beam through the window to capture in its light the two people who faced each other across the room.

John Lockley stood bare-chested.

Phoebe smiled and moved towards him, her body covered in dusky pink lace, her burnished hair brushed out and falling to her shoulders. 'So, my husband, we only have one night together.'

He looked at her: little Phoebe grown into a voluptuous, desirable woman. 'Yes, my darling, just one night. I love you, Phoebe.' He raked his fingers through his hair and then extended his hand to her. 'I can picture you now on the *Regent Three*, with your bright eyes and your infectious laugh. I can see you as a schoolgirl in your long white dress in Cape Town and as a teenage girl at the Tugela farm; and, too, as the young woman on the veranda at Bishopstowe when I came back from Ceylon . . . and now, I see you as my wife. Perhaps I've always loved you.'

She came to him and took his face between her hands. 'I know I've always loved you.'

And as the sensuous ripple of love and excitement extended up through her body to tingle in her very fingertips upon his face, he bent to kiss her waiting mouth.

CHAPTER THIRTY-NINE

It was late afternoon and the rain had stopped. It had been raining heavily on and off since the British advance into Zululand on 11 January.

A breeze was drifting from the flooded Buffalo River towards the little mission house at Rorke's Drift where the boundary commission had made their decision for the Zulus and against the Boers nine months before. John Lockley stood on the veranda, where all semblance of the missionaries had gone, though the missionary himself, Otto De Witt, had been reluctant to leave and had only been accompanied away this morning. The house was now a hospital, and the chapel a commissariat store. Tents and men and oxen and wagons and the accoutrements of the soldiers were all about.

They had been moving supplies in wagons up to Lord Chelmsford's camp at Isandlwhana Mountain all day; a slow, wearying process.

John Lockley had seen Phoebe two weeks before in Greytown, where she and Coral-June were organising a military hospital. She intended moving on to her second hospital in Newcastle at some time and he didn't know when he would see her again. She had been brave when he took her in his arms to say goodbye. He pictured her face and remembered her last words. 'My darling, please come back safely to me.' They had parted with smiles on their faces, but each knew that it was only a show of unconcern.

He was aware now that Phoebe was his lasting love; his adult love. He had cared deeply for Jettama, but she had been the passionate love of his youth; and Kate? He now acknowledged that poor Kate had been merely passion. He sometimes wondered what had become of Tom King; there was a rumour that he had gone to Australia. His father, Jonas, was a decent old man and had written John Lockley a letter of abject apology for the actions of his son.

John Lockley crossed his arms in thought and moved over to lean on the veranda upright. Fires were appearing between the tents, and the men were organising themselves for the night on the damp ground.

John Lockley's own men and two units of mounted Natal Natives were waiting six miles west at Robson's Drift. They were part of Anthony's support column, and John Lockley had ridden over when he received word that Anthony was coming up from Krans Kop near Middle Drift with some of his Durnford's Horse, as his own NNC, Natal Native Contingent, were known. John Lockley smiled to himself. Anthony amazed him. He had raised a native army of some four thousand men, all of whom were loyal to him, the Basutos and Putini being especially devoted. Mind you, he and Anthony treated all men under their command the same; unlike some other commanders.

John Lockley recalled the day in Pietermaritzburg when they had been organising their support column and he and Anthony had addressed all ranks. Anthony had said: 'In this column, we expect that every man will do his duty. I will treat you fairly and so too will my second-in-command, Lieutenant-Colonel Harrison, and all other officers. In return we expect you to treat us fairly. There will be no flogging and no corporal punishment. Those types of discipline merely degrade. There is one thing we will not tolerate and that is the use of the word "nigger". I never want to hear it said, and it will be a most serious offence to use the word.' He had raised his good arm to heaven as he finished with the words, 'At all times we must be able to rely on one another. I trust each one of you to give me your best.'

The cheering had been deafening.

The orders to cross into Zululand had been given thirty days after the ultimatum had been read to Darlengi and the other Zulu chiefs near the old Settlers' Drift on the Natal side of the Tugela River. John Lockley had been there as an interpreter. It was the day that the decision on the disputed territory had finally been revealed to the Zulus.

He thought of it now. It was the last time he had seen Darlengi. Fifty attendants had accompanied the three chiefs

557

and eleven subordinates. The indunas all arrived wearing mutyas of monkey skin, lion-claw necklaces and ivory bracelets; each with his bone knife – to scrape his face in the heat – tucked in the top of his mutya. Darlengi had stood beside Chief John Dunn throughout the reading, which had taken place underneath a wide canvas canopy slung between trees.

John Shepstone read out the award in English, then he and John Lockley translated it into Zulu. The Zulus were naturally pleased with the findings, for the territory was returned to them; though Sir Bartle Frere had added that any Boers who opted to remain living in the area would come under the jurisdiction of the British resident in Utrecht and not Cetshwayo.

They broke for luncheon, and in the afternoon John Shepstone read a second long message from the High Commissioner, Sir Bartle. It was read first in English, and John Lockley watched his brother's face as the points were announced. Darlengi was immobile but the tightening of the muscles of his jaw announced to his brother what he thought. Then John Lockley translated the message into Zulu and the other chieftains turned to Darlengi with growing apprehension on their faces.

There were nine main points in the message, two to be complied with by the end of the month, and the other seven within thirty days. These were followed by a number of reforms. It took some hours to read and translate. The demands made would reduce Cetshwayo's powers to such an extent that even as John Lockley reached the fourth point, which was in essence the disbanding of the Zulu army, he knew the Zulu king would never comply.

When the Zulu deputation was about to leave, John Lockley took Darlengi aside.

'It would seem that Sir Bartle has decided to bring your king to heel. He's totally committed to a federation of southern Africa. But I know for a fact that he doesn't have the sanction of the home government. I was at Government House with Anthony just before I came here and we know he's received repeated warnings against conflict with you. Hicks Beach deprecates it.'

Darlengi shook his head. 'Hicks Beach is in England, my brother, and Sir Bartle is in charge here.' Then he rested his hand on John Lockley's shoulder. 'There are many young men on both sides who will greet the news with joy. The Zulus are ready for a war; and, to be truthful, want one. It is just ironic that it is you we fight.'

John Lockley nodded his head. 'Yes.'

'I go home, Lockley, to deliver the message to Cetshwayo . . . and then no doubt, to begin conducting war rituals.'

They said no more, they had said it all weeks ago in the little bedroom at the Mullers'. They clasped hands in a sustained grasp and hugged each other briefly before they turned in opposite directions.

As John Lockley remembered all this he left the veranda of the hospital at Rorke's Drift and headed down towards the tents. He had not gone far when he heard a call from behind him.

'Colonel! Colonel!' It was little Shakes, the youngest drummer boy with the 24th Regiment. He was a nine-year-old army orphan who would join as a regular when he turned seventeen. John Lockley smiled as the child ran up to him. 'Yes, Shakes, what is it?'

'Reckon as there's men comin', sir. See'd them wiv me own eyes from that old Oskarberg.'

'Why, Shakes, what good eyes you have.'

The child smiled widely, glowing at the compliment.

Then John Lockley saw Lieutenant Chard of his Royal Engineers hailing him. 'Lookouts tell us Colonel Durnford's coming, sir, with part of his force.' He pointed to the south-east. 'Looks like about five hundred in all, half mounted.'

John Lockley ruffled the child's fair curly hair. 'So young Shakes has just informed me. Sergeant-Major Rama's here somewhere, Chard . . . rode over with me. Ask him to bring up Horatio; I'll ride down to meet Colonel Durnford.'

When John Lockley saw Anthony, he was astride Chieftain and looking like some marvellous stage brigand arriving at the head of his black, mounted, mountain warriors. He wore his usual outfit: shining brown boots to the knee over dark cord breeches; a serge patrol jacket; a broad belt bandolier over his shoulder which held a revolver; and a wide belt round his waist holding a hunting knife and ammunition pouch. On his head was his wide-awake felt hat, the crown wrapped around with the inevitable crimson puggaree that all his Natal Native

Contingent wore round their foreheads. His stiff arm and gloved hand simply added to the romantic picture.

Behind him rode his three shadows: Simeon Kambula, Jabez Molife and Induna Hlubi, two of whom had been with him since their skirmish in seventy-three in the Drakensburgs. Then came a convoy of mounted Basutos and amaPutini, whom Durnford called 'my clan', followed by some of Langa's old tribe.

As Anthony came closer he called, 'Hallo lad, I was told I might find you here,' maintaining his hold on Chieftain with his knees and lifting his right hand to wave.

'Evening, sir,' John Lockley called, smiling at his eccentric looking friend. Anthony's brevet had arrived in December, so he was now a full colonel in all but pay, and that would soon come.

'Any orders to move on further into Zululand?' Anthony asked as he halted beside John Lockley.

'No. My battalion's back at Robson's Drift, waiting. The General, Lord Chelmsford, and the headquarters' column with the first and second battalions of the Twenty-fourth Regiment moved up from here this morning to Isandlwana Mountain. We've been sending wagon loads of supplies there all afternoon. They're camped under the eastern base of the mountain. There's some word from the scouts that they believe there's an impi further out.'

'I see. My men are exhausted, lad. The wagons move at a snail's pace and stick in every damp spot; ten tons of equipment on the leading wagon. We've crossed two flooded rivers on our way here and been on forced march. How far's the Buffalo?'

'About half a mile, and it's flooded too. But it's not too bad at the drift.'

Anthony shrugged. 'Thank goodness it's no further, for we'd better cross tonight and camp over there.' And he signalled for his men to move on. 'Who's here at the mission?' Anthony asked as they rode along.

'A company of the Twenty-fourth under Lieutenant Gonville Bromhead. He's actually quite deaf, so he's better in support. And I'll leave one of my Engineers, Lieutenant John Chard. In the hospital there are thirty-three sick and there're a few native soldiers and a Swiss corporal. That's about it.'

That night in the camp on the Zulu side of the river, the two friends sat near the fire. Little Shakes poured them more coffee and moved away to help the cooks.

'Well, lad, we've done a bit of this camping out together in our time,' said Anthony, looking across the flames. 'The worst being in the snow of the Drakensburgs when we were closing the passes.'

John Lockley smiled. 'Yes. Doubt we'll ever forget that; but they've all been good times. I've enjoyed every one.'

'So have I. And now it seems we have a real war to fight together, eh?'

'Yes, it does.'

They were both silent for a time, drinking their coffee. Then Anthony looked up, his pale eyes glinting in the firelight. 'I'm smarting a bit, laddie, for when I was down at Middle Drift, I crossed over into Zululand on some information received from Schroeder, the missionary we met at Cetshwayo's coronation. He said the Zulus were massing there. The General didn't approve, told me I was too headstrong.'

John Lockley weighed this for a few moments. 'I see. It would seem to me that as commander of the second column you had the right.' Then he pushed his hand back though his hair. 'Perhaps he thought you were taking his initiative away. But I'll tell you something, Anthony, I have reservations about our Lord Chelmsford. I don't say he's not competent but I fear he isn't taking the Zulus seriously enough. Yesterday I was explaining some of their strategy to him, and the need for caution when dealing with them. I mentioned trenches and laagering and throwing out vedettes many miles from camp once he crossed over into Zululand. He took it all pretty casually, too casually. Said our ox wagons were larger than the Boer wagons and too unwieldy to be constantly laagering. I'm told he actually laughed at the cautious way Wood moved over the border on the eleventh. And one of his staff, in talking to me about crossing the border, used the words "this promenade into Zululand". I'm concerned.'

Anthony frowned. 'I've noticed the same thing with many of the newly arrived officers. Perhaps Lord Chelmsford is mistaking the Zulus for the Gaikas and the Gcalekas whom he trounced.'

John Lockley agreed. 'Yes, I'm afraid so.'

'And remember, laddie, ten days ago the centre column under the command of Glyn successfully attacked Chief Sihayo's men in his caves and kraals. It probably made them feel that the Zulus were not the great fighters that we say they are.'

'I know, Anthony, I know. But I've lived here most of my life. I've known about the deeds of Shaka and Dingane and their Zulu killing machine since I was a boy; and it's been stirred into action again ... damn it! Lord Chelmsford's staff have just arrived. They have no experience with Zulus. While we have superior weapons, they have massive numbers and they'll be prepared to die. Life's cheap to them, and they're courageous, beyond Chelmsford's comprehension. Anthony, you've been here long enough to know that a Zulu impi is not the same as a few of Sihayo's men hiding in caves.'

Anthony swallowed his coffee. 'That's all true. We'll just have to try to impress it upon the General when we catch up with him.' Then he put down his mug and his pale eyes shone again in the glow from the fire. 'Exactly how far is Isandlwhana Mountain?'

'Eleven miles by the wagon route and eight on the bridle path.'

'What does the word mean?'

'Indlwhana means "little house". So the literal translation in Zulu means "something like a little house". They think the mountain looks like one. It's sort of conical with a long ridge, actually looks a bit like a sphinx. Funny, for the badge of the Twenty-fourth Regiment has a sphinx on it! And they're up there. Isandlwhana's north from the Tugela farm across the Mangeni River. I was there years ago when Uncle Chris took me on a trip up to Utrecht; odd sort of place, lots of tall grass and broken stony ground and a view over the plain from the eastern side of the mount.'

Anthony gestured to the north-east with his coffee mug. 'I suppose Darlengi has his regiment somewhere out there in Zululand.'

John Lockley stared into the fire. 'Yes. I suppose he has.'

'Ah, lad, he's as much a professional soldier in his way as we are. And professional soldiers cannot complain when they are presented with a war.'

562

John Lockley closed his eyes. 'No doubt you're right, my friend.'

Then Anthony threw the dregs of his coffee into the fire and asked, 'Have you seen your wife?'

'Yes, she's in Greytown, soon to move up to the hospital in Newcastle.'

'A marvellous girl,' Anthony said.

John Lockley smiled. 'I'm coming to realise just how marvellous. With Phoebe I've found what I've never had . . . a sense of permanence, of reliability. So . . . how are things with you and Fanny?'

Anthony pulled on his long whiskers. 'I love her deeply, lad. I'm thinking of retiring soon. Get out of the army first. Then . . . well, we'll see.'

Cetshwayo's royal taster passed him the calabash of food, and the king dug his fingers in and began to eat.

Opposite him sat two elderly indunas.

There was a sound at the opening to the Great Hut and a third aged induna, Meleseli, came crawling through. 'Baba, a runner has just come in. Our main impi under the supreme command of Tshingwayo, Mavumengwana, Vumandaba, Darlengi and Mundula is hidden in the valley of the Nxcata stream, east of Isipezi Mountain. We have more full regiments there than there are fingers on both hands: more than half the warriors in all of Zululand. Our spies tell us there is a force of British red-coated soldiers camped under the Isandlwhana Mountain. They raised up white little houses and have many oxen and big carts, but they have put up no earth in banks, nor have they put their carts end to end as the Boers do.'

'So, they have not laagered?' The king shook his head in thought. He remembered what Darlengi had said to him: 'Our traditional methods will not work against fortified positions. The British will laager and hold an all-round defensive square, and we will never beat them. We need new methods.' Cetshwayo had not wanted to hear that. 'Our traditional methods will be used,' he had replied. 'We will draw them away from their fortified laagers and our superior numbers will overcome. This way was good enough for Shaka, it will be good enough for us.' But now his messenger was telling him that the British were not fortifying their position at Isandlwhana

563

Mountain at all. 'How strange,' he said, almost to himself. 'Are they so confident that they grow stupid like the old ox when it has lost its horns?'

Cetshwayo thought for a moment. He was sure Darlengi had equivocated about his feelings on the war. But even so, Darlengi was a Zulu, and had led his regiment out to do battle.

The king motioned for the newcomer to sit, and then Meleseli said, 'When the sun rises it will be the day of the new moon. As you know it is the custom to avoid combat on this day, but if any of the British leave and the soldiers are divided, we will attack no matter what day it is.'

Cetshwayo nodded. 'The impi that sits now in the Nxcata valley is the largest the Zulus have ever formed. Far greater than any of my Uncle Shaka's.' He said it with satisfaction and put down his food. Now he stood up as if he were addressing his whole council instead of just three elderly warriors. 'Send a runner back and tell him to repeat again to my warriors, as I told them before they left here . . . Leave none alive who wear red coats!'

As dawn broke over Rorke's Drift reveille sounded and the cooks began to prepare breakfast. Little Shakes was there, sleepy-eyed but pouring out the tea. John Lockley drank a cup. 'Good tea, Shakes.'

'Goin' back to Robson's are ye, Colonel?' the child asked.

'Yes, son.' And then he winked. 'You take care of things here, won't you?'

'Yes, sir!' The child grinned widely as John Lockley and Anthony moved over to Tenny Rama, who stood holding Horatio and his own horse, Nebus.

'So lad,' said Anthony as John Lockley mounted up. 'If I hear anything or have anything to report, I'll send a rider on over to you.'

They were riding away when Anthony called after them, 'I'd rather be doing something than sitting here waiting. I don't believe in battles, but if there's going to be one, I want to be in the thick of it.'

When John Lockley returned to his own camp all was quiet. That afternoon, he spent some time overseeing the earthworks and then with his second-in-command, Captain Timothy Pudney, and Tenny Rama, he did some scouting around the base of Nsugangeni Hill, a few miles to the north-east of Robson's Drift. Later he wrote some letters, and at about ten o'clock he took a turn round the camp and spoke to the sentries. Then after a final cup of coffee, and a chat with Tenny, he went to bed.

He was woken by reveille and was eating his breakfast when Captain Pudney came hurrying to him.

'Rider just in from Rorke's Drift with a message from Colonel Durnford, sir.' He handed him a piece of folded paper.

It read:

> 22 January
>
> Smith-Dorien has brought a message from the General. I have been ordered up to the main camp at Isandlwhana Mountain. The General has moved out to attack an impi of Zulus ten miles distant. You are to follow me with all force available.
>
> Anthony.

John Lockley leapt to his feet. 'Rally the men. We're to move up to Isandlwhana Mountain immediately.'

Intongalu sat eyeing Darlengi with ill-concealed hatred as Darlengi, Tshingwayo, and Mavumengwana stood together in the early morning sun. Intongalu was here with his regiment but he knew he should have been in command with the other great chieftains ... *would* have been in command if he had not been reprimanded by Cetshwayo because of Darlengi. All his life Darlengi had thwarted him. He even believed that Veele, his own Great Wife, would have preferred to marry Darlengi over him. How he hated Darlengi ... and all his ancestors.

The immense impi spread out along the great curving valley: thirteen full regiments, all twenty-five thousand of them, sitting shoulder to shoulder. It was an astonishing sight. They had lit no fires last night but had sat waiting silently only miles from the British Isandlwhana Mountain camp.

Tshingwayo was now in his seventies, and while he had marched with the impi would stay back from the battle; he was here to share his experience. He turned to listen as a young induna came up to him and Darlengi and Mavumengwana.

'Our spies tell us that Matshana ka Mondisa led a small force of soldiers who followed him yesterday to the Hlazakazi Heights. As the soldiers camped across the valley from him last night he lit many, many fires so they would think his force was very large. It seems they have sent back to the main encampment for reinforcements, and half of the British have marched and ridden out from Isandlwhana Mountain camp before dawn this morning.'

Tshingwayo smiled at the messenger. 'In which direction do they head?'

He pointed. 'Past Matshana's stronghold.'

This was to the south-east. Tshingwayo looked round his companions. 'Let us wait until this force which has moved out is led far away beyond Matshana's. Then we will attack.'

'Today is the day of the new moon,' Mavumengwana said.

Tshingwayo shook his head. 'It does not matter; we will attack if the time is right. Many of our warriors grow impatient and hard to restrain, like the baboon when he sees his arch enemy, the leopard.'

Darlengi asked the young induna, 'Has the main encampment dug any holes in the ground yet?'

'No, and their big carts are not laid end to end together as the Boers do.'

'Good,' said Tshingwayo.

At Isandlwhana camp the morning had begun normally: reveille, breakfast and allotted duties.

The commanding officer, Brevet Lieutenant-Colonel Henry Burmester Pulleine of the 1st Battalion of the 24th (2nd Warwickshire) Regiment of Foot, moved through the camp. On the previous day they had seen various small groups of Zulus on the distant hills and Major John Dartnell and Commandant Lonsdale and some volunteers, plus some Natal Native Horse, had ridden out towards the stronghold of a Zulu chief called Matshana ka Mondisa. Then Pulleine had been woken when a message had come in at two o'clock that morning from Dartnell informing the General that he had encountered Matshana, and found the large Zulu impi they were looking for.

Lord Chelmsford had taken half the force and ridden out with Colonel Glyn, before dawn. A message had been sent to

Durnford and Harrison to reinforce the Isandlwhana camp, and then Pulleine had caught a couple more hours of sleep and risen for breakfast.

He was returning to his tent in company with Captain Degacher when a reconnaissance rider came in.

'There's a large force of Zulus to the north-east, sir.'

'How many?'

'Hard to say, sir, but six hundred maybe. They advance on the north side of the mountain.'

Pulleine took the news quite calmly. 'Here, wait, I'd better inform Lord Chelmsford.' He scribbled a note and handed it to the man. 'Ride out to him with this.' Then he turned to Degacher. 'Sound a stand-to and draw the troops up in the direction of the Zulu approach.'

An hour later the troops stood down from the alert, as none of the enemy had appeared. And an hour after that Anthony rode up over the stony ground of the rise leading up from the Rorke's Drift track towards Isandlwhana Mountain. Beside him rode Captain George Shepstone of the Natal Native Horse, his political assistant; behind came five troops of his mounted Basutos; and some way back marched his foot soldiers and rocket battery, about five hundred men in all.

He spurred by the wagon park and the oxen, loomed over by the strange sphinx-like shape of the mountain, and arrived in the main camp which stretched for a mile along the eastern side of Isandlwhana. He spoke briefly with an interpreter, Paul Brickhill, who told him where the camp commander was. When he found Pulleine, he asked about the General's movements, and the Lieutenant-Colonel advised him. Then Pulleine told him, 'We've been getting reports since dawn about various Zulu movements in the hills all around and there have been small advances over the Nquthu Plain all morning which we're repulsing, but we're very depleted here now. At eight hours I sent a message out to the General informing him of a considerable Zulu force to the north. There are supposed to be other sizeable parties of Zulus out that way.' He pointed east. Then his voice dropped as he eyed Anthony uncomfortably. 'I suppose I must release my command to you,' he said.

Anthony did not reply immediately. In the note Smith-Dorien had brought him that morning relaying the message straight from the General, there was absolutely no mention of his taking over the camp. The two battalions of the Twenty-fourth were Pulleine's men; Pulleine was their commanding officer, and while he had never seen active service, from the way he was speaking he certainly didn't want to relinquish command.

Through Anthony's mind fluttered many sensitive phantoms, the most recent being the reprimand from the General for crossing over into Zululand. He rubbed his stiff arm as he shook his head and answered, 'No, Lieutenant-Colonel Pulleine, I will not take your command from you. I'll ride out to the east and look for this large body of Zulus which is reportedly there. And I'll send my men, Captain Shepstone and Captain Barton, out to reconnoitre to the north-east.'

The relief showed on Pulleine's face as Anthony turned from him. Then, when Anthony was a few yards away, he looked back. He was thinking of what John Lockley had said, and he raised his good arm to motion across the camp. 'You've only got about six hundred infantry and they're pretty spread out. The camp's totally unprotected, and while it's time-consuming, I suggest you bring down some wagons and make at least one or two defensive squares; and use some of the rocks that are strewn about for breastwork if the ground's too hard to dig into.'

Pulleine watched him go. Durnford was probably right, but Lord Chelmsford hadn't seen the need to laager or to entrench. This was a temporary camp after all. And apparently there were no large impies of Zulus in the vicinity, so why should he worry?

Anthony found Shepstone and Barton and sent them, along with Lieutenant Raw and the rocket battery and three troops of mounted Basutos – about a hundred and fifty men – out on to the Nyoni Heights to the north-east. Then he took Simeon Kambula and Induna Hlubi and his remaining two troops of Durnford's Horse, and rode out to the south-east.

When Lord Chelmsford received Pulleine's 8 a.m. message it was approaching ten o'clock. It read: 'Report just come in that Zulus are advancing in force from left front of camp.' Chelmsford's ADC, who was from the navy, took his telescope and climbed a tree to look at the camp which was about twelve miles range. He reported that all appeared calm.

Chelmsford looked round his officers. He had already sent a message back to Pulleine telling him to break camp at Isandlwhana Mountain and send on supplies in the wagons. 'There's no urgency in this message from Pulleine, and even if we returned post-haste it would be after noon before we got there. I think we'll push on and find a position for a new camp.'

It was about midday when Lieutenant Raw and some of his troopers chased a few Zulus driving eight head of cattle up a long, stony hill. They were five miles from camp and Captain George Shepstone followed closely. At the crest of the hill Shepstone saw Raw wheel around and fire a couple of shots. He rode swiftly to the brow to see what it was the Lieutenant fired upon. His eyes widened in disbelief and a ripple of shock ran through his body. 'Oh no!' he whispered.

There below him, in a valley that stretched away forever, were more Zulus than he had thought existed. 'Lord in heaven, we've found the impi!'

For some seconds he was transfixed as he watched them rise up and begin to pour up the hill towards him.

'uSuthu! uSuthu!' they yelled, spreading up the hill, a massive fury unleashed.

Shepstone brought himself back to life, fired a few bullets from his pistol, pulled his horse round, and charged down the hill, shouting to Raw, 'Send a man out on the plain to warn Colonel Durnford and ride before them. Harry them if you can! I'll warn the main camp.'

When the troopers suddenly appeared at the crest of the hill across the wide valley from him, Darlengi had been talking to Kayo.

'uSuthu! uSuthu!' the warriors screamed as they leapt to their feet, scrambling up and over the hilltop in a mighty mile-wide wave where they spread even wider, swarming over the undulations of the plain.

The chieftains had no hope of checking their warriors. Throughout the morning they had been restless and hard to hold and now they ignited like gunpowder.

Darlengi's regiment had charged away to become part of the left horn of the impi, and he ran to follow, calling to Tshingwayo to attempt to restrain the four regiments who had been bivouacked farthest back along the valley.

The chieftains did manage to hold those regiments and they were brought up in orderly fashion and marched off in the rear of the army, down a huge declivity to become the right horn of the impi. This horn came around the western side, or the back, of Isandlwhana Mountain.

John Lockley arrived at the camp just after noon. As he rode up the stony slope and past the wagon park he looked up at the mysterious looming shape of the mountain. He shook his head as he rode further into camp and it became obvious that there had been no laagering and no defences raised. He spurred forward with Captain Pudney and Tenny Rama on his heels and saw Lieutenant Pope of the 2nd Battalion of the 24th coming through the horse yard. Pope wore a monocle and was a happy, popular man.

They could hear firing to the north of the camp out on the Nyoni Heights above the Nquthu Plateau.

John Lockley reined in and hailed him. 'Where's Colonel Durnford?'

'He left camp, sir, with a couple of troops of his mounted Basutos. He rode out towards that conical hill.' Pope pointed miles away to the east. 'I think a company of the volunteers went out to join him. There've been reports all morning about parties of Zulus out there and to the north.'

John Lockley was surprised. Anthony should be commanding. He was the highest-ranking officer. 'Who's commanding the camp?'

'Colonel Pulleine, sir. Has been since the General left.'

John Lockley lifted his eyes to the row of hills far to the north-east. He drew in his breath in amazement as he saw the line of the horizon change. It began to ripple and move and he realised it was a wave of Zulus swelling over the horizon and spreading steadily wider, and wider, and wider, an inexorable flood of humanity streaming down over the slopes, coming straight for the camp.

His pulse quickened. 'That'll be the head of the buffalo,' he thought aloud. He turned back and looked to the south-east.

Anthony was out there with only a couple of troops of Basutos. *That's where the left horn will come. Straight at Anthony.*

At that moment the alarm sounded and Pope looked around nervously. 'I'd better get to my unit, sir.'

'Yes, all right. Where's Pulleine?' John Lockley called as Pope moved away.

'He was over there in the headquarters' tent earlier.' Pope pointed.

John Lockley turned to Captain Pudney. 'Our infantry will be along soon. Leave a lieutenant to bring them up in support of Pope, then move our mounted men up here and wait for me. I'll try and find Pulleine and see what's happening first.'

Bugles sounded and men were reacting to the alarm and hurrying by in all directions as John Lockley rode past the tents. He could not see Pulleine anywhere, but he spotted Captain Barton of the Natal Native Horse hurrying towards him. 'What orders has Pulleine given?' he said, holding him.

'He's sent Mostyn and Cavaye and their companies up the spur. Smith's two seven-pounder guns are over there, between Porteous and Wardell's companies.' He pointed to where John Lockley could just see them facing the advancing enemy, who would soon be boiling across the plain towards them.

'What about the others?'

'We were drawn up earlier this morning, sir. Strung out in a line from here right round the north of the mountain. After Cavaye there're Mostyn and Shepstone and Erskine, then Younghusband, I think.'

'Have any messages been sent out to the General?'

'I believe so, sir.'

It looked to John Lockley as if there were thousands and thousands of Zulus coming at the camp ... maybe tens of thousands. The most they had here were about eight hundred regulars, and even with Anthony's men out on the plain, and the mounted police, and volunteers, and native soldiers, perhaps only another thousand! He couldn't find Pulleine and it was too late to pull back the companies now. He sent the Captain off. 'Thanks, get back to your men. I'll see if I can move out and help Colonel Durnford hold. He'll be facing the left horn of the impi.'

Now came sounds of heavy firing to the north, and as John Lockley rode back he saw little Shakes standing with a sergeant by the ammunition boxes. The child must have come up with Anthony's infantry from Rorke's Drift.

'Colonel, Colonel, the Zulus are coming!' the child shouted excitedly.

He leaped down and patted Shakes on the head. 'Yes, son, but don't you worry.' He looked meaningfully at the sergeant. 'Look after him, Sergeant.'

There was constant firing now to the north front of the camp. He remounted Horatio and looked back. The head of the buffalo was surging across the plain. It appeared that the companies of Cavaye and Porteous were about to take the brunt of it.

His own troopers were gathered at the edge of camp and he rode over to them. Looking south, he thought he could see the left horn of Zulus pouring across the plain. They were coming round the conical kopje miles away. He thought there was a small British force riding ahead of them. *That must be Anthony.* If he could get to him they could make some sort of a stand.

He raised his hand and rode out, followed by his Natal cavalry thundering across the rocky and broken ground. As he came closer he could see the horn of the impi flooding in its thousands round the conical hill towards Anthony and his rocket battery, which had crossed the plain and rejoined him. They were riding hard and then he saw them retiring into a donga. John Lockley realised with a shock that there must be twenty or thirty Zulus to one of Anthony's men; and as Anthony deployed his men along the donga he was actually holding the main thrust of the Zulu left horn.

As Anthony held the donga and John Lockley moved in to join him, a wing of the uMbonambi broke off from the left horn of the inGobamakhosi regiment that Anthony fought and bore down on John Lockley's troop, separating the two.

John Lockley looked anxiously around and saw another crevasse in the ground ahead. 'Here . . . into this!' he shouted as he rode down and dismounted. He was about three hundred yards from Anthony, and as a bullet thudded into the bank in front of him, he aimed his Martini-Henry and brought down a Zulu.

No one really noticed that the sun disappeared at that moment as a partial eclipse began covering the plain in an eerie light.

Then ensued the same holding action that Anthony was fighting. John Lockley knew Tenny was beside him, but for every Zulu they shot, ten more appeared.

He looked back to camp. There was so much smoke and noise he could not tell what was happening, but they seemed to be holding, thank God. Why the devil hadn't Pulleine secured the camp? Even his defensive line of troops was too damn long and thin!

Wave after wave of Zulus fell before their fire. It was the main Zulu impi all right and Chelmsford was probably a dozen miles away.

Perhaps it was close to three-quarters of an hour later when John Lockley noticed that some of his men were restless. They were looking round and muttering to each other. He faced round to Captain Pudney, who uttered the chilling words, 'We're running out of ammunition, sir.'

'Haven't you sent back to camp for more?'

'Yes, sir.'

'Well?'

'None has come. The two men I sent came back saying they're asking for official requisitions.'

'God in heaven! Don't they realise what's going on out here?'

'Apparently not, sir.'

'Send more men in immediately. We'll have to retreat to camp soon.' That was when he saw Anthony's rocket battery head back to camp, and a couple of minutes later some of his Basutos came riding out of the donga fighting a rearguard action and followed by some volunteers.

'They must be out of ammo too, sir,' said Pudney.

John Lockley stood up, ignoring the occasional bullet whistling by. 'All right men, mount your horses and retire back to camp! Slowly. Ride steady, steady. Fall back slowly. Make each bullet count. Take aim . . . fire . . . and fall back while you reload.'

So, pulling his men in formation about him, and withdrawing in line with Anthony a few hundred yards to his right, John Lockley and Anthony and their men attempted to stem the tidal wave of Zulus.

Suddenly John Lockley saw some of his own NNC break away and gallop back towards camp.

'What the bloody hell are they doing, Tenny?'

'They frightened, Colonel. They out of ammunition and retreating to camp.'

'I gave no order, damn it, they . . .' but a bullet slammed into the top of his helmet and knocked it to the ground and brought his attention back to where some of the Zulus were trying to outstrip them.

'Aim at them!' he shouted, pointing. 'Keep retiring at a steady pace. Come on, boys,' he continued to shout as he took aim and fired, then turned Horatio in retreat again. 'Mark your man and don't miss!'

So they continued withdrawing under the relentless Zulu onslaught, and, as they came closer to camp, John Lockley thought that the British lines were holding. About two hundred yards out, there were masses of Zulu dead lying along the front of the camp like peppercorns. Yet still they came. They would lie down and inch forward, then jump up and run at the guns.

They were, just as he always knew they would be, fearlessly brave, ignoring the dead in front of them.

John Lockley and his Basutos came charging in to the southern edge of the main camp now, and he shouted to Tenny, 'You go for ammunition too. Get any you can! Don't worry whose it is! Take it!'

The Zulu horn was spreading out now, getting wider and wider and only a few hundred yards away, coming inexorably forward towards them. He could see Anthony's men moving steadily back to the saddle of ground between the mountain and a stony kopje to the south, but he lost sight of Anthony for a time. And then he thought he saw Simeon Kambula and Jabez Molife riding back towards the wagon park. Some minutes later he noticed Charles Pope was moving his men in, and John Lockley signalled that if they could join up with Durnford they could make a stand.

He turned to his second-in-command. 'Pudney, retire slowly back to the rising ground behind the hospital tents. Tenny's getting ammunition. We'll make a stand there. I'll try to get over to Colonel Durnford.'

'Right, but I've only three rounds left and I think there are Zulus at the back of the camp now, Colonel,' shouted the captain, pointing over the wagon park.

'Hell, the right horn must have come round the mountain. Do what you can, Captain. I'll come back to you.'

John Lockley looked around and saw Anthony come riding down from the main camp. He must have gone up to look for Pulleine. Most of the men with Anthony seemed to have carbines and were using them, so they must have some ammunition. Anthony had his good arm raised holding his revolver and rallying his men.

John Lockley looked back along the line of the camp. Suddenly things seemed to be in disarray. The seven-pounders had stopped firing and now there were Zulus much closer to his left.

Where the devil was Tenny with the ammunition?

Then he saw men from the native contingents fleeing towards the nek between the mountain and the stony kopje. The Zulus had broken through the lines! The natives were running away!

As a head induna, Darlengi was not in the attack; he watched from a distance and gave orders on strategy. When his regiment in the left horn of the impi had gone in towards camp, he had followed.

The sudden and disorderly way they had risen up out of the valley had altered their tactics, and the regiments that were to form the two horns and chest of the buffalo lost their positions: what was to be the left horn became the right horn; what was to be the right became the centre; and the centre, the left.

He had seen his warriors run down across the great plain and meet up with an advance party of mounted Basutos and volunteers under their British officers. They had been joined by a rocket battery and some survivors of a vedette on the conical hill and had held a running battle with his own regiment and the mighty inGobamakhosi and the youthful uVe until they took shelter in a donga about a mile and a half out from the camp. There were only about two hundred of them and yet they held up the thousands of warriors in the left horn for over an hour. Darlengi watched his warriors go forward in waves to be continually repulsed.

A second small force attempted to join the first about half an hour into the battle; but Darlengi turned a wing of his own regiment and thus put a wedge between the two forces so they could not join up. The second British force held in a smaller donga some three hundred yards to the north of the first. Darlengi could see that as long as they had ammunition they would hold these positions and it was taking a massive toll on his warriors. Some of his men had guns but they were not good shots; most were using the traditional weapons: each man having two or three izijula – throwing spears – and the iklwa, the short stabbing spear. Some had knobkerries and axes. All were ineffective against the Martini-Henry when in a fortified position, and the donga was acting like one.

Kayo had been standing near him when a stray bullet had thudded into his throat and brought him down.

Darlengi knelt down beside him. 'Kayo, Kayo, you did not even need to be here. You should have remained back with Tshingwayo.'

Kayo had tried to smile up at him. He could not speak and he was bleeding profusely. But his eyes spoke, and they said he had wanted to be with Darlengi.

Dear Kayo had been loyal to him all these years, right from when he was a boy. *Oh no, Kayo. Not you. Of all the Zulus, not you.* Darlengi smoothed the old warrior's brow and looked at the injury. It was bad, but he might just live. 'Kayo, I am sending you back to safety. You wait for me. I will come and get you.' He hailed two of his warriors. 'Take Induna Kayo back to Tshingwayo.'

Kayo lifted his hand and Darlengi took it briefly before they carried the elderly induna away. He moved a little further out of the range of fire and was considering withdrawing his men from the terrible beating they were taking when he saw the British forces mount their horses and exit the dongas almost in unison. They must be running out of ammunition! This was the chance for the left horn to push on, no matter what. As the British force came out of the first donga he saw who led them. It was Anthony! His good arm raised in the air, rallying his men, holding on to Chieftain with his knees. Darlengi felt very odd, watching Anthony ride away, as he forced himself to lift his own arms to signal to his warriors to press on after him.

Then the second shock! Not only did he recognise the man who led the other troop out of the smaller donga, but again he recognised the horse. It was John Lockley on Horatio!

He watched his brother ride into the distance, followed by the immense mass of his own warriors ... watched John Lockley as he turned to fire every hundred yards or so ... watched his red coat until it disappeared into other red coats back near the camp.

John Lockley had tried to reach Anthony. At one point in all the noise and fury he had seen Anthony about two hundred yards away. He had dismounted and was rallying his men around him, laughing and holding a rifle between his knees and clearing the jam with his good hand then handing it back to a soldier and taking out his own revolver from his bandolier.

Bullets buzzed by John Lockley and some soldiers called out to him. He shouted, 'Retreat to the higher ground!' and began to ride towards Anthony, but suddenly there was a mighty Zulu surge forward.

God! They were surrounding Anthony!

A bullet thudded into the cantle of his saddle and Horatio reared.

His own men had moved back to the higher ground, he would get up to them, make a stand. But all organised resistance seemed to have gone. A hundred yards away there were Zulus running between the tents! He saw Horace Smith-Dorien, who had brought the orders down to them this morning, riding through the far side of the tents, firing over his shoulder.

Then he saw little Shakes. The child was running, screaming, in front of a Zulu. John Lockley aimed and fired. The warrior fell dead to the ground. He urged Horatio forward to the child.

'Colonel! Colonel!' The terrified child ran towards him, arms uplifted. He leant down to pick up the boy, and as he enfolded him, raising him to safety, the child screamed again. John Lockley could not believe it. There was a battle-axe right through little Shakes's back. The child was dead in his arms, his blood running everywhere. John Lockley held his Martini-Henry in his right hand and, swinging Horatio round, he fired point-blank at a tall Zulu, who dropped right in front of him.

He let the small body slip to the ground, Shakes's tiny pale face staring up at him in death. He had just a moment to spend on the child, then he reloaded. He had only four rounds left, and now there were Zulus everywhere shouting *'uSuthu!'* He heard a cry, 'Every man for himself!' Then another, 'Warn them at Rorke's Drift if you can!'

He looked across to where Anthony was making his stand with the last of his volunteers and Durnford's Horse. He had no hope of getting to him, and he knew his friend was out of ammunition now. He could just see Anthony through all the writhing bodies, right in the middle of his men, now on foot and fighting hand to hand.

Turning back further into camp, another bullet whistled by his head. Suddenly there was a shout beside him and he turned as a knobkerrie whizzed over Horatio's mane. A Zulu was running at him ready to hurl his spear, and John Lockley used one of his last precious bullets to bring him down.

He looked back towards Anthony but could only see Zulus now. He heard Anthony's voice ringing in his head ... *I'm thinking of retiring soon. Get out of the army ... but if there's going to be a battle I want to be in the thick of it.*

With a shudder, he drew his hand across his eyes then, dragging it back through his hair, pushed Horatio though the tents towards the nek of Isandlwhana in an attempt to find his men.

Darlengi had seen his warriors take a shocking beating at the hands of Anthony and John Lockley's force, falling dead in their hundreds on the plain back near the dongas. Yet still they had risen up and made rush after rush. After that Darlengi had followed his warriors in towards the camp.

And now it was different.

The uMbonambi, the inGobamakhosi, the uMcijo, and the uVe were already in the British camp and moving between the tents, stabbing everything in sight, even the mealie bags.

Darlengi had seen Anthony surrounded and it had surprised him how some of the Natal natives had fought with him to the death. They must have worshipped him to do that, for there had been chances to ride out. Darlengi had watched from a safe distance. He was an induna and did not fight these days. He was glad of that, for he had no heart for this. He saw his warriors throwing their own dead on the British bayonets to bring them down. In the end Anthony and his men had fought using anything ... even their fists. He could not help but picture Anthony standing beside him at the altar as John Lockley married Phoebe. He could almost feel Anthony's presence beside him now. Darlengi shivered, and he turned away.

Maphoko had come over to Darlengi afterwards. 'We did not want to kill the one with the long whiskers, Baba. He had only one arm but he fought like a lion to the end.'

'Yes, I know he did.'

He looked left and right. There had been small British enclaves all around the mountain that had held out like Anthony for hours. They were so damn brave ... these British and these Zulus. They should not be fighting each other. He was of them both; and yet understood neither. Two warrior races, one sophisticated, the other savage; yet both with their irrational reasons for being ready to die. He looked around. They had done just that; the camp was littered with black and white corpses. He shook his head. It was bloody pointless ... literally so; there was blood everywhere.

Now he was scanning every dead man's face. Most of the British corpses had been stabbed multiple times: a Zulu custom of honouring a greatly admired, mighty and formidable foe. And already he could see his warriors disembowelling the corpses along what had been the defensive line. He shook his head when he saw a little drummer boy lying dead with an axe through his back.

Intongalu was running through the tents slashing them and shouting, '*uSuthu*, kill the red coats!' Warriors followed him, killing horses and oxen, looting the tents, breaking open officers' trunks and smashing anything and everything.

Darlengi ran up over the saddle of ground at the southern end of the mountain and through the wagon park. The whole camp was now in total chaos. Anyone on a horse was fleeing to the south-west towards the Buffalo River, and those on foot were being brought down by the warriors chasing them.

There were stray animals wandering about in the smoke and dust, and Darlengi was aware that the partial eclipse of the sun was making the day even murkier.

Then at last he saw John Lockley. He was alive! Thank God. He was beside an outcrop of rock down past the stony kopje that was south of the mountain. He was still on Horatio and fighting two warriors with his bayonet. Beside him was one of his native contingent fighting a third warrior. Six or seven Zulus lay on the ground, and in amongst them a few native soldiers and some British.

As Darlengi ran over the hundred yards between them, John Lockley bayoneted one of the warriors at the same time as the native soldier smashed a warrior with the side of his rifle then drew his pistol and shot him. The third Zulu threw his assegai from only yards away as John Lockley wheeled around to face him. It caught him in the shoulder and as John Lockley teetered on Horatio's back and the warrior rushed in to finish him, the mounted native shot the warrior dead with his pistol.

'John Lockley!' Darlengi shouted as he appeared through the smoke and came running up to him.

Tenny, who had found ammunition and had also found John Lockley, aimed his pistol at Darlengi but John Lockley shouted, 'No! Don't shoot, he's my brother!'

This was an amazing revelation to Tenny, but he did as his Colonel bid and held his fire.

John Lockley, who had blood on the side of his face where a bullet had grazed his temple, tried to pull the assegai from his shoulder as Darlengi shouted, 'Take off your jacket, Lockley, quickly. Orders have been given to let none survive who wear red jackets.'

John Lockley slipped out of the stirrups and dismounted beside Horatio, and Darlengi took hold of the assegai and pulled it from his brother's shoulder. Tenny watched in amazement as the Zulu warrior helped John Lockley remove his coat. Then he witnessed the unbelievable as the two men embraced each other.

Blood seeped down John Lockley's shirt as he awkwardly reloaded his Martini-Henry. Darlengi pointed to the Buffalo. 'You must ride to the river, it's the only...' but he got no further, for suddenly a warrior of the uVe came rushing up over the stony ground, shouting 'uSuthu!' He threw his knobkerrie and it thudded into the side of Tenny's horse's head. The horse fell to its knees and Tenny came off on to the ground.

Darlengi turned to face the uVe warrior. 'Forget these men! Go away!' The stunned warrior came to a halt as Darlengi raised his assegai and pointed back at the camp. 'I order you to go over there. Go, now!'

The young warrior could not disobey Induna Darlengi, and he faded into the murky light and the noise and smoke.

But another Zulu had witnessed all this. Down in the smoke and confusion beyond the edge of the wagon park Intongalu saw what had taken place. And Intongalu swiftly realised who John Lockley must be.

He ran back and called three of the inGobamakhosi who were looting the wagons. 'Come! There are two British still up here.'

As the warriors made a charge up the hill, with Intongalu behind them, they screamed, '*uSuthu!*' and Darlengi turned round and lifted his hand, shouting, 'These do not wear red coats,' but then he recognised Intongalu, and he moved forward to intercept the oncoming warriors. He saw that Intongalu carried a rifle with fixed bayonet, and as Darlengi shouted Intongalu halted . . . smiled . . . raised his rifle . . . and fired.

Darlengi staggered three paces and dropped to the ground.

John Lockley froze as he saw his brother fall and the warriors come charging over the top of him. Now Tenny was on his feet, and as the first warrior threw his assegai at him Tenny ducked and shot him. But on came the second and third warriors and Tenny closed with the second as Intongalu threw the used rifle to the ground beside Darlengi and ran in behind them screaming the war cry.

John Lockley was still in shock, but he realised he had no time to reload. He took his Martini-Henry in his left hand and, drawing his pistol in his right, shot the third warrior who wielded his knobkerrie ready to throw.

But Intongalu was upon him now. As John Lockley faced him, the Zulu thrust his iklwa in and John Lockley leaped sideways in an attempt to avoid the spear, but it met the pistol barrel in his hand, and knocked it to the ground.

John Lockley still held his rifle in his left hand, with the bayonet attached. He swiftly brought it into both hands and up to counter Intongalu's second thrust. The assegai slid along the blade. Intongalu could see that the soldier he fought was wounded, and as he thrust again and again John Lockley parried each blow. Neither man had ever seen the other, but both knew who they fought. The violent hatred between them was as tangible as the smoke and the haze of the day.

Intongalu yelled, and jumped forward, plunging in with his blade, and once more John Lockley countered it, but he was losing a lot of blood from his wound now and he staggered slightly as he moved back from Intongalu's next thrust. As he regained his balance Intongalu stabbed in and up, and the tip of his spear pierced John Lockley's side.

Intongalu shouted with glee as John Lockley went down on one knee, and he raised his assegai high in the air to ram it down into his enemy. Through John Lockley's mind flashed the time once before when he was near to being killed this way, and even though he knew it was useless, he struggled to rise and to bring his bayonet round in defence.

Then, suddenly, Intongalu's face stiffened and blood spurted from his mouth. He gave a guttural sickening growl as he let go his spear and abruptly pitched forward on to his knees, dropping dead to the ground.

Darlengi had killed him.

Mortally wounded in the chest, Darlengi had forced himself to stand and lift Intongalu's discarded rifle with bayonet secured. Then, with a mighty effort and the last of his ebbing strength, he had raised it over his shoulder and hurled the rifle like an assegai; the twenty-one and a half inch long bayonet smashing straight through Intongalu's back under the left shoulder blade, breaking his rib cage, slicing through his lung and heart and out of his chest.

At that moment Tenny, who was grappling with the third warrior, managed to draw his knife and thrust it into him. The man fell and Tenny picked up his fallen pistol and shot him.

Darlengi stood in the swirling smoke. He was a wonderful, wounded image as John Lockley staggered across to him. A smattering of gunfire sounded in the distance as the two brothers sank to their knees, side by side, with noise and dust floating all around.

Then, as Darlengi's black eyes met his brother's for the final time on this earth, John Lockley whispered, 'My brother, my Zulu, myself.'

Darlengi smiled. It was a perfect smile, saying all the things that they had ever said to each other; and bearing all the love they had ever borne.

As they slipped to the ground together, Darlengi thought of his beautiful Thulile; but he felt warm and almost comfortable here in his brother's arms . . . *How brightly the sun shines. Where did Isiwukulu come from? Oh, yes, I see, we're riding along the Tugela again. Look at Isi's hooves thundering through the long grass. Hey, John Lockley! I'll show you how to find plovers' eggs. Who is that? It's my Ice Princess over there, waving, and look . . . Jettama too, and Thulile . . . all together. Why are you laughing, John Lockley? Now you are making me laugh . . . We're laughing . . . laughing . . . laughing . . .*

John Lockley was so tired; so damn weary. *It's all over. It doesn't matter. I want to stay here. Here with Darlengi. We can sleep.*

He heard Mattana's voice croaking out of his long ago . . . 'I see a time when you both face death . . . face it as brothers' . . . Yes they would . . . here, now, together . . . They would sleep.

But stridently came the insistent voice of Tenny in his ears. 'You come with me, Colonel, you come. We must go. Quick! Your brother is dead. You come now. Please.'

'No, Tenny . . . you go.'

'I no go. Not without you. You come now.' And Tenny pulled him from Darlengi's embrace, up, on his feet. That was when John Lockley lost consciousness.

Tennyson Rama loved his Colonel. His Colonel had given him dignity. He had always treated him like a man . . . like a friend. Some of the commanders had spoken roughly to him and called him 'nigger', but never his Colonel. His Colonel put men in the lock-up who used that word. His Colonel always talked to him and asked him how he felt. His Colonel even asked him *what he thought*.

Tenny was powerful and he lifted John Lockley and laid him across Horatio. Nebus, his own horse, was too badly wounded from the knobkerrie blow, they would both have to ride Horatio. He looked anxiously back towards the wagon park. Through the smoke he could see a lot of Zulus, but they were busy looting. Then he took a thick thong from his saddle bag and strapped his Colonel to the stallion. He knew he could not hold the Colonel, and the reins, and a rifle, so he dropped the rifle and took his Colonel's pistol and pushed it into his belt; then loaded his own and held it in his right hand. Now he turned back to the man his Colonel had called brother. Even in his haste Tenny noticed that the man somehow resembled his Colonel. Round his neck were two chains; one with a diamond and one with a locket. He took them for his Colonel. Then he mounted behind him.

As he did there was a shout from above him and dozens of Zulus came running down towards him from the stony kopje. He fired two shots, and turned Horatio, urging him away as one fired at him and missed.

He had taken an assegai thrust in the flesh of his upper arm and a slash in his cheek which was bleeding profusely. He would have liked to wrap his handkerchief round his face before he set off for the Buffalo, five miles away, but that would haveee to wait.

He took Horatio down over the stony ground; there was no path, and boulders were everywhere. Men were fleeing and the ground was covered in shields, assegais, clothing of all description, hats, even saddles. Oxen were intermingling with Zulus and mules and fugitives on horses. There were spiny trees and date palms and aloes blocking the way, and wait-a-bit thorn bushes down sudden ravines. It was dangerous, broken ground where a horse could lose its footing easily, but Horatio kept on, almost as if he were aware of the task he was performing. For some time he followed a number of native soldiers in the Edendale contingent who were making a mass break for it to the Buffalo, then they went down a wide donga and he lost them. When Zulus approached him, Tenny shot at them.

At one point he saw ahead of him the colours of the 24th being carried by a soldier, the flag flapping in the wind as he went down a ravine and disappeared. He did not see him again.

It was a dangerous and ghastly ride over rocks, along dongas and up steep sides of ravines, and when at last he reached the Buffalo there was no time to choose where to cross; there were Zulus running in long lines further up, shouting and yelling.

The river was in flood, six feet higher than normal, with the water rushing, gushing, boiling round rocks hidden from view. It was a daunting sight, but Tenny trusted Horatio. He said, 'We swim, Horatio,' and plunged in.

CHAPTER FORTY

John Lockley stirred.

He could hear rain pattering on canvas and voices around him. He opened his eyes and saw a vision of his wife Phoebe. He must be dreaming. Then the vision began to weep and it leant over him and kissed him and called him by name. He realised she was real.

'My darling, my darling,' she was saying.

He went to lift his arms to clasp her to him, but he could not move. Then he became aware of the pain in many places all over his body: his right shoulder ached and so did his entire left side, and his head, and his back. He managed to smile and to whisper, 'Phoebe.' And she smoothed his brow and called him 'darling' again before he slipped back into the darkness.

The next time he opened his eyes she was still there. And now he remembered everything: the ghastly battle . . . Darlengi was dead; Anthony was dead; so many of his men were dead.

'Where am I?' he asked, and his beautiful Phoebe leaned forward and said, 'In Helpmaaker, sweetheart. Tenny brought you in.'

'Then you know?' he asked.

'About the battle at Isandlwana Mountain? Yes, we do.'

And a tear rolled from his eyes as she kissed him again. He turned his head and saw Tenny in the cot next to him.

'Tell me what happened,' he asked.

So Phoebe told him how Tenny had saved him and brought him across the flooded Buffalo and over ten miles of rugged country here to Helpmaaker.

She would never forget Wednesday night. She had just arrived here with Thulmi and Sergeant Gardiner on her way from Greytown to Newcastle when Captain Stafford, one of Anthony's commanders of the native contingents, had ridden in exhausted and covered in dust. He cried out, 'We were wiped out, I tell you. We fought them off for hours. There were Zulus everywhere . . . must have been thirty thousand of them! A massacre at Isandlwhana Mountain.'

A lieutenant asked, 'Where was the General?'

'He'd left the night before . . . off with half the force. We didn't realise the enormous impi was so close.'

Everybody looked disbelieving and the lieutenant protested, 'But surely the whole camp can't have been overcome.'

The man's voice rose hysterically. 'I tell you, it's gone. There're some survivors . . . we got across the Buffalo . . . but the camp's taken. Any man who got out had to have a horse!' Then he pulled his animal's head round. 'Look, I'm going on . . . must warn the farms and settlements . . . you should laager here. They may cross the border. There are tens of thousands of them! Must get to 'Maritzburg and tell Sir Bartle Frere.' And with that he spurred away.

And then, as the soldiers at Helpmaaker laagered and put up defences, and waited for the worst, the survivors had trickled in. When the sun set, they could see fires all along the horizon in the direction of the Buffalo. The Zulus were setting fire to kraals and homesteads along the river.

Phoebe had gone about saying the prayer her mother had taught her as a child. 'Peace I leave with you, my Peace I give unto you: not as the world giveth give I unto you. Let not your heart be troubled, neither let it be afraid.' But it wasn't comforting her the way it normally did.

The little force at Helpmaaker remained alert, and at about nine o'clock that night Major Spalding, the officer in charge at Helpmaaker, returned. During the afternoon, he had ridden off to Rorke's Drift with a company of the 24th Foot. He brought more terrifying news. The mission station at Rorke's Drift was surrounded by thousands of Zulus. He had not been able to get near it and had watched the onslaught impotently from a distance. Then, fearful that the Zulus would flood on further into Natal, he had returned to Helpmaaker.

Phoebe had gone about helping with the defences and attending the sick soldiers, but the fear that John Lockley would have been at the battle was constantly on her mind. Then, at about ten o'clock, Horatio had limped in, bringing Tenny and his unconscious Colonel.

She felt so guilty at her joy, when she knew how many would be mourning.

John Lockley had remained unconscious and had only woken once briefly since then. Now, thank the Lord, he was fully awake.

'What day is it?' he asked.

She leaned forward and kissed him. 'It's Friday, the twenty-fourth.'

Just then they heard raised voices and someone shouted, 'Two riders coming in along the Rorke's Drift road!'

Four minutes later they rode in: Theopolis Shepstone's son, Theopolis Junior, and Charles Norris-Newman, war correspondent for the London *Standard*. They were on their way from Rorke's Drift to Pietermaritzburg with official letters from the General, Lord Chelmsford, to Sir Bartle Frere.

Phoebe rose and went to the hospital tent flap and opened it wide. John Lockley lay with closed eyes listening as Theopolis Junior looked round the gallery of anxious listeners and told them, 'Between four and five thousand Zulus crossed the Buffalo River and attacked Rorke's Drift the night before last. A hundred and fifty of our lads, thirty-six of them sick cases in the hospital, held the Zulus off all night. I tell you, it's black with Zulu dead up there. They're burying them right now. The impi finally retired as dawn broke yesterday.'

Theopolis went on, 'Lord Chelmsford and Colonel Glyn led us down from Isandlwhana Mountain where we had returned on Wednesday night and where we made a ghastly and miserable bivouac during the hours of darkness. We were risen before dawn. I do believe the General did not wish for us to see what we had slept surrounded by – and so we left Isandlwhana and marched to the Drift.' He looked over to Norris-Newman, who nodded soberly. He continued, 'As we came towards Rorke's, we passed the Zulu impi that had attacked it. It was the weirdest experience I've ever had, for it was in the grey breaking of the dawn light. And I tell you, they passed us, and we passed them, thousands of Zulus ... with not more than a hundred yards between us, and nary a sound was made by either side.'

'How could that be?' asked Major Spalding.

'Both sides exhausted ... mentally and physically ... couldn't have fought each other even if we'd wanted to.

'I was back up at the battlefield yesterday afternoon ... looking for my brother George,' he closed his eyes as he recalled it, 'whom sadly I found. It's a hideous sight up there ... bodies disembowelled everywhere. Some even beheaded and hacked to pieces. There'd be as many Zulu dead as ours, to be honest; perhaps more.' He drew his hand across his brow. His face was white and drawn. He looked quite desolate.

'How many do you think have died?' called a soldier.

He did not reply, and Norris-Newman answered for him. 'About seven hundred regulars, we think, and then about a hundred or so officers and NCOs of the native contingents. Plus about the same number of native soldiers. All brave men.'

Before Theopolis went on his way Phoebe brought him in to the hospital tent to see John Lockley.

'I'm glad to see you alive, sir.'

John Lockley nodded his head to Tenny. 'I wouldn't be but for my sergeant-major, Tenny Rama.'

Theopolis greeted Tenny. Then he turned back to John Lockley. 'I'm sorry to tell you Colonel Durnford's dead.'

John Lockley closed his eyes. He was very slow to answer. 'Yes, I know.'

'When I was at the battlefield yesterday I recognised him by his whiskers and his watch and pocket knife. The knife had his name on it and the watch his initials ... I know he was very close to you, sir. Do you want them?'

John Lockley looked at Phoebe, whose eyes were filled with tears. Anthony had been such a wonderful man ... She was thinking about poor Fanny and how heart-broken she would be. It was all so devastating.

John Lockley looked back to Theopolis and shook his head. 'No, give them to Fanny Colenso and her father, the Bishop.'

After Theopolis had gone, John Lockley turned, as well as he could, to Tenny. He remembered how he had fallen beside Darlengi, quite prepared to die there with him. 'I can never repay you,' he said softly.

Tenny answered, 'Inkosi, I could not have done it without Horatio.'

And then John Lockley remembered the day Anthony had praised Chieftain, saying that to a soldier a horse could make the difference between life and death. He answered, 'My dear friend, I could not have done it without both of you.'

It took him many days to finally be able to speak of Darlengi's death, and when he did Phoebe's face paled. She would not accept it. Darlengi dead? She sat down on the edge of his bed and held his hand, just staring at him for a long time. Later she walked along the laagered wagons and she cried. Dear Anthony gone ... Darlengi gone too ... with his astute mind, so rational and discerning ... his limitless understanding gone ... it did not seem possible. He had always seemed somehow invincible. She pictured him loping across the veld. She saw him winking at her at the altar the day she married John Lockley. She remembered the Christmas Day she had said goodbye to him and how he had told her she was Africa's and must return. She imagined his dark eyes looking down at her as he took her in his powerful arms to hold her close to his heart. She relived the day so long ago when he had told her of Ellen's death. He had kissed the palm of her hand that day ... somehow she felt his lips on her hand again.

And now she shivered as she leaned on one of the large wagon wheels and wept for the other woman who had loved him, the one she had never seen and yet felt akin to ... Thulile.

Thulile wandered along the hill above the Umlatoosi River, her fingers playing with the imPangele – a necklace of triangular beads – that she wore. It was a hot, steamy day, and it had been some weeks since she had seen her beloved Darlengi. And what wonderful news she would have for him when he came home.

At last, after all these years of marriage, her ancestors had heard her incessant prayer and answered it. She was to bear his child. She glowed with the treasure of the thought she carried: of the child she carried. It would be beautiful and strong and good, like its father.

Darlengi knew so much. He was brave like the lion and strong like the buffalo and good like the rain to the mealie field. He was so different from all the other men of their kraal; different from all the men of all the kraals. She was so proud to be his. So proud to lie with him, and call him husband.

He had gone to fight the British. She thought in his heart he had been as loath to go as the red-billed ox-pecker is loath to leave its host, the rhinoceros. But he had gone, for Cetshwayo.

He had whispered to her as he lay with her the night before he left, 'I love you, Thulile, you have brought me great happiness.'

Oh, how wondrous it was to hear him say that. She had kissed him many times and whispered, 'What does it mean, this war with the British?'

She could hear his answer now as the wind played in the long grass of the veld beneath her feet. She did not quite understand his reply. He had said, 'It means that most men are greedy.'

'Do you mean Cetshwayo too?'

'Yes, I mean most men,' he had replied.

There had been a great battle at Isandlwhana Mountain far away across the plains. They were expecting their warriors home soon to ritually cleanse themselves. Zulu runners had brought the news yesterday. There had been many killed and many wounded but it had been a victory for Zululand. Everyone had rejoiced. She supposed Darlengi would have been there. But she was not worried. He was an induna and indunas did not fight, they told the warriors where to go and what to do.

She had sensed that Darlengi had been worried about his British brother. But he was an induna too, so she supposed he would not fight either. She recalled the one time she had seen him. It had been when the Magic One, Mattana, had died. It had greatly surprised her when she saw that Logley had the same face as her husband. She knew how her husband loved him; and how important he was to him. She fancied she would like to see Logley again when the baby came. Yes, of course they would see him often, for Darlengi would want Logley to know his child well. What a happy family they would all be.

She smiled tenderly as pictures of Darlengi floated through her mind and she turned her footsteps up towards his kraal . . . their kraal. She was imagining how Darlengi would run down this slope, laughing with their child at his heels.

She was picturing placid, lovely, perfect days together, once this war was over. Perhaps it was over now; for they had won the battle. Yes, Darlengi should be home soon.

Then into her daydreams came the unaccustomed sound of raised voices wafting down the slope to her. She looked up and now she hurried, beginning to run up the hill. She knew before she reached the kraal that something was very wrong.

As she came through the gate the hubbub of voices became louder. The people were in the cattle kraal. She ran by the huts to the centre pen. There she saw Maphoko, Darlengi's young induna, and Kayo with a great wound in his throat, and several other of the warriors. All the kraal people were talking at once.

As soon as she came in, they turned round to her and silence fell. She looked questioningly at Maphoko.

'What is it?'

Maphoko came forward two paces. She knew by his face what had happened before he said the words that chilled her.

'Thulile, our great chief, Darlengi, has gone to his ancestors. We have brought his body home to you.'

Thulile heard nothing after that. Except for the scream that exploded through her head. She did not even know that it burst out of her mouth as the whole kraal went black and all the people disappeared.

EPILOGUE

It was a cold September day some weeks after the end of the Zulu War. Cetshwayo had been taken away from Ulundi in custody on Sunday, 31 August, and the Zulu people had begun the wearying task of trying to return to normality after over seven months of life-draining war.

The afternoon sun threw an insipid light across the kraal above the Umlatoosi River, as a man wearing mufti and a wide-awake on his head rode steadily up the valley to the gate. The brilliant colour of his eyes had not altered and he was as handsome as ever; the scar on his temple somehow enhancing his looks as he gazed down at the kraal people congregating about him. Yet when he dismounted he moved carefully, like a man who must, for a time, remember his injuries.

He was surprised; for when he asked in perfect Zulu to see the woman Thulile, the widow of the great Induna Darlengi, they acted as if they had expected him. There was whispering and then muttering amongst the people, for they noticed that the white man's face was like their dead induna's; just as Thulile had told them it would be. Fenni, the witch doctor, began to throw green powder about as the man came towards the entrance in the palisade.

He took off his hat and pushed his hand back through his thick hair. 'Where is the woman, Thulile?' he asked again as the people pressed around him. A young induna stepped forward. It was Maphoko; he had fought many battles for Zululand, and while he had been wounded, had lived through them all. 'She lies beside her husband in the valley below.' He pointed, and John Lockley looked down through the long grass and the trees.

There was infinite sadness in his voice as he said, 'She is dead too?'

'Yes. She lived only to give birth to his son. Then she joined him. Her spirit was always with her husband.'

'Son?' John Lockley swung his eyes around to the induna.

'Yes. Thulile told us all that you would come for the child. She said we were to wait for you, and to give him to you. She said when

592

you came we would know you, for your face is the face of our great Induna Darlengi ... and it is so.'

The people separated and a woman walked forward with a baby wrapped in skins. It was only perhaps three weeks old.

Maphoko took it from her and handed the child to John Lockley. 'We have been waiting for you. Thulile said to tell you, his name is the name of his father ...'

John Lockley looked down at the tiny face, and his eyes brimmed with tears. There was the slightest tremor through his hands as he took the child, for he was overcome by the thought ... *You hold Darlengi's son.*

He mounted Horatio and said to the people, 'I live at the Tugela farm near the Intalalala River. My name is Harrison.' And even though he knew they would not understand, he added, 'Darlengi was my brother.'

He waved once as he rode slowly down the valley to the burial place. There he dismounted, holding the newly born in his arms, and stood before the mound near the cluster of wild date palms, deep in the heart of Zululand.

He thought about Thulile ... and for the first time John Lockley knew who she was. She was the beautiful, willowy girl who had taken him to the dying Mattana and stood near the gate and watched him ride away from the kraal all those years ago. Yes, he knew her now, and felt her presence. 'I accept your gift, as you knew I would,' he whispered.

He put his hand in his pocket to touch the chain and the diamond that Tenny had removed from Darlengi's body. He would keep these for the child.

He stood there in front of the graves as the chill evening breeze found him and shadows lengthened about him. He relived days and nights gone by ... saw his brother's black eyes ... heard his steady voice ... felt the strong grip of his hand ... imagined his smile ...

The baby stirred in his arms.

He looked west to a kraal on a distant hill. He would make for that and spend the night there. He smiled gently as he thought of Phoebe. Tomorrow he and the little one would be home with her; with her love and her dependability. There was much to do at the Tugela farm. And much to do in Natal and Zululand: rebuilding and restoring: the country and the people.

Slowly, holding Darlengi close to his heart, he mounted Horatio, and, with a last lingering look back to the burial place, rode away through the long grass of the veld.

AUTHOR'S NOTES

Simeon Kambula, Jabez Molife, and Chieftain, Colonel Anthony Durnford's horse, all escaped from Isandlwhana.

The battles of the Zulu War, in chronological order, were:

Isandlwhana	Wednesday, 22 January, 1879, afternoon
Rorke's Drift	Wednesday, 22 January, 1879, evening and night
Nyezane	Wednesday, 22 January, 1879
Ntombe Drift	Wednesday, 12 March, 1879
Hlobane	Friday, 28 March, 1879
Khambula	Saturday, 29 March, 1879
Gingindlovu	Wednesday, 2 April, 1879
Siege of Eshowe	Thursday, 23 January to Thursday, 3 April, 1879
Ulundi	Friday, 4 July, 1879